THE REMEMBRANCER'S TALE

After majoring in, at various times, philosophy, anthropology, linguistics, and physics, David Zindell graduated from the University of Colorado with a degree in mathematics. He was nominated for a Hugo Award for best new writer, and his best-selling novel *Neverness*, a cosmic SF epic, was shortlisted for the Arthur C. Clark Award. A successor trilogy, A Requiem For Homo Sapiens, came next, followed by the four-book Ea Cycle, a Grail quest to end all Grail quests. David lives in Denver, Colorado, and you can find out more about him at his website: www.davidzindell.com.

By David Zindell

Neverness

A REQUIEM FOR HOMO SAPIENS

The Broken God
The Wild
War in Heaven

THE EA CYCLE

The Lightstone
Lord of Lies
Black Jade
The Diamond Warriors

The Idiot Gods

THE REMEMBRANCER'S TALE
DAVID ZINDELL

HARPER
Voyager

Harper*Voyager*
An imprint of HarperCollins*Publishers* Ltd
1 London Bridge Street
London SE1 9GF

www.harpercollins.co.uk

HarperCollins*Publishers*
Macken House, 39/40 Mayor Street Upper,
Dublin 1, D01 C9W8, Ireland

First published by HarperCollins*Publishers* 2023
This paperback original edition 2023
1

A catalogue record for this book is available from the British Library

ISBN: 978-0-00-849569-5

This novel is entirely a work of fiction.
The names, characters and incidents portrayed in it are
the work of the author's imagination. Any resemblance to
actual persons, living or dead, events or localities is
entirely coincidental.

Set in Sabon LT Std 10/11.5 pt by Palimpsest Book Production Limited,
Falkirk, Stirlingshire

Printed and bound in the UK using 100% renewable electricity by CPI Group (UK) Ltd

To Maryann,
who has stuck with me through everything and all

Part One

Into the Inferno

1

In Neverness they called Thomas Rane 'Lord Remembrancer' or sometimes the Remembrancer – the man with the perfect memory who could never forget.

On the evening before the day of Maria's funeral, Rane stood on the shore of the frozen sea, remembering. How very much he remembered! How Maria had loved watching the seals sun themselves on the rocks of North Beach and listening to their barks and moans! With deep winter now taking hold of Neverness Island, the sleek grey seals had sought shelter down in their holes beneath the ice, leaving their favourite rocks and the whole of the beach deserted. With only some birds for company, Rane kept his vigil alone. He called to mind the times when Maria had stood here with him, waiting for supernovas to appear out of the sky's glittering blackness much as cave dwellers on Old Earth had long ago watched for shooting stars. It was a very human thing to do. In a time when many peoples across the galaxy were leaving their humanity behind them, or trying to, Maria had reminded him how much he relished being a man and how very good it was to be alive.

She had touched others in similar ways. His favourite student, Sunjay, had concocted a little fancy about Maria: the whirling spiral arms of the Milky Way could be seen as the centre of the trillions of galaxies around it because from the very stuff of the galaxy's stars had evolved the human race. And the Civilized Worlds were certainly the centre of the galaxy, for on the three thousand or so planets from Yarkona and Urradeth across the Stellar Fallaways to Kittery and Kirdun, humanity had reached its finest flowering. And Icefall, upon which Rane stood looking up at the bright constellations, had long been recognized as the topological nexus of the Civilized Worlds, indeed of the entire galaxy: in the deep space above his cold planet, many billions of pathways through the manifold converged into a singularity, a sort of way station that opened upon countless other stars. And Neverness was the centre of Icefall (though the planet's original people and animals spread out across many frozen islands might dispute this belief). And the Order, which had put down roots in the spires, libraries, and halls of the Academy pushed up against the mountains to the east, centred the life of the City of Light and gave Neverness its purpose. And Maria had come to this axis mundi as from out of nowhere bringing her own dazzling light. And so she had become, in a way, the centre of the Order and of the whole universe itself.

How quickly her brightness had called the Order's and historians, its eschatologists, notationists, and all the others, to gather around her! And how that had always seemed to Rane so strange! For he was of the Order of Mystic Mathematicians and Other Seekers of the Ineffable Flame, and the pilots who plied the most difficult of mathematics in guiding their lightships from star to star had always been seen as the soul of the Order. The pilots, though, explored the galaxy's physical spaces only. Whereas Maria, in the poems that she composed on beaches such as this and then recited in the Hofgarten or the Fravashi Green or in other public places, sought a much deeper kind of discovery. She spoke to the most ancient longings of the Order's academicians and high professionals, the pilots, too, and it was as if the warmth of her musical voice held the secret of kindling that mysterious, ineffable flame.

Sunjay's sister Chandra had upbraided Sunjay for centring all things around humanity and Maria in particular, and she was right to do so, even though he had offered his conceit in the spirit of play. One thing, though, Rane could not deny: in little time, Maria had become his centre. If the Star of Neverness ceased exerting its force of attraction, Icefall and the other planets orbiting it would spin off into the emptiness of space. So it had been with Rane. Over the days since she had gone away, all his thoughts about returning to his duties as a remembrancer and resuming his life had spun off into a meaninglessness as black and cold as an interstellar void. He had no idea what to do with himself day by day or even moment by moment.

What was there to do, now? He watched a flock of kitti-keesha, perhaps startled by the cry of a snowy owl, leap up off the beach in a burst of white wings throwing off the day's fading light. His life had blown up into a similar white cloud of chaos, and in the end, he had no more control over it than he had over the pretty, panicked birds.

When simple remembering failed him, when deep winter's cold worked its way through his thick furs and underclothing into his bones, he tried to knock away the pain of his numb fingers so that he could pick up one of the beach's rounded grey stones and keep it as a memento of one of Maria's favourite places. He turned and hiked up the path cutting a steep diagonal in the cliff above the beach. Twice, he slipped on frozen rocks, and the second time he struck his head against the side of the cliff.

At the top, at the kerb of the street that ran along the edge of North Beach's quiet neighbourhoods, he fumbled about with his frigid steel skate blades, trying to snap them into his boots. At last, metal clicked into metal, and he struck off down the North Sliddery, skating along the street's orange ice with great force in order to warm his legs. He turned south onto a green glissade, toward the moonlit spires of the Old City. He crossed one of the city's two yellow streets before turning west again onto a purple gliddery that gave out onto a red lesser gliddery only a couple of blocks away. By the time he reached his house, the wind had come up, freezing his face and driving icy needles into his eyes. He decided that he'd had enough of cold to last a lifetime, and he had lived more than one lifetime in this dark, bitter city.

His chalet overlooked North Beach, though the curves of the cliff on which his house was built obscured Seal Rock and various features of the shoreline. He took no thought of this now, for other sights he wished to behold. He went inside by way of the back door, and he hung his furs on a peg in the skate room and took off his ice-encrusted boots before stepping with numbed feet through the kitchen out into his fireroom. The big windows facing the ocean had gone dark for the night; the granite walls, stripped of artwork, rose stark and grey from

the wood floor. Columns of red jewood framed rectangles of
stone and supported the chalet's great slanted roof beams. With
the tapestries and paintings that Maria had loved packed
away, the barren walls reflected the slightest of sounds and filled
the whole house with echoes.

It didn't take Rane long to light the many candles in their
bronze stands and get a fire going. He sat as close to its cracking
orange flames as he could bear, letting its heat flow into him.
Soon, he began to sweat, and he took off his thick wool sweater.
He unbuttoned his shirt. Maria, he remembered, had come to
Neverness owning little besides a blue dress and a scarf. He
wore that scarf now, tied around his neck. Even a strong wind
could scarcely move it, for it had a startling heaviness. Its shimmering fabric might have been spun of silver or iridium or gold.
Its silky texture, however, felt the opposite of metallic. Incredibly
soft it was, softer than shagshay fur and seemingly as delicate
as a fire rose's petals. Whenever Rane put his fingers to the scarf,
he could not tell where his flesh ended and the scarf's substance
began. How strange then that its crimson and violet threads
paradoxically wove themselves into an inexplicable hardness.
The mechanics to whom Rane had taken this artefact had not
been able to cut or pierce it, even with diamond drills. They had
failed completely to analyse it, and they had pronounced it a
work of made matter, crafted by one god of the galaxy or another
or perhaps by an alien race. How Maria had come by such an
amazing thing, he thought, was a mystery.

In memory of Maria, he pressed his nose down into the scarf's
folds. It still held her scent, the fragrance of her skin and her
hair, the sweetness of her breath, her mysterious Marianess. He
couldn't help drawing this essence in and in.

'Maria, Maria,' he whispered.

He closed his eyes, meditating in preparation for remembrance. Light and dark in the shifting shapes of flames played
across his eyelids. He breathed long and deep.

Maria, Maria, Maria . . .

Which memory should he choose in summoning Maria to
him on this cold, dark night? With red-hot logs popping and
hissing on the fireplace's andirons, he thought about the nature of
choice and fate. The cantors had their Axiom of Choice, one
of the keystones in the edifice of set theory. The cetics, too,

had a similar axiom, though they applied it to their science of soul and mind and not to mathematics. So it was with the economists and the eschatologists, too. The Axiom of Choice of the remembrancers differed from these others. As Rane had long ago been taught, and as he taught Sunjay and Chandra and all his students, it was axiomatic that one could choose any memory in trying to recreate a totality of being and occurrence, for every event and thing in spacetime interconnected with every other and was recorded in the One Memory. In theory, at least, this was true. In practice, Rane's ancient discipline would always remain an art in which one should take great care in choosing what to remembrance.

Many memories built inside him, a seemingly infinite number of Maria moments. Once, when they had been out skiing through the forest on Neverness Island, they had surprised a snow tiger beneath a great yu tree even as the tiger had surprised them. And Maria had stared the great white beast down. That is, she had gazed into the tiger's yellow-green eyes without the slightest fear, and something great and wild had passed between them. The tiger had taken nearly forever to drink in the sight of her before moving off deeper into the forest without a sound. Another time, Maria had spent a happy few hours with some autists camping out in the City Wild. She had shared her poems with them as they had shared laughter and lice with her, and when she returned home, Rane had taken great care in picking the little insects out of her hair before Maria had practically leaped into his arms to begin an evening of the most gleeful lovemaking. That memory recalled the time in false winter when they had taken a schooner far out to the south of the city and had spread out a blanket on the frozen sea. With the cold ice beneath them and the hot sun above, they had made love with a zest as fresh and strong as the wind.

One memory above all, though, Rane decided he wished to revisit on this most desolate of nights: the day when Maria had taught him to play with poetry. It was his favourite memory of Maria, or rather, of the lovable Maria.

Rane chose to enter the memory through the attitudes of olfaction and gestalt. With his eyes still closed, he held Maria's scarf over his face and breathed in deeply. Her scent excited nerves connecting directly with the centre of smell deep within his brain. Memories cascaded inside him like a waterfall striking rocks and coming apart into a brilliant spray. He entered gestalt then, and reassembled the billions of glittering water droplets into a larger whole. After this pattern had set, he moved into the difficult attitude of recurrence, in which he did not merely recall the manifold details of his Maria memory but rather relived the experience.

When he opened his eyes, the windows facing west shone with strong sunlight, for night had become day. Rane still sat on furs by the fire, but he wore different and fresher clothing, and his mind filled with new thoughts that were also old. He waited for Maria to join him there. Her soft footfalls sounded against the polished wood floor in the hallway, and she walked into the fireroom. As was her wont, as much as possible, she went about the house naked, as if she couldn't bear the burden of the garments that civilized people forced upon their bodies. When he had pointed out that she had come to the wrong city for a nudist, she had said, 'Just keep your fires lit, and I'll be happy.'

How happy it made him whenever Maria walked into a room! She moved with an animal's ease with herself, a fully embodied grace that he had seen in Sunjay and Chandra and their father, Danlo wi Soli Ringess, and only a few other people. Neither tall nor short, she filled the space around her with a well-muscled curvaceous body and a sense that at that moment she could belong nowhere else in the universe. Her hair rippled in black sheeny waves across her shoulders and halfway down her back; her eyes were black diamonds set into a tawny face that he thought of as both earthy and lovely and most others simply called beautiful.

'Have you been writing?' he asked her.

She sat down beside him, kissed him, and then twirled her finger about in the fabric of the scarf that she now wore and he did not. In the attitude of recurrence, in the intense experience of reliving the past, the scarf's colours came alive with an intensity that seemed almost too real: blue blazed into a shimmering cerulean and green into viridian as the scarf's red fibres deepened into blood crimson.

'I've been reading,' she said. 'From a book of poems written on Old Earth. Would you like to hear one?'

Without waiting for an answer, she recited:

'Tyger! Tyger! Burning bright
In the forests of the night,
What immortal hand or eye
Could frame thy fearful symmetry?'

'It is important,' she explained, 'to rhyme eye and symmetry.'
'I know this poem!' he said. 'I know this tiger of Blake.'
'You are my tiger,' she said, 'my beautiful tiger. You will devour me utterly, as I will you, and we will become part of each other and grow infinitely vaster in the becoming. We will feed each other, as fire does fire: so bright, so bright! So beautifully, beautifully bright!'

He laughed at this because her innocence pleased him so much. She often said such impossibly romantic things that no one else would say. He looked at her and murmured, 'No one has ever called me beautiful before.'

'But you are! So utterly, utterly beautiful.'

Then she drew in a deep breath and said:

'He walks in beauty, like the night
Of cloudless climes and starry skies;
And all that's best of dark and bright
Meet in his aspect and his eyes.'

He laughed again at this, for she thought nothing of altering the words of hallowed ancient poems in order to suit her purpose. And that purpose, he wondered, was . . . what? And then came the answer, gathering like a flame in her eyes: to affirm every aspect of him, with a blazing totality and an unswerving delight. And that pleased him even more.

'Have you no respect?' he asked her. 'What would Lord Byron think of you for mutilating his poem?'

'Lord Byron is long dead, but Lord Rane sits with me now. Don't I honour Lord Byron all the more by enhancing his poem to tell the truth about you?'

And with that, she drew in a breath and let it out in a stream of musical words:

'Rane, my Ranelight, burning bright
In the starscapes of the night . . .'

Sometimes, she called him by such terms of endearment as 'my heart' or this new play on his name. There was sunlight and moonlight and starlight, and each illuminated the world in its own way. And now there was Ranelight, a word and a substance that Maria had called into being to suggest that he not only filled her life with radiance but caused it to blossom as with showers of warm rain. Why did she reverse the way things really went between them?

> What immortal hand or eye
> Dare frame thy fiery symmetry?

She laid her hands on his cheeks, then moved them down the column of his neck, across his shoulders and down his arms to his sides. Her fingers pressed into him as she drew him closer and kissed him again.

'Now it's your turn,' she said.

'My turn for what?'

'To adapt Blake's poem.'

'I can't do that.'

'Why not?'

'Well, to begin with, you haven't recited all of it to me. Why don't you, and then you can adapt more lines so that I can get a better idea of how this playing with poetry works.'

He kissed her mouth, then edged his lips between the scarf and her skin to kiss her neck. His hand framed the fullness of her large, brown breast.

'Oh, no!' she laughed out. 'You are just hoping to buy time and distract me.'

'Well, that has worked before.'

'Not this time, *mi ardu*. Which lines of the poem do you want to adapt? You said that you know the poem – don't tell me that you haven't memorized every word.'

'I've never written a line of poetry in my life.'

'Then this will be good practice.'

'For what?'

'I've written poems for you. I want you to write a poem for me.'

What she suggested filled him with terror, as might the

prospect of trying to fall naked from one star to another through the vacuum of space.

'But I'm a remembrancer.'

'You're a poet, too. I knew that the first moment I saw you.'

'But I would feel . . . silly.'

'How could you ever, with me?'

She kissed his neck, pressing her full lips against him and murmuring sweetly as if trying to awaken his voice with the warmth of her own.

'All right,' he finally said. And he drew some air, and with it, a bit of her breath, which he boldly let out:

'In what distant deeps or skies
Rose the sunbirds of thine eyes?
With what wings dare thou inspire?
What the song, dare pass the fire?'

She laughed in great gladness, and then she went to work on the poem's third stanza, likening Rane to a star. And so it went, the two of them alternating stanzas of William Blake's immortal poem. She felt her way into the rhythms and rhymes much more quickly and easily than he did, for despite what she had said, he was all mind and memory whereas she was a woman of poetry and power. He had much trouble adapting Blake's *In what furnace was thy brain?* He wanted to know, as reflected in the words he struggled to find, what star had formed her soul? Who had made Maria and could ever dare to grasp her fearful love of life? From where had she come? Why did she make of herself such a mystery? Why did life itself have to be such a mystery?

'Beautiful!' she said after he had uttered the last word of the last line. 'Now you can make a poem for me.'

'Now? Here?'

'You can start it here.'

'I don't know how I—'

'Please, *mi ardu*! Just one line. Or one word. The rest will come from it.'

In a way, this was her Axiom of Choice: that one could always choose poetry as a doorway to the miraculous. And always choose miracles over the mundane. And that also seemed to him utterly strange. For he had always sought meaning through remembrance: somewhere in the One Memory must lie the great secret of all things. Maria, though, had reminded him from the first, with a single smile that emanated both from eyes and heart, that life was not a puzzle to be solved but a mystery to be lived.

'All right.'

He closed his eyes, and he concentrated on a word that she had spoken more than once that afternoon: beautiful. He recalled the first time Maria had looked at him. Like shooting stars in the sky, more words came to him. He opened his eyes and said:

'You beheld me beautiful
Born in splendour . . .'

He stopped and said, 'I'm not sure I can compose any more right now.'

'I'm not sure I want you to.'

'What *do* you want?'

'You know,' she said, her voice as soft as her scarf. She touched his hand and looked at him. 'You always know.'

And so the making of poetry moved naturally and inevitably into the making of love. She helped him get his clothes off, and they lay back onto the furs. Their mouths pressed together as their fingers began a dance more exquisite and pleasurable than any poem could ever be.

This reliving of the past always went exactly the same way. Of the many times they brought body and soul together, this was not to be the longest or the fiercest, the tenderest or the most playful. They were not to call out of each other the wildest gush of ecstatic energies. However, in one short hour, all their ways of merging as one combined into a perfection that opened them into the greatest possibilities of eros and love.

How he always thrilled to the touch of Maria's fingers and the pressure of her hand around him! How she loved the way that he touched her! He could not get enough of her murmurs of contentment as he discovered once again the smoothness of her breasts and her belly. In the firelight and the deeper radiance of recurrence, the whole of her skin from toe to brow glowed. Its light brown colour pulsed with deeper tones of ochre, umber, and burnt almond. It was as if he could see and grasp the life of her every cell. Even the parts of her that the biologists called dead – her black shimmers of hair, the bronze calluses of her feet – seemed to him just the opposite. When her fingernails dug into his back, pulling him into her, those ten curves of hardened keratin fairly quivered with an ancient and vital purpose.

How naturally, how fearlessly, Maria opened to him her legs, her heart, her eyes! How deeply she looked at him, as if calling him out of himself, or rather, into himself – into a Rane made new and more alive with every breath she breathed against his face! There could be no escaping her beautiful black eyes. He could find nowhere to hide, and that was the hell of it but the heaven, too. For in the way she looked at him, with no shame but only her great faith in him and all of life, she made him want to stand with her forever as beneath a warm sun utterly naked in the soul.

After a long while, they lay nearly still together, breathing deeply. Maria had a way of resting her head against his chest, over his heart, as if trying to take shelter there. Could she hear its wild, rhythmic beats? How could she not? For he could still feel the urgent calling of hers.

'I love you,' she said.

But what did she call him *to*? Only joy, and nothing less. However, as his joy in being with her again in remembrance built like a soaring mountain, so did his grief deepen. For the more vividly that he brought her back through remembrance so that she might live again, the more that he longed to hold her again in real life. This only inflamed his grief like a fire's ember working its way into a wound. How he needed to close that wound! But doing so would close him to Maria and leave only a cold, hard scar. Nothing of Maria would remain.

'Love is infinite,' she had once said to him.

Love might indeed be infinite but so was pain. As Rane's longing built into an agony of emptiness, he could find no help for it. Only one thing could he think to do. And so he said goodbye to the Maria who now slept peacefully with her head against his chest. His closed his eyes to begin another remembrance. When he opened them, he saw that the windows facing west shone with strong sunlight, for night had become day. Maria's soft footfalls sounded against the polished wood floor in the hallway, and she walked into the fireroom. She sat down beside him, kissed him, and then twirled her finger about in her scarf. Soon would come poetry and passion and a joy too great to bear.

Five times that night he entered into the recurrence attitude of remembrance. And each time, his grief grew worse until he thought he might die. Not so easy was it, however, to get away from pain that way. He could escape it only for a while. For inevitably, with his final remembrance of her, it blew through him in a storm so deep and terrible that his fireroom and Maria and the whole world vanished into a cloud of blinding whiteness, and he could remembrance no more.

In the darkest hour between death and morning, Rane found himself sitting alone before a cold fire. He wore the same clothes that he had put on to venture out on the frozen beach. Something in his pocket, pressed between thigh and floor, hurt him. He drew out a grey rounded stone, of the kind that the sea washes up upon the shore. He could not recall how it had come to be there.

'Rane,' a voice called to him.

He looked up to see Maria standing by the fireplace. She wore her favourite blue dress and her scarf. He could not understand how she had come to be there.

'You are bleeding, *mi ardu*.'

Never, in any recurrence, had Maria said such a thing to him. Nor had she ever in waking life.

'Doesn't it hurt?'

He pressed his hand to his forehead, which caused the gash there to sting. He looked at his fingers, sticky and red with blood. There came a faint memory of his striking his head against the side of the cliff.

'You are shivering,' she said.

Yes, he was. Violent spasms ripped through his belly and chest, and he recalled the terrible cold of the time when he had got lost while ice schooning on the frozen sea. Cold it was near his chalet's floor, and there he had sat for most of the night.

'I just need to eat,' he said.

He could not remember the last time he had, and his body needed food to warm itself as the fireplace needed new logs to begin throwing out fire again.

'I can't cook for you,' she said, standing as straight as one of the wooden pillars that held up the roof.

'Come sit beside me, and I'll be warm,' he said.

Maria, though, usually so kinetic that chairs could not long hold her, didn't move.

'It *does* hurt,' he said as he pressed his hand to his head again.

'Do you remember what I told you once about that?' she asked.

Did he remember? Words came to him, perhaps lines from one of her poems or her quoting of another poet, long dead: 'Suffering carves hollows in the soul that make room for more joy.'

'I know you know,' she said.

Yes, she always had known all the most important things.

'You are my joy,' she said.

And she was his fountain of life, from which he must drink or die. But when had he ever been able to hold so much life?

'I cannot live without you,' she said.

She was like a rainshower that soaks a seed. But the seed couldn't germinate and grow into a great tree without destroying itself.

'Why can't you,' she asked him, 'remember that?'

'I remember the feel of your fingers over my eyes the first time you tried to sing me to sleep. I remember everything.'

'Do you?'

She looked at him in her gentle, searching way, as no one ever had before.

'You beheld me beautiful,
Born in splendour,
Naked in my soul . . .'

'Do you,' she asked, 'remember this?'

In the light of the last candles that remained burning, she stood above him, biting her lip. A single drop of blood welled up from the slight wound that her teeth had torn into living flesh.

'No!'

A red rain fell upon him, and he raised up his hands over his head as if to cover himself. And he shouted, 'Go away!'

When Maria started crying, her tears poured out bright and
clear. And she said to him, 'Come find me.'

Then she was gone. Rane sat gazing through empty space.
He didn't want to know what she meant.

2

A few hours later, Rane stood on the bare ice of the Hollow Fields, staring at the coffins and blinking against a storm of wavering images. The wind off the frozen sea drove cold nails through glazy eyes straight into the soul, and he could barely make out the multitudes gathered around him. Hundreds of them there were, swaddled in their hooded furs: men, women and children who clung to the very human need for an explainable world. For as long as they could bear it, until long after the rockets fired, they would hold hands and shiver and weep. They would deliver orations and try to extract meaning from the clouds of unknowing that darkened their lives. They would look to Rane to tell of Maria. They would expect him to share out a perfectly preserved part of her, some pure Maria essence, like a radiance that would lighten their grief. He was to delve deeply into his phenomenal memory and call forth so vivid a remembrance of her that they, too, would never forget.

What a mystery, he thought, that anyone should remember anything at all! What would he remember in future years about this day, if any future remained in which to remember it? To the east, the great mass of Mount Urkel overshadowed the runs and ships of the Hollow Fields; the mountain's gleaming curves of snow and conical symmetry suggested an underlying order to the world that should have given him comfort. To the north, the spires of the Old City split the gelid air. The streets of the Farsider's Quarter, off to the west, wove together like strands of green and orange, purple and red. The sheen of their tinted ice recalled the colours of Maria's scarf – as well as the shimmer of something much deeper and brighter inside her. South of Neverness, over the dead still ocean, the golden-banded sky opened out into a deep blueness almost as beautiful as the centres of Maria's brilliant eyes.

'Lord Remembrancer.'

A voice murmuring along the wind compelled him to look in another direction. Ten yards from him, his friends and students huddled together like sea birds using each other as shields against the sudden gusts. Kolenya Mor smiled at him, her fat, friendly face turned toward him with all the intensity of a full moon. Kiyoshi Telek waited next to her, as did Jonathan Hur, Poppy Panshin and others of the old Kalla Fellowship. The massive Bardo, who had astonished everyone in becoming Lord of the Order at the end of the war fifteen years before, seemed as solid and reassuring as a mountain himself. His thick black beard blended into the ruff of his sable furs, and he evinced no sign of minding the cold. He stood with one huge, gloved hand covering the shoulder of Sunjay and the other clasping the arm of his older sister, Chandra. Everyone said that their father, Danlo wi Soli Ringess, had gone off to become a god like his father before him.

'Lord Remembrancer.'

Rane could almost feel the pull of the many eyes hooking expectations into him. What could they really see as they gazed at him? How many perceived him as a youngish man, with the first grey frosting his temples? How few knew that he was on his fourth and final rejuvenation, with only one last life to live?

'You look much as you always do, young or old,' Kolenya Mor had once said to him during a time of calm between Maria and him. Then she had gone on to describe him as handsome, noble, sensitive, decent, and demanding.

How many had the desire to go beneath the surface of things to get at their essence? Some people used aromatic drugs that infused the blood and the sweat so that the body gave off pleasant or subliminally potent fragrances. Maria had laughed at the use of such technologies, saying that he naturally smelled of kindness and goodness – as well as passion and a terrible pride. Well, he thought, she had certainly been right about the pride.

'Lord Remembrancer – it's nearly time.' Rane forced his attention back to the long object that froze so many pairs of weeping eyes. The coffin, crafted of polished shatterwood, gleamed upon its stand of mounded ice. He could almost hear the sound of its hard, hinged cover locking shut. He could not believe that Maria lay inside the coffin's cold and dark.

How many similar coffins were arrayed upon the acres of the Hollow Fields that morning? Rane looked up and out – and out and out. He saw coffin after coffin, each with its own gathering of friends and family, each one a bit of wood and metal marring the glossy ice for half a mile in any direction. How many people, he wondered, died in Neverness in a season? How many died each year on the thousands of the Civilized Worlds and on those countless planets on which men and women strived to become more than human? From the beginning of human time on the burning grasslands of lost Old Earth, down through the tens of thousands of years and out across the starry expanses of the universe, how many people had ever lived and died?

Just then Bardo cast him a long, penetrating look. He disengaged from Chandra and Sunjay, and he made his way toward Rane. He moved across the ice with slow, powerful steps. As he drew close to Rane and mumbled soft words, his voice recalled the tremors of a soon-to-be erupting mountain.

'What will you say?' Bardo asked him. 'Have you decided?'

A sea of memories abided inside Rane, and Bardo's innocent question caused a million images to begin forming up, like white-capped waves in a storm. He slowly shook his head.

'Can you speak, then? I will if you cannot.'

Rane drew in a deep breath in an attempt to blow the images away. He looked around him and said, 'Most of these people are Ringists. I'm sure they would rather hear from you.'

'No, no, I am Lord of the Order now, and I have nothing to do with Ringism.'

No, Rane thought, nothing more than playing prophet and telling everyone that they should follow the way of Mallory Ringess. He smiled at this. He remembered tutoring Mallory, the curious and often confused boy, the proud and brilliant journeyman pilot with the cold, sparkling blue eyes. Could he have guessed that Mallory would have taken the lead in the quest to find the mysterious Elder Eddas, which Mallory had characterized as instructions to human beings on becoming gods? Could Rane have ever prophesied that Mallory would set off the Pilots' War and the much greater War in Heaven that had followed? Bardo, like others, sometimes seemed to believe that Mallory had gained powers of mind so great that he might as well be called a god. But what did that really mean? Surely Mallory had remained a man of blood and blazing passions, a man who longed to hear a beautiful poem or to clasp a woman to him even as Rane did Maria.

Bardo, a man of deep intuitions, waved his hand out across the ice and said, 'You had a part in all this, too.'

Yes, he had. In how many ceremonies had he measured out the remembrancer's drug kalla to the seekers who had joined together into what came to be called the Kalla Fellowship?

'I wanted only,' Rane said, 'to teach them to remembrance.'

To remembrance the deep things, he mused – what Mallory had called the Elder Eddas and others believed to be the One Memory.

'You *did* teach them,' Bardo said.

'Perhaps. But I never saw that we'd be starting a *religion*.'

And over the years, the Way of Ringess had grown and grown – and quickly grown corrupted. The passion for believing the unbelievable had precipitated the great, bloody war, which some said had purified and changed forever this popular religion. Ringism drew thousands to Neverness each year. Rane thought that it had drawn Maria from somewhere in the stars.

'We made this,' Rane said, looking at the people clumped around the coffins.

And Ringism, like all new religions, had made a new ritual. At the centre of the Fields stood a great silvery sunship, its spun-diamond hull gleaming and waiting, its nose pointing straight up toward the white fire of the Star of Neverness, which blazed in empty space so many millions of miles away.

'You blame yourself for too many things,' Bardo said softly.

The wind scraping over the earth sucked away Bardo's words and whisked them up into the air. Rane did not want to summon the effort to hear what he said. At the moment, he could scarcely hear at all, for the cold caught him and he began to shiver. He had to lay the whole of his will upon his body to control the chattering of his teeth.

'Shall I,' Bardo said, looking back across the ice, 'send Sunjay for hot coffee?'

Rane shook his head at this. Why he should he warm himself when others, too, must endure this frigid day?

Impossible it was that Sunjay should hear what Rane said in such a cruel wind, and yet Sunjay seemed to hear him all the same. He shot Rane a look of unnerving empathy. He began moving toward Rane and Bardo, with Chandra gliding across the ice right behind him.

In the boy's tallness, Rane thought, in the hawklike fierceness of face and in his bold blue eyes, he favoured his father and grandfather. (And even his great-grandfather, the preeminent pilot, Leopold Soli.) But where others of the Ringess line tended toward coldness of countenance and a chilling clarity to the depths within themselves, Sunjay seemed to turn all his awareness outward toward the world. And today, toward Rane. Rane could see it, like the fire of suns, pouring out of Sunjay's large eyes. Even more, Rane felt it flowing through his insides and warming him in a way that coffee never could.

His older sister possessed all of Sunjay's gifts, and more. Although her blonde hair and dark brown eyes recalled her mother, Tamara, she shared not only the Ringess genes but the family talent for pushing through the impossible into the miraculous. She smiled at Rane, her expressive mouth conveying to him a hundred shadings and colours of warmth.

'I brought the flower,' she said to him.

'Thank you, Chandra,' he replied with a bow of his head. 'But maybe you should hold on to it for a while.'

'Will you not speak, Lord Rane?'

'Why is it that everyone assumes that I cannot say what needs to be said?'

'But what will you say?'

'What should I say?'

Gazing into Chandra's eyes just then was like watching an infinite flower opening out its petals toward the ends of the universe.

'Will *you* speak?' he asked her.

She glanced at Sunjay and then back at Rane. 'One of us should. We haven't decided, but Sunjay wants to recite a poem.'

'Which . . . poem?'

'You know which one,' she said. 'He doesn't want to recite it without your permission, but I've tried to persuade him that it belongs to everyone, now.'

She leaned closer to Sunjay, and whispered something that Rane could not hear. Then it came time for Kolenya Mor to address Maria's friends, and Chandra could not continue talking. That is, she could not exercise her vocal cords, lips, and tongue in order to utter the sounds making up most human speech. She, like Sunjay – like other girls and boys whom Rane taught – spoke another language altogether. Although sometimes incorporating sounds, it was an intricate composition of gestures, touches, blinks, expressions, and all the quanta of meaning that could be bound up in the radiance of a knowing look. It partook of the beauty of music and made metaphors the way evolution brought forth novelties of life. It had a million 'words'. Or perhaps a million million – Rane could not be sure. For this strange new language never held still, but rather flowed like water in a stream, here dividing into separate rivulets, there eddying or circling like a whirlpool or breaking upon rocks and being cast up in a spray as uncountable numbers of sparkling droplets. Only one versed in the remembrancers' art, it was said, could develop the capaciousness of memory needed to hold such a language.

While Kolenya forced her dulcet voice to do battle with the wind, Chandra said things to Sunjay in silence. They spoke so quickly that Rane couldn't quite follow the fluttering of their eyelids, the widenings and narrowings of their pupils, the flickering of their eyes, left and right. And that otherness of suggestion that warmed their faces with such a heartbreaking eloquence.

'What are we going to miss most about Maria?' Rane heard Kolenya call out this lament to the hundreds packing the ice. 'What is it that she most wanted, for herself and for the world? What is it that we will all remember?'

. . . *her dharma-as-destiny, like the way of the warrior-poets, the highest art* . . .

So completely did Sunjay and Chandra seem to understand each other – and so completely opaque was their lightning-quick communication – that their speech might as well have been called telepathy.

. . . *the highest art, in fearlessness/flawlessness/flowingness always and only through the will to* . . .

Some of those present couldn't help stealing glances at Sunjay and Chandra. It was said that Danlo wi Soli Ringess, in fathering them, had created something new that had never been in all the universe. People called them, along with others of their generation, the *Asta Siluuna*: the Star Children. They revered such lovely sprigs of humanity almost as much as they feared them. They asked a question, sometimes openly, sometimes only in the look of longing and dread that filled their eyes: were these children still really human?

As Rane remembered how Maria had practically adopted them for her own, Chandra came up close to him. She opened her furs, and from an inner pocket drew out a fire rose. Long-stemmed and fragile, its petals still retained a crimson-orange glow. No other flower could defy a Neverness winter by blossoming in midwinter spring. No other flower, Maria had remarked, held so much beauty or so much life.

'We've decided,' Chandra told him in their silent, secret language. She slowed her movements so that he would understand her. 'Sunjay will recite the poem . . . unless *you* want to.'

She held the flower out to him. The sight of it exploded through Rane's visual field like the flash of a bomb. He couldn't help staring at it, for it burned with a terrible brilliance. Quickly, though, in the icy air, the flower began to freeze. Its colours began die into a dull blood-red. There was no help for that. Rane looked at Chandra. Her eyes filled with tears, and there was no help for that, either, for she shared moments of 'telepathy' with him, too. One tear built large and lustrous, and rolled down over her dark eyelash and beaded upon her cheek. There it froze, a little drop of hardened water and salt and anguish.

It froze *him*, fixing his gaze and paralysing his eyes. It captured his consciousness, as a butterfly might be imprisoned in memory's cold, clear ice. The images came flooding in then: smiles and scowls, looks of agony and bliss and every shade and colour of human expression. The images, in all their dizzying millions, drew him in and in and in. They seemed always pulled toward a singularity in space and time. They seemed always to constellate around it, as stars swirl around the galactic core.

'Maria.'

Rane couldn't help thinking of a concept of the cantors and other pure mathematicians, for he had their talent and might have become one of them. As he had done so many times, he watched the images form up as points fractalling toward a manifold that he thought of as a strange attractor. There could be no escaping this memory and this moment. He always found himself getting closer and closer to it.

'Maria – why?'

The attractor embraced him and pulled him even closer. It pulled him into the softness of Maria's breasts and belly, and into the glory of her black hair. He felt again her heart beating too fast and her throat catching with words she tried to force out but could not. And the sobbing, sobbing, sobbing . . . the tears frozen like diamond drops to the tawny skin beneath her eyes.

And always, the other words – the words he had heard ten thousand times: 'Leave me alone!'

Through the force of will, he drove the images away. A sudden stillness came upon him. Now he could see again and hear again. Now he could feel Chandra pressing the thorny stem of the rose into his gloved hand. She wept freely, and more tears froze beneath her eyes. This, too, would become an image bound up with all the others. This, too, in the coming days, he would need to make die.

'I found this at Arabella Tevor's shop,' Chandra told Rane in a flurry of eye flicks and taps on the back of his hand. 'She grows the most beautiful roses.'

The memories, of course, would never really die. He might encase them within the hard shell of his bitterness and his need to forget, but like seeds trampled into the ground, they would inevitably open up at the right touch of moisture and warmth, and spring into new life.

'Thank you,' Rane whispered to her.

She cast him a long, knowing look, as Maria had often done. Compassion, he thought, could be a very cruel thing.

As Kolenya stood near the coffin recounting Maria's love of poetry, Rane tried to calculate the number of steps needed for him to join her there. He watched the play of the clouds' shadows lightening and darkening the coffin's polished wood. How was it possible that Maria could lie within such a cold, sunless place? What did it even mean to think that she was there? What did it mean, he wondered, to say that anyone is or is not? Couldn't he still see the amazing *isness* of Maria in her eyes whenever he allowed himself to look? How could Maria ever be anything other than utterly and ecstatically alive?

Certainly, he thought, Maria's things had been set inside the coffin: her blue dress and her blue coffee mug; the books of poetry and an adjal and her flute. And much else. That was the custom of the Ringists, now, to entomb the effects of a dear one in case no body could be found to be buried. And, according to an impulse that mirrored the anxieties of the ancient Egyptian kings and queens, if not their practices, these things would be preserved for all eternity in a spectacular way.

One possession Rane had *not* allowed to be buried. He put his hand to Maria's scarf, which warmed his neck. It felt soft and alive.

With Kolenya now reciting one of Maria's poems, Rane breathed in the scarf's scents, and the memories came:

In that hour, taste of tea, scent of sadness,
At a table topped with black stone . . .

Like spinning diamonds, words of the poem that he had finally written for her tumbled out into the air. Soon, Rane thought, he must step forward and recite a poem himself. He must say *something*. How could he not satisfy the expectations of the followers of the religion that he had helped to create?

'Lord Rane.' Sunjay, a couple of yards away, began speaking to him in the silence of his language. He moved closer, so that Rane could read the inklings of his eyes. 'Will you give them your poem?'

You beheld me beautiful,
Born in splendour,
Naked . . .

'According to your sister,' Rane said, 'since I once gave it to Maria, and she gave it to a hundred friends, the poem is no longer mine to give – or not to give.'

Sunjay smiled at this. 'And a hundred times that number of people now remember it, yes? Have you not said many times, sir, that a man may make the moments of his life, but that the remembrance of them belongs to the universe?'

Impossible it was to win an argument with Sunjay. Like the other children of the *Asta Siluuna*, he possessed a system of mores that Rane could not quite grasp. Then, too, Sunjay spun out the words of his language so quickly and so adroitly that in trying to follow them Rane always felt a little dizzy.

'Would you like to give them the poem?' Rane asked.

'I'd like to give them Maria – isn't that what remembrancers have always done?'

Although Sunjay hadn't attained his full growth and stood somewhere in that wild borderland between boy and man, he sometimes seemed a million years old. Rane saw in his too-wise aspect the stern face of Rane's own father, who had taught him never to cry. He saw, as well, the faces of his father's fathers, perhaps imagined, perhaps recalled by some arcane power of memory, back across the light years of the Stellar Fallaways, all the way back to the millions of faces of his ancestors who had lived and died on Old Earth.

How many of those ancestors had been remembrancers, however rudimentary in their skills? As Rane often had, he reflected on origins. Hadn't *the* Remembrancers, as few remembrancers now knew, begun in ancient times as an obscure religious sect? Hadn't they invented their liturgies and their eidetics as a way of preserving the dead? For they had believed that as long as someone remained to preserve with memory everything about those who had departed – their smiles, their words, their deeds, their dreams – then they could not really die. Through faith, zeal, and a bone-deep fear of extinction, the fallen would be embalmed in the brains of those making a remembrance. Thousands of years before the Remembrancers had purged themselves of such superstitions and had joined the Order as a new discipline, their most powerful practitioners had thus tried to keep their dear ones alive.

In that hour, taste of tea, scent of sadness,
At a table topped with black stone,
When I wept to know it glorious
Strange to know you not strange . . .

The scent imbuing the folds of Maria's scarf suddenly called up the tastes of gall and spleen. How strange, how tinged with irony and excruciation, that Bardo and Kolenya – and now even Sunjay! – should want Rane to regress ten millennia in order to re-enact the mythos of a Venerable Remembrancer!

'You may do as you wish,' Rane told Sunjay. 'As you have said, the poem does not belong to me.'

A few minutes later, Kolenya finished her recitations and her paean to Maria. Sunjay bowed to Rane, and then moved over to the coffin to tell everyone how he had met Maria. He extolled her wit and her gentleness in teaching him to make poetry, as she had so many others. When he chose to speak in the Language of the Civilized Worlds, Sunjay had a powerful voice that belied his youth. It rang out across the ice, and for a while Rane lost himself in its sound. Then he realized that Sunjay was reciting Rane's poem:

'In that hour waking wonder,
Tender of touch,
Wet sweet burning eyes,
You looked without cover
Into the inferno – into myself.'

Had Rane, Rane wondered, *really* written those words? He stared off through the haze of his eyes. Life teemed everywhere around him: in the crowds of people exhaling their steamy breaths into the air; in the yu trees bright and green upon the mountains; in the flocks of kittikeesha beating their wings across the blue sky; in the triptons and the vacuum flowers and the other newly evolved organisms of the Golden Ring high above the world.

Could all this immense vivacity ever be enough to overcome its countervailing force? For death, too, laid its hand upon all things. The deep winter wind would kill many animals with bitter cold, and the scavenger birds would hunt their corpses in the snow. The faces of his friends held a foreboding of the inevitable, even as the coffins dotting the ice held what remained of glorious treasures that had been dear to them.

Who could ever help that? Rane pressed his fist to his throbbing forehead. His memory, he thought, was a bone coffin containing dead people. His mother. His father. Ali Alesar of Urradeth and Paloma the Younger and other friends killed in the war. Maria's unborn and perhaps never-conceived child.

And most of all himself.

Where is the life we have lost in living?

He wanted put this question to Kolenya and to Bardo, to Jonathan Hur, and even to Chandra and Sunjay, who would have thought it both sad and strange.

'On that day dreaming darkness,
Solace of steel,
Hot quick ripping veins,
You walked with life
Into the Hofgarten – into my life.'

Although Rane did not want to hear these words he had once written for Maria – the only poem he had ever written in his life! – he could not *not* listen to them. Sunjay kept finding more words to say, and it seemed that he continued on for ten thousand years.

At last, however, he finished and fell into a strange silence. At last it came time for Rane to speak. He forced himself to move forward. He pushed his feet across the ice, so cold that any slipperiness had given way to a gritty friction more like that of sandpaper. He positioned himself behind the coffin. He paused, unable to set the frozen fire rose upon it. He faced Sunjay, who had again taken his place beside Kolenya, Bardo, and Chandra. What should he tell the many hundreds of people gathered to mourn Maria? What *could* he tell them?

'Maria . . .' he began with a whisper.

Everyone stared at him. He tried to clear his throat, but it seemed that a lump of coal was stuck there. His voice was as dry as coal, and he could not get his vocal cords to vibrate.

Maria.

He began to remember. He *wanted* to remember, needed the torment of memory as a man lost in a blizzard needs the pain of almost-frozen feet to reassure himself that blood still pulsed within and that his flesh had not completely hardened into ice. There came a warming, a softening, a burgeoning of moisture. He felt it as a hot, sweet burning in his eyes. He knew that he could not allow a single tear to form up upon *his* cheek. One drop of water, falling, might prove the first of ten or ten thousand more. Then would come the storm. Then would come the deluge that would sweep him away into a bottomless sea.

> In that moment, open gaze, pools of light,
> When I plunged into that sacred sea . . .

Rane knew that he must search for a safe memory, one that would warm his eyes and bring a comfortable smile to his face. But there were no safe memories.

> In that moment, open gaze, pools of light,
> When I plunged into that sacred sea
> Down through a bottomless pain carved joy
> To find you, wisest child of the deep . . .

In his years as the Order's foremost virtuoso of the art of memory, Rane had again and again instructed his students in the sixty-four traditional attitudes of Remembrance. There was eidetics, of course, along with olfaction and mnemonics. And fenestration, plexity and portraiture. And the new attitudes such as hologic and inherence, which he and a few other mavericks had pioneered and elaborated – but which the masters of his discipline had yet to accept as part of the remembrancers' canon. How many ways were there, really, to remember?

As he tried to find his voice and to address the multitudes, he looked down in horror at the coffin. How had it become spotted with so many bits of scarlet? He realized that he had gripped the fire rose's stem with such force that one of its thorns had ripped through his glove and punctured his palm. The glove's soft leather had soaked through with blood, which continued to drip down upon the coffin. One of the drops seemed to take a million years to freeze into a little ruby. In this foreverness of time, he felt himself pulled into a frozen moment. He heard once again Maria sobbing, and he saw her biting her lip. A drop of blood welled up from it – a single drop of red blood that rolled onto the white snow beneath her. It stained the world's whiteness in a haemorrhage that swelled out and out, engulfing the snow-shagged mountains, sweeping across the sea's ice and colouring crimson all that he looked upon, without and within.

'No!'

He could never, though, keep this memory from coming. He kept gazing down at the coffin. Beads of blood rolled down its smooth shatterwood and fell through the air like a red rain. They melted little holes through the ice – and burned a hole straight through him. He felt one bit of blood quivering inside, down beneath his heart, all hot and vital and sweet with something purely and only of Maria. With all the terrible urge of an embryo to quicken and take hold, it sprang into life, and it grew and grew and grew.

Maria.

He tried to keep her from taking hold of *him*. How could he bear such a gentle but ultimately cruel touch? How could he let her make him so bone-meltingly weak?

Maria, now fully formed, stood with him on the ice beside the coffin. Her eyes were like dark, deep wells.

'You mustn't blame yourself,' she said to him in a voice as warm as liquefied pearls.

'Why, Maria?'

'Because I have enough blame for both of us.'

At this, he pressed his palm to the cut above his eye and slowly shook his head.

'You mustn't try to keep me either,' she told him. 'The Maria you have made.'

'But I haven't—'

'You know who I really am.'

'No, I don't—'

'You know *where* I am,' she said. 'Come find me.'

She reached out to embrace him. She pulled him into the softness of her breasts and her belly, and into the glory of her black hair. He could not tell where his flesh ended and the substance of her being began. Her heart beat too fast, as one with his, and her throat caught with desperate words as she began to sob.

'Maria – why are you crying?'

He almost knew why, could almost feel the answer to this question calling to him in a strangle of voice and breath as she sobbed and sobbed and sobbed. Then his belly seized up with a sickening tremor. It clutched at him deep inside, all the way up through his heart and his throat. All that kept it from breaking out into a sob of his own was his stony will – and against the ocean he now felt boiling through his eyes, that was no will at all.

No – leave me alone!

How many ways were there to forget? Few among the normally memoried appreciated the importance of forgetting. For in the same way a dreamer could become trapped within a nightmare, a remembrancer could become lost in a hell of images, smells, and sounds. The words of a poem might devour one's consciousness. The murmured endearments of an *amorata* could build into a raucous and infinitely looping song that could bounce back and forth between the bones of the skull, pounding at the mind and making a man mad. As he often had, Rane summoned within himself a great blue star. The Architects of one of the Cybernetic churches, defeated in the War in Heaven, had learned how to detonate the galaxy's stars into supernovae, and so had created that hellish, blasted-out region of the galaxy known as the Vild. Rane took his inspiration from them. He applied the entire force of his mind, all the great gravity of his will, toward making this star collapse upon itself. Its swirling plasma began to fuse with what would become in moments a hundred billion degrees of heat. Then, as it had a thousand times, the star rebounded in an explosion of fire and light.

'Maria.'

This trick of his should have been enough to blast Maria from his memory: the flush of her lips; the golden tones of her hands; the sable softness of her eyes. She had been made of so many bright colours! Her whole being had blazed like a rainbow lighting up the sky. He needed to burn all that away, every bit of her. He needed to burn away the longing that bound him to such beauty. Most of all, he needed to annihilate the deep, delightful feeling that Maria had been made for *him*, that the underlying purpose of the universe was to bring to everyone a bright and bottomless joy.

He expected this proven remembrancing technique to result in quiet, calm, the cessation of motion that is absolute cold. Not nothingness, exactly, but rather that pure and perfect neverness underlying time and pain and all created things. The Buddhists, of course, for ages had tried to describe the indescribable quality they called Emptiness. The ancient Kristians had spoken of the

'peace that passeth understanding'.' Rane dreaded the impulse
to entertain such religious fancies. He just wanted *peace* – whatever that really was. When the blinding brilliance subsided, an
afterimage of charred skin and melted-out eyes remained for a
moment to grieve him. Then that, too, faded away. He found
himself standing alone behind Maria's coffin – standing and
staring down at the drops of blood that still stained it.

'Maria,' he whispered, calling out to the wind.

Did memory record reality or remake it? Did a man make
memories of his life or did memories make a man? How many
stars could he explode before he destroyed the very best part of
himself?

Maria.

He looked up and out at Sunjay, at Chandra and at Bardo
and all the others still waiting for him to speak. In the vast
silence that fell upon the Hollow Fields, he tried to project his
voice out to all of them.

Leave me alone!

Finally, it began to rain. This seemed to him impossible on
such a frozen winter day – until he realized that the drops of
water pouring down upon the coffin had their source in his
blurry eyes. Who could hold very much of it? Who could hold
such a volatile substance *within*?

Finally, too, he found his voice, raspy and too deeply pitched
though it might be. He looked out over the coffin at Kolenya
Mor, who stood gazing at him as she wept along with him.
Bardo, next to her, did likewise, for he had always been a watery
man, and so did Sunjay and Chandra and others of the *Asta
Siluuna* whom Rane had instructed. Many, many people wept
that day, too many to count. They wept for Maria, he thought,
a woman so beautiful that she could have caused the sky itself
to break open and weep.

> In that time of no time, perfect and clear,
> When I walked with you
> Through a bright infinity in marvel
> Of seeing myself in you seeing me . . .

How could he tell them the most basic thing about Maria,
the wondrous thing that no poem could ever evoke? How could

he convey his sense that she had conceived of *herself* as a kind of poem, that the highest of all arts is self-creation? And that what she had wanted to create was a woman utterly faithful to life, a woman so full of praise and splendour that the earth's flowers and trees and stones would sing her into life again and again for a million years, long after mere human beings had grown into gods and had forgotten who she really was.

'Maria,' he finally called out with a cry of anguish and wrath, 'cannot be here!'

He tightened his belly in an attempt to still the tremors ripping through him. A thousand people, it seemed, gazed at him in confusion – and with confidence that he would soon make sense of this strange protestation. They waited for him to speak of Maria, to tell them comfortable and good things about her so that they could feel comfortable and good about themselves. The tide of great emotion flowing across the Hollow Fields suddenly angered him. It reminded him of the sentiments that Ringism's mass gatherings and rituals had unleashed. Why couldn't these believers of miraculous things *really* believe? Why did the faithful followers of a religion that preached a personal evolution into infinite possibilities refuse to accept the wild chance that Maria might somehow remain alive?

'She cannot be here!' he told them.

And with that, he made his bloodied hand into a fist. He brought it down upon the coffin with so much force that it seemed the shatterwood might be riven into splinters. Kolenya and his other friends stared at him in dismay, and everyone seemed stunned.

'She cannot be here!' he shouted out a third time.

Decent, Kolyena had called him, and noble and sensitive. Maria had thought him kind. Again his fist crashed down against the coffin. How he despised both decency and decorum – and all other such civilized traits! A wild man he really was! A man of both passion and pride!

'There are a thousand dead men and women here today!' he said. His arm swept out across the Hollow Fields. 'Children, too – all dead! Go mourn one of them!'

As a wave of shock spread over friends who thought they had known Thomas Rane, he felt sick at what he had said. But it was too late to unsay it. So it always was. Through the mysterious power of time, which moved in one direction only, the impulses and acts of the present became frozen in a bitter past that might be remembered but never changed.

And so Rane bit back his remorse, and he whirled about with a wrenching pivot of his neck and his hips. He strode off across the ice. He walked as quickly as his shaking legs would carry him. So startling had his outburst been, so filled with a fearful aloofness, that no one dared to follow him.

It seemed that he walked for hours. He walked through icy air that cut his face and through a grief that cut much deeper. He walked and walked, and he found himself moving east toward Mount Urkel. At last he reached the edge of the Hollow Fields, where its runs, glissades and acres of ice come up against the base of the great mountain. He started stumbling up its frozen slopes. He pushed his numbed feet against rocks and wind-packed snow. He wanted to climb and climb forever, to climb right up to the peak of the mountain and then off into the coldness of empty space. But he had no strength left for such an escape. Soon he collapsed against a snow-packed boulder in sheer exhaustion.

Only then did he turn and look back at the Hollow Fields. The many funerals held that day must have concluded, for the hundreds of groups of mourners gathered around the individual coffins had broken up. Men, women, and children, holding hands, now formed themselves into a great circle many miles in circumference. At its centre stood the sunship. He couldn't make out the long box containing Maria's effects, of course, for all the coffins had been loaded in the ship's hold.

Come find me.

He listened as the wind whipped at his face and whispered to him. He could almost see Maria standing next to the ship far below him. He needed to ask her a question: a single, simple question. Why, he wondered, could he not recall the answer to it? To forget what he wished to forget when he needed to forget it was necessary, if he was to remain sane and alive. To forget those things most vital and dear to him was a sacrilege of his soul.

Come find me!

'All right,' he said, 'I will.'

He waited a long time for the rockets to explode into life.

Gouts of orange and red gases roiled out in a cloud of flame that nearly enveloped the ship. At last, it rose an inch into the air. And then two inches, and then twenty more as the ship accelerated toward its eventual velocity of many miles per second. Soon the ship streaked like a diamond needle up through the atmosphere. In how many seconds would this quickly shrinking bit of matter pierce the blackness of space? How many thousands of seconds more would it take for the ship to reach the corona of the Star of Neverness and then pierce through to its fiery heart?

And how long would it be, Rane wondered, before the star's fusing hydrogen vaporized diamond and shatterwood in a hellish blaze of annihilation – and the ship and all its contents were no more?

3

The days following the funeral grew shorter and the nights longer as deep winter darkened toward its coldest part. Rane tried to isolate himself inside his chalet in the Pilots' Quarter overlooking the ocean. For decades, this heap of cold stone had been a place to work and eat and sleep but never a home. Then Maria had come to live with him. She had relished sitting by the big bay windows and looking out at the colourful sails of the ice schooners that raced across the frozen Sound. Sometimes she drank her coffee and wrote her poems; sometimes she played her bamboo shakuhachi, perhaps in emulation of Danlo wi Soli Ringess, who had inspired many to take up this ancient and difficult instrument. A radiant music had often brightened his house's contemplativeness – even as Maria had taken charge of brightening his life. Rane recalled how she had overcome his reluctance to let her decorate his austere rooms. One evening, he had returned from the Academy to find rich, red carpets lining the cold wooden floors. Maria had festooned the walls with tondos and tapestries, and had filled the sunroom with blue vases full of freshly cut fireflowers. And she had said to him with great delight: 'See how beautiful our house is!'

So irresistible was her happiness that he had not been able to refuse her, any more than he could refuse the rising of the sun. And she had known that her enthusiasm would melt away his obduracy, that her desire would dissolve his dislike of the new – and perhaps, through that strange alchemy of endearment that he both feared and longed for, transmute it into a golden enthusiasm of his own. That was one of the most amazing things about her, he thought, that her essential innocence somehow fused with a deep, deep knowingness. Indeed, in a way that he still could not understand, her shrewd insight into him had seemed to flow *from* a pure and perfectly simple source.

Now, of course, the tapestries and the tondos (all save one), along with the dreammakers and the Darghinni sculpture and the other things piled into the coffin, were burning up in Neverness's sun. Rane might have welcomed the return of his house to its old severity if not for the fact that nothing had really changed. For he could still see Maria's favourite tapestry, the sheen of white and blue woven wool that had hung on the wall above the bed. With an immense clarity, he could still make out the warp and woof of each individual fibre. Even as he could still *see* Maria and him twined together on that bed. Such sights finally drove him away from the fire's crackle and heat out into the cold. He needed to rip himself free from the past, even as he did not dare to think about the future. And so he sought out blood-pounding experiences that forced him into a total consciousness of the present: he journeyed to the far side of Neverness Island and skied alone through the forests where snow tigers prowled; he climbed unroped the great icefalls above the Elf Gardens; he took flimsy schooners too far out into the emptiness of the frozen sea. For many, many sun-filled days, he found a strange peace in the terror of imminent violence.

Inevitably, however, at the fall of dusk, he had to return to his chalet. Then, at night, with the sound of the shakuhachi echoing off the bare walls, Maria came for him. She haunted his dreams and slipped down next to him beneath the soft furs of memory. Her hands caressed every part of him; her fingers locked with his fingers, and her heart beat close to his. When he awoke sweating in the middle of the night, he could feel her warm, sweet lips pressing her breath into him.

Here I am!

There came a moment in life, he thought, when a man had to accept the truth he heard whispering inside or he must abandon the purpose of that life. And more, accepting it, he must affirm it and act upon it. So it came to be that after many days of venturing into the borderlands of death, he decided to seek a more perilous thing. He put away his ice axe and his spiked crampons and his skis. He strapped on his skates, and he went out into the streets to look for Maria.

On the first day of this new quest – or to be more precise, a new phase of a lifelong pursuit – he ranged the city from the Tycho's Green and the Ring of Fire down along the Serpentine, where that great boulevard of orange ice twists west past the Hollow Fields and cuts through the Farsider's Quarter. He took in the sight of wormrunners hawking Yarkonan bluestars in the Diamond District and the aroma of caramelized sugar-cakes that the alien Friends of Man liked to eat. These furry evangelists sang to the many passers-by in sprays of rank speech molecules, even as long-fingered minstrels from Kittery plucked the strings of their gosharps and made a more apprehensible music. Rane might have paused to listen to their ancient ballads, if not for the pull of an even more timeless song that he heard sounding upon the air from somewhere deeper into Neverness.

He had no idea, really, where Maria might be – or how he might go about finding her. He spent hours skating randomly, picking his way around the Winter Ring, then venturing up to the East-West Sliddery and over to the Long Glissade. He made excursions down side streets in the Ashtoreth District, packed with young astrier women doing their daily marketing at shops selling exotic fruits from a dozen planets, cultured meats, and freshly baked bread. In the faces of all of them, he looked for a certain flash of dark eyes and an exact curve of lips. He looked and he looked, and he skated and skated. The sharp steel of his blades cut into the streets with a clacking pressure that melted watery grooves in the very cold ice upon which he glided. After a while, the colours of the slidderies, the glidderies, and the glissades coalesced into a fabric as seamless and multihued as the scarf tied around his neck. When he skated at speed, it flapped in the wind and streamed out behind him like a banner. When he made his way more slowly through the multitudes crowding the Great Circle near the Hyacinth Gardens, the scarf gathered about his cheeks and mouth, and filled the air with Maria's scent.

How to describe this singular scent which burned straight up his nose and seemed to ignite each cell of his body? Impossibly sweet it was, yet not cloying, like the too-thick aroma of a roasting sugar-cake. Arousing it was, yet it did not incite sickening lusts as did the erotic perfumes; rather, it infused the blood with a deeper drive. Intoxicating he found it, too, yet drinking in Maria's essence in no way stupefied him but somehow made him more clear-headed and awake.

The sense that Maria would leave some telltale of her presence in the streets – as she left an indelible delight on those who had known her – drew him on and on. Inevitably, the fragrance wafting off the scarf swept him into the remembrancing attitude that he called olfaction. The human brain's biology connected smell to memory, for the olfactory bulb had evolved in close association with both the emotion-laden amygdala and the hippocampus, which mediated the recall of moments long lost to time. Thus a hint of cinnamon infusing the scarf's fibres caused Rane to remember a day in deep winter when Maria had been sipping from a cup of cinnamon coffee in the Hofgarten. At a nearby table, a visitor from Summerworld had voiced concern over the extraordinary dangers to be found in Neverness: for each year when the bad storms came, a number of people made wrong turns on the streets and became lost in the blinding snow. The howling wind obliterated their cries for help. They quickly weakened and died of the cold – sometimes within yards of a building in which they might have taken shelter. The snow buried them beneath drifts that didn't melt until late in midwinter spring. Only then would the bodies of these 'Lost Ones' be found.

'But that is too terrible!' Maria had protested. 'The most terrible way to die, I think.'

Rane had often wondered what Maria had meant by that. Had she merely been referring to the panic of being trapped within a cloud of devouring whiteness and the pain of freezing flesh? Or had she somehow sensed the deeper agony of lost people dying alone in darkness when someone should have come to their rescue?

Now, in the cold, cold time after Maria's funeral, after a season of many deadly storms, Rane recalled that day in the Hofgarten. He did not want to believe that Maria could have strayed off into a *sarsara*, perhaps to collapse beneath the snow-encrusted yu trees in the desolate acres of the Tycho's Green or another park. In city as old as Neverness, weren't there other ways to become lost? What if, he speculated, she had become infected with a rare memory virus used in some ancient war? What if that virus had destroyed her sense of herself, and she now wandered the city unable to remember who she really was?

Such worries caused him to think of Tamara Ten Ashtoreth. In her early career as a young courtesan, many had pursued this now-famous woman. Tamara, though, had reserved her passion for one man only, Danlo wi Soli Ringess, who had pledged himself to her. Their rare affection for each other had aroused the rancour of Hanuman li Tosh: Danlo's dearest friend and deadliest enemy. Rane recalled the story of how Tamara's memories had been destroyed, not by a virus, but by Hanuman. Out of jealousy and a poisoned soul, upon the pretext of recording Tamara's perceptions of the One Memory, Hanuman had fitted a mirrored metallic heaume over Tamara's head and had then proceeded to use this disguised cleansing computer to unmake all of her memories relating to Danlo. Afterwards, she had wandered through her life haunted by her total adoration of Danlo – and by her total inability to re-experience it.

Because Rane hoped that Tamara might be able to help him, he decided to call upon her. After the war, she and Danlo had taken a large chalet overlooking the Tycho's Green. The crimson ice of the gliddery fronting the house brought out the hues of the red granite and the sweeping shatterwood beams with which it had been built. It had a sunroom and a fireroom, a tea room, a music room and a huge kitchen. Five sleeping chambers, two on the first floor and three on the second, provided plenty of space for the family that Tamara and Danlo had raised. Their first child, Jonathan, had starved and died in the war, and had never known the comfort of the chalet. The three adopted girls, however – Miwa, Julia, and Ilona – had played games of hide-and-seek throughout the house for many years before developing into beautiful women and moving into their own apartments in the Old City. Sunjay and Chandra had grown up there, too, and they still came home for extended visits during the Academy's many holidays. Now, though, most of the time, only the laughter of the six-year-old Tavio filled the house's rooms with the sounds of a happy childhood – in addition to the coos and cries of the newborn Alasharia.

Tamara received Rane in the tea room, whose frosted windows afforded a view of the park's great yu trees rising up from the snow like emerald spears three hundred feet in length. She directed him toward a table set with a big white pot and little blue cups. A tall woman with blonde hair and coffee-coloured eyes, Tamara retained a voluptuousness that had once unbalanced Hanuman li Tosh. Rane held in his mind's eye a clear picture of the younger Tamara, and he thought that her beauty, like the flush of a red yu berry, had only richened and deepened over time.

She seemed as well to radiate an ever-intensifying sexuality. The loose sable gown she wore did nothing to cover or contain it. From where, he wondered, did this magical heat arise? Did it result from her long practice of ancient arts designed to excite the fires of pure consciousness bound into the body's billions of cells? Or did it have more to do with her union with Danlo and its consequent triumph: Sunjay and Chandra, Tavio and Alasharia, the children called the *Asta Siluuna* who had taken life out of a blaze of cosmic couplings and who had given the blind, orgiastic power of the sexual instinct both purpose and a gloriously awakened new form?

Whatever the source of Tamara's allure, Rane could not doubt his good fortune in being able to enjoy it in person. The wife of Mallory Ringess's son had to be careful whom she admitted into her house. And in any case, since Alasharia's birth she had seen few visitors. As she sat opposite Rane at the table and poured him a cup of jasmine tea, she cradled her baby in her arm and apologized for missing Maria's funeral.

'I wanted very badly to say goodbye with everyone else,' she explained, 'but with Shara only three days old, I couldn't take her out in such cold weather.'

Rane looked at the sleeping baby, whose tiny black-haired head rested against Tamara's belly. He sipped from the cup of tea, so hot that it burned his lip. To Tamara, he said, 'I'm glad you decided to stay home.'

Had she heard the story of how he had scandalized Maria's friends with his outrage and his howl of denial of Maria's fate? How could she *not* have heard?

'Bardo,' she said, 'told me that you haven't been home very often since the funeral. He's concerned about you.'

He thought of the snow tiger that had surprised him in the rolling forest east of Mount Atakel: the way that the animal had appeared like a ghost upon the snow and had crouched and quivered as it fixed him with its great, golden eyes. Why, he wondered, had the tiger not sprung upon him?

'I've been very busy,' he said.

'I'm glad that you could come by today. It's been too long.'

How long had it been since he had last seen Tamara? A year? Two years? He thought that it might have been as long as seven years, when she had been pregnant with Tavio.

'I'd forgotten,' he said, 'how much I enjoy having tea with you.'

She smiled as if he had made a little joke, as if it was impossible that he could ever forget anything. 'It's too bad that Danlo couldn't have been home, too. I'm sure he'd like to see you.'

Where was Danlo? Rane wondered. For years, he had frequently left Neverness on journeys across the ocean to the islands of the west where the Alaloi people built houses of snow and hunted seals for food in their devotion to living lives as purely and simply as they could. A generation earlier, however, their primeval innocence had come to an end when an ancient virus called the 'Slow Evil' infected them. The tiny munition engineered long ago on Yarkona during the War of the Faces had awakened in people a terrible frothing fever that savaged human flesh. It reduced strong men and women to bleeding skeletons, and had wiped out the whole Devaki tribe. Danlo had made missions to the surviving tribes to teach them how to control the virus and keep it from exploding through the cells of their bodies.

'Is he back with the Alaloi?' Rane asked.

Tamara took a long sip of tea but did not answer his question.

'I'd heard that the *Snowy Owl*,' Rane said, speaking of Danlo's lightship, 'remains in Neverness. So he can't be out in the stars.'

Her full lips broke into a smile that hinted of secrets and mysteries. 'You know how Danlo is. He comes and goes, like the wind.'

'That must be hard for you. It's not every man who goes off to become a god.'

She set her cup down into its saucer with just a little too much force. The hard ceramic sent a ringing tone out into the air.

'But what does that *mean*, to become a god?' she asked.

'Who really knows? That's a question for the eschatologists.'

'Who study these things as astronomers look up through their telescopes at the stars.'

'I'm sure they would be happy to study Danlo in the flesh if he would stay in one place long enough to talk to them.'

Her mouth filled with a musical laughter, and she said, 'They might as well try to lay hold of the wind.'

'Can you blame them? They know something happened to Danlo. And continues to happen with his children.'

He glanced at Alasharia, sleeping beneath the shelter of Tamara's large breasts. Tamara looked down, too, then back up at him.

'Danlo,' she told him, 'is a *man*. Totally and beautifully a man. Like the first man, I think, the first true man. A man as men should be.'

Her voice vibrated with a rare combination of passion, gratitude, and contentment. It resonated with the quiet anguish knotted up in his own throat. Maria, he remembered, had once spoken with a similar adoration of him.

'You used to talk about that,' he said. 'There was that night at Bardo's house, at the joyance on the eighty-first of false winter. It was snowing, the kind of light, fluffy snow that Danlo calls *soreesh*. We stood next to one of the diamond windows, drinking wine and watching it come down. And you told about your order's secrets, what your Society of Courtesans had been teaching for ten thousand years.'

'And what did I tell you?'

'Do you want the exact words?'

'Do you have them?'

'Yes, I do.' Then he drew in a breath and quoted: '"Each cell of the body has its own consciousness, a cellular consciousness of electron transport chains and protein synthesis and DNA. The whole past and all the memories of the future are bound into the DNA. We call that the 'Sleeping God'. And we can wake it up. We can wake up, and through consciousness will our own evolution."'

She held him in the softness of her gaze as she waited for him to say more.

'You told me this, too,' he added: '"Someday, perhaps

farwhen, perhaps tomorrow, man and woman will come together to give birth to the first truly human being."'

She seemed to drink in his words the way that some people listened to music. Light danced in her eyes. Her excitement must have communicated to Alasharia, for the baby stirred and let out a couple of low, urgent cries. Almost without thinking, Tamara loosened the fold of her gown and freed one of her milk-swollen breasts. The baby's lips locked around the brown aureole and nipple, and she began nursing. With each hungry gulp, a murmur of contentment sounded from deep within her throat.

'She looks like you,' Rane said. 'And Danlo, too – she has so much *animajii*.'

'Would you like to hold her?'

Rane sat shaking his head as if her words made no sense to him. 'Oh, no, I couldn't, she's so little and I've never—'

Tamara, however, had already pushed her chair back from the table and stood up. She took a step toward Rane, disengaging Alasharia from her breast as she did so. With great gentleness – but also with an insistence that could not be denied – she lowered Alasharia toward him. He had no choice but to reach out and take the baby in his arms.

'She's so light!'

The whole of Alasharia's body moulded to his forearm, with the nape of her neck fitted into the crook of his elbow. She seemed as weightless as *soreesh* snow. And yet he could feel her heart beating against his arm veins like the pulsing of a hot, massive star.

'What a beautiful child!' he said softly.

Alasharia's perfectly formed head, covered with a dark down, turned toward him, and he couldn't help smiling at her. As babies often were, she seemed possessed of great presence and sense of being. He could feel her bright eyes looking right into him. He could see her astonishment at seeing the world, newly, as well as her infinite gratitude at *getting* to see it. And more, her gladness of just being alive. And she had, he thought, no self-consciousness of this grace – not this perfect, bright, little Buddha baby.

When he could bear it no longer, he indicated that Tamara should retrieve Alasharia. For a moment, it seemed that Tamara would deepen her cruelty toward him by making him hold the child all morning. Finally, though, Tamara relented. She took her daughter back into her arms, sat down, and resumed nursing.

'That night at Bardo's house,' he managed to say, looking back at Tamara, 'you talked about a new symmetry of the body and mind that people dared not dream of. A new purpose for the human race.'

'I did say that, didn't I?' She enunciated these words as if trying to convince herself that she had. 'It would have been something that I would have said.'

'You don't remember?'

'You're the one who can capture the past so perfectly.'

'Yes,' he said with a fierce curve of his lips, 'I'm Thomas Rane, aren't I?'

At this, Tamara returned his smile, but with compassion replacing the irony.

'You teach my children,' she said. 'You taught me.'

'Did I? I thought perhaps it was Danlo who really did.'

'Well, in a way, he's taught me everything.' Her smile flowed upon her face with all the ease of the summer sea and seemed to invite him into its warmth. 'But you're not speaking of *those* things, are you?'

Again, he looked down at the baby, then back up at Tamara. 'That day when the war ended, in Hanuman's sanctuary, something happened to Danlo, didn't it? And in the days that followed, something happened to *you.*'

'Many things happened to me,' she said.

'Somehow,' he continued, 'you remembered. All that Hanuman had taken from you, the memories that had been annihilated – were somehow restored.'

'Why should that be such a mystery?'

'*Why?*' he breathed out. 'What could be more mysterious than memory?'

'What I mean is: why should that be such a mystery to *you?*'

She went on to speak of the One Memory, which the remembrancers had sought like a holy grail for ten thousand years. She related this conception to the ancient Hindu philosophy of *Samkhaya* and the idea that all human knowledge – and indeed, the whole history and experience of the cosmos – was bound into a non-material intrinsicality called the Akashic Records. Over the millennia, she said, many times and in many places, people had elaborated and transfigured their intuition that the essence of existence should be forever preserved. The Kristians of the Society of Kristoman the God had cherished their notion of heaven and the resurrection of dead, decayed bodies into glorious, golden forms. The mechanics had their Unified Field; the Librarians of Babel believed that the story of all creation had been written in an uncountable and uncollectable number of 'books'; the Architects of the Cybernetic Universal Church saw every bit of matter as part of an infinite computer that stored each quantum event in spacetime as pure information. Even the archaic Australians, long, long ago on Old Earth, had dwelled in their *Altjiranga Mitjina*, the Dreamtime, in which the eternal era of their ancestors and their waking dreams became as one.

Tamara, of course, did not tell Rane anything fundamentally new or that he did not already know. But she told it in a way that enchanted him. She had a rare talent for weaving together arcana and the long-accepted canon of the Order into a beautiful tapestry of ideas that seemed to come alive with new meaning. And more, she had her art of embodying the ideal in the intensely physical and even the carnal: her hands made a dance of emphasis and nuance to the accompanying music of her words even as her eyes caught him up in her passion for intelligent conversation. She conveyed her experience of intellectual excitement in quick, in-drawn breaths that lifted up her breasts and seemed to send a burst of energy down her spine into her belly and loins with so great a heat that he could almost feel it, too. Aside from her mastery of all matters sexual, this fire for true learning was the first of the qualities that had made her a great courtesan, for she had always been able to engage minds with the most erudite of academicians as a prelude to a deeper joining of beings.

As well, she had another purpose in charming and singing him into her web of words. She wanted to remind him of his place in a great and age-old journey.

'No one,' she told him, 'has explored the One Memory with your power of perception. No one has understood it as have you.'

'And yet I do not *really* understand it.'

'You are the greatest remembrancer the Order has ever seen.'

'So they say. And yet Danlo has had the greatest remembrance.'

'But how could one possibly measure such things?'

'By their result. Look at Danlo. Look at you.'

At this, her lips broke into a smile that seemed to say: 'Look at you, too!'

'I know,' he said, 'that Danlo helped you recover the memories that Hanuman destroyed. But they weren't *really* destroyed, were they?'

'Can the universe itself be destroyed?'

'Perhaps,' he said, 'you should be teaching remembrancing to me.'

Her eyes seemed to search his eyes for the chasm that led down through darkness into a raging sea. She spoke soft words to him then. 'No, you are the Remembrancer. You teach my children – the other children, too. It's you who will find the way into the One Memory and show it to everyone else.'

She said this with an unshakeable certainty, as if stating an episteme or a prophecy that could not be circumvented. That was her gift and her grace, her most profound quality, the way she could make a man feel *valuable*. It partook of a primeval eros that transcended the sexual. Something within her called to the deepest part of him. He felt it as a fundamental force validating all that he was, wanting and needing him – and thus fusing his purpose with the universal urge to bring into the world something marvellous and utterly new.

'If I do find my way,' he said to her, 'it will only be with your help.'

'But how can I help you?'

'The One Memory,' he told her, 'is like a dark continent. Few can journey there. Fewer can find their way to return in complete possession of their senses. And yet you came back with a buried treasure.'

She nodded her head slowly, then closed her eyes. After many moments, she said, 'It *is* like a dark continent – so totally, totally dark. Like a dark *world*, lost in the emptiness of the Adal Vun where there are no stars. And yet somehow, at the centre of that world is the sun itself. If you look for it, really look, its radiance blazes up through earth. The light touches everything. Everything comes alive. It's all golden and impossibly bright, and everywhere there are diamonds – and rubies and sapphires and pearls. All the treasure we bury when we forget. Or, I think, when we die. It's all there, waiting to be found.'

As she fell into silence, he gazed at the black pearl that hung on a twining of black hair that circled her neck. He thought of Maria, lost in a desolation of her own and perhaps adrift on the frigid streets of Neverness – even as he sat by a nice fire enjoying the sweetness of jasmine tea and a little conversation. Could what Tamara had just told him, he wondered, be true? How could it *not* be true?

'I think that Danlo,' he told her, 'is a better teacher than I could ever be.'

'No, that's not so – he does not have your mastery of the remembrancing techniques that people will need.'

She articulated the word 'technique', however, as he might speak of the ratio of gears in one of the old Timekeeper's clocks or the thrust delivered by the burning of so many grams of hydrogen in a fusion rocket.

'But people,' he muttered, 'need more than just techniques, don't they?'

Her eyes flashed with an intense radiance. 'I didn't say that.'

'You say it in the way you look at me. You say it in what you don't say.'

She shook her head sadly, then turned away from him to fix her attention on her nursing baby. After a while, she picked up her cup and pressed its blue rim to her lips. Finally, she told him, 'Maria once said that you helped her remember moments from her childhood that she had thought forever lost. So many moments, so much joy. She said that you even brought her back to her birth – and that she was born laughing.'

'Maria said that?'

'Yes, she did. She said that she came to Neverness because she had heard of the Way of Ringess and a great remembrancer who could teach people to know who they really are.'

A tightness in her throat alerted him to an ache in his own. Who *was* Maria, really? Did she really still live? Did she still laugh, know happiness, cry out in delight? Or did she cringe in some abandoned building in the Farsider's Quarter like a frightened animal lost in an incomprehensible darkness? Or worse, did she remember the other moments and *the* moment, that terrible moment of frozen tears and blood and dead white flesh? A time not for laughing at all, but only for sobbing and sobbing and sobbing . . .

'Maria,' he said, 'wanted never to forget a single thing.'

'How should she?'

'How should she *not*?' Then, as Tamara's baby stopped nursing with a smack of lips breaking suction, he added, 'You should know. When your memories returned, all these diamonds and rubies, were there not firestones among them? Did they not burn you with their flames?'

She draped a towel over her shoulder and lifted up Alasharia in order to pat a few burps out of her. She studied him with a practised sympathy to what a man or a woman really wanted.

'Why do you ask now about matters we might have discussed years ago?'

'I've only recently realized what must have happened to you.'

'But you must have suspected?'

'Even if I did, some things require the passage of time before people can gracefully speak of them.'

'You are too kind. And too, too sensitive.'

'Only a few,' he murmured, 'have ever said that of me.'

'What's wrong, Rane?'

He watched her hand beating gently against the baby's back, and she watched him. What could he say to her? How could he admit that he hoped find Maria wandering the city's darkest streets – or perhaps even the abandoned alleys of the mind? That he *did* dream of laughing with her again? And yet how could he deny what Tamara so obviously perceived glistering behind the frosted windows of his eyes?

'You see,' he said softly, 'I have buried gems of my own.'

While still holding the baby to her shoulder, Tamara reached out to touch his hand. Her fingers slipped down to the inside of his wrist. She seemed to search in his pulse for a warmth that the cold set of his face usually concealed.

Finally, she told him, 'The firestones *do* burn. But they also give such a bright, bright light.'

'Could that really be true?'

'Danlo once said that suffering carves hollows in the soul that leave room for more joy.'

'I don't like to think,' he said, 'of what Danlo suffered.'

'Sometimes I can't think of anything else.'

'I don't like to think of what he suffered over *you*.'

She bent down her head to kiss Alasharia's temple. Then she cast him a long, deep, beautiful smile.

'When the memories returned,' she said as if his words had set off an avalanche of revelation, 'at first I couldn't bear some of them. When I'd met Danlo, I still had my duties as a courtesan, you know. I still had to be with other men, sometimes with women, even though I wanted to *be* only with Danlo. It's *hard* to be a courtesan. Sometimes, it almost killed me. And yet, how should I have wanted to forget this pain, as its poignance only made me more aware of what Danlo and I had together?'

What, Rane asked himself, had Maria and he had together? How could he ever be sure?

'In a way,' Tamara continued, 'what Hanuman did to me is not so different from what some courtesans and many women in the streets and brothels do to themselves.'

'What is that?'

'You really don't know?'

'I'm sorry,' he said, 'but I have little experience of that world.'

'Sometimes,' she said, 'a woman does need to forget – or she feels that she does. After a bad night, or a bad man, she will drink a nepenthe to wipe out the sensations and to forget.'

'Nepenthes,' he said, speaking in his professional capacity, 'are dangerous. Very dangerous.'

'Some men are very bad – very, very bad. The procurers down near the Slizzaring. The wormrunners who kidnap women off the streets.'

Tamara's sad, simple statement sent a burst of adrenaline shooting through him. 'What do you mean, they kidnap them?'

'They take them and imprison them. In the secret brothels.'

'What?'

'How is it that you who know so much do not know this?'

Who, he wondered, *would* want to know such a thing? How could he reconcile his need to idealize Neverness as the City of Light with the dark reality of sexual slavery?

'Some wormrunners,' she said, 'actually force their women to take nepenthes. Not as a kindness. They do not want them talking about what goes on inside the brothels.'

The adrenaline caused his heart to pound in quick, painful

beats. 'How is it that you know so much about these criminals and their crimes?'

'It's more than just a crime. The wormrunners, the worst of the worst, force the women to be with the *Gorgorim*.'

Rane, who knew a million words in fifty languages, said, 'I am not familiar with that term.'

'*Gorgorim* – the Horrible Ones. Men who have sculpted their bodies into the forms of beasts. Derelicts. Lepers. Hibakusha. The autists, with their filthy clothes and their lice. Men with whom no woman would willingly consort for any amount of money. Sometimes, they are not even men.'

'What do you mean?'

'Sometimes, in the brothels south of the Slizzaring, some of the *Gorgorim* are aliens.'

His eyes filled with so great a pounding pressure that he could hardly see.

'Aliens! Which aliens?'

'Does that matter? The Elidi. The Darakhun. Sometimes, rarely, one of the ronin Fravashi. Even the Scutari, if that can be believed.'

Rane recalled his first sight of one of the cannibalistic Scutari, with its white, wormlike coils and dark red mating claw. The adrenaline poisoning his blood sent the organs of his body into sickening paroxysms. Wrath grieved his brain; spleen burned through his belly; his throat choked with the bitter taste of hot, black bile.

'That cannot be!' he called out.

But he knew enough about human beings to know that it *must* be.

'And you tell me this,' he continued, 'to persuade me that we should cherish even the horrible memories?'

'No, not just. Maria and I talked about this, once. I can't help thinking of what she said.'

'About those aliens?'

'About *you*.' She drew in a long breath as she met eyes with him. 'When things became difficult for you and Maria, she said that consorting with a Scutari was just about the worst thing in the universe that she could think of – but that it was nothing next to the pain of losing you.'

Now he could see nothing at all. Or rather, he could see only one thing, a darkness so completely black that it formed inside him with a substantiality more tangible and real than that of teacups or fireflowers or any other fashion of matter. It gathered in the soft centres of Maria's eyes as she looked at him so desperately and hopefully, and never stopped looking and looking and looking . . .

'She would never,' Tamara said, 'have wanted me to tell you something like that. But now that she's gone, I had to.'

'*Is* she gone?' he said.

She stared deep into him, and then spoke of her firstborn son, many years dead: 'During the worst part of the War, when Jonathan's feet froze, the cutter had to amputate them to save his life. Surely you have cut out the memory of Maria's death to save yourself.'

'No, I—'

'You found her dead in the snow.'

'People say that, people who sit safe and warm indoors and couldn't possibly know.

'You helped place her body in the coffin.'

'Everyone tells me I did, to spare me.'

'To spare you what? What could be worse than the pain of losing someone you love?'

'The pain of hope,' he said.

To distract himself from Tamara's gaze, he picked up his cup and took another sip of tea. Its steamy scent overpowered the much fainter jasmine fragrance bound up in Maria's scarf. With each breath that he drew in, he felt more and more certain that Maria could not possibly be gone.

'I should leave,' he said. He set his cup down against the hard table. He tried to smile as Alasharia, up near Tamara's neck, fastened her tiny fingers in her mother's hair. 'You must have things to do – but thank you for talking with me.'

'Are you going home? You *should* go home and rest.'

Where was he going? he wondered. He recalled the words of an ancient poet, lost to history, who had written these lines:

Where are we going?
Always home . . .

He pushed back his chair and stood up so abruptly that the force of his feet against the wooden floor vibrated the table and caused the teacups to rattle. Somehow, he thought, Tamara's and Maria's past confidences concerning such bizarre and horrible matters might have set into motion an even more dreadful future. Words could work as incantations; thoughts entertained too intensely could fix the mind and conjure stark realities. Maria's own will to test her compassion against human cruelty might have caused her to venture into the last place in Neverness that she would wish to be.

'Goodbye, Tamara.'

He would go down deep into the Farsider's Quarter, into the maze of streets of the Slizzaring. He could not waste another moment. If Maria had never stopped looking for the brightest part of him, how could he cease trying to find her – even if his search should lead through unknown and darkly remembered gates?

4

And so on a day of bright blue skies tinged with the auric sheen of the Golden Ring that encircled the world, Rane skated south by way of the Old City Glissade. He passed by Bardo's old mansion, with its hand-hewn stones and diamond windows. Here Rane had once led hundreds of men and women deep into the attitudes of remembrance, and the religion now called Ringism had begun. Not far from this shrine, scarcely three hundred yards down the street, he paused in front of the Light Pavilion. He watched people coming and going between the twelve great pillars that supported an immense clary dome. He and Maria had rendezvoused beneath that dome on the first of their trysts. On cloudless evenings, the forged clary let in the radiance of the stars and magnified it so that any sector of the sky that one studied opened into a whirl of constellations and a dance of light.

The Pavilion's clary had other powers. If one spoke the name of any of a thousand worlds, the dome would instantly switch perspectives and display a vista of the galaxy as seen from that world. Rane remembered standing wordless and wondering in the middle of this great show – standing so close to Maria that he could almost feel the breath that steamed out of her mouth. He stood at the centre of a golden circle of silence that encompassed Maria and him as people called out with longing the names of their birth worlds: Kittery. Vesper. Nish. Solsken. Yarkona. Urradeth. Sometimes the dome whispered names back to them. He could barely hear all these voices, for he had ears only for what Maria would say to him.

'Where were you born?' she asked him.

'Darkmoon. And you?'

'Faraway.'

'Is that a planet? Like Farfara?'

'It doesn't really matter where I was born.'

'It matters to me. Because the matter of that planet makes up *you*.'

'That's a poetic thought. I think at heart you're a poetic man.'

'I wish I were. But if I ever wrote a poem, I'd want to praise the planet that gave birth to you.'

She laughed at this and kissed him. 'I was born on Earth.'

'Earth? Which Earth? There are hundreds of them.'

'It doesn't matter,' she said again.

'But don't you want to see?'

She shook her head, and this little motion sent a wave of lustre shimmering through her dark hair. 'I know what my stars looked like. I want to know about yours.'

He took her hand, and this touch of fingers pulling at fingers thrilled his blood with a sparking fire. It passed back and forth between them with each beat of their hearts. An impossibly sweet warmth seemed to melt out his insides and fill them with something bright and good.

'I want to know about our star,' he said. He told her, so new to the city, of an old Neverness tradition: when a man and a woman felt moved to join their dreams, they would come to this place and pick out a star. Sometimes they chose one of the galaxy's double stars: Darvening or Sirius, Acrux or Shams or Eluli. When they spoke together the star's name – and spoke their own names, too – the dome would highlight the star so that it stood out in a blaze of radiance from all the others. Ever after, that star would be theirs.

'You are a romantic,' she said to him with a quick, easy laugh.

'Only with you.'

'You have so much hope.'

'Only because you make me that way.'

'Do you believe,' she asked him, 'that our future is written in the stars?'

'I believe in us,' he told her.

He told her more than that. He spoke of the distant past, faraway and long, long ago, when a certain star somewhere in the galaxy had ended its life by exploding into a supernova. The impossible heat of this conflagration had fused hydrogen into more complex forms of matter: carbon and oxygen, iron and iridium and gold – all the elements that composed Maria's and Rane's bodies.

'The stars made us,' he said. 'They destroyed themselves to become us, stars of a new kind.'

'You really *are* a romantic – and that has nothing to do with me.'

'The stars remember us,' he went on. 'And we remember them.'

Her hand tightened in his and seemed to draw him into her.

'Are these the memories of the future that you Remembrancers speak of?'

'Present, past, and future – to a star, there is no difference.'

'I want to find our star,' she said.

She told him that she wanted to journey with him to the far end of the galaxy, looking and looking for the star that they would make theirs, and theirs alone. And so they began calling out names of the constellations: old ones such as Orion and Aries, and new ones named Ahira, Kalkin, and Ars Siluun. And with each name, the dome loosed a burst of light as stars flared into prominence and they fell across the Milky Way. Star after star illumed the clary, in streamers of white, orange or red flames that swirled around each other. In this way, standing hand in hand and giving voice to their secret hopes, they searched for a long time. Finally, in the blazing deeps out beyond the Morbio Superiore, they came to a little-known star that the dome named as Jerushin.

'Oh, look at that one!' she said. 'It is very beautiful, no?'

'Beautiful, yes,' he said, looking up.

The two suns orbited a common centre in the space between them: spheres of brilliant blue doing a cosmic, fiery dance. They whirled so quickly around each other that all the other stars in the galaxy spun off into emptiness.

'Are they taken?' she asked. 'I couldn't bear it if they were taken.'

Rane said a few words, and the dome informed them that the star remained unclaimed.

'May we rename it?' she asked. 'It's the star of our souls, and I think it should have a new name.'

Rane closed his eyes as he looked into his memory. He searched through the words of the impossible language called Tlönish for one that could be approximated in sounds that Maria's lips and tongue could shape.

'Let's call it Val Adamah,' he said.

'Val Adamah,' she repeated.

She raised up his hand and pressed it against her breast. They spoke inviolate words to each other then. With the star raining its blue light upon them, they promised always to remind each other who they really were and what they were made of. They promised, too, to create something new together, something marvellous and bright that had never existed anywhere in the universe. They pledged themselves in fire, fire feeding fire, to breathe life into their secret dreams. The clary above them blazed with the incandescence of their star, but they had no care for this little miracle of technology. Through the dazzling domes of each other's eyes, they looked for a deeper kind of splendour.

Later that evening, after they had lain together and spun sparks of joy into the night, she began writing him the first of many poems:

Star of my soul,
How you shimmer
Behind the midnight sky . . .

How many poems had she made for him in those first days they dwelled together? How many more might she compose if he found her and reminded her of their star?

He thought about this as he left the Light Pavilion and searched Neverness's streets that day. Poem after poem cascaded through his memory like a waterfall composed of the onstreaming notes of Maria's voice. Strange it was that natural, animal sounds shaped by lips and tongue into words could encode the deepest utterances of her soul.

Any other man might have worried that he thus would become lost within his mind – and simultaneously lost in the maze of streets twisting through the Bell or in the even greater

Gordian knot of glidderies that formed the twisted heart of the Slizzaring. Rane, however, prided himself in the knowledge that he could not become lost. For if he saw a street a single time, its turns and topology would sear a clear map of coloured ice into his mind's eye – in much the same way that he could recall the curve and tangle of each of Maria's tens of thousands of black hairs.

And so he continued on, and he crossed the Street of Master Courtesans and the Street of Imprimaturs, skating due south. As he edged around Rollo's Ring through the Diamond District, he watched neurosingers, cutters, tubists, and farsiders from fifty planets gliding across the big ring and taking their exercise in defiance of the cold. Nearly everyone wore furs or kamelaikas of various colours, though only a few had deemed it bitter enough to put on face masks. Their thousands of mouths moved even more frenetically than did their limbs. At the rim of the Ring, a sharp-featured woman stood hawking cilka with a rude supplication that shrilled out like the screech of a bird of prey; nearby, a wormrunner darted along at a reckless speed as if he owned the ice of the street, and he brayed at slower skaters to get out of his way. There another man called for a sled, all the while stamping his feet and glancing at his timepiece as if he had an appointment he needed to keep. Fifty yards from him, others stood screaming and cursing and gambling silver City Disks over the outcome of a game of hokkee. So loud was the cacophony of people bleating and bawling out their desires that it drowned out the music of Maria's poems.

With the Ring's murmuring throngs pressing in on all sides, Rane pushed off deeper into the district. On the Street of Stalls, he came upon a shabbily dressed man who had a woman backed up against a building. He groped beneath her opened furs, then took her by the arm and led her off to one of the street's hour hotels. Nearby beckoned a well-known restaurant at whose tables obese people gorged on fairy foods composed of left-handed molecules that would neither nourish their bodies nor add a millimetre of adipose to their girth. Next door, at a sense shop, men and women paid shining coins to revel in their ecstasy of choice; then they took a nepenthe to purge themselves of their experiences so that they could re-experience each novelty again and again. They reminded Rane of the ancient plutocrats who jammed tufted sticks down their throats and vomited up thirty courses of delicacies, course after course, and then returned hungry to the feast.

Upon witnessing such activities herself, Maria had once exclaimed, 'Oh, they're like animals!'

As Rane kept on skating, he tried to recapture the tone with which she had said this. He skated all that day, eventually coming out onto the glazy, goldish ice of the East-West Sliddery. Then some lenticular *haruteth* clouds came up and obscured much of the sky. A tinge of moisture hardened the air and stung his face. As he worked his way down the Street of the Ten Thousand Bars, the very buildings and the patrons who entered them seemed misted with a frisson of danger. The menace of the district became more tangible when he turned onto the narrow Street of the Common Whores, where numerous women stood waiting and meeting eyes with those who passed by. Their tattooed faces assessed Rane, even as the smell of their pheromone perfumes sweetened the air. Although most of the street's women remained independents or had joined the street's various clubs and associations, a few had hired wormrunners to procure for them or to 'protect' them. These lurking men seemed always to be cut from the same chromosomes, for they were invariably big, bearded, and belligerent. On account of the wormrunners – and other outlaws – Rane had warned Maria never to venture into certain parts of the Farsider's Quarter.

'But I want to see!' Maria had protested upon Rane's description of this district.

'There are other sights in the city I should show you.'

'Are you trying to protect *me*?'

Maria had laughed off his concerns for her safety and had insisted on the freedom to venture wherever she wished to go. Rane had counter-insisted that if she wanted to waste her time on a fool's tour, he must accompany her. In the end, she had agreed to this compromise.

And so, only a few years before, he had escorted her down this very street. When they came upon a nearly naked woman collecting a platinum coin from a well-dressed and handsome man, she clapped her hands together and exclaimed: 'But this is wonderful! When a woman feels kemmish, she can not only lie with as many men as she wishes but can gather money for doing so!'

Rane remembered smiling at this because he felt sure that Maria was making a joke.

A few moments later, five young men had staggered around the curve of the street. They wore rich fur capes and ermine hats. One of them called out in a drunken voice to the woman hurrying off with the astrier man. Another – the apparent leader of the quintet – fastened his gaze on Maria, and let loose a sharp whistle.

'Come, let's go,' Rane said to Maria.

He had heard of these men, who called themselves the Rakehells – and were called by those who tried to avoid them the 'White Hats'. Each year, across the Civilized Worlds, wealthy families sent their sons to Neverness to petition for admittance to the Order. Only a few very fortunate boys, however, found places among those wishing to become cetics, horologes, and other sorts of professionals. The White Hats recruited from the many failures who couldn't bear the shame of returning home. Though far from the worst of the city's gangs, they had been known to corner women at random, then to beat them down to the ice and to kick their skate blades into their faces, sometimes slicing off noses and scarring the women horribly.

'Let's go!' Rane said again, reaching for Maria's arm.

But she astonished him by bringing her fingers up to her mouth and whistling right back. The men quickly skated over to them. Their leader looked Maria up and down, and in a voice full of wine and intimidation, he said, 'Are you wanting to play?'

'What do you mean?' Maria said. 'I was only returning your greeting.'

'I'm Artulio – I keep a room down the street. I'll pay you twenty City Disks.'

'Do you mean, to *couple* with you?'

She seemed to study Artulio's eyes and the long, shiny scars cut into the patch of his forehead that showed beneath his fur cap. More scars – upraised keloids, probably resulting from habitual ingestion of jook – pocked his cheeks and his weak chin. He stank of toalache smoke and, Rane thought, of self-pity and resentment. Rane's heart began beating furiously and pushing blood up into his brain. Then he felt Maria loop her arm around his arm, and she laughed sweetly. 'I already have a man.'

Artulio, however, didn't even look at Rane. To Maria, he said, 'Yes, I will swive you – if you're not too fat beneath those furs.'

Rane didn't really think that these youths would attempt an abduction or any violence on a busy street in the clear light of day. But how could he be sure? He cast about, looking for anything that might be used as a weapon. His gaze fixed upon a huge icicle hanging from the steep eaves of the building behind him. Would it, he wondered, crumble into bits if he stabbed the point into Artulio's throat?

'But I couldn't swive you!' he heard Maria say. 'You're so ugly!'

'Suppose we take you to my room, and I pay you nothing?'

Maria looked straight at Artulio.

'Suppose I *make* you put your pretty lips around me?'

'Then,' Maria told him, 'I would bite off your testicles and claw out your eyes.'

At this simple statement, Artulio let loose a short, nervous laugh, which cued the other men to snicker as well. They obviously thought that Maria must be joking. And yet. And yet. Maria spoke with such an ease and a naturalness that it was unnerving. Rane was reminded of a *morateth*: the death wind that begins to blow from out of the west with a susurrant gentleness but quickly builds to so great a ferocity that it can flay the flesh from a man's face.

'I'd like to give you the opportunity to try that,' Artulio said with a false bravura. 'But I would wager that you really are as fat as a pig.'

His friends laughed again, this time with an almost tangible relief. One them shouted out to Artulio: 'Come on, let's go find that new place that you told me about. What did you call it?'

'The Bar of the Three Kindnesses.'

Without another word or another look at Maria, Artulio clapped his friend on the shoulder, and then led off across the ice. As quickly as they had come, the five White Hats skated down the street.

'Animals,' Rane said after they had vanished altogether. 'They *are* like animals.'

'Of course they are. But they're like angels, too – they just don't know it.'

Her remark had sparked the first of their arguments. Rane shook his head at what she had said, and then quoted from the Pascal: '*L'homme n'est ni ange ni bête, et le malheur veut que qui veut faire l'ange fait la bête.*'

'But what does that mean?' Maria asked him.

'"The more men try to be like angels, the more they wind up like beasts."'

'Perhaps that was true once,' she said, touching his face. 'But now there is the Way of Ringess.'

Rane shook his head more vigorously. 'You have too many hopes for this *religion*.'

'Perhaps it is you who has too few.'

'Do you know how many religions men have made in the last thirty thousand years?' He continued shaking his head. 'Do you know how many have begun with the highest ideals and designs for human perfection, only to inflict upon humankind the most murderous of wars and the worst kind of degradation? I *saw* this happen with the Way of Ringess.'

'That is because Hanuman li Tosh—'

'If it hadn't been he who debased Ringism, it would have been another.'

'But Danlo restored the Way of Ringess to a true *way*, didn't he? Things will be different this time.'

'Why should they be?'

'Because Danlo is different, as was Mallory Ringess before him. Because Neverness is like no other place in the universe. And because—'

'In Neverness, men pay impoverished women to—'

'And because *you're* different,' she told him. She touched his cheek to turn his face toward her, and then kissed his lips. 'I came here because of you.'

She kept touching him and kissing him, and the gentle calling of her fingers and her lips drove all dispute from his mind. And yet his doubts had soon returned, as they did now on a cold day in deep winter years later. Now, with the sounds, sights, and smells of the Street of the Common Whores assaulting his senses and driving him back to the present, he continued his journey into the Farsider's Quarter, this time alone. As he often had, he tried to let Maria's zest for life carry him over into an affirmation of her beliefs about life – but how could he deny the protest of his eyes? For as he skated down through the city, he saw everywhere about him human beings busy being all too human. On a frozen corner east of the Merripen Green, he watched an avid-eyed man trying to recruit 'fresh fish' into an aggressively revanchist sect of Tychism while on the opposite corner, an Architect of one of the Cybernetic Universal Churches sold glittering strands of precious and probably purloined Edic lights. Many peddled supposedly valuable information, bound into crewelwork or coded into City Disks. Wormrunners dealt in jook and jambool, kalla and toalache and dozens of kinds of euphorics. Would-be prophets promised people easy exaltations in exchange for their devotion, which in the end amounted to the same thing.

On the Street of Dreams, one of these charlatans – the self-appointed Theorarch of the newly formed True Way of Ringess – tried to capture Rane's attention by asking him: 'Have you looked within to remember the god you really are?'

They called Neverness the City of Light or the City of the Stars, but was it really so exalted or different from the cities of Old Earth in the dark ages of humanity's childhood? Rane moved ever deeper into the Farsider's Quarter, and names came tumbling into the quiet rooms of his mind: Alexandria; Gomorrah; Hyung Kung; Lone Dune; Samarkand; Rome. He thought of these cities' souks, citadels, and star chambers in which men had vied for money or power. He lingered over images of temples, cathedrals, opium dens, brothels, and bars. In how many millions of stone houses and mud huts had men tried to beat their wives into servility even as women had met their truculence with a coldness of the heart and perhaps poisoned cups of wine? In how few dwellings had the two halves of the human race come together with the kind of joyous accord for which they had been born?

Wasn't it always easier, Rane asked himself, to descend into the blood-heats and blindness of the low instead of reaching up for the shining possibilities of the very highest things? He couldn't help seeing, in his memory's eye, women and men clawing at each other on their sweat-stained pallets, gobbling down sweetmeats and whipping the flesh off the backs of their slaves – and always and everywhere, filling their living spaces with tapestries and tondos, with fine furniture and showy ceramics and every conceivable fashion of pelf and plunder. Human beings had never minded taking from other human beings, both pleasure and pain. He recalled the burning sands of ancient arenas in which gladiators had plunged razor-sharp swords into living flesh even as good citizens wagered on who would die and pocketed gleaming coins; he summoned a scene of the Aleksandar's armoured phalanxes marching out toward the Hellespont to conquer the world; he listened to the Holy Inquisitors of the Kristian Church condemn men's bodies to death by fire so that their souls might be saved. How it sickened him that his bloody kind was always so greedy for gold, greedy for glory, greedy for God!

When he considered the matter most profoundly, it seemed to him that people had always been driven by a desire to grasp the ungraspable glimmer of an unneeded hypothesis. The resultant frustration – felt as an unbearable, pounding pressure deep within – twisted them. It besmirched even their highest aspirations. It drove the poetry from their blood. And so, in their torment of hunger, avarice, and lust, they tried to lay hold of more apprehensible things. Rather than meditate on the shimmering infinities of the mind, they cannibalized each other's consciousness and life energies; they hoarded knowledge in place of seeking mysteries; they accumulated orgasms as a substitute for true transcendence and joy. Human beings had never 'found' God and never would, but for millennia they had succeeded in loosing upon the world a devil's sick of sin.

On the Street of Wombs, halfway down the block in front of one of the shops, he came upon a heavily bearded astrier man and his daughter. Like others of his sect, the man had turned himself out nicely in rich sable furs clasped with a heavy gold chain. The daughter, minus the chain, was dressed likewise. A veil draped down from the hood of her furs; this flimsy piece of black silk, however, did little to shade her face, for anyone could see that she was a beauty. Rane couldn't help being caught by the gleam of white teeth and the flash of eyes that lit up the veil. He couldn't help overhearing the astrier man hawking his daughter's wares and calling out to the passers-by that this gorgeous young woman had eggs to sell.

'You, sir,' the man said to Rane, 'must be of the Order, yes? A remembrancer? Perhaps even a master remembrancer?'

Rane silently chided himself for not changing his clothing after leaving Tamara's house. His silver robes, he thought, gave away his profession to anyone who had the eye to look for such things.

'What is your name?' the man asked him.

What should he tell this acquisitive astrier? In the ordering of names most commonly used in the Civilized Worlds, the personal name came first, followed by that of one's family. On Darkmoon, where Rane had been born, it was the reverse. When Rane had come to Neverness as a callow youth so many years before, however, the Master of Novices had failed to account for the Darkmoon custom and had recorded Rane's family name first. And so, in one of the many ironies of his life, the novices had called him Thomas Rane, even as his parents had – and in so doing, got his name wrong.

'Thomas,' he told the astrier, not wanting to give out a name by which he might be recognized (and the name that Maria had called him). 'I'm known as Thomas.'

'And I am Georgios Donashan.' The astrier moved a step closer to the woman standing next to him, and he laid his heavy arm across her shoulders. 'This is Cornelia Twelve Donashan – my twelfth-born. Have you ever seen a comelier woman?'

'She is very attractive,' Rane agreed. His eyes felt like daggers ripping through her veil. 'In fact, I am trying to find someone who closely resembles your daughter. Her name is Maria.'

'Maria . . . who?'

'I believe she might be living in this district.'

Georgios's thick black eyebrows pulled together into a frown. 'Why look for gold buried in the dirt when diamonds are arrayed before you?'

His arm tightened around Cornelia, and he smiled at Rane.

'I thought it was eggs you were offering,' Rane said.

'And what perfect gems they are,' Georgios countered. 'There are many who would give much for a single, sparkling one of them.'

He went on to tell of the neurosinger Nyeshia, who had paid the astounding sum of a thousand City Disks for the privilege of implanting one of Cornelia's fresh young eggs in her old and hitherto barren womb.

'And what a fine baby it was that Nyeshia bore!' Georgios declaimed. 'Bright! Beautiful! A prodigy in music and mathematics! Healthy as a dolphin and strong as a bear! Shall I show you a foto of this blessed boy?'

'No, that won't be necessary,' Rane told him, shaking his head.

'A truly phenomenal boy,' Georgios went on. 'We Donashans have chromosomes, for twenty generations now, that have warranted the highest possible rating.'

'Warranted by your church?'

'As you can see,' Georgios continued, ignoring Rane's question, 'what the genes impel proper nurturance compels.'

He beamed at his daughter as an artist might exult in a great painting.

'I cannot see very much,' Rane said, looking at Cornelia.

'Daughter!' Georgios barked out. 'Remove your veil so that Master Thomas might see!'

As Georgios's arm dropped away from Cornelia's shoulders, she touched her hands to her veil and lifted it back over her furs' hood. She stood staring down at the street's red ice, and Rane could almost feel the heat pouring out of her eyes.

'Behold!' Georgios called out. 'Behold and extol a face that could launch ten thousand lightships!'

As Rane gazed at this striking woman, whose skin seemed as rich as coffee with cream, he decided that she looked only *something* like Maria.

'Such lips!' Georgios said proudly. 'Red as apples and sweet as bloodfruits! Such eyes, such a fine nose, such perfect cheeks! Such a face might have been sculpted by the Master of the Universe Himself!'

'She is very attractive,' Rane repeated, not knowing what else to say.

'You cannot imagine how attractive she really is. Many would pay much just for a glimpse of the most perfect figure that the Wise Lord has ever made.'

Rane shook his head slowly, for he did not want to believe what Georgios was saying.

'How much would they pay?' he heard himself ask Georgios.

'Ten City Disks would not be too much to make your eyes sing.'

This time, Rane shook his head in bitter blame.

'Two disks, then.'

'We of the Order,' Rane said, 'do not carry *money*.'

'You don't carry money? How do you *live*, then?' Now it was Georgios's turn to shake his head. 'Well, no matter. It would be unfair for you to be deprived of a golden opportunity due to a temporary lack. Daughter!'

Again, Georgios's voice boomed out above all the other voices filling the street.

'Daughter – open your furs that Master Thomas might *see*!'

Cornelia, her head still lowered, undid the fasteners of her heavy garment. She left it to Georgios to reach out and pull the gleaming sable folds away from her body.

'Such breasts!' Georgios called out. 'Round as melons and sweeter than milkfruits! Such a belly, to quicken and bear the finest seed – such hips, made for birth. Such a body might have been created by the Lord of a Thousand Delights Himself.'

As Georgios proclaimed his daughter's glories, Cornelia's body seized up against the shock of the cold air. Only a thin white gown, Rane saw, now covered the front of her. Beneath its translucent silk, he made out the heavy breasts, perfectly formed, with brown aureoles as large as City Disks. He noted the nipples, hardened as by the touch of ice. Her belly curved down into her full hips with a soft voluptuousness, while below beckoned the dark fur of her sex.

'Tell me, my Master Remembrancer,' Georgios continued, 'have you ever seen a body such as this?'

Yes – yes, I have, Rane thought as he closed his eyes. On a quiet street somewhere inside the darkest quarter of his mind – in that softly lit room where Maria always waited for him – he looked upon her nakedness for the ten thousandth time.

'Have you a wife, perhaps, who could make use of such a beauty's eggs?'

'No,' Rane said, forcing open his eyelids so that he could gaze at Cornelia. 'I have no wife.'

'Not even a single wife? But who will bear your children then?' As Rane drank in the sight of Cornelia's bountiful body, he heard Georgios add: 'My first wife, Cornelia's mother, bore *me* twenty-nine.'

Plant your seeds in all soils on all worlds . . .

Words from the *Arda Sophar*, the astriers' sacred work, came tumbling into Rane's mind. Once, long ago, in his fascination with the origins of religion, he had familiarized himself with this vast corpus of writings. In an age in which most people absorbed information by kithing the jewel-like ideoplasts that computers infused directly into the visual cortex of the brain, Rane sometimes preferred to seek out ancient wisdoms bound up in physical books. He took a strange pleasure in sitting down with dusty old relics and letting his eyes play over yellowed pages in exercise of the barbaric and nearly lost art called reading.

Plant your seeds in all soils on all worlds that you might bring forth a garden and live in eternal paradise with your Lord.

Astriers, he recalled, must dedicate themselves to ensouling new beings, transforming as much of the universe's dead matter into living flesh as they possibly could. With each child born, an astrier earned a credit toward realizing the divinity bestowed by the Wise Lord. If he gained enough credits, upon his death, he would be ensured rebirth and everlasting life on a newly created world, which he would fill with ever more children.

'What do you say, Master Thomas?' Georgios's loud voice blasted Rane back to the present moment. 'I would be pleased to offer you my daughter's services. For two thousand City Disks, you may not only purchase the finest egg that you will find in Neverness but you may make use of my daughter's womb.'

Rane gazed at the now-shivering Cornelia.

'For that price,' Georgios went on, 'I will include the right for you to fertilize the egg *in utero*, personally. Take as many times as you wish to make sure that my daughter is impregnated and then – by the grace of Lord of Life! – and then, a short three seasons later, she will present you with the most beautiful child you have ever seen.'

Rane ground his teeth together until his jawbones hurt. He couldn't make himself look away from Cornelia.

'And if you're a follower of the fashions, I can make arrangements with a splicer who is a friend. A little crewelwork along the chromosomes, and your child will be born with a fur coat of his own, as proof against this world's abominable cold.'

Cornelia's body tensed as from a blow to her belly; Rane could not imagine such a child emerging from this beautiful, brown-skinned woman.

'If you'd like, for only ten thousand disks,' Georgios said, 'you may take Cornelia as your concubine – or even as your wife. She will bear you many children, I promise you.' Rane's breath seemed to explode from his nostrils; the gelid air sucked back into his windpipe scorched his throat – even as the sight of Cornelia shivering in cold burned his eyes like a golden fire.

'If you are unsure,' Georgios added, 'my daughter keeps an apartment nearby. For only twenty disks, you may take an hour to assure yourself that she is everything you might wish her to be.'

Rane finally summoned the will to take a step closer to Cornelia. He reached out his hand toward her. Then his fist closed around fine sable fibres, and he pulled her furs closed about her trembling belly and breasts. As she lifted up her head, he finally met eyes with her in a silence so profound that it seemed he would never be able to speak again.

And then a rage ripped words from deep within his throat, and he shouted at Georgios: 'What is wrong with you, that you would sell your own daughter?'

Rane felt his hand again form into a fist, which he wanted to smash into Georgios's greedy face. At this, Georgios fell quiet. He eyed Rane as he might a wolf that has come out from beneath the cover of a sheepskin.

'How could an Orderman such as yourself,' he said, 'know what it costs to raise a family?'

Rane stood so close to Cornelia that he could feel her breath puffing out against his face. Without looking away from her, he quoted words to Georgios: '"The cost to those who sell their dreams for money shall be their immortal souls."'

At his recitation of the twenty-third line of the eighty-fourth chapter of the seventh volume of the *Arda Sophar*, Georgios stared at Rane in surprise.

'You have read our book?'

'I have read many things,' Rane said.

'Well, you shouldn't have!' Georgios countered, his voice

filling with anger. 'Our scripture cannot be understood by those not raised in our ways!'

'What is there to understand about such a simple statement?'

'Well, nearly the whole of the ninth tractate of the *Revisioning* deals with the complexities of money mentioned in the *Arda Sophar*.'

'Yes, and the commentary to the forty-fourth chapter of that tractate, written by the Exemplar Awan Javaris, unravels the strands of these complexities, in regard to procreation and sex.'

At this, Georgios's arm jerked up, and his fat finger described a circle in front of his face: a sign meant to ward off the evil eye or the second sight that can peer into another's mind.

'These matters *are* complex,' Georgios said, 'and only an exemplar who devotes his life to their study can fully explain—'

'Do you mean, as the Exemplar Florian Davos Narashan has explained?' Rane closed his eyes for a moment. 'Isn't his side note to Exemplar Javaris' note – on page 1,746 – the final word in such matters?'

Georgios's finger trembled in the air as he stared at Rane.

'"And so it has been proved through the natural deduction calculi from first principles",' Rane quoted, '"that for a man or a woman to offer sexual favours in exchange for any sort of financial consideration is a first degree sin."'

If Georgios had ever read Exemplar Narashan's side note or even knew of it, he gave no indication. Instead, his face lit up like that of a man stranded on an icefall who has been thrown a rope.

'"For a man to commit a sin",' he quoted back to Rane, '"in avoidance of a greater sin is no sin."'

He shot Rane a look of triumph, and added, 'And no greater sin can there be than wasting the life that the Wise Lord has given us.'

Now it was Rane's turn to fall silent; he looked back at Cornelia yet again.

'In any case,' Georgios said, trying to secure his victory, 'although prudence demands that we pass on the cost of verifying my daughter's quality, we are offering only eggs.'

Rane shook his head slowly back and forth. 'But you also offer to cark your own daughter's chromosomes, that your grandchildren will be born clad in fur like animals!'

'The Wise Lord has said that we must live in harmony with our environment. And that we must populate all worlds.'

'That cannot mean what you construe it to mean. For twenty thousand years, it has been agreed that a man may do with his flesh as he pleases, but his DNA belongs to his species. That is the Law of the Civilized Worlds.'

'We follow a higher Law.'

Cornelia surprised Rane by reaching out to take hold of his hand. Through her naked flesh, he felt the tremors ripping through her body as she stood there shivering in the cold. He felt something else, too. Beneath the pain and the pressure of her nearly frozen fingers, an ardent force seemed to pull at him with an immense gravity. It formed up in her eyes as an urgent plea. She embraced him with a look that promised pleasures almost beyond bearing if only he followed his heart and lost himself in the wonder of what their joining would create.

'Please, please!' she seemed to whisper.

Maria, he remembered, had looked at him in exactly the same way.

'Please take me away with you!'

How, he wondered, could he leave such a beautiful woman on this frozen street, to stand here hour after hour with such a venal father?

'Come, let us not argue!' he heard Georgios say. 'Let us be friends and find a warm café, in which we might enjoy a friendly cup of tea and talk further.'

For 'only' ten thousand City Disks, Rane thought, he might buy Cornelia away from this man. He could find a nice apartment in the Pilots' Quarter and instal her in rooms filled with beautiful tapestries, tondos, and fine furniture. He would come to her only on those nights of despair, when the loneliness hollowed out his insides as a wolf tears the entrails from a carcass. Or, if he felt compelled to try to be noble (as he knew he would), he would somehow find another thousand City Disks so that she might purchase a little restaurant or café near the Academy. She would spend her days serving spiced breads and hot cinnamon coffee to eschatologists, librarians, haikuist and other professionals, one of whom would surely be happy to make her his wife.

'Come, now!' Georgios said.

As Rane looked at Cornelia yet again, he felt himself falling through the black holes at the centres of her eyes: falling down into a dazzling darkness without end. Each of the countless trillions of atoms making up his being began dissolving into a wrath of terror that shimmered off into a negative infinity.

'I can see how much you desire my daughter,' Georgios said. 'Since you are momentarily bereft of funds, I will accept a promissory. You may take my—'

'No – go away!' Rane shouted out these words with so loud a howl of denial that people up down the street stared at him. 'We of the Order do not deal in money!'

Georgios, pushing out his hand as if to ward off a blow, casting nervous glances at the other astriers and egg sellers who watched him, finally lost his patience. He told Rane, 'You do not deal in the truth. You are afraid, aren't you, of giving up your privileges in order to have what you really want? You are like the sun which hoards its own radiance: you refuse to bestow a single ray on the most promising of buds, that it might blossom into the most beautiful of flowers.'

This pronouncement caused Rane's fingers again to contract into a fist. He wanted to whip it with all his strength into Georgios's face. He felt a terrible, seismic force working at the tissues of his soul, like a crack running down through layers of sea ice.

Please!

What would happen, he wondered, when the crack finally opened? Rane knew he could not remain to find out. And so, with a final glance at Cornelia – who stood blinking the tears from her soft eyes – he backed away from her. Like a drunkard, he stumbled across the sidewalk. He managed somehow to turn around. Then his legs and arms fell into furious motion, and he joined the throngs of humanity skating down the street.

5

As Rane struck his skate blades into the frozen street with a desperate savagery, the click-clack of steel against ice ripped out like the chopping of an axe. He gasped for breath against the intense coldness. His throbbing lungs pushed reheated air steaming from his mouth, and from his throat sounded a moan of outraged membranes. Men and women, in all their hundreds and thousands, blurred past his stinging eyes. He turned right, and left, then right again. He quickly found himself on streets unknown to him, full of unknowable people. He found himself a stranger to himself. Everything about that forbidding being hurt, and in his wrath to escape his essential affliction, it seemed that his bones might shiver into splinters. He wanted to skate and skate forever, right down the streets' red ice and off the edge of the world.

What was wrong with people? Why, he demanded of the sky, did they act as they did? How could human beings bear their folly, their madness, their low estate?

The truth was, he thought, as the wind bit patches of numbness from his face, they couldn't. And so they drank and drugged and buried themselves in purchased flesh. They looked for transport from the agony of incarnation through the fantasy of surrealities, simulations, and other cybernetically created worlds. They meditated and chanted and fasted and prayed. To any number of deities, imagined or real, they begged for deliverance from exploding stars, murderous artificial intelligences, and an ever-growing number of cosmic calamities. The worst sculpted their bodies into the shapes of animals or embraced with

passionate intensity the rough Beast from which the human race
had evolved. The best applied every technology and technique
toward transcending their humanity in becoming gods.

Long ago, Jin Zenimura had told his followers that the human
soul existed only in those who knew themselves to be more than
human. The poet Avangel had written that apprehending the
soul was like trying to lay hold of starlight. A cynic might have
agreed with the Exemplars of the Fostora Redemption Fellowship
who stated, simply, that human beings had lost their souls.

With the memory of Cornelia searing his optic nerves, what
could Rane say to this? As a remembrancer – as Lord
Remembrancer – he knew what his office required of him. For
ages ago, on Old Earth, his Order had accepted a fundamental
charge. After the Holocaust Centuries, at the beginning of the
Swarming and the Clading, with human beings tampering with
their chromosomes and carking their shapes into those of
dolphins or winged beings, as had the Agathanians and the Elidi
(or trying to cark their consciousnesses into their computers in
anticipation of Nikolos Daru Ede and a thousand billion
members of the Cybernetic Universal Church) – in that existentially shocking and terrible storm of technology that threatened
to sweep away all of time and history, the Remembrancers had
been formed as anchors for humanity. As one of Rane's distant
ancestors had taught, the Remembrancers were to be the
preservers of the truly human; they must always and forever
keep alive the soul of the human race.

Rane, however, knew that such a glorious ideal would remain
beyond anyone's reach. He could keep nothing alive – and so
how should he wish to preserve anything? He called to mind
things preserved: fruits in jellies; information in silicon; ants in
amber; mummies in gold-painted sarcophaguses. Who was he
to delimit humanity's soul by shutting it into the frozen crypt
of his memory?

The best he could do, he thought, was to understand. As he
skated ever deeper into the Farsider's Quarter, he moved into
the twenty-eighth attitude of remembrance, which some called
gestalt. This was not a matter of reviewing recordings of the
past as an historian might and trying to order millions of chaotic
data into a coherent whole. Nor did his integration of lost eras,
zeitgeists, and primeval impulses depend on the accessing of the

akashic registry (or universal memory) in the form of individual recollections of those who had died – or not just. To those not of his profession, Rane most often used chess as a metaphor to describe the twenty-eighth attitude. Grandmasters did not decide whether to move queen or pawn through the mere calculation of possibilities, as computers did; rather, they used their memory of the positions of pieces in millions of games to apprehend critical patterns. These patterns they then matched against ever-arising new positions on their ebony- and ivory-squared boards in order to envision how the game might best play out.

What patterns, Rane asked himself, did he apprehend on his journey down toward that torment of twisted streets known as the Slizzaring? What shapings and deformations of the soul of humankind? Rane sometimes called upon Tlönish or Moksha to describe his perceptions to himself. More often, though, he used the Language of the Civilized Worlds to put names to his gestalts. There were, of course, the simple patterns: decadence, dominance, and the worship of death. And the old, old 'sins' that the ancients had characterized as anger and greed, gluttony and envy – also pride, lust and sloth. There was vanity, too, always vanity, and all the many isms: barbarism and sadism, cynicism and egoism, along with solipsism, narcissism, and atheism. Rane saw everywhere (especially in the reverence accorded computers) the human race's fundamental philosophical mistake of trying to divorce 'good' spirit from 'evil' matter, which took on its most recent form in what he called cybernetic gnosticism. This error related to the Fravashi concept of *prenune*: the compulsive viewing of reality in a way that split subject from object – and the resultant sickening of the mind.

Rane had words for more subtle and complex patterns. He thought of *bika-pelau*, the 'truth-that-everyone-knows-but-fears-to-say'; also *schadenfreude*, the 'taking-joy-at-another's-misfortune'. There were the annihilation words, too: *ilnorn*, *furanorn* and *vashnorn*. And the old dynamic of *carita pelosa*, which meant something like generosity springing from the ulterior motive of gaining favours that must be returned. He reflected on the Fravashi term *glavering*: assuming that one's assumptions about the universe must be true solely upon the basis of having the good fortune of being born into a people favoured by nature, vocation or the grace of God. Or, as the Fravashi Old Fathers liked to say: 'Human beings can't help prettifying their inherited worldviews and flattering themselves with a presumed superiority – despite overwhelming evidence to the contrary.'

Then there was the master pattern, the one centring impulse from which arose all the others, and that was fear. Out of the primeval fear (which itself sprang from the sense of separation and perishability experienced by every bit of matter in the universe), men fashioned idols and sky gods requiring supplications and bloody sacrifices; they made men themselves into messiahs or buddhas or prophets; they created the white-bearded, muscular being they dared to call God. Always, they sought deliverance from suffering and death. Always, too, however, they secretly agonized over the certain ending that awaited them. Their fear of their fate left marks of weakness and woe that Rane perceived in people's faces, much as a cetic was said to read a man's or a woman's 'programs'. For tens of thousands of years, on a thousand worlds from Old Earth to Arcite to Neverness, the patterns engendered by this existential terror had played out in people again and again. Sometimes, he saw these patterns as mathematical attractors: topological basins that forced the chaotic sets of human possibilities into order. In a way, they were like racial memories steened into cytoplasm or grooves worn deep into the human psyche. They caused all desires and deeds to settle naturally toward a low point of actualization, even as water is pulled down into a drain.

In Rane's worst moments – and the time he spent skating away from Cornelia and her greedy father had to count among these – he switched metaphors. He envisioned a region of space so dark and heavy with emptiness that it sucked down even light. He saw all the manifold motifs that made humans so hopelessly human as black holes in the soul.

How many such points of neverness annihilated the promise of his kind? Ten thousand? Ten million? As many as the number of stars that brightened the night-time sky? How many ways were there for people to go wrong?

On the infamous Scarlett Street – a tube of red ice and red granite buildings winding like a blood vessel into the heart of the Slizzaring – Rane came upon a wormrunner procuring patrons for the women he claimed to protect. Rane stopped to make inquiries of this angry-eyed man. It turned out that this particular panderer had only two women to offer, at a very reasonable hourly rate. He refused, however, to offer them to Rane.

'You're in the wrong district,' he growled out, eyeing Rane's silver robes. 'You Ordermen do better to keep to the Street of Courtesans – or even the Street of Common Whores.'

'I'm afraid that on those streets, I won't be able to find what I am looking for.'

'And what is that?'

Rane glanced at the panderer's women, who stood with their backs up against a ruddy stone wall. Gusts of air blowing out of a warming press tousled their dark hair and heated their exposed skin. That included most of their bodies, for except for their black, thigh-high boots and red scarves, they were naked. Flesh frescoes writhed beneath their epidermides; these moving tattoos made of colonies of varicoloured bacteria had been programmed to paint the most lurid and lascivious of scenes.

'I am looking,' Rane told the wormrunner, 'for those places in which a man might find whatever he is looking for.'

He smiled at the wormrunner, as much to reassure this criminal as to congratulate himself on what he considered a cleverly coded response. The wormrunner, however, glared at Rane with an instant suspicion.

'There are no such places in Neverness!' the wormrunner informed him.

'Are there not? I heard of a hibakusha with burns over most of his body and a melted face who paid a hundred City Disks to be with a Jacarandan woman – I don't remember her name.'

'Do you have such a sum?'

'I'd heard,' Rane said, evading the question, 'that the Jacarandan worked out of a brothel not far from here.'

The telling of lies, he thought, was an old, old pattern seared deep into the soul of humankind.

The wormrunner's hand slipped down into the opening of his brown furs as if to grasp a weapon. His suspicion deepened to brazen animosity as he shouted at Rane: 'You've been mis-informed! There are no brothels in this district! Now go away before you find what you are certainly *not* looking for!'

With a storm of violence perhaps ready to break out from the centre of the wormrunner's tensed body, Rane decided to skate away immediately. His clumsy foray into the Slizzaring had forced him to face three unpleasant truths: first, without money, he would not go very far in a realm ruled by currency and coin. Second, his manner of dress gave him away as belonging to the Order, and the district's denizens might therefore naturally regard him as an official who would make report on a riot of very unofficial activities. And most importantly, how was he to find one of the city's secret brothels if it was truly secret?

That evening, he returned to his house and went to work solving his problems. From the wall of his sleeping chamber, across from the bed, he removed the tondo that had been so dear to Maria. For a while, he studied this illumination of the Great Mother nursing her child. Although he perceived some of the same power in the piece as had Maria, he had never warmed to the magnificence of these two beings, for they seemed lost in their love of each other even as they shared some incomprehensible secret bound up their bold black eyes. Such mutual regard did not pull him into its wonder; rather, it seemed to create an entire world too beautiful and bright for him to touch. When he sold the tondo the next day on Socorro Street, two things surprised him: that a painting he had considered a minor work by a little-known artist fetched a thousand City Disks – and that he felt a strange and terrible sadness at parting with it.

He did not, however, allow himself to savour such emotions. He immediately took a fraction of this money and went down to the Palashin Market, near the Street of Fumes, where he purchased the brightly coloured pantaloons, vest, and cape of a harijan. That these garments were tattered and soiled accorded with the carelessness toward materiality which the harijan sects affected, though Rane could not abide the lice that usually infested these people and would have added authenticity to his new guise. It was hard enough to remove his remembrancer's robes and to bear the touch of silken fabric stained with another's sweat and stench.

With the pockets of his pantaloons stuffed with gold – and with his unshaven cheeks showing the stubble of a dense black beard – he congratulated himself on his resourcefulness and his willingness to bear the nearly unbearable. The third of his problems, though, proved more troublesome. He decided that if he wished to enter the sink of secret brothels hidden away in the Slizzaring, he must first make acquaintance with the smugglers, slel neckers, panderers, and whores who dwelled there; then he must somehow win their trust.

The first of the women he solicited introduced herself as Magda, though he never learned her real name. He found her through a wormrunner who sold authentic ermine hats, made from pelts poached in the forests north of Neverness: real flesh and fur ripped away from the bodies of once-living animals. Rane bought one of these hats and seated it upon his head like a gleaming helm; thus accoutred, he called upon Magda in a windowless room above the wormrunner's shop. Though too dark to show all the cracks and stains that marred the obscenely painted walls, the tiny chamber held the distinct scents of incense and oranges, toalache smoke and rat droppings and sex. Each of these noisome odours keyed off a distinct memory of another time and another place. Rane told himself that he wished to be in any of these places, instead of standing there at the room's threshold, with the snow melting off his boots and running down onto the warped wooden floor. He couldn't help inhaling Magda's fermy fragrance and staring at the silk-draped bed, which beckoned with a compelling obviousness beneath a stand of softly glowing Edic lights.

Rane had hoped that he might just sit on the bed's red fabric and ask Magda a few questions, then pay out her ten City Disks upon receiving a satisfactory answer. However, Magda – a big-boned, blondish woman with an air of exhausted competence – had other plans. She demanded her fee, and directed Rane to set the coins on her dresser, nearly covered with a debris of cosmetics, jewellery, undergarments, razors, jambool boxes, orange rinds, triya seeds, and twists of charred toalache. She told him to remove his clothing. As she waited for him to comply with this unexpected command, he read impatience on her ruddy face, along with a flush of suspicion. His fingers began fumbling at the fasteners of his cape and his pantaloons. As he stripped himself in front of her, he asked her if she knew of any brothels nearby in which a man might have a choice of women as pulchritudinous as she. He implied that he desired to enjoy two or more of these women at once. Magda did not answer him. She waited and she watched him make himself nude before finally saying to him, 'Am I not woman enough for you?'

The chemise that she wore did little to conceal the fact that she was more than enough for any man. Soon enough, though, she pulled off even this insubstantiality of black gossamer and stood revealed in all of her overwhelming nakedness. Her huge, blue-veined breasts drooped down upon her belly, swollen with fat. Her heavy hips might have been the envy of an ancient fertility goddess; yards of creamy, delicate skin encased her body, from her painted toenails to her pretty face. Her pinkish pallor recalled the misty northern forests of Old Earth that had engendered this genetic affliction of extreme fairness shared by so few members of the human race. Some men referred to such yellow-haired, blue-eyed women as angels, and sought them as they might living gold. To Rane's eye, however, Magda's body seemed like a white canvas that too easily displayed the insults that grieved the human hide. The translucent scars of stretched skin lined her hips, buttocks, and belly; the reddened papules of ingrown hairs erupted across her shaved pubes. This wanton depilation made her genitals appear too large, too vulnerable, and much, much too stark.

He expected a ritual of examination and washing now to ensue. This would be followed by the placement of prophylactics or pessaries: the artificial tissues that would line their most sensitive bodily parts. Rane certainly wanted some sort of protection from Magda's burgeoning flesh. She therefore surprised him at how quickly she laid hold of him and got her painted lips around him. It fairly astonished him how readily he responded to the slipping softness of her tongue. When he protested their recklessness and called for precautions, she pulled away from him and sat back upon the bed. Her face clouded with a returning suspicion.

'You're the first man who has asked me to use a pessary,' she told him.

'Can that be? Surely most men would wish to safeguard—'

Her sudden laughter, high and harsh, cut off the stream of his words.

'But surely,' he began again, 'you must have asked them to—'

'Am I a courtesan, then, to make such demands of men?' Her eyes grew tight and troubled as she regarded at him. 'And are you an arhat with money to waste on such things or are you a harijan?'

He opened his mouth to try to reason with her, but then decided that he had already said too much. Only later would he learn of the immune stimulants and antibiotics that the creatures of the Slizzaring consumed by the cupful as proof against the viruses, bacteria, fungi, prions, protozoa, and yeast that infect the body. Only later, when it might already have been too late, out of remorse and fear, would he stop by the vaccine-seller down the street and drink such a chemical cocktail himself.

'Are you ready?' she asked him. She lay back upon the bed's red covering and opened her legs. The smell of sex drove like a red-hot spike up through his nostrils straight into his brain. He stared awestruck at the glisten and gravitas of her waiting body. How, he asked himself, could he possibly think to join his body with hers? What would be the resultant record of the press of their skin and the pull of their limbs: all the many movements of matter and energy which would become bound into the fundamental unity that underlay spacetime? Why was he about to commit an act that would be preserved forever in universal memory – and therefore in his own?

Rane suddenly did not want this moment with Magda to dwell side by side with all the millions of moments he had spent with Maria. But then the smiling, blonde-haired woman he had paid held out her arms, grasped hold of him, and pulled him into her. There came a shock of flesh shivering into flesh, along with a torment of ecstasy and dread. Why was it always so *startling*, he wondered, when he found himself within the wild, wet clutch of a woman's body? Why was this rapture always so overwhelming and strange? Because, he thought, a woman was the Other, the great unknown, and a very special part of it. No other place in the universe would he dare to enter in such intimate embrace. No other work of creation was more like a man – and yet so utterly different. Who needed the thrill of coupling with an Elidi or other alien female when one had a woman such as Magda? As he began to lose himself in the rocking rhythm of Magda's body, he tried not to take *too* much pleasure in this moment of clenching muscles, hot sweat, and quickened gasps of breath. For Maria lay there, too, and he couldn't bear for her to look over at him, forever watching what he did. He told himself that this urgent copulation with the now-moaning Magda would help him in his quest. Was not his reckless exposure of himself and his loss of faithfulness a sacrifice he needed to make? Did he not need to do very hard things in order to find Maria?

Soon enough, he found that moment when bliss and dread, movement and memory, became as one. He felt his ecstasy rip a terrible cry from deep within him. For what seemed an eternity, he entered into a blindingly brilliant space in which he forgot everything that was or had ever been.

And then he opened his eyes, and the world reformed and rushed back in. The colours of the sexual scenes painted on the wall above the bed seemed too vivid and much too real. He nearly gagged against Magda's sour stench. He felt her hand pressing hard and hurtful against his chest. As he rolled away from her, he listened to their sweat-slicked skin become unstuck. He watched her rise off the bed in a bounce of breasts and big white buttocks and cross the room so that she could wash his secretion out of her. In the end, she did not really want any part of him to contaminate her tissues or to linger inside of her.

In the days that followed, Rane found other women to solicit. There were Genita and Taqqwa, Jardena and Karah and Iris. And Gura and Viola, who joined him in the same bed. He recorded in his memory the exact timbre of Tatianna's voice as she moaned obscenities in his ear and the precise position of every bit of bristle that shaded the skin of Onora's dark *mons veneris*. It seemed that there could be no exhausting the number of available women in the district surrounding Scarlett Street, any more than there could be an end to memory itself.

Rane recalled sitting in a café a hundred and twenty-eight years before on a warm winter day and listening to an historian declaim that it was just as hard for someone to descend in the societies of man as it was to rise. Had this plump historian, Rane wondered, ever got out from beneath his records, tractates, simulations, and computer models in order to put this theory to the test? For Rane did not find it very difficult – at least practically difficult – to go down through the layers of the morass of humanity that made up the society of the Slizzaring. He needed only to push aside his aspirations and his sensibilities and let his atavistic instincts guide him in his descent.

Meeting the desired people, he discovered, depended on two things: reputation and referral – and the latter largely depended on the former. With the weather worsening toward the awful storms of midwinter spring, Rane established a reputation as a whoremaster capable of swiving a great many women, sometimes six or seven in a single night. Although he could not claim any sort of record in the number of his debaucheries – not in a populace in which more than one profligate drank jambool in order to pour fire into his loins – he gained renown for his prowess of arousal and his willingness to lie with almost any woman.

This included the fat and the thin, the blind and the burned, the deformed and the ugly and the old. He accomplished his feats by means of a simple trick that he revealed to no one. It all began on the night when he took to bed Ysabel, the third of the women who succeeded Magda. When he had set his hands on Ysabel's brown skin, pocked with scars caused by the red-hot tips of burning cigarettes, he had found himself unable to tumesce. And so he had employed his remembrancing powers to call up an imago of Maria, complete down to the exact curve of Maria's black eyelashes and the suppleness of her shoulders. He had then superimposed this imago onto Ysabel's mutilated form, in essence transforming her into Maria. Ysabel's arms became Maria's arms; her sad, pained words filled with the richness of Maria's voice. In this way, Rane managed not only to ignite his desire but to convince himself that he still remained at least partially faithful.

Inevitably, it seemed to him, one stormy night he found himself in a dimly lit room in a dark stone building tucked away behind the apartment blocks that lined a snow-choked alley giving out onto Scarlett Street. After his congress with a woman named Ailieyha – a small-boned, black-skinned beauty as different in form from Magda as a woman could possibly be – he tried to relax back against the sweat-soaked sheets. He tried not to listen to the cries that sounded out in the other rooms up and down the brothel's main hall, outside the thick wooden door.

'Do you have to leave?' Ailieyha asked this of him as she moulded her tiny body into the space between his chest and curled arm.

'Our hour is almost expired,' Rane told her.

'Can't we go once more?'

'Aren't you exhausted? I don't want to make you sore.'

She laughed at this as if he had made a great joke. From the room across the hall came a wail of pain that caused Rane's belly muscles to tighten and his jaws to clench. The patrons of this brothel paid good gold so that they could savage raw tissues or deflower virgins or cut open the sutures in women whose genitals had been sown shut.

'You *could* stay,' she said to him.

'No, I really do have to leave.'

'But the woman you're looking for has never worked here.'

'In another brothel like this, then.'

'There are no other brothels like this.'

'Are you sure?'

'Why do *you* seem so sure that the one you seek would be here?'

How could he explain to her his intimation that Maria, the highest and the best of the human race, was destined to experience the lowest and the worst? He could not explain what he regarded as the fundamental perversity of life even to himself.

'Perhaps,' he said, 'they keep her in one of the secret rooms that Iris told me about.'

'But there are no secret rooms here!'

'How would you know? Since they keep you locked inside?'

'They do let us out, sometimes. We . . . tend to each other.'

And by that, as Rane had learned, she meant that the brothel's dozens of imprisoned women not only salved each other's wounds but too often wreaked the harm that had caused them in the first place. For such was the way of human cruelty that the very women who had been cut open many, many times became the most expert in the violence of needle and thread.

The wrath that this thought called up in Rane caused him to want to tender to Ailieyha the opposite of pain. And so he gave in to her imprecations, and he stayed much longer than he should have. He lost himself in the openness of her flesh and in her eyes' silent suffering, which he only inflamed the more gentle he tried to be. Time evaporated in the way that the steam of one's breath vanishes into an endlessly deep blue sky.

There came a distant thump of heavy footfalls in the hallway outside the room. Then the sudden pounding of a fist against the door jolted Rane out of his pleasure with Ailieyha – and the pain of his remembrance of Maria. A voice as big as thunder struck the door, too, and shook its timbers.

'You're past your appointment!' a man called out. 'This is *my* time!'

'Go away!' Ailieyha said, pressing herself up against Rane's side. 'I've a client who has paid for another hour.'

She looked up at Rane with her soft brown eyes as if to plead with him to go along with her lie. He nodded at her as his arm drew tighter around her shoulders.

'I've paid for *three* hours with you,' the man called out again, 'right now! Open the damned door before I break it down!'

The violence of the man's voice impelled Rane to sit up and reach for his clothing. He began pulling on his pantaloons as Ailieyha murmured to him, 'It's Batar Bulba. Please, I can't see him now!'

Rane knew of this name by reputation only – but it was a terrible, ferocious reputation. Batar Bulba, a huge wormrunner who was said to do murder for a big enough fee, had apparently once killed a harijan by forcing handfuls of snow into the man's nostrils and mouth. He often misused the five women he kept out on the Slizzaring's frozen streets, though he visited Ailieyha's brothel when he really wished to hurt a woman. 'He thinks he likes me,' she said to Rane. As Bulba continued pounding at the door, she explained how he called her 'Sweetness' and always brought her flowers or perfume or other gifts. 'But he really loathes me – someday, he'll pay for my death.'

Her eyes filled with a strange, sad longing, and she seemed to accept this inevitability and even to look forward to it. Rane hated it that she retained so little will to live – and that he understood her resignation too well.

'Go away!' he shouted toward the door. 'We're not finished here!'

What happened next would forever leap out among his many millions of memories as one of the most vivid and intense. Bulba must have thrown his immense body against the door, for the great slab of oak suddenly burst inward in a shriek of twisted metal hinges and splintered wood. And there, framed by the doorway, stood a man thicker of limb than any man that Rane had ever seen. Bulba couldn't have weighed less than four hundred pounds, with this mass of muscle packed onto a frame about six and half feet in height. And all of this quivering, brutal flesh Bulba proudly displayed. For it was his wont, after he had taken his pleasure in one chamber of the brothel, to go from room to room, strutting the brothel's halls and intimidating the other patrons with a horrible nakedness.

Rane would later learn that Bulba exulted in being one of the *Gorgorim*; in fact, he had paid various cutters and splicers a great deal of money to cark his form into that of a creature that seemed as much animal as human. Bulba's body hair – so thick that it might almost have been called a pelt – covered most of his skin, from his big feet to the black beard that bristled from his face. The cells of the bones just above his overhanging forehead had been engineered to produce layers of keratin, which projected out from his hairline as two upcurving horns. To gaze at Batar Bulba was to realize that a human being really could call up the traits and temperament of a satyr.

The astonishing tuber of flesh that jutted out from Bulba's loins reinforced his guise of rampant bestiality. Rane had never seen so large a phallus attached to a man; indeed, such a tumescence did not seem possible. Its garish colours burst out into the room and grabbed hold of the eye: the bright blue of the long, thick shaft gave out onto the bulging tip, tinged a flamboyant red. Rane couldn't tell if such unnatural hues had been the work of a splicer or of a talented tattooist. Or perhaps it had been a work of teleogenesis. Certain sects, he remembered, practised *narachastra prayoga* and bred for great size and brilliance of the male sexual organ. Over generations, the men of these sects had vied with other men to see who could sport the most impressive phallus. The results of this evolutionary 'arms race', like the huge antlers that encumbered the heads of the mountain elk, had little to do with actual sex or the pleasing of females. One might have supposed, though, that the upper limit in size would be constrained by the capacity of women to accommodate such monstrosities – and supposed wrongly. For Bulba clearly gave the lie to this sentiment. As Ailieyha had confided to Rane, Bulba exulted in the fact that very few women could take such an organ into themselves without sustaining damage. Indeed, Bulba gained his greatest pleasure in causing pain: in using his sexual parts to violate the most tender of tissues and to batter, to bruise, and to rend.

'Go away!'

More booming words broke from Bulba's thick lips, stained red like the skin of a yu berry: most likely from drinking jambool. Certainly, Rane thought, Bulba must have drunk a good few drams of this evil potion in order to harden himself and to maintain his state of priapism. Jambool could also madden a man and cause him to wreak mayhem; this realization drove Rane finally to leave the chambers of mind and memory and to deal with the deadly danger at hand.

'Go away, now, I say!'

Bulba raised a mightily muscled arm and pointed a massive finger at the shattered door. Ridiculously, it seemed, in his other hand he held a bouquet of pink and white tulips.

'It's all right,' Ailieyha said to Rane, nodding her head in defeat. 'You should go.'

Why, Rane wondered, as he stood to face Bulba, *shouldn't* he leave? How could he think to protect Ailieyha from this monster of a man? And what would be the point in doing so even if he could? For if Bulba did not slay Ailieyha on this evening of snow and bitter cold, then surely he would on some other night. In any case, Ailieyha would soon enough die: of some mutilating disease or of a fall on the ice or in the hell of an exploding star – or even of the ravages of old age. Life consumed life nearly as quickly as a match flaming into fire and then burning out into black char. Why couldn't people just embrace their fate, with all its resultant painlessness and peace, and make a dignified end to things?

And then something happened, a seemingly small thing, that opened a door to the deeps containing Rane's own fate. Bulba lifted back his arm and flung the tulips at Ailieyha's face. His contempt for such a bright flowering of womanhood enraged Rane. He realized that he could not leave Ailieyha. How could he *not* protect her? What did it mean to be a man and not be willing – or even joyously eager! – to give up one's safety and self in order to save another?

'No!' he called out.

Bulba turned to look at him in amazement. Though Rane

was a tallish man with a body hardened from climbing rocks and ice, he stood half a head shorter than did Bulba and weighed half as much. As Rane shook his fist in the air, Bulba's eyes flared and his face flushed with what could only be called the lust for battle. For it must have been obvious to Bulba that in only moments, it would be he who destroyed Rane.

Rane felt certain of this, too. He no longer cared. He took a step toward Bulba, and then another. As he fell into a full-out charge, the floorboards creaked beneath his bare feet. From far away came the sound of a woman's whimpering.

'No, no!'

He knew that if Bulba laid hold of him with his monstrous hands, he would break Rane's bones or perhaps simply tear off his limbs. Therefore Rane had to deliver a disabling blow before Bulba could close with him. He had no idea, however, how he might do that. For even in the dormitory brawls of his youth and in the many violent hokkee games – and in all the years of three long lifetimes between then and now – he had never struck another human being.

'Rane!'

Memory called to him. It spoke in the voice of a woman, like that of his mother – and like Maria's voice, too, along with the voices of all women, melded into one. At first soft, sweet, and musical, it quickly grew deeper and richer until it rang out like the voice of the earth itself. Rane heard in it the murmuring of that which had formed the earth and the name of the unnamed intrinsicality behind and beneath the world. He had never been able to say this name. It hid somewhere in his memory, though, like the name of a childhood friend that he felt ever trembling to break out into a blossom of recognition but could never quite recall. He always heard it whispering. A man, he knew, a remembrancer, had only to listen and he might apprehend all things.

'Rane!!!!'

And so it came to be that on a night of deep snow and savagery, with a man called Batar Bulba reaching out his hands toward Rane and Rane's life perhaps about to end, he listened with a terrible will to really hear. And one voice, in all the myriad millions of voices bound up in the One Memory, called to him. He knew, somehow, that the voice belonged to a warrior-poet

– a *woman* warrior-poet, for its timbre was feminine, rich, vibrant, and strong. Her words echoed in his ear and reverberated in his head. Her words weren't really words at all, but rather an utterance of the warrior-poet's being bound up in bone and blood. Rane heard this great cry ringing through his own blood. Through their childhoods and all the days of their lives, the warrior-poets practised their killing art, driving the memory of deft motions deep into muscle and nerves. And deeper still, the rush of cytoplasm and the explosions of epinephrine, histamine, and all the other molecules that caused the firing of neurons – like the long, dark roar of the universe – gathered in a single sound.

The memory of all things is in all things!

The memories of the warrior-poet were in him; in a way, the memories of the warrior-poet *were* him. And so Rane found the memory he needed not in a set of instructions or tondo-like images playing out in his mind, but in the sudden knowingness that poured through his body with the firing of his nerves and the beating of his heart. His blood filled his muscles with an urge to move with a terrible, quick grace. And so move he did, almost more quickly than the eye could see.

As Rane flew in close to Bulba, he dropped down low, onto one knee. The immense mass of Bulba's body loomed above him; Bulba's hands closed on empty air. His grotesque phallus still jutted out, like a spear painted blue and red – now only inches from Rane's face. Rane drove the heel of his hand up beneath it with a shockingly savage but precise force. Bulba's testicles smashed up against the harder tissues of his pelvis and ruptured like bloodfruits caught in a juice press. The huge man let loose a horrible shriek. Rane couldn't bear that. With Bulba doubling over and continuing to scream, Rane rose up off his knee in a single, fluid motion. He felt his fingers coursing with a will to make murder. A darkness opened before him, and through him, and he felt himself falling into a bottomless pit.

Much later he would remember the bones of his fist smashing into Bulba's throat – and the cartilages cracking like eggshells as Bulba's larynx broke and he began to cough and gasp for air. The thud of Bulba's body dropping to the wooden floor would pound at Rane's recollection of this moment, along with the sounds of Bulba wheezing and whimpering and choking to death.

Worst of all, however, would be an engram graved into the heart of his memory: Bulba's great, colourful phallus deflating like the rubber of a punctured balloon even as a primeval terror of nothingness filled Bulba's black, bulging eyes.

'Oh, my God – you killed him!'

He would hear, and hear again, Ailieyha crying out in astonishment and relief (and dread), even as he would feel once more her snapping closed the fasteners of his cape and frantically pulling this garment tight around him.

'Go – please!' she said to him. 'If they find you here, they will kill you!'

The unexpected anguish in her voice would remain with him forever. Then at last he turned and fled; with his cape billowing out behind him, he rushed out of the room and ran down the brothel's halls like a madman. In his fury, he broke open four doors to rooms that had always remained locked.

'Maria!' he cried out. 'Maria, Maria!'

But he did not find her in any of them. Finally, he had to give up. When he reached the door to the street and opened it, a blast of bitter wind carried him away into the blackness of a raging storm.

6

Rane skated without plan or purpose into a wall of moving air and particles of snow. Cold it was, so deeply cold that he instantly felt the water in the skin of his face hardening into ice. He whipped off his gloves and pressed his relatively warm hands against his cheeks. Then he tied Maria's scarf around his head so that it covered his face from his chin to his stinging eyes. The wind rose like the scream of a dying man and drove the scent of Maria from Rane's nostrils.

I have murdered a man!

He could barely hear the staccato of his skates striking the street beneath him. Soon the storm piled up layers of snow that muffled that metallic sound, even as it rimed his eyes with icy crusts. He could barely see, barely think. A frenzy of tiny, six-sided ice crystals scattered the light of the glowglobes. Through the clouds of snow swirling through the darkness, he had a very hard time making out the course of the street as it snaked its way through the Slizzaring's nearly invisible buildings. He turned right, then left and left again. He turned a hundred times through a maze that often defied even those who dwelled in this district – turned and turned and turned until he felt the fluids in the curved canals of his inner ear circling around and around and spinning him off into a dizzying emptiness that made him sick.

After a while, the snow driving down from the sky thinned out and then stopped altogether. At the same time, though, it grew even colder. Rane remembered a word, *morakaleth*, which the Alaloi used to describe the kind of killing cold that sometimes follows in the wake of such initial icy precipitation. Rane determined to get home quickly; failing that, he would have to seek shelter wherever he could.

Why, he asked the buildings around him, couldn't he manage to orient himself? No one, of course, knew the city completely, but shouldn't the greatest of remembrancers have learned the streets of Neverness? As Rane skated and skated, and turned and turned, it seemed that he had plunged into a topological nightmare. He recalled what he knew of the mathematical spaces of the manifold. Many of these – such as the torsion and the klein spaces – twisted and turned with a similar confusion. And many a pilot venturing into the space beneath realspace had become lost within such mathematical mazes, not because no clearly defined pathway or exit into the universe existed, but simply because they could not find their way out. So far as Rane knew, no pilot had ever accessed the manifold's ripples and contortions without the aid of a lightship's spacetime perturbing engines, which opened windows into a world at once wondrous and hideously complex. With the storm's coldness confusing both his brain and his body's sense of itself, however, more than once it seemed to him that he had skated down a chute of ice and plunged right through black space into the strange and unknown pathways of the manifold.

How long he struggled thus, he could not say. On whatever snow-choked gliddery or alley Rane turned down, he found himself alone. He encountered no one; of neither man nor alien passing by could he ask his way. He should have pounded on any of the streets' closed doors and asked directions. Even more, he should have located one of the district's numerous brothels and taken shelter by a crackling wood fire, if not within a woman's deeper warmth. He should have done whatever he needed to do in order to get out of the storm and to keep its terrible cold from ripping through his garments and piercing straight through to his heart.

I have murdered a man!

The chain of memory seemed to tighten around his chilled throat. It caused him to remember even more terrible things. His recollection of the redness of the tip of Bulba's sexual organ called up the hues of fire roses and Maria's favourite dress. He saw again Maria's beautiful, bitten lip and the drop of blood that welled up from it – the single drop of red blood that had rolled onto the white snow beneath her. He remembered her fingers curled into the scarf's colourful fabric as if she were trying to keep a hold of it. Then the image storm blowing through him became clouded, as with a billion particles of snow. *Had* Maria been wearing the scarf that day? Surely Rane must know if she had or had not been.

He realized with a sickening tightness in his belly that he could not bring to mind the threat that Maria had delivered to the leader of the White Hats, Artulio, or the last words that Maria had spoken to Rane. He couldn't say why she had written poetry or which dish at their favourite restaurant she had liked the best. He could not recall a single time of kissing her red lips. Why *had* she wanted to be with him? Which planet had been the planet of her birth?

Then a panic seized hold of him as he tried to remember the name of the planet on which he himself had been born. Adrenaline squirted in his chest, and his heart started thumping so wildly that he couldn't dare to try to count the beats. In what year had he come to Neverness? *Why* had he wanted to join the Order? What year was it now? How old was he?

I have murdered . . .

If Rane had no idea how old he was, something within him did. For it came to him that his body kept a record of such things even if his mind did not. The cells remembered their true age. If the body was brought back to youth too many times, the cells rebelled at the urge to hubristically (and hopelessly) remain forever young, and they began demanding to die.

'Why can I not find my way out of this damned district!' he shouted to the wind.

Surely the memory of how to free himself from the hell of the dark, twisted streets of the Slizzaring still dwelled somewhere inside him, as vivid and inviolate as the shining peak of a mountain. Or did it? For even mountains, he reflected, through gravity, wind, and rain, one grain of glittering sand at a time, eventually wore away.

As he kept on skating, he drew no closer to the secret of escape. The cold deepened. He felt his limbs clutching at a desperate fire as he shuddered and stumbled and tried to keep on moving. Finally, though, his exhaustion grew so overwhelming that he could not take another step. In a dark alley behind a building, he collapsed into a drift of snow. Soft it seemed, almost as soft as a feather bed. He wanted to sink down into its fluffy comfort and sleep forever.

Now, crudely sheltered from the wind, he could once again breathe in the scarf's piercing scent. He closed his eyes, breathing in and breathing out, hundreds of times and perhaps thousands. Memories filled him. He heard for the millionth time the piping of a shakuhachi and the beautiful melody that Maria had adored. He heard the sweet sound reverberating in his heart and pouring through his ears into his brain. It seemed to him that the scarf itself somehow made this music, for he felt its silken fabric fluttering and vibrating against his face. The pure notes of Maria's bamboo flute seemed to flow outward, too, and to echo off the alley's cold stone. He thought then that he must be caught in a hallucination, hearing the unhearable in a final derangement of his senses that would hurl him into death.

For a long time he lay listening to the scarf's arias and lullabies, lost in a mysterious music. When the wind howled down the alley's tube of stone, it would sweep away the plangent tones for a while, but always the scarf continued piping and singing, and always its music returned. In those welcomed moments, it seemed the only sound in all the universe.

At last, however, in the middle of the night, there came a different sound, and Rane thought that he hallucinated that, too. The noise of skate blades striking ice clinked out along the frozen air. A voice called out through the darkness – called out *for* him by his name:

'Lord Rane!'

He had neither the strength nor the desire to call back. He lay deep in his bed of snow, listening and listening.

'Lord Rane – I'm coming!'

He knew that he very well knew the person to whom the voice belonged, but he could not quite connect it to any of the faces of the tens of thousands of human beings he had ever met. Then his rescuer turned into the alley and skated right up to the snowdrift. He cried out, '*There* you are!'

He waded through the drift, and knelt by Rane's side. Rane felt a gloved hand brushing the snow from around his head; a distant glowglobe cast just enough light that he could make out the aquiline features of Sunjay's face.

'How?' Rane forced out. His voice wavered somewhere between a croak and a whisper. 'How did you find me?'

'How could I *not* find you?' Sunjay said.

Then he smiled, and Rane recalled how Sunjay always seemed to dance through life so lightly, as if life were a performance that demanded the utmost of his skill and attention, but nevertheless remained only part of a great Show that should not be taken too seriously.

'If you were any colder,' Sunjay said, pressing his ungloved hand to Rane's forehead, 'you'd be an icicle. Here – drink some coffee.'

Sunjay produced a thermos and unscrewed the top. He slid his arm behind Rane's neck, cradling his head and helping him to sit up. He held the rim of the thermos to Rane's lips. The dark, delicious waft of Summerworld coffee enveloped Rane's nostrils. He took a sip of the rich, extremely potent coffee, and then another. He burned his tongue and his throat but he didn't care. He kept on drinking and swallowing as the hot liquid poured new life into him.

'No, really,' he finally said to Sunjay. 'How could you possibly have found me here?'

'It wasn't so hard,' he explained mysteriously. 'We were to have met last night at your house for a review of the thirty-third attitude, do you remember? When you didn't come home, I went looking for you.'

Which, of course, was no explanation at all.

'Come, Lord Rane,' Sunjay said.

Sunjay, who had attained much of his adult height and had grown into the same sort of preternatural strength that had powered the bodies of Mallory and Danlo wi Soli Ringess, practically pulled Rane up out of the snowdrift to his feet. He hauled Rane's arm around his shoulders, the better to help him stand and skate through the Slizzaring's wind-blown streets.

'I can't,' Rane said.

'Of course you can.'

'I have . . .' he began. He took a deep breath. 'I have murdered a man.'

In the glowglobes' soft illumination, Sunjay's expressive face and eyes spoke a flurry of words of the *Asta Siluuna*'s strange, silent language. Then he said, 'Of course you have. But we'll talk of that later, if you'd like, sir. Right now, we've got to get you home.'

'But I don't remember. I don't remember how to go home.'

Sunjay's face broke into a smile as if Rane had made a great joke. 'Oh, that isn't so hard. It's *this* way.'

With his arm now locked elbow to elbow with Rane's, he led off through the Slizzaring. They passed dark lanes and drifts of snow. It didn't take long for Sunjay to guide them out of the district, into the slightly straighter streets south of the Merripen Green – only a quarter of a mile from the East-West Sliddery. Once they reached this great boulevard of orange ice, even Rane could have pointed the way back to his house.

Three times along the way to the Pilots' Quarter, they had to stop at warming pavilions. With gusts of hot air melting the ice crusted to Rane's hair and making the scarf billow out like a banner, Sunjay insisted on tending to Rane's frostbitten fingers and face. He called for torrid gel packs, which he applied to Rane's throat and armpits. He made sure that Rane finished the mugs of hot chocolate that Sunjay ordered for him.

In this way, they made their way back to Rane's house, where Sunjay put him to bed. He stood guard over him for the rest of the night. In the morning, he made Rane a breakfast of Summerworld coffee and buttered cinnamon toast. When he saw that Rane was out of danger, he said goodbye, for Rane wanted to think, to remember, and to be alone.

I have murdered . . .

The practical ramifications of his encounter with Bulba bothered Rane the least, though they tormented him enough that he couldn't stop sweating and shaking. The more that he considered the matter, the more it seemed to him unlikely that he would be connected with this crime. Ailieyha did not know his real name, and probably would not tell it to anyone even if she did. The owner of the brothel – a greedy, ravaged harridan called Suva – would not want to draw attention to the even greater crimes that occurred inside its locked rooms. Most likely she would find a circumspect way to dispose of Bulba's corpse: perhaps by dumping it into a snowdrift, where it would not be discovered until the thaw of midwinter spring uncovered the bodies of many other Lost Ones.

Rane thought that he would do best to forget about Ailieyha

and her squalid, perilous life, but of all the things that seemed to be slipping from his memory, the image of a shocked Ailieyha standing over Bulba's broken body was not one. How *could* he forget her? How could he just abandon her to the next Batar Bulba who decided to batter down her door?

After half a morning of thinking through things – and after drinking five cups of strong coffee – he devised a plan to rescue Ailieyha. He put on his furs and his skates, and he went out into the cold to pay Tamara a visit.

'I need to ask you a favour,' he said to her in the privacy of her tea room. Then, as Tamara's baby sucked the milk from her breast and met eyes with Rane, he told Tamara all that had happened.

'Oh, God, you are lucky to be alive!' she said.

'You might put it that way. Do you think you can help me?'

Because he had spent nearly all his money on the many women of the Slizzaring, he could not buy a restaurant for Ailieyha, as he had considered doing for Cornelia. In any case, Ailieyha remained imprisoned within the brothel. It had occurred to Rane that he might use what little gold he had left to buy Ailieyha from Suva. He could not, of course, make this purchase himself. Therefore he had devised the following scheme: he would donate the gold to the Society of Courtesans, whose agent would approach Suva to make arrangements. The Society would then protect and employ Ailieyha, as either a servant, a paranymph or an aspirant courtesan.

'Does she have a calling?' Tamara asked.

'I have never met a woman who worked so hard to please a man.'

'Oh?'

He did not need a cetic's talent of reading faces to determine what she was thinking. He said, 'Maria did not have to work to please me.'

Did the sun have to work to shower its radiance upon the earth? Did the earth need to labour to bring forth beings that basked in the sun's sweet heat? Maria, he remembered, had taken so much delight in delighting him that she couldn't help giving of herself, without measure or restraint, as an infinite ocean pours itself out only to replenish itself from a mysterious source – and so becomes vaster and ever deeper in the pouring.

'I will see what I can do,' Tamara told him. 'Please give me a few days.'

And so as Rane wished, it came to be. The Society's agent made the short journey to the brothel and bought out Ailieyha's 'contract', as Suva euphemistically referred to Ailieyha's bondage. He escorted her across the city to the Courtesan's Conservatory, just south of the Street of Embassies. On those beautiful grounds shaded with lilac trees, in one of the pretty old buildings that housed the Society's novices, Ailieyha was given a room full of rich fabrics and fine furniture, sweet air, and freshly cut flowers – a room whose door locked only from the inside. Rane visited Ailieyha in that room as soon as he could. He desired not her erotic company, however, but only conversation.

Within moments of their meeting, he learned something that astonished him: Batar Bulba was not dead! Rane sat in a comfortable chair by the room's windows as Ailieyha took the chair opposite him and told him the incredible story:

On that bitterly cold night, after Rane had fled in one direction down the halls of the brothel, it seemed that Ailieyha had rushed into another part of the brothel, where she had retrieved a jambool pipe and a small but exceedingly sharp fruit knife. Upon returning to her room, she knelt over Bulba's massive form and put the knife to his throat. Instead of slashing the arteries there to ensure Bulba's quick demise, however, she made a deft incision through the tissues below Bulba's crushed larynx so as to expose his trachea. Into this gaping hole in his flesh, she inserted a cut piece of the jambool pipe. Bulba's lungs spasmed to pull in air through the pipe and the wound's bloody red suck, and to push it out, again and again, in a desperate rattle and wheeze. But at least Bulba could breathe again.

'I'm sorry,' Ailieyha said to Rane. She felt it necessary to apologize for the great distress that the iniquity of Bulba's continued existence would cause him. 'Batar Bulba was the most horrible of men, but I couldn't just let him die by my bed.'

As Rane considered the implications of what she told him, he tried to swallow back his first three impulses, which were shock, fear, and anger at Ailieyha for saving the life of a man who no doubt would now try to hunt down Rane and destroy him. Then it came to him that Maria likely would have done exactly the same thing as had Ailieyha – and so Rane surrendered to his fourth impulse, which was compassion.

'It's all right,' he said, touching Ailieyha's cheek. 'You acted out of kindness, and you shouldn't feel sorry for that.'

'I don't think that Bulba will find it so kind.'

'Why not?'

'I don't think, either, that he will try to hunt you down.'

What she related then caused Rane to shudder and to exult – and to waver between the sadness of compassion and the satisfaction of revenge. For it seemed that Bulba would never be the same man again. The blow that Rane had delivered to Bulba's testicles had crushed them beyond repair, and Bulba had needed to visit a cutter who had amputated the twin nuggets of ruined flesh and had implanted new ones that did not work as well as they should have. Bulba's magnificently coloured phallus no longer worked at all, due to damage to the nerves of Bulba's groin that the cutter could not ameliorate. Bulba might have bellowed out his outrage and grief over losing the use of his most precious parts, except that he had lost the power of speech as well due to the death of billions of his neurons during those moments of choking when his blood could not oxygenate the language centres in his brain. He walked now (he could not skate) with a limp, his half-numbed body listing to the right. Most of the time, however, he avoided the Slizzaring's streets altogether, hiding in his jambool-tainted room instead. For the word had got out that Ailieyha was being protected by a ronin warrior-poet, who had a contract to slay Bulba on sight.

'You are cruel in your compassion,' Rane said. 'Not that Bulba doesn't deserve it – I have never known a man more worth hating.'

'But I never hated him!'

'No?'

'I . . . dreaded him.'

And that, he reflected, illustrated the difference between Ailieyha and Maria. For in all the universe, Maria had feared only one thing – and that was not a man such as Batar Bulba. She would certainly have hated him, though, and with passion, as naturally and as easily as she breathed or made poetry or cried out in gladness whenever Rane brought her flowers. Maria, like a Fury, would have trembled to use Ailieyha's fruit knife to slash Bulba's throat and thus complete the destruction that Rane had begun. Even more, her darker angels would have impelled her to want to castrate Bulba, severing his sexual organs down to the root so that there could be no hope of a cutter someday restoring him. That she would not have completed such a savage act, he could not ascribe to her compassion – nor to respect for the law nor to any sense of doing wrong, and certainly not to a fear of retaliation. No, he thought, Maria would have spared Bulba the mutilation he deserved only because of the dream she had for herself (and for everyone) of becoming what she called a true human being.

'You're thinking of her again, aren't you?' Ailieyha said to him in the quiet of the room.

'Yes, I am.'

And the more he thought and remembered, the more it seemed to him that Maria might have saved Bulba's life as Ailieyha had – and then used the knife to castrate him after all. For although Maria had called Rane a romantic, it was she who entertained a great romance with the possibilities of humankind. Maria might have hoped to use shock and pain to make Bulba aware of the agonies he had inflicted on others, thereby awakening him to his innate empathy and to the suffering of the whole human race.

'I had hoped, somehow, through all of this,' Ailieyha said to Rane, bringing him back to her little room, 'that we might find a way to be together. But that's not possible, is it?'

Was that possible, he wondered? Why shouldn't it be? Why couldn't he be happy with this lovely woman, as much as he could be with anyone?

'No,' he finally said, 'that is not possible.'

'You won't find her, you know, in any brothel.'

'Probably not.'

'Where will you look, then?'

'I don't know.'

She stood up and walked around the table to his side. She took his hand. 'Well, I hope you do find her. I would like to thank her for inspiring the man who saved my life.'

She kissed his forehead, and he held her close like a treasure that he didn't want to surrender. Then he said goodbye and went outside into the cold, clear air.

7

After that, Rane ceased his excursions into the Farsider's Quarter. Although he refused to believe that Maria could be dead, he no longer hoped that he would find her imprisoned in one of the Slizzaring's brothels' filthy rooms. He denied as well the impossible conception that his memory could be failing him. He simply could not picture himself as one of the poor, befuddled wretches suffering the senile dementia, the angslan, of those who had pushed the body's ability to rejuvenate past its natural limits. Might he not have just exhausted himself during the many days since Maria's funeral? Could not the extreme distresses inflicted upon him have loosed torrents of cortisol and other hormones that had poisoned his brain and temporarily impaired his ability to remember? Did he not just need to rest, to recuperate, and to return to his familiar life? Wouldn't it all come back – every sparkling memory – if he did?

He could scarcely remember his old life before Maria, however, much less resume it. Even so, he tried. He took up again the mantle of Lord Remembrancer and submitted himself to the often tedious duties of his office. He made daily journeys to the Academy, where he sat within the draughty, cold halls of the College of Lords and listened to crusty old men and women hold forth about all matters of state, from the continuing war between the Solid State Entity and the Silicon God to speculations about the evolution of the Golden Ring and the *Asta Siluuna* and other eschatological concerns. He had tea with the Order's masters and other high professionals. He lectured novices about the fundamentals of the Remembrancers' art, and he instructed journeymen in more advanced techniques.

He never, though, begrudged the time he spent tutoring his students. He especially enjoyed the company of the *Asta Siluuna*. One of the Children, Binah Jolatha Alora, a girl with fine, delicate features and golden hair, had been orphaned even as he had long ago. The recent war (recent as Rane thought of things) had left her physically maimed: the blast of a hydrogen bomb had driven burning bits of stone into her eyes, which the cutters had needed to remove. Three attempts to regrow these bright blue orbs had failed. Sometimes that happened, for the complexity of the nerve connections of eye to brain challenged the skills of even the finest of cutters. She never seemed to regret what had happened to her. Rane thought that her misfortune had left her with a double disability, for being as eyeless as a scryer, she could not participate in the intricate and nuanced eyetalk of the Children. She faced the future, though, with what seemed to Rane a preternatural equanimity, even a panache. One day, he overheard her whisper to Sunjay: 'I can talk in other ways, and someday I'll talk the *Asta Siluuna* into entrusting me with much of their *chith* and you into marriage.'

That Sunjay had fallen in love with this pretty girl he never admitted, though he didn't deny it either. Rane met with him every five days or so at Rane's chalet above North Beach. There, in the meditation room – a glorious, quiet place of shatterwood beams polished with lemon oil and aglow with the reflected radiance of many lit candles – he helped Sunjay master the Remembrancers' art. One evening, when Sunjay was having some difficulty with the nineteenth attitude of mythopoesis, Rane bade him lie back on one of the room's tatami cushions. He instructed him to concentrate on the sound of the shakuhachi music that filled the room.

'We could skip mythopoesis, if you'd like,' Rane said to the boy stretched out before him. Rane sat cross-legged in the lotus position by his side. 'Sometimes open-waiting is a better beginning of the sequencing toward the sixty-fourth.'

Thus did he like to refer to the final remembrancing attitude that encompassed and made sense of all the others. Some called the sixty-fourth the 'One Memory'. Rane himself believed that the Elder Eddas sought by the entire Order in the time of Leopold Soli and Mallory Ringess might be a doorway to this universal memory that must underlie all things and make sense of and record every event in spacetime that had ever occurred. Rane had spent much of his life exploring and articulating this mysterious One Memory.

'But, sir,' Sunjay said, 'don't you still believe that mythopoesis is a better beginning for me?'

Rane considered the various forms of racial memory and archetypes that came so easily to Sunjay, only a generation removed from Danlo's adoptive Devaki tribe and all their rituals and myths. He said, 'It doesn't matter what I believe, only what you choose.'

'I wish other remembrancers thought as you do. Why can't they trust the deviations from the formulae?'

He spoke of the many established sequences of attitudes thought to most effectively lead a remembrancer toward the One Memory.

'The formulae,' Rane said, defending his profession, 'have proved very effective for very many people.'

'Why can't they trust *me*?'

Rane looked down at him. 'I'm sure they would, if they knew you better.'

Sunjay seemed to take great encouragement from Rane's smile, as he might soak up sunshine on a warm day in false winter. He smiled back at Rane. 'I wonder if we might try something altogether different.'

'What are you thinking?'

'It might take up too much of your time.'

Rane smiled again, now at Sunjay's concern for *him*. 'How better could I spend my time?'

'Thank you, sir. Perhaps, then, we could begin with olfaction.'

As Sunjay listed a sequence of remembrancing attitudes that he wished to try, Rane listened intently, not just with ears and nerves and three lifetimes of experience, but with his heart, as Maria had taught him. He placed his hand on Sunjay's chest, not only to help steady Sunjay's breathing but as if to dip into the torrent of words that poured out of him, as if his fingers could make better sense of his student's enthusiasm than could the auditory lobes of his brain. He could almost feel the wisdom of innocence bound up in Sunjay's hot young blood, along with the preternatural instinct toward the highest of things that had been a gift of his remarkable family. Although Rane often denied it, he felt this same gift inside himself, and he found his greatest satisfaction as a teacher when he called upon the best of himself to act as a sort of mirror for all that was brightest in another.

And so from a wooden box filled with trays packed with vials containing essential oils, pheromone suspensions, and the like, he removed a little bottle of green glass and unstoppered it. The pungency of peppermint wafted out into the air. He didn't need to hold the vial very close to Sunjay's nose for him to begin recalling the aroma of the peppermint tea that Tamara Ten Ashtoreth had often drunk while nursing him. That smell connected to the sweetness of his mother's milk and the sweetness of life itself as the chain of olfaction pulled Sunjay deep into memory.

After a while, Rane guided him through the irregular sequencing of synaesthesia, dereism, and gestalt before helping him pass deep into recurrence. There Sunjay remained for most of an hour, reliving moments of his own life – and perhaps the lives of others. Rane continued holding his hand lightly against Sunjay's chest. He could almost feel him opening out and inward upon that same brilliant memory that shone through all things.

At last, though, Sunjay opened his eyes and sighed. He clasped his hand over Rane's. 'I went deep, sir, so deep. Deeper than I have ever been.'

His huge smile seemed a reflection of Rane's own.

'But I must go deeper. All the way to the centre.'

'*Is* there a centre? I think the One Memory is like an infinite sphere whose circumference is nowhere and centre is everywhere.'

'Then I must go everywhere, no matter how hard the journey.'

'We can try again tomorrow, if you'd like,' Rane said.

'Can we try something else now?'

'What do you have in mind?'

'Do you still have time?'

'As much as you need.'

Sunjay outlined a sequence of attitudes that seemed to Rane so unlikely as to be both dreadfully difficult and nearly nonsensical. Did he *really* trust Sunjay to experiment on himself this way?

'And after sanaesthesia, sir, I would like to try to enter the One Memory with the help of kalla.'

Rane's smile died, and his face grew stern. 'Hasn't it been only a few days since I last gave you kalla?'

'It's been six, sir. I am more than ready again.'

'You think so?'

'Haven't you said that I have a knack for making kalla my friend?'

'All right, then.'

Again, he placed his hand over Sunjay's heart. He told him to delve down through the layers of deep meditation. When he felt sure that the room's gleaming surfaces and murmuring echoes of shakuhachi music had slid away from Sunjay's consciousness, he brought out a small bottle made of blue glass. It held an ounce of kalla, as clear as water. Those of Rane's profession sometimes used kalla to 'remember down the DNA' – down and back and through the dark, roaring rivers of genetic memory toward the One Memory, said to be not only the final cause of all consciousness and the chemical workings of the bodymind but the source of all things. With Sunjay's eyes lightly closed and his breath flowing in and out as soft as a whisper, Rane unstoppered the bottle and held its rim near Sunjay's motionless lips.

'Take one sip of kalla, and flee God,' the remembrancers say. 'Take two sips to see God. Take three sips and *be* God.'

From the first, Rane had disapproved of such deistic characterizations of remembrance's most profound and ineffable experience. And for many years he had insisted that no one should take more than two sips. Hadn't Hanuman li Tosh, in emulation of Danlo wi Soli Ringess, sipped three times of the prepotent kalla, and hadn't the resultant descent into delusions of divinity driven him mad? Yes, it had, and in his monstrous inflation of his self-conception, Hanuman had brought war and ruin to Neverness, and had set loose an insane mechanism of cataclysm that might have destroyed the universe. And yet Danlo, whom they called Danlo the Wild, had also taken three sips – and he had broken through the sky to a new universe of powers and possibilities for the human race.

In certain ways, Rane partook of Danlo's essential wildness and even intensified it. In the reactionary pendulum that swung back toward safety and rigidification of custom naturally ensuing after the War's chaos ended, there came a time when Rane cast off the constraints that the Order and his fellow master remembrancers imposed upon him. Because the *Asta Siluuna*, such as Sunjay and Chandra, seemed to possess a radiant sanity and a rare talent for exploring the ancient caverns of memory within themselves, Rane had experimented by administering to the brightest of them a higher dose of kalla. It had become his practice to give Sunjay and certain others such as Binah three sips.

Or rather, three drops. In the mass ceremonies of remembrance that had fed the fanatical fires of the Way of Ringess, the kalla had been diluted with water so that it could more easily be drunk by hundreds and then thousands from a common cup. Now, in the stillness of Rane's meditation room, he used a more precise measure. From the blue bottle he drew out a pipette full of pure kalla. It exuded a fragrance recalling hyacinth and mint. He touched open Sunjay's lips and let three drops of kalla roll into his mouth. Then he set down the bottle and waited.

And while he waited, he recalled other evenings in which he had given Sunjay three drops of kalla – even as he had Maria. When he closed his eyes, he could see Maria stretched out on the tatami cushion beneath him, her heavy breasts rising and falling with her breath. He remembered an evening when Maria had moved her head toward him as he had touched her lips, which had caused the pipette to knock against her *labium inferium* and to release prematurely a single drop of kalla. He watched as this shimmering drop, five one-hundredths of a millilitre, beaded up upon her lip. It captured his gaze, as might a scryer's crystal. Through the kalla's fathomless clarity he perceived another drop of liquid, coloured red. The bit of blood welled up from Maria's bitten lip and drew him down and into a sea of flowing red that tasted of iron. The sound of the sea caught him up in its rhythmic and sempiternal sobbing and sobbing and sobbing.

When he had fought back the one memory that he could not bear, he opened his eyes to see Sunjay lying nearly motionless on his tatami. The flickering candles seemed to lick his face with yellow tongues of fire. In Rane's confusion of space and time, person and place, it seemed to him that Sunjay had long since reached that perfect moment when the deepest level of meditation would prepare him both to endure and to exploit a full dose of three drops of kalla. He seemed to be waiting and waiting, patiently and peacefully. Rane reached down toward the glossy wooden floor and grasped the blue bottle.

Fifteen-hundredths of a millilitre of the Remembrancers' drug dropped down between Sunjay's open lips. The scent of hyacinth and mint sweetened the air and sparked memories of other moments when Rane had administered kalla to Sunjay. The scent suddenly pierced straight through Rane's nose and mouth to his stomach and made him sick, for a ghost memory of giving Sunjay his dose of kalla only a short while earlier haunted him. Or *was* it a ghost memory? He blinked his eyes, staring down at Sunjay. The candlelight made everything in the room seem uncertain and fuzzy. *Had* he in fact already given Sunjay his three drops? And then three more? No, no, that was impossible! – the Lord Remembrancer could never make such a terrible mistake. Thomas *Rane*, the decent man, the sensitive and noble man who had a perfect memory and a perfect hope for Sunjay and Sunjay's future could never have done such a thing. But what if his ghost memory was real?

As Rane watched and waited, Sunjay's breathing began to slow down. Four drops of kalla would kill some people; few could live after drinking five drops, and no one had ever survived six. Rane pressed his fearful fingers to Sunjay's throat and felt the arteries there pulsing at a rate of perhaps fifty times in a minute – then forty, thirty, and twenty. His own pulse, tight and choking in his throat, began to quicken until it seemed that his heart beat like the wings of a frightened bird. The acids of undigested coffee ate at his stomach. Sweat broke from his forehead and face. For although remembrancers sometimes joked of an anti-remembrancers' drug called akalla, there existed no antidote that could bring back a person who had poisoned himself by drinking too much kalla.

Soon enough, Sunjay's breathing stopped altogether and so did his heart. The room fell quiet. Sunjay's face relaxed into an eidolon of complete acceptance, deep peace, and the bliss of nothingness. The coldness of time, Rane knew, would preserve him this way forever in eternity – and in Rane's memory.

With this hateful thought, Rane fell into a fury of motion. He locked his hands together and pressed down in violent rhythms against Sunjay's chest. He opened Sunjay's mouth, and breathed hot, hurting breaths through Sunjay's unmoving lips. He breathed and he breathed, dozens of times, and more – and he would gladly have breathed his last breath into Sunjay then have given up breathing altogether and forever if only Sunjay might return to him.

And while he performed such futile protestations against fear and fate, he remembered: Sunjay hungrily and happily drinking life from Tamara's breast; Sunjay's tentative, toddling first steps; the way Sunjay had called flowers 'flowwows' in his first word spoken in the Language of the Civilized Worlds (at only half a year old!) and his even more precocious mastering of the finger inflections and the eye speech of the *Asta Siluuna*. He remembered sitting Sunjay on his lap and telling him stories of gods and goddesses, of dragons and demons and bright, shining, magical swords. How bright and beautiful Sunjay had been! How radiant his eyes, how incandescent his smile! How could Rane let such splendour die from the world? How could he bear for Sunjay to die – and even more, how could he ever excuse himself for causing Sunjay's death?

No, no, he never could, never *would*, and in his despair over the ruin of a life he valued more than his own, he let his head fall down onto Sunjay, and he wept. The sobs torn from his insides vibrated Sunjay's still body; his tears soaked the scratchy wool of the kamelaika that covered Sunjay's chest. He wept and he wept, and his lungs clutched at the room's death-poisoned air.

I have murdered a boy!

He sat up straight and grasped the bottle of kalla. Again he unstoppered it. As he had many times, he held the cool glass pipette to his lips. He let fall onto his tongue six drops of the magical, murderous kalla. He swallowed, and he waited.

I have murdered a boy!

He fell down to the wooden floor with a thud that he did not hear. He fell through the universe. There planets and stars and entire galaxies spun about their centres in whirlpools of hard matter and fire. There, too, in the universe inside him, haemoglobin and serotonin and DNA and all the other soft, moist matter of his body whirled and streamed in perfect consciousness of itself. How could Rane not be conscious of this infinitude of shimmering, magical stuff? How could he not make pure magic out of the substance of himself? How could he, as a teacher, not share the intense knowingness of this new art with this beloved boy, even if he could never explain it to him, or even to himself? And so he found himself reaching out to Sunjay, not with his hand but with something else, something mysterious, neither completely felt nor seen. He reached out, and in, and what moved inside him modelled the way that Sunjay needed to know and move himself.

I have . . .

Rane sat up, and wept to see Sunjay lying so still. He pressed his hand close to Sunjay's quiet heart. Then he gasped in astonishment to feel Sunjay's lungs explode into life and gasp in a breath of their own. He shook his head in shocked bewilderment as Sunjay's heart began beating again, like a great booming, indestructible drum. He lived! He lived! Impossible it was to survive drinking six drops of kalla, yet inexplicably and rejoicedly, Sunjay somehow had returned to life!

And Rane himself had survived drinking six drops of kalla, and he did not know how that could be.

After another eternity of waiting, Sunjay finally opened his eyes and looked up at Rane. He smiled at Rane in a glory of triumph, gratitude, and understanding. Rane might have hoped that Sunjay would be amnesic of the moments he had spent in the land of the dead, as of a man coming out of a coma – but Sunjay seemed completely aware of his descent into the underworld and of what had happened to send him there.

'That was wild!' Sunjay murmured with a huge grin. 'And yet pure and perfect, too.'

His smile deepened as he looked at Rane. He knew, Rane thought, that Rane had given him six drops of kalla – and he knew that Rane knew that he knew. The *Asta Siluuna* had a word, *awarei*, which meant something like radiant awareness, as of a beam of light shone down through layers of deep understanding or reflected back and forth between a tessellation of mirrors until it grew almost impossibly bright. *Awarei* was at once the highest of human faculties and an expression of that glorious urge which sought out and pushed at the bounds of those faculties – and Sunjay possessed it in abundance.

'I went so far out,' Sunjay said. 'And . . . in. Almost to the centre. Almost.'

'I was afraid you wouldn't come back.'

'You, afraid, sir?'

'Only a little,' Rane said with a smile. *Awarei* was also a game, which Rane played poorly, and sometimes it took on the lineaments of war.

'But you must have often visited the same place yourself.'

'Oh, yes, many times. Sometimes I can't wait to go back for an extended holiday.'

'How not – it was so clear there!' Sunjay said. 'I could see everything, *be* everything. I wouldn't have minded remaining myself, but I heard you calling me back.'

'But how could you have heard anything at all?'

'How could I not?'

'How *did* you return?'

'That wasn't so hard once I realized the nature of the test.'

'I see, I see,' Rane said. The test? What test? What was Sunjay talking about?

'Thank you, sir, for having so much trust.'

Then, through the corneas of Sunjay's blue, brilliant eyes, he perceived the glimmer of what the boy had meant. Rane had the sensation of a lightship passing through a window to the manifold – or rather what he imagined that sensation might be. He suddenly began passing through windows of perception, window after window, in an accelerating interfenestration that opened into the dazzling depths of Sunjay's design. It became pellucidly clear to him that Sunjay meant to act as if Rane's giving him six drops of kalla was nothing more than a test of his remembrancing prowess – and that Sunjay expected Rane to agree to this pretence. And why did Sunjay do this? Only because he couldn't bear for Rane to lose face.

'How could I not trust you?' Rane said to him.

How could he not honour Sunjay, which meant honouring their little lie? And how could Rane determine that he hadn't been testing Sunjay after all? Perhaps some silent part of him had somehow known that Sunjay would not only survive the overdose of kalla but would return from neverness bearing jewels of light in his hands.

'Thank you, sir.'

'You're welcome. Now can you tell me how you came back to this room?'

Rane could not tell of his own journey toward the core of himself and back.

'But you must have returned many times yourself.'

'One would hope so,' Rane said. 'But one would also have to admit that I lack your talent with language and so lack your ability to describe what for many would seem indescribable.'

'Only because you haven't had time to practise speaking with Chandra and me, and the others.'

Rane fought back a smile. 'A person not experienced in consuming the higher doses of kalla would ask how anyone could survive such a test.'

'But that is not so hard to describe! Could you not simply say that one needs only to isolate the molecules of kalla in the blood and metabolize them more slowly, thus deepening the experience while eliminating the risk?'

'Oh, is that all?'

'What more should there be?'

'But how does one isolate these molecules? And control their metabolization? The inexperienced would want to know such a thing.'

'By . . . reaching inside and taking hold of them.'

'But how could anyone do such a thing?'

'Just as you showed me.'

'Please say more.'

'How could one *not*? Can *you* not, Lord Rane, at this moment, conceive that you will your hand to open or close? Does not that wish impel the firing of your neurons and the electrochemical impulses that shoot down your nerves into your fingers? Do not these impulses cause your muscles to contract and enable you thus to move the molecules of which you are made?'

Sunjay reached out and offered his hand to Rane. 'Can you not take hold of whatever you wish?'

With a smack of skin upon skin, Rane clasped hands with Sunjay. Many things passed between them then: forgiveness, affection, understanding. *Awarei*. For a moment, Rane felt an incredible strength coursing through Sunjay's fingers – and through his own.

'Perhaps that is as good an analogy as anyone could make,' Rane said, 'for what must be an ecology of causation and actualization that is too complex to describe.'

'Or too simple, sir.'

Sunjay smiled again, and Rane felt his desire that Rane should grasp hold of this miraculous and terrifying new power. Rane, however, had to look away from Sunjay. He let go his hand, and he pressed his fingers to his face to try to scrub the exhaustion from his eyes.

'We should both rest now,' Rane told him. 'Return in five more days, and I'll help you continue to explore the sixty-fourth attitude.'

'I should like that, sir.'

'But this time, we'll need to limit the kalla to three drops.'

Sunjay's lips turned up, and his eyes brightened. 'But there's no need for kalla at all any more.'

'What do you mean?'

'The same way that one can take hold of the kalla, inside,' Sunjay said, 'one can learn to synthesize the molecules themselves. *Create* them from the neurotransmitter precursors or the peptides and the amines, even down to the individual atoms. It is the next step, yes?'

'The next step,' Rane said softly.

After Sunjay had said goodnight and had skated off singing happily, Rane returned to the meditation room, for he could not sleep. He sat for an hour, gazing at the candles and replaying the recent events in his mind. He couldn't decide which troubled him more: intending to kill Batar Bulba and failing or not intending to kill Sunjay and very nearly sending him on to the other side of day. Surely his criminal negligence in giving Sunjay six drops of kalla, he told himself, would never be repeated, with any other student or in any other situation that tested Rane's abilities. In the end, things had come out well, hadn't they? Wasn't that all that *really* mattered?

He sat for more hours contemplating the answer to this question. Then he considered what would have resulted had not Sunjay been ready to take his 'next step'. He envisioned Sunjay lying cold and still inside a coffin on the Hollow Fields, and he again brought out the bottle of kalla. The blueness of the glass drew him into the even darker blueness of Sunjay's eyes, so full of trust, hope, and faith in life. Once, he himself had possessed such faith – and faith in his own ability to venture deep into the heart of the One Memory, as deep as anyone could go. How *had* he, really, made the journey nearly to its centre? What would happen if he dared once again to put the rim of the bottle to his mouth and take six long, deep, delicious sips?

8

Truth can be a difficult thing, pregnant with subtleties and bitter ironies. The telling of it can prove treacherous. Rane recalled the ancient saying: 'The truth that is not heard is not the truth.' In the days following Sunjay's experiment with the deadly dose of kalla, Rane came to formulate a newer and perhaps more profound saying: 'The truth that is not told is not the truth.' For he realized that if no record was made, and made formally, of his nerve-shattering evening with Sunjay, time and the nearly infinite power of self-deception might lead Rane to soften his culpability and so possibly to repeat it. He knew that he had to tell *someone* what had happened.

He met with Kolenya Mor at her house only a few streets away – a granite chalet that Rane knew too well. His old friend's taste ran toward the opulent, and Kolenya had covered the walls of her home with vivid Solsken frescoes and the floors with Fravashi carpets. Into her small rooms she had crammed many rare plants and flowers, collected from across the galaxy but most of which had originated on Old Earth. Rane noted the dwarf rubber trees and the ostrich ferns, the dahlias and the daisies and the pretty jonquils, which seemed to crowd her fireroom and give the impression that one had entered a greenhouse. Kolenya had acquired her passion for cultivation from Leopold Soli, Sunjay's great-grandfather. After all these years, Rane still wondered if Soli and Kolenya had been paramours, in violation of Kolenya's understanding with Rane – not to mention Soli's marriage vows.

Kolenya invited Rane to join her on the Fravashi carpet,

woven from the long white fur of a famous Old Father. He sat across from her, close to the smouldering fire, and too close to memories that came flickering back into his mind. He sipped from a cup of jasmine tea that Kolenya prepared for him, while she socialized with a twist of toalache. The tip of the burning herb flared into a bright orange as Kolenya puffed and drew in the fulsome smoke. He disapproved of her fondness for toalache, as he always had. And he tried to disregard the carelessness with which she settled down onto the carpet and the resultant flash of flesh as the silk of her blue eschatologist's robe pulled back to reveal her bare, voluptuous legs. He had always thought of their colour as alabaster.

'Now tell me, dear Rane,' she said, puffing at the toalache, 'why you've been ignoring me.'

Kolenya, who could be a subtle thinker in her professional capacity as an eschatologist, rarely exercised finesse in her dealings with others. She prided herself in being honest and direct, and she took on the pose that people appreciated her gems of advice when too often they felt burdened by the sheer weight of the treasure that she lavished upon them – or worse, felt brutalized by insights almost too brilliant to bear. She had a good heart, however, and that, allied with her intelligence, her sweet smile, and her pretty face, had won her many friends, if not paramours. Few there were who were willing to bask in the deepest intimacies of the soul and who really desired to have a light shone upon their character, their motivations, and their deepest deceptions.

'How could I ever ignore you?' Rane said to her with a smile. 'That would be like ignoring the sun.'

'Well, each evening the earth turns its face away into the night.'

'And each morning turns back.'

'Is this morning for you, Rane?'

'Are we to speak in metaphors the whole time of my visit?'

'Wouldn't you be more comfortable if we did?'

'Perhaps I would,' he admitted.

'Perhaps you'd rather we spoke of the weather. It has been unusually snowy and cold, don't you think?'

'Oh, yes, snowy, to be sure. And very, very cold.'

After some rounds of artificial small talk in which Kolenya

provided many openings for Rane to divulge the reason for his unusual visit, she began asking him pointed questions, trying to pierce the tough skin of his natural reticence:

'You have been absent from the College of Lords these past ten days – have you been ill?'

'No, just very busy,' he said.

'You look very tired – I've been worried about you.'

He rubbed his burning eyes, then waved his hand in the air. 'Thank you, but I'm fine.'

'Are you still climbing icefalls by yourself?'

'How did you know that?'

Because Kolenya felt more comfortable asking questions than answering them, she smiled at him and said, 'A journeyman holist, I can't say who, saw you skating through the Slizzaring – and wearing the rags of a harijan!'

Rane said nothing as he took a long sip of tea. Was she referring to Sunjay? No, no, he thought, Sunjay was a journeyman pilot, and he would never tell Kolenya or anyone of rescuing Rane from the snowdrift the night of his fight with Bulba.

'Whatever were you doing in such a place?'

'What was your journeyman doing there?' he countered.

'I know that with Maria gone, it must be terrible for you in many ways, but you can always come—'

'In fact, I was looking for Maria there.'

'What do you mean, you were looking for her?'

'Looking for the missing piece of the puzzle: who she was and why she did what she did.'

'But why should that be so hard to understand? Your puzzle is a puzzle only if you break it into pieces and try to fit them back in a way that they don't fit.' Kolenya sighed as if her blue robe had suddenly grown too tight around her heavy breasts. 'Maria was very simple, more so than anyone I've ever known. Everything that she did, she did *for* one reason and *from* one desire only.'

'Must I hear of that again?'

'When have you *heard* it at all?'

An oyster, drawing in a grain of sand along with the water that it filters for food, builds up layer upon layer of iridescent nacre in order to protect its tender tissues from the sand's irritating sharpness. So it creates a pearl. And so, metaphorically, did Rane protect himself from the sharpness of Kolenya's tongue. He sat staring at Kolenya, even as he built a shining sphere of obduracy that she would have needed a hammer to crack.

To break the uncomfortable silence, Kolenya tried a change of subject. 'How is your work going?' she asked him.

'Very well, I think.'

He wanted to blurt out a confession of his near-disaster with Sunjay, but he had always counted on Kolenya to draw such serious confidences from him. Then, too, now that it had come to it, he didn't know if he should tell Kolenya that he had given Sunjay such a monstrous dose of kalla.

But he had to say *something*, so he explained: 'I've been busy trying to articulate a model for how best to enter and negotiate the sixty-fourth attitude.'

'Oh? Is there a best way?'

'The One Memory might enfold more possibilities than I had thought.'

'Do you mean, the possibilities that Danlo began to explore when he became a god?'

He smiled at this. 'Whatever Danlo is, he's still a man. Even if what he accomplished in overcoming the poison that Hanuman gave him is something no one yet understands.'

'Not even you? Aren't you *the* Remembrancer?'

'Many outside our profession,' he said, smiling, 'are in awe of the nearly perfect memories of some of our practitioners. They wonder, for instance, how we can see every brushstroke of a tondo – each striated swirl of colour – with our eyes closed, or *hear* each note of a symphony as we replay it inside our heads.'

'I have wondered the same thing myself,' she admitted.

'Of course, how not? But if one thinks deeply enough about the matter, one is led to the fundamental question of how we remember anything at all?'

'Of course, of course.' She looked deeply at him. Then she said, 'Which naturally opens up the question of why we forget.'

'Naturally,' he said.

'I've often wondered what it must be like for you, forgetting nothing.'

'Oh, but I do forget some things, sometimes.'

'Yes – you forgot my hundredth birthday.'

'And you still remember that? I'm still sorry, Kolenya.'

'That's all right: to know you is to learn how to forgive.'

He rubbed the aching arteries of his throat as he looked away from her.

'What other things have you forgotten, dear?'

'Ah, trivial things, such as where I set down a book or whether I've added a spice to a dish that I've been cooking.'

'But you don't cook!'

'Well, I've begun to—'

'Or were you speaking metaphorically? Tell me about these delicious dishes you've prepared.'

'I'm sure it would bore you if I were to recount their recipes in detail.'

'But you do remember?'

'Why wouldn't I?'

'Because you've had a lot on your mind.'

'Yes, I've had a lot on my mind.'

'Such as articulating this new model for the sixty-fourth attitude?'

'Yes, among other things.'

'Can I assume that the model concerns the essential nature of memory and its preservation? Which would lead to the nature of the One Memory itself?'

'What other problem should concern a remembrancer more?'

'Perhaps the problem of how a human being can make sense of the One Memory.'

'You're very perceptive,' he said with a smile.

He went on to explain that the new model could be viewed as a precise navigation system through the stormy sea of the One Memory. Or, in a change of metaphors, he described the model as a sort of perfect translator, which rendered the universal and the absolute into the personal and the specific.

'Or,' he said, 'you could think of it as a blueprint instructing a person how to recreate individual memories from the infinitely vast store of raw material that is the One Memory.'

'I see, I see.' Kolenya relit her twist of toalache, which had gone out. She sat puffing at it, drawing in smoke and blowing it out in perfectly formed rings that floated through the air. 'So if someone forgot something – let's say whether or not he had added saffron to a chicken curry – he could find his way through the One Memory to the exact time, place, and perspective in which that event was recorded.'

'Yes, something like that.'

'But isn't that just what Mallory Ringess and Danlo did? And what the *Asta Siluuna* are doing?'

'Yes – but they are-doing it haphazardly and imperfectly.'

'You should be doing it, Rane. You should be leading the way in this.'

'I used to lead the kalla ceremonies for the Way of Ringess, do you remember?'

'The Children need you – and their children will as well. Bardo and the Order need you. And so do I, dear one.'

I need you, Maria had said to him.

'We're not ready,' he said. 'Don't you remember how the One Memory destroyed Hanuman? And nearly overwhelmed Danlo, too? We first need a map, lest we sail off the edge of the world.'

'Maps! Models! Attitudes! I think you'd rather spend your whole life bending over your precious blueprint than building a glorious cathedral that points toward the stars.'

'Each man has only one destiny,' he said.

Kolenya blew a smoke ring straight toward his nose. 'You're like the philosopher of a revolution who cannot abide the revolution he begins.'

'Revolutions are dangerous,' he said, coughing at the acrid toalache smoke. 'Even more dangerous is the co-opting of revolutions that one such as Hanuman stands ever ready to make.'

He thought he had scored a good point, for Kolenya sat in silence contemplating the smoke rings that widened through the air before evanescing into nothingness. Then she called out, 'Dangerous! Of course they are! Was it not dangerous for the first fish that left Old Earth's oceans to crawl up on dry land? And for the birds that took wing into the sky? And for our ancestors who left the forests to stand upright and to look out over the herds of antelope and the prides of lions that roamed the burning veldt of Afarique? And the pilots! They who made new mathematics and dared the burning black spaces of the manifold in their flimsy lightships – did they not open the human race to whole new sets of dangers never dreamed before? Revolutions are always dangerous! But, dear friend, *Homo sapiens* has been itself a revolution. *We* are, Rane. It's *here*, right now, in us, in this very room.'

As Rane looked away from Kolenya's fiery blue eyes to study the fronds of a fern that probably looked little different from the ferns of the Cretaceous Era a hundred million years before, he listened to her preach about her favourite subject. She spoke with a passion with which she rarely invested romance or eros. Sometimes he thought of her as a true scientist, in the ancient and best sense of that word, though often she betrayed scientistic (and even religious) tendencies, wanting more to know the absolute truth than desiring to search for it meticulously and endlessly, for the sake of the satisfaction that came from the search itself. Still, how could he not honour anyone who possessed such a great fidelity to the third of that triad of fundamental forces that the Plato had identified as Beauty, Goodness, and Truth? In this, she embodied the soul of the Order, for she had always wanted to stand at the very centre of an age-old and very noble enterprise. And of all the things that she wished to know, foremost was a picture of the way that the universe would unfold. Although he felt loath to put things in such terms (and she would never do), what she desired most deeply was to apprehend God's design.

When she had finally finished her declamations as to the glories and the infinite possibilities of the human race, he said to her, 'Aren't you conflating human-made revolutions – dependent on their technological tools of mathematics, physics, chemistry, and biology – with the natural Darwinian evolution that led those first fish to claw their way onto land and the first birds to fly?'

'*Am* I conflating? Very well, then I happily conflate. Revolution and evolution, technology and teleogenesis – *this* time, there is no difference.'

Rane's eyebrows pulled tight as he considered this. 'But haven't you eschatologists always explored that very connection? Haven't you in fact defined your discipline as an exploration of technology's effect on evolution?'

She puffed out another smoke ring, then waved her hand to disperse it. 'But there is strong and weak eschatology, old eschatology and new. And holistic eschatology and—'

'I always thought of you as mostly orthodox.'

'Well, I mostly was. But then I drank kalla along with Danlo wi Soli Ringess.'

At the mention of this dangerous drug, Rane's eyebrows pulled even tighter. Kolenya, he thought, could shift beliefs as easily as a flea hopping from one host to another. She had been born on Fostora as an Architect of the Cybernetic Universal Church, one of the many branchings of Edeism. At an early age, she had abandoned the older church in favour of the less stifling Church of Ede. Upon her emancipation at age eighteen, she had joined the mystical Elidis on Urradeth and then defected to the Danladis, who attempted to explain the uploading of Nikolos Daru Ede's mind into a computer and his subsequent divinization in purely rational terms. At age twenty-one, she had cast off Edeism altogether, in favour of the deep study required for admission to the Order. Miraculously, she had won admittance to the novitiate at the unheard-of age of twenty-three. For many years after – long after she had become first a journeyman, then a full professional and then a master eschatologist – she had cleaved to the more technological and therefore genetic and cybernetic extrapolations of human destiny. In this, she had stood in fierce opposition to the old Timekeeper and to the two most important Laws of the Civilized Worlds: that a man might do with his flesh as he pleased, but his DNA belonged to his species. And that Man could not stare too long at the face of the Computer and still remain as Man.

Then, upon her elevation as Lord Eschatologist, she had perforce joined her discipline's orthodoxy. Most of her peers held that human evolution was still unfolding as it had been for millions of years. And civilization, they taught – contrary to the position of many ancient transhumanists and singularitists – rather than clamp a brake on human biological evolution had actually accelerated it. In the forty thousand years since humanity's primeval hunters had settled down to farm the land and had built the first great civilizations on Old Earth, the pressures of this new way of life had produced profound Darwinian effects. The rate at which genes were positively selected to engender in humans new features and forms had increased as much as a hundredfold. The biological eschatologists had shown that at least three genes linked to brain size were rapidly evolving, as were others that were changing the way the brain interconnected with itself. And this whole process was entirely natural, in some sense coded into the possibilities of human DNA. The eschatological orthodoxy believed that human beings should not tamper with this unfolding in any way. To do so would be to tamper with the essential ordering of the universe.

'And so with two sips of kalla,' Rane said, smiling, 'you saw fit to throw off thousands of years of the accumulated wisdom of your profession.'

'How you put things! And what a hypocrite you are! You have less sympathy with eschatological doctrine than I do.'

'Yes, but I'm not the Lord Eschatologist.'

She blew a smoke ring directly at his face, and smiled to see it break upon his nose. 'I think it's now absolutely and incontrovertibly clear that what happened to Danlo and is happening to the Children must be seen as the natural fulfilment of eschatological understanding.'

She went on to emphasize that the old scientific technology had not superseded biological evolution, nor had it acted as evolution's tool, in the sense of allowing human beings to engineer their DNA. What had happened instead – starting millennia ago in the city of Ur near the mouth of the Euphrates River on Old Earth – was that technology had relentlessly altered the environments in which human beings had lived, which in response had spurred the creation of ever more powerful technologies and ever more complex and challenging environments. Human beings, to survive the drifting of deserts or ages of ice, had needed to adapt to these environments. It was this basically Darwinian engine that drove the accelerating evolution of the human race.

'We simply *cannot*,' she reiterated, 'see our future as the creation of these endlessly Faustian technologies that deform the human body and soul.'

'But that has been our future for thirty thousand years,' Rane said. 'And now it is also our past. How many peoples have carked their genome so that their children might have bigger brains or other body parts? How many human beings have sprouted wings so that they could fly?'

'But are they really *people*, Rane? Are they still human?'

'I wish I knew.'

'And what of the neurosingers and the cybershamans?' she

demanded of him. 'And the symbionts, such as Mallory Ringess himself? And the gods! The April Colonial Intelligence, Enth Generation, and the Solid State Entity? What of Ede the God and all those who have tried to cark their consciousnesses into computers?'

As Rane had no answer for her, he sat staring into the centres of her bright blue irises. 'And the pure AIs,' she continued, 'such as the Silicon God itself – are such monsters really to be considered the children of humanity?'

'We did create these beings,' he said. 'If not from our loins, then from our minds.'

'But they are not really beings at all!'

She argued that no artificial intelligence could ever be really alive and conscious; only organic life, she declared, could contemplate, reflect, and feel. Life had developed this capability through the layers of billions of years of evolution – in a way, life remembered itself and possessed true memory as no AI ever could.

'But no one knows what memory really is,' he said softly.

'Do you really think that cold silicon circuitry or hot blood beating through fins or wings is the future of our kind?'

'Aren't those questions for an eschatologist?'

'Or for a remembrancer – aren't remembrancers supposed to keep alive the soul of the human race?'

As she looked at him pointedly, he murmured, 'Sometimes I have trouble enough keeping my own soul alive.'

At this, she covered his hand with her warm fingers and looked at him in a way that he could not abide. To divert her attention, he tried to return to the topic under discussion, saying, 'So, this radical teleogenesis that you advocate would be—'

'We might as well call it a saltation, Rane. The great juncture for the human race.'

'So you would contend that this teleogenesis is the natural progression of phylogenesis? And that what evolution took billions of years to build will be utterly transformed overnight?'

'Yes!'

She went on to say that teleogenesis was just an intensification and awakening into full consciousness of the universe's fundamental force, which had been working to structure matter into ever more complex forms since the first atoms coalesced out of the fireball at the beginning of time. She squeezed his hand as if wishing to impart to him some of the excitement that she could not contain.

'You could think of it,' she said, 'as the technology of a willed and directed consciousness. The true human evolution. And what we are about to will into being are the first true human beings.'

Why, he wondered, must she feel compelled to think in singularities? Why must there be one religion more veracious than all others, one science, one true way? (Or, he thought, smiling to himself, One Memory?) Who was to say which was the *real* evolution? *The* path for humanity, the most truly human? Which opened up the greatest possibilities? Perhaps the future of *Homo sapiens* belonged in the hands of those who engineered obscenely large brains, even as Batar Bulba had cultivated other body parts. Perhaps the artificial intelligences – frozen into their cold circuitry that whipped information about at the speed of light – should be seen as the real Children of the human race. As he considered his discussion with Kolenya, he realized that he mostly agreed with her, though he cared little for her arguments. For Rane, the future form of their kind should not be a matter of proof, power or possibilities; it should be a question of aesthetics. In his mind's eye, he saw Sunjay's face lighting up with triumph upon surviving the kalla. Such zest for life was not only good and true but beautiful. And this was the future that he wished to be.

'Aren't you contravening,' he said with a smile, 'your discipline's central dogma?'

'*Which* central dogma?'

'The old central dogma, elucidated by Crick.'

He referred to the belief that environmental or organismic information could not be transferred back from proteins to nucleic acids – or, in other words, that information could get *out* of DNA but not back in.

'Oh, but exceptions to *that*,' she said with a wave of her hand, 'were found ages ago.'

She went on to describe instances of transgenerational epigenetic inheritance, such as the phenomenon of paramutation in maize.

'Doesn't that crack open,' he said, 'the door to Lamarkian evolution? And aren't you now flinging that door wide open?'

He talked about Old Earth's giraffes, which had fed on the leaves of acacia trees high above the ground. Had these strange creatures really developed their ridiculously long necks through purposing through successive generations to stretch just a little higher so that their lips could reach these leaves? One might just as easily believe that human beings could lay hold of the stars and fall through the universe merely by reaching out with their minds and their mathematics. Such was the snare of Lamarkian thinking.

At this, Kolenya shot him a fierce, knowing look, as if to say: what a trickster you are to use that term pejoratively! How dare you play such rhetorical games with me!

Instead, she exclaimed, 'Yes – I am in fact proposing a marriage of Lamarck and Darwin. Lamarck knew well enough that all beings have a purpose, as does evolution. His problem was that he could never explain how an individual organism's experiences and purpose might be transmitted to its offspring. He offered only mystical explanations of this mechanism.'

'And now you offer much more.'

'No, you do,' she said.

She added that remembrance would be *the* critical discipline needed for the new evolution. Evolution built upon prior forms, and remembrance preserved what had been built. Even more, at its most powerful, remembrance showed what *could* be built.

'It is you, through the technologies of remembrance that you are "articulating", who will develop these mechanisms. It is your fate, dear friend, to put the tools of evolution into the Children's hands.'

And not only Rane would do this, she added, but other remembrancers would, too. The cetics, of course, with their meditations that slowed the heart while quickening consciousness, would also play a central role in the coming saltation. So would the pilots, whose mathematics opened the brain to new perceptions and complexities, and opened the manifold to the diamond-hulled lightships that streaked across the universe. The cantors and the akashics would contribute to this great enterprise, along with the holists, the scryers, the neologicians, and the other academicians and high professionals of the Order. Those of the old Kalla Fellowship who had left the Order – Jonathan and Benjamin Hur and the Nirvelli – would join with others such as Malaclypse of Qallar in providing instruction first to the Children and then to the citizens of Neverness and the many peoples of the Civilized Worlds.

In this, they would follow the path blazed by humanity's great eschatologists: Anaximander and Zhuangzi, Nietzsche and Teilhard de Chardin. And Aurobindo, of course, and Nils Ordando and Jin Zenimura. From the Third and the Fourth Mentalities of Humankind to the Fifth Mentality and the Age of Simulation and beyond, through the waves of the Swarming and the seven Greater Dark Ages and numerous lesser ones, such visionaries had dreamed the possibilities of the human race. And now, after thirty thousand years, here on a small, cold planet spinning in the blackness of space – beginning first with Danlo wi Soli Ringess and his children but quickly spreading like a wildfire – their dreams were about to be fulfilled.

'"And God",' Rane said, quoting from an old, old source, '"shall wipe away all tears from their eyes; and there shall be no more death, neither sorrow, nor crying, neither shall there be any more pain: for the former things are passed away."'

Kolenya sat shaking her head as if she couldn't believe his gall. 'Oh, how impossible you are! I'm not talking about divinity or any sort of human perfection.'

'No?'

'No!' She told him that she had only scorn for the misty-eyed idealists who thought that evolution made things 'better', as in more moral or more free from suffering. 'Do you see the Children as perfect beings? I'm afraid they will find within themselves new and ever more powerful means to be bellicose, cruel, and depraved.'

She mentioned the *Asta Siluuna*'s development of *awarei*, which could be seen as both a higher faculty of perception and as a game that too often left one or more of the Children in tears.

For a moment, Rane distracted himself from the intensity of Kolenya's gaze by considering the etymology of this word. Chandra wi Soli Ringess had coined it as a sort of pun playing on three ancient sources. The was the Old Anglish '*aware*', of course, whose connotation the Children had expanded to mean something like 'the awareness of being aware' – or even the awareness of that awareness. In the most sentient moments, this deepened into an infinite recursion of seeing that grew ever vaster, deeper, and brighter. Too, there was an Afariquen game, *awari*, whose movement of seeds or beads around a wooden board may have inspired the later creation of the famous Glass Bead Game. In this great synthesis developed in ancient, doomed Castalia, the interconnectedness of all art, science, music, mathematics, and higher human endeavour had been illustrated by the placement of glass beads that symbolized subtle and often dazzlingly complex patterns. (The Glass Bead Game had in turn inspired the creation of holism and the Second Science, which certain master holists viewed as the highest possible understanding of *lila*, the divine play of the universe itself.) The final derivation of the word came from the Old West Japanese, *mono no aware*. This concept had been invented by the scholar Motoori Norinaga, and it signified a profound empathy for all things, particularly in the sense of openness to the poignance and therefore to the deep beauty of life's ephemeral nature. One needed such sensitivity to appreciate the true spirit of the *Asta Siluuna*: the immense sadness they felt at the passing of the human race coupled with an even greater joy.

At last, however, he had to return to the fierce inquiry of Kolenya's eyes, as cutting and concentrated as the coherent light of a laser. He saw in these twin cerulean jewels the hint of a suggestion that he himself should employ his highest human powers to become the opposite of bellicose, cruel, and depraved – even as Maria had made use of her darker angels to bring people poetry and something much more profound. For Kolenya, too, possessed *awarei*, which could often play out as a sort of reading of minds.

'I think you are being coy,' he finally said to her. 'I think you actually believe that the Children are developing a higher morality, as far above that of most people as human morality is above the behaviour of apes.'

'Perhaps the Children are. Because they *must* – because their capacity for the lower things will be much greater.'

'But the more men try to be like angels, the more they wind up like beasts.'

'Please don't be more cynical than you need to be, dear. You don't really believe that.'

'I don't?'

'And please don't play your *awarei* games with me.'

'Do you think I'm playing now?'

'Do you ever stop playing?'

'How can I play at all, since I am not one of the *Asta Siluuna* and I have not been apprised of the new rules?'

'But isn't the first rule that one may make one's own rules?'

'Yes, but—'

'And isn't there much, much more to *awarei* than the playing of a game?'

'How should I know? I have so little—'

'A cantor must learn a great deal of mathematics before he can appreciate how much remains to be learned. It is precisely in such protestations that you reveal your true capabilities.'

'But I don't—'

'Why do you think the Children look to you as they do? When you wish to, you have more *awarei* than anyone I've ever known.'

For a moment, he looked at her in silence. Then he said, 'Except for Maria.'

Maria, he thought, had the softest and loveliest eyes in all the universe. Black as night they were, and yet so deep and full of light that to gaze into them was to fall through immense spaces full of stars. Although she had little formal education (as he thought of things) or concern with matters of the intellect, she always seemed to *know* almost everything that really mattered. And she *knew* that she knew, and she took the greatest delight in passing on this intense knowingness to others in beautiful, blazing looks that pierced to the heart of things and that Rane thought of as the quintessence of *awarei*.

'Maria was Maria,' she said softly. 'And you are you.'

'That is the sort of statement that says almost nothing.'

'Or almost everything.'

'Maria,' he said, 'like a child hoping for presents on Last Night, believed in—'

'Look at yourself, Rane!' In the dark, mirrored centres of Kolenya's eyes, he caught a glimpse of a grim, guilt-ridden man whose hopelessness he could not abide. 'Why can't you believe what should be as real to you as the beating of your own heart?'

He smiled at this. 'Didn't Danlo say that beliefs are the eyelids of the mind?'

'Why can't you embrace what Maria really was? Why *couldn't* you? The bright thing, dear one, the really beautiful thing – why couldn't you just hold on to it?'

Could a man, he wondered, embrace a star? Could he hold a moon-shimmered ocean in his hands?

As if Kolenya could read his thoughts (and maybe she could), she said to him, 'Maria was just a woman, you know. A woman as women could be, perhaps, in certain ways, but a woman all the same.'

'Do you think I don't—'

'I think that in eschewing objective teleology, you looked to Maria for your private purpose. In rejecting any sort of deity, you made her your personal god.'

Yes, he thought, and Maria's eyes were windows more beautiful than stained glass, her whispers were sacraments, and her heart was the altar at which he still worshipped.

'What will you do about that?' Kolenya asked him.

'I don't know,' he said.

'What will you do about what is troubling you so badly right now?'

'But nothing is troubling me more than—'

'Something brought you here today, sweet friend.'

'Well, I told you that little things had been slipping from my mind.'

'It's no little thing that eats at your eyes that way. You've got guilt graved into every line of your face.'

He scurfed his hand across his temple and jaw as he looked at her. 'Is it so obvious? The truth is, I've actually been forgetting a great deal. I don't know why.'

'What have you forgotten, dear? Didn't you come here to tell me?'

Yes, yes, of course he had – but now that the moment had come, he found his throat and tongue searching for words. What was the truth about his evening with Sunjay and the kalla, anyway? As Maria had once said: the truth that can be told is not the truth.

'Rane?'

Could he trust her, he wondered? Despite her volubility, when it came to things that he had confided concerning Maria, she had never betrayed a single secret.

And so he drew in a deep breath and said, 'I nearly killed Sunjay.'

In the quiet of the room, acrid with toalache smoke, it seemed that he could hear the quickened beating of Kolenya's heart. She gazed at him as if bewildered by a blow to the head.

'I gave him too much kalla,' he explained. 'Six full drops.'

'Oh, no!'

'I held him in my arms for I don't know how long, and all the while he remained a glimmer of a whisper of a thought away from death.'

In quiet tones that did nothing to soothe the rage boiling up behind his eyes, he told her what had happened with Sunjay.

'But that is terrible!' she said, taking hold of his hand. 'And yet wonderful, too!'

'More the former than the latter, I think.'

'In time it might not seem so.'

'Time will do nothing to erase the look I saw on Sunjay's face.'

'Don't hate yourself, dear. You will only make things worse.'

'How should I not blame myself for what happened?'

'I did not say don't blame yourself. You'll need all the blame you can summon to keep such a thing from happening again.'

'But I can't keep anything from happening. Maria—'

'No one blames you for that – no one. The day she died—'

'*Did* she die?' he blurted out. 'Could she really be dead?'

The alarm that flushed Kolenya's face deepened to a pure, carnelian shock. 'What do you mean?' she asked him.

His tongue seemed frozen to the back of his teeth as she fixed him with a horrified look. Finally, he explained his theory of how Maria might have disappeared in some dark, cold corner of Neverness, forcing her friends to bury an empty coffin.

'Oh, dear one, you can't really believe that!'

'Did you see her body, Kolenya? Did you see her put in the coffin?'

'Why, no. But you must have—'

'I have no memory of that,' he said softly. 'No memory of that day.'

'Nothing?'

'No, nothing at all. When I try to remember, it's like looking into a black hole.'

'But surely Bardo would have—'

'Bardo surely believes that she is dead. He wouldn't want me to keep alive a false hope.'

'Why don't you just talk to him?'

'How can I do that? I would have to tell him that my memory is failing.'

'Well, he is the Lord of the Order – and more, your friend – and he should know.'

The tension in her voice disquieted him. 'You mustn't say anything to him, Kolenya.'

'Well, I wouldn't—'

'Please promise me you won't.'

She hesitated longer than he would have liked before saying, 'All right, I promise.'

His lips let loose a relieved sigh. 'It wouldn't do any good, anyway. No matter the truth, Bardo would tell me that he saw Maria in the coffin.'

'But what *would* do you good, sweet friend?'

Nothing, he thought. One's memory eventually began to crumble until only fragments remained to haunt and to distress, as cracked Doric columns called to mind the glories of abandoned cities and doomed civilizations.

Instead, moved by the great concern he saw gathering in Kolenya's eyes, he told her, 'It has been a great help just sitting with you today. I'm sure I will be able to figure something out.'

'Oh, good!' Her sudden happiness made him happy.

'It's getting late,' he said.

'Not *too* late,' she said. 'Do you have to go?'

'I'm sorry – I'm so tired.'

'But will you come again soon, then?'

'Yes, if you'd like.'

'Do you promise?'

'I promise,' he said with a smile.

She smiled back at him, and covered his hand as if to seal their mutual pledges with a pressure of her warm fingers. Soon after that he finished his tea and said his goodbyes. In the end, he thought, he had told the truth as well as he knew how to, and he should feel glad for that.

9

Early the next morning, Rane sat down to coffee in his tea room by the window overlooking the still-frozen Sound. Maria came for him then as she often did. In one moment, he watched large, fluffy snowflakes sift down from a whitened sky, and in the next, Maria appeared out of the room's air and settled down into the chair opposite him with what seemed an infinite gentleness. She wore a robe as white as snow and seemingly as soft. It clung to her full breasts and her hips, and he felt his fingers aching to touch it. He knew that he mustn't, however, so clamped his hand around his coffee mug and held it there until his skin began to burn.

'Good morning,' he said to her.

'Good morning – did you sleep well?'

'I dreamed too much; it seemed I was dreaming all night long.'

'Of what did you dream?'

'You know,' he said softly.

'I dreamed, too. I dreamed I woke up to see you happy again.'

'I'm always happy when I can be with you.'

'You certainly seem so today. That makes me happy.'

'Well, I feel better than I have since . . .'

'You still can't say it, can you?'

'Since you . . . went away.'

'They had a *funeral* for me, Rane!'

'It doesn't matter,' he said. 'No one could ever bury you.'

'At least not as long as you are alive.'

'Well, I'm very much alive, aren't I? I can ski all day and still climb an icefall afterwards, if I want to.'

'Can you still remember everything you wish to remember?'

'I remember everything about you.'

'Everything?'

'At least all the things I ever knew.'

'Is that really true?'

'I remember every word you ever spoke to me.'

'But what are words? What do they really matter?'

'You, a poet, ask that?'

'Can you remember what was *behind* the words? Did you ever really know?'

'I can still hear the exact timbre of your voice as you spoke the words of the second poem you wrote for me.'

'Can you remember the words of the only poem you wrote for me?'

'Of course I can.'

He took a breath of the coffee-scented air and said:

'In that moment, open gaze, pools of light,
When I plunged into that sacred sea
Down through a bottomless pain-carved joy
To find you, wisest child of the deep . . .'

'But you never,' she said, 'really understood that, did you? The light—'

'I remember the moon's reflection in the centres of your eyes on the deep winter night you wrote your last poem for me.'

'You still can't call it my death poem, can you?'

'Warrior-poets write death poems. Your poems were all about life. And something else.'

'And what was that "something", Rane?'

'Am I a poet, to be able to describe it?'

'Yes, *mi ardu*, I think you are.'

The way she spoke those words made him want to stand up and clasp his arms around her. He knew, however, that he must never do that.

'I can hardly describe to myself,' he said, 'how it was for me, before I met you and then the day after.'

It had been, he thought, as if all his life he had dwelled on the edge of a cold continent of mists and ice fogs, in which all the forms and features of the world manifested in various shades of grey. The flesh of his fingertips had been too numbed to perceive much more than gross changes of pressure, temperature, and texture. His lips had existed only to pull bland foods into his untasting mouth, while the odours that his nostrils gathered to his brain smelled mostly of the salt air driving in from over the sea.

And then Maria had come to him. Colours had blossomed across creation, as fire roses and sunflowers give their glory to a new spring. Their hues of red, yellow, blue, and violet astonished the eye with their individual perfection. And yet, when he had looked deeper – as he had been impelled to look at Maria – he had been pulled into what seemed a more fundamental colour, so vivid and intense that it could only be an outpouring of the world's essential unity. Likewise had his other senses awakened. Maria's mouth had brought to his mouth the tang of oranges and had put fire and poetry to his tongue. The scent of her soul had interpenetrated his soul with such a poignant sweetness that he couldn't help knowing himself to be ecstatically alive.

'I think you described it well enough,' she said to him, 'in the poem that Sunjay recited at my funeral.'

'Did I? Did I?'

'The problem is, you don't believe your own words.'

In the silence of his sunroom, he stared at Maria's black hair arrayed so perfectly against her white robe.

'You can't,' she accused him, 'feel the flame that forged the words inside you.'

'Can't I? Can't I?'

'You're as numb as if your heart itself froze into a lump of stone. You let my death kill the best part of you.'

'But you cannot die!'

He leaped out of his chair and moved a couple of feet to where she sat gazing at him in accusation. He flung his arms toward her, thinking to clasp his hands around her shoulders and pull her up to his lips – and yet not really thinking at all. His fingers closed around empty air. For as suddenly as she had come, she was gone.

'Maria!'

His voice shook the timbers of the ceiling above him. He

cried out for Maria to return to him. But his little sunroom replied to him in emptiness and silence.

'I won't let you go!'

Even though he closed his eyes and tried to recreate her, however, down to the one eyelash that always grew out longer than the others along the lid of her right eye, he could not summon her back.

He might have stood there all morning, clenching his fists and staring into the whirlpool of memory, if some listening part of him hadn't perceived the stuttering click-clack of skate blades striking the ice of the walkway that led up to his house. He listened more intently as he waited for Maria to return, and there came a knocking at his door.

'Go away!' he whispered.

But he might as well have commanded the last half year to go away, and the knocking of knuckles against wood sounded out louder.

And so he trudged through his sunroom and then down the short hallway that led to his front door. When he opened it, a short, youngish man beamed a smile at him from out of a kindly face the colour of mahogany. A mantle of snow clung to his sable furs, beneath which showed the orange robes of a cetic. Rane realized that he knew this man slightly: he was called Cyril Bramani, a meditation master of excellent repute.

'Yes?' Rane said. The jolt of being interrupted by this unwelcome visitor caused him to retreat into a cold formality. 'How may I help you?'

He stood blocking the threshold and blinking against the snowflakes that drove in from his opened door. He could not imagine why a little-known master cetic should wish to see him.

'May I come in, Lord Rane? There is something I need to discuss with you.'

'May I ask what that is? I am very busy.'

'It is a sensitive matter. It would be best if we might discuss it in private.'

Rane looked up and down the snow-choked street, lined with little stone chalets similar to his. No one as yet on this early morning had ventured out into the cold.

'Perhaps,' Rane said, 'another time would be more conducive to—'

'I must tell you that this is the time suggested to me that I might find you at home.'

'Suggested by whom?'

'By the Lord Pilot and the Lord of the Order,' Master Bramani said, returning Rane's formality, 'who has asked me to talk to you.'

'Why would Bardo ask that of you?'

As soon as Rane said this, however, he understood the impulse behind Master Bramani's insistence on talking to him: for Kolenya Mor must have betrayed Rane to Bardo after all, and Bardo must have sent this cetic to make inquiries.

Damn Kolenya and her fat, gabby lips!

As soon as this thought burned through him, however, he felt shame flushing his face to cool the rage. Kolenya, he realized, would have gone to Bardo only after a fierce debate with herself as to the best action to take concerning Rane. Out of duty to the Order – but even more, out of concern for him – she would have told Bardo about Rane's problems and asked him to help Rane. Why hadn't he anticipated that she would do this? Why must he remain caught in the unalterable events of the past rather than try to foresee how the vagaries of chance and character might play out in the future? Well, he hadn't, and so he had done what he had done. And now Bardo knew what he knew. Rane also realized that Kolenya would be agonizing over her perceived need to intervene in this way. Good, then let her stew in her perfidy! But because this thought, too, shamed him, he dug deep to find his more tender feelings for Kolenya. She would want and need his understanding, and so he must find a way to understand. The next time they met, she would ask for his forgiveness, and so he must reassure her that she would remain his dearest and most trusted of friends.

As if Master Bramani could tell exactly what Rane was thinking, the cetic flashed a sympathetic smile, then said, 'Perhaps we might discuss this over tea. I will try not to take up too much of your time.'

'Very well, then – why don't you come inside?'

Master Bramani ejected his skate blades and stepped into the hallway, where he took off his slush-encrusted boots. He gave his sable fur to Rane, who hung the garment on a wooden peg beside his own furs. Rane led Master Bramani through the house into the tea room. He asked Master Bramani if he would share a cup of coffee with him, but the clear-eyed cetic asked for herbal tea instead – in a tone that hinted of a disapproval of coffee and other such drugs. Rane went into the kitchen to prepare the tea. When he returned with a blue pot full of steaming peppermint tea (the same sweet tea that Maria had loved so much), he found Master Bramani sitting in Maria's seat. He found, too, that his coffee had grown cold. He resolved to drink it even so rather than to make a new cup and thereby prolong this bothersome cetic's visit.

'The Lord of the Order,' Master Bramani said, 'has had reason to become concerned about the Lord Remembrancer's . . . ah, health.'

The Lord of the Order, indeed! Rane thought. He had first known this 'Lord' as Pesheval Lal, a nervous young novice who had shared a dormitory with Mallory Ringess and had wet his bed at night. He had known him for many years as the man who had transformed himself into Bardo: a reckless pilot and profligate, whose feats as a discoverer of new stars and new pathways through the manifold nearly matched his reputation as a whoremaster and a drunk. When Bardo had transformed himself yet again to become the prophet and founder of the Way of Ringess and had gone on to inspire Danlo wi Soli Ringess to elevate him as Lord of the Order, he had completed a career only slightly less unlikely than the divinization of Nikolos Daru Ede as Ede the God.

'My health is good!' Rane wanted to insist. 'I can ski all day and still climb an icefall afterwards, if I want to.'

Instead, he decided not to play games with this cetic. Master Bramani certainly knew what had happened with Sunjay and would easily perceive that Rane knew that he knew.

So instead, Rane declaimed, 'I've excellent health, other than a few lapses in memory, of which you've no doubt been made aware.'

'Just so,' Master Bramani said, holding his blue teacup close to his lips. 'And it is those lapses that much concern the Lord of the Order.'

'If Bardo is so concerned, then why did he not tell me so himself?'

'I'm sure he would have, if he were not also concerned with pressing matters.'

He spoke of the mission to find Old Earth, which had not only failed as had previous missions, but which appeared to have claimed the lives of the five pilots sent out into the Orion Arm of the galaxy, in the spaces too near the dark region claimed by the Silicon God. Perhaps, Master Bramani opined, the pilots had been caught in the war that still raged between that purely machine intelligence and the somewhat human Solid State Entity. The repercussions of the war necessarily concerned the Lord of the Order, as did the thousands of petitions for emigration to Neverness that arrived daily from Ninsun and Avalon. The citizens of those planets feared the approaching wave front of radiation blasted out into space by one of the exploded stars of the Vild; it didn't matter that this killing light would not fall upon Ninsun for another century and upon Avalon for twice that span of time. People always looked to the safety of their progeny, and Neverness, shielded by the radiation-devouring organisms of the Golden Ring high above the atmosphere, appeared to many as a haven in an otherwise deadly universe.

'Then, too,' Master Bramani continued, 'a rumour has been circulating concerning the children you call the *Asta Siluuna*. It's said that the Order has finally discovered the secret of immortality, which has been bestowed upon these youths.'

'That might not be so far from the truth.'

'Yes, but the Lord of the Order has had to meet with delegations of astriers, Tychists, and even Architects, who have demanded that this secret should be made available to them. As if it could be passed out to the populace like a magic pill.'

'Well,' Rane said, 'Bardo passed out pills and toalache – and much else – when he tried to persuade the people to follow the Way of Ringess and become as gods.'

Master Bramani wrinkled his face at this. 'That was a different time and a different man.'

'Bardo, I think, is still Bardo.'

'You will not mind, will you, if I continue to refer to our superior as the Lord of the Order?'

'Not if *you* don't mind,' Rane said, 'if I exercise my perceived dwindling powers in recalling a man who offered triya seeds to beautiful young women so that they might more easily follow him to his bed.'

'You are cynical for one who is effecting the very kinds of transformations that you seem to deny.' Master Bramani took a long sip of tea and fixed Rane with his quick, dark eyes. 'I understand that Sunjay wi Soli Ringess, under your tutelage, achieved a . . . new level of mastery.'

'It is kind of you to put it that way.'

'Of course, it appears that Sunjay had to overcome certain dangers in his hyper-metabolism of the extra kalla that you gave him. It is thought by the Lord of the Order that perhaps these dangers are too great.'

'I think that myself.'

'Yes, but the Lord of the Order must necessarily protect the safety of novices such as young Sunjay – even as he must try to protect the health of great lords such as you.'

'I've already told you that my health is excellent.'

'I'm sure it is, but it is thought that I might help you with the aforementioned lapses, which must disturb you deeply.'

'Thank you for your offer, but I don't see how you can help.'

'It is not really an offer.'

So saying, Master Bramani shot him a hard, knowing look. The cetics, of course, had long ago developed the eyetalk which the *Asta Siluuna* had transformed into a speech that no cetic could any longer comprehend. Rane couldn't comprehend much of it himself, but the meaning of Master Bramani's classic eyetalk was all too easy to make out: Rane was the Lord Remembrancer of the Order, and he had taken a vow of obedience to the Lord of the Order himself.

'And so,' Rane said, 'this Lord of the Order whose great wisdom has prompted your visit today believes that you will teach me a few incantations and my problems will go away. Isn't that like sending a witch doctor to cure cholera?'

'Are our disciplines so different?'

Master Bramani formed a smile that seemed composed equally of a desire to win Rane with an easy camaraderie and an anticipation of imparting persuasive information. He cited the great Nils Ordando, who, in the year 19,459 CE, on Simoom, had assembled groups of yogin, neurologicians, cybershamans, scryers, and even remembrancers to form the Order of Cetics.

All these disciplines, Master Bramani said, had made common cause in seeking the source of the ineffable flame of pure consciousness. For a time, they had worked together like the fingers of a hand.

'To this day, for example,' he added, 'we of the yogin rely on the imaging attitudes that you remembrancers pioneered, just as you learn our eighty-one meditations.'

'*Are* you of the yogin?' Rane asked. 'I had thought you a neurologician.'

Although Nils Ordando had supposedly abolished all distinctions among the five disciplines, distinctions had remained and had led to disputes. While the traditional yogin remained devoted to mastering the science of meditation, the neurologicians had sought to define and control what they termed the 'programs' of the human brain-mind. Over the centuries of the Fifth Mentality, the neurologicians had refined this control. Some had become so adept rewriting their master meta-programs that it was said they not only could perform such ancient tricks as stopping the beating of their hearts but could also delve into different consciousnesses at will, from alpha bliss to beta fugue to deep delta sleep. Others had made an art of this reprogramming, shaping their minds as a sculptor does ice; they took pride in being able to mime the bizarre worldview of the autist or in adopting for a few hours the berserker mindset of the outlawed sect that called themselves the Warriors of Ede the God. The neurologicians had attempted to decode the programs that ran alien minds such as those of the Darghinni or the Scutari. One neurologician, Adamak Li, had even tried to mime the Scutari master program in his own mind – an experiment that had either succeeded wildly or failed horrifically, depending on one's point of view. For Adamak, as Rane recalled, had applied Scutari mores to the bad chance of a child infected with a mutation virus inherited from the War of the Faces: when his own son had been born without arms and legs, Adamak had smothered and eaten the baby out of the oxymoronic Scutari sensibility that might be translated into human speech as something like 'compassionate cannibalism'. In this, Rane thought cynically, the Scutari weren't so far from the devotees of certain ancient Kristian sects, which had believed in devouring the body and the blood of their god. And poor Adamak hadn't been so far from the more adventurous of the neurologicians, who had believed in rewriting all human impulses, sensibilities, and mere mores as a new and more universal design for the human race.

'I began my studies as a neurologician,' Master Bramani finally said to Rane, 'but my penchant for meditation led me to sit with the yogin. In any case, we cetics are not so divided as those of other disciplines think.'

Was that true, Rane wondered? He thought of the cyber-shamans, who practised illegal continual interface with their computers, even as they hid from the sight of the rest of the Order within secret grades of the secret society that they had created. Hanuman li Tosh had been a cybershaman, and he had used his great insights into the human psyche to beguile, to befoul, and ultimately to betray the people who had made him powerful. While many looked to the yogin to help heal broken minds, nearly everyone dreaded the cybershamans (and many of the neurologicians), who got into others' brains like drillworms.

'I hadn't heard,' Rane said, 'that the cetics had become masters of memory.'

'We do not need to be. It is enough that we have mastered meditation.'

'As you observed, we remembrancers learn your eighty-one meditations, and I have not been negligent in practising them.'

'There are meditations and meditations,' Master Bramani said.

Rane smiled at this. 'Spoken as cryptically as any cetic.'

'There are always *new* meditations, and variations on the old. And, of course, nothing can replace the efficacy of guided meditation.'

'Perhaps, but I prefer to be my own guide.'

'Isn't that like trying to pilot a lightship blind through the stars?'

'I am not without insights into my problem.'

'Can the eye ever see the eye?'

Could the 'I' ever really see the 'I', Rane wondered. That was the better question, the deeper question and, in a way, the neces-sary question. How was it possible not only to be conscious but to be blazingly conscious of that consciousness? How, in that infinite regress of *seeing*, could one glimpse the soft, golden shimmer of the ultimate source of consciousness itself? How was it possible to know, to feel, to ache, to remember?

'If one has a mirror, one can see.'

'Just so,' Master Bramani said. 'And I am here to be your mirror.'

No, Maria is my mirror!

Words rushed like an ocean into his mind:

In that time of no time
Perfect and clear
When I walked with you
Through a bright infinity
In marvel
Of seeing myself
In you seeing me . . .

'It's kind of you to offer such a service,' Rane said, 'but I'm far from the help of such charity.'

'In my experience, no one is beyond help.'

'In your experience,' Rane echoed softly. 'And you have been a master cetic . . . how long?'

'Almost seven years.'

'I have lived almost one hundred and sixty-seven years – can you help that? Despite rejuvenation, the brain eventually begins to wear out and die, does it not? The angslan—'

'Do you really believe the angslan is causing your forgetfulness?'

'Do you believe that it is not?'

'At this point, I neither believe nor disbelieve. Let us say that I am here to determine a basis for belief.'

'Please pardon me if I show little enthusiasm for that determination.'

'I wish only to make you well.'

'By invading the solitude of my mind?'

'Let us just say that a great remembrancer needs help in remembering and that a simple cetic was glad to help.'

Rane tried to keep a cynical smile from souring his lips. He thought that Master Cyril Bramani would be glad to use this occasion as an opportunity to re-establish the cetics' ancient precedence over the remembrancers.

'And so after your meditations have laid me open,' he said, 'you'll use this cetic's eye of yours to look into my soul.'

'That is not a word we use. And as for my cetic's eye, it will be aided by a brain scan, to determine if you are suffering from the angslan after all.'

'You mean, to rip from me any secrets I might be keeping from you.'

'Let us rather say secrets that you might be keeping from yourself.'

Rane's inner smile deepened. If he really had secrets to keep, then shouldn't they remain secret?

'I was as sorry as anyone,' Master Bramani said, appearing to change the course of the conversation, 'at the death of your paramour.'

'Oh, did you know her?'

'I met her once, after one of her performances. She was extraordinary – not a woman one could easily forget.'

'No, no one ever forgets Maria,' Rane said with a smile.

'At least not the overall gestalt that she impressed upon one's mind. And certainly not the . . . how would a remembrancer say it? . . . not the scent of her soul.'

Rane had knotted Maria's colourful scarf around his neck, the better to keep away the chill of the early morning. From the clutch of the fabric's soft rainbow twists, he could still wrest the faint scent of Maria's skin.

'But perhaps,' Master Bramani said, 'it would be all too easy to forget certain other things about her. The small things, the jewels of the heart, that one would wish to keep bright and inviolate within.'

'You speak poetically, for a cetic.'

'I am trying to imagine what it must be like for you in this most difficult of times.' His face seemed to soften and melt and envelop Rane in a sea of sympathy. 'It must be very, very difficult, even after all these days.'

The anguish in Master Bramani's large brown eyes called up a moist burning in Rane's eyes, and he had to look away from him.

'In fact, it must be like . . . hell.'

Rane wanted to rush out of the room, out of the house, out into the cold and driving snow. Instead, he pushed himself back in his chair and forced himself to look at Master Bramani. The cetic had a sort of practised kindness, so different from Maria's natural compassion. It seemed to come all from his head and not from his heart. No, that wasn't quite right, Rane thought, looking more closely: it was as if Master Bramani's head commanded his heart to be kind, and out of many years of servitude, his heart did as it was bidden, to sometimes profound effect.

'I would guess that even the greatest of remembrancers,' Master Bramani said, 'might have one or two jewels, as brilliant as diamonds, that have been mislaid. Surely he would wish to recover them and keep them safe.'

So, Rane thought, changing metaphors, this was how Master Bramani would dulcify the bitterness of Rane's submitting to a course of guided meditations. Such a sweet, sweet fruit Master Bramani offered him – and how could Rane's fingers not ache to reach out and take it?

'I have often wondered at the mystery of your cetics' brain scans,' Rane said.

'That is a strange word to use for a technology that is ancient and well understood.'

'But the brain itself is still *not* understood. The mind isn't. How can it be, for instance, that a scan can determine if a man is thinking of the colour red or blue, but it cannot uncover a single recollection before it is called up from memory and brought to mind?'

'I suppose you remembrancers would say that memory is a mystery.'

'We do say that.'

'Well, mystery or no, is it not possible to use thought keys and images to open the door to rooms of memory that usually remain locked?'

'Yes – and a remembrancer would call that not technology but art.'

'Whatever one calls it, what we cetics do is not so different from what you do, as I have said.'

'There is a crucial difference.'

'How so?'

'When we go down into the association attitude,' Rane said, 'we choose which image keys and mnemes to apply. And the memories that arise are our own.'

'I understand that one wishes to keep certain images to oneself. These colours of blue and red.'

Rane looked down past his coffee up to the folds of the scarf gathered upon his chest. So many bright colours had been woven into its mysterious fabric! A flash of red opened windows upon the past. He saw again Maria's beautiful bitten lip and the drop of blood that welled up from it – the single drop of red blood that had rolled onto the white snow beneath her.

'And it is only natural,' Master Bramani continued, 'for one to feel a certain reticence before undertaking a course of healing.'

'Your scans would necessarily image the limbic brain, would they not?'

'We would need to look everywhere.'

No, Rane thought, you would not! He glared at Master Bramani. It would avail him nothing to see the beads of sweat that gathered along Maria's neck as she tore blood drops from savaged skin and clawed deep in a sweet, screaming fury. Neither did he need behold the wildness that flashed through Maria's eyes. And this sly cetic could never understand Maria's urge to pour out this basic, beautiful thing and to share it ecstatically and freely with—

'Of course,' Master Bramani said, 'I would keep my findings to myself. We cetics are nothing if not circumspect.'

—without reserve or possession, to open herself unrestrainedly, and to share and share and—

'Then, too, as the healing progresses, you will likely experience your reluctance to uncover your personal life transforming into the kind of profound relief that comes from sharing your deepest—'

'No.'

The single word broke from Rane's throat like the crack of melting sea ice. How could he ever submit to Master Bramani's probings and humiliations? How could he go on living a life robbed of simple dignity? He stood up from his chair, accidentally knocking against the table with sufficient force to rattle the teacups and the coffee pot. To Master Bramani, he rudely commanded: 'Wait here.'

He paced quickly across the floor and went into the small sleeping chamber that had served as Maria's writing room. Positioned near the window overlooking the Sound was the curious construction of rosewood and inlaid onyx that she had called a desk. He sat upon a dusty chair, which fitted beneath the desk's gleaming surface; he might as well have been taking his place at an altar used by some strange and archaic religion. From a square, open wooden box filled with many sheets of paper, he removed a single sheet and set it down carefully on the writing pad. A tapered cylindrical shaping of cerulean jade still sat upon its little stand, like a relic of a shrine. Rane picked it up, unscrewed its cap and touched its pointed gold nib against the paper. Nothing happened. So he put the cold nib to his warm tongue, licking gently. He tasted graphite, iron, and burnt bones. When he pressed the nib to the paper a second time, the ink inside the jade cylinder, like black blood, began to flow from the nib and to mark the paper with little lines and curlicues. In this way, he formed the glyphs that encoded the sounds and words of the Language of the Civilized Worlds. Thus had Maria composed her poems, before committing them to memory, as Rane had taught her – even as she had taught him the ancient art called writing.

When he was finished, he folded the paper and sealed it with blotches of melted wax, as Maria had also taught him. Then he went back out to Master Bramani.

'Here,' he said, standing above the table and thrusting out the paper to the obviously dismayed and curious cetic.

'But what is it?' Master Bramani asked, taking it in hand.

'It is a letter.'

'A . . . letter?'

Rane began to explain what he had done in Maria's writing room, but then Master Bramani chopped the air with his hand and said, 'Oh, that.'

He wrinkled up his face and shook his head in disbelief. Rane might as well have presented an account of lighting his stove by striking sparks from stones.

'Please give this to Bardo,' Rane said, 'after you give him my appreciation for sending a cetic to look after my health.'

'Then we are agreed that we should appoint a daily time for our work?'

'We are not agreed. There will be no work, thank you. So you will please also give Bardo my regret that I cannot do what he has suggested to you.'

'Have I failed to point out that it was not a suggestion? You are the Order's Lord Remembrancer, and you must—'

'No, I am no longer that,' Rane said, tapping the letter with his fingernail. 'Please give the Lord of the Order my resignation.'

For as long as it took Rane to draw in a long breath and let it out, Master Bramani sat staring at him in dumbfoundment. He might have applied the stealthier and less ethical of his cetic's powers toward persuading Rane to reconsider such a rash decision if he hadn't read the adamantine resolve that hardened Rane's face. Although Master Bramani also kept his face cold and stony, it seemed to Rane that he struggled to keep from lashing out in a defeated rage.

'As you wish, then,' Master Bramani forced out. He stood up and jammed the letter down into his pocket. 'I shall continue to hope that you find your way toward the return of your memories.'

After he had gone, Rane sat back down at the table. He waited for Maria to reappear, but of course she did not. Although the day had scarcely begun, he felt exhausted.

'Maria, Maria,' he murmured as he let his chin sink down against the incredible softness of the scarf.

He felt the fibres of the scarf begin vibrating, a thousand times more softly than the oscillations of the strings of a gosharp. Sweet musics of many melodies, colours, and counterpoints seemed to touch his lips and conduct through flesh and bone up into the listening centres of his ears. He heard the harmonies of various voices; he heard chants and lullabies and prayers. When he listened hard enough, he thought he could make out a deep and dulcet voice singing the most beautiful of poems.

'Maria, Maria,' he said to the scarf, 'why must you always go away?'

For the next hour of the cold morning, the scarf seemed to answer him in a stream of soft words that he could not quite understand.

10

The next day, Bardo summoned Rane to a late-afternoon conference in his offices in the College of the Lords. Rane, however, decided not to wait for the appointed hour. In the strong light of a crisp, clear morning – the previous day's snow had blown away – Rane skated down through the Pilots' Quarter. He moved quickly and rhythmically, sucking in lungfuls of refreshing air. He crossed the Tycho's Green, whose acres of spruces and yu trees were powdered in white. He entered the Academy by way of the West Gate and proceeded straight to the Morning Towers. Various novices, journeymen, and full professionals, wearing robes of dozens of colours, bowed their heads to him as he glided past them at speed. They must have wondered at his hurry, for Rane had a reputation as a patient and a deliberate man. They couldn't have guessed that Rane, who thought he knew Bardo's habits, wanted to catch the Lord of the Order in his private rooms as he was taking his morning coffee.

On this day of fancy and fate, however, Bardo surprised him. When Rane reached the North Morning Tower, he learned that Bardo had left early to hold a breakfast conclave with some of the members of the old Kalla Fellowship: Poppy Panshin, Jonathan Hur, Kolenya Mor, the Nirvelli, and Malaclypse of Qallar. New ring masters of the Way of Ringess were also to attend the conclave, to be held in the chapter house of the magnificent cathedral that Bardo had purchased years ago. Why had he himself not been asked to attend this gathering? Although he had distanced himself from the Way and had made his disdain for the Way's rites and rituals plain, he had never formally broken with the new religion. Therefore, he *should* have been invited to the conclave; that he hadn't been suggested more than simply a fall from Bardo's favour occasioned by his letter of resignation. For the Order and the Way, even if intertwined in an unhealthy manner, remained in theory two separate entities. Rane suspected that Bardo had not informed him of the day's discussions for the excellent reason that Rane's dangerously failing powers were to form at least a part of those discussions.

Rane knew that he should have waited for his appointment with Bardo, perhaps by spending time in the library or in whiling away the hours in meditation on the silvery trees of the Shih Grove. He was a patient man, was he not? A man of decency and decorum? Instead, he found himself skating once more through the Academy grounds, this time retracing his path back toward the West Gate. The Rose Womb Cloisters flew by him; so did Ordando's Dome, Kirin Hall, and the dormitories of Upplyssa College. The men and women whom he sped by gave him a wide berth, dancing out of the way across the glidderies' red ice, for they did not wish to risk a collision with such an impetuous man.

Soon he put the Academy behind him and passed into the Old City. In this most ancient district of Neverness, buildings faced with living stone refracted the morning sun into dazzling variegations of light; spires made of spun diamond ten thousand years before pointed the way toward a sky so perfectly clear that it seemed to draw all sight and aspiration up into its azure deeps. One such tower had once topped Bardo's cathedral, whose sweeping arches of stone and perfect proportions made it the most graceful and magnificent of buildings. Bardo, however, had ordered the tower to be taken down and to be replaced by a clary dome. He had wished not so much for a display of the symbolism of humanity's transcendent urges but rather a view of the heavens – more specifically, of the stars that he had jour-neyed among so many times. It was the golden glimmer of the great cathedral's dome that guided Rane that morning – no less the memory of little winding streets that *he* had journeyed down too many times.

The circular chapter house occupied the centre of a group of small buildings, courtyards, and gardens attached to the cathedral's north side. It had once served as a meeting place for the bishops of the Kristian sect that had originally constructed the cathedral – and for the elders of the New Day Saints and for the readers of the Universal Church of Ede, who had acquired the cathedral in succession before Bardo purchased it for the Way of Ringess. During Hanuman li Tosh's time of power, Hanuman had used it as workplace, but upon his death, Bardo had restored it to its original function. Now, instead of mantelets, sulki grids, and tables piled with neurologics, the chapter house held a long table and a dozen padded leather chairs, upon which occasionally sat the luminaries of the Way of Ringess.

When Rane came up to the chapter house's carved door, he hesitated, debating the merits of knocking or not. Then he drew in a breath of air and opened the door. A ring of scalloped arches and pillars made a stone panelling that encircled the room. Above, the long windows cutting into the curves of the room's granite dome let in streamers of light that fell down upon the room's single table and the women and men seated around it. At the creaking of the door's hinges, everyone turned toward Rane. Bardo, dressed in his formal black pilot's robes, cast Rane a startled look that conflated the emotions of guilt, embarrassment, and outrage.

'My apologies for being late,' Rane called out, 'but I had a pressing matter that I had to attend to.'

He had decided against an open accusation of being slighted by Bardo's failure to invite him to this conclave. Although everyone present would see through his ploy, at least Bardo would have the chance to save a little face.

'Ah, well, at least you are here now,' Bardo said, glaring at him with his large brown eyes. 'We were just about to break for coffee.'

Some of the others glanced at Bardo, as if looking for a cue as to how they should comport themselves. Kolenya's moon-shaped face seemed to reflect Bardo's embarrassment, while Malaclypse of Qallar tightened his gaze as if in anticipation of needing to escort Rane from the room. Jonathan Hur, however, as impish as always, smiled in amusement while the icily visaged Nirvelli observed the potential drama with the dispassion of a scryer. The ring masters – Li Jasmina, Braham Liuz, and Poul Porfirio Diaz – seethed with displeasure at Rane's sudden appearance. They had always envied his powers of remembrance, even as they resented the very prominent part he had played in Ringism's beginnings.

As Bardo waited in the silence that opened through the room, he pulled at his black beard with the fingers of his left hand while he pressed the knuckles of his other hand against the table's chatoyant surface. One of the varifunctioned devices made on Silvaplana, the table could display a hologram as easily as it could serve as a portal to the shih spaces of the ontic realm; its powerful field, as with a heaume, could infuse the ideoplasts of many languages (along with almost any image) directly into the brains of those who sat around it. At the moment, though, the table was being used for more prosaic purposes. Pots of tea and coffee had been set upon its centre; there, too, were little plates and bowls of butter – and baskets heaped with hot breads and pastries. One other object rested upon the table. In front of Bardo, next to his mug of steaming coffee, the letter that Rane had written lay open, with its wax seals broken and the little black letters standing out for anyone to see.

Before Rane could sit down, Bardo scooped up the letter and stood away from the table. He hurried across the room over to Rane. Resting his massive arm around Rane's shoulders, he said, 'You have missed the first hours of our meeting and need to be apprised of what we discussed. But let us not bore the others with a recapitulation of that. Come, walk with me, and we shall talk.'

While the others cast them curious glances, Bardo urged Rane toward the chapter house's inner door. Bardo opened it and steered him into the hallway beyond. The footfalls of their hard boots echoed off ancient stone. They walked down dim passageways past the library and the sacristy, then crossed cloisters and walled gardens. The door to the cathedral proper opened upon a long aisle bordered with statues and granite columns. Past the red-carpeted altar they proceeded, and Rane noted the golden urn and the blue bowl used in many kalla ceremonies – before kalla had been deemed too dangerous for the many godlings who flocked to Bardo's church and Hanuman li Tosh had substituted the false remembrances induced by computer simulation in its place.

As they moved deeper into the cathedral's nave, various

godlings went about their business, sweeping floors or polishing statues or setting out vases of flowers for the evening ceremony. Without being too obvious, they positioned their bodies as if hoping to catch a few words that Bardo or Rane might speak even as they cast Rane a reverent look that sickened him. Then Bardo thanked them for their devotion, and suggested that they take a break from their work and go off to do other things. As soon as Rane and Bardo were alone, the air seemed to fall colder and quieter. The great dome above them let in the gold-tinged radiance of the Star of Neverness; the windows set into the high, graceful walls had been made of bits of coloured glass that depicted the great moments from the life of Mallory Ringess. Because Bardo had played a part in more than one of these moments, an artist had fashioned his likeness into one of the glass panels. Rane looked up to see Bardo's brutal but intelligent face glowing in the sunlight streaming into the cathedral. Agony wracked that face, for a spear stuck out from Bardo's blood-stained white furs. All gazing up at this scene would be forever reminded of how Bardo, out on a frozen island west of Neverness, had sacrificed his life for Mallory Ringess and had thus died his first death.

Bardo paused before one of the great fluted pillars that supported the walls. Above them, many tons of stone seemed have been flung up and suspended in space. Bardo, however, had no eye that morning for the cathedral's glories. He glared at Rane as he waved his letter in the air and half-shouted: 'Why could you not wait for our appointment later? Why must you make things so difficult for me?'

His voice boomed out with a tectonic force that seemed to shake the very walls and to send sound waves reverberating through the cathedral's millions of cubic feet of contained space. Rane, however, had never allowed himself to be disconcerted by this huge voice or by the huge man behind it. Should he be intimidated by a volcano just because it rumbled from time to time?

'Why did *you*,' Rane countered, 'not invite me to the conclave?'

'Ah, I suppose you know why.'

'And why did you send your cetic to humiliate me?'

'Humiliate you? I wanted to *help* you.'

'Did you? Did you?'

'Of course I did! Of course I do!'

'I don't need help. What I need is a little time to—'

'You nearly killed one of my novices! Danlo's own son!'

There, Bardo had said it, the incontrovertible thing, and thanks to Kolenya's indiscretion, no equivocation that Rane might make could alter his terrible negligence.

'And don't blame Kolenya,' Bardo continued. Ever a man of loose emotions and empathy, he often seemed to possess the mind-reading powers of a cetic. 'She still cares for you more than you know.'

'I don't blame Kolenya – I blame myself,' Rane said. He flicked his fingernail against the letter that Bardo gripped in his massive fist. 'Why do you think I wrote this?'

'Ah, yes, ". . . for the good of the Order",' Bardo quoted as he unfolded the letter with a loud rattle of paper. He had learned the art of reading from Mallory Ringess, who had begun a small revival of this ancient form. '". . . for the good of my students, for the good of myself, I tender my . . ."'

For a few moments, Bardo went on reading out loud. When he had finished, he refolded the letter and looked at Rane. Then he thundered, 'Nonsense! I can't tell you how it pained me to read such a rot of rigmarole and stultiloquence.'

Rane fought back an amused smile. 'And here I'd thought I'd put things rather clearly and well.'

'All right, then, let's discuss these points that you think you made so well.' Bardo loosed a long, troubled sigh. 'How about if we begin with "the good of the Way"? For years, you've had little to do with the Way of Ringess – as little as possible.'

'But I am still officially the Way's Honoured Remembrancer.'

'Then do you hope to resign that position as well? Your letter didn't make *that* clear.'

'Since Danlo remains the official head of the Way, I can resign my position as Honoured Remembrancer to him only.'

'That does not answer my question.'

'The Way of Ringess has no need of me.'

'You still think not? Did you not see the way those godlings regarded you a few minutes ago? They look to you lead them in the great remembrances that will enable their evolution.'

'Am I an alchemist, that I can transmute base metal into gold? They should look to Danlo, if it's magic they want.'

'Well, Danlo has left the city, and as long as he is gone, the Way of Ringess must be looked after by Kolenya and the others – and by you.'

'And most of all, by you.'

'I am only one of many who offer Danlo counsel.'

'Don't be modest, old friend – it doesn't suit you.'

'Well,' Bardo said with a smile, 'water will seek its own level, won't it?'

'I must tell you how much I loathe the interpenetration of the Way and the Order.'

'You *have* told me that, old friend. And I would think that your best personal solution to such sentiments would be to resign your position with the Way instead of the reverse. Then you may continue to concentrate your talents on those such as Sunjay, whose golden possibilities need only to be polished a little brighter.'

'You think too much of my talents.'

'Do I? You could train a whole new generation of remembrancers. Ah, a whole new generation . . . of human beings.'

Could he, really? Rane wondered. Could any man make such a miracle?

'This teleogenesis that Danlo teaches is a terrible thing,' Rane said. 'His own children are taken with the dream.'

'A dream, you say? You who are the greatest dreamer of all.'

'So Maria called me. But she was wrong about that, as she was so much else.'

'Was she wrong about the Children? Tell me you don't believe they can transform themselves, even as Danlo has begun to make the journey we all could make.'

'I think you have come to believe the very doctrine that you helped to invent.'

'Chandra and Sunjay, the other *Asta Siluuna*, too – they could live as no men or women have ever lived, not even the gods!'

'Perhaps,' Rane said, remembering. 'Or perhaps they will all die in the trying.'

He gazed up at the colourful panel that dramatized the day of Bardo's death. In a way, the entire cathedral was a monument to death – or, rather, to the very human urge to deny death's horror and finality. The first owners of the cathedral had celebrated the Kristoman's bloody torment, death, and resurrection;

the Architects who later acquired the cathedral believed that when Nikolos Daru Ede had carked his consciousness into an eternal computer, thus destroying his physical body, the essential part of him had lived on. And how many had actually died within the cold crypt of the cathedral itself during the final battle of the War? And over the years since then, how many thousands of Ringists had been laid to rest in coffins gathered in front of the altar before being transported to the Hollow Fields for burial in Neverness's sun?

'No, no, no.' Bardo's voice rolled out into the air. 'If we are careful, why should the Children die?'

Why should *anyone* have to die? Rane wondered. He rested his hand on the nearby pillar; the ancient stone sucked the heat from his palm even as it seemed to impart to his flesh memories of events that had occurred within the cathedral's nave over many years. He heard again Bardo preaching sermons to assemblages of godlings even as he himself gave voice to the dangers that the godlings would face during the kalla ceremonies. *The memory of all things is in all things*, he thought. In a way, stone itself lived and remembered. And it spoke to those who knew how to listen.

'And we will be careful, won't we?' Bardo said. 'I will not be the one to tell Danlo that his son or daughter died from drinking too much kalla, and neither will you.'

But what, Rane asked himself, did all the cathedral's stone and stained glass have to say to him? What did he hear through this remembrancing sense of resonance when he listened right *now*? Nothing but murmurs of eternal lamentation, and a terrible sobbing and sobbing and sobbing . . .

'No,' Rane agreed, 'I will not suffer anyone to put Sunjay into a coffin and fire it into the heart of a star.'

Images from the morning of Maria's funeral coalesced within Rane's mind. He saw for the millionth time the shatterwood coffin and the diamond-hulled ship pointing up toward the sun. To distract himself from these memories, Rane looked at Bardo and added, 'Not everyone can return from such an ordeal.'

'What do you mean, return?'

Rane pointed up toward the stained-glass panels. 'I always thought it curious that you chose to portray your first death but not your second.'

'Yes, that day, that star, that moment of my . . . ah, death.'

It was said that during the Pilots' War, out in the Orion Arm of the galaxy near Perdido Luz (and too near the nebula claimed by the Solid State Entity), Leopold Soli had used the spacetime engines of his lightship to hurl Bardo and the *Blessed Harlot* into the inferno of that star. According to one version of the story, the Solid State Entity had resurrected Bardo from what should have been an instant and final annihilation. For at the moment that the star's fierce heat disintegrated Bardo's blood and bones, the Entity had used Her unfathomable powers to remember the configuration of every atom that composed his body. She had then used other atoms to recreate him – and his lightship. And so the *Blessed Harlot* had fallen back out into realspace containing the newly made and living being called Bardo.

'But I do not really know,' he admitted. 'The informational incompleteness, you see, the quantum uncertainties – unless our science has been wrong for thirty thousand years, there is no way that the Entity could have *exactly* remembered and remade me. So perhaps I really did die.'

'Perhaps you did.'

'That's the hell of it: perhaps I am not really I.'

'But does that matter?' Rane asked. 'From moment to moment, with every thought and action, with every breath, the atoms of your being reconfigure themselves anyway. And yet you perceive yourself as still you.'

'It matters to me,' Bardo said softly.

'I suppose you will never really know.'

'*Won't* I?'

The gleam that brightened Bardo's brown eyes caused Rane to ask, 'How could you know?'

'There has always been another possibility,' Bardo said. 'After the battle, when I became aware that I had somehow survived, the Entity told me that She had recreated me. But what if She lied? What if She had only rescued me, somehow reaching out Her mighty hand to perturb spacetime and pull my ship from the heart of the star at the very instant that I fell *into* the star?'

'What if She did? One could ponder such ontological mysteries forever and still come no closer to the truth.'

'Or,' Bardo said, 'one could simply ask the Entity what really happened.'

'I suppose one could, if one could get close to Her – and if She deigned to talk to a human being.'

'Mallory Ringess got close to her – very close. And She did talk to him.'

'But Mallory is dead.'

'Dead,' Bardo murmured, rubbing at his beard. 'I suppose he is. But as part of his bequest to me, he left me a letter. In it, he hinted that others would need to talk to the Entity, too.'

'But the Entity has killed people as easily as She might flies.'

'Hitherto, She has. But Mallory believed that the war She waged – and still wages – with the Silicon God has changed her.' Bardo waved his hand in the air like a magician conjuring coins. 'She is cleaving closer to humanity. Why do you think I mounted the mission to Old Earth?'

'But what does the Entity have to do with Old Earth?'

'I don't know, with certainty. But Mallory also believed that the Entity had found Old Earth. And had taken up residence there.'

'How does the being the size of a nebula reside on a small planet ten thousand light years from that nebula?'

'But that's just it: we don't really know *where* Old Earth is to be found.'

'We certainly know that the Star of Earth must lie in the galaxy's Orion Arm, near the Rainbow Double.'

'Yes, but "not far" can mean a region of space encompassing twenty million stars.'

'So many? Well, you are the mathematician, not I.'

'I am the Lord of the Order and the Lord Pilot,' Bardo said, 'and it should have been *I* who led the mission.'

'Then you would have died, too – again.'

'Are you so sure of that?' Bardo loosed another deep sigh. 'In any case, we do not know the pilots I sent out are dead.'

'But you suspect they are?'

'Yes, I suspect. The Entity slays those whom She deems unworthy of survival. She is a veritable engine of Darwinian evolution.'

Rane smiled grimly at this, but said nothing. He gazed up at the bits of coloured glass in one of the panels high upon the walls. The scene depicted the Entity in Her human incarnation called Kalinda of the Flowers. Rendered brilliantly as a golden-skinned woman wearing a blue dress, She held out a godly hand to pull Mallory Ringess up through an archway of glittering stars.

'Someday,' Bardo continued, 'I will mount a new mission to Old Earth – a mission led by pilots whom the Entity *won't* destroy.'

'And who might these pilots be?'

'You know,' Bardo said. 'Sunjay and the other Children will return to Old Earth in a great flocking of lightships not seen since the War.'

'The old dream. And you would sacrifice the lives of our best just to try to realize it?'

'No, no – I will sacrifice nothing. The *Asta Siluuna* will do what they were born to do. That is, they will if *you* do what you should.'

Bardo glanced at the letter that he still clenched in his fist, then he turned his gaze upon Rane. His large eyes seemed to fill with an intense heat.

'I see,' Rane said, nodding. 'I see why we spent so much time discussing matters that seemed to have digressed from the reason for my coming here today.'

'Then let us return to the matter at hand. You are important to the Order, important to *me*. I cannot accept your resignation.'

So saying, he thrust out the letter toward Rane. Almost without thinking, Rane's fingers closed around it.

'You have had a terrible time,' Bardo said. 'Anyone with eyes can see that.'

The crinkle of paper against Rane's palm made him almost regret writing the black letters inked into the white sheet.

'And it's a terrible passion you had for Maria,' Bardo continued. 'Terrible, but beautiful, too, and who could blame you for that? I think Maria was the most beautiful woman I've ever known.'

Bardo's eyes, like dark pools, began filling with water as he gazed at Rane. So much pain this sometimes brutal-seeming man held inside! Rane could hardly bear to look at him.

'Too, too beautiful, too bad,' Bardo said. 'The loss of such a woman could undo any man.'

Undo? Rane thought. His outrage stiffened his back, tightened his jaw, and made his eyes lock onto Bardo's. Was he truly *undone*? No, no, he could never be so long as Maria murmured in his ear and sang to him soft songs – and how could the shockingly alive Maria whom he had held so close to himself for so long ever be done?

'I have lost nothing,' Rane said softly. The stone walls around him seemed to devour his words, which vanished into the cathedral's vastness.

'What? What did you say?'

'Nothing is lost – nothing can ever be lost,' he whispered.

'I'm not a cetic, you know, and I cannot read lips,' Bardo chided. 'Will you please tell me what you said?'

'Only this,' Rane whispered again. Then he drew in a great bellyful of breath and shouted out as loud as he could, 'MARIA CANNOT BE DEAD!'

It took many moments for the echoes reverberating from the cathedral's walls and windows to fade away. Rane wanted to shout again, but his throat felt like a wound ripped open, and his eardrums pulsed with pain. Bardo stood gazing at him in dismay – and in sadness. So terribly, terribly sad he seemed! The sentiment poured out him with a palpable force, like water from a broken dam.

'I had heard you might think that,' he said to Rane.

'Yes, from Kolenya.'

'You must know that Maria cannot be alive.'

'But I *feel* her alive. When we speak of her, when I touch her things, when I close my eyes and—'

'I had heard that you might hope that she is lost somewhere in Neverness.'

'Why couldn't she be? What if—'

'But we buried her!' Bardo said. 'You and I, in this very room, on the night after you found her in the snow – we washed the blood from her lips, and we put her body into the coffin.'

Rane shook his head as he looked about the candlelit cathedral. Its curving stone surfaces gleamed and recalled many things that had occurred in this huge mausoleum. For how long now had the Way held the first part of its funerary rites here? He saw open coffins arrayed before the altar and too many men and women set out for viewing by their fellow Ringists who would mourn them – but none of these cold, closed-eyed corpses was Maria.

'You would say that,' Rane murmured. 'To spare me the anguish of hoping—'

'I am not that compassionate,' Bardo said.

'Aren't you?'

'I am not that cruel.'

Bardo, he could see, was struggling to hold Rane's gaze within the crushing truth of his own.

'And cruel it would be,' he continued, 'for me to perpetuate a fantasy in order to spare you grief.'

'But I—'

'You know,' Bardo said. 'I know that you know.'

'No, I do not! I do not remember the night that you speak of.'

'But you know that I would not lie to you – not about this.'

In answer, Rane could only stand there shaking his head as he tried to blink the hot sting of reality from his eyes.

'Maria *is* dead,' Bardo said softly. 'You kissed her lips, then closed the coffin yourself.'

'No, she cannot be—'

'You watched the ship's rockets fire. She has been cremated in the sun.'

Rane said nothing as he looked at Bardo.

'She is gone,' Bardo said. 'You must know that she is gone.'

If a man floating in the warm, salty waters of a tropical ocean became caught in a riptide, Rane thought, should he swim hard for his life or let himself be swept out to sea? He blinked, once, twice, thrice, trying to dry the moisture in his eyes. Feeling his chin begin to tremble, he clamped down so hard with his jaws that his teeth pushed painfully into bone. The force of his fisted fingers drove nails into his flesh as he fought against the current – and fought and fought and fought.

'I'm sorry,' Bardo said.

He laid his hand on Rane's shoulder, but Rane jerked backward, lest Bardo pull him into a shared suffering that truly would undo him and leave him quivering like a worm.

'I'm sorry, but what else is there to do but to go on?'

'I intend to do just that,' Rane forced out. The coldness of his voice helped still the hot rush of emotion tearing through him.

'To go on denying that Maria is dead? To go on refusing help for your forgetfulness?'

'I do not need help.'

'Yes, you do. And I find myself in the unfortunate position of having to insist that you accept all the help the Order has to give you.'

Rane noticed that he still gripped his resignation letter in his fist. He reached out and handed it back to Bardo.

'But I do not want this!' Bardo shouted at him. He shook the letter close to Rane's face. 'And I do not accept it!'

So saying, he strode off a few paces, over to the nearest candelabra. The stand's intricately carved iridium seemed to be tinged with a saffron sheen, and its seven candles were arrayed in an arc of flame and light. He thrust the rolled-up letter into the fire of the highest candle. The paper ignited and began to burn. He positioned it so the orange wreath of the tiny conflagration ate its way up toward his fingers, then he dropped the smouldering black remnants upon the floor.

'I do not accept your resignation,' he said formally. With a loud slap, his boot stamped down upon the smoking ashes.

'Who is in denial, then?' Rane asked.

'Tomorrow, I shall send someone to you. If you cannot abide Cyril Bramani, then I shall ask another cetic to attend you.'

'But I need no such attentions.'

'You are the Order's Lord Remembrancer, and how can you help others delve their memories when you cannot help yourself?'

'No, I am only Rane – Thomas Rane.'

'Protest all you want, but you are still the man who led Danlo wi Soli Ringess to his first remembrance of the Elder Eddas.'

'No, I am no longer that man.'

'I know that your heart belongs to the Order. And you still wear the robes of the Lord Remembrancer.'

In silence, Rane stood there staring at Bardo. Then his arms and his fingers fell into furious motion as he bent and twisted and pulled, ripping at zippers and fasteners, shrugging out of his uppers and sliding off the pantaloons so that he completely divested himself of his remembrancer's robes. When he had finished, he backed away from the grey garment crumpled upon the floor. Except for his boots and the scarf tied around his neck, he stood naked, trying not to gasp at the cold knives

that the air currents dragged along his spine. He felt the tiny
muscles around his body's hair follicles tighten as his skin horrip-
ilated and he fought not to shiver.

Bardo, who had once transformed his flesh into the form of
a Neanderthal and had taken part in atavistic orgies, who had
fought in wars and had died two times, was not a man to be
easily shocked. But he did seem surprised – and even more,
saddened. He shook his head at Rane and muttered, 'Ah, then
I have lost you after all, too bad.'

'I'm sorry, Bardo.'

'All right, you've made your point.' Bardo motioned down
at the heap of clothing. 'Now cover yourself before the godlings
return.'

'No, I told you – I will not wear the robes of a remembrancer.'

'What will you do, then? Skate out into the streets like a
bare-bellied whore?'

A wildness came upon Rane, and his eyes gleamed. 'Yes! I
will do whatever I need to do, for as long as I need to do it.'

'To do *what*, then?'

'To find Maria,' Rane said simply.

At this, Bardo grimaced as if stunned by a blow. He shook
his head. 'I do not understand.'

'I will go out into the stars,' Rane said. 'To the very ends of
the universe, if I must. Even to Old Earth. I will go to the Solid
State Entity and ask for Her help.'

'But how can She possibly help you?'

The wildness blowing through Rane intensified, as a *sarsara*'s
whipping winds and particles of ice build into a great mother
of a storm that sweeps everything away.

'I will lay my mind open to Her,' Rane said. 'As you wished
me to do with the cetic, I will uncover every thought, image,
and feeling I ever had relating to Maria. Then I will ask the
Entity to recreate Maria from my memory.'

Bardo stared at Rane in dumbfoundment, then shouted out:
'You're mad! What you want is impossible!'

'The Entity recreated *you* from what She saw in your brain
and in your memory. Can She do less well upon looking into
my memory?'

And with that, he reached out and clasped Bardo's hand.
'Farewell, old friend.'

Rane turned and began walking toward the cathedral's doors. He flung them open with a crash of wood, and a blast of cold air shocked him down to his bones. He didn't care. Neither did he heed the disbelieving stares of the godlings who had hurried back into the nave at Bardo's shouts nor mind the astonished men and women skating down the street outside the cathedral. He casually clicked in his skate blades as if he had all the time in the world. It occurred to him that no law had ever been made against skating naked in public only because no one had ever thought that such a prohibition would be necessary in a city so frigid as Neverness.

'Farewell!' he heard Bardo call out to him.

Then he touched the scarf that he always wore now (and was now *all* that he wore). As soon as his fingers brushed the silken fabric, a voice rose with the wind – a strong, plangent, and beautiful voice that he recognized as Maria's. She whispered to him and sang to him and called to him with a deep urgency, all at once. He began skating through the multitudes of onlookers who had converged in order to witness the spectacle he provided. And with every swing of his arms and genitals left and right, with his skate blades striking out bullets of ice, with the scarf flapping out behind like a colourful banner, Maria's voice grew stronger and stronger: *Come make me, come take me and hold me in your arms again!*

Could he really do such a mad, magical thing? Why couldn't he? Was he not Thomas Rane, the Order's former Lord Remembrancer – still and always *the* Remembrancer, the man with the perfect memory who could never forget? How could he *not* find Maria and clasp her to his heart again?

Such thoughts put fire to blood and drove him through the streets of Neverness at great speed. His newly found zest seemed to create around him a sphere of diamond that shielded him from the stares of the passers-by no less the wind. And so he skated and skated, up through the Old City and the sparkling red glidderies of the Pilots' Quarter.

And up through a rising current of hope, as well, up through the deep blue sky and straight into the stars.

Part Two

The Bright Infinity

11

It is one thing for a man to announce a dream to himself (and to the world), but it is quite another to bring the dream to fruition within the constraints that both the world and the man's talents place upon it. In Rane's case, his dream of clasping Maria to him again could better be characterized as a mad fancy, having little real hope that he would ever realize it. And yet, he knew that if he was to do anything at all in pursuit of her, he must do it as if he really intended to succeed. And that meant planning, scheming, finagling, and following the possibilities open to him – and all with the tenacity and the logic needed to accomplish real things in the realspace of the universe, in which human beings lived and breathed.

The logic of his quest led him to face certain vexations and to make many decisions, in relentless succession. First, he needed to vacate his house. He did not own the little chalet, with its gleaming wooden beams and shining memories; no member of the Order owned his residence, for such possession would violate an Orderman's vow of poverty. His position as Lord Remembrancer entitled him only to lifelong tenancy of his house, and now that he had resigned from the Order, that tenancy no longer officially existed, for he was 'dead to the Order', as Kolenya lamented when she heard the news. Bardo extended him a measure of grace in allowing him to stay in the house for thirty days from the day of his disrobing. And that wasn't very long at all for him to make the preparations for his journey. He began to sense the passage of every day, every hour, every minute and second, and almost to hear it, even as he recalled the ticking of one of the old Timekeeper's clocks.

His second decision sprang from the first and highlighted the most pressing of his needs: he would sell nearly every item of his personal property, even the tondos, books, cookware, and writing materials that had been dear to Maria. Only the scarf and a few items of clothing and other necessities would he keep. He would liquidate this meagre wealth for the few City Disks that it would fetch. He would then use the money to purchase passage on a ship that would take him out to the stars.

After some days, however, of venturing into the Farsider's Quarter and haggling with one flea merchant or another over the price of his silver tea service or his chipped ice axe, it became clear to him that he would not be able to acquire enough money even to take passage on one of the deep-ships plying the Fallaways that formed the great arc of stars giving radiance to most of the Civilized Worlds. And, in truth, he knew that such a passage would not suffice to take him anywhere close to the end of his journey. A deep-ship, after all, might fall as far as the Fayoli or Redstar, but what deep-ship pilot would ever consent to approach the spaces of Perdido Luz, much less journey on to the Eta Carina Nebula? And had Rane really settled on the stars of the Solid State Entity as his destination? He couldn't decide. For if the Entity had somehow abandoned those stars and had taken up residence on Old Earth, then he must search ten thousand light years away along the galaxy's Orion Arm, in a region of space too near the Silicon God, where no deep-ship would ever go.

No, he thought, he needed a lightship and a *real* pilot willing to dare the unexplored regions of the galaxy. Where might such pilots be found? A few of the merchant pilots of Tria might undertake such a venture, but who among them had the skill to guide a lightship through the wild spaces outside the Fallaways? And for their doubtful services, they would likely charge him a fortune that he did not possess. After a little thought, it occurred to him that he knew very well the finest of pilots, who might relish a mission such as his, who might take him out to the stars of forbidden nebulas just for the sheer fun of it. And these were called the Pilots of the Order of Mystic Mathematicians and Other Seekers of the Ineffable Flame.

Three days after Rane had rid himself of his robes, he skated over to the Gallivare Green to meet with Cristobel the Bold beneath the great yu trees whose millions of needles sparkled with verglas from a recent ice storm. Cristobel, who had survived both the Pilots' War fomented by Mallory Ringess and the much greater War in Heaven ended by Mallory's son, fairly reeked of an odour of cockiness that seemed to permeate every particle of his being, from the mane of reddish-grey hair that framed his large head to his restless green eyes that had looked upon too many ships incinerated in the fusion fires of stars. He had proved the tricky Crystal Conjecture and had been the first to map the spaces of the Blue Blue Twins. Many counted him among the ten greatest living pilots. He counted himself in this way, for his self-assurance nearly matched that of the Sonderval, whom Leopold Soli had once characterized as 'more arrogant than God'.

Strangely, however, he had great respect for Rane, possibly because Rane was (or had been) one of the few of the Order's professionals outside the pilots to have learned a considerable body of mathematics. Then, too, he displayed something resembling awe of Rane's phenomenal memory, probably because that was one accomplishment that he did not deem himself to possess.

'What you propose,' Cristobel said to Rane as they sat side by side on a wooden bench, 'does appeal to me.'

'It would be a quest unlike any quest a pilot has ever made,' Rane said.

'Yes, an impossible quest, I'm sure most everyone would say. Even a suicidal quest – ha!'

Cristobel looked down at the gleaming band of spun diamond that encircled his middle finger. Upon this nearly indestructible bit of carbon, he had once vowed to seek wisdom and truth, even though his seeking should lead to his death and to the ruin of all that he held dear.

'I have often longed to talk to the Entity face to face, even as did Mallory Ringess. There are questions I would ask of Her.'

'I couldn't pay you much,' Rane said. 'So far, I have managed to amass only—'

'Pay?' Cristobel spat out. 'What am I, a merchant pilot to whom you should have to pay *money* for rendering a service that should be considered as a sacred duty? What pilot worth his lights would accept *pay* for having so much fun?'

Rane smiled to see Cristobel's cool green eyes come afire with enthusiasm. What a fine day it was, he thought, with the sunshine pouring down in hot, sweet torrents and the blue sky swelling into a gold-tinged infinity!

'Then, too,' Cristobel continued, 'how many times, in how many kalla ceremonies, have you done *me* the service of helping me pilot through the torsion spaces and black holes of my own mind?'

'I only helped you journey through difficult places,' Rane said. He decided to speak in terms of the mathematical metaphors that Cristobel liked to use. 'But it was you yourself who discovered the mappings and fell out among the most brilliant of inner lights, as only the greatest pilots of the mind can do.'

Rane hated flattery, both in the giving and the taking, but he couldn't help feeling gratified at the effect that his unwarranted praise obviously had on Cristobel. The grizzled pilot seemed to devour Rane's words as a fat bear intent on growing even fatter might feast on shiny yu berries.

'Mallory Ringess,' Cristobel said, 'sought the Elder Eddas along with the rest of us, but what did he really find? A puzzle that not even he could solve. But what is the greatest mystery of all? I cannot tell you how eager I am to journey back to the Entity, with you – and to discover the *real* secret of life.'

'It may be that we wouldn't journey to the Entity's nebula, but rather to Old Earth.'

'Better still. What better place to bring back to life a human being than the world that gave life to humanity in the first place?'

'What better place, indeed!'

'I can only hope,' Cristobel said, 'that fate will allow me someday to make such a journey.'

'What do you mean, *someday*? Did I not make it clear that I need to leave—'

'You *did* make it clear. And your need might be more pressing than your imperative to draw breath, but sadly, I cannot take you where you wish to go.'

The sick feeling that gripped Rane's belly made him recall

the shock of a climbing accident many years before when he
had fallen off a cliff and plunged through empty space.

'But I thought we were practically agreed! And I thought a
pilot could journey wherever he—'

'A pilot usually *can* journey wherever he will, wherever he
has the genius and the jewels to journey.' Cristobel's large hand
gripped his groin, and he grinned in order to emphasize his
point. 'But a pilot of the *Order* must obey the commands of
the Lord of the Order, and Bardo has forbidden me to make the
very journey you wish me to make.'

'But how would he know that I would ask you?'

'I must tell you that he's far more cunning than you: upon
anticipating that you would ask *some* pilot to further your quest,
he has forbidden *all* pilots to do so.'

Rane tried to read the complex of emotions stirring in
Cristobel's green eyes, but it was like looking for currents a
mile deep in the sea. He recalled the stories told of the Battle of
Mara's Star, in which Cristobel had nearly thrown the battle to
the enemy in order to further his own vainglory. He recalled
as well, however, that in the end Cristobel had deferred to
Bardo's leadership, and had gone on to play the crucial role
in the much greater Battle of Ten Thousand Suns that had
ended the War.

'I see,' Rane said, feeling his voice grow icy. 'I can only hope
that fate *does* allow you to make a journey which perhaps only
you could make.'

'Not only I.' Cristobel tried to force the contours of his proud
face into a semblance of humility; however, the unfamiliar effort
served only to lend his visage the aspect of a sardonic clown.
'There are other pilots.'

'Yes, the merchant pilots, whose services I cannot afford.'

'No, *not* the merchant pilots. There's not one of them who
has the jewels to journey to the Solid State Entity, much less the
genius. Then, too, Bardo has arranged with their prince that no
merchant should give you passage.'

'My resignation must have greatly embarrassed Bardo, but I
didn't realize that he hates me so much.'

'It is just the opposite. He esteems you so highly that he will
go to great lengths to keep you here in Neverness.'

'It's beginning to seem that he will succeed.'

'If you would give up your quest so easily, then perhaps you were not meant to fulfil it.'

'I did not say that I was giving up. But a man can't fall across the universe merely through the power of his own desire, can he?'

'As I said, there are other pilots. The ronin pilots who—'

'Who are outlaws!' Rane said. 'Outcasts, exiles, and oath breakers who—'

'Some of our finest pilots who could not abide the rule of the Ringess dynasty, or that of Bardo, have gone ronin. Along with a handful of the merchant pilots who aspired to higher things. And perhaps a score of the pilot-poets who survived the breaking of their order when Aoide was destroyed.'

Rane thought about this as he ground his knuckles into the wood of the weathered, splintery bench. 'I have not heard that the ronin pilots are moved by charity. Would they not charge one such as I even more than would a merchant pilot?'

'At least their courage – and their skill – would be commensurate with the sum that you paid them.'

'But I have no money! Nearly no money!'

'Then get it. Anyone with the intelligence to become the Lord Remembrancer can figure out how to acquire money, which those outside the Order excrete almost as readily as they do dung.'

Cristobel the Bold formed a smile that was one part sympathetic and one part conspiratorial – and wholly sceptical of Rane's success.

Those who have not made their fortunes in the world of men and women often assume that they could duplicate the success of others, if only they *really* tried. Rane, however, had neither the time nor the ruthlessness that a career of gaining wealth required. He had nothing more than his gift for remembrance and a burning need to find Maria – and at first he could not see how either compulsion should gain him money.

His conundrum led him to entertain certain rogue thoughts. He couldn't help considering how he might go down into the Farsider's Quarter and rob one of the diamond merchants who foisted on unwary buyers manufactured carbon crystals in the place of authentic Yarkonan bluestars. Or he might even use to advantage the savage reputation he had won upon his battle with Batar Bulba: it might be possible for him to extort one wormrunner or another of City Disks amassed through selling juf, smuggled goods, or enslaved women. The readiness with which he turned to his darker angels shamed him almost as much as it shocked him, for he had always wanted to think of himself as basically honest and good. A wild man he might be, a man of both passion and pride, but he could never become a thief and a murderer – or could he?

As the day approached when he must leave his house and wander the streets in search of lodging, he met with Sunjay for a final remembrancing lesson. They spent an hour deep in the first attitude; it occurred to Rane that he insisted on this review out of nostalgia more than need. After their work had been completed, they skated down to North Beach and sat on the rocks as they watched heaving grey clouds move in over the Sound. They listened to the raucous cries of the seagulls fighting over bits of smashed clams; not far away, a dozen seals flippered about on their rock and barked out some sort of dispute as well.

'I'm sorry that today must be our last time together,' Rane said. He felt cold and exposed to the wind in the plain racing kamelaika that covered his limbs. Never again, he thought, would he wear the thick silver furs that he had sold on Sulki Street. 'I am going to recommend that you continue your study with Master Apatow or Master Shang.'

'As you wish, sir,' Sunjay said. His usual smile failed to break the seriousness of his winsome face.

'They are both great masters of our art; I'm sure you would do well to sit with either of them.'

'As you wish, sir,' Sunjay repeated.

'In any case, you are approaching the moment when you must be your own master.'

'Do you really think so?'

'Yes – yes I do. Were it otherwise, I would not have been able to leave the Order.'

'I've heard that you are planning to leave Neverness.'

'And from whom did you gain this bit of gossip?'

'Everyone knows what you vowed to Bardo that day in the cathedral. It's been the talk of all the godlings – now the talk of the Order.'

'Do they talk of just *how* I am going to leave this planet? I can't grow wings and fly up to the stars, can I?'

He explained his difficulties in the acquiring the funds needed to buy passage on any sort of ship, and then added, 'I might be stranded in Neverness until I die.'

'Perhaps you should wait, sir, until my father returns.' Sunjay's hands pulled in toward his chest, as if he were summoning a lightship down from the sky. 'Bardo has no say over him. He has journeyed to the Entity once before. Perhaps he would take you back to Her.'

'No, he would never approve of what I need to do. And he has other concerns.'

'You might be right about my father. On his journey, when he reached the false Earth that the Entity had made, She reached into my father's own memory, and from the images there and from the elements of that Earth, She created a *doppel* of my mother, whom my father had thought dead to him.'

'Yes, I have heard that story.'

'But have you heard my father's response to the Entity's temptation? As he beheld the *doppel* for the last time, he said that he did not want to be desired by a being that was only the ghost of his own memory.'

'I think you share your father's belief.'

'It doesn't matter if I do or I do not. I would help you, if I could.'

'Truly? But I thought you wouldn't want—'

'I would give you all my money, if that would help.'

Rane smiled at this. How much money could a poor journeyman such as Sunjay possess?

'Have you violated your vow of poverty, then?' Rane asked him.

Sunjay smiled back at him. 'Not in spirit, sir. The only money I have is of the sort that would be useless in acquiring things or compelling services – at least within Neverness or on the Civilized Worlds.'

'But what sort of money is *that*?'

'We call it *chith*, sir. Have you not heard of it?'

'No, I haven't,' Rane said. 'I've been much too busy to keep myself apprised of all the coinages you and your friends have added to your language.'

'It is your language, too.'

'Do you think so? Well, I've no idea how you came up with the word.'

'I'm sure you would if you thought about it. *Chith* derives from both the Chinese concept of life force and the ancient Hindi term for a promise to pay. It's easiest, however, to think of *chith* as mental money.'

He went on to inform Rane of the evolution of this peculiar form of currency. About a year ago, Sunjay said, the *Asta Siluuna* had issued to each of themselves ten thousand *chith*. Since that time, they had used it in various transactions among themselves: buying and selling personal items such as flutes and fantells; compensating for help on academic assignments; trading for sexual favours. *Chith* also served as a prize in the *awarei* duels that children sometimes fought with a sort of elegant savagery. No coin, gemstone or other physical object denoted the amounts of *chith*; no written, electronic or quantum records were kept of *chith*'s transfer or accumulation. The essence of *chith*, as Sunjay explained, was that each of the *Asta Siluuna* was bound to keep a strict mental accounting of his or her own wealth.

'As of yesterday,' he said, 'I have a total of 23,852 *chith*.'

'Then, ineluctably, your gain has been another's loss.'

'Yes,' Sunjay said with an enthusiasm tinged with sadness. 'Is that not the nature of money?'

'Perhaps it is,' Rane said. 'But I would suppose that those who now find themselves with less than their initial ten thousand units would be tempted to augment their store of *chith*.'

'Do you mean, to counterfeit it?'

'What would stop them?'

'Honour would, sir.' He went on to explain that *chith* also meant honour.

'And all of your friends possess such fine qualities?'

'They try to. The price for failure . . . is very high.'

He told Rane of Marcus Sheikman, who had been caught cheating in a very small way, counterfeiting an extra twenty-five *chith* which he had not earned. The other *Asta Siluuna* had stripped him of all his wealth and redistributed it among themselves. In order to regain a little *chith*, Marcus had thereupon been reduced to selling his body to the more vindictive (and kemmish) of the *Asta Siluuna* girls, who had relished teaching him a lesson.

'I see,' Rane said. 'I see why I, along with most of the Order, have disdained money.'

'You disdain it, but in one way or another, you use it. Money is as natural to human beings as language itself – and as inevitable.'

Money, Sunjay said, predated civilization by many tens of thousands of years. The essence of money could be seen as promises – and obligations – to return accrued favours. This essence had persevered through millennia of refinements and complications. What meaning had money outside of a society's promise to return goods and services in exchange for whatever coin, credit or quantum of currency that an individual might pay out? A rich man marooned on one of the uninhabited islands west of Neverness must learn to gather or grow food – either that or starve to death, unless he could persuade a snow tiger to hunt for him in exchange for City Disks. As the old saying went, one couldn't eat money.

'All right,' Rane finally admitted, 'money might be natural, but the money system is cruel.'

'Cruel, perhaps, but wonderful, too. Like life itself, yes?'

Because Rane did not know what to say to this, he said nothing.

'It is too bad,' Sunjay said, 'that my friends and I possess nothing that the ronin pilots would wish to redeem for our *chith*, otherwise we would take up a collection.'

'But I would not want you to. I have done nothing to earn such largesse.'

'On the contrary, sir, you have given us more than we could ever repay, even with all our *chith*.'

Rane took this sentiment with him as he bade Sunjay goodbye and went off to consider how he might acquire a large sum of real money. That night, as he recalled the faces of every one of the *Asta Siluuna* whom he had taught, it occurred to him that he had given them a great deal – and that certain men and women outside the Order might pay City Disks or Darkmoon eagles or the coins of any number of the currencies of the Civilized Worlds to likewise study with the greatest of remembrancers.

So was born his brief and frustrating career as a tutor to

those seeking the ineffable flame of remembrance. He would draw his clientele from the narrow intersection of two sets of people: those desirous and disciplined enough to sit with him during many difficult remembrancing sessions and those wealthy enough to afford his services. Once he committed himself to this course, he pondered the question of just how he was to find such people? The answer came to him as he considered what resources he might devote to his goal; with an almost gleeful irony, he realized that he might turn what had hitherto been a bother into a boon. His dear friend, Kolenya Mor, knew many, many people, both inside the Order and without. All he needed to do was to inform her that he had opened for business, and Kolenya's quick tongue and fluttering lips would do the rest.

And so it happened. Word of Rane's new career spread quickly, from the halls of the Academy to the Diamond District to the mansions lining the edge of the Ashtoreth District along South Beach. Arhats, artists, wisdom brokers, Architects, cutters, and ambassadors – and many others – vied to reserve time with the great Thomas Rane. And after skating across the city to one fine house or another and sitting through a number of sessions with such students, Rane always felt enervated, as if a vampire bat had let the blood from his veins. Indeed, he felt as he supposed a whore must feel about her profession: he performed a needed service for a high rate of pay, and sometimes, with an exceptional student, he actually enjoyed his work. But he would never do what he did if not for the bitter necessity of earning money, which he acquired in exchange for pieces of his soul.

'I was born to teach,' he confided to Kolenya after a particularly trying day, 'but this, with students who are mostly dilettantes or dullards, hour after hour, all day long – it's astonishing what people have to do for money.'

And just how long must he continue doing it? He had only so many weary hours in a day, and although the money poured into his palms and enabled him to rent a nice apartment near the Fravashi District, it did not seem to amass very quickly. How much would he need to persuade some strange pilot to set off on a journey in which the probability of returning to Neverness might be as low as one chance in ten? He didn't really know. He considered making inquiries of the city's ronin pilots; however, he thought that doing so himself would betray his desperation, thereby resulting in an inflation of fees. And so he asked Cristobel if he would query one ronin pilot or another in Rane's stead.

Cristobel, feeling guilty for having already failed Rane, seemed glad to oblige him. After some days of waiting impatiently for Cristobel to name a sum, Rane met with the pilot for coffee at the Hofgarten and received the bad news: 'A hundred thousand City Disks – and that is the lowest figure that anyone quoted me.'

'A hundred thousand disks! But it would take me years to gather such an amount – and that is if I did not spend a single disk to eat!'

At this, Rane fell into a black despair. He cancelled his appointments for the next five days. What was the point in working if he must work nearly forever and not realize his objective? Why should he venture out of his apartment when all that awaited him was another day of dreary skies and a return to his barren rooms? Why should he bother eating when all the food that passed between his lips tasted like chalk? Indeed, what sense did it make to go on living if he must live without hope of having that which made life sweet and good?

He might have remained in his rooms for many more days, sulking and wasting away, if an old acquaintance had not come to visit him. One morning, on a day of spiky winds and heavy grey clouds that perfectly suited his mood, he broke off drinking his fourth cup of coffee to answer an unexpected knocking at his door. Upon viewing the small, dark woman who greeted him with the warmest of smiles, it took his caffeine-drugged brain some moments summon up her name: it was Ailieyha, whom he had not seen (or much thought of) since he had last visited her at the Courtesan's Conservatory.

'Come in,' he told her after a few stunned moments of silence. He couldn't guess why she should have showed up unannounced and unwanted on this miserable morning, but how could he forget his manners and turn her away? 'Would you like some coffee?'

Upon ushering her inside, however, he almost immediately regretted his reluctant hospitality, for he realized that the only place they might sit comfortably enjoying their coffee was on top of Rane's futon, in the middle of the main room's polished jewood floor. As he prepared yet another pot of pungent Summerworld coffee, he looked out at the seamless white walls of his empty apartment as with new eyes. Perhaps, he thought, he should have spent a little money on furniture or paintings that might have lent this cold-looking cave of a dwelling space some modicum of grace. After all, he might need to stay here much longer than he had initially hoped.

After they had settled down onto the futon's raw cotton surface facing each other, Rane realized that he had nowhere to set the coffee pot and the hot mugs other than at the edge of the futon, on the floor. Although he had become inured to such barbaric severity, Ailieyha would have grown used to the Conservatory's luxuriousness – and so how could she abide remaining in such a barren place, in such dubious company?

Ailieyha, however, had not taken up residence with the courtesans in vain. She applied all her newly won talents at pleasing men (along with her natural kindness) to put him at ease.

'This is nice,' she said, looking up at the beams of the room's vaulted ceiling. 'It wants only a woman's touch to make it beautiful.'

Did Ailieyha, he wondered, think to be that woman? How could she? Did she not remember where his heart dwelled?

'How did you find me here?' he asked between sips of coffee.

His words – sounding more like the gutturals of some alien language than human speech – echoed off the stonelike walls.

'Oh, it was your friend, Kolenya,' she said. 'Kolenya told Tamara Ten Ashtoreth, who told me.'

'I might have guessed,' he said with a sigh. After closing his eyes for a moment to summon up a bit of will, he looked at her and continued: 'Well, you are here, and please forgive me for not remembering my manners. It is good to see you! How do things go at the Conservatory? Have you been happy there?'

'Yes, I have been. I've only another year as a paranymph – it's been decided that I am to become an aspirant.'

'I think you were born to be a courtesan.'

'I'm not sure about that. But I do know that I find myself in accord with what the courtesans say about a calling.'

'And what is that?'

'That the greatest pleasure is in bringing others' pleasure.'

So saying, her ebony fingers began undoing the buttons of

her white shagshay furs, which Rane had neglected to take from her, as he had no place to hang them. His arm shot out to arrest her motions. His hand pressed down gently on hers, and he murmured, 'No, no, please.'

'Oh, no, I don't think you—'

'I have made myself a promise. I will never again be with another woman except Maria.'

She smiled as if amused by his naivety. 'I know that. That's not why I've come.'

'Then why, Ailieyha?'

'To give you *this*,' she told him.

Her fingers eased his hand aside, and she unbuttoned her furs. From an inside pocket, she drew out a red silk purse, small but bulging to its capacity. It took only moments for her fingers to tease open the drawstring, then she emptied onto Rane's futon ten sparkling diamond disks. Into each was graved the star wreathed in flame of the Great Seal of the City of Neverness, and each one bore a glyph representing the number ten thousand.

'I . . . don't understand,' he said, not wanting to understand. 'Have you robbed the Conservatory of its treasure?'

A hundred thousand City Disks! A hundred thousand City Disks! Even in his relatively benign neighbourhood, she might easily have been murdered for such a sum.

'Do I look like a thief?' she asked him.

'I've never seen a ten-thousand disk before.' He touched a finger to the cool diamond of one of the disks as if to reassure himself that it was real.

'I've heard,' she said, 'that you will need all ten of these to buy the passage you seek.'

She told him then that twenty-three master courtesans had pooled their wealth and had charged Ailieyha with the pleasure of giving it to Rane.

'But why? Why would they do such a thing?'

'They want to help you.'

'Many need help much more than I do. Why should they give their money to a stranger?'

Her full lips opened as if she wanted to say something, but then she shrugged her shoulders and sat looking at him.

'Kolenya,' he said, 'would never have thought of this – neither would Tamara. This was your idea, wasn't it?'

She smiled and nodded her head. 'You saved my life, so how should I not want to bring hope to yours? Then, too—'

'Yes?'

'What you want to do, your fire for doing it – it's so *romantic*. What woman wouldn't want a man to want her so badly? So beautifully, like a poem. I think the others would like to play a part in a story that will be told for ages.'

He glanced down at the diamond disks and said, 'I could never repay such a sum.'

'But you don't have to – it's a gift.'

'Then the other courtesans would ask nothing of me when I return?'

'Oh, no one thinks you will return – almost no one.'

'Except you,' he said softly.

She looked at him as with utter faith in his ability to find his lost love, and that was the greatest gift of all.

'I cannot accept this money,' he said.

He noticed that she had pressed her fingers against his palm, and the pressure of her warm skin felt more real than the ten glittering diamond coins.

'Yes, you can,' she told him. 'You owe it to the others.'

'Owe? What do you mean?'

'In giving you these,' she said, flicking a fingernail against the tinkling coins, 'they have gained the satisfaction of taking part in a great dream. Would you deny them that?'

'But how can I—'

'Would you deny *me*?' In her soft, dark eyes murmured a plaint which he could not refuse. 'Someday, you *will* return with Maria. And then I'll get to ask her a question.'

'What question, Ailieyha?'

In answer, she only smiled at him. And that was all the answer he needed.

'Here, these are yours,' she said.

She scooped up the disks and dropped them back into the purse, which she held out to Rane. He hesitated for a few more moments, then his fist closed around the treasure.

'I have to go,' she announced. 'Come say goodbye to me when you're ready to leave the city.'

'All right,' he promised her, 'I will.'

She closed her furs, stood up with him, and kissed his lips.

And she told him, 'You know, in your heart, where she is to be found. Have the courage to follow her.'

'All right,' he promised again, even though he thought that was a very strange thing for her to say.

After she had gone, he stood staring out of the window at the cloud-shrouded mountains north of the city, and he considered what he had said to her. He *would* follow his heart, he promised himself, out into the one place in the universe where Maria awaited him. How could he not always follow his heart?

With that resolved – and with a smile on his lips – he stuffed the red purse into his kamelaika's pocket. Then he went out to hire himself a pilot.

12

Rane spent the next five days down on the Street of the Ten Thousand Bars, mostly in the scacchic bar frequented by the ronin pilots. He interviewed pilot after pilot. In order to adjust his level of consciousness to theirs and so win a shared conviviality and trust, he downed thimble after thimble of scacch. This very potent drug supposedly enabled its drinkers to apprehend the ever-fluid patterns of the manifold with the sort of virtuosity of a chess master grasping in a single gestalt the multitudinous possibilities of a chess game; in truth, however, aficionados of scacch drank the bitter blue liquid because it afforded them a clear-eyed and concentrated euphoria.

After his seventeenth interview, however, Rane realized that it was going to be much more difficult to conclude his business than he had supposed. One of the bar's habitués, a hoary old merchant pilot from Darkmoon, negotiated with Rane down to two hundred thousand City Disks, a sum that would enable the pilot to retire in glory on the pleasure planet of Ojo Azul. A second, younger man, demanded a flat fee of a million disks, paid in advance, so that the pilot could establish a trust for his wife, who, he said, was certain to become his widow when he did not return from their suicidal journey. A third pilot seemed inclined to agree to Rane's terms, though he changed his mind when he discovered that Rane intended to search for Maria at Rane's whim, with no time constraint placed upon the quest. Yet another pilot, the infamous Kennett Hiu, had been dismissed from the Order for cowardice during the Battle of the Ten Thousand Suns, and he wished to redeem himself by displaying the sort of recklessness that he supposed Rane's mission would entail. Hiu did not smile once during his two-hour talk with Rane; the stony-faced man would not look at Rane directly, and Rane immediately disliked him. Following his gut, if not his heart, he reluctantly decided not to contract with Hiu, who drank so many thimbles of scacch that sweat beaded up on his face and his eyes jumped about like angry sleekits.

When Rane left the bar after that meeting, he flirted again with desperation – and then had to fight off an even deeper level of hopelessness at his lack of faith. What was wrong with him? He carried a fortune in his pocket, a plan in his brain, and a fire within his heart: why shouldn't that suffice to sweep him along past any obstacle toward ultimate triumph? As he skated past the well-tended trees and the pretty acres of the Fravashi Green, part of his awareness noted that it happened to be a warm, clear day; the abominable weather of midwinter spring seemed to have finally given way to false winter's radiant blue skies and the thousands of fritillaries sipping nectar from the season's first wildflowers. Rane, however, perceived the vivid hues of the insects' flitting wings to be tainted, as if some filter between his eyes and his brain dirtied the brilliant blues and the flaming reds and smeared them with shadow. Likewise did he perceive the exuberant people skating along the glidderies of the Old City to be disfigured by the very phenomenon of that exuberance. Arhats, ambassadors, new mothers, courtesans, students, icemen, workmen, and would-be godmen – why should they beam back smiles at the sun just because they got to whip along the ice unencumbered by their heavy winter furs? Wasn't their gaiety doomed to be fleeting and therefore somehow false? No, he thought, when he looked more deeply, he could see the frights and rots that ate at this stampede of humanity. What was wrong with *them* that they should try to slip on a mask of happiness to conceal the reality that in the most fundamental of ways they were all so hideously, so hopelessly, and so irre-deemably ugly?

As he passed by the tenements of the autists along Armoury Street, constructed of the most ancient and therefore colourless organic stone, he asked himself why these buildings seemed so disproportioned and drab? Who had designed such monstrosities and why hadn't they been torn down? No wonder that so many autists preferred to live on the streets or to camp out in the city's many greens! Why couldn't passers-by drop a couple of coins into these ragamuffins' outstretched hands? Why must life be so uncaring and cruel?

Such unanswerable questions, like lead boots too tight around his feet, weighed him down and impaired the pained pumping of his legs. As he crossed the green ice of Old City Glissade then turned down a red, lesser gliddery, it seemed he had slowed nearly to a crawl. The sounds of the city oppressed him and lent even more gravity to his motions. And yet somewhere in that great noise, in all its multitudinous but distinct shrieks of dissonance, he became aware that the click-pause-clack of his skate blades found echo in the skating of someone else on the street. He looked ahead of him, at the sinuous swarm of people out for their exercise; he turned his head, but all he saw was a continuous mass of swaying arms, colourful fabrics, and cheerful faces. He began moving a little faster then, and the impact of steel against ice beneath him rang out in harmony with the clamour of another's skate blades behind him. He quickened his pace even more, and, with a perfect synchrony, so did whoever was following him.

So, he thought, someone must have learned of his offers to the ronin pilots and had pursued him across the city from the bar. Or perhaps one of the very pilots he had queried had turned rogue and was out to rob him. His hand moved down to press the pocket of his kamelaika, where he had stashed the diamond coins. Well, what good had this wealth done him? Why shouldn't he just cast the purse down upon the ice and be done with it?

No, no, he raged against his defeatism, *these coins are ten steps toward the lightship that will take me to Maria!*

And with that thought, the flame smouldering in his heart burst into a great fountain of fire. This blazing substance put life to his limbs and burned away the pessimism clouding his head. He would not let anyone take his treasure! He would kill any man who tried to rob him or he would be killed fighting him off! A murderous man he really was, a man of both wrack and rage!

It occurred to him that he did not want to be caught on a crowded street. In the press of jostling bodies, his pursuer could sidle up next to him and slip a needle through the wool of his kamelaika into his flesh. Curarax, jejex, galladeth . . . he could think of half a dozen poisons that would paralyse him immediately and drop him to the ice as if he had been felled by an aneurysm or a stroke. How hard would it then be for his assassin, under the guise of offering aid in catching his fall, to rifle through his pocket and make off with his purse before any of the shocked onlookers realized what was happening?

And so, only a few blocks from the Ringists' cathedral, Rane turned north down a narrow gliddery lined with old apartments faced in red granite. Scarlett Street, they called this chute of well-travelled ice, one of at least three streets in the city to be so named. The hues of both the buildings and the ice seemed to melt beneath the hot sun and flow before his eyes like blood. He hastened his pace, and in only seconds, it seemed, he came upon an open space of silvery shih trees and lawns of dreamgrass spangled with flowers. His skate blades sent out showers of chopped ice, and he turned onto one of the many winding paths that led through the City Cemetery.

Here were many graves, thousands of years old. In the cemetery's western tracts, the markers were arrayed in a hatchwork of neat lines, while closer to the Academy, to the east, concentric circles of white, red, and black stones predominated. Marble, granite, and basalt hewed out of the rocky earth of Icefall – and even minerals such as hot slate and precious soul stone imported halfway across the galaxy from Vesper – formed the substance of many thousands of headstones. Rane well knew the way down a spiralling path through the shih trees toward his favourite stone: a simple and rather small shaping of black diamond that had been set in the centre of one of the circles for any to see. Its graceful lines curved upward, and into its sheeny surface had been etched a few dozen characters of Old West High Japanese. Somewhere in the ground beneath this stone, Rane thought, lay the bones of Ringo Zenimura, discoverer of kalla and the first remembrancer to have survived the dangerous thirty-seventh attitude.

Here, on the emerald dreamgrass by this grave, Rane stopped and waited. Dozens of people milled about other graves and glided down nearby paths. None pressed closely enough to shield the actions of an attacker, while most were close enough to witness an attack should one be made.

A few moments later, a man appeared, skating along the very path that had brought Rane to this spot. His forceful limbs moved him closer and closer across the ice toward Rane. He stood middling tall, and he looked to be somewhere between youth and middle age – perhaps his first youth and his first middle age. A mass of curly black hair fell in ringlets about his large head, and his skin, like burnished copper, picked up the redder hues of the sun. A man of beauty he was, a man of power and a rare, easy grace. A man of danger, too, Rane thought, for as he drew up close, Rane looked into a pair of soft brown eyes that seemed utterly devoid of hesitation or fear.

'Thomas Rane,' he called out, 'I learned of your quest in the bar, where you talked with many pilots. I would talk with you, too, but that was not the place.'

'And so you followed me, like a thief?'

The man's eyes flicked in the direction of Rane's pocket, where Rane had stashed the disks. 'Perhaps I wished only to guard you from your own rashness,' he said with a smile.

How, Rane wondered, could this stranger possibly perceive what his pocket contained? Rane had showed the ten coins to no one. And yet, the man seemed to *know* – to sense Rane's secret wealth and his vulnerability in the same way that a white bear sniffs out a seal's lair beneath the frozen snow.

'And rash it would be,' the man added, 'for you to enlist the aid of the wrong pilot. Your quest is rash enough, as it is.'

'You followed me to tell me that? Or is it that you wish me to enlist *your* aid?'

'That is what we need to determine,' the man said. Then he bowed his head to Rane and told him, 'I'm called Nikolandru – formerly of Aoide.'

A pilot-poet! Rane thought – and one of the few to have survived the destruction of Aoide in one of the battles fought between the Solid State Entity and the Silicon God. Then Nikolandru must have been out sailing the stars somewhere when the Silicon God caused hellfire to rain down from the skies of Aoide, incinerating the biosphere and killing all living things on this pretty planet under the Solid State Entity's protection.

'That was a terrible thing,' Rane said. 'Did you have family there?'

'My brother and sister pilots,' Nikolandru told him. 'And my mother.'

Rane recalled that the pilot-poets did not marry, though no rule of their order prevented a poet from enjoying the succour of a paramour. Indeed, the poets had been encouraged to seek such cosmic couplings as a source for their poetry.

'I'm sorry,' Rane wanted to say. But then he recalled how terribly such condolences had weighed on him during the dark days following Maria's death. And so instead, he asked, 'How long have you been in Neverness?'

'Only twenty-three days,' Nikolandru said. 'I've just returned from a journey out to Jewel's World – and beyond.'

'Jewel's World! That lies past the stars of the April Colonial Intelligence, does it not? Only a few of our pilots have ever journeyed so far coreward.'

The Sonderval, he supposed, had once broached those uncertain spaces – as had Delora wi Towt and Richardess and John Penhallegon, better known as the Tycho. And, of course, Leopold Soli, who had ventured deeper into the galaxy's core stars than had any other human being.

'Then only a few of your pilots,' Nikolandru said, 'ever had the chance to behold the most wondrous sight in all the universe. On Midgard, where the lights—'

'But Midgard and Asgard are only myths,' Rane said. 'Long ago, Ishi Mokku made much the same journey as you claim to have made, looking for Asgard in order to prove or disprove the myth.'

Nikolandru smiled as if to say that perhaps Ishi Mokku did not look hard enough. 'I have stood on the ground of Midgard – it is as real as the ground beneath our feet.'

He pointed down at the millions of blades of dreamgrass, at once as faceted and sheeny as emeralds and as soft as feather moss.

'I have stood on Midgard,' Nikolandru repeated, 'drunk with the fire of the great bridge Bifröst that connects Midgard to the heavens.'

And Bifröst, he said with a warm smile, was nothing more – but nothing less! – than the greatest and the most resplendent of all the galaxy's many auroras.

'Midgard,' he said, 'is a rocky planet of little distinction otherwise. And yet, its magnetic field is nearly powerful enough to pull the iron out of your blood. There, high in the atmosphere, the solar wind blows like a cosmic storm, like the breath of the gods. And the nitrogen and oxygen atoms, ionizing, the photons pulled down to earth like the clasp of a woman's arms – the colours! Shimmering archways of light, the greens and pinks and pure, pure blues and a secret colour that blazes only in the mind, or perhaps in the soul's imaginings and deepest dreams, which is at once a union and fulfilment of all the other colours – that impossible, ravishing, beautiful colour which I call glorre. No words exist in any language to describe it.'

His smile caught up Rane in its brilliance, and Rane couldn't help smiling back at him. How like a pilot-poet! To describe the gorgeously and gloriously indescribable through a protestation that no description could be made!

'I would warrant,' Rane said wryly, 'that you *have* described it, in a poem.'

Why else, he wondered, did the pilot-poets exist? For each of them, at the completion of an education hardly less rigorous than that of the Order's own pilots, took a vow to seek the beauty and the truth of the stars and to sing of it across the universe.

'Indeed I have,' Nikolandru said.

He cleared his throat, and in his poet's deep, rich, sweet voice, he began to recite:

'Behind the cool and fiery sky,
Behind the mind and brain and eye
In Midgard's cool and fiery sky
There burns a colour . . .'

Rane listened as Nikolandru sang out his poem. In the flowing blues and golds of the nearby fritillaries' wings, Rane could almost make out this colour that Nikolandru called glorre.

When he had finished, Rane gazed at him through a strangeness that seemed to sweeten and intensify all that he looked upon. 'The one I seek would have liked that – she made poems, too.'

'I have heard that,' Nikolandru said.

'Where your words, however, were fire and ice, hers were moon-silvered water.'

'I have heard that also.'

Rane studied Nikolandru's handsome face, as open as that of a child and seemingly without hesitation or guile.

'Listening to you,' Rane said, 'made it easy to believe that a colour such as glorre might really exist – and so with Midgard.'

'It is easy to believe, but not for one who finds it hard to believe the simplest things.'

'Have you heard that, too? What other investigations have you made into my life?'

'I don't need to investigate what I see before my eyes.'

'Oh, am I so easy to read then? Or do you claim the skills of a cetic, along with those of a poet?'

'One doesn't need to be a cetic to know what moves you.'

Rane didn't want to ask this stranger's opinion of his deepest motives. Still, it always surprised him to learn how others perceived him. And so he said, 'Tell me about myself then.'

'I can tell you in a single word.'

'And what word is that?'

'You know,' Nikolandru said.

'Do I? How would *you* know that?'

Nikolandru's long, beautiful fingers slowly closed. 'How do I know the air warms as we speak?'

'I do not believe,' Rane said, 'that a single word can encompass anyone's purpose. Unless you have also invented a word for that which is complex and fathomless beyond understanding.'

'Or so simple that even a child knows it, as he knows the sun, even as a fritillary knows the same thing – as does a blade of grass and the soil from which it grows.'

Because Rane did not like the turn of their conversation, he said, 'You are skilled with words, and you have a silver tongue.'

'Thank you.' Nikolandru smiled as if Rane amused him. 'But you didn't mean to pay me praise, did you?'

Rane fell into silence as he stared at him.

'One can't help recalling,' Nikolandru said, 'the line from Ede's *Algorithm*, from the *Iterations*, in the third Trigon: "Beware the man with the silver tongue who has a heart of iron."'

'Are you an Architect, that you quote from the *Algorithm* so readily?'

'No, of course not. But we of Aoide take inspiration wherever we find it.'

'Few outside the Cybernetic Universal Church find it easy to wade through Ede's interminable ravings. We should add pertinacity to your list of skills.'

'Thank you again,' Nikolandru said, making a slight head bow. 'But in the end, only one of my skills should concern you. And that is my skill as a pilot.'

'As you say, that does concern me. If I am to place my life – and even more, my purpose – in your hands, then I will need to be persuaded of those skills.'

'Have I not already done that with my account of my journey to Midgard?'

'Have you proofs of such a journey?'

'The proof is in the poem.'

'But what kind of proof is that? Words—'

'The words of the poem tell true. I know that *you* could tell they were true.'

Rane didn't like the intensity with which Nikolandru peered into his eyes just then, so similar to the way that Maria, with the simplest of looks, had laid him bare.

'I can tell that you have beheld glories,' Rane said, 'perhaps of the stars, perhaps of the soul, and have made words to describe them. That is what poets do, yes?'

'What kind of proofs do you need then? In my lightship, there are the computer's logs. There are holograms, too.'

'Such records could be fabricated.'

'Yes, they could be, couldn't they? Which is why I said to you that the proof is in the poem. You either heard the truth of it, or you did not.'

'I heard you sing of impossible—'

'And you either heard or did not hear the truth of the tongue that made the poem – do you not trust what your heart tells you must be true?'

Follow your heart, Ailieyha had said to him.

'In the end,' Nikolandru said, 'all affairs among human beings come down to trust. And so I must ask you to ask yourself: do you trust me or do you not?'

Did Rane trust this persuasive man? He wanted to. Rane had often shared the company of great pilots, who had a certain essence of being – the same scent of self-command and pride that caused Nikolandru to emanate an almost impossible equanimity. However, because Rane was so adept at hiding things from others, he could tell that Nikolandru must be concealing something from him. Beneath Nikolandru's flawless presentation of himself, Rane sensed anguishes and suppressed passions flowing like a dark underground river. Could it be that Nikolandru had suffered grievances too outrageous to bear? Perhaps he, too, had lost a paramour and wished to recreate her, even as Rane did himself.

'Let us suppose,' Rane said, 'that for the moment that I choose to take you at your word, though I would still want to see your ship's logs and the holograms you spoke of. Even so, we would have to determine that we would make suitable companions for a very long journey.'

'What will suit you best,' Nikolandru said, 'is a pilot who can take you where you wish to go. And what will suit me best is a passenger who remembers that I am the pilot.'

'And that is all?'

'It is the most important thing – other than the price of your passage.'

'Money,' Rane said, with a tightness in his throat. He slowly shook his head as he recalled the first rule of commerce that he had learned negotiating the price of a woman's body: never be the first to mention an amount. 'How much would you require?'

'How much can you afford for a journey to the end of the stars?'

In Nikolandru's steely gaze, he saw razor-sharp daggers of resolve, and he knew that the pilot would prevail in this waiting game.

'Well,' Rane finally said, 'I can pay you forty thousand City Disks.'

'That is not enough.'

'How much would be enough?'

'More.'

Rane could almost feel the purse of diamond coins burdening him like the weight of the world. He said, 'Fifty thousand, then.'

'That is still not enough.'

'You should tell me what you need.'

'You have not yet told me exactly what *you* need. It's said that your paramour is lost somewhere in the stars, perhaps in the spaces near the Solid State Entity. And that you intend to search for her until you find her.'

'What could be clearer than that?'

'The truth could be clearer. It's also said that she died last winter in Neverness and that you hope to ask a goddess to recreate her.'

'I have no certain proof . . . that she died.'

'But you believe that she died? Or perhaps you don't?'

'What is death, then?'

'Only the dead really know. It is strange to me that you strive so diligently to become one of them.'

'I wish only to ask the Entity a favour.'

'Is that not the same thing?'

'Perhaps,' Rane said. 'Or perhaps the Entity will be moved to do as I ask. Mallory Ringess told that the goddess esteems poetry above almost all other things. And Maria was a poet above almost all other poets.'

'I see,' Nikolandru said with a smile. 'And upon this one silken strand of possibility you hang the great weight of all your hopes and imaginings?'

'Not just. I have intelligences that the Entity has been experimenting with just such projects of resurrecting human beings. My favour might appeal to Her.'

Nikolandru seemed to stare right through the centres of Rane's eyes as if he intended to force his way through the twin black openings right into Rane's brain. 'What you propose *does* have appeal: to journey into a nebula that has killed a hundred pilots.'

'But we do not know that the Entity remains in Her old nebula beyond Eta Carina.' Rane found himself telling Nikolandru what Bardo had told him in the nave of the cathedral. 'It may be that the Entity – at least the human part of Her – now resides on Old Earth.'

'Then you propose that we search for Old Earth?'

'I'm not sure. The Entity really could be anywhere within a region of space encompassing more than a billion cubic light years.'

'So many? And how many stars lie within this region?'

'Billions, I'm sure.'

'I see, I see. Billions. Yes.'

'We will find a way to reduce the volume of that search. Somewhere in the galaxy, people must remember where Old Earth lies.'

'And how will you find these people?'

'I do not need to find them – only their memory.'

'Now you speak in riddles that I cannot solve.'

'That doesn't matter. All that should concern you is that I *will* find her – I know I will.'

'Do you mean, find the Entity or find Maria?'

Rane, staring at one of the gravestones behind Nikolandru, found that he could not answer him.

'How long, then,' Nikolandru asked, 'do you suppose that will take?'

'I'm not sure – perhaps a year.'

'An Icefall year or an Old Earth year?'

'An Icefall year.'

'I don't think you really believe that.'

'Two years, then. Perhaps three.'

'Perhaps a billion, no?'

'No! No more than four years, I should think.'

'That is a long time to search with perhaps no end in sight.'

'It will take as long as it takes.'

'Yes, but I can't allow this journey to take up all the years of my life.'

'How long, then?'

'Three years,' Nikolandru said, 'is all that I can afford.'

'Really? To take part in a quest of which you will sing for the rest of your life?'

In Nikolandru's eyes glittered cold steel, while his smile opened with the warmth of a sunny day. 'Possibly, I might commit to five.'

'If you would do so, I would pay you sixty thousand City Disks.'

'Yes, I have heard that you offered such a sum to Kennett Hiu.'

'It is all the money I have.'

Nikolandru's smile widened. 'Does it not also say in the *Iterations*: "Who builds a house on a lie, builds on sand"?'

'Perhaps,' Rane said, 'I could find a way to borrow another ten thousand – seventy thousand disks total.'

'That is a great sum, but it does not interest me.'

'Eighty thousand – somehow I will obtain eighty thousand.'

'And that is all you would give to find your sweetheart?'

'What would you have of me, then?'

'I would have you give your life to hold once more the woman who *was* your life. Failing that, I would have you give all that you possess. How else will I have something worthy of which to sing?'

Rane swallowed hard against the dread knotting up in his throat. If he paid every coin he had to this merciless pilot-poet, he would have nothing should some emergency arise upon their journey.

'Ninety thousand!' he cried out. 'Ninety thousand City Disks!'

A knowing laughter broke from Nikolandru's full, sensual lips. 'I will accept a hundred thousand disks, and not a single disk less.'

'But ninety thousand is all that I can pay you, and not a single disk more!'

'Must we haggle like merchants?' Nikolandru aimed a muscular finger at Rane's bulging pocket. 'I'd wager that you carry a purse containing a hundred thousand disks.'

Rane's hand, as with a will of its own, drew down to cover his side.

'I'd wager the price of your passage. Show me what your purse holds, and if it is less than a hundred thousand disks, I will take you out to the stars for free.'

Rane hesitated. In the stillness of the cemetery, he could hear the pulsing of his heart and the beating of the fritillaries' wings. 'And if it holds more?'

Nikolandru laughed harder. 'It does *not* hold more. The courtesans made you a gift of exactly ten ten-thousand disks, did they not?'

'You knew!' Rane cried out. 'All this time, you knew!'

'Of course I knew.'

'But how?'

'Did you suppose that before I committed to risking my life on this crazy quest of yours I wouldn't make the proper researches?'

'Those there are who wouldn't call consorting with courtesans "proper".'

'Perhaps not. But I assure you that my short stay with a courtesan named Jerusha was as pleasant as it was illuminating. She told me of the gift that Ailieyha made to you on the courtesans' behalf.'

'That was supposed to remain a secret!'

'Yes,' Nikolandru said through a rolling chuckle, 'a secret that half the city will soon share. A secret that half the galaxy will someday talk about, for I shall sing of it, along with the rest of your story.'

Rane clawed the fabric covering the purse and its ten diamond coins. 'Then all this time you were playing with me!'

Nikolandru's eyes caught up Rane in their sparkle. 'Perhaps someday, I'll get you to play, too.'

As anger stiffened Rane's body, Nikolandru slid closer on his skates and touched his hand to Rane's shoulder. 'Easy, there, Lord Remembrancer. For what might be five years, our lives will be joined together, and I had to know who will be sharing my lightship.'

'*Will* I be sharing your ship?' Rane said as he knocked Nikolandru's hand away.

'A question only you can answer.'

For an uncomfortably long few moments, Rane locked eyes with this strange, unfathomable man. Then he drew out his purse and gave it to Nikolandru.

'For a passage, anywhere in the Milky Way galaxy that our quest might lead us. For a journey as long as five years.'

After Nikolandru had stowed the purse in his own pocket, he held out his hand to Rane, who clasped it with an almost desperate ferocity.

'I will find her,' Rane promised. '*We* will.'

'Yes, I believe we will.'

Nikolandru smiled then, and Rane could almost hear him composing the first lines of a great poem that told of dreams, impossible passions, and the defiance of death.

13

Travellers in many times, climes, planets, and places have extolled travel as being both exciting and romantic. Perhaps, Rane thought, locked within the passenger compartment of Nikolandru's lightship, a pilot found that to be true. Only once before had he ventured inside the pit of a lightship, when Danlo had given him a tour of the *Snowy Owl*. Most of the soul and substance of a lightship's pit form up in the neurologics woven into the pit's black shell. These information-rich logics connect to the ship's computer and model a pilot's brain functions holographically. Thus the computer 'reads' the pilot's mind even as it infuses the pilot with images of stars and jewelled ideoplasts: the three-dimensional symbols that the pilot will kithe and arrange so as to work the mathematics of the manifold. In the moment that a pilot 'faces' his ship, the interface between man and machine becomes so profound it is as if they are almost one living thing. And so a pilot could float free in the dark pit of his ship and spend endless hours, days, and years looking outward at the fire of the stars and turning inward to behold the brilliance of the pure topological mathematics by which he guided his ship along the spiral arms of the galaxy.

A passenger aboard the *Asherah*, however, had few such pleasures. A hull of black spun diamond shielded Rane from cosmic rays and other radiations even as it denied him a clear view of the galaxy's many nebulas and constellations. A great round panel of diamond more impenetrable than the Great Wall of China separated his tiny compartment from the even tinier pit that Nikolandru claimed as his own. Anchored to the hull was a padded chair into which he might strap himself during the dangerous accelerations of take-offs that might otherwise crush him. Cabinets fixed to the walls held stores of food, water, medicines, and other necessaries such as Rane's wooden remembrancer's box and his personal effects. Lights could be called on or off to illuminate or darken different parts of his living space. Indeed, to call Rane's new dwelling a living space was to highlight its single virtue, for within its curving hollow Rane breathed in tepid, recycled air, even as he consumed insipid rations and excreted and used the compartment's null gravity machines to exercise so that the muscles and bones of his weightless body did not completely waste away. Only the noisome odours of his body and the too-loud beating of his heart (and his thoughts of Maria) reminded him that he remained alive. He could die of the smothering boredom of such an existence, and then his quarters would become a dark, silent, moving coffin.

He might have done what most travellers in such circumstances chose to do, which was to enter into that state of semi-hibernation called quicktime. Would it not be a simple thing to interface the neurologics woven into the black diamond surrounding him and let the ship's computer dampen the firings of his brain? Could he not then glide dreamily through the endless hours as his inner clock slowed down and time thus seemed to pass more quickly? Rane, however, mistrusted such mechanical manipulations of the mind, and he particularly disliked computer-generated quicktime.

And so he found other means by which to pass his journey. He allowed himself the lesser interface of delving into the computer's myriad data pools. To find his way through a near-infinity of information, he employed one or more of the cybernetic senses that he had learned from the cetics long ago: iconicity, shih, hallning, syntaxis, and most of all, kithing. Like every member of the Order – and like most people living in the Civilized Worlds – he had long grown used to a computer's infusing his visual cortex with vivid ideoplasts encoding the morphemes, words, and ideas of one language or another. To interpret such crystal-like three-dimensional symbols through the sense called kithing was to practise a basic skill that had occupied human beings for a much larger span of history than had the even more ancient art known as reading. A cetic who had studied such matters once calculated that a man could kithe information five times more quickly than he could read it – and his understanding would be more complex, more interconnected with previous layers of knowledge, and thus more profound.

Rane, of course, had always been quick at kithing, and as the *Asherah* fell through the manifold from star to star, his astonishing memory enabled him to absorb a great deal of information. For many years, he had meant to study physics, chemistry, biology, geology, and all the other ancient disciplines in the context of the great revolutions of holism and the Second Science that had superseded them. He took a particular interest in Omar Narayama's creation of the universal syntax during humankind's Fifth Mentality. It amused him, for instance, to explore a very old conundrum: did the universal syntax represent a mathematization of language or a linguistic reformalization of mathematics? His duties as the Lord Remembrancer had long precluded such arcane ponderings. Now, though, in the inky darkness of the *Asherah*'s passenger compartment, it seemed that he had an infinite amount of time.

It occurred to him to look for the *ratio cognoscendi* that supported a triad of possibly related disciplines: the universal syntax, the language of the Children, and the art (or sense) that the *Asta Siluuna* called *awarei*. How much, in the way of 'words' and concepts, had their language taken from the universal syntax? Could the universal syntax ever model the depth and complexity of concepts that only the *Asta Siluuna* seemed to understand? And could *awarei* help refine both the universal syntax and the Children's language so that either could serve as sort of Rosetta Stone enabling human beings finally to speak the one secret and true language of the universe?

When Rane tired of learning – and learning and learning and more learning – he faced away from the ship's computer and he slept. Sometimes, upon awakening, he composed poems to Maria. More often, though, he exercised one or another of remembrancing's sixty-four established attitudes to enter into memory space. He tried to recall everything about Maria: every curve of her face and her body, every glint of her eyes, every word that she had ever spoken to him, every heartbeat and breath.

In this effort he found unexpected aid in Maria's scarf. Sequestered in the privacy of his little compartment, he had no need of clothing, and so he made his way through the manifold in nakedness – a nakedness that would have been stark but for the scarf that he refused to take off. He used the scents of Maria embedded in the scarf to enter the attitude of olfaction perhaps more than he should. How could he help himself? His living space, no matter the freshets of air pumped into it, began to smell of a thick stew of substances: apocrine sweat and the rank butyric acid excreted by the axillary bacteria that fouled his skin oils; the taint of the esters and ammoniums cooked into the chemicals with which he tried to sanitize himself; the ketones of his breath, reeking from the acidosis of his body's burning too much protein for energy because he had too little appetite to eat enough food. More subtle aromas bothered him even more, and these were the smells of deep space: blackness, loneliness, emptiness, and the concomitant odour of hopelessness that too often seeped into Nikolandru's ship. To filter out this omnipresent stink, Rane took to tying the scarf about his face so that instead he could breathe in Maria's essence. He fancied that it took only a single sweet molecule that had once been a part of *her* body to shoot straight up his nostrils into the hippocampus of his brain, there to set loose a cascade of vivid memories that swept him away into a better time and a better place.

Somewhere in the manifold between (or beneath) the real-space of Ninsun and the hot blue stars of the Aud Cluster, the scarf revealed in fullness a new property. One day – or one night, for in the manifold it was always night – the silken fibres of the scarf began vibrating to new rhythms. Even as Rane floated in a delicious reliving of the first taste of Maria's lips, he heard her singing out the words of the Blake poem that she loved so much. It took him some time to realize that this sound came not through olfaction and the subsequent attitude of recurrence that he had entered, but through his ears and his auditory nerves. Maria's words took form close to him, as close as if her lips had pressed them into his:

Tyger! Tyger! Burning bright
In the forests of the night,
What immortal hand or eye
Dare frame thy fearful symmetry?

'You try to frame me,' she said, 'but you still haven't framed your own fearful symmetry.'

'What do you mean? Why do I never quite know?'

'Why do you never quite dare?'

'I've dared everything to have you again. Where are you?'

'I am right here, my Ranelight.'

After Maria went away, he lay in silent darkness of the lightship breathing in the rainbow fragrances of the scarf. One particular fragrance seemed to overpower the others and push them from his mind; or perhaps it was his mind that did the pushing in his desire to identify a strange new scent that beguiled him. It emanated from near the scarf's centre; it had the tang of oranges and the sweetness of hyacinths, all submerged beneath a more fermy aroma of sea spray on raw toalache. He allowed this fragrance to sweep him from olfaction into the attitude of association memory. From there he entered into quantum memory, so named (or misnamed) according to the discovery millennia ago that either of a pair of polarized photons will instantaneously 'know' the polarity of the other no matter how far they become separated in spacetime.

From this fundament of the cosmos, the ancient mechanics had postulated the interconnectedness of all things, an understanding that Omar Narayama had formalized in the universal syntax. The great remembrancer Arshan Prem had experienced intimations of an analogous property in Rane's own art: that small amounts of various substances might be used to trigger recollections of other substances with which they had once been associated. Not until the apotheosis of Mallory Ringess, however, had Prem's intimations proven to be true. From the taste of the aldehydes and iodine in a single sip of golden skotch, it was said, Mallory Ringess could call up images of fields of golden barley from which the skotch had been fermented – and he could 'see' as well the planet in which the stalks of barley had taken root. It was claimed, too, that he could sense the very atoms of carbon bound into the barley's germ, atoms that had once swirled in the exhalations of men and woman who had originated on Old Earth. The tree of matter and memory grew out through space and time into a sort of fractalling infinity. Or, as the remembrancers said: *The memory of all things is in all things*.

Rane would soon put a name to the new scent bound into the fibres of Maria's scarf: askling. The naming came about in this manner: as he held the essence of askling somewhere between the olfactory bulb and the deeper, blood-pink folds of his brain, images began flickering through him, from amygdala to memory to mind. In his mind's eye, he saw a great mountain, whose northern face showed miles of glaciers, granite crags, and cracks. As seen from the right vantage, the mountain took on the aspect of a sad old woman, and Rane thought of it as the Weeping Widow. He looked upon an entire range of mountains that ran like a broken backbone down a rugged coastline. He saw sediments of silt layered deep down into a grey-blue ocean; he saw forests and deserts and verdant grasslands broken with strange, golden-leaved trees nearly quarter of a mile high. A hundred landforms and seascapes took shape, along with thousands of kinds of fish, birds, barloches, and other phyla of animals. A million features of what might have been a single planet sprayed out into the blue-black panorama of quantum memory. They were like multicoloured shards from a shattered stained-glass window. All he needed to do, if he wished to apprehend this pattern, was to reassemble the shards and put the window back together again.

This he did through the aid of the ship's computer, though it pained him to do it and required a long time. How easy his search would have been if he had been able to iconize the millions of his mental images and infuse them into the computer! For then it would have been a simple thing for the computer to match the images with fotos and holograms of the galaxy's millions of planets, which formed a tiny fraction of the computer's data pools.

Computer memory, however, was not like that of a man; a computer encoded information as bits of energy bound into silicon or neurologics or some other material substrate, whereas after thirty thousand years of brain scans and theories, no one really knew what a man did when he remembered. A few of the cetics still had faith in programs that ran the machinery of the mind; the neurologicians, in particular, continued their millennia-long search for the master or meta programs that would at last enable them to control every aspect of consciousness and memory. Some of Rane's fellow academicians spoke of memory as an outfolding of explicate representations of a deeper, implicate order. A man's memory, according to others, was only part of a universal hologram formed as the universe evolved and recorded all events occurring in spacetime. Many remembrancers believed, more simply, that matter was in some deep sense nothing but pure memory – and that the meaning of evolution was to be found in the way that the primordial particles of matter generated out of the universe's fiery explosion into being had learned over billions of years how to assemble themselves into progressively higher and more complex states. The more mystical of Rane's brethren thus viewed reality as matter's remembering the fundamental purpose with which it had been imbued.

For many years, Rane had debated with himself, and with others, the validity of the various positions. Privately, he held great sympathy for the mystical viewpoint, while publicly, in his office of Lord Remembrancer, he had favoured the Fravashi ideal of plexure: simultaneously holding *all* positions (even if contradictory) to be valid and weaving them together to form a colourful tapestry that revealed a higher pattern of truth. In his depth and breadth of philosophical equability, he had often congratulated himself – that is, he had until Maria had ridiculed his hypocrisy.

One day in false winter, with the yellow-winged bluebirds back in Neverness from the southern islands and the fire roses in full flower, Rane had skated with Maria through the Hyacinth Gardens adjacent to the Great Circle. Maria was new to the city and new to Rane – but not so new that she couldn't see through him, as one could make out the blue veins of the millions of white blossoms of the shih trees along the icy garden paths. As it often did, the subject of remembrance came up for conversation, for Maria insisted on discovering everything that she could about Rane's difficult art. And Rane had told her of the different philosophies of remembrance.

'Of course the eschatologists,' he said, 'agree with those remembrancers who see the universe as evolving through matter's progressive memory of itself toward a certain end.'

Through a soft rain of white petals falling from the shih trees, Maria looked at him in wide-eyed wonder. 'And what end is that?'

'Who can really know?'

He went on to say that he cared little for determining the ontological likelihood of this view; his concerns tended toward a more phenomenological nature, and because he sometimes did experience a purpose to memory, he flirted with embracing the eschatologists' teleology. Most of the time, however, he proudly declaimed, he took the stance that all views of memory must be given fair weight and pleached together with the others, even the belief of the formalists that memory was nothing more than a symbolic inner representation of outer events.

'Phenomenology, ontology, eschatology, teleology – I hardly know what these words mean!' she said to him.

As the wind shook loose flowers from the tree, whitening their hair and covering their shoulders with fragrant petals, Rane delivered a lengthy discourse on the philosophy of remembrance.

'Words,' she said to him. 'You are so full of words and more words.'

'And you, a poet, are not?'

'A poet uses words to reveal the hidden reality of the world; you use them to obscure what is in front of your eyes.'

'But what is real? Is that not the point of this conversation?'

'Memories are real. And, of course, the universe remembers to a purpose – as do we.'

'But such teleological thinking has always been dangerous. And unnecessary.'

'As your esteemed Omar Narayama showed, it is logically no simpler to assume that matter is not imbued with purpose than to assume that it is.'

'In the sense of formal logic, that might be true. In the sense of science, which should be a practice of the possible, teleology has always been seen to be—'

'Why can't *you* see?' she challenged him. 'When will you have the courage for what you know?'

'But that's just it, I don't know what remembrance really is. No one knows.'

She plucked one of the shih blossoms from his hair and held it up to the sun. The strong light illuminated the flower's whiteness and revealed the cerulean veins and filaments of an infinitely intricate texture.

'If I asked you what a flower is,' she said, 'you could talk about stamens, anthers, pistils, and the pigments of the petals. Or deeper, the molecules of which the carpels are made. Or deeper still: down to the configuration of atoms, quarks, strings, and infons. But, sweet Rane – is that really what a flower *is*?'

They stood beneath the shih tree gazing at each other and savouring the blossom's sweetness.

'How can you doubt what memory is?' she asked him.

When she looked at him that way, her eyes full of hope and light, he couldn't doubt, and that was the great and wondrous thing about Maria. From the moment they had met, she had made him ecstatically aware of life's mighty purpose. When he looked through the fire of Maria's eyes to find his own secret splendour, he *knew* that they both remembered something deep and eternal that they both shared, as they shared the air they breathed. This vast, inextinguishable thing called them to dream, to desire, to do: to remember who they really were and why they had been created.

In the quiet of Nikolandru's lightship, a fifty-yard-long diamond needle stitching in and out of the manifold's opalescent fabric, Rane thought about that day in the Hyacinth Gardens. He couldn't help trying to apprehend the mystery of memory through various ideological lenses, just as he couldn't stop asking himself the question of how he could ever know memory's true nature. After a while, though, he returned to the more practical problem of how the memories that the scarf incited in him could be put to use. Certainly, no matter the ontological status of his memories, no computer known to the Order's professionals could reach into his mind to read them. But with his inner eye he could descry the images of various planets that the ship's computer infused into the visual cortex of his brain. As fotos and holograms of at least fifty million planets had been encoded into the computer's data pools, however, it took Rane many, many days to match his memories with the images flooding through him like an ocean.

He would surely have failed in this project had he not designed a sorting system to reduce the volume of his search. Maria, he remembered, had come to Neverness on a deep ship by way of Ninsun and the August Cluster. Very well, then, he would begin by matching images of the planets that circled the stars along that span of the galaxy's Sagittarius Arm. He would then sweep

coreward and back outward in arcs of ten, twenty, and then
thirty parsecs – and more, if needed. He would also, at least at
first, concentrate on the three thousand Civilized Worlds and
those planets associated them, with a lesser priority given to the
Japanese Worlds and those of the splinter factions of the
Cybernetic Universal Church. Lastly, he would follow the scent
of the scarf in opening himself to a deeper sense that could
divine Maria's plan in coming to Neverness and could 'smell
out' her purpose.

And so forty days and some 512,677 images later, he came
upon a hologram of the very mountain that he had named the
'Weeping Widow'. Of course, he had asked the computer to
show him images of mountains in particular, in the hope of
getting a quick and easy match. But nearly all the planets that
he studied had mountains – there were millions of them – and
his characterization of this one mountain as a grieving old woman
relied on his own sentiments and idiosyncratic perceptions, which
the computer's AI programs failed to duplicate. Once he had
made the match, however, the computer identified the mountain's
planet in less than a nanosecond: it was named Askling. It was
indeed one of the Civilized Worlds, and it lay along the Stellar
Fallaways just beyond Maniwold, Batunde, and Jocacia.

Rane wanted to announce this discovery to Nikolandru immediately, but how could he? No sound, no ray of light, no particle
of oxygen could penetrate the diamond panel separating Rane's
compartment from Nikolandru's. Another pilot might have
consented to sharing some small sliver of his computer's thought-
space with that of his passenger, perhaps through iconicity,
perhaps through syntaxis, instantiation or even one degree or
another of computer telepathy. Thus a man travelling as Rane
did could inform his pilot of various needs or alarms. Nikolandru,
however, insisted on a strict partitioning of his computer. They
would be journeying *not* just through the older, well-mapped
regions of the Fallaways, he had explained to Rane, but through
the manifold's wild torsion spaces, klein inversions, quandles,
and seifert subspaces, whose hideous complexity and ever-
shifting, ever-fracturing patterns would demand Nikolandru's
utmost concentration. A single moment of inattention might
result in the *Asherah* being flung into an infinite decision tree
from which there could be no escape – or the ship might fall

out into realspace, right into the heart of a hot, blue giant star. In such circumstances, Nikolandru would need silence and a deep clarity unbroken by the faintest whisper of another's mind.

And so Rane had no choice but to wait. How long he waited in the inky, rank darkness of his compartment he did not know, for time is relative, as the horologes like to say. Time can also be confusing and cruel, and journeys across the stars wreak upon body and mind various time distortions, both on outtime and more subjective intime: there are the Einsteinian contractions of realspace, along with the manifold's temporal telescoping and the effects of computer-generated slowtime and quicktime. No horologe who might compute the resulting net time gain or loss accompanied Rane. Rane estimated that from the time he identified Askling as a planet that he must explore to the time that he informed Nikolandru of his desire, nearly ten days passed.

Their meeting took place on an unnamed planet that orbited an unnamed white star about the size of Old Earth's sun. It had become part of their procedure for Nikolandru to put down from time to time on one planet or another just so that he could confer with Rane. And so somewhere beyond Agni Lux, the *Asherah* fell out of the manifold into star-studded realspace and then glided down through the planet's atmosphere and came to rest on a vast plain of grass. The sparkling greenery curved outward in all directions into a pure blue sky. Rane stood on this grass, breathing in fresh air and resting his hand upon the *Asherah*'s hard hull so as to steady himself. His leg muscles had grown so weak that he feared to walk more than a few steps lest he collapse.

Nikolandru, younger than he, had suffered less wasting of his body, and he stood at ease within the black uniform that he wore in emulation of the black garments worn by the Order's pilots. He, too, drew in breaths of cool air as if grateful for the chance to leave his ship. His quick brown eyes scanned the horizon as if looking for herd animals that grazed on grass – or the inevitable predators that attended such herds.

'I would like us to journey to Askling,' Rane informed him.

His legs trembled as he said this; he felt certain that the planet beneath him had a higher gravity than that of Icefall.

Nikolandru reached out and gripped his shoulder as if to steady him. His muscular fingers dug right down to Rane's bones.

'You are too thin,' Nikolandru said. 'You need to eat more – and to exercise.'

'I've been making researches,' Rane replied. He told Nikolandru about the scarf and how he had come to identify Askling.

'Strange,' Nikolandru said. His fingers moved from the wool of the kamelaika that Rane had donned to the scarf tied around Rane's neck. He caressed the scarf as he might a woman's skin; the features of his handsome face pulled into a frown of puzzlement. 'There is something very strange about this frippery that you're so fond of.'

'Yes,' Rane said, pulling back from the other man's unwanted touch. 'I have often thought that myself.'

'Of what material is it crafted? I've never felt its like.'

'The mechanics of my Order believe it might be a work of made matter.'

'Made by whom?'

'Certainly not by any peoples we have knowledge of. Perhaps it was made by an alien race – or by one of the galaxy's gods.'

'But made of *what*? That is the better question.'

Rane shrugged his shoulders. 'Who knows? It's said that the gods can disassemble matter down to quarks and strings – and build it back up into new elements more different from the matter that we know than carbon is from cobalt.'

'Strange, strange,' Nikolandru murmured. And then, 'You claim that the scarf's fabric has the propensity to hold smells?'

Yes, Rane thought, and other things, too. Because he did not want to tell Nikolandru about the way the scarf made music and recited poems in Maria's voice, he said no more.

'And to retain these smells long past the time that they would have dissipated from another material?'

'The scarf grabs and holds molecules as surely as a black hole captures any bit of matter falling within its event horizon.'

'An unusual metaphor, that.' Nikolandru studied Rane's face. 'But the strangest thing of all, I think, is your claim that you can detect these molecules – are you a bloodhound or a man?'

'I am a remembrancer,' Rane said. 'We spend a great deal of time training our sense of smell.'

'If what you say is true, it seems that you have developed a new sense far beyond anything that could be called smell.'

'It *is* true. We have only to journey to Askling and look for proofs of Maria's having been there.'

'What proofs do you hope to find?'

Rane drew in a breath and savoured the molecules that pricked his nose. As soon as they made planetfall on Askling, he hoped, the scent of the air would be all the proof he needed.

'Askling,' he said, 'still counts itself as one of the Civilized Worlds. Surely there will be immigration records. Perhaps an imago or an eidolon, too – we might even be able to find someone who knew Maria.'

'I thought you wished to find Maria herself. To bring her back from the dead.'

'I do. I . . . will. But in order to accomplish this, I must first remembrance her as perfectly as I can.'

'I've heard it said that your memory is already perfect.'

'Well, there are things about her that I don't know.'

'What things?'

'The world of her birth, for one. And her mother – she said that her mother still lives, somewhere. Maria would never speak of such things, however. She always made a mystery of herself.'

And what greater mystery could there be than the one, secret, vital thing about Maria that had always eluded him?

As if Nikolandru could hear his thoughts, he said, 'But the self is always a mystery, even to oneself, is it not?'

'Maria was a child, somewhere,' Rane murmured, evading the question. 'And is it not said that the child is the mother of the woman?'

'Then you would seek Maria's real mother, that you might know the child?'

Rane nodded his head. 'There are things that I would ask of her.'

'It seems that you have a quest within a quest.'

'I would call it more of a bending on a path that leads in one direction only.'

'Why did you not tell me of this before we left Neverness? You reveal the truth to me in layers, as a flower unfolds itself.'

Even as I reveal it to myself, Rane thought.

'Then is it your plan,' Nikolandru asked, pointing at the scarf, 'to use this strange new sense of yours to follow Maria back to her planet of origin?'

'My plan is unfolding even as our journey progresses.'

'It might unfold more gracefully if I were apprised of your thinking.'

Yes, yes, so it might, Rane thought. How simple it would be to take Nikolandru into his confidence, as he might Sunjay or Kolenya! Simple, but not easy: Rane had deeply trusted only one other human being, and then never completely. Nikolandru, smiling at him so openly and kindly, inspired a great deal of trust, but the very force and seeming artlessness of his charm disquieted Rane. He recalled the story of an Architect who had smuggled a string of Edic lights into Malbring, an ugly, oppressive city in which any theistic profession or possession of religious artefacts incurred a penalty of death. The Architect, who claimed to be a merchant-prince of Tria, had ingeniously woven the diamonds of the Edic lights into the golden fabric of the gown that he wore, thus hiding the jewels of his holy computer in plain sight. It occurred to Rane that Nikolandru did a similar thing.

What, though, did Nikolandru hide that Rane could easily see? He was friendly, self-assured, and playful, often with a touch of irony that coloured many of his communications. He seemed brave and bold. And curious and intelligent and creative, and much else – and that was the problem, for so much about this pilot-poet beamed so brightly that Rane had a hard time identifying the single thing that worried him even as it bedazzled him. And what was that thing? Rane thought he perceived it as desire, a blazing desire nearly as incandescent and powerful as his own. Whenever they spoke of the purpose of their journey, Rane felt a fierce longing come alive within Nikolandru and light up his eyes, and Rane did not know why that should be.

'I would like,' Rane finally said, 'to explore the same planets that Maria visited on her journey to Neverness.'

'But there might be a hundred such planets. And many of them might have sheltered Maria no more than a day or two while her ship took on supplies. They cannot all be worth an investigation.'

'But some of them will be.'

'How will you know which ones? Will your scarf tell you *that*?'

Rane considered this. 'Perhaps, then, we will have to explore all of them.'

'The span of five years,' Nikolandru said, 'delimits the time of our searches. How much of it are you willing to waste?'

His words seemed to stab into Rane's chest, causing a sharp pain that spread up through his throat.

'Five years,' Nikolandru repeated in a softer, kinder voice, 'may seem like a long span now, but it will pass quickly. We should find a way, ourselves, to delimit the space of our search.'

'What do you suggest?'

Nikolandru's smile broke upon his face with both reassurance and a great force. He gazed out at the vast green plain surrounding them as if he could look off the edge of the world to identify the very stars that they must find.

'Ultimately,' he said, 'you plan to stand before the Solid State Entity and ask Her a great boon. When you do, most likely She will either help you or destroy you.'

'She will help me – I know She will.'

Nikolandru's smile widened. 'I am gambling a great deal that you are correct. All right, let's say that you are. Then if your purpose is to become Hers and your woman is to be remade, would it not make sense that She would help you in your searches?'

'Help me how?'

'She is a goddess, isn't She? It's said that the gods keep watch on all that occurs within the galaxy, especially on the worlds of man.'

He drew in a breath as if oxygenating his brain with this idea. Then he continued, 'It may be that She will be able to point you to the planets upon which Maria spent the most time. *Then* we could journey to them, that you might perfect your memories of her.'

Rane stood looking up past the sun, whose xanthic dazzle obscured the twinkling of the stars to which they must journey.

'So,' Rane said, 'we are to proceed straight to the galaxy's most powerful deity, a being known to slay seekers like us as we might squash an annoying fly. We do not know whether the human part of the Entity resides within the nebula She took over or on Old Earth, wherever that might lie among billions of stars. Suppose we journey first to Her nebula. Then, assuming we can survive the deadly maze of the manifold that this being distorts through the very nature of Her beingness – we are somehow to communicate with Her. And to ask Her to bring one of the dead back to life. But before She grants this impossible grace, She is to forgive our laziness and supply us with intelligences that we should have gained for ourselves. We'll have to pray that She won't send us off to some spectacular doom for the presumption of begging of Her multiple boons – and for the even greater presumption of reducing Her to the role of a travel guide. Then, when we return to Her after some years have passed, we must find our way through the ever-shifting manifold beneath the realspace near Her once again. And we must hope that a goddess known for Her capriciousness and lethality will wave Her magic wand over a cauldron of amino acids, lipids, and DNA, infused with a few of my memories, and out will step the same beautiful woman who died on an icy planet ten thousand light years away.'

His little soliloquy caused Nikolandru to smile. 'When you put things that way, journeying twice to the Entity *does* seem utterly mad.'

'Yes, it does.'

'Of course, journeying to Her a single time is mad enough – why did you not put such objections to yourself before we began this journey?'

'Why should you think that I did not?'

'Because there is only a thin sliver of a particle of a chance that we will succeed.'

'That may be true. But why, then, split that chance into yet smaller slivers by visiting the Entity two times?'

'Because half of an infinitesimal is still an infinitesimal. Your chances of gaining what you desire are so small as to approach zero. In such circumstances, we might as well put probabilities aside and rely on other factors.'

'What factors?'

'Well, fate. Either you are fated to reunite with your woman, or you are not.'

'I suppose a poet would argue that. Do you really believe in fate?'

Rane burned his eyes by looking up again too near the sun. *Fate and chance, the same glad dance* – hadn't Mallory Ringess been fond of saying this?

'Do you believe in fate?' Nikolandru asked him.

'I believe what I must believe. And I believe that we should look for Maria *before* journeying on to the Entity.'

'It is too bad that belief will not open windows to the manifold and take you where you wish to go.'

'No,' Rane said, slapping his hand against the *Asherah*'s diamond hull, 'but your lightship will. Have I not paid you a hundred thousand disks for a passage?'

'For a passage, yes. And that is exactly what I propose: to pass through the galaxy to the Entity as quickly as we can.'

'But I propose something different. Did we not agree that you would take me anywhere in the Milky Way galaxy that our quest might lead us?'

'It leads to the Entity.'

'In the end, perhaps. But also, in the end, this is *my* quest, not yours.'

'Only one of us can pilot my lightship.'

'I would not think of suggesting *how* you should pilot your ship – however I must insist on *where* we must go.'

'If you were a pilot,' Nikolandru said, 'if you understood the mathematics of the manifold, you would know that the "where" and the "how" are fitted together like a lock and a key. One can't simply look at a hologram of the galaxy and decide to journey from Arcite to Askling, for instance, by a straight light route, as one would skate across Neverness from the Sound to the Old City by way of the East-West Sliddery. It might be a shorter journey, timewise, depending on the perturbations of the manifold, to fall out first near Darkmoon – which lies spacewise in the opposite direction – before making a mapping directly to Askling.'

'I *do* know that,' Rane said. 'A child knows that.'

'No child has ever found his way through a serpentine space. It takes *years* to master the manifold.'

Why, Rane wondered, was this pilot-poet proving to be so difficult? Was it pride that impelled him to insist on his prerogatives as master of his lightship? Did some unexpected cheapness of character lure him into wanting to make the most of the hundred thousand disks in the least possible time? Or did something else altogether call him to rush headlong into the heart of the Solid State Entity, as a moth is drawn to a flame?

Maria had often accused Rane of having deep intuitions –

and then ignoring them in favour of glittering golden chains of reason that dangled so appealingly before his mind's eye. Was that really true? All right, Rane thought, suppose it was true, for hadn't Maria been right about so much? What, then, could Rane sense about Nikolandru in this moment, with a strange sun burning their faces and the smells of grass, earth, and something sublimely alien hanging in the air?

Rane could *almost* see it, the way that one could almost make out the dark portion of a waxing moon by using the eye to fill in the curves of the crescent. And what he saw was this: Nikolandru *would* honour their agreement by consenting to take Rane where he wished to go. He would use the mystery of his mathematics, however, to justify deviations in their route. If Rane sensed in the scarf the piquancy of passionwood, for instance, he would insist on journeying straightaway to Ars Ananda, the single place in the galaxy on which the purple amorgenic passion trees grow. And Nikolandru would counter with the claim that due to some unverifiable distortion in the manifold, they should first fall out near Rosh Mayim before kleining back toward Ars Ananda. But having reached that world of ten-mile-high mountains cut with sparkling rivers and spectacular waterfalls, Nikolandru would no doubt find a reason to make a mapping directly to Aotearoa or some other planet that Rane also wished to visit – planets closer to the galaxy's Orion Arm and to the presumed location of the Entity. Nikolandru would speak of infinite serpentine spaces and zero-point storms and other dangers of the manifold. How would Rane ever know which of these objections was reasonable and which was not?

As he had so often, Rane put the scarf to his nose and inhaled the scents born years before on a planet upon which stood a mountain shaped like a grief-stricken old woman. He stood on the sweet grass by Nikolandru's ship, and he pointed up into the sky.

'Let us first journey to Askling,' he said, 'and we shall see what we shall see. We can determine the next leg of our journey then.'

As Nikolandru's face fell too easily into a mask of blithe acceptance, Rane made himself a promise: as soon as the *Asherah* rocketed up into space, he would use the endless hours he spent floating in his stinking quarters to begin a study of topology, non-Euclidean geometry, Lavi algebras, and the other mathematics a pilot used to navigate the manifold. Such study, Nikolandru had warned him, would take years to complete. Very well, then, in front of Rane lay a vast expanse of stars separated by the galaxy's long, dark, endless miles – and years and years of precious time.

14

And so it came to be. For many days (or what passed as days), he floated naked in the warm, dark, nidorous bowels of Nikolandru's ship. He faced his part of the ship's computer, and he looked upon the billions of glittering glyphs into which thirty thousand years of mathematical ideas had been encoded. He rather quickly verified what he had always been told was true: that mathematics was like a golden, infinite tree of knowledge that opened outward in all directions forever. A single branch, such as classical geometry, might send out a shoot of a new postulate that questioned the assumption that parallel lines never meet; the shoot would then engender new axioms that vivified such glories as elliptic, hyperbolic, Riemannian, kinematic, and other non-Euclidean geometries – and each of these shoots, in turn, would become mighty branches of their own that grew and grew and grew. As Rane climbed higher and higher up the tree, for instance finding his way from geometry to topology to the generalized Poincaré conjecture (that every homotopy sphere is isomorphic to the standard N-sphere), he felt much like a monkey who could only appreciate the vastness of the canopy above him the higher that he climbed. There were two kinds of vertigo, he realized, and the lesser came from looking down dizzily from a great height to the ground. The greater vertigo – the cantors called it the *vashnorn* – was to feel oneself pulled ever upward into a bottomless blue inner sky, past theorems and fancies and realizations that streaked by like whirling stars, straight into the mind of God.

How easy it would have been for him, he knew, to fall – and

fall and fall and fall! Hadn't it always been that way with him, in whatever endeavour caught up his passions? Hadn't he, above all others of his profession, plunged through veritable pools of cool blue kalla deep down toward the One Memory that held the knowledge of all things? Hadn't he likewise sought to be annihilated in Maria, melting into the soft sweetness of her body and disappearing into the bright black centres of her adoring eyes? Yes, yes, he had. Yes. Hadn't he, however, also inevitably panicked and fled at the precise moment that he might have passed through this infinite knowingness to become everything by becoming nothing? What a cruel paradox it was that a man's greatest rapture should also be his greatest terror!

When it came to his new exploration of mathematics, Rane told himself that he must dampen his exhilaration by surrounding himself with a closed horizon. He would not allow his gaze to drop down the infinite tree toward the ground, and he certainly would not stare rapturously upward. Neither would he swing monkey-like from branch to branch, here looking for a juicier fruit or a more perfectly formed leaf. He had a purpose – very well, he would cleave to that purpose. He would confine himself, at least at first, to comprehending continuous mappings, differentiable manifolds, quaternionic projective spaces, and other basic maths that the Order's pilots learned in the first of their journeyman years.

Rane, in a flaring up of an essential hubris that he had always tried to conceal from Maria, flirted with the notion that he could someday pilot a lightship. His more rational parts, of course, realized that such imaginings made him very much of a fool. Pilots studied things besides mathematics: astrophysics, quantum mechanics, nucleosynthesis, exobiology, exoecology, exopsychology, and much else. They spent long hours in the Rose Womb Cloisters, floating in darkness and breathing highly oxygenated water in preparation for the spacetime-annihilating experience of the manifold. They had to learn not only the generalized cybernetic senses such as iconicity, shih, and hallning, but others peculiar to the pilot's art: stivance, gyrance, fractation, figuration, and fenestration. And after years of demanding preparation that many failed to complete, a journeyman pilot had to put all the maths and everything else to the test through action. Even under the tutelage of master pilots, nearly a third of all journeymen died in their first dozen forays into the manifold.

When Rane tired of mathematics – and tired of freefall, preserved foods, recycled water, and the other bothers of stellar travel – he sometimes chided himself for creating unnecessary dissension with Nikolandru. Had he, particularly in their last conversation, been too secretive? Too insistent, too stubborn, too harsh? So he had been with Maria. Why must it always be this way when he considered himself, at heart, to be a such a reasonable and congenial man?

Rane felt glad to put such questionings behind him in his inevitable turn of thoughts toward the memory of Maria – and he felt gladder still when they finally reached Askling. After ten days or so of hurtling through the manifold, the *Asherah* fell out into realspace above a brown and blue planet about the size of Icefall. Its three highly desertified continents sheltered a small population of only twenty million people. Nikolandru put down on a runway of the fields outside of Sallhet, a city built on a great shelf of land above the ocean in Askling's small but verdant tropical belt. As soon as Rane stepped from the hold of the lightship, a thickness of warm, moist air seemed to wrap itself around his face and nose like a sopping blanket. He looked upon the tumid and too-green vegetation that choked the misty, rolling foothills of Askling's greatest mountain range. And he inhaled the tang of oranges that perfumed the orchards; he smelled, too, the sweetness of hyacinths, all submerged beneath the more fermy aroma of sea spray on raw toalache that wafted up from the ocean.

In a smile of triumph and validation that he could not hold in, he looked at Nikolandru and said, 'Maria stood on this very planet, even as we do now.'

If Rane needed confirmation of this, he found it later at a white-washed hostel on Sallhet's greatest boulevard. The hostel's owner, a large man with flowing flaxen hair and ice-blue eyes, recalled Maria very well: 'An alluring woman who unfortunately arrived without a parsig in her purse. I let her stay here in exchange for entertaining the other guests. As I remember, she had a voice like an angel.'

She hadn't, he added, remained very long, a fact that Rane verified when still later he bribed one of the keepers of the fields where lightships, longships, and deep-ships from across the Stellar Fallaways put down: the keeper produced the log containing the dates of Maria's arrival on and departure from Askling, and he showed it to Rane for a 'consideration of only twenty City Disks'.

'Very well, then,' Nikolandru said to Rane. 'It seems that your "nose" has pointed you true after all. To where does it point next?'

'Farsheyden,' Rane said, sniffing at his scarf. 'Let us journey to Farsheyden.'

They returned to the *Asherah* and rocketed up through Askling's atmosphere. After perhaps twelve days of intime, they reached Farsheyden, a rather small, watery world not far from Pushkin's Star Group. There Rane learned that Maria had not stayed long either, for she had been deported for breaking several of Farsheyden's sumptuary laws: chief among her violations was her insistence on wearing her favourite blue dress, as only Farsheyden's perfecti class were allowed to wear garments the colour of the sky.

The theme of Maria scandalizing others or outright breaking laws continued as Rane furthered his explorations, naming the planets they must visit and seeing to it that Nikolandru guided them along the Fallaways. On Kamadhluk, as Rane discovered, Maria had broken the modesty laws by wearing that same sleeveless blue dress, and worse, by going about barefoot on her browned and thickly callused feet. And on Marklig, she had nearly been executed for the crime of casting off her dress altogether and swimming naked in the Moon River, which runs through the centre of Marklig's greatest city. That here, too, she had only been deported Rane attributed to a rumour that Maria had made a temporary friendship with a powerful Marklig aristocrat.

Rane's journey into greater knowledge of Maria and her past continued as the *Asherah* journeyed on through the endless present of stars and yet more stars into the uncertain future. Rane and Nikolandru fell from planet to planet as they might hop from island to island in crossing a vast ocean. Moksha, Samtal, Singularis, Tormentare – on most of these Rane discovered clues as to who Maria really was. On Newvannia, it seemed, Maria had gained fame for winning a poetry competition, while on Alumit, she had temporarily adopted a motherless child.

Somewhere beyond Treblinka Luz, where the stars of the galaxy's Sagittarius Arm grow thin but bright, the *Asherah* reached Aracelli, the Dreaming City. Its name meant, variously, Altar of the Sky or Flame of the Sky, and many called it simply Flame. Some visitors, however, chose an ugly nickname for the vast megalopolis that covered most of Aracelli's single small continent: instead of Flame, they called it Phlegm, for according to Ali Easwaran, one of the first pilot-poets to range the spaces between Treblinka Luz and Sheydveg, the ugly planetary city was like a 'stinking excrescence coughed up from the diseased lungs of history'. Nikolandru, following his predecessor's sensibilities, did not want to put down on Aracelli, but Rane insisted that they must.

After making the usual inquiries, Rane and Nikolandru travelled by tube five hundred miles to a broad boulevard that ran straight through the heart of Aracelli. The owner of a dirty hostel off one of the boulevard's side streets had a record but no memory of Maria's having stayed there. As the small, glassy-eyed man put it to Rane, 'A thousand strangers stay here each year – why should I remember any single one of them?'

Rather than look at Rane directly, he kept glancing up to his left, as if finding the answers to Rane's questions inscribed in the air. He seemed distracted and uninterested in Rane's quest, and apparently cared little for the bribe that Rane practically had to force upon him.

His apathy found echo in the vacuous stares of the people who plodded down the sidewalks of the boulevard. Rane and Nikolandru watched this clutch of humanity from beneath a soot-smeared yellow awning outside a dress shop. Although it was a cloudless day, they needed no protection from the sun, for the many fumes that poisoned the atmosphere formed a protective bubble above them nearly as dense and impervious to sunshine as gaseous lead. Rane could hardly breathe for all the ozone, benzene, perchloroethylenes, sulphur dioxide, and formaldehydes that each inflection of his diaphragm sucked into his lungs. He could hardly think through the tremendous noise that over-clamoured the more natural and human sounds of the city. From somewhere nearby, a siren screamed and the blast of a concrete cutter shook the air. Down the street in numerous lanes rolled an endless succession of vibrating metal choches, most occupied by single passengers fighting their way to appointments or duties, or more likely, to shops where they might purchase some superfluous and shoddily made thing. Unbelievably, each of these noxious machines burned hydrocarbons for motive power! Rane had no idea why. Who could live amid such torment? How it degraded the Aracellians to abide such miserable lives, for miserable far beyond need the Aracellians seemed! Although they crowded into restaurants and shops little different to those that lined the streets of Neverness – jewellery sellers and spice shops and sculpting parlours – they took no pleasure in strolling along their great boulevard, at least none that Rane could perceive. What he *could* see was a myriad of men and women passing by, their sad, sallow faces betraying an inner decadence. The Aracellians seemed to Rane a sickly people: sick not just in their enervated and often bloated bodies, but morbidly ill to the core of their souls.

'Let us leave now,' Nikolandru said to Rane. 'This Phlegm is a bad place – surely Maria would not have remained here.'

Rane easily enough surmised the cause of Aracellians' collective torpor, for accounts of visitors told of a populace which had scorned one of the three laws of the Civilized Worlds: that they must not 'gaze too long into their computers'. Many Aracellians interfaced their ubiquitous machines to one degree or another continually; the most habituated of them spent long days lying on soiled beds in the darkened rooms of their tiny apartments – and all the while they lost themselves in the cybernetic spaces generated by the neurologics woven into the very sheets and blankets that covered them. These Dreaming Ones, as they were called, vacated the limitations and dullness of the real world in favour of entering into the scintillating vistas of what they called the Real Real, or sometimes, the Dreaming. In this, Rane thought, they conflated ideas held by contemporary autists no less than the ancient Australians. In their stinking and immobilized way of life, he mused, they nearly recreated the hellish existence of a passenger on a lightship.

'No, this is the Dreaming City,' Rane reminded Nikolandru. 'If Maria came here, she might have dreamed, too.'

'Why should you care if she did?'

'It may be,' Rane said, 'that if Maria made a dreaming, it is still preserved.'

'How likely is that?'

'I have often wondered,' Rane murmured, 'what it would be like to make a dreaming. It's said that of all the simulation computers on the worlds of man, the Aracellians' are the most powerful.'

'Powerful, yes. So is opium, so is the Song of the Sirens – so is a sorceress's enchantment.'

'But what man doesn't long to hear the Sirens' Song at least once in his life?'

With that, Rane led off down the crowded street, smeared with exhaust residues and oil that leaked from the choches; they walked past dilapidated shops with cracked windows and alleys rife with garbage and the stench of rotting urine. Excrement fouled the sidewalk, and they had to wave away the big black flies that buzzed around their heads. From the rusted grates beneath their feet issued sewer gases and the effluvia of a thousand chemicals dumped down the Aracellians' drains. A couple of blocks farther on, across from a large concrete structure that housed the public toilets, they came to a dreaming pavilion, which was set back from the boulevard. A dozen benches blemished with brown peeling paint encircled the pavilion; Nikolandru positioned himself on an unoccupied bench even as Rane brushed the dirt from one of the pavilion's reclining chairs. He sat down and looked up at the heaume attached to the back of his chair. Like a hollowed-out metal moon it was – and he could almost feel the neurologics within pulsing with electrons and generating the noetic field that would descend upon his brain like a black hood and cut off the sights, sounds, and smells of the real world. All he needed to do was to reach out to the heaume with a few sharp, clear mental commands, and he would almost immediately fall out into the vivid thoughtscapes of the *real* real world.

'You've paid me well to take you this far,' Nikolandru called out to Rane, batting at the flies that came too near his face. 'How much more will you pay for me to keep these vermin from you as you dream?'

Rane glanced around him at the handful of people occupying a few of the pavilion's twenty chairs. Only the poorest Aracellians, of course, used the public dreaming stations; those with more means entered the Dreamtime by way of metallic skullcaps welded to the bones of their heads or even through neurologics expensively (and very carefully) implanted into their brains. Being poor, the men and women who joined Rane at the pavilion that day could not afford a personal tender to fend off the numerous banes of life in Aracelli, though the old woman in the chair next to Rane employed her grandson (Rane guessed) to stand by her chair while she dreamed and to fan away the city's omnipresent flies. The five others near Rane, however, had no such good fortune, and flies buzzed around their nostrils and crawled across their twitching eyelids and faces. The ragged man beside Rane lay as one dead, his fly-sucked eyes staring straight up at nothing. One had to be tough to be poor in Aracelli, Rane thought; he soon learned that many of Aracelli's lowest orders took a special pride in being able to endure any hardship of the outer and far lesser world without show of complaint.

'Who ever died of a few flies?' Rane said to Nikolandru with a bravura at odds with the twitching sensation that pulled at his skin. Then he looked up at the shiny waiting heaume and added, 'One can hope, however, that our hosts take better care of their simulation machinery than they do the rest of their city.'

Some said that the Aracellians had hollowed out the core of their planet in order to build a computer vaster and more powerful than any extant outside the realms of the gods. Rane knew that to be untrue, of course, for the core of Aracelli was made of a ball of blazing nickel-iron nearly as hot as the surface of a star, just like the cores of Icefall and Old Earth and the other planets on which human beings lived. What the Aracellians *had* done was to expend most of their wealth on fabricating humanity's most sophisticated computers and then building an array of these supposedly intelligent machines beneath the city, deep down in the ground below even the layers of the tube tunnels, the sulki grids and the sewers. Smaller computers connected to this system through various tachyonic radiations and were integrated into the walls and floors of the Aracellians' homes, into their light fixtures, into their choches, into their clothing and even skin – into every aspect of their existence and their lives.

'How long,' Nikolandru asked Rane, 'will you give yourself in this surreality looking for Maria?'

'As long as it takes. If you grow bored, I'm sure you can wander off and find some amusement.'

'Ah, yes, I could always watch a man being sculpted into a yeti or I could bed one of these cankerous Aracellian women.' Nikolandru looked around them and slowly shook his head. 'No, I will remain here. If I can't keep the flies off you, at least I can fend off the thieves. You're too well dressed to be lying insensible on the street.'

Rane fingered his rather worn racing kamelaika and smiled at Nikolandru's hyperbole. 'No one is going to rob me,' he said.

How could anyone safely rob anyone in this most peaceful of cities in which every human action and interaction (and practically every thought) was recorded by some computer eye or sensor?

'Well, what about the dogs?'

Nikolandru referred to the feral dogs that ranged the alleys of Aracelli and befouled the sidewalks. He implied that a pack of the hungry beasts could possibly descend upon Rane while he was dreaming.

'All right,' Rane said, his smile growing wider. 'Please stay and protect me from the dogs.'

And with that, he reached up and pulled the heaume down over his head. As the machine's field caught him up in its rushing, rainbow-coloured totality, he asked himself yet again what he *really* hoped to gain by entering this unfamiliar ontological space. As always, of course, he wanted to grasp the ungraspable thing about Maria. Sometimes he even put a name to this truth of Maria's being: *sawol* – an old, old word, older even than 'soul'. Did a person really have a soul? Or was it more as the Buddhists had once believed with their concept of *anatman*: that a man or a woman was nothing more than a swirl of sparkling consciousness that gathered for a moment like a storm to break forth its lightning upon the universe for a few glorious moments before it dissipated into darkness and died back into stillness and peace?

He knew he would never answer such questions, for they would remain always unanswerable. What he could do was to settle a matter that had been tormenting him: could he use his once-superb memory to recreate a Maria so faithful to the real Maria that he could not tell the difference? And if all this fell out just as he hoped, would his experience of her convince his senses not just visually and aurally but tactilely, olfactorily, and even thermally? In the end, he knew, he just wanted to hold Maria all warm and sweet in his arms again.

It would have been simplest if he, godlike (or like Hanuman li Tosh), had been able to create his own edenic world and populate it with two perfect beings called Maria and Thomas Rane. Aracellian laws, however, forbade the simulation of private paradises. The Aracellians had devoted their vast arrays of computers to the articulation of an even vaster communal dream. Each person who entered this single surreality could add to it, as an artist might contribute colourful dabs of pigment to a group painting – but the painting itself was to be shared by everyone and to continue to grow ever more elaborate and textured through time.

This ideal necessitated (or so the Aracellians believed) many laws and rules: no one could instantiate into the Dreaming as an alien or an animal – or even as a particularly unsightly human being, for it was thought that any sort of ugliness or deformity would disturb one's fellow dreamers and mar the beauty of what they co-created. There could be no doppelgängers either, for running various versions of oneself could confuse the self as much as it did other people. As well, one's diseases and upsets could not be brought into the simulation, and this included the scourge of obesity which afflicted so many Aracellians. Various rules governed people's dress as they did their speech; name-calling in the heat of argument, for instance, was punished by a suspension from the Dreaming – as were public displays of almost any sort of ism, not just the obvious ones such as sexism, ageism, and racism but also negativism, absolutism, thanatism, and any sort of egoism. More minor rules identified which words currently had the approval of the censors and which had become offensive. Rules concerning behaviour ranged from a ban on eating meat to an admonition against looking at anyone in a manner that engendered feelings of discomfort. The Laws of the Dreaming, as they were called, aimed not just at the ordering of a good and just world but at the creating of a world from which suffering had been eliminated altogether.

After Rane had passed through the heaume's prismatically scintillant window, he fell out into the crystal-clear, almost too-real space of the Dreaming. He stood on the same great boulevard down which he and Nikolandru had walked only a short while before. Nikolandru, however, had vanished, as had the pavilion itself and the adjacent toilets. Gone as well were the poor people who had plagued the streets of the other Aracelli – along with the garbage, the dog droppings, and the flies. The terrible smog had lifted like a filthy veil from a woman's face to reveal the fairest city that Rane had ever seen. For the first time, in the pure light that poured down from a perfectly blue sky, he took note of the fine, classically balanced architecture that recalled the symmetries and beauty of lost Xanadu; it seemed that some invisible hand had scrubbed the buildings clean of their layers of grime. The awning above the dress shop gleamed with an immaculate yellow tone like that of a newly unfurled flower.

It took Rane a moment to realize that he could now hear the conversation of his thoughts and even the whisperings of his soul, for the cacophony of machines and choche engines had also vanished from the street, along with the choches themselves. The great, greasy boulevard's black surface had been torn up and replaced with fitted red bricks, upon which a parade of people moved. All wore clean, colourful garments; all of them – the men, women, and children – seemed handsomely made, or nearly so. The great Aracelli simulation computers did not completely resculpt one's form and face according to some ideal of perfection, for doing so would render a person unrecognizable to his friends and his family. Rather, the figuration programs accentuated the stronger and more comely features in order to create a balance with the inevitable flaws, in much the same way that the ancient Japanese potters sought to realize the beauty of imperfection.

Rane watched people going in and out of the shops: an art gallery, an ice cream parlour, a spicery, a sound chamber. Children ran screaming through jets of water that erupted from one section of the bricks, while their parents looked on from the little green patches of lawn that dotted the boulevard. One strikingly svelte woman paused before a planter full of tulips; she inhaled the flowers' fragrance and seemed to revel in the way that the petals, like translucent yellow cups, caught the light of the sun. To Rane's right, a diva plucked the strings of a gosharp and sang out the most mellifluously sweet aria that he had ever heard; to his left, an acrobat entertained a crowd of onlookers by dancing across a tightrope stretched between two light poles. A smaller group encircled a portraiture artist who created likenesses of men, women, and children through the unlikely technique of suspending tiny globules of paint in the air like a cloud of colours. All the people – there must have been ten thousand of them packing the boulevard for miles east and west – appeared to be completely engaged in their pursuits. All of them appeared happy to share with each other this impossibly rich and textured phantasm, and Rane thought that Aracelli could truly be called the Dreaming City.

Rane finally moved out into the street himself, for not to join the great Show, as the great gathering of humanity was called, would be considered as isolationism, one of the very worst isms forbidden in the Dreamtime. He made his way past a sandpit full of granite boulders that children climbed. No one paid him any particular attention. He noticed that instead of his tattered kamelaika, he now wore a pair of fine cotton trousers and a flowing blue shirt, much like the garments that the other Aracellian men sported. He walked toward a large upraised planter constructed of the same red bricks that lined the street. Several shih trees grew from it. Beneath the trees – this section of the boulevard was like a miniature park – red roses grew in well-tended flower beds while a small fountain built into the shelf of brick that formed the planter's edge sent up silvery sprays. Water tinkled back into the fountain in pleasing tintinnabulations. Women and men sat on the planter's brick shelf in the shade of the trees, talking and laughing.

For some reason, Rane felt drawn to the fountain. When he stepped closer to it, he noticed that its centre was made of an upraised medallion of bronze and cast into the shape of a tiger's head. The sprays shot up from the tiger's mouth and fell back into the fountain's pool. He watched as a boy about nine years old climbed up on the planter's shelf and manoeuvred one of his bare feet past the pool directly over the tiger's mouth. The boy managed to divert a pulse of water and squirt the two women sitting closest to him. They screamed in startled glee, as did the boy. Their white dresses soaked through in moments, revealing comely bodies that seemed toned by a lifetime of focused exercises. Although they scolded the boy away from the fountain, they seemed as happy with his petty misdemeanour as he did.

And then Rane saw that the people nearby him appeared to be paying scant attention to this little scene; rather, they had turned their gazes to the opposite edge of the planter, to Rane's left. Rane looked in that direction, too. And there, poised on the brick shelf, resplendent in a flowing blue dress, stood a barefoot and beautiful Maria.

'Look, it is she!' the man next to Rane cried out.

Rane needed no such encouragement to look and look and look. He stared so hard that he feared the people in the crowd would notice his rudeness and chastise him. He drank in Maria's browned legs, the swell of her hips beneath the dress, her large breasts, her lithe arms, the strong but fine column of her neck. Her hair fell down in sheeny black waves upon her naked shoulders. Her eyes, as deep and beautiful as he remembered, seemed like infinite pools of light.

'Her nose is too large, though,' he murmured.

Though not so aquiline as the bold noses of Mallory, Danlo, Sunjay, and others of the Ringess line whom Rane had known so well, he thought that the Aracellian computers had erred slightly in rendering this instantiation of Maria. Or perhaps it was he who had erred. Could he really be sure that he exactly recalled the proportions of Maria's face? Perhaps he had mismade this simulation of Maria, and the computers had only painted her according to his specifications. Another possibility, however, occurred to him: what if the woman perched on the planter was the original simulation that Maria had constructed and the computers had preserved – what if Maria had misremembered *herself*? And how was Rane to know what part of this simulation to attribute to Maria and what part he created?

The man next to Rane – he was so tall and blond that he might have been a brother of Tamara Ten Ashtoreth – apparently overhead Rane's remark about Maria's nose, for he frowned the moment that the words left Rane's lips. He looked at Rane and shook his head. He must have taken Rane's simple statement as a criticism, or even as a judgement. The Aracellians counted criticism as a dangerous ism – and judgementalism was even worse. The man backed away from Rane, still shaking his head. Then he made an obvious effort to compose himself and ignore Rane. Apparently he did not want to allow himself to judge what he construed as Rane's egregious judgementalism.

'It is she, it is she – look, look!' someone else called out, picking up the man's cry.

Even as Rane watched, the silken folds of Maria's blue dress burst into flames.

'It is the Burning Woman!'

Rane jumped forward to cover Maria's body with his own so that he might extinguish the fire; however, a wall of people separated him from Maria, who seemed neither alarmed nor anguished by the hot indigo flames enveloping her. The dress burned and burned, but the flames did not seem to burn or harm Maria. She just stood on the edge of the planter, smiling and waiting.

'It is the Burning Woman! It is the Burning Woman! It is the Burning Woman!'

The crowd of people surrounding Rane pressed toward her and packed the red-brick boulevard even more densely. It occurred to him that Maria was like a star that must burn brightly and shower its radiance on others – either that or die. He could not tell if this thought came from his own mind or from the computer's program which moved his mind, though he wanted to believe that he was its creator. In the same way, he retained an almost mystical belief that he could use his memory to reveal the secrets of this ontological space at once a part and *not* a part of him. He felt sure that some deep place within him had captured the essential Maria, whom he would soon meet.

He noticed that some of the people near him had turned around to look away from Maria, back into the crowd. He looked that way, too, and he noticed a ripple in the sea of Aracellians who gathered on the boulevard. The ripple grew into a wave that seemed to agitate the sea and to divide it; people began shifting to the right or to the left as if making way for someone or something that moved toward the planter. Rane felt the crowd's excitement. The blond-haired man's face had tightened with a sort of fear-tinged anticipation of witnessing a dangerous but beautiful thing.

Rane sensed rather than saw something move down the aisle of the parting crowd, for too many people stood in front of him to allow him a clear vantage. He waited a few moments as the Aracellians filled the air with their sighs, whispers, and murmurs of hope. The rippling of people pointed straight toward the planter. When Rane turned back in that direction, he saw that the Burning Woman had vanished, or rather, had become a pillar of fire that gave off a blinding blue light. He had to look away from this intense illumination, and when he did so – now gazing at the opposite shelf of the planter – he saw the aisle open and a flash of orange and black burst from the crowd like a bolt of lightning. Then, to his astonishment, a beautiful tigress leaped onto the planter.

'It is She! It is She! It is She!'

Rane immediately recognized this powerful being as Maria, but he could not say how he knew this. Somehow, Maria had instantiated into the Dreaming as an animal – had been *allowed* to instantiate as one of the forbidden forms. He watched as people cleared away from the planter's shelf and the tigress settled down by the rim of the fountain. Her face – a glory of black and orange markings, with white around the great golden eyes – turned toward Rane. The fur along her lithe body seemed to blaze, not in the way of the Burning Woman, whose blue flames still shivered the air, but rather as a fire rose infused with a deep and inextinguishable light. Her glorious covering reminded him of the scarf's shimmering substance. It seemed to invite him to reach out and touch it, to stroke it, take it, and hold it clenched between his adoring fingers.

Before he could rush forward, however, many of the people between him and the tigress began forming themselves into a queue that led up to the planter. He became aware of many little conversations around him. He learned that the tigress had appeared in this part of the Dreaming City perhaps a dozen times before. At the tigress's first instantiation, people had fled in a panic. They demanded that the computer's master program should cast the tigress back into the pit of the defiance of their laws from which she had emerged, or worse, they called for her to be killed.

And then a miracle had occurred. A little girl had burst from the crowd, running not away from the tigress but *toward* her. Before her frightened father could stop her, she bounded up the planter's steps and threw her arms around the tigress. She kissed the great beast's dappled head, and the tigress returned her affection by licking her face. All looking on later claimed that they felt pass through them a wave of gratitude at the immense beauty and greatness of life. Women and men remarked that the tigress had been sent to them to remind of their own splendour.

And that, Rane thought, gazing at the tigress who opened her jaws to lap up a bit of the fountain's water, must have been why the master program running the Aracellians' surreality computers had not intervened to erase Maria's instantiation as an animal. For the animal was also an angel who continued to exalt and enchant the Aracellians – anyone gathered in front of the fountain could see that. Rane saw it himself; Maria's violation of the law, he thought, was like a flaw in a teacup which pointed toward a greater perfection that could not only bear the flaw but make use of it toward creating a higher beauty.

'Momma – may I pet the tiger today?'

Behind Rane, a girl about five years old put this question to her mother. That motivated him to join the queue, for he realized that if he was to greet the tigress as he hoped, he could not simply hurry up to the planter elbowing people out of his way. If he was to take the tigress in his arms and put his lips to hers, he would have to wait.

How long he waited, he couldn't say. In the Dreaming City, time seemed even harder to measure than in a lightship suspended beneath space. The bluebirds perched on the limbs of the shih trees twittered out their songs as the sun hung like a yellow jewel in the sky, and Rane took a step forward and another – and the queue in front of him shortened person by person. And then, finally, it was his turn to greet the tigress.

He stood before the brick shelf upon which she lay, belly down, head held up high. She gazed at him. He had never seen such great golden intensely aware eyes – except of course for Maria's, although her eyes had been nearly as dark as the night-time sea. As it had been with Maria, the eyes drew him in. He had a sense of falling, as into the corona of a star. Strangely, however, the heat of this terrifying event did not completely consume him, for time slowed down like a strand of gold drawn out to an almost infinite length, and the moment seemed to last forever. And in that moment, he saw something that he had somehow always missed, or rather, had looked away from, for how can one truly look at a star? He saw it in the tigress's wild, beautiful eyes: her limitless, tender, terrible ferocity to achieve her purpose, whatever that might be.

He panicked then. He turned to run away from this fearful being. However, it was too late. With a gathering of muscles and a sudden release of tension, the tigress exploded from her crouch and sprang upon him. Her jaws closed upon his shoulder from behind, and he felt the three-inch canines tear into the skin, muscles, and ligaments. He *heard* the crunching of his flesh, even as the tigress's claws hooked into his sides with a shock of fire. The tigress began dragging him back upon the planter. Although he struggled like a madman – lunging right and pulling left, trying to pivot so that he could strike his fists against the tigress's face or gouge out her eyes – his fury accomplished nothing, for the tigress met his fury with her own. She bit him, again and again, piercing, slashing, and tearing him.

And all the while, above all the gore and the agony, he smelled the fermy sweetness of her fur and the acrid stink of his own sweat. The tigress's hot breath burst from her nostrils in deafening pants next to his ear. Her saliva (or perhaps it was his blood) stained his shirt and plastered it to his chest. He himself gasped for breath in between his spitting out of curses and trying again and again to tear himself free. Inevitably, though, the tigress dragged him back toward the planter, for against her incredible power he could do nothing.

Finally, he collapsed against the bricks, with the tigress's weight heavy upon him. He had once learned that the ancient spear and shield battles of Old Earth had lasted only minutes due to the exhaustion that quickly overcame the limbs and bodies of men fighting all-out. He understood this now. His belly pulled in lungfuls of hurtful air, and his heart beat so hard that it seemed it would burst – and these spasmings of his autonomic muscles seemed the only way his body might ever move again. Even so, after a few moments of near-motionlessness, he burst once more into a violent struggle. And again he emptied himself of all strength and resistance, and again he lay helpless beneath the tigress. This cycle repeated many times. The tigress, though, continued to hold fast as growls of anticipation rumbled deep in her throat.

Embraced by her claws, he took inventory of the damage she had wreaked. He could no longer have stood in order to run away because the tigress seemed to have hamstrung the tendons of his left leg, rendering it nearly useless. His left arm was broken, and a jag of bone stuck out from the torn skin above the wrist. His right arm did not work at all: most likely one of her fangs had ripped through the nerve complex of the brachial plexus beneath his collarbone. His back burned. He felt a lump beneath him, as if he were lying back upon a bed whose blankets had been bunched into a knot of fabric. He realized that the lump, however, was mostly likely a flap of bloody skin that had been torn loose and was pinioned between his ravaged body and the planter's red bricks.

It came to him, beneath his rage and terror, that the tigress had never before done anything like this. He heard the people on the boulevard crying out exactly this sentiment; he heard them screaming and saw them stampeding across the red bricks in their frenzy to get away from the now-bloody fountain and the terrible beast that had defiled it. How, he wondered – as the Aracellians must have wondered – had the simulation programs allowed such an event to occur within the Dreaming? *Why* did they allow it to continue? Had the censors not been alerted to the crime being committed in bright daylight on one of Aracelli's greatest streets? Or was it that they did not care?

More time passed, five hours or ten – or perhaps it was only five minutes. Now the boulevard had emptied of almost everyone, excepting the boldest or the most bloody-minded who remained to witness a primeval spectacle.

'No, no!' Rane shouted to the tigress. 'Go away!'

But she did not go away; he knew that she never would. She began eating him then, eating him while he remained stubbornly and hopefully alive. So it went with animals. Once, in the forests east of Neverness, he had watched a snow tiger devour a young shagshay bull. Like Rane, the bull had been felled by wounds and exhaustion but from time to time would loose a bellow of pain as the tiger pulled at parts of the bull's body and jerked free gobbets of flesh. The tiger had seemed in no hurry to complete its meal, but rather ate with a practised casualness that told of savour and pleasure. Rane doubted that predators such as tigers and thallows had a killer instinct; they had an *eating* instinct, and they simply did not care if their prey screamed and twitched and bled. Or perhaps these great beasts relished feasting on agony as much as they did flesh.

'Go away! Go away! Go away!'

The tigress began with his manhood, ripping away the last tatters of his clothing to get at this morsel. Her teeth snipped through it as easily as he might have chewed the tenderest cut of a cultured meat. She gulped and bit again, this time tearing off his testicles. And again she swallowed, and her pink tongue flicked out to lap at the blood that flowed from the gape of his body. Her tongue felt at once soft and raspy as she licked away bits of tissue. Murmurs of contentment sounded from within her throat. Then she used her claws to rake open the skin and muscles beneath his ribs. She pushed her bloody snout deep into his belly so that she could work at his liver. She bit and tugged and ripped again, and then, with a couple of snaps and gulps, she consumed this great purplish organ.

Strangely, during this ordeal, as shock took hold of him, Rane experienced little pain. No, that wasn't quite right: he felt every rupture of muscle and shriek of nerve fibre with a jolt of excruciation, but it was as if the terrible sensations did not matter – almost as if all the outrage and agony was happening to someone else. He had the curious sensation of simultaneously suffering his devastation from within even as he moved outside himself to witness it. He seemed to have become two beings: one was a helpless animal, a still-living assemblage of bones and meat. The other stood always beside him, and would always remain – watching, waiting, knowing, remembering – even after he died.

But he didn't die, and that was the hell of it – the heaven, too. As he lay with his belly nearly hollowed out, more a carcass than a man, he gazed into the tigress's eyes. So bright they were, so full of life! He looked and looked, and suddenly he knew that he *could* look into a star; he could plunge deep into its heart, into all the fire and anguish, and he would be consumed yet somehow remade.

Even as the tigress (or Maria) now remade him. Her eyes fixed on his from only a few inches away. Something warm and good passed from her to him. Then his liver regenerated itself, and his other organs grew back, and the skin of his torn belly knitted into a seamless whole. His broken arm healed, and so did his shoulder and his leg, and strength poured like a flooding river into his body. When the tigress's grip upon him relaxed, he jumped up and stood on the planter across from her. He felt more robust than he ever had, more awake, more powerful, more alive. The tigress's golden eyes continued to draw him in. In their sparkle and dance, he could almost see a great thing, could almost apprehend Maria's purpose. He felt Maria calling to him, wanting him to nourish her, to fill her up and give her life.

Again he panicked. And again he tried to flee, and the tigress sprang upon him and dragged him up to the planter's shelf by the fountain. She devoured him as she had before, beginning with his genitals and progressing to his liver and his other organs. And again his liver grew back, and he stood to regard her, and he panicked and he fled. This cycle repeated many times as the sun hung hot and nearly motionless in the blue Aracellian sky. And at the end of each cycle, Rane returned to himself feeling greater than he had before. As the tigress feasted on his flesh again and again – and renewed him each time – his agony grew so deep and excruciating that it became a kind of rapture of power and increased life. Death *became* life, and life became death, and his cold, hard self-conception as Thomas Rane, the Remembrancer, gave way to a vaster sense of himself coupled with an ecstatic oneness.

'I could stay here forever,' he said to the tigress at the end of one of their cycles. 'Maria, Maria, it could all end, here and now.'

He knew that he *could* stay. To be sure, as the hours or days passed in the real and lesser world, Nikolandru would eventually tire of his vigil of standing guard over Rane's paralysed body in the dreaming pavilion – either that or he would become concerned. He would pull Rane free from the heaume enclosing his head and thus tear him from the grip of this surreality called the Dreaming. It wouldn't matter. For Rane could declare to Nikolandru that he had finally found Maria after all. He could bid Nikolandru farewell; he could take refuge in Aracelli and return to the great boulevard with its bloody, beautiful fountain. And he could remain with Maria forever.

'Maria, Maria, Maria . . .'

The tigress crouched by the fountain, her orange and black fur wavering in the sunlight. So mysterious she was, so dreadful, so beautiful, so bright! Why *shouldn't* he remain? Here at last, in this strange ontological space called the Dreaming, he could tell himself that he was giving himself to her completely as she had always wanted him to give, as she needed him to – he could persuade himself that it was safe. What was so wrong with being happy?

'No, no,' he murmured, 'go away!'

He could not determine if he spoke to the tigress or to himself. The effect of his words, however – the effect of his will – seized hold of him and pulled him free from the Dreaming. The sunny boulevard with its flowers, magic shows, and blissful people vanished, and he found himself hurtling through a tunnel of fire. So frightening was this plunge back into the mundane and the ugly that his hands spasmed into fists. He noticed clenched in his hand a bit of orange and white fur: he must have torn it loose, he thought, during one of his struggles with the tigress. He pressed this treasure against his heart; he promised himself that he would never forget whence it came or the ardour that burned in the tigress's eyes.

And then he fell out into the dreaming pavilion and into the dirty padded chair that supported his limp body. The stench of smoky air, garbage, and sweat replaced the sweet scents of tulips and the tigress's hot breath. He looked down at his hands. His left hand had spasmed so tightly that his fingernails had torn bloody marks into his palms. And so it was with his right hand, in which he expected to find the bits of fur that he had brought back. Instead, he saw clenched between his fingers Maria's scarf and nothing more. Its fiery fibres, however, seemed to burn into his blood a secret that he would never reveal to anyone, perhaps not even to himself.

15

During the days that followed, as Rane resumed his role as a passenger in the *Asherah*, he savoured the memories of his extraordinary experiences on Aracelli, and he tried to take meaning from them. Why had the Aracellians, he wondered, *really* abided the breaking of their laws in allowing Maria to instantiate as a tigress? Why had the censors not put an end to Rane's bloody evisceration? Surely they had a purpose; people always did. Often, though, women and men did not always know what drove them the most deeply, and so the overseers of Aracelli's simulations might have deferred to secret programs encoded into their Dreamtime computers long ago. Perhaps Maria, with her incredible sensitivity, had somehow divined the nature of these programs and had made use of them in seizing the workings of the computers to render the censors as helpless as the tigress had him.

This notion, however, called up another question: *why* would Maria have infused her sensibilities into the Dreaming as a sort of sleeper program, which might or might not ever awaken as it had with Rane? Maria had come to Aracelli long before she had emigrated to Neverness and met Rane. How could she have known that Rane would someday enter the Dreaming in search of her? Was she secretly a scryer who could behold the future as he might skip through the pages of a book? Or was it that she had conceived the tigress as a gift to the staid Aracellians should anyone *like* Rane ever come to Aracelli and incite the tigress to unfold all her terrible powers and possibilities?

Although Rane favoured the latter hypothesis, doing so

brought him face to face with its disturbing implications – and even more disturbing memories. He recalled words that Maria had spoken to him in Neverness's Light Pavilion, centuries ago now, it seemed:

'I've finally found you,' she had said to him beneath the bright sprays of stars. 'I've been looking so far, looking so long.'

He had supposed that she spoke poetically, as she often did, but what if her sweet, simple statement had expressed a literal truth? He'd always had a sense that Maria found in him at least a partial realization of an ideal man whose image she had long held inside, but her gladness at their first meeting seemed to go beyond the satisfaction that comes from serendipity fulfilling expectation. What if he, he mused, was not just *like* this man she hoped he might someday become? What if she had journeyed across the stars and come to Neverness looking for *him*?

Memory alone, he thought, as he floated naked in the passenger compartment of Nikolandru's lightship, would never suffice to pull back the layers of wants and needs that concealed Maria's most essential desire, but what else did he have? One memory above all others seemed to hold the truth of what he sought: the tigress's golden eyes. Rane still could not look away from them. In all their fire and ferocity, one simple thing blazed forth – so simple that Rane could neither name it nor grasp it, any more than he could lay hold of the sun's light. Maria's deepest purpose still eluded him, even as his own reason for living remained a mystery.

Strangely, however, he felt that unknown purpose pulsing within him, just as he felt that he now understood Maria in a way that he never had. Maria – the real Maria – called to him with each beat of his heart and from every cell of his brain and his body. Her voice vibrated each atom of his being and bathed him in a sound like the long, dark roar of the universe. It frightened him; even more, it filled him with an intense loneliness.

He might have palliated the sting of this most bitter of emotions by sharing his concerns with Nikolandru. How he longed for the comfort of conversation, the communion that came from a few relaxed moments exchanging words with a true friend! But how far he had journeyed from Kolenya Mor, Danlo, Tamara Ten Ashtoreth, Sunjay, and others who remained dear to him! How many hundreds of planets and trillions of miles! How long had he now holed up in the dark, dirty den of Nikolandru's lightship? A year? Two years? How could he measure time without a horologe to compute the temporal distortions that such an endless journey in and out of the manifold effected? And not even a master horologe could speak to Rane's subjective sense of time's passing. As he fell across the galaxy farther and farther from Aracelli, the loneliness took hold of him and grew like a black malignancy inside him – and each moment of listening to Maria's plaintive voice seemed to last forever.

Finally, on a dry, cold little planet called Lazuris, Rane decided to break the silence with which he had enveloped himself in the time since Aracelli. He stood with Nikolandru upon the rim of a great gorge carved by a winding river millions of years before. The river had long since evaporated into Lazuris's thin atmosphere or else had vanished into the desiccated soil. All that remained of the river's passing were layers of blue and red rock cut out of the earth down to a depth of two and a half miles.

'It's always good to breathe real air again,' Rane said after filling his lungs, 'even air so thin as this.'

'Thin but sweet,' Nikolandru agreed. 'Especially when compared with the miasma of Aracelli.'

'Aracelli,' Rane said, looking down into the gorge.

'What foulness human beings wreak upon their worlds when they have care only for otherworldly concerns!'

'The Aracellians,' Rane said, stamping his boot against the ground, 'do not think of the Dreaming as another world. For them, it is as real as the rock beneath our feet.'

'So it was with the heaven of the ancient Kristians, and so with the Cloud of the Architects of the Cybernetic Universal Church. So it always is with those who cannot abide the real world.'

'In a way,' Rane said, 'the Dreaming is *more* real. You cannot imagine.'

'Ah, but I can. Did you think I would remain content to stand over you shooing away the flies as you screamed and writhed in your chair like a prisoner being tortured?'

He explained that he had taken the chair next to Rane's in the dreaming pavilion and had then joined Rane in the crowds on the boulevard near the fountain.

'I was afraid that whatever was happening to you in the Aracellians' surreality,' he said, 'would kill you in the real world.'

Rane smiled at this. 'The Dreaming is not real in that way, despite the old myth of the cyberneticists. And *that* myth harks back to an even more ancient one: that if you die in your dream, you die in your life and do not wake up.'

'I was afraid that you would never wake up; I thought to tear you free of that damned chair, but I thought that doing so might damage your brain.'

'Thank you,' Rane said. 'Did it not occur to you, though, that if I *had* died, you could have gone off with your hundred thousand disks and been done with this endless quest?'

'I promised you a passage. So long as you are in my charge, you are under my protection.'

'I did not feel so very protected. All those people, leaving me to the tigress. Were you among those who fled? Or did you remain to watch what she did to me?'

'I arrived just as the beast – or something – remade you. You did not seem to need protecting.'

'Then you watched as she tore me apart . . . again and again?'

'I watched you, yes. You endured your agony well.'

'I never stopped screaming!'

'So it must have seemed to you. And yet, there were quiet moments when you looked upon your death with open eyes and did not blink.'

'Only because I knew that I could not die!'

'Yes, you knew. You reached a moment, did you not, which you knew could never be destroyed, even as you knew that *you* could not be destroyed. The eternal moment, which exists outside of time, in which all things become possible.'

As Nikolandru spoke, Rane closed his eyes and journeyed through vivid interior landscapes, looking for the memory, trying to recapture the moment.

'Six times, the beast mauled you,' Nikolandru said, 'and six times you stood back up as if you had become a god. You seemed enthralled – happy, even. How should I have thought to protect you from that?'

Rane said nothing to this as he turned away from Nikolandru and stared down at the blue and red strata of rock that formed the walls of the gorge.

'The beast,' Nikolandru said, 'was Maria, wasn't she? Somehow, she was Maria.'

'How did you know?'

'You kept saying her name. Every time she came for you, you called out, "Go away, Maria, go away!"'

'I thought it was Maria, yes.'

Rane sighed, then told Nikolandru all his thoughts and hypotheses as to what had occurred by the fountain in the Aracellian otherworld.

'In a way, then, you found her after all,' Nikolandru said. 'Why did you not deem your quest fulfilled and remain on Aracelli?'

'Because I want to hold Maria in my arms again, not a tigress!'

'Are you sure there is much of a difference?'

'I want to marry Maria and give her what she always wanted.'

'I'm sure you could have done that in the Dreaming. You could have transformed the beast into Maria, couldn't you?'

'Perhaps.'

'You could have met her, again and again, all the days of your life. You could have *made* a life with her, just as you wished.'

'Yes, I think I could have.'

'Then why didn't you?'

Rane considered this as he tried to make out the shapes in the darkness that filled the bottom of the gorge two miles below. He stamped his boot down upon the grit-covered rock beneath him. 'She would have been a string of information coded into a computer and instantiated as an imago in my mind. She would not have been real.'

'Will the Maria you hope the Entity will recreate from your memories be more real?'

'I don't know,' Rane said with all the honesty he could summon. 'When I feel her heart against mine and her breath upon my lips, then I will tell you.'

After that, they returned to the *Asherah* and continued their journey. They made the long, long passage from the Sagittarius Arm of the galaxy to the Orion Arm. The stars grew thinner, but still many millions of sparks glittered out of dark, empty reaches of space. And still Rane 'followed his nose', drawing in the aromas embedded in Maria's scarf and following his sense of which planets Maria had visited on her own stellar crossing. Or rather, he told the names of these planets to Nikolandru, who piloted their silver-diamond lightship past Sheydveg and Sahasrara and Jonah's Star Far Group. They avoided the blasted, burned-out region of the Götterdämmerung, where, it was said, the August Colonial Intelligence had once destroyed the ten billion godmen of Austricess who had tried to build a dyson sphere around their beautiful star. Nikolandru and Rane came upon numerous planets that Maria had visited, and on most of them Rane uncovered some record, testimonial, or clue as to who Maria really was.

Much of what he learned only reinforced his conceptions of her or coalesced cloudy suspicions into suppositions that he thought to be true. Many facts and rumours seemed trivial, though when it came to shining a light on the human soul, one might see that a score of *seemingly* trivial traits or habits were really windows to a much deeper and more significant self. On Nilevist, for example, it appeared that Maria had danced naked in front of a crowd of men in exchange for a large sum of money, which she had then either given to Nilevist's poor or gambled away, depending on which of two witnesses told true. On Petra, she got drunk on many glasses of potent firewine and curled herself up in a dog's bed. When she had come to Arpont, it seemed, she had smiled everywhere at all the dour Arpontians, who considered such spontaneous displays of happiness to be the affect of a child or a fool.

Some of the stories people told of Maria simply could not be believed: on Blueworld, more than one person regaled Rane with an account of how Maria had swum with dolphins for ten days far out in the Night Light Sea and had learned to speak the unspeakable cetacean language. And on Roshava, an old woman claimed that Maria had healed a blind man by laying her hands upon his dead, milky-white eyes.

Other stories Rane did not *want* to believe, such as the gossip that on Principio Luz she had consorted with one of the alien Friends of Man sent to civilize that profligate planet. And what was he to make of the wild slander that an exemplar on Zallning related? According to this obviously unreliable man (who took the account from the brother of the wife of a game master),

Maria had gambled away all her money in one of Zallning's dice dens. Destitute and hungry, she had then stolen into the Aldholm Game Preserve, whereupon she had promptly stalked an infant tamarin monkey, had torn it from its mother's breast, strangled it, and had begun devouring it – before realizing that it was still alive and dashing out its brains upon a rock. Could this possibly be, he wondered, the same woman who had once given her furs to a freezing autist on an icy street on a cold Neverness day – and had then wept because she could not do more for him?

Such ponderings exhausted Rane, as did Maria's incessant calling to him coupled with the loneliness that the calling engendered. So when the *Asherah* fell out above a pretty blue and white planet named Nepenthe, Rane considered trying to relax on one of Nepenthe's many tropical islands and taking a holiday from his interminable quest.

This would have been easy to do. Nepenthe's peoples lived on the thirteen thousand islands spread out in a vast archipelago for three thousand miles along Nepenthe's equator and two thousand miles either to the north or the south. The archipelago's shape reminded Rane of the ancient Sanskrit letter र, ra, with perhaps three quarters of the islands pushing down into the southern hemisphere. Some islands were tiny, no more than fern-covered sandy dots upon a single worldwide ocean. Other islands rose up out of the blue waters in expanses of mountainous earth a few hundred miles in breadth, and there most of the population made their homes.

Upon researching this unusual world, Rane had thought at first that each island formed its own polity, but that proved not to be true. In fact, Nepenthe had no polities, as most people of the Civilized Worlds usually conceived that term; neither did it have rulers, meritarchs, theocrats, councils, direct democracies, or any of the usual organizations of political power that could be called a government. As far as Rane could determine from his study of the *Asherah*'s information pools, the Nepenthians had succeeded in what many others had dreamed of but never achieved, which was to live in a wild but peaceful planetary anarchy.

Nepenthe's informality made it easy for the *Asherah* to put down on almost any beach of any island; the same lax customs, however, made it difficult for Rane and Nikolandru to determine which of the islands might prove fruitful in Rane's quest. The Nepenthians kept no records as to who visited their planet, nor did they much care who journeyed to which island once a visitor arrived. Rane had to resort to the painstaking process of flying from one island to another and asking people if they had known or heard of Maria. With more than thirteen thousand islands on which to make inquiries, however, chance alone would likely not avail Rane – not unless he wished to remain on Nepenthe for a hundred more lifetimes. As it turned out, the *Asherah* skipped like a silver stone from island to island for twenty-two of Nepenthe's long days before Rane gained his first word concerning Maria.

On an island called Jardajeen in the southern tropics, Rane found a man who thought he might have recalled hearing a rumour of an unusual black-eyed woman who had created something of a disturbance on one of the Poetry Islands. He could not say which island, but he guessed that it might have been one of the more westerly ones, in the northern hemisphere near the point of the ⲅ, which comprised the two hundred or so Tragedy Islands. It frustrated Rane that he could not easily locate these places on a map, for such names were informal and referenced only the artistic 'theme' that gave meaning to the lives of the people who dwelled on any particular island. The Nepenthians had various names for these themes: not only Poetry and Tragedy, but Aria, Canticle, Origami, Shanfrieze, Raku, Fresco, Glypto, and many, many others.

'They live for art,' Rane had said to Nikolandru when Rane had first begun to make sense of Nepenthe's strange society. 'They try to live their lives *as* art.'

At first, Rane had thought that the Nepenthians were like so many millions of seeds scattered across their world at random. Their society, however, as anarchic as it seemed, did not lack organization. On each island (at least the smaller ones), a single grouping of people held sway. These thousands of groups each had something about them that recalled the functions of an art movement, a set, a league, a coterie, or a society. The Nepenthians called them royads, each of which to Rane's untutored eye seemed more like a cross between a family and an orgy club.

On one of the Poetry islands, the *Asherah* put down on the

soft white sands of a broad beach. Turquoise waters rippled off into the western horizon, while green-shagged hills rose up like a series of steps toward the east. The south part of the island gave out onto a massif of rock called the Elephant's Head, whose sheer cliffs overlooked the sea. The moist, warm air smelled of tangerines and tamarind, of zinnia, moonflower, and Ede's tears, along with other scents that Rane had discerned in Maria's scarf. Thousands of squawking parrots befeathered in reds, yellows, and blues made their homes in the forest that edged the beach. There, in the meadows between the lemon and the sandalwood trees, the ninety men and women of the royad who had feted Maria during her stay on Nepenthe made their homes as well.

When the Nepenthians learned the nature of Rane's and Nikolandru's visit, they called out the entire royad for a feast on the beach. At dusk, with the last of the sun melting like a great orange candy along the rim of the world, Rane and Nikolandru joined their hosts on blankets arranged around five bonfires made of driftwood gathered from the strand beneath the beach dunes. They ate roasted crab and conch, half a dozen kinds of fish, seaweed soup, greens spiced with pepper and cubeb, pecan pastries, yam stew, plumcots, and pomegranates, and much else. Rane could not remember when he had enjoyed a more delicious meal. He enjoyed the company of the Nepenthians, too, though much about their ways seemed to him disquieting and strange.

'We rejoice in celebrating with two travellers who knew our beautiful Maria,' a slender man named Julior said to Rane. His golden eyes twinkled and made a stark contrast with the mahogany skin that covered the fine bones of his sensitive, delicate face. 'Maria was poetry transformed into corporeality, the Song of the Earth written into flesh. She left the best of herself everywhere on our island. Do we not all still hear her beautiful singing?'

Rane sat between Nikolandru and Julior, who cocked his head as if listening for something intangible but profound. Rane listened as well (or pretended to), but the sounds that came to him were the rhythmic pounding of the ocean's waves, the chattering of the night birds, the clicking of insects, and the buzzing of the Nepenthians' voices as the ninety women and men of the royad sat around the crackling wood fires and cast long, curious looks at their guests.

'We rejoice with Maria's beautiful, beautiful friends,' Julior said. 'You are welcomed, welcomed, welcomed!'

He leaned over to kiss Rane's cheek for the third time, then he turned his attentions to Nikolandru, kissing his face and hands, and brushing his fingers through Nikolandru's curly hair. Nikolandru, following the ways of the Nepenthians, sat cross-legged and naked on his blanket, and he seemed as comfortable in his bare skin as their hosts seemed in theirs. Most of the islanders displayed garish flesh frescoes: living tattoos that swam beneath their skin and took on the shapes of snakes, sharks, orcas, and other sea animals, or formed up as birds painted in crimsons, indigos, magentas, and similarly bright hues. Julior looked at Rane as if waiting for him to disrobe as had Nikolandru. Rane, however, continued to wear his old kamelaika. The sultry air, coupled with the fire's heat, caused him to itch and sweat. Of course, he felt out of place wearing clothing at all; he wished to divest himself of his kamelaika but would not allow the Nepenthians' expectations and seeming guilelessness to impel him to do so – in the same way he had never allowed himself to cast aside his foibles in order to dwell more harmoniously with Maria. Why, he wondered, had he never quite been able to shed his demur, doubt, and pride, though such barriers to happiness had bound him as surely as did his scratchy wool garments?

'Thank you for your hospitality,' Rane said, forcing himself not to wipe at his cheek. Julior's broad lips, glistening with fish fat, had left a greasy impression upon it. 'I've never eaten so well.'

Julior smiled at this compliment. 'And you haven't yet eaten one of our sugarfish. We save the best for last.'

So saying, he clapped his hands. From out of the darkness near the line of trees above the beach, a shadowy form flapped through the air straight toward them. When it drew near the fire, Rane saw that it was a large bird, with red feathers, a hooked beak, and yellow talons as pointed as needles. Except for its colouring, it had the appearance of an osprey. Rane started at the approach of this dangerous-looking raptor, but Julior held out his arm and allowed the bird's talons to close harmlessly around it. The bird's jewel-like eyes fixed on Julior's. Only then, at such a close distance, did Rane realize that the bird's feathers seemed made of some kind of spun metal, as its beak had been cast of a material resembling black jade. The 'bird', Rane realized, was not a bird at all, but only a cleverly contrived robot.

'Bring us a sugarfish,' Julior said to the robot. Then flung up his arm. 'Hunt!'

A whoosh of air fell upon Rane's face as the robot beat its wings and burst into flight. It flew across the beach, then out over the frothy white crests of the breaking waves. Two of Nepenthe's moons were out that night, and they illumined the sky with a purplish glow even as they cast great lanes of light upon the ocean's wavering surface. Rane watched the robot swoop down toward the dark band of sea between these lanes and disappear into the rolling waters.

It remained submerged for quite a while, long enough for the voluptuous, blonde-haired woman sitting next to Nikolandru – her name was Thena – to feed him at least fifty pomegranate seeds through the time-consuming process of pressing each seed one by one between Nikolandru's lips. Finally, the robot breached the ocean's surface. It clutched in its talons a large, silvery, writhing fish. The mechanical osprey flew back across the beach, and when it reached the edge of the bonfire where Rane and Julior sat, it stopped in mid-flight and hovered in the air in a way that no real osprey ever could.

With a smile, Julior held out his arm again. This time, however, he gripped a wood skewer. Then the robot bird went to work: its underside split open from crop to vent, and from the gape of its metallic body, various knives emerged and flashed in the moonlight. The knives whirred and whittled and cut, and in almost no time at all, the robot reduced the fish to two fat fillets of meat, the first of which it impaled on Julior's skewer, and the second on a similar skewer that Thena gave to Julior. Julior then set to crisping the fish over the fire's red-hot coals. Its flesh, when Julior had finished his cooking and pressed flaky, white morsels into Rane's mouth, proved to be as sweet and succulent as Julior had promised.

'Maria favoured sugarfish over all others,' he told Rane. 'Though she would not let me cook it as I have for you. She preferred instead to eat it raw and shaved into slices so thin that the moonlight shone through them. What a strange, strange, beautiful woman!'

'You must remember her very well,' Rane said.

'As well as anything or anyone should be remembered.'

Rane's brows knitted in a frown. 'Shouldn't all things be remembered as well as they can be?'

'What a strange thing to say!' Julior said, looking at Rane. 'I think you are strange in many of the ways that Maria was strange.'

Rane savoured the taste of the sugarfish that clung to his mouth. 'Yes, she also had a passion for remembrance, though she kept too busy composing poems to formally practise the art.'

At the questioning look that brightened Julior's golden eyes, Rane recounted something of his life and his calling to enter the Order as a remembrancer.

'Oh, oh, the Order of Mystic . . . ah, the Order on Inverness, ah, oh, . . .'

Although Julior shook his head to indicate that he had forgotten most of what he had obviously once learned about the Order, he did not seem at all dismayed at his failure. Rather, he loosed a tiralee of sharp, piercing whistles and smiled. A few moments later, a blue and red parrot flew out of the forest and alighted on Julior's shoulder. And Julior said to the bird, 'Tell me of the Order of Mystic . . .'

'. . . Mathematicians and Other Keepers of the Ineffable Flame. Founded by Sarojin Noy (also known as Rowan Madeus) during the Fifth Mentality of Humankind and re-established in the city of Neverness on the planet of Icefall in the eightieth year of the Sixth Mentality (or 24,790 AD in the old Gregorian calendar), the Order pledged itself to expanding all spheres of knowledge toward the end of illuminating, touching, and expanding the One Radiant Sphere, whose boundaries are nowhere and whose centre is everywhere. The Order's motto translates as: to begin; to journey; to learn; to illuminate. The Order's first Lord Pilot, Rollo Gallivare, led a fleet of one hundred lightships to—'

'Less depth,' Julior said with a snap of his fingers. He turned up his head toward the bird perched on his shoulder. 'Summarize the Order's history and then tell me of the remembrancers.'

'The history of the Order,' the parrot said, 'intertwines and sometimes fuses with the histories of the Order of Cetics, the Order of the Warrior-Poets, and the Order of Remembrancers . . .'

The bird then delivered a squawking account of the Order's early history, from its informal beginnings on Arcite in 9061 AD to its absorption of the Order of Cetics eight hundred years later and the refusal of the Cetics' founder, Nils Ordando, to accept the rule of the Order's Timekeeper. Ordando had led a group of schismatic cetics to Qallar, where he established the Order of Warrior-Poets to breed a new race of human beings who would live upon the razor's edge that separated life from death – and therefore would come to understand existentially all artificial antinomies, especially the seeming illusion that split matter and consciousness into two opposing forces. The quest to understand – and more, to control – the material universe through the force of consciousness had absorbed the passions of both the Order and the warrior-poets, though the pilots and professionals of the Order had tended more toward under-standing while the warrior-poets had sought mastery of every aspect of their bodies and minds. They sought to reform them-selves as perfect shining swords that would pierce straight through all life's sloppiness and suffering and touch upon the eternal state of pure being that they called the Moment of the Possible.

'In their desire to master time,' the parrot called out into the tepid air along the beach, 'the warrior-poets employed many of the techniques developed by the Remembrancers millennia before. The Remembrancers . . .'

Through the sounds of the ocean's roaring and the monkeys' howling in the forest above the beach, Rane concen-trated on the vibrations of the mechanical speech organs welded into the parrot's throat. He listened as the bird told of how the Remembrancers had formed on Old Earth as a cult that sought through rites of memory to resurrect the billions incinerated during the Holocaust Centuries. The Rememb-rancers, too, desired to annihilate time. Unlike the warrior-poets, however, who sought to dwell always in perfect awareness of the eternal Now-Moment, and unlike the men and women of the Order who studied the way that the mind produced such glories as music and the mathematics of piloting through the manifold, the Remembrancers looked to the far, far past all the way to time's beginning in order to apprehend the One Memory and how consciousness folded upon itself to remember all things – and thus to *unfold* the great purpose infused in matter's fiery heart. Each of these three very different groupings of seekers, the bird said, though at times separate and opposed, shared the common cause of using consciousness to sculpt the human soul.

'Throughout the millennia of the Sixth Mentality,' the parrot informed Julior, 'the Remembrancers prided themselves that they held the soul of humanity in their keeping.'

The parrot's words caused Rane to beam in approval of the essential majesty of his calling. And then the bird added, 'The same pride pervaded the entire Order on Neverness, as well as the Order of Warrior-Poets. The seeking of power over the self degenerated into the exercising of power over others. While never descending so far as the warrior-poets in coming to relish murder and death, the Order froze into a kind of empire of the mind that built fortresses of theories and traditions around its professionals and kept them walled off from life. The Order forbade any venture of technology that might threaten the Order's control. The Order's eschatologists, committed to exploring the ends of evolution as an idea, grew fearful of evolving in themselves. The Order's pilots kept secret their art, which if shared might have united the peoples of the galaxy toward the cause of attaining the Order's exalted but insincere ideals. Hypocrisy engendered inauthenticity, which in turn led to disillusionment, alienation, bitterness, and solipsism. Out of this decadence that weakened the Order came a conflict that . . .'

With the ocean's waves pounding out a rhythm that measured the passing hours of the night, Rane listened to the robot bird deliver an assessment of the Order that might as well have been a critique of Rane's own life. He did not think that the bird told true – not exactly. If one held a ruby crystal to the eye, he mused, one would perceive the world as fragmented into many facets, each coloured red. While the Order had indeed fallen into decay and eventual war, even as the bird now related, there dwelled at the heart of the Order a living flame wrought of a pure splendour that the bird (and apparently the Nepenthians) could not see. The hue of the lens that the bird held up to history overcoloured this glorious crimson flame, which Rane sometimes felt smouldering in his own heart – and which had drawn Maria to Neverness like a bright butterfly flitting across the dark emptiness of space.

When the parrot had finished its discourse, Julior sat regarding Rane with tones of condescension and pity tarnishing his golden eyes. What did he see as he studied Rane? Through lenses of what colour did he view him? Rane had always felt that others misperceived him, even as Rane had trouble looking upon the core of his innermost self. Only Maria, he thought, had ever seen him clearly. It seemed to him that she saw *all* things clearly, although his sense of her perspicuity was obviously distorted by his reverence of her. Could it possibly be, as he wanted it to be, that unlike others Maria had been born with a natural (or perhaps preternatural) purity of vision?

'My friend here,' Julior said, flicking his eyes toward the parrot, 'spoke of the Elder Eddas. That is an ancient poem of Old Earth, yes?'

'Actually, a series of poems,' Rane said. 'Among other matters, they concern the nature and the struggles of the old Norse gods.'

'But what has that to do with your Order?'

'Some years ago, before the War,' Rane said, 'Leopold Soli piloted his lightship close to the galactic core. From out of the singularity there, he received a communication declaring that the hope for humankind lay in Man's past and future. If we searched for the universe's fundamental mystery, according to this communication, we would find the secret of life.'

'And what is a singularity?' Julior asked Rane, depending on him to augment his knowledge as he had depended on the parrot.

'It is a point in spacetime in which the gravitational forces of collapsed stars grow so great that they crush matter to an infinite density and a volume of zero.'

As a comely young man named Naveek got up to heap some more wood on the fire, Rane explained something of the physics of singularities and black holes. And Julior said, 'But if light itself cannot escape the grip of a singularity, how could any signal have done so?'

'Many of our Order asked that very question,' Rane said. 'It was thought that an ancient race of gods – we called them the

Ieldra – had somehow fused their consciousness with the singularity and had used it to generate the signal in a way that we still do not understand. In consideration of the signal's source, our Order's eschatologists named the secret for which our pilots quested "the Elder Eddas".'

'Ah, oh, hmmm,' Julior said, 'I think I understand.'

Some believed, Rane remembered, that the Ieldra could also move from one world to another merely by wishing it so as he might move from one room of a house in order to retrieve an adjal or set down a flute that he had been playing. He didn't, however, want to burden Julior with such myths and speculations.

'It was thought that the Ieldra, who had supposedly seeded the galaxy with their DNA, had somehow carked the Eddas into the oldest human genes. Encoded the secret into the nucleotides.'

'Ahhhh . . . and what is DNA?'

While Rane kept his face an immobile mask in order to hide his scorn, the parrot answered Julior in Rane's stead.

'And did your Order's eschatologists,' Julior asked, 'ever *decode* the information that you call the secret of life?'

'It was Mallory Ringess who first understood the Eddas, at least in part.' Rane gazed off at the moonlit sea. 'The Ieldra had indeed carked the seemingly superfluous part of the human genome – the so-called junk genes – with information. Mallory employed the remembrancing attitude called molecular memory in order to activate these genes and call up the message of the Ieldra.'

Along with Thena, Naveek, and other Nepenthians sitting near the fire, Julior waited for Rane to say more. Finally, he asked, 'And what was the nature of this message?'

'The Eddas can be thought of as instructions for becoming gods.'

'For evolving, as humans should evolve, yes?' Julior smiled at Rane. 'I *like* these Ieldra, whoever they are.'

'The Eddas, though,' Rane said, 'are also something more. Something deeper. Mallory's son, Danlo wi Soli Ringess, was the first to apprehend the true Elder Eddas.'

At the look of polite interest that warmed Julior's face, Rane went on relate words that Danlo had once related to him. The Eddas, he said, were really universal memories, part of the

One Memory that was just the memory of the universe itself: the way the universe evolved in consciousness of itself and caused itself to be.

'"We are just this consciousness,"' Rane quoted, '"nothing more, nothing less. We are the light inside light that fuses into the atoms of our bodies. We are the fire that whirls across the stellar deeps and dances into being all things."'

'Oh, those are beautiful, beautiful words!' Julior said. 'Then Danlo wi Soli Ringess is not only a pilot but a poet!'

'He never thought of himself as such,' Rane said.

'But what is he if not a poet of the possible?'

A human being and nothing more, Rane thought. *Perhaps the first true human being.*

'Your Order, I think,' Julior said, 'would do well to look toward future possibilities rather than to try to recall lost memories of the purpose of the past.'

Rane smiled at this because it seemed to him that Julior's observation could serve as a censure of his own life. Then he said, 'Are not the two really one and the same?'

'Memory is a chain that binds us with iron links to our bloody, barbaric past.'

'There are those who say that we should remember this past lest we repeat it.'

'Memory binds our race, but even more it binds us as individuals. It keeps us locked in engrossment with the urges, prejudices, and conceits of our smaller selves.'

Julior paused to smile and to ascertain if Rane might be open to further instruction in what Julior obviously considered as basic wisdom. Although Rane felt as closed as he always had been to any sort of sentiment that hinted of dogma or consensual truth, he kept his face impassive. He looked off toward his left, where still another of a species of mechanical bird hovered in the air. This creature defended the people on the beach from mosquitoes. Every minute or so, the bird's eyes would flare into a bright crimson as beams of laser light flashed out and crisped the hapless insects that whined through the dark.

'We must forget our smaller selves,' Julior said, 'that our greater selves can be born. Is it a crime upon the coconut that it destroys itself in becoming a palm tree?'

'No, it is not,' Rane replied, looking upon the line of trees above the beach. 'But the tree remembers the nut. All things remember all things.'

Julior smiled at Rane with a pained forbearance, as a father might regard a wilfully obtuse child. Then he tried to be gracious: 'Of course, your Order has its own way of looking at these matters, and that must be respected. But we of the Poetry Islands have found great freedom in turning away from the destructive memories created by the actions of the dark, destructive parts of ourselves. It is as salutary to forget these monsters of the past as it is to expunge selfishness, aggression, cruelty, and all the other atavisms that keep human beings so stupidly and painfully human.'

The bird with the laser eyes burned to a blackened husk a mosquito hovering only inches from Rane's face. The dead insect plummeted earthward like a tiny meteor, and disappeared into the darkness of the sand beneath him. Little lights streaked out again as Rane listened to Julior speak of the engineering of Nepenthian children and the ideal of expunging from them lust, gluttony, greed, sloth, wrath, envy, and pride – what the ancients had identified as the Seven Deadly Sins. Although Julior, who knew nothing of DNA, lacked the expertise to describe the techniques used by the island's robots to edit the Nepenthian genome, he stressed the role of forgetting in this ongoing and glorious program for improving oneself:

'Is it not, in the end,' Julior asked, 'a matter of freeing ourselves from the primeval impulses with which we are born?'

He nodded his head toward Thena, who smiled back at him in agreement of the most basic things. Then Julior quoted the wisdom of an ancient, honoured Nepenthian poet whose name, if not words, had been forgotten:

'You are what your deep, driving desire is:
As your desire is, so is your will;
As your will is, so is your deed;
As your deed is, so is your destiny.'

While Julior paused to take a drink of a gourd full of a potent brandy distilled from the essences of passionfruit, armital leaves, and one of the *Psilocybe* family of fungi that Julior praised as a 'magic mushroom', Rane again affected a stony demeanour.

For he knew well enough that the aphorism Julior extolled had not issued from the lips of any long-dead Nepenthian poet. Rather, it came from a source much more ancient, more than thirty thousand years old: the Brihadaranyaka Upanishad, whose author truly had been forgotten.

Because Julior obviously thought that his quote needed elucidation, he said to Rane, 'Our actions spring from those matters upon which we focus our attention then will to be. And our will at its bottom takes form out of the desire to be and thus to dominate part or all of the universe, which afflicts all living things. And what is the result of this deepest of all impulses? Discord. Hatred. Murder. War. Agony. Death.'

Julior took another drink of his brandy, then went on: 'Memory chains us to the dark desire that would destroy us. We must forget this bane that has so nearly ruined our kind. When we do, we forget our will to obtain power over others that has led so many billions of people to a million years of grievous acts. Then we forget that we seem to be doomed to suffering and death but instead know that we are fated to enjoy a wondrous destiny.'

And with that, he pressed the gourd into Rane's hand. 'Drink, friend, and be at peace. Drink, delight, forget – forget those things that torment you.'

Nepenthe, Rane suddenly recalled, was an ancient Greek word meaning 'that which chases away sorrow'.

Rane looked down at the gourd full of a liquid whose ochre hues seemed so different from the clarity of kalla. Then he handed the gourd back to Julior and said, 'I cannot give up my painful memories – they're all I have.'

Julior, who was neither a callous man nor an unkind one, smiled at Rane in a mutual understanding of just how deeply and wilfully Rane lied to himself.

'Yes, so many memories you have,' Julior said. He touched his fingertips to Rane's brow and smoothed out the wrinkles there as if he could massage away all Rane's sufferings. 'All right, my strange, beautiful man. If you would not expunge the old memories, then why not create new ones?'

He looked down the line of fires toward the dark part of the beach nearer the ocean.

Although he made no gesture nor change of expression,

something about his desire seemed to communicate to the others of his royad as the perfume of violets might excite honeybees. Some of the other Nepenthians turned toward the ocean, too. Rane watched a woman rise and give her gourd of brandy to the man next to her. The moonlight bathed her dark skin as she stood on the beach's sugary sands smoothing back her hair. The curves of her form against the glowing sky reminded Rane of something.

> Like a ripe passionfruit
> Held to a hungry man's lips,
> Her sweetness revived . . .

Rane listened as Julior intoned words to a poem that he composed in the moment, either as augur of an important event soon to occur or as a commentary upon it. Rane tried to pay him no attention. As well, he tried to ignore the other Nepenthians who disported themselves around the bonfires, though this proved more difficult to do. Firelight seared burning images into Rane's eyes even as it inflamed the naked flesh of men and women kissing and caressing. Next to him, Thena knelt on all fours as she ran her reddened lips up and down Nikolandru's engorged manhood – even as a small, blonde-haired woman parted Thena's plump thighs and licked her yoni from behind. Closer to the ocean, the handsome and young Naveek drew a lithe woman named Sariah away from their fire, and he pushed her back upon the sand and fell atop her in a moaning frenzy as if it had been years (and not hours) since he had copulated. As the brandy took hold of the people around Rane, a blast of pure eros fairly scorched his lungs and drove deep into his core; it seemed that he had been forced to swallow red-hot magma arising from the vent of a volcano.

She is for you, she is for you . . .

Julior continued composing his poem while the woman of whom he spoke walked up the beach toward Julior's and Rane's fire. Now Rane's gaze moved from the familiar voluptuousness of the woman's body to the beauty of her face. He studied the strong nose that led down from her thick eyebrows to her wide and sensual mouth; her lips were like scarlet ribbons that he could almost feel impressing their silk upon his lips. Her eyes, bright and black, found his eyes with an open invitation to ecstasy that caused him to gasp for breath and his heart to leap into flight.

She is for you, and you are for her, and . . .

'Who are you?' Rane cried out into the night.

The woman moved right up to Julior and Rane. Julior took her hand and pressed it into Rane's hand. And he said, 'Is she not glorious?'

Rane sat frozen to the beach sands as he continued gazing up at this woman who seemed nearly identical in form to the Maria he had known. A wild thought flashed through his mind: that upon Maria's visit to the island, the Nepenthians had slelled and cloned one of Maria's cells, and had used it to quicken a zygote that had somehow in only a few years grown into the gorgeous woman who smiled down at Rane and squeezed his hand. The Nepenthians, after all, lived far from the laws of the Civilized Worlds and might be wont to commit such abominations.

'Peace!' Julior exclaimed as he tried to touch a little solace to Rane's face. 'Can you not, friend, allow yourself a moment of peace?'

But Rane knocked his hand away and said, 'Are you slel neckers then, that you would steal a woman's DNA to fashion a plaything for your amusement?'

His accusation seemed to wound Julior. He called over his parrot who spoke to him for a while. Then Julior said to Rane, 'But my dear friend, we've done no such thing!'

He went on to tell of the origin of the woman whose hand Rane could not seem to let go, despite his outrage and his horror. Julior explained that after Maria had said goodbye to the royad and had left the Poetry Islands, this woman had decided to change her form to resemble that of Maria. And so she had gone into the forest, and she had swum out into the Pool of Transfiguration, which most Nepenthians visited many times during their nearly immortal lives. There the woman had floated in warm, dreamy waters as robots a quadrillionth the size of Julior's parrot had swarmed around and in and through the tissues of the woman's body. Over forty days, the woman had undergone a complete transformation of her physical self, and when the robots had finished whittling and steening and sculpting, out had stepped the woman who now looked nearly identical to Maria.

'It must seem to you,' Julior told Rane, even as he smiled at the woman, 'a remarkable coincidence that she chose to look like Maria. But your Maria was one of the classical forms, and so how should anyone be surprised when one of our women chose to remake herself in her image?'

'But her image . . . is so nearly the same!'

'How not? We of the Poetry Islands can remember well enough, if there is need.'

'But why not just remember yourselves as you were born and as you are and be content with that?'

'Because we are meant to be more. It is a noble thing to compose words into verse that exalts the soul; but it is a beauty beyond beauty to shape the self into a poem through which the universe itself sings.'

Rane stood up so that he could more easily make out the woman's face. He listened to the sound of her breath streaming past her brandy-stained lips.

'But what is your name?' he asked her.

And in a musical voice set at a higher pitch than that of the voice he most remembered, she said to him, 'I am Maria.'

'No – what was your name before? The name with which you were born?'

'Does that matter?'

'I'd like to know.'

'Well, I don't really remember.'

'Truly?'

'Do you remember the first moment your mother spoke your name?'

Rane fell silent as he gazed past her at the sparkling ocean.

'I've had many names,' she told him. 'I am Maria now – isn't that enough?'

Her fingers tightened around his fingers. Her breathing quickened, and her lips parted in a smile of blood-surging lust that found reinforcement in the thick, musky scent emanating from the dark patch of hair below her belly. A highly evolved human being she might have been, a pure poem of a woman singing out with all the rhythm and beauty of the moonlit sea – but just then she seemed even more an animal in heat. Although her fierce concentration on Rane made him feel as if he were a god, he thought that she would just as easily have mated with a baboon.

She is for you, and you are for her,
And the two of you are
That the world might cry out
Your names and sing with glory.

The beating of the waves counted out the passing moments of Rane's life. He tried to look deep within himself to behold that primeval desire with which he had been born. Then he looked at the woman who faced him across two feet of space, and he drank from the dark, dazzling liquid of a different kind of desire that bubbled up from the black centres of her eyes.

16

As Naveek had done with Sariah, Rane led this new Maria off a few paces and pulled her down to the sand. He suddenly *did* want to forget his woes and his old, anguished self; even more, he wanted to cast off all the constraints that people (and he above all) had placed on him all his life. Although he had taken not a sip of brandy, the potent liquor of an insane and insatiable urging poured down through his belly and into his sexual organs. He couldn't remember having ever grown so hard and huge so quickly. The new Maria took hold of him with a greed for the impossibly carnal that hurt him almost as much as it inflamed him. She pulled him deep inside her. How wet she was, how fervidly hot, like an ocean of magma that sucked him down and burned him – burned him ecstatically and completely away! Their screams of pleasure joined with those of the others on the beach as he disappeared into the long, dark roaring of an inward sea. It seemed that they flowed into each other forever.

She is for you, she is for you, she is for you . . .

During the blissful days and nights that followed their first joining, Rane coupled with this lascivious woman many, many times. They lay together beneath the palm trees covered in warm breezes blowing off the ocean and in the cool canopy of the starry night-time sky. When the fire in his belly inevitably cooled, he consented at last to drinking the Nepenthians' powerful brandy – and then he coupled some more. Time seemed to vanish like honey dissolved into a cup of warm wine.

As much of himself as he forgot, however, he never quite

fooled himself that the woman he took into his arms was the
real Maria. Her voice vibrated at a slightly higher pitch than
had Maria's, even as her heart seemed to pulse to a different
purpose. She spoke of different things and in a different way,
often complaining of a sunny day that turned cloudy or criticizing
another member of her royad whose poetry she found lacking.
In her sex with Rane, she usually insisted that he mount her
from behind and thrust into her with a strenuousness that
approached the savage; Maria, he recalled, had thrilled in clasping
him close face to face as she held his gaze into the infinite deeps
of her eyes. The Nepenthian woman smelled different, too. This
disparity, he thought, came not so much from the fragrance of
the crushed orchids that she rubbed into her lustrous hair or
from the somewhat cloying and oversweet musk emanating from
her yoni; in the end, what he found most unalike about her was
the scent of her soul.

Even so, she pleased him in many ways, and he discovered
many things in her that he came to relish. She composed poems
for him, as Maria had, and she cooked him succulent meals of
fatfish and pomegranates; as well, she gave freely of a mellif-
luous laughter that bubbled up inside her with an assurance
that life should be an endless transport of enchantments and
play. After the gravity of his dark existence in the time since
Maria's death, he felt like an uncaged bird set free to soar
across a dazzlingly blue sky. He took to wandering the island
with her, and he joined his body with hers atop the torrid
beach sands and in the ocean's shallows and beneath the lianas
and flowers of the jungle's trees. He wanted to be alone with
her as often as he could.

Their intense regard for each other, however, upset many of
the royad. One day, with the tropical sun throwing golden arrows
straight down upon the beach, Julior took Rane aside to talk
to him.

'Ah, my beautiful friend,' Julior said, taking Rane's arm, 'we
all rejoice that you have found such succour and release from
your sufferings. And you are welcome to stay with us as long
as it pleases you and pleases us. During those few moments
when you are apart, Maria sings your praises!'

Rane tried to match the ease of Julior's smile, but something
in Julior's voice disquieted him.

'It is good for you to enjoy her, of course, very good, but perhaps it would be better if you would not go off together as much as you do.'

'Better for whom?'

'Better for the others, and better for you, too.'

'We only wish to be with each other.'

'And you *should* be with each other, as much as you wish, but you should not be with each other so often alone.'

'But we have a way with each other.'

'Yes, but it is not *our* way. It is not seemly; it is not sociable; it is not generous.'

'But you said that she is for me, and I for her.'

'Yes, you are. But you are both for everyone else as well.'

At these words, Rane wiped at the sweat beading up on his forehead.

'On the world where I lived,' he said, 'men and women share physical union with only one other at a time.'

Julior smiled in a kindly way at this shameful lie, but he did not call out Rane for it. Instead, he stroked Rane's hand and said, 'Sometimes, two people burn for each other for a while, like torches feeding each other's fires. And so you and Maria may share your union exclusively as much as you wish, but it would be very bad for you to share it in secret.'

As a man of culture and refinement, Julior made no ostensible threat; even so, Rane read a stern warning in Julior's friendly words. Rane had to remind himself that he had come upon a people who were really barbarians at heart despite seeming hyper-civilized on the surface. He knew that the Nepenthians could be cruel – as they had proved in the ugly affair that had unfolded around Naveek. After Julior had gone off, Rane thought about Naveek, for he saw something of himself in this energetic young man. Only ten days before, Naveek had offended the others of the royad. Although Rane had not witnessed Naveek's disgrace and the ensuing discord that it fomented, he got a good account of both from Maria, who loved to gossip.

In preface to her story, she had told Rane something that he hadn't known: that Naveek was not only the youngest of the royad but the only truly young Nepenthian on the island. The Nepenthians, it seemed, allowed themselves to procreate only when one of their number died. Given the care that

Nepenthians took with their persons, however, and given the Pool of Transfiguration capable of bringing one back to youth many, many times past the three times permitted in the Civilized Worlds, death occurred only rarely – and almost always as a result of an accident or a suicide. The accident that had opened the way to Naveek's quickening and birth had taken place some eighteen years previously, when a man named Lemuel had been out swimming in the ocean. Two tiger sharks had surprised him at the same moment that the guardian robots that attended dangerous activities such as water sports had been called away to watch over Thena, who had decided without notice to climb a palm tree in order to gather coconuts. Lemuel's screams had not summoned the robots in time. Before the robots (they took the form of giant eagles with razor-sharp steel beaks) could fly across the beach, the sharks had torn Lemuel into bloody pieces. Although the robots drove off the sharks and gathered Lemuel's remains, too little of him was left to transport to the Pool of Transfiguration. And so the royad had been forced to hold their first funeral in perhaps a hundred years.

'After that,' Maria had informed Rane, 'we gave permission to Karina to bear a child, and we all swam out into the pool to share ourselves.'

And in the Pool of Transfiguration, the robots swarmed into the Nepenthians' bodies, and they snipped and pasted and rearranged the combined germ plasm of the entire royad into order to form the fertilized egg that the robots implanted in Karina's womb. Three-quarters of a year later, Karina had given birth to Naveek.

'He is still so young!' Maria had said to Rane. 'Practically a baby – I can't even remember what it is like to have only seventeen years!'

What it was like for Naveek, of course, was that he wanted to spill his seed night and day. He accomplished this on the beach frequently with women such as Sariah; however, being so young and as yet unbroken to the ways of the royad, he had a particular taste for amusing himself. So it came to be that one day – some thirty days after Rane and Nikolandru had arrived on the island – Thena had come across Naveek alone in the woods. She caught him under a tree, with his engorged manhood in hand, jelqing away with abandonment.

Such an act, as Rane discovered, the Nepenthians regarded as a great transgression: not as a sin against God, exactly, as the Kristians castigated onanists, but rather as a violation of the royad's trust. To masturbate was to scorn the affection of the men and women of the royad, to announce to them, in effect, that they could not fulfil one's sexual needs. Even more, to avoid physical pleasure with one's paramours and friends was to admit dislike of the forms they had shaped for themselves and to criticize in the most hurtful way the artfulness that had gone into that shaping. In that sense, to deny another was to deny Poetry itself – and the Nepenthians regarded that as worse than a sin.

Things would have gone better for Naveek if he had simply bowed his head in shame at his disgraceful act and acquiesced to the royad's ways. Wasn't he very young, after all, practically a baby? And weren't his brothers and sisters willing – no, eager! – to forgive the youth and to instruct him in the art of being human? Naveek, however, had not been able to bring himself to submit to Nepenthian mores, which he ridiculed as being both arbitrary and stultifying. And so he had defied the others, and he had announced that he would jelq as often as he pleased, wherever he pleased, and in whatever circumstances that he found pleasing.

In response, Julior informed him of the decision of the royad: Naveek was of course free to jelq night and day and to spill oceans of seed in the jungle or up and down the beaches; however, if he did so, the royad would have to shun him. Because Naveek was so young and artless, Julior had to explain the meaning of this old, old word: if the royad shunned Naveek, no one would be permitted to talk to him, nor would the others sit with him at feast or share food. When he beckoned to Sariah or another woman, they would close their legs to him and turn away. In effect, he would become invisible to the only human beings he had ever known; as long as the shunning continued, he would live as one who is dead.

Faced with such an unimaginable fate, in the zealous way of youth, Naveek had decided not to live. He would swim out far from the island, he announced, miles and miles out into the open ocean where the sharks hunted in packs. When the great beasts had finished with him, not even a fingernail would remain to be buried.

At this threat, Julior had countered with one of his own. In his affectionate but implacable way, he had assured Naveek that he would not be allowed to kill himself: an entire cadre of guardian robots would be assigned to watch over him day and night and to keep him from harm. The huge birds, with talons that could serve as leg irons, would hover over him wherever he went.

In contemplation of such restriction and humiliation (and estrangement from people he cherished despite their bullying of him), Naveek had finally given in. He had broken down weeping and wailing out that he could not live without the care of the men and women of the royad. He would, he promised, jelq no more. And why should he, as Maria had put it to Rane?

'Naveek is such a beautiful man,' she had told him. 'He can plant his root inside Sariah anytime he needs to – or, for that matter, inside Thena, Narmada or me.'

Rane wondered if the Naveek story had truly come to an end with the young man's acquiescence, just as Rane often contemplated his own fate. Why, he asked himself, did he linger on the island? He had already learned a great deal about certain aspects of Maria that had hitherto remained opaque to him – did he really desire to learn more? Why shouldn't he return with Nikolandru to the *Asherah* and rocket up away from this soft, watery world so that he could complete his quest?

Although he resolved to do just that, he found himself once again thinking about Maria, or at least the Nepenthian woman who called herself by that name. Late in the afternoon of the day on which Julior had spoken to him, Rane found Maria in the forest harvesting coconuts. Although she could have summoned a robot to do such hard work, she liked to pit her muscles and skills against the tough coconuts, which did not surrender their sweet treasure easily. He watched as she used a steel machete to shred off a coconut's tough green outer husk. The day's heat had gathered among the fronds of the ferns and the palm trees that arched above them. Maria seemed to revel in this invisible, almost viscous substance, even as the late sun danced along the beads of sweat that sheened her tawny skin. She smiled when Rane appeared and walked up to her. With a dozen deft blows of the machete, she split open its shell and held the coconut up high so that its fragrant water ran into

Rane's open mouth – and over his lips and chin, too. She laughed and kissed him, then licked his face with all the greed and exuberance of a dog.

'Julior spoke to me earlier,' he said to her. 'He disapproves of our being alone.'

'I knew he would talk to you. I don't know why it took him so long.'

'Perhaps he disliked having to tell me things that he shouldn't have told me.'

'No, he is right. We have made a sweet, sweet thing together, and that has been a great pleasure, but does one keep such goodness to oneself?'

So saying, she used the machete's sharp edge to sheer away the coconut's shell from the creamy white meat within. She broke off a bit of the meat, then pressed it into Rane's mouth.

'I've no liking to share you with the others,' he told her, chewing away at the fibrous coconut.

'You liked it well enough that first night.'

'That was different,' he said. 'It had been a long time for me. When I saw you, touched your hand, it was like being pulled into a tunnel of fire. The rest of the world burned away.'

She laughed at this, and fed him another chunk of nut.

'Now, if we were to join with each other while the others looked on,' he said, 'I would be too aware that they *were* looking on.'

'But in looking at us, our passion would ignite their passion, which they would then give back to us in their regard, and with their hands, and we would pass this fire back and forth, forth and back, like burning archangels of bliss.'

He smiled at this, then kissed her hand, all sticky with coconut juice. 'As Julior said to me, your ways are not my way.'

'Have you never, then, been with more than one other at a time?'

Rane thought back to the wild, wanton days in the Farsider's Quarter when he had taken to bed the pink-skinned Magda and other women he had bought with cold coins. And he said, 'Never with women *and* men.'

'But what does one's sex have to do with it?'

'I was made to be with women,' he said.

'Who has asked you to be with anyone else?'

'I *saw* what was happening around the fires, that first night on the beach.'

'I thought that you were so enamoured of me that you couldn't see anything else.'

'Well, a part of me saw and remembered.'

'Yes, you're a remembrancer, and you remember all sorts of things, don't you?'

'I remember that everyone was touching everyone.'

At this, she traced her sticky fingers along his chest and down through the fine hairs of his belly. 'I've never heard you object to being touched.'

'Not by you. But I don't wish to be touched by men.'

'But flesh is flesh, is it not? And the fire that feeds it burns just as sweetly in a man as it does in a woman.'

'Perhaps it does,' he said. 'But it burns *differently*.'

'How so?'

'I don't know, it's just different,' he said. Then, as her fingers moved down to his loins and he gazed at her eyes to behold the ardour that moved her, he had an inspiration. 'In a man, the fire is of magenta, crimson, and chrome red. It's like iron heated red-hot, then quickly flaring white hot and throwing out sparks. Ah, but a woman's colours! On the outside, they're all burning blue, as if she were dressed in cerulean silks that had caught fire. And deeper, as if the silks had fallen away to reveal a bright, blazing orange, like the raiment of a tiger burning through the night.'

She laughed at this and clapped her hands with amusement. 'Tell me more, my beautiful, poetic Rane!'

'Each woman,' he said, looking at her intensely, 'burns with a pattern of purpose and possibilities unique to herself – and so with each man. The pattern of flames sears our beings with the memory of who we really are.'

'Good! Good!' she said. 'Then I am some combination of cerulean and sapphire, of indigo, cobalt, and azure! And the orange hues! Carnelian, copper, and marigold!'

'Something like that,' he said.

'Then you can *see* these flames of my being?'

'I can see you,' he said. 'Julior was right: my Maria was one of the classic forms, and so are you. You are a woman as woman was meant to be: purely, beautifully, and totally woman.'

'Thank you,' she said, 'I am now – it was what I intended to be.'

Rane's belly tightened as his breath caught in his throat. 'What do you mean, you are now?'

'Well, in my last incarnation, I was a man. My name was Henri.'

Rane stared at her, dumbfounded. He did not want to believe what she had told him. 'What do you mean, you were a man?'

He shook his head because his words seemed idiotic to him, but he couldn't have helped saying what he had.

'Well,' she explained, 'in my incarnation before my last one, I was a woman named Clarissa, but I tired of her, and so I decided I wanted to walk the world as a man again.'

'Again? But you can't just change sex like someone taking off one garment and putting on another!'

'Why not? Don't tell me on your world that people never change sexes!'

'Ah . . . they do. That is, they change their gender. Sometimes one will be born with the identity of a man but the form of a woman – or the reverse.' He took a breath of the jungle's warm, sticky air, then added, 'Or sometimes people are just curious. They go to cutters who transform them, at least on the surface.'

'I see. Then a man would become a woman without a womb, and the woman a man without viable seed?'

'Yes, something like that.'

Maria whistled for a parrot, which appeared from out of the canopy of green leaves in the trees above them. She spoke with the blue and red contraption, all the while tapping the machete's steel edge against a coconut as if she had need but little patience for this conversation.

'Henri stepped into the Pool of Transfiguration as virile a man as you,' she told him. 'And the Maria who stepped out is as much a woman as the one you still yearn for, complete with all a woman's organs – and with two X chromosomes in every diploid cell of her body.'

Rane gazed at the beautiful woman who stood before him, smiling at him with invitation. Beads of sweat dripped down her heavy breasts and gathered on her nipples like a clear milk. When he closed his eyes, his nose became more sensitive to the scents hanging in the heavy air, and he tried to fight off the overpowering sense that she smelled very much like a woman.

'Ah, your cells, yes, your DNA,' he said, grasping for words. 'But deeper than that lies—'

'Are we going to talk again about these pretty flames of yours?'

She rested the machete against the base of the palm tree behind her. Then she turned and drew closer to Rane; she took his hand and pressed it to the moist fur between her legs.

'Tell me,' she said, 'that I have been less a woman to you than your old Maria, and I shall leave you alone to go back to your search for her.'

He sucked in a huge lungful of air as she pushed his fingers inside her, then he gasped out: 'Tell me how you were when you were born!'

'Does that really matter?'

'Tell me what your first name was – you must remember your name.'

'I've already told you that I don't.'

'But how is that possible?'

She took his hand in hers and put his fingers to his lips. 'You are a remembrancer who can recall all things, but is there nothing you wish to forget?'

At this, he pulled free his hand and stared off at the huge greyish-white rain clouds that gathered to the west, over the ocean. 'I would not want to forget who I really am.'

'But who you were is not who you are. And who you are is not who you might be.'

'But who I am contains who I was, just as who I was born to be pulls at me with all the gravity of a star.'

'But your *conception* of all those I's weighs you down as if you'd donned a suit of armour as protection against sharks in order to swim safely in the sea.'

'But we can't simply forget those I's, can we?'

'We *must*,' she said. 'The memories of our many selves are like links in an iron chain fastened to our throats. Thus bound, how can we breathe freely?'

Rane did not know how to respond to this. Everything seemed to confuse him: the jungle's moist heat; the stillness and pressure of the air that presaged a thunderstorm; the delicious but oppressive smell of sex. Not far from him stood a mango tree hung with fruits so garish and tumid it seemed that they might at any moment burst. A smear of red in the skin of one ripe mango recalled a similar hue that he could never quite forget. Suddenly and inexorably, this carmine colour pulled him into the past with an attractive force so great that he felt his very cells being crushed. It pulled him into the softness of Maria's breasts and her belly, and into the hot, sweet agony of her body. He felt again her heart beating too fast and her throat catching with words that she tried to force out but could not. And the sobbing, sobbing, sobbing . . . The tears frozen like diamond drops to the tawny skin beneath her eyes. He saw again Maria's beautiful bitten lip and the drop of blood that welled up from it – the single drop of red blood that had rolled onto the white snow beneath her. Why could he never look away from that terrible drop?

'Rane?'

And why, he wondered, could he never look *through* it in order to perceive the deep and terrifying source from which it had come?

'Rane,' he heard a voice say as if from far away, 'what have I said to distress you?'

He felt a hand upon his arm, and his eyes focused upon the gorgeous and suddenly worried Maria who stood beneath the palm tree.

'All right,' he said to her softly, 'then you've forgotten who you were – you're right, everyone forgets something.'

'What is it *you've* forgotten, sweet man? What is it you wish to forget?'

Her eyes drilled into him like obsidian needles. Where she cast him piercing looks that threatened to lay bare his thoughts, the real Maria had enveloped him with her heart, as if feeling out the tissues of his being from within.

'I forget,' he said, in order to distract her, 'the ending to a poem I once wrote.'

'But what was the beginning of the poem? Perhaps if you recite it, the rest will come to you.'

'I think,' he said, 'it went like this.'

'On that day, dead of winter, ice and cold,
  When I walked with the dead . . .'

He continued speaking for a while, but soon enough the words seemed to dry up like water running through a ditch carved out of the desert.

'I'm not sure what comes next,' he said.

'So much pain in your poem! But pain must always give way to pleasure. Is there no joy in your poem?

'Yes, there is.'

'In that moment, open gaze, pools of light,
When I plunged into that sacred sea
Down through a bottomless pain carved joy
To find you, wisest child of the deep . . .'

He spoke more words, which dried up, too. He did not want to look at her just then, but couldn't help doing so.

'Julior was right about you,' she finally said. 'You *do* belong with us.'

'Why, because I can stack a few lines of verse together?'

'Is that all you think we do here on our island?'

'No – you're all busy shaping yourselves as if you were living poems.'

'But what else is one to do with one's life?'

She sat down on a carpet of ferns, and pulled Rane down beside her. Then she elaborated on the Nepenthian ideal of self-creation as the highest art. She observed that all high art should aim at a totality in which none of its elements stood out but rather worked together as an integrated whole: instead of a gaudy garment studded with brilliant opals and rubies, one should make of oneself a rich tapestry of multicoloured strands woven together with such art that its viewers would be moved by only the beauty of the entire composition.

After she had finished her disquisition, Rane said to her, 'I thought you of the Poetry Islands made *poems* of yourself.'

'Poems and paintings, it is all one,' she said. 'Other islands have other modes, but we have chosen the poem as our muse here.'

And for those of the royad, she added, the fulfilment of the poem could not be found in any individual person but only in the royad as a whole. Words, she said, were analogous to one's traits and talents; lines took their shape in the form of a person.

'We use poetry to exalt, focus, and shape our persons,' she told him. 'This is our way, our tao. But what good are words, no matter how brilliant, which grind and tear at each other? It is only in the creation of the royad that our highest poetry sings.'

As she stroked his belly, he couldn't help recalling words that Maria had once spoken to him, by way of Danlo wi Soli Ringess:

Our lives are the songs that sing the universe into being.

He began stroking her, too, and soon he found himself slipping into her as he kissed her succulent lips. Their sex that day seemed to him sweeter than their many other couplings, as if he had bitten into a new species of mango perfumed with a heavenly scent. They rocked together atop the rattling ferns almost like one perfectly coordinated organism, like a song of ecstasy that could go on forever.

17

So began a new phase of Rane's stay on the island. The warm days passed in pleasure, and gave way to nights of fire and poetry and a passion with Maria that the two of them did not try to contain within themselves but rather shared with the others of the royad as they might have circulated a cup of wine. Beneath the canopy of bright stars that were strange to Rane, he lay with Maria on soft sands as women and men joined in a never-ending, orgiastic communion. As much as Rane disliked that word, he felt forced to use it, for he discovered that the nightly revels on the beach only partially concerned sex. Much more, the royad's gatherings acted as a sort of subterranean heat that melted the shells of people's exteriors and fused them into a new and splendid substance. Often, Rane noticed, various members of the royad participated in the orgies through little more than the tendering of massages or touches or songs. Indeed, two men – Rikyu and Koffi – could hardly be thought of as men at all, for they had chosen to incarnate into forms that were smooth between the legs. They each wished to live at least one life free from the throes of sex. They derived their greatest satisfaction in exploring deeper means by which to strengthen the royad's bond.

While Rane only slowly habituated himself to the cries and the caresses of the nightly orgies, he found himself astonished at how readily Nikolandru took to the Nepenthian ways. On many a balmy evening – with the beach bonfires blazing and crackling and spitting out sparks – Nikolandru joined with naked women whose sun-browned bodies quivered around him like a ball of flesh. Sometimes, he enjoyed the communing with men with an almost equal abandonment. It seemed to Rane that Nikolandru had forgotten his purpose and might be content to remain on Nepenthe for a hundred years.

This worry, however, proved to be unfounded. One day, as Rane sat on the wet sands by the ocean's edge letting gentle waves wash over him, Nikolandru walked across the beach and came up to him.

'I think this island,' Nikolandru said, 'has enchanted you.'

'Enchanted *me*? Every night, night after night, the Nepenthians swarm around you like bees that have found a new source of honey. They adore you.'

'They adore you, too.'

'No, they don't,' Rane said, staring across the beach at the char that filled one of the fire pits. 'But they are coming to accept me, I think.'

'Nearly as much as you have accepted them. A stranger visiting this place would believe that you were born here.'

Rane looked at the verdant jungle above the perfectly white beach and the undulating hills above that. Then he gazed at the sparkling ocean and said, 'Who wouldn't want to be born in such a beautiful place?'

'It's too beautiful,' Nikolandru said. 'When will we be leaving?'

'I'm not sure. As soon as I find what I came here to find.'

'And what is that?'

How could Rane reply to this? How could he explain to this pilot-poet with the black curls and easy laughter that the Nepenthians had called him to question what it was to be a man or a woman – and thus to question the very nature of selfness and identity?

'If I am ever to recreate the real Maria,' he said, 'I must better understand who she was – at the bottom of who she really was.'

'*Are* you to recreate her?'

In answer to this question, Rane gazed out at the bottomless blue ocean.

'Why are we here, Rane? Why are we still *really* here?'

What could Rane tell this popular and unrestrained man who yet kept secrets of his own? That the endless travel across the stars had exhausted him and he wished to rest? That the Maria he had met on this timeless island bathed his body in a paralysing narcotic which also numbed the anguish in his soul? Could Nikolandru, who laughed and communed with people so easily, ever understand the soul's fundamental discord with others and the even more fundamental longing for an impossible peace? How could Rane explain the urge to lose oneself in another and to dwell together as one despite the terrible, terrible price?

'There is something about Maria,' he said, 'that the Nepenthians have yet to reveal to me.'

Whatever Rane confided to Nikolandru, he knew that he could never tell him the deepest reason that had marooned him on the island: the dark, unmentionable thing that he could not even tell himself.

'Let us hope that they reveal it soon,' Nikolandru said, 'else the time for which we contracted will expire. We've been here nearly a year.'

'So long? I haven't counted the days.'

'Perhaps you should.'

'I don't wish to,' Rane said. He realized that his worry over Nikolandru's frolics on the island had masked his own reluctance to leave it. 'I don't care if I spend another thousand days here – or the rest of my life.'

'You can't mean that. How will you ever find your woman?'

'Perhaps I already have, in a way.'

'But is it a way that will satisfy you?'

'Why should that matter to you?'

'Because we have made a contract to—'

'If you are so concerned about honouring your contract with me,' Rane said, 'then why don't you consider it dissolved?'

'You can't mean that.'

'I do. You are free to seal yourself in your ship and leave whenever you wish.'

So saying, Rane pointed down the beach where the silvery *Asherah* sparkled like a huge diamond cast upon the bright beach sands.

'I think you've drunk too much of the royad's drug,' Nikolandru said, shaking his head at this.

'You've drunk as much as I.'

'I am not speaking of the brandy.' Then Nikolandru looked at Rane with an unexpected kindness, and clapped him on the shoulder. 'Have pity on me, friend. If you do not continue your quest for Maria, how will I ever be able to compose the greatest of poems, the poem I was born to write? If you remain here, I will have no great saga of which to sing.'

'But you will have a fortune with which to pursue other inspirations.'

'Do I have to drug you, for real, and abduct you to get you off this island?'

'Would you truly do that?'

'I won't leave you here. If you stay, I stay.'

Rane scooped up a handful of wet sand and let it dribble out so that it quickly dried into a shape that resembled a granular, lumpy spire of a castle. 'I just want to be happy,' he said.

'No, that is *not* what you want,' Nikolandru said, shaking his head, 'not really.'

'What is it you think I want then?'

'To wake up,' he replied, 'as from a dream remembering who you really are.'

After that, Nikolandru stood up and left Rane to sit in the sand and build up the walls of his castle. Rane spent the following days in such indolent pursuits – and in his blissful exploration of Maria's body and soul. The world turned, and the sun rose out of the eastern ocean each morning and made its fiery arc across the sky with a hypnotizing rhythm.

Early one evening, as Rane was wandering the beach looking for shells near the *Asherah*, Naveek came out of the jungle and caught him up in conversation. With his straight black hair and lively eyes, the handsome lad looked somewhat like a masculine version of Maria. He seemed at once overly friendly and doubtful, vainglorious and secretly nervous, like many another male throughout time and space who faced the difficult passage to young manhood.

'You call your vessel a lightship, yes?' Naveek said to Rane. He moved over to the gleaming needle, fifty yards long. He rapped his knuckles against the *Asherah*'s hull and added, 'Is it really made of diamond?'

'Yes, of spun diamond,' Rane said, stepping close to the ship. He slid his gritty fingers across the smooth hull.

'And lightships such as this one dance across the stars, yes? You have visited many stars, it is said.'

How many stars *had* Nikolandru's ship visited, Rane wondered? The *Asherah* had fallen out around so many that he had long since lost count.

'One of the parrots told me,' Naveek said, 'that two stars once collided, creating a nebula with three rings.'

'That is true,' Rane said. 'It happened long ago in the Magellanic Cloud many thousands of light years from here. The rings are of magenta and violet, with crimson arms spiralling out as if to touch other stars.'

'You have seen such things yourself?'

'Yes, I have.' He told Naveek of the Dragon's Eye Nebula in the galaxy's Sagittarius Arm and the Opal Vortex out beyond Sheydveg. 'In this galaxy alone, so many glories.'

'I want to see them, too,' Naveek said.

'Then you should ask your robots to make a telescope.'

'I want to see them as you have seen them.' Naveek again rapped his knuckles against the ship. 'Will you take me with you when you leave this world?'

The intensity with which Naveek forced out these words surprised Rane as much as it pained him.

'But this is your home,' Rane said, motioning toward the island's misty hills. 'Julior, Thena, Hakainu, Sariah – they are your people.'

'They are a prison, as is this island. I cannot *breathe* here.'

He went on to explain how the expectations of the royad were strangling him like so many hands gripping his throat. He wanted, he told Rane, to live according to his purest and truest impulses and so to be free.

'I understand,' Rane said. 'But the kind of freedom you seek does not exist. No one has ever lived that way.'

No one except Maria, he thought. *And hadn't such living in the end destroyed her?*

'On all planets and in all places,' Rane continued, 'all peoples must make accommodations to the societies in which they live.'

'But I live *here*, where one is supposed to be free to create oneself – unless a gaggle of old men and old women do not approve of one's creation.'

'You'd encounter worse restrictions elsewhere. On Summerworld, and on other planets, too, they keep slaves who stoop to satisfy their masters' whims.'

'And what are slaves?'

As if Rane were a parrot disgorging information that too many had known too intimately and viscerally for fifty thousand years, he explained how human beings had used torture coupled with the threats of mutilation and death to compel other human beings to do their bidding. On Old Earth, he said, kings had clipped off the genitals of war captives so that they could safely attend their women or sing with the beautiful voices of young boys. Naveek's eyes went wide with horror even though it seemed that he could not quite bring himself to believe what Rane had told him.

'Even if what you say is true, are things much better here?' Naveek waved his hand toward the jungle that sloped up from the beach. 'I am a slave to those who say they cherish me even as they clip my wings so that I cannot fly.'

Rane smiled at the boy's hyperbole, then asked him, 'Do you know the story of the camel, the lion, the dragon, and the child?'

Naveek shook his head, and he asked Rane to explain these words. After Rane had done so, he continued: 'The Fravashi Old Fathers tell a parable, adapted from a much older source dating back to Old Earth.'

'And what is an Old Father?' Naveek asked.

Rane told him something of the huge, white-furred aliens who taught their philosophy of cosmic freedom in such cities as Neverness. Then he said, 'You chafe at the restrictions that Julior and the others place upon you, but you should accept them like a camel enduring a heavy load. No, not just accept them: you should *ask* for increasingly heavy loads. Indeed, you should exult in such burdens, for if you are truly to create yourself you must someday make new laws and values for yourself that will weigh you down even more. How could you ever hope to bear *that* burden unless you had become as strong as a camel?'

Naveek kept his eyes locked on Rane's as Rane spoke. Then he said, 'But I have had enough of being a camel! The royad's rules are meaningless to me.'

'Then the day will soon dawn when you must become a lion,' Rane said. 'And on that day, you will face a great scaled

dragon whose name is Thou Shalt: for every scale covering
the dragon's mighty body glitters golden with the words "thou
shalt". A thousand "thou shalts" must the lion slay before slaying
the dragon itself.'

'And what is the lion's name?'

'His name is "I Will". But the will alone cannot suffice to
create new values by which to live. The lion cannot. And so he
must become a child.'

'A child? What sort of child?'

'Well, *not* a labourer – the camel laboured mightily,' Rane
said. 'And not a hero, for the lion took on that role in slaying
the dragon. No, he must become something you might call a
star child.'

In the silent intensity with which Naveek gazed up at the
sky, Rane quoted from an old, old book: '"Innocence is the child,
and forgetfulness, a new beginning, a game, a wheel rolling out
of its own centre, a first movement, a holy Yea."'

'I know those words!' Naveek shouted, turning to Rane. 'I
was very young, but I remember Maria, *your* Maria, the one
you came here to find, saying something like that.'

This revelation surprised Rane only for a moment, for he
recalled that it had been Maria, in Neverness, who had given
those words to him.

Maria was such a child, Rane thought.

He, too, now gazed up at the sky. From what planet around
which blessed star had Maria really come? What had made
Maria so wise but so impossibly innocent? Like Sunjay and
Chandra and all the others of the *Asta Siluuna*, Maria lived to
play a strange new game whose rules were nowhere written
down, whose strategies Rane had never quite been able to
comprehend.

'Then Maria,' Rane said to Naveek, 'would have advised you
to bear your burden as long as you can. And when you have
finally become a lion, to fight with skill as well as with ardour
– and then to create new values of such grandeur that the others
of the royad will make them their own.'

It pleased Rane to tender advice that this troubled young
man so badly needed. Rane wanted, in a way, *needed* to help
him. So it came as something of a plunge into cold water when
Naveek said, 'No, Maria would not have advised that.'

'You think not?'

'Maria's ways were not our ways,' Naveek said. 'Not wholly, not at first. I have talked to Sariah about this. If the royad changed after Maria's coming, it wasn't due to Maria's values but to Maria herself.'

He went on to tell Rane something that Rane had suspected but had never quite articulated to himself: that within half a year of her arrival on the Poetry Islands, Maria had become nearly the most powerful member of the royad.

'Everyone loved her,' Naveek said. 'She gave so much to everyone! Kindness, laughter, tears, passion, hope! And she gave not as Julior does, to impress others with his magnanimity, or as Damiana does, to hand out favours that must later be repaid twice over. No, Maria couldn't help giving of herself – and giving and giving and giving! – because it delighted her to please others. It was as if she were so full of life and goodness that she needed to share it with the whole world – or else she would swell up and burst into a million parts and die.'

Rane stared out at the ocean, remembering. He stared so hard that he had to blink several times at the burning in his eyes.

'Maria made herself *necessary* to everyone,' Naveek said. 'If she had stayed here another year, I think she would have become the motif.'

'Motif?' Rane asked.

'Are you not familiar with the word?'

'I am, but I usually associate it with music. And sometimes with poetry.'

'Just so. As a sonata or a poem turns about a thematic centre that gives it movement, so with the royad. Right now, Julior centres the royad with his idea of who we should be, and so we call him the motif.'

'I have never heard that,' Rane said.

'Have you heard, then, that Julior was jealous of Maria? That he feared her dream of what the royad might become?'

'And what was that?'

'I'm not sure – the others don't talk about it, and I was very young.' Naveek, naked and tattooed, kicked his bare toes into the beach's sand. 'I think, though, that it was something wild. It might have had something to do with her wanting a baby.'

This statement caused Rane to tighten with remembrance. 'But she couldn't have borne a baby here unless one of the royad first died.'

'Just so. I think Maria might have tried to persuade the others to let themselves die when their time came, instead of seeking endless lives of renewal in the pool.'

Yes, Rane thought, *Maria might have said something like that.*

'I have a distant memory of Maria telling Julior something once.' Naveek looked at Rane with sad, beautiful eyes. 'She said that the life he would lose in embracing death would be restored a hundred times over in the creation of a child. Do you think that could be true?'

To live, I die – Rane recalled this saying of the warrior-poets.

'I believe that some of the others thought it was true,' Naveek added. 'It was a new idea for the royad: that one could do more living in a moment of perfect splendour than in an endless expanse of pleasurable but ultimately meaningless days.'

'Not everyone,' Rane said, 'sympathizes with such sentiments.'

'Julior doesn't. Neither does Rebecca or Eliahu. But what if they did? I might have a younger brother with whom to race by the water. When I mate with Sariah, we might make a child of our own.'

'Are you so ready to be a father?'

'I am ready to leave this island, this world. Please take me with you.'

The yearning in Naveek's voice pained Rane and felt like a lump stuck in his own throat. How could he do as the young man asked? He couldn't bear the thought of returning to the stars. He wished for nothing more in life than an endless expanse of pleasurable and peaceful days.

He patted the lightship and said, 'I can't take you with me – there is not enough room for two passengers.'

He described the cramped, stinking quarters that he had endured on the *Asherah*'s journey out from Neverness. However, Naveek did not seem dismayed.

'You speak of a long journey in grim circumstances,' he said. 'But I could comfort you and ease your loneliness.'

He touched his hand to Rane's shoulder and looked deep into his eyes.

'No, Naveek, it would be impossible to—'

'*Please* take me with you!'

'I can't,' Rane said, peeling away Naveek's fingers from his skin. 'I have decided to remain here – and so has Nikolandru.'

Years ago, during the war, Rane had watched the collapse of the Penhallegon Tower, weakened by the blast of a fusion bomb. Naveek now appeared to collapse in a like manner, from within, as if his interior supports had weakened and then broken. He slumped, then fell weeping against Rane and gripped him in his arms. His belly pressed against Rane's belly, and its spasming impressed waves of despair into Rane and touched off a barely controlled quivering in his own muscles. Maria had once accused him of being born with a great capacity for empathy and an even greater will to deny this gift – as he denied it now. How could he not? Should he let the tremors that shook Naveek's belly and chest invade his own body? Or choke for breath as he was washed away in a flood of tears? How could he just melt into another's anguish and the terrible sobbing, sobbing, sobbing that accompanied it?

'I'm sorry,' he said, patting Naveek's back. 'I'm sorry.'

He stood for while stroking the back of Naveek's head and pressing his closed eyes into Naveek's hair. Then he managed to break from him. He watched as Naveek slunk off down the beach, head drooping, like a lion shorn of all its strength along with its glorious mane.

The next day, as Rane crouched on the beach inscribing mathematical figures in the wet sand, a hideous shriek split the air and obliterated the patter of the lapping waves. Rane sprang to his feet, for in all his time on the island, he had never heard such a sound. He ran down the beach, toward the huge Elephant's Head which jutted up out of the jungle and dominated the skyline to the south. Julior, Narmada, Thena, and others came out of the forest running, too: everyone running and running toward the wailing that grew louder and louder. In little time, the entire royad converged at the base of the Elephant's Head. The tide had pulled back to reveal jagged rocks slimy and green with algae; wedged between two of the rocks lay the body of Naveek, all broken and bloody. Sariah knelt by his side, wailing and kissing his blue lips, then wailing some more as she whipped her head back and forth in outrage and shook her fist at the sheer rock face rising straight up above them. She pulled at his body, too, as if to scoop up Naveek in her arms and rescue him from the rising tide. The rocks, however, held him fast. It took the hard work of Sariah, Julior, Thena, and Nikolandru to free the body and bear Naveek to the soft sands farther up the beach, where they laid him out beneath the morning sun.

When the waves of weeping had subsided, Sariah told what had happened, as much as she knew: 'When I awoke, our bed was empty. And that was strange, because when had Naveek ever risen early? I followed his footprints down the beach, to the base of the cliff. He must have climbed it hoping to gather condor eggs – you know how he enjoyed eggs for breakfast.'

She pointed up at the cliff's white-spattered rocks and the birds' nests that the condors had built into the cliff's many rocky shelves. Naveek, of course, had never exerted a moment's effort in the getting of food, leaving such work to the robots. Everyone knew that he had not come here to collect condor eggs.

'He fooled me,' Julior said, wiping tears from his eyes. 'He only pretended to accept our rebuke, while all these days he must have been contemplating this.'

Hearing these words, Rane realized that Julior could not bear to accept any part of the blame for Naveek's death but instead felt compelled to shift it onto Naveek. Julior's denial should have outraged Rane; instead, it only saddened him.

'He made me believe,' Julior added, 'that we no longer needed the eagles to watch over him.'

Rane turned his gaze from Naveek's battered body to the rocks of the Elephant's Head high above the beach. An image came to him: Naveek, standing at the edge of the precipice and spreading his arms wide to embrace the sky as he launched himself into space, and, for a moment of perfect splendour, flew like the great bird he wanted to be.

After some rounds of discussion, the royad determined that too much time had elapsed from the time of Naveek's death for him to be resurrected in the Pool of Transfiguration: his brain cells would have died and begun their decay. The most that the royad could do now was to bury him and then do their best to forget this horrible day.

Naveek's funeral recalled to Rane the cold, cold day on the Hollow Fields when Maria had been interred in the Star of

Neverness. Some of the particulars, of course, varied as much as they could: in the heat of the blazing afternoon, the royad lowered Naveek's body into a deep hole dug out of the ground near the base of one of the waterfalls that cascaded down the Elephant's Head. They filled it with a mound of earth, which they covered with colourful flowers. Then the men and women of the royad, working as a whole, composed a poem that Julior recited. They wept together, too. In the end, Rane thought, all funerals were really one and the same.

Ten days after that – days that Rane spent in wandering the island or staring up at the stars or in drinking bitter brandy from the cup of forgetfulness – Maria found him alone deep in the jungle lying on the band of grass that encircled the Pool of Transfiguration. So entranced was Rane by the jewel-like reflections dancing along the water's surface that he hardly took notice of her until she sat down next to him.

'It has been decided,' she told him, 'that there is to be an addition to the royad – and I am to bear the child.'

Rane sat up and looked her, but said nothing.

'Will you be one of the fathers?' she asked him.

'How can I be a father? I am not of the royad.'

'We've decided that you should join us – Nikolandru, too.'

He had long been hoping for such an invitation, but now that it had come, he took no pleasure in it.

'How can three more,' he asked, 'join the royad when only one has died?'

'We will carry Nikolandru's and your addition as debts to be repaid in the future. When the next two of the royad die, no children will replace them.'

Rane shook his head at this suggestion, for it horrified him. 'Then you would steal the lives of two children which you might create so that Nikolandru and I can continue drinking brandy and copulating in the sun for centuries until we've forgotten our names?'

'Do not put it so! We need your poems, your wisdom, your life! *I* do, Rane! Will you make a child with me?'

Will you make a child with me?

These seven simple words called up a deeper horror along with a terror so vast and bottomless that it pulled him down into the dark, dark pool of his most painful memories. *Will you make a child with me?* How easy it would be to say yes to this simple question! How easy, how natural, how gratifying!

'Please!' Maria said, grasping his hand.

His fingers pressed against her sun-browned wrist, and he felt the life that pulsed within her – the life that seemed so like that of the real Maria but yet so utterly different.

'Please, Rane!'

He gazed at the pool, at the rippling reflections of the leaves of the trees above them. All he needed to do was to wade out into the pool's cool waters with this Maria – and with the others of the royad – and he would make her happy. And then, in the millennia to come, as he plunged into the pool in cycle after cycle of renewal, he would live nearly forever.

'No, I cannot.' His words rang out into the quiet air like struck gongs. He pulled himself free from her grip. 'I'm sorry.'

'But I've never told you how much—'

'I will leave your world as soon as the ship can be made ready.'

'But why must you go?'

'You know why,' he said softly.

For a while, he let her rest against his side as he stroked her hair and listened to her muffled weeping. She asked him to speak the poem that he had once recited for her, but he told her that he had forgotten the lines. Then he stood up to go to find Nikolandru.

The next day, at dawn, in a blast of fire and radiance coruscating from the *Asherah*'s diamond hull, the lightship rocketed up away from the island, and Rane continued his journey into those parts of the galaxy where he had no wish to go.

18

And so the stars flew by in pulsations of light that illumined Rane's eyes for a moment or two before giving way to the gloom of forgetfulness and yet another burst of radiance in the seemingly endless cycle of falling out around star after star. So tired of such travel had Rane become that he hardly bothered to remember the names of the planets they visited: Mansurmal, Karkur Yang, Sapphire, Theodora's Paradise, and all the others. He continued gathering what clues about Maria that he could. On Godsward, it seemed, Maria had taken part in the religious frenzies of the annual Festival of the Ten Earth Angels. On Wehiland, she had suffered a gash to her forearm while breaking up a dogfight, while a hundred light years away in the Oxblood Nebula, she had lost herself in the data pools of Amaranth and had nearly starved to death. There seemed no end to the aspects of Maria that he might discover, trivial though many of them proved to be.

After nearly a year had passed since Rane's stay on Nepenthe, the *Asherah* put down on a fat, pretty world known as Kailash Poru. Rane had not wanted to visit this place, for the perfecti, as the ruling class called themselves, strenuously defended their right to keep slaves. This barbarism affronted Rane's eyes from the moment that he and Nikolandru left the safety of their light-ship and walked through the marble passageways of Kailash Poru's single star port: various perfecti, resplendent in jewel-studded robes, met friends or family returning from journeys to nearby worlds such as Caritas, Redemption, or Azul Amor. And every one of these proud men and women were attended by one or more naukars wearing the golden collars of enslavement. The naukars bent beneath the loads of the luggage that they bore and followed their masters as if they were dogs. Of course, the perfecti could have fabricated robots to do such work or employed wheeled carts, but they preferred the service of human beings. Indeed, they took their own measure from their mastery of others, as if their elevation to the heights of the humanly possible depended on the debasement of human slaves.

Rane hadn't taken ten steps through the port before two terrible sensations set upon him: the first tingled up his spine in a thrill of déjà vu that left him trembling with a sense that he had passed this way once before; the second burned through him in a red rage that made him want to strike out at the fabulously accoutred perfecti and shout out to their slaves that they should rise up and slay their masters. Had he done so, however, it would likely have been *he* who was slain. Dozens of proclamations – etched in big black characters into the port's white marble walls – warned that those who broke Kailash Poru's laws concerning slavery should expect to suffer various punishments: mutilation, enslavement, and death. Additional caveats advised those visiting Kailash Poru to turn back immediately if they felt that they could not abide by these cruel laws.

As Rane had long practice in biting back the words that he most wished to say, he and Nikolandru managed to leave the port without incident. Trouble came, however, almost as soon they began travelling through Kailash Poru's cities and villages along the main continent's western coast and made the usual inquiries concerning Maria. It took less than a day for Rane and Nikolandru to determine that Maria had visited this world; indeed, she had left her mark on Kailash Poru, becoming in a little time well remembered and much reviled for her infamy.

In the city of Easwaran, famed for its broad boulevards lined with pearl-blossomed trees, a perfecti lord named Silas Inay sent a cadre of armed slaves into the city's central square to summon Rane and Nikolandru to tea in the lord's palace. They had no choice but to comply with this peremptory meeting, and the slaves marched them through fragrant streets to the palace in the hills above Easwaran. One of the slaves advised Rane that he should have a good answer to the question of why he and Nikolandru had been asking after a notorious outlaw, for Silas Inay was the city's Lord Examiner.

In a cool room of marble floors and high white walls set with triangular blue tiles, Silas Inay greeted Rane and Nikolandru and invited them to sit at a teak table inlaid with gold. With his own hand, he poured them cups of jubol root tea, famed for its subtle aromas as well as its ability to facilitate conviviality by loosening the tongue. Silas, a hawk-faced man with hair as yellow as saffron, wore a magnificent blue caftan trimmed with a silver border into which thousands of sparkling diamonds had been sewn. When he caught Rane staring at this fabulous garment, he said, 'My seamstress, Kiki, spent a year making this for me. If you are too hot in your, ah, woollens, I can have her fetch something for you that would be more suitable to our climate.'

Rane, sweating in his kamelaika beneath the gaze of this sharp-eyed Lord Examiner, said, 'No, thank you. I am comfortable as I am.'

'Good, good!' Silas said with doubt fairly dripping from his words. 'I would like you to feel perfectly comfortable so that you might clarify a mystery that puzzles me.'

'I have trouble,' Rane said, 'clarifying the mysteries of my own life, but how may I help you?'

Silas looked more intently at Rane. 'My captain tells me that you are of some mythical Order on a planet called Neverness.'

'Neverness is no myth, Lord Inay, and neither is my order.'

'You are some sort of historian, then?'

Rane nodded his head in silence, for he could not bear to lie out loud. Of course, in a way his masquerade could be seen as a kind of the truth, for wasn't it a remembrancer's task to try to recall the deep history of every aspect of the universe?

'And you,' Silas said, turning to Nikolandru, 'are a pilot-poet of Aoide? I have not heard of that order, either.'

Nikolandru regarded Silas with his soft, fearless eyes. 'We are few, and my world was destroyed. I have since ranged the galaxy seeking wonders of which to sing.'

'An interesting profession. I have a passion for poetry, and have written some myself. Perhaps if you remain here, I can share a few lines with you.'

'I would like that,' Nikolandru said. He had a much easier time lying than did Rane. 'Unfortunately, we have come to your world on business, not pleasure.'

'Yes,' Silas said, turning to Rane, 'please say more about the nature of your business, for I admit it makes little sense to me.'

Rane drew in a quick breath, then confided to Silas Inay the story that he and Nikolandru had concocted: he told of a famous poet, Maria of the Roses, who had enchanted the entire city of Neverness with her brilliant verses before suffering an untimely death. Rane had devoted himself, he told Silas, to researching and then writing a history of Maria's life.

'I see,' Silas said. 'Then you have travelled halfway across the galaxy merely to gather facts concerning the life of a poet? That is part that I do not understand.'

'You might if you knew more about the Order. It's not unusual for our professionals to spend their lives illuminating fine points of their disciplines.'

'Is that why you've undertaken a journey that will likely require years to complete? Or do you have more personal reasons for making such researches?'

Rane didn't like the way that Silas Inay scrutinized him, so he resorted to an evasion: 'Well, Maria's words have touched me deeply, and so I would like to know more about the forces and events that shaped her.'

'Nothing more than that?'

Silas clearly didn't like Rane's dodging his inquiry, and he revealed his anger in the way that he brusquely poured some tea for Rane and practically shoved the little blue teacup under Rane's nose.

'What more should there be? Maria was a very great poet and—'

'She was an outlaw!' Silas snapped out, interrupting Rane. 'She scorned our codes, and was involved in the death of a great perfecti. Do you intend to put *that* in your history?'

'I will record the truth, whatever that might be.' Rane took a sip of the bittersweet jubol tea and looked at Silas. 'But what do you mean that Maria was involved in the death of a perfecti?'

'I was hoping you might illumine that matter.'

'How so? I know nothing of what you've just said.'

'No? Then please tell me of how you happened to come to Kailash Poru?'

Again, Rane felt forced to lie. 'Maria kept a journal in which she named all the planets that she had visited on her journey to Neverness.'

'Her journey from where?'

'I don't know,' Rane said. 'She never mentioned the name of her birth world, and that is one of the major mysteries about her that I would like to solve.'

'But what did she say about Kailash Poru?'

'Very little, actually. She said that yours was a hot world, at least in those climes in which most of your people live, and that you—'

'Did she mention that we keep slaves?'

'I'm sure that everyone who knows about Kailash Poru knows that.'

'Yes, of course. But did Maria tell in her journal that she had wantonly broken our laws and therefore suffered enslavement herself?'

No, no, no! These words sounded in Rane's mind, even as a great force seemed to push the air from his lungs. *No, Maria, you never did tell me that!*

'What laws did she break?' he managed to ask.

'She wrote poems promulgating the absurd proposition that all people are created equal, at least equal in the natural freedom with which they are imbued. In effect, she incited slaves to overthrow their natural masters. She shared these poems with slaves in secret – or so she thought.'

Silas went on to relate the story of Maria's stay on Kailash Poru, as much as he knew. After Maria's arrest in the city of Onklash, he said, she had been condemned to death by impalement. Just before she had been set upon one of the red-encrusted spikes in Onklash's central square, however, a visiting perfecti named Armas Sarkissian had taken note of her. He offered to buy her from Onklash, which had acquired all rights to her person and property upon her condemnation. Onklash's Lord Examiner advised against such a purchase, citing Maria's essential unruliness and bellicosity, no less her power to suborn people with her various charms. Armas Sarkissian had insisted even so; he offered Onklash's Lord Examiner ten thousand gold eagles for her. Because Onklash happened to badly need money for the construction of a new amphitheatre, the Lord Examiner had agreed to the sale. He ordered a gold collar locked around Maria's throat. Armas Sarkissian then chained Maria's wrists together and led her away.

He took her to his palace, the Karadan Adri (or Eagles' Aerie), built on top of a great cliff overlooking the western ocean. There, Armas instructed her in her new duties as his body servant and commanded her to compose poems that pleased him. There, too, according to Silas Inay, Armas had become enamoured of Maria and had taken her to his bed. Armas Sarkissian's enemies even prattled that Armas would have married Maria, had he not somehow plunged off the lip of the cliff and fallen to his death.

Silas Inay finished this account, poured a cup of tea, then looked at Rane to see what effect his words might have. Rane, however, kept his face as cool and stonelike as the marble from which the walls of Lord Inay's palace had been made.

'An inquest was conducted, of course,' Silas said. 'Although the truth remains opaque, the examiners determined that one way or another, Maria caused Armas's death. Before his body was discovered, she made her escape.'

Rane watched as a naukar – a flaxen-haired boy about twelve years old – arrived with a fresh pot of tea and a tray of honey cakes. The gold of his collar threw out tiny spears of light which grieved Rane's eyes.

'How is it that Maria was able to escape?' he asked after the naukar had left them alone again. 'I understand that you can instantly locate any slave through his collar – and if necessary can explode the collar remotely.'

For the first time during their tea, Silas Inay looked embarrassed. 'You see, we have a law that no perfecti may lie with a slave. Sometimes, of course, a master will desire a naukar's sexual services. In that instance, he will issue a temporary manumission and remove the slave's collar. So it was with Armas and Maria. While thus freed, before her manumission expired, Maria ran away.'

'She ran down the cliffs of this Eagles' Aerie and all the way to the star port without being detected? And then simply boarded a ship and left Kailash Poru?'

'No, of course not. One of the merchant pilots who did business with Armas happened to be visiting the Karadan Adri. Maria seduced him, and he stole her away.'

'That is a fantastic story.'

'I believe,' Silas said, 'that most of it must be true.'

'Most of it,' Rane muttered, shaking his head.

He happened to look at Nikolandru, who had so far remained nearly silent. But now Nikolandru said to Rane, 'Then you have the necessaries to record in your history – and I have a new romance of which to sing.'

This glib statement, however, seemed to satisfy neither Rane nor Silas. Rane turned to Silas and asked, 'You say that Maria caused Armas's death – how?'

'I wish we knew. Accounts of his last days differ.'

'Whose accounts?'

'Primarily, those of Armas's son and daughter.'

'What do they say, then?'

'This is a matter of some importance to you?'

'I would like to know the truth of what happened and then record it.'

'Yes, of course you would. But it may be that you know as much of the truth right now as you ever will.'

'I would like to speak with Armas Sarkissian's son and daughter.'

Silas's brows wrinkled as he stirred some honey into his hot tea. He looked at Rane; he looked at Nikolandru. Then he looked out of the window and up at the sky. Finally, he turned back to Rane and fixed him with his cold blue eyes.

'On one condition, I shall inquire of the son and the daughter if they are willing to speak to you.'

'And what is that condition?'

'That you *do* record their report in your history.'

'You trust me to do that?'

'Are you not a man of honour? Is your word not the seal of that honour?'

Rane considered this. 'All right, whatever the son and daughter say, I will record.'

'Thank you.' Silas clapped his hands, and a huge guard armed with a singlestick appeared. 'Little Mouse will show you to your rooms, where you will remain until the Sarkissians have made their response.'

Silas stood up with a suddenness that indicated the tea had come to an end. Little Mouse closed in on Rane and Nikolandru. With his large, hardened muscles and fierce visage, he reminded Rane of Batar Bulba.

'Aren't you afraid,' Rane asked Silas, before being led off, 'to put weapons in the hands of your slaves?'

He pointed at the naukar's black ebony singlestick, shod in steel.

'Only one who doesn't know slaves would ask such a question,' Silas said. 'No, I am not afraid. What do you suppose a slave desires more than anything in the world?'

'Freedom,' Rane said without hesitation.

'Just so. And to those slaves who have proved their worth,' Silas said, 'we offer freedom, after they have completed a period of service as enforcers of the law. I assure you that they enforce it more faithfully than any free master ever would.'

After that, Little Mouse led them through the halls of the palace to rooms which proved to be as large as they were luxurious. By Silas's orders, Rane and Nikolandru were denied no comfort: over the next two days, Silas sent them slaves bearing silver trays laden with delicacies and cakes – and with carafes of wine and liquid toalache and other imbibables. A harpist arrived to sing for them, and a blind old naukar set ivory and ebony pieces on a marble and jet chessboard and then proceeded to defeat Rane nine games out of ten. Four pretty young slaves, two by two, massaged the knots out of Rane's and Nikolandru's bodies and afterwards offered their sexual services. Rane declined, turning his energies instead to his study of mathematics. Nikolandru, though, gladly took all four of the naukars to his bed. He was not a man to pass up pleasures offered so enticingly, if not entirely freely.

On their third day as 'guests' in the palace, Lord Silas Inay arrived to inform Rane and Nikolandru that the Sarkissian children had invited them for a visit. Silas wore a golden caftan set with emeralds; as well, he wore a white bandage around the knuckles of his right hand, most likely necessitated by a collision with the face of some hapless youth. As Rane had learned from the blind chess master, Silas liked to beat his slaves.

'I'm sending you in my shuttle,' Silas told Rane, 'to the Karadan Adri. It lies only two hundred miles from here.'

'Very well,' Rane said, with a slight head bow. He could not bear to thank a man whose hospitality derived from the coercion of human beings.

'After you've spoken with the Sarkissians, you'll be taken back to your lightship. Before you leave Kailash Poru, however, I'll expect you to send me a synopsis of what you intend to write in your history.'

'Agreed,' Rane said.

He couldn't wait to get off this hellish planet.

19

The flight from Silas Inay's palace in Easwaran to the Karadan Adri took little time. Sealed within the fuselage of the rocketing shuttle, Rane looked out over the undulating greenery that carpeted the rugged terrain beneath them. The Karadan Adri – constructed of white marble cut from the same quarries that had supplied the stone for Silas's palace – had been built on a shelf of land that gave out upon a high cliff overhanging the blue waters of the ocean. The great three-tiered house was itself nearly a palace, and groves of orange trees and gardens surrounded it on three sides. With all the gentleness of an alighting mosquito, the shuttle set down on a broad expanse of grass in the middle of one of the gardens. The fragrance of flowers – orange blossoms and roses and the strange, thousand-petalled lotus that grew only on Kailash Poru – filled the air. Through the thick perfume, Rane caught the salty scent of the sea smashing against the rocks at the base of the cliff five hundred feet below.

Armas Sarkissian's son, Santuu, met Rane and Nikolandru on the lawn. His intelligent blue eyes seemed ill-fitted to his jet black hair and ruby brown skin. His voice, too, seemed at odds with his slight body, for it boomed out of him in the kind of deep baritone that Rane had associated with large, fat men such as Bardo. Armas moved with a quickness and sureness that suggested his wiry limbs contained more strength than a casual observer might have supposed. The features of his handsome face might have been chiselled by a master sculptor, though Rane thought that the mouth was all wrong. The full lips should have been turned up in happiness at Santuu's many gifts and advantages; instead, they pressed together in a hard line of barely contained fury.

'Welcome to my home,' Santuu said. 'I am Santuu Sarkissian, son of Armas Sarkissian. I have arranged a luncheon on the veranda.'

He escorted Rane and Nikolandru down a cobblestone pathway around the side of the house. Flowers had been planted everywhere, and Rane took note of the roses, irises, and tulips familiar to him, as well as the blossoms with names like eustilla and the purple, nine-petalled pindara, which were strange to him. A broad veranda – roofed in blue stone held aloft by pillars thirty feet high – fronted the house's western side. It looked out over a well-trimmed lawn planted with more pindara bushes and a dozen orange trees. The lawn came to an end a hundred feet from the house, where the grounds of the Karadan Adri gave way to the edge of the cliff on which the estate had been built. From the veranda, Santuu explained, one could enjoy entire days of fragrant breezes and the vista of the western ocean far below.

Rane followed Santuu up a few shallow steps onto the veranda. The day's heat immediately seemed to bleed away into a delicious coolness emanating from the veranda's white marble flooring. A great black stone table inlaid with lapis, onyx, sugi-lite, and mother-of-pearl had been set with bone china and silverware as for a feast. As Santuu showed Rane and Nikolandru to their places, the feast began arriving on platters of food borne by naukars wearing white cotton chitons and the inescapable gold collars. There were sushis cut from the living bodies of molluscs such as clams and the simpler native cephalopods. There were soufflés and rice dishes bathed in sauces of wine and bubbling cheese – and caviar, curried lentils, salads, pistachio nut pâtés, and pastries. Rane couldn't imagine how twenty people could eat so much food, though he noticed not a single meat dish at the table. Santuu explained that he could not countenance the eating of anything that 'had a face'. To slaughter an animal for its flesh, he said, was as barbarous as it was bloody.

Just as a naukar pulled out Rane's chair, a young woman wearing an iridescent caftan came out of the house and strolled onto the veranda. Her face seemed cut from the same chromosomes as Santuu's, though she had dark eyes and fairer skin: when one rolled the genetic dice, Rane thought, it was hard to say how they would fall. Santuu introduced this striking woman as his sister, Tajasha. She sat at the table next to Santuu, who faced Rane.

After Santuu said a prayer thanking the Four Architects of the Harvest for the bounty they enjoyed, he passed Rane a dish of salmon caviar, and said, 'Please tell us about yourselves and the Order on Neverness.'

There ensued a round of pleasantries and polite conversation as the Sarkissians made acquaintance with Rane and Nikolandru. When the forms of hospitality had been observed, Santuu looked at Rane and said: 'Lord Inay informed me that you have very personal reasons for making inquiries of the slave Maria.'

Rane shifted in his chair, and he said, 'I never told Lord Inay that.'

'You didn't have to. Do you think our Lord Examiner is a fool?'

'Well, you could say that I knew Maria somewhat. In Neverness, we were part of the same circle of—'

'Do you think *I* am a fool?' Santuu said, most inhospitably. 'Our conversation will go better if you admit that you were enamoured of Maria.'

'I wouldn't quite put it like—'

'It is all right. Maria bewitched men with her charms, and my father was one of them.'

'Lord Inay suggested that your father wanted to marry Maria.'

'I am sure that he suggested no such thing. My father had enemies, and it is they who spread that slander about him.'

Santuu shot Tajasha a sharp, imperious look as if to warn her to silence. In the quiet that fell over the table, Rane said to Santuu, 'Is it a slander that your father forced Maria to his bed?'

Santuu waved his hand at this question as if shooing away a fly.

'My father had a weakness for beautiful women, and Maria was as ripe as a plum hanging overlong on a tree.' With his lips pressed together even more tightly, Santuu stabbed his knife through one of the fat, glaucous plums that sat on a silver plate near him. Juices spurted from the plum's broken skin, and he conveyed the speared fruit onto Rane's plate. 'I would not say, however, that my father had to *force* Maria. That is not the word I would use.'

'No? Then what word would you use to characterize the way one human being coerces another to his will?'

Again, Santuu waved his hand. 'Of course, you do not approve of our ways. Few do. And even fewer understand them.'

Rane took a drink of wine that one of the naukars serving them had poured into a crystal goblet near his plate. He said, 'I am one of those. We have visited a hundred planets on our journey here, and on not one did people think they could own each other.'

At this, Nikolandru shook his head slightly, and Rane could tell that he did not want Rane to broach the subject of slavery. Rane, however, couldn't help himself.

'Then more pity those people,' Santuu said. 'They would serve themselves better if they "forced" slaves to serve them.'

Rane watched as three young women wearing golden collars moved around the table, filling glasses and taking away plates. He said to Santuu: 'But why use human slaves when robots would work just as well?'

'Would they really?' Santuu caught the hem of the chiton of a black-haired slave named Uma and pulled her close to him. He took a soiled plate from her, set it down on the table, and grasped her wrists. 'Can you really say, Master Historian, that you would find it as pleasant to be served by a robot's hands as by these?'

Santuu pulled on Uma's wrists, the better to show Rane her opened hands.

'Can *you* really say,' Rane countered, 'that it is pleasant to rob human beings of their freedom and terrorize them into cleaning your dirty dishes?'

'No, you're right – pleasant is not the word I would use.'

'Then what is?'

'Satisfying – it is deeply, deeply satisfying to gain and exert mastery over another.'

Santuu's words boomed out, startling Rane with their naked brutality. 'At least you're honest,' he said.

'I will be as honest with you as I can, though I doubt if you will grasp the truth of what I will tell you.' Santuu took a long drink of liquid toalache as he regarded Rane. 'You are a great lord of the Order of Mystic Mathematicians and Other Seekers of the Ineffable Flame, so you claim – and you call many of these seekers novices, journeymen, and full professionals. Has it then never occurred to you that the world involves a natural order in which the few are elevated above the many?'

'We have a hierarchy, yes, but some would say that all men and women are created equal in their essential—'

'Only a fool,' Santuu interrupted Rane again, 'would believe that one man is equal to another. A fool – or one who is weak and powerless.'

'That is easy for you to say, since you were born to power.'

'You misunderstand my estate. I was born to position, not power. Real power cannot be inherited but only achieved.'

Rane loosed a long sigh. 'You're not the first to devote himself to such pursuits.'

'Of course I'm not. Human beings have always wanted what is good.'

'You equate power with goodness?'

'Of course I do! Look around you!' Santuu commanded. 'Is it not good to sit here on a pleasant day in this beautiful place that my grandfather's father's slaves built with the toil of their bodies? Is it not even better to eat the delicious food that *my* slaves have grown, harvested, cooked, and served out on our plates? Tell me that you do not think that it would be very good to take for yourself the beautiful Uma, whom you have been eyeing ever since you sat down to my table?'

Only then did Rane realize that he had looked once too often at Uma, whose deft motions and easy sensuality caused him to think of Maria. He scrubbed his fingers across his eyes, and said to Santuu, 'You mistake the good with the pleasurable.'

'What is good, then?'

'People have asked that question for thousands of years before Plato.'

'And who was Plato? A lord of your Order?'

'In a manner of speaking.'

'Then did this Plato ever declaim that what is good is all that heightens the experience of power, the will to power itself in man?'

'No, another of my order said that – and tyrants across a thousand planets and thirty thousand years have misconstrued the sentiment.'

'And how do you construe it, Master Historian?'

'How can power be called a good if it is not used to create the good?'

'But is it not good that we should feel coursing within ourselves the full force of life?'

'Can you not feel that without imposing your will upon others?'

'Not to its fullest extent,' Santuu said. Again, he took hold of Uma's wrist and pulled her closer to him. 'Only in the resolve to master others can we know the infinitely greater mercilessness of mastering ourselves. And only in this way can we develop our will.'

'Toward what end?'

'Toward being noble, wise, beautiful, and strong.'

Santuu began musing upon the great labour that only the rarest of men and women were able to undertake. He told of how a true master – one who had mastered himself – must ever strive to become vaster and deeper, like an ocean that forever fills itself from the infinite possibilities of its own being. A man should make of himself the one perfect expression of life that he, and he alone, was born to create.

As Santuu spoke, Rane couldn't help agreeing with much of what he said. Even more, he found himself softening to the *way* that Santuu told of his highest aspirations and thereby opened himself to all Rane's scepticism and scorn. So much yearning poured from Santuu, so much desire for the one beautiful thing that all people sought! And why shouldn't Santuu seek it too? Was he not at heart as human as anyone else? Wasn't there good in everyone? Didn't all women and men sense within themselves the same great swell of hope that swept across the universe like a single onstreaming wave?

Despite the savagery of slavery that had deformed Santuu's sensibilities, he yet retained something wondrous and childlike – or so Rane wanted to believe. Surely Santuu must long to cut away the leaden collar of conditioning that had constrained him and so escape the whole vile system of slavery! And then, just as Rane found himself wanting to like Santuu instead of hating him, Santuu finished his disquisition by embracing slavery ever more fervently:

'We might wish the world were other than it is,' he said, 'but it is only through the cruel necessity to exercise the full force of our will that we can take our place at the apex of life and so bring forth life's purpose.'

Rane rubbed his temple against the pain throbbing there. 'You think life's purpose is to torment your slaves and live off their sweat and blood?'

'Life itself is torment,' Santuu told him, 'and all life lives off other life.'

'That does not imply that humans must live off other humans. Are we cannibals, then?'

Santuu laughed at this at this, and he brought Uma's hand up to his mouth and nibbled along the fat part of her thumb. Then he pinched her cheek. 'I did not suggest eating one's slaves. Especially not one with a face as pretty as hers.'

'No – you speak of eating their souls.'

'How easily *you* speak hyperbole,' Santuu said.

'Do you deny that you cause your slaves great suffering?'

'No, I do not deny; I celebrate it.' Santuu pointed at the translucent spheres of golden-red caviar that clung to the tines of Rane's fork. 'The anguish of a slave is validated in the exaltation of her master in precisely the same way that these eggs torn from a salmon's living body have nourished you.'

'But how can you bear to inflict such anguish?'

'How can I bear *not* to?'

'Have you no compassion?'

'Look around you at the natural world. Where do you see compassion?'

'That is an old, old justification for cruelty.'

Santuu smiled at this. 'Power needs no justification – nor do the powerful.'

Rane took a sip of water, hoping to cool his anger. He breathed in and out slowly as he listened to the susurrus of the water running through pipes beneath the marble flooring: the clean salt water pumped up from the ocean that cooled the veranda's hard white stone.

'I wonder,' he finally said to Santuu, 'if you would speak such words if you or your beautiful sister had been made a slave.'

Tajasha, happy to have an entrée into the conversation, smiled at Rane and said, 'I'm afraid I would prove a very poor slave: I would poison my master's wine if he commanded me to serve him or I would slit his throat as he slept if he took me to his bed.'

'Would you really?' Rane asked. 'Then you would be impaled or crucified.'

'No, I would not: I would cut my own throat first. I am not afraid to die.'

'And that is precisely the point,' Santuu added, beaming at his sister. 'No one can *make* another a slave. It is fear that makes slaves of us, not other men.'

Rane did not know what to say to this. He took a long drink of toalache to wash the salty-slick taste of caviar out of his mouth.

'And that is why I have no compassion for slaves,' Santuu said, heedless of the naukars that brought out sherbets to clear their palates. 'They could have their freedom whenever they wish, but they choose servitude instead. They are slaves – heart, mind, and soul – and so why should I not rejoice in taking mastery over them?'

'I think we are beginning to argue in circles,' Rane said.

'Why argue at all? Did you come here to scold me for owning slaves?'

'No, I want to discuss Maria.'

'Then please do.'

Rane paused only a moment. 'Can you tell me how your father died?'

'I can tell you as much as I told the examiner who conducted the inquest, as much as I know, for my sister and I were five thousand miles from here at a friend's wedding when my father was murdered.'

'Murdered!' Rane called out. 'Lord Inay said nothing of that!'

'Did he not tell you that Maria was involved in my father's death?'

'Yes, but he provided no more details.'

'Then I shall.'

Santuu looked across the lawn and pointed at the waist-high stone wall that snaked along the edge of the cliff. Beyond the wall was empty air and miles of blue ocean.

'My father was last seen standing by the wall arguing with Maria,' Santuu said. 'That was some years ago, on the tenth day of the Feast of the Five Avatars, early in the evening.'

'What were they arguing about?'

'I don't know. As I told you, I was not there.'

'Strange,' Rane murmured to himself. And then he said to Santuu: 'Don't you think it's strange that a master should argue with a slave?'

'It is impermissible,' Santuu agreed. 'If Maria had been mine, I would have cut out her tongue the first time she disputed me. I would have blinded her the first time she cursed me with her evil eye.'

'Do you really think she had such power?'

'You never saw the way my father looked at her: it was as if a rakshashi had eaten his soul.'

'Surely it is you who now speaks hyperbole.'

'You think so? From the moment my father first saw Maria, about to be sat upon the spike in Onklash's central square, she cozened him with her lascivious smiles and her lying eyes. Then after, when he could not help himself, she used every wile and all her sex to enrapture him.'

'It sounds as if,' Rane said, 'it was she who enslaved him.'

Without warning, Santuu hammered the edge of his fist down upon the table with so great a force that his wine goblet toppled over and shattered into a thousand glistening fragments. Uma hurried up to clean up the broken glass, but Santuu turned in his chair and slapped her away. His face had flushed purple-brown, and red wine stained his caftan.

'Maria was *his* slave!' he shouted. 'He should have had her chained to the rocks on the beach so the crabs could tear her apart!'

Tajasha, sitting next to him, reached out to stroke his bruised hand as if he were a little boy who needed soothing. When he had calmed down, he croaked out, 'Instead, my father allowed Maria to murder him. He should never have removed her collar.'

'Are you claiming that she pushed him from the cliff?'

Santuu looked at Rane. 'They found my father's body on the shingle of the beach below. As he fell, he struck a rock, which decapitated him. The gulls had gone to work on his head, and the examiner had to do a DNA test to certify that it *was* my father.'

'Perhaps he only stumbled – why shouldn't you think it was an accident?'

Santuu pointed across the lawn at the stone wall that edged the cliff. 'The wall is too high to just *stumble* over.'

'Perhaps he sat upon it and lost his balance.'

'No, my father forbade anyone to sit on the wall – even himself. Maria must have grabbed him and heaved him over. She was strong, Maria was, in the body and the hips.'

'You mentioned a groundskeeper who witnessed them arguing – did he witness anything more?'

'Apparently not.'

'May I speak with the groundskeeper?'

'No, you may not. Unfortunately, he did not survive the questioning that attended the inquest.'

'Unfortunately, indeed,' Rane said. 'Then no one actually *saw* her push him?'

'What else could have happened?'

Just then a naukar appeared with a bag of ice that Tajasha had ordered. As Santuu took a drink of wine from a newly filled glass, she wrapped the ice around his now-swollen hand. She seemed ready to say something, but Santuu silenced her with one of his disapproving looks.

'What about the other naukars?' Rane asked.

'They worshipped him. My father treated slaves better than did anyone on Kailash Poru – much better than he should have.'

'Perhaps one of them did not think so.'

'No, it is impossible. The naukars' collars track their every movement.'

So saying, he hooked his finger through the collar of a naukar named Ananda and pulled her close to him. 'Every word they speak, every step they take – all is recorded.'

Ananda, fat and old and wise to Santuu's ways, smiled to convey the impression that she appreciated his attentions.

'Lord Inay mentioned,' Rane said, 'that Maria fled with a merchant who was a guest in your—'

'We have a record of that, as well,' Santuu said, releasing his hold on Ananda. 'The cameras hidden in the merchant's room recorded that Maria rendezvoused with him around the time my father would have fallen. Less than an hour later, they fled.'

'That must have required perfect coordination and a cold heart: Maria would have had to murder a man and then moments later knock on another's door.'

'Yes – she had the sangfroid of a snake.'

'Are you saying that in a matter of minutes, she seduced the merchant, coupled with him, and persuaded him to—'

'She had already seduced him, with those damn eyes of hers. And how much persuading do you think is necessary for a man who is bewitched?'

Because Rane could not answer this question – or rather, did not want to – he took solace in sipping at his wine. Santuu smiled a cruel, triumphant smile as if he was happy indeed to have proved his point.

That might have been the end of the conversation, or at least of Rane's inquiries, if Rane hadn't recalled just then the precise wording of something that Lord Inay had said to him. He now regurgitated these words: 'Lord Inay informed me that one way or another, Maria had caused your father's death. We have discussed the one way – what do you suppose might have been the other?'

Again, Tajasha looked at Santuu with doubt and plaint filling her dark eyes, and again Santuu flashed her a scowl that commanded obedience. This time, however, she did not surrender to silence. Perhaps she could not bear the way that Santuu had gloated over the deflection of Rane's questions; perhaps she could not bear to bite back words that she so obviously wished to say. Whatever her reasons, she now spoke – and so from the ancient grudge of childhood hurts and Santuu's lifelong domination of her, she broke forth to perhaps her first mutiny:

'There might be,' she said, 'another possibility.'

Again, Santuu hammered the table, this time with his other hand. 'Do not bother our guests with speculations that might only confuse—'

'My father,' Tajasha said, speaking over him, 'kept journals. Most concerned—'

'Uma! Ananda! Lalita!' Santuu shouted out the names of the naukars serving them and waved his hand at them. 'Leave us!'

After they were alone, Tajasha continued: 'Most of my father's journals concerned his thoughts on his life: a record of problems with slaves, arguments with family, finances, his difficulty in limiting his wine-drinking – that sort of thing. He spent thousands of pages analysing his actions and making resolutions as to how he could perfect himself. One of the journals, however, was devoted to Maria. We found it under his mattress after his death.'

'May I see this journal?' Rane asked.

'Sadly, no. The examiners took it away for the inquest.'

'Did you never ask for it back?'

'We did, but our request was denied. I'm sure the examiners destroyed it.'

'Why?'

Tajasha glanced at Santuu, who sat in his chair sulking and glowering at her. He clearly wished to muzzle her, but short of clamping his hand over her mouth, there was nothing he could do.

'My father wrote things that no owner of slaves should ever write. Earlier, you asked my brother if he had no compassion for slaves. Well, my father had too much.'

'You think so?'

Tajasha nodded her head. 'He said that any punishment a master inflicted on a slave, he inflicted on himself – only magnified ten times. He wanted to free all our slaves, but of course he couldn't do that.'

'Why not?'

'Why, how would we live?'

Rane pointed out across the lawn. 'You could pluck oranges from your trees and gather crabs on the beach. They don't have much in the way of faces.'

At this, Tajasha waved *her* hand in the air, a gesture that she must have learned from Santuu.

'My father,' she continued, 'wanted to free Maria – and not by just a temporary manumission. He *did* want to marry her.'

'That is a lie!' Santuu thundered.

'It is not a lie!' Tajasha looked from Santuu back to Rane. 'He wrote of his feelings for Maria, how he thought about her every moment of every hour – and how each moment he couldn't be with her seemed as long as a year.'

'He was mad with desire!' Santuu said. 'Swiving that witch had rotted his brain.'

'Calling her a witch does not change the fact that she had a great deal of charm. And there was a gentleness about her that—'

'Were she here now, I would crucify her just so that you could feel the venom she would spit into your eyes.'

'Well, I would not.' She turned toward Rane, and said, 'My father wrote that if Maria did not return his affections and agree to be his wife, his life would be meaningless.'

Rane turned these words over and over in his mind as he sipped his bittersweet toalache. He wished he had a stronger drug to drink: something that would paralyse the muscles of his face so that he would not betray what he was thinking.

'Then Maria,' he finally said to Tajasha, 'was not enamoured of your father?'

'Oh, no – she was wild about him! Lack of affection had nothing to do with Maria's refusal of my father's wish to marry her.'

'Then what did?'

'Three things above all, I think.' Tajasha held up a finger. 'First, Maria abhorred the idea of becoming a perfecti herself and owning slaves. And second, she very badly wanted children.'

These words slid into Rane's ears with all the sear of molten silver. He managed to force out, 'And your father did not?'

'He thought it would be disrespectful to Santuu and me.'

Rane smiled grimly at this. Santuu probably would have strangled any Sarkissian baby that came out of Maria's body.

'You mentioned a third reason?' he said.

'Yes – my father wrote of his sense that Maria had a purpose that had impelled her journey and had impassioned her, though apparently she never mentioned what that might be.' Tajasha looked off at the sky. 'He said that he feared that Maria could never be happy with him – and so all the days of his life would be a torment.'

'He used that word?'

Tajasha nodded her head. 'His last journal entry told of his despair. He wrote that he did not want to live without her.'

'I understand,' Rane said softly. 'Then you think he took his own life?'

'I am sure that he did – right after the argument with Maria of which my brother has spoken.' She pointed at the white stone wall at the edge of the cliff. 'No one had to throw him over.'

Rane turned in his chair to gaze at the wall. Perhaps the wall's white stones, he thought, held a memory of what had happened on that evening years ago.

'I would like to look at the wall,' Rane said.

Without waiting for Santuu's permission, he stood up and strode across the lawn. Santuu and Tajasha followed him. Nikolandru, pausing to refill his wine glass, did too. When Rane reached the wall, he planted his hands on the top and moved as if to mantle himself up upon it.

'We still have a rule that no one may sit here,' Santuu warned him.

With a set of smooth, coordinated motions, Rane vaulted himself up so that he stood upon the wall. Tajasha gasped in fear as Rane steadied himself and looked down. The mass of the cliff supporting the wall mostly overhung the cliff's base: it would be nearly an unimpeded fall to the broken grey shingle of the beach five hundred feet below. Only a few sharp rocks jutted out into space to keep one from plunging straight down. Armas Sarkissian must have struck his head on one of these.

'I'm not sitting,' Rane said to Santuu.

And Santuu replied: 'Come down immediately!'

'Yes, please come down!' Tajasha urged him.

Rane continued gazing down at the beach and ocean's incoming tide which sent waves roiling and frothing across the beach rocks. He listened to the white gulls cawing out warnings to each other as they hunted for clams and other shellfish churned up by the surge of the sea. After a while, he hopped down from the wall. Santuu, he thought, was right: Maria could have easily taken hold of Armas and heaved him over it.

'It is a difficult decision you must make,' Santuu said, 'is it not? Was the woman you've pursued across half the galaxy a murderer? Or did she surrender her heart to another?'

Rane whipped about to face Santuu. He had tried very hard not to hate this cruel, contemptuous man; as he stared at the mocking smile that deformed Santuu's lips, however, he finally failed.

Perhaps thinking that it would be easier for Rane to know

that Maria could not have murdered her father, Tajasha said, 'There is a record that I think makes things clear.'

'What sort of a record?' Rane asked.

Tajasha glanced at Santuu. 'We never told the examiners about it, but my father made a visual record of his and Maria's private moments together. There are solidos.'

'What are those?'

'Moving holograms. Anyone viewing them would see how passionate Maria was and that she obviously cared about my father.'

'It was not obvious to me,' Santuu said, smirking at Rane. 'She was *too* passionate – no woman could be so inflamed. To her talents of witchery and bloodlust, we must add the skills of a consummate actress.'

Rane looked back and forth between Santuu and Tajasha even as with another sense he gazed inward at the images that flickered through his mind more vividly than could any hologram.

'You don't believe me?' Santuu said to Rane. 'Would you like to see the solido?'

'No!' Rane croaked out.

'Are you sure?'

Rane stared at the Adam's apple that bobbed up and down in Santuu's throat as he spoke. How easy it would be, he thought, to strike out and crush it, as he done with Batar Bulba.

'Come,' Santuu said, 'why don't I see if I can find the solido?'

Upon considering that the naukars might succour Santuu before he choked to death, Rane suddenly changed his plan. He would reach out across the two feet of air that separated him from Santuu, and he would grab hold of him. He was taller than Santuu and more heavily muscled, despite the depredations of journeying through space. It would be an easy thing to push him back toward the wall – and then to heave him up and over it.

'Of course,' Santuu added, 'we should really review it together in private. You've never heard a woman scream as Maria did. It was enough to have awakened the—'

'No!'

No, Rane suddenly decided, he would *not* heave Santuu over the wall. He would clasp his slight body close, chest to chest, so tightly that it would crush the air out of him. Then he would throw both of them over the wall together. His eyes burned to see them plunging through empty space together, the rocks of the cliff flickering by in a blur, the little stones that carpeted the beach growing bigger and bigger and ever closer. Every cell in his body cried out for him to do this bitter deed. Every muscle quivered to fire into contractions: the deadly and final motions that would put an end to two hateful lives.

And then Nikolandru, taking a step toward the wall as if he wished to look over it, stumbled and fell toward Rane as he called out, 'Oh, damn wine! I've drunk too much!' Without thinking, Rane took hold of him to keep him away from the wall. Spilled wine doused Rane's kamelaika even as Nikolandru grabbed onto Rane's arm with a surprisingly fierce and powerful grip. Rane could hardly move, much less close the distance between himself and Santuu.

'Why did you let me drink so much?' Nikolandru asked Rane. 'Have you no pity, friend?'

Santuu, as Rane saw, had started back toward the house – probably to follow through on his threat to retrieve the solido. Although Rane still trembled with a wrath to kill, he realized that the moment was lost.

'No, I don't want to see the damn solido!' he called out. 'And I don't want to see any more of your damn world. Thank you for lunch and all your hospitality.'

He turned to walk across the Sarkissian estate to the waiting shuttle. As soon as its shiny aluminium doors sealed themselves around him, he would begin composing a report for Lord Silas Inay. One question burned in his mind: what would he say?

20

And so once again, Rane returned to the *Asherah* and consented to confinement within the coffin of Nikolandru's lightship. In the peace of the passenger compartment, Rane floated in silent darkness, and he tried to make sense of what had occurred on Kailash Poru – and along the way of his journey leading up to that hateful planet. With the remembered smells of oranges and sea salt vying with the reality of the stench of stale air, he tried to escape from the chains of physical sensa into contemplation of a different sort of bondage. He turned over and over in his mind a question that resonated with a conundrum that he sensed lay at the heart of his quarrel with life: what did it mean to be a slave?

The word had many connotations; the most obvious concerned those aspects of the world that brutally constrained one's physical freedom. Of course, it was a terrible thing to have a golden collar locked around one's throat and to tremble every day under a perfecti's threats of torture and death – but wasn't it worse, in a way, to dwell in a lightless prison cell of one's own making, where the simplest motions of the inner life became impossible because one had amputated vital parts of the soul? And what cruel master executed such punishment? Had the Buddha been right, after all, in attributing the bondage of being attached to one's unquenchable desires?

Armas Sarkissian, he thought, had certainly been enslaved in a very real way by his desire for Maria, even as Santuu Sarkissian's urge to control and torment the people around him clipped his wings and kept him shut away within a gilded cage. On a higher plane, men such as Bardo could never be happy without enjoying all the pleasures of the body and the mind, while Nikolandru needed to compose sublime verse, a desire that impelled him on a journey to an almost certain death. The gods of the galaxy cast aside every scruple and the last vestiges of their humanity in their rage to work their will upon creation and so become more. Even the rarest of beings – Rane thought of Danlo wi Soli Ringess, who wanted to become a sort of infinite sky where others might soar like great white thallows – were limited by their very desire to free themselves from all limitations.

And what about Rane himself? For what did he most yearn? What force impelled the atoms of his body to align in one direction only and to move as with a purpose that he could not resist?

You are what your deep, driving desire is . . .

Such questions led him to others and inevitably brought him face to face with the spectre that had haunted his dreams for many millions of miles. It fought its way up from the blackest pools of mind and memory into the light of cold consciousness that he now shone upon it. Why, he asked himself, had he *really* wanted to remain on Nepenthe? What was the dark, unmentionable thing that he had not been able utter, even to himself?

I want to die, he finally admitted. *I desire death*.

The whales of Agathange, he remembered, speak of quenging from star to star as they might swim from one island in the ocean to another. How much simpler it would be for Rane (and for everyone who knew him) if he could just quenge *into* the fire of one hot blue star or another and be done with things!

Hadn't he always known, in his blood, that his quest to have and to hold Maria again was hopeless? Hadn't he undertaken it only because he couldn't end his life by his own hand? Yes – yes he had, for he lacked the courage for such easy liberation. Ah, but what if the dangers of his headlong plunge into the galaxy's deadly stars did the killing for him? Or what if the Solid State Entity, outraged at the hubris of his request, simply annihilated him with no more qualm than She would have at squashing a worm? Then who could say that the great Thomas Rane had become a suicide and therefore disgraced himself as the most cowardly kind of murderer?

With this realization, Rane called for a consultation with

Nikolandru. They put down on the very civilized world of Gavriel's Gambol, although they avoided the resorts along the Gold Coast, with their famous restaurants and pleasure domes. Instead they camped out in a wooded mountain meadow far from this pretty planet's concentrations of population. Around them, they had acres of green grass and a clear line of sight of the snowy peaks of the Pearl River Mountains. After the stultification of the *Asherah*, Rane almost rejoiced in the breathing of crisp, sweet air again.

In the cool of a starlit evening, Rane found a pair of boulders on which they could sit face to face and discuss things. He said to Nikolandru, 'I'm finding it harder and harder to be shut away.'

'After Kailash Poru, who could blame you? That planet is like a prison.'

'Yes, and in their fear of their slaves, the perfecti make prisoners of themselves.'

'I think Santuu Sarkissian would have done well to fear *you*. I've never seen anyone hate another so much.'

'Was it so obvious?'

'I was sure you were ready to throw him off the cliff.'

Rane stared at the palms of his hands. 'Well, I wanted to.'

'I was sure that you were going to throw yourself off with him.'

'Ha!' Rane called out. 'Why would I do that?'

His words thundered out across the meadow and found echo in the rocks that surrounded them. The question seemed to answer itself.

'I'm sorry,' Nikolandru said, 'for splashing wine on you, but I've grown much too fond of you to let you go over the wall.'

'I assure you that I was in no danger.'

'Really?'

'Really.'

'All right then, I'll have to trust your word.'

'All right. Yes. Good.' Rane grew quiet for a moment as he looked at Nikolandru. Then he asked, 'Are you a cetic, that you can descry the intentions of others by reading their faces?'

'No, I'm a pilot – and a poet who must at least try to look into the hearts of those he would sing about.'

'Well, don't worry about singing of me. The journey is over.'

Nikolandru picked up a stone and cast it at a slender aspen

tree twenty yards away. It was a lucky throw, for the stone hit the trunk dead centre with a thunk that reverberated through the still air. And he asked, 'What do you mean, the journey is over?'

'I want to return to Neverness. There's nothing left for you to sing about.'

'How wrong you are, friend!'

'Will you sing of a coward who abandoned his quest before reaching the hardest part?'

'*Have* we yet to reach the hardest part? On Kailash Poru—'

'I've learned as much about Maria as I want to. I've also learned that what I have wanted all these days and light years is impossible.'

'But how do you know it is impossible until you've explored all the possibilities?'

Rane smiled grimly at this as he recalled something that Danlo wi Soli Ringess had once said: *How is it possible that the impossible is not only possible but inevitable?*

'If there is no more you wish to learn about her, then why not proceed to our ultimate objective?' Nikolandru's smile brought out the gleam in his eyes. 'By great good fortune, your search for your lover has taken us closer to the Solid State Entity. The goddess lies there.'

He pointed up above the Pearl River Mountains, whose white snowfields shone in the light of the thick swathe of stars of this part of the galaxy's Orion Arm. He identified for Rane the brilliant bit of fusion fire known as Perdido Luz. Beyond that famous yellow star glowed the polychromatic gases of the Eta Carina Nebula. And very close to that celestial wonder, the cloud of stars taken over by the Solid State Entity's millions of moon-brains beckoned like a beguiling artwork painted with a hundred thousand points of light.

'I will sing of this beauty to any who will listen,' Nikolandru said.

'That beauty, as you call it,' Rane said, 'has killed the pilots of my order as we might mosquitoes. Mallory Ringess told of this.'

'She did not kill Mallory. She did not kill Danlo wi Soli Ringess.'

'Am I Danlo? Am I Mallory Ringess?'

'No, you are the Order's greatest remembrancer, and it is said that She has devoted Herself to exploring the mystery of memory and creation.'

'Then let Her continue Her explorations without my assistance.'

'Don't you think it's possible that your desire to revive Maria would excite the Entity's curiosity?'

'That is what I once told myself.'

'From curiosity, it is but a small step to understanding and another to compassion.'

'The Entity will kill us,' Rane said, 'most likely long before I can speak to Her, if one can really speak to a goddess.'

'I can't let you give up,' Nikolandru said.

'If you're so eager to die, you should have waited for me to go over the wall and *then* taken hold.'

'It is you who are eager to die. But not as much as you are to live.'

Rane gazed at Nikolandru through the dark air. 'I'm eager for *you* to live. You have much to live for.'

'I will live as I never have if we go to a place where no poet has ever gone. So will you.'

'A casual observer of our discussion might think that it was *you* who was making a quest to the Entity.'

'I am,' Nikolandru admitted. 'It is thought that the Entity was once a warrior-poet and still lives by poetry. I wish to discuss with Her the essence of the poetic.'

'Nothing more?'

'I would ask Her if She had ever come across Placida Lovita's lost poems, said to be the most beautiful ever written.'

'Nothing more?'

'What more should there be? Of course, I would have you complete *your* quest so that I can sing—'

'No, there's no chance of that.'

'There *is* a chance,' Nikolandru said. He pointed up at the sky some thirty degrees above the ghostlike peak of the mountain to the west of them. 'The brightest of chances.'

Rane looked along the line of Nikolandru's finger. The stars above this wilderness stood out brilliantly against the blackness of space, and there were many of them, thousands and thousands of fusion fires throwing out sparks into the emptiness of space. Where Nikolandru pointed, the stars thickened into a fountain of light, and sprays of pink, turquoise, and blood red drew Rane's eye and all his hopes up into the stars' swirling centre.

'The Solid State Entity, at last,' Nikolandru said. 'Shall we come so close and go no farther?'

'But what if the Entity really has taken up residence on Old Earth?'

'What if She has not? What if She has moved Old Earth here?'

'I'm sorry, but I've lost my desire.'

'Your *desire*? Can you lose your brain? Your heart? Was it or was it not you who wrote these words?

'In that forever rising radiance,
You showed me the sun,
And my star blazed in your fire,
And I knew myself alive.'

Had he really written the lines that Nikolandru recited, Rane wondered? How could Nikolandru have known if he had? Had his researches into Rane's and Maria's lives really gone so deep?

'I won't let you turn back,' Nikolandru said. 'It's become my desire to see your desire fulfilled.'

He stood up from his rock, and stepped up to Rane. He beamed a smile at him. He reached out to clasp Rane's shoulder as if to impart to him his certainty that the deepest desire of the universe could be nothing other than the brightest of love.

'All right,' Rane said, smiling back at this warm, lively man, 'then we'll go on.'

They returned to the *Asherah*, gleaming in the dark meadow like a huge needle of spun diamond. Their quest resumed. As Rane floated in the lightship's passenger compartment, he could only guess what mathematical theorems and topological puzzles Nikolandru must find his way through in navigating the strange spaces of the manifold. In their long, long journey across the Sagittarius and Orion arms of the galaxy, Rane had learned almost all of the arcane mathematics that the pilots call upon in practising their beautiful but nearly impossible art. That the pilots' prowess in falling from star to star through all the twisting torsion spaces, fragmenting fractals and such should be called an art and not a science Rane deeply appreciated. For it is one thing, for instance, to prove by simple calculus that launching a stone at a given velocity into space at an angle of forty-five degrees will carry the stone the maximum distance; it is another matter altogether to feel out with eye, muscle, and nerve the precise angle with which to make such a throw. How many years did the arduous training of a journeyman pilot take? What was it like to immerse oneself for many days at once in the spacetime-annihilating tanks of the Rose Womb Cloisters in order to get a feel for piloting a lightship through the manifold? Journeymen had to impress into nerve and the mind's eye the hideously complex rules of interfenestration so as to open and pass through the manifold's windows at a speed that would have disoriented or blinded the uninitiated. They had to make many, many journeys across the well-known pathways of the Stellar Fallaways before daring the much wilder spaces of the unmapped part of the galaxy.

And even so, as the saying went, journeymen died. So, too, did pilots. Even the best of them might make a mistake mapping through an especially treacherous part of the manifold and fall out into realspace into the hot, hellish heart of a blue giant star. And some of the best of the best had died in the manifold beneath the stars of that very nebula toward which the *Asherah* now hurtled. They had died because the Silicon God's attacks upon the Solid State Entity in the war they had been waging upon each other for three hundred years had deranged the manifold beneath the stars of the Entity: some said that a chaos space might someday propagate outward from the centre of the Entity and render the entire manifold unmappable. And the pilots had also died because the Entity had killed them: when Wicent li Towt and Erendira Ede attempted the manifold beneath the spaces of Her moon-brains, She ensnared them within the branchings of a decision tree from which they could never escape. So it had been with Alexandravondila, Ishi Mokku, and the great Ricardo Lavi. And with Jemmu Flowtow and Atara of Darkmoon. And even the Tycho, whose brain She severed so that She could copy every synapse and molecule and absorb his consciousness into a memory space, there to savour and enjoy for as long as the stars whirled and shone.

And so while Rane floated and waited and imagined what sort of mathematics Nikolandru plied in the pit of the lightship, the pilot-poet mapped his way from Perdido Luz to Vajra to the twin blue stars known as Athena's Eyes and then on to many others. At last, they penetrated the outer veil of gases enveloping the many stars and moon-brains of the nebula that the Entity had taken over. The *Asherah* fell on, deeper into the Entity's lightsome and intelligent substance, for the whole of the nebula could be thought of as a living, superluminal organism a-shimmer with thoughts and conceptions of the universe measureless to any man. They fell along streams of radiance in realspace, and they tunnelled through the torsion spaces beneath, and Rane thought that it was as if their diamond lightship was a bacterium burrowing deeper and deeper into a brain made of spherical neurologics the size of Old Earth's silvery moon – and all the many millions of moons pulsing, gathering in the energy of a hundred thousand stars and intercommunicating with each other through bursts of tachyons that streaked through the Entity nearly infinitely faster than light. How easy it would be, Rane thought, for the Entity to destroy the *Asherah*, as his immune system might eradicate an invading *Streptococcus*! But how easy to overlook a single small lightship and the two determined men inside.

After many days (or what passed as days in the time sickness of too many days aboard a lightship), Nikolandru and Rane put down on a little planet that orbited a huge red star known as Kamilusa. Mallory Ringess had once visited this lost world, whose know-nothing peoples had no idea that they lived out their inane lives within the corpus of the galaxy's greatest goddess. Because Rane wanted to be alone with Nikolandru, they stood on a cold, dark plain empty of human habitation as they discussed what to do next.

'Well, here we are, and here we still live,' Nikolandru said to Rane with a smile.

Rane wore a thick wool kamelaika against the wind cutting through the evening. Above them, in the black dome of the sky, many stars twinkled.

'So it was with Mallory Ringess when he, too, stood on this planet,' Rane said. 'Then, when he tried to penetrate into the centre of this nebula, the Entity nearly killed him.'

'But at least She first spoke to him. Isn't that what you desire?'

'You know what I desire.'

'It would seem that the Entity can speak to anyone within these spaces whenever She desires. Why not, then, make toward the Earth that Danlo wi Soli Ringess told of?'

He pointed up a sector of the sky sixty degrees from the nebula's centre. His finger nearly touched a yellow-white star that he called the sun. 'You said that Maria claimed to have been born on Earth. Haven't we been seeking her birth world as well all these many light years?'

'She can't have been born on Danlo's Earth. He reported that the planet he visited was uninhabited.'

'Would he have known what secrets an entire planet can hide?'

Through the dark air, Rane looked at Nikolandru. 'There are at least 361 Earths in the galaxy. Maria might have come from any of them.'

'But there is only one *Earth*. Didn't Danlo also wonder if the Entity had moved the sun and the solar system of Old Earth to this nebula?'

'It's known that Old Earth occupied the spaces not far from the Rainbow Double and the Silicon God.' Rane shook his head. 'It's not possible that the Entity could have moved the sun and nine planets across nearly ten thousand light years of space full of stars.'

'Who knows what is possible? You thought we had no chance of coming this far.'

'But why, even if She could, would the Entity do such a thing?'

'Well, there's something fabulous, isn't there, about moving an entire star?'

'I think you like the idea of adding the discovery of Old Earth to your epic.'

'It would be a great thing to sing about, wouldn't it? Almost as great as the great Thomas Rane's recovery of his lost love.'

'Now you're mocking me.'

'No, I'm encouraging you. Don't you long to stand before the goddess and look into Her eyes as you ask Her to make your miracle?'

Rane gazed up at the stars. 'Who said anything about looking into Her eyes? I might as well wish to be blinded by looking into the sun.'

'Then you don't wish to behold the goddess in Her human form as Kalinda?'

'We don't know that She still *has* a human form. That might be a myth.'

'It's known, isn't it, that the Solid State Entity began as a warrior-poet who created the Entity's moon-brains to amplify the power of Her own?'

'That is *believed*. But even if true, that warrior-poet might have died long ago, leaving only the machine part of Her substance.'

'But what if the warrior-poet still lived?' Nikolandru smiled mysteriously. 'What of that poet part of her? The *woman* part? How might she feel about your desire for Maria to be restored to you? Don't you think you would have a better chance of charming her if you stood before her face to face?'

'I might. I just might.'

'Shall we then make for that star and determine if it really is the sun? And then see what we see?'

'All right,' Rane said. He smiled at this strange poet he had come to like if not entirely trust. 'Who knows what secrets we might uncover there?'

They returned to the lightship and resumed their journey. For three days straight, whatever a day really was, Nikolandru piloted the *Asherah* through dangerous, shifting inversion and jellyfish spaces unseen by Rane but strangely sensed through his deepening feel for the mathematics of the manifold. It seemed to Rane that any of these spaces might engulf or outright kill them at any moment, especially the chaos spaces that broke apart like shattered stained-glass windows only to be reassembled a moment later into patterns that only the finest of pilots such as Mallory Ringess or the Sonderval had ever been able to perceive and therefore escape. For most of this time, Rane vacillated between the cold fear of annihilation and his burning memories of Maria, which anchored him to life. Adrenaline poisoned his brain and exhausted him, and yet he could not sleep. Finally, however, as his naked body floated sweating and stinking in dead-still air, his mind floated off into unconsciousness and the realm of dreams.

Rane.

In dreaming as in waking, sounds come to life within the auditory cortex buried deep within the temporal lobes of the brain. There a voice murmured to Rane, and in its sweetness and musicality, no less its warmth and strength, he recognized the essence of Marianess that could belong only to a single person. In his dream, as in his memories of his life, Maria asked him once again what was wrong. She promised merely in the ardour of her voice to take him into an earthy yet cosmic place where nothing could ever be wrong again. Hers was the voice of a healer, an adventurer, a lover. He wanted to remain inside this dream listening to Maria forever.

Then, however, the voice grew colder and clearer – too clear and purpose-driven to have come from Maria, who had flitted from one experience to another like a golden-winged butterfly whose deepest purpose was to gather nectar from an endless succession of fireflowers and savour all the goodness of life. And, of course, to share that life with others and wake them up with sheer wonder. In the call and command of the voice that now sounded behind Rane's ears, he heard little that he would call the good. The voice grew louder and more irresistible, with an insistence on its inherent right to demand from him all and everything.

Rane Thomas, Thomas Rane Rane Rane – why have you come here?

His whole body jerked awake to the power of this voice, which seemed to pummel him from within and without. He blinked his eyes against the fur-like darkness that cloaked him. He shook his head. He listened. The passenger compartment filled with this new voice as if it had been taken over by another. That other moved the compartment's gaseous interior in precise patterns of air molecules making up the waves of sound that beat against his chest bones and eardrums. It was as if an unseen pair of lips moved and made of rushing breath simple words and meaning.

Why, why, why . . .?

Rane thought about this, and he wondered if he should state the truth and be done with it. But what was truth, really? Could he ever *really* know his deepest reasons for why he did what he did?

'If you are the one known as the Solid State Entity,' he said, 'then can you not look into my mind and tell *me* why I have come?'

You are like Danlo wi Soli Ringess and his father before him in that you answer questions with questions. I like that. But I will not permit that. Do you understand?

'What if I understand but don't consent?'

And again you ask when you should just respond. Are you so eager to die?

'Are you so eager to slay?'

Again, the molecules inside the lightship's passenger compartment moved, only this time those molecules were also inside Rane: for they jangled within the cornea, sclera, retina, and optic nerve of his eye. Rane's hand clamped hard over his forehead and face as he screamed. It felt as if a red-hot spike had been driven straight into his brain.

You are not here to test me. You are here to be tested.

Although Rane's agony did not lessen, his screams died within his throat and gave way to a gasping for breath. And in between gasps, he managed to force out, 'Good . . . then at least . . . I know . . . why I am here.'

The agony vanished into whatever willed hell from which it had come, though an after-burning of outraged nerves filled his eye like hot blood. Nothing but blackness could he perceive, and he worried that the Entity might have blinded him. Then he remembered that he had drifted off to sleep in the dark, as he always did.

You jest while dwelling deep inside your pain, and that is a rare thing. You make me smile.

'Can a goddess composed of computer circuitry that fills an entire nebula truly smile?'

What do you know of me?

'I know that now it is you who answers a question with a question.'

That is permitted, brave man, whoever you are.

'But you must know who I am. You called me by my name.'

Did I? Or did I only speak to your soul, which you heard as your name?

'But does anyone really have . . .?' He started to ask if the soul really existed before realizing that again he was about to answer a question with a question. As he was not eager to experience his head exploding into bloody bits, he choked off his words in mid-sentence. Then he said, 'I don't know what you spoke to or how I heard you speak.'

Not knowing is the beginning of wisdom.

'I have always found such sayings the beginning of triteness, if not outright mystification.'

That, too, is true.

'I have never claimed to be wise, otherwise I would not have journeyed here.'

The Shakespeare said this: a fool thinks himself wise, but a
wise man knows himself to be a fool. Tell me, my veracious,
foolish man, who are you?

'Who is anyone?'

And that is the truest question anyone can ask, though you
ask it as a rhetorical question only, and therefore I shall
regard it as a mantra originating in wisdom and not as
another invitation to pain.

'Thank you.'

You like to play, and I like that. Your pilot-poet likes to play,
too. At this moment, I am torturing him to reveal your name,
but he insists that it is not his to give. He insists on answering
my questions with poems meant to charm me.

'Please stop! My name is no secret. I'm called Thomas Rane,
though Rane is my given name.'
     Rane expected a more or less instantaneous response from
this unseen Entity jiggling the air molecules inside the *Asherah*
in order to speak with him, for it took less than an instant for
a million moon-brains to process the aesthetics and intricacies
of all the philosophies that human beings had ever conceived.
He had a strange sense, however, that he had startled Her and
made Her think before answering him. And in that pause which
hung suspended in time like a great frozen moon, he asked Her
this: 'You really didn't know my name?'

I have a new game that I play: except at need, I will listen to
another's thoughts only if freely offered to me.

'I can't . . .' When had he ever been able to let another inside
himself? Hadn't his self-containment always been Maria's
main trouble with him – almost the worst of Thomas Rane?
'I can't let you roam my mind, if I have any choice in the
matter.'
     In truth, the cetics (and Danlo) believed that the Entity could
not just rip into a man's brain and dig out all the secrets buried

there. No, it was said that She could perceive a thought, emotion, or memory only at the moment of one's thinking, feeling, or remembering.

There are many Thomas Ranes in this galaxy. But you are the Lord Remembrancer of the Order of Mystic Mathematicians and Other Seekers of the Ineffable Flame, are you not?

'Then you *have* looked into my mind. Or Nikolandru told—'

Given your name, the rest was easy to deduce. I know of Neverness. Tell me why you have journeyed from the City of Light across half the galaxy?

Against this very moment, Rane had prepared to obscure at least part of the truth through the practice of various cetic and remembrancer's attitudes of controlling the mind. Perhaps the Entity did play a game of not listening to his thoughts or perhaps She really couldn't until he had thought them. But he wanted to take no chances. And so he meditated even as he spoke, and he simultaneously entered the attitudes of imaging, gestalt, and dereism, where fancies become as if real while thoughts are directed away from reality. Through this prowess of mind and memory mastered by only one remembrancer in all of history, he hoped to confuse or evade the Entity if She *should* violate the most inviolate part of him.

'I am seeking,' he said, 'a woman named Maria.'

The silence that fell over him seemed deeper than the great emptiness between the stars. He had a strange sense that he had again given the Entity pause. She could think a trillion trillion thoughts in a nanosecond; he wondered if She could feel a feeling nearly as quickly.

Describe her to me.

And so he did. He spoke of Maria's radiant eyes and thick hair framing her lithe shoulders like a black mane. Her skin, he said, gleamed like amber but took on the darker tones of fireflower honey in false winter when touched by the sun. And her smile . . . her smile, so easy, so innocent, so wise, her glorious smile had always invited him into a place of warmth and delight, like a chalet's door opened in a storm to reveal the blaze of the hearth fires inside. Maria, he said, like the Entity Herself, liked to play. In Maria, the eternal cosmic game of *lila* played itself out in her purpose to live her life with both the zest of a wild animal and the exaltation of an angel and always – always, always, always – to bring to others the deepest of love.

'She is like no woman . . . I've ever known.'

Your Maria is less like a woman than a fantasia of one. Why are you seeking her?

'Who wouldn't seek such a woman?'

Why are you seeking her *here*?

'I'll gladly tell you, but only in person.'

You are inside my person, and cannot get further than that.

Rane let the aftersounds of the Entity's voice play through him. Did he sense in Her words the faintest tone of fear? As he knew very well, as Maria had taught him, fear could dwell close to desire.

'It's said that you incarnated as a tiger to test Danlo wi Soli Ringess and then took form as Tamara Ten Ashtoreth.' He took a deep breath in preparation for what he willed himself to say next. 'It's also said that you, a part of you, still live as the woman once called Kalinda. If I could stand before *that* woman on Earth as Danlo did Tamara, I would tell her anything she asks me to tell.'

You would place conditions on *me*? No, you will tell me all, here and now.

'I'm sorry, but I can't.'

Do you truly wish to test me?

'I've journeyed thousands of light years to ask a favour of Kalinda of the Flowers.'

Speak, man, of your purpose, or journey no farther.

'Then kill me if you wish. I'm not afraid of death.'

Brave man! Then let us find out what you do fear.

The instant the Entity spoke this word, pain exploded through Rane's chest as if a bomb had burst into fire there. He broke out into a sweat and gasped for breath, but that helped not at all, for the pain built into an agony. No matter how hard he tried to enter the nineteenth attitude of sanaesthesia and change this horrible experience into a sort of continually remembered dream, he could not escape his excruciation. Neither could he escape the certainty that, despite what he had said, he was horribly, terrifyingly afraid to die.

Men believe that heart attacks kill in a moment or debilitate before eventual death. But I can attack your heart forever.

'I don't . . . care.' How had he managed to force his racked breath past his grinding teeth in order to form these words? How could he bear another moment of such torture? 'What is that pain . . . against that of a heart already broken?'

And with that, the pain was no more. He floated sweating and coughing in his terrible remembrance of what he had just endured. He had the strange sense of someone watching him through an impenetrable darkness.

'If you do kill me this way,' he said, 'or keep me alive to wish for death, Nikolandru will sing of it, and that song will live in eternity.'

The memory of all things is in all things.

He went on to tell the Entity this; he said that the tale of his quest to ask a simple favour of a goddess would live on within the One Memory, there someday to be recovered when Sunjay or one of the other *Asta Siluuna* mastered the sixty-fourth attitude and told everyone about Thomas Rane and what he had dared to dream. His beloved students he called the Children would know all; the universe itself would remember.

He had little hope that he might persuade this unseen being

known as the Solid State Entity. He wanted, though, at the least, at perhaps the ending of his life, to tell the truth.

Lord Remembrancer, I would know more about this art of yours, for in a way, remembrance is everything.

Rane waited in the dark, listening to his still-ragged breathing. Had Maria been afraid of death? How could she have been?

I would know more about *you*, my poetic man, and how you have made of your life a poem. And so I will meet you as you wish, and you may ask your favour.

'Thank you! Then I will be the happiest—'

I did not say that I will grant your favour. You must continue to please me. Consider well and deeply how you may best do that.

'And if I do, then you will—?'

If you do, then you will live – until you do not.

'Do not what? Do not please you?'

He waited in the dark, silent deeps of the lightship for the Entity to say more, but no more did She have to tell him just then. The quiet surrounding him like an arctic night went on and on unbroken. Soon, perhaps tomorrow or the next day, Nikolandru would land the *Asherah* on a planet that might be Old Earth and then Rane would stand face to face with a living goddess.

Part Three

Wisest Child of the Deep

21

Nikolandru put the *Asherah* down on a broad beach on the coast of one of this Earth's northern continents. How many times had the lightship come to ground on some beach, meadow, desert, plain or star port? How many more times would it do so again? Perhaps never, Rane thought, for although he had deceived himself about many things, he did not want to fool himself into believing that he stood a good chance of charming the Entity to give him what he wished. Probably She would kill him for failing one of Her infamous tests, Nikolandru too, and that would be the end of the *Asherah*'s journeys.

Rane stood with his pilot-poet on hard-packed sands near the ocean's edge gathering strength into his wobbly legs. Although the gravity here was perhaps a shade more powerful than that of Neverness, it somehow felt just right. The whole Earth smelled right, as if something deep inside him recognized his ancestral home.

He looked around at the features of this part of the world. To the north, the beach curved off into a rocky headland. Beyond it, out in the water, a monolith of basalt rose up out of the waves like a great black lightship pointed always at the sky. To the east opened grassy dunes that gave out onto a coastal plain covered with grasses, bushes, and stands of trees. The Entity had provided Nikolandru with precise directions for their meeting: they were to walk from this spot across the plain toward the wooded foothills that rose in the east, orienting in a straight line toward a great snow-covered mountain shining in the distance.

This they did. It was a fine day of fresh breezes off the ocean, neither too hot nor too cold, and Rane felt comfortable wearing his black kamelaika and his scarf. The smells of salt, seaweed, and some almost imperceptible thing brought out identical scents from the scarf's rainbow substance, and Rane knew with a shock of recognition that this scarf had resided in this very place once before. He didn't quite know how he knew, and he doubted that he knew, for didn't many seashores smell very much the same? Still, he would have liked to linger on the beach, breathing in the same air and gazing at the same sparkling sands that he felt sure Maria had once known.

Their short journey took them along a path through shrubs and trees not nearly so tall as the oaks and pines that predominated in the foothills beyond them. From images that Rane had studied while aboard the *Asherah*, he identified pomegranate and cannabis, and fig trees, almond, persimmon, and tamarind. He saw kei trees, too, bearing round yellow fruits blushed with red, and many moringas, the so-called 'miracle tree' – the tree of life. He doubted that what amounted to a miles-wide orchard had come to grow here naturally, though what nature might mean on a planet such as Old Earth nearly once destroyed by megatons of poisonous chemicals, clouds of radioactive dust, and killer heat storms he couldn't say. He couldn't say why he believed this planet to *be* Old Earth. Maybe he just wanted it to be. Or maybe some deep part of him reached out as with fingers evolved here millions of years ago and through the sense of an inner touch remembered.

After a while, they came into a grassy clearing where many flowers grew. Songbirds warbled in the fruit trees to the music of a clear brook running over round rocks. The air smelled of ripe oranges. The Entity had bidden them to wait in this place. At the edge of the clearing, in the shade of a great moringa tree, stood a stone table around which had been set four stone chairs. Rane considered collapsing onto one of these chairs, for his legs hurt, and the short walk from the beach had tired him. He didn't, though, want to be caught slouching in a chair when a goddess walked into the clearing – *if* anyone came at all and this was not just some sort of a silly test.

'Are you all right?' Nikolandru took hold of his arm as if

to help him stand. The two men had hardly talked to each other since their last planetfall on one of the worlds that orbited Kamilusa. 'You look tired and hungry.'

'Are *you* all right? The Entity said that She tortured you.'

'No more, I think,' Nikolandru said with a smile, 'than She tortured you. We should consider well what we say to this woman, should we have the chance to say it.'

'*Is* She a woman then?'

'The one I spoke to certainly was. She had a woman's voice and a woman's ways. A woman's *soul*.'

Rane thought about this as he remembered the agony that had nearly ruptured his heart. 'Then we should also consider very well what we *don't* say.'

He eyed a fat, round fruit hanging from one of the lower limbs of a nearby orange tree. He badly wanted to pluck it, bite into it, and savour its sweet citrus tang, but he didn't want to be caught with a juice-smeared beard and sticky fingers in case the woman that Nikolandru had described really did show up. And it was a good thing he didn't, for that woman, whoever she really was, as much as she might like to play, did not keep them waiting long.

She came to them from out of the trees along the brook that flowed down from the foothills to the east. Her body – well-muscled, curvaceous, and rather short – moved with the same measured grace as did the great black-and-orange-striped tigress that padded along by her side. The woman had black hair and blazing black eyes that reminded him of Maria, though her skin was much darker, more the hue of a baru nut than Maria's honey-like covering. A lei of woven flowers sat upon her large head like a violet and red diadem; she wore a many-coloured dress that seemed wrought of the same chatoyant substance as the scarf tied around Rane's neck. A belt of black leather cinched the dress tight around her small waist, and from that belt hung a long, sheathed dagger: the exceedingly sharp and shining killing knife of a warrior-poet.

At the sight of that knife and, more, the tigress, Rane wanted to turn and flee. He noticed Nikolandru, too, eyeing both knife and beast. The woman walked right up to Rane and stopped, even as the tigress settled belly-down onto the grass, with her furry orange, black, and white head held up erectly. Both tigress and woman looked at Rane as if they could tear him apart with their eyes alone to look inside him.

'I am Kalinda,' the woman said, reaching out her hand toward him. He took it in his; her dirt-stained hand seemed both soft with invitation and yet hard with callus and healed cuts that hinted of a terrible power. 'They used to call me Kalinda of the Flowers.'

With a second shock of recognition, he realized that he had heard her voice before: in that evil room with Batar Bulba when the woman warrior-poet had spoken to him out of the universal voice of remembrance and had instructed his body in the terrible motions needed to nearly kill the awful Bulba. He listened now as this woman named Kalinda spoke to him in a clear, commanding voice at once feminine, rich, vibrant, and strong.

'You must be hungry, so we'll share a meal together and talk. Please sit down.'

She held out her arm toward the table as if by the force of muscle and hand she might ease Nikolandru and Rane into their chairs. They all moved through the clearing and sat, Kalinda between the two men. The tigress lay down again by Kalinda's side, watching and waiting – perhaps waiting for the food to arrive, for on the table was nothing more than four stone goblets and some plates woven of leaves, along with settings of chopsticks and steel cutlery.

'Tell me of your journey,' she said to Rane. 'Leave no detail out of your account.'

'I am a remembrancer, madam. If I recount every detail, we will be here many years.'

'I have been here three thousand years. I have all the time I need.'

'I, unfortunately, do not. My contract with Nikolandru will soon expire, as will I, for I have lived three lifetimes and cannot be brought back from senescence again.'

Rane felt proud of himself for being so forthcoming. Surely his honesty must have a good effect, mustn't it?

'You cannot be brought back by any art your people possess,' Kalinda corrected. 'But let's not speak of that now. Tell me of the planets you visited and why you did so.'

Rane couldn't do as she asked without mentioning the smells

embedded in Maria's scarf and the mechanism he had crafted out of human and computer memory to point the *Asherah* toward the planets that Maria had walked upon on her journey to Neverness.

'Remarkable,' Kalinda said, looking at Rane with a new curiosity. She fingered his scarf as if remembering. 'And resourceful. Now go on.'

And so he told about Parsig and Cilehe; he described the horror of the filthy streets of real Aracelli and the wonder of the nearly perfect dreamworld that the Aracellians had made from their computer simulations of the real. Of Kailash Poru, he said only a little. That little, though, Kalinda focused on like a hawk swooping down from a great height to seize a rabbit trying to hide in a bush.

'Clearly you agonize over whether your Maria pushed Armas Sarkissian over the wall. Is Maria a murderer? I wonder why that it so important to you.'

'I didn't say that it is.'

'Your eyes say all. So does your heart.'

'You gave me to understand, madam, that you would not look into my mind without my permission.'

This short woman who may or may not have been the living core of the goddess known as the Solid State Entity did not like to be reminded of her assurances to Rane. Quicker than he could have believed, her hand whipped down to grasp the carved bone hilt of her killing knife. He noticed the red ring encircling her hand's little finger. Only the most deadly of warrior-poets ever earned the warrior's red ring.

'I haven't looked into your mind, but your eyes tell entire epics of love and hate, and it would be a pity to cut them out. As for your heart, that is easy to feel.'

Rane's smile seemed to put her at ease, and her hand relaxed, opened, and slid off the knife's hilt onto the head of the tigress. The huge cat made a happy chuffing sound as her fingers caressed orange and black fur.

'I'm not sure,' he told her, smiling again, 'that Maria would have said that about my heart.'

'No? You loved her very much, and she loved you even more.'

'I never said that.'

'Don't play games with me, Rane.'

'I thought you liked to play.'

'Don't play with the truth. You might not like that game.'

Some pressure of her hand must have communicated to the tiger, for the beast let loose a great rumbling growl and sat up. It trembled as with a terrible tension as it stared at Rane. He remembered too well being torn apart in the Dreaming City by a different kind of tiger. If now this very real tiger smelling like sour butter and wrath clawed the liver out of his belly, he didn't suppose that it would grow back again.

'Of course they loved each other,' Nikolandru broke in. 'And a cosmic love it was, and is, like double stars sharing light – the same light that has called us on through much darkness.'

Kalinda's hand lifted off the tigress's head and came to rest on the table. Her other hand reached out to touch Nikolandru's face. It lingered there as if savouring the feel of his beauty. Then it slid down over his jaw, and came to rest lightly upon his muscular neck. A second red ring encircled that hand's little finger: the ring of a matchless poet.

'You have a lovely voice,' she said to him. 'It's been a long, long time since I've heard such a voice.'

Her fingers caressed his throat as if she might pull from him and hold onto that loveliness of sound. She smiled at him, lifted away her hand, and kissed her fingers.

'Brave pilot-poet,' she said. 'Lonely pilot-poet. I'm sorry that I could not keep Aoide from being destroyed. Your family—'

'Still lives because I live to sing about them. As they always will live in my poems.'

'Yes, you write lovely poems, and you might have been a warrior-poet except that you are too lovely to kill as we must kill.'

She looked at him for many moments as if searching in him for an innocence she longed to find within herself.

'I would like,' he told her, 'to hear the poems you have written.'

'They might be too terrible for you to hear.'

'Or too beautiful?'

'Is there a difference?'

'That,' he said, 'I would like to discuss with you.'

'You have come a long, long way to discuss it.' She reached

out to lay her hand on top of his. 'Is there nothing more you desire?'

'Only to ask if you know of Placida Lovita's lost poems.'

'Have you asked Rane how poems or anything can truly be lost?'

'I wasn't speaking mystically or metaphysically,' Nikolandru said, returning the clasp of her hand. 'It's said that these poems are like pearls of sound sparkling with the greatest of beauty.'

'Beauty,' she said, gazing at him. 'Beauty too rich for use?'

'If you know of these poems, I would give a great deal to hear them.'

'Would you give your life?'

'In a way, I already have. I've spent years of my life just so I might hear Placida's poems.'

'I thought you journeyed here so that you could sing of Rane's "cosmic" love.'

'That, too, is true. Isn't beauty just an emanation of love?'

Kalinda smiled at him. 'Your answer pleases me, beautiful man. Let's eat together and see if you and your heartbroken friend can please me even more.'

Rane studied the empty table, and he wondered if Kalinda might simply instantiate food upon their plates, even as the Entity had caused the *Asherah*'s air molecules to move or the Aracellians had made of computer code and memory the iced creams and other delicacies that the Aracellians liked to eat. But no food appeared by such technological magics. Instead, many edibles arrived by much more ancient and simple means: a troop of thirty or so bonobos, some bearing baskets beneath their long hairy arms, made their way through the woods toward the clearing. Their chattering drew Rane's attention, as did the naturalness of their gaits, for they moved much more easily on their long legs than did their close cousins, the chimpanzees. A few babies clung to the hair of their mothers' undersides while older juveniles rode upon their mothers' backs. Rane had only kithed the ancient accounts of these nearly bipedal apes, for unlike the many holograms made of the chimpanzees who had accompanied various human groups out into the stars during the Swarming centuries, no such visual record of bonobos existed for anyone to study. Rane had supposed these creatures who shared so much genetic material with human beings to have long been extinct.

'Shimuri, what do you have for us today?' Kalinda called out.

One of the adult females, her large clitoris waggling between her legs as she walked, came up to the table and set down her basket. It was half-full of moringa leaves, cattails, pine cones, and acorns gathered in the woods or the foothills above. Other apes, who had ranged down by the ocean, presented a bounty of mussels, clams, abalone, and seaweed. Kalinda kissed each of the bonobos in turn. Some desired more intimate connection than this, and these she touched between the legs, here caressing a moist vulva, there wrapping her hand around a stiff, skinny, pink phallus. Shimuri, her black fur gleaming in the light filtering down into the glade, apparently felt free to touch Kalinda at her pleasure, and this she did. Then Shimuri turned her attentions to Nikolandru, kissing his lips before running her fingers through his hair as if searching for lice. The other bonobos must have taken this as a signal that they should also make acquaintance with the two men. Rane couldn't guess if they were used to such company or whether Kalinda had somehow communicated to them that they needn't be afraid of these human strangers. Various bonobos – females and males, old and young and very young – came up to Rane and showered him with kisses and stroked his thick beard as if marvelling that hair could grow over his upper lip and his chin. For a moment, it seemed that they were back on the beach with Julior, Thena, and all the others of the royad again.

Rane couldn't understand why none of the bonobos seemed afraid of him, for hadn't human beings hunted their brother and sister apes nearly to extinction for the sake of a little bush meat? As well, it made no sense that one of the juveniles, a hairy imp whom Kalinda called Jimomo, felt free to hop on the tigress's back and bounce about before stroking the happy cat on the sensitive fur between her golden eyes.

'Jimomo, that's enough for now,' Kalinda said. She pulled the little ape onto her lap and kissed him. With her fingers, she made signs that Rane could not interpret but Jimomo seemed to comprehend. 'Yava has work to do.'

She set Jimomo on the ground, then reached down to tap the tigress on her side. 'Hunt,' she commanded.

With an explosion of muscles and bunching black and orange fur, the tigress rose from the grass and bounded off through the trees.

'Let's make our meal,' Kalinda said.

Why, Rane wondered, didn't this prepotent woman simply summon robots to prepare any number of savoury dishes that might have been assembled from the foodstuffs that the bonobos had gathered? Or, she could have imported the humans who lived their pampered lives on Kamilusa; she could have put golden collars around their necks and turned them into chefs and servitors. Instead she set to, building a fire from river rocks that she stacked and deadwood that the bonobos collected. She put Nikolandru and Rane to work, too. Pignolis needed to be got out of pine cones, oranges peeled, and flowers, stems, leaves, and seaweed mixed with a herb and quail-egg dressing to make a salad. Roots had to be roasted, and so did the clams and mussels, which Kalinda arrayed on the hot stones around the fire until they cooked through and opened.

The bonobos took charge of collecting most of the fruit, for they were great tree climbers who brought down from bough and branch the ripest of tamarinds, figs, persimmons, grapes, and other succulent sweets that made up most of their diet. However, upon occasion they also relished meat, and many of the younger apes specialized in collecting insect larvae and earthworms dug from moist soil. Much of this fare did not entice Rane, especially the fat, wriggling caterpillar which little Jimomo insisted on pushing between his lips. He was happier with the guava that an ape named Oma presented him, for he was very hungry, and he felt free to munch on such appetizers while working, as did the bonobos and Nikolandru and even Kalinda herself.

He had some doubts when the main course arrived: for Yava padded into the clearing with a bleating baby rock goat clamped between her jaws. He almost couldn't watch as Kalinda took it from the tigress and used her killing knife to slit the goat's throat. He hated the way she drank the fresh blood from the opened throat arteries then quickly cut the poor animal into pieces. And he hated most of all that the aroma of roasting meat smelled very good to him.

The preparation of their feast seemed to go on for hours,

but Kalinda had little care for time and less for any impatience that her guests might feel. At last, though, she deemed everything ready. She waved her hand, and the air moved, and a sweet music of flutes and strings filled the glade. Rane sat at table with Nikolandru and Kalinda. He still had many questions to ask of this mysterious woman, and he reminded himself to be careful of how he asked them.

22

Rane ate some more of the succulent rock goat, while the bonobos enjoyed their food sitting or lounging on the grass. He watched a mature male named Aluino use his long fingernail to split open a prickly pear and then turn back the skin to get at the sweet, juicy pulp inside.

To Kalinda, flashing signs back and forth with nearby Shimuri, he said, 'You must find these apes' company very comforting.'

It was his way of asking why she didn't make company of men and women. He didn't want to put too many direct questions to this prickly woman.

She continued her sign talk with Shimuri even as she said to him, 'I have not had many deeper conversations with most human beings.'

Just how deep, Rane wondered, could an ape's thoughts and therefore conversation really go? He eyed the table's unused fourth setting. Were they to be joined by another, perhaps some man or woman captured within the Entity's unexplored spaces – perhaps even a pilot of the Order, whom Kalinda had made her lover?

'Danlo wi Soli Ringess,' he said, 'told of meeting a woman who resembled his lost Tamara on the coast far to the north of here. Other than her, however, he reported this Earth to be uninhabited.'

'*This* Earth?' Kalinda said. Her arms swept out as if to embrace the whole of the glade and the planet beneath it. 'Or do you mean *the* Earth?'

'That I would like to know.'

'Would you?' She smiled at Shimuri and the other apes, then stroked the head of the tiger, again sitting by her side. She looked up at a bird twittering in the tamarind tree. 'Then in answer to your implied questions, let's just say that *my* Earth has all the inhabitants She needs – almost all.'

She looked at Rane provocatively as he regarded her in silence. From her leaf plate, she plucked a piece of greasy goat meat and put it to her teeth. After she had eaten it, she said, 'Once ten billion people inhabited my Earth and nearly destroyed Her. Would you have me allow human beings to walk my Earth again?'

'You allowed me to. And Danlo and Nikolandru.'

At his mention of the pilot-poet, she handed Nikolandru a kei apple and smiled at him.

'It's thought,' Rane said, 'that you once made the acquaintance of Mallory Ringess, too.'

Kalinda's eyes lit up with fierce little lights. She seemed to look off far into the past – and perhaps far into the future.

'And Maria. We more or less followed her here. She once lived on *your* Earth, didn't she?'

Now Kalinda looked at him.

'Who is she, madam? Why did she leave this place to go to Neverness?'

Her hand dropped down to clasp the hilt of her knife. She gazed at Rane for a long time, then said, 'Maria was Maria, and you are you, and my Earth is not for human beings as our kind have been for two hundred thousand years.'

'Our kind? But are you not a goddess?'

She laughed at this as her hand came off the knife and swept her thick black hair away from her striking face. She had a lovely laugh, full of irony and self-reflection and a strange, sweet innocence.

'Don't I look like a woman, Rane?'

Nikolandru answered for him: 'You are as woman might be if our kind survived another two hundred thousand years.'

She smiled at this. She seemed to relish the affection he offered her as if he had dropped a juicy grape into her mouth. Then her face grew hard and frigid. 'No, I am old, and my Earth needs that which is new.'

'Isn't that,' Rane said, 'the very essence of being a god or a goddess? To remake oneself according to one's own design and become forever new? To evolve into that which the universe has never—'

'To evolve, yes, my memoried man, but to evolve *how*? Isn't the memory still fresh for you, of how Hanuman li Tosh tried to break out into godhood and started a war that might have destroyed the universe?'

As Rane and Nikolandru listened with a rare and fraught attention, she told of how human beings and therefore many of the galaxy's gods had evolved to gather to themselves greater intelligence, everlasting lives, and above all more and more power over the material universe. Most had done so, as Kalinda herself had, by accreting and reshaping matter to form into the extensional arms and hands called robots and vast 'brains' such as the moon-sized computers that filled the Solid State Entity's nebula. This 'god' impulse or program could be seen at least in part as a reification of a very natural human vulnerability and fear of death. And even more, as the driver of the age-old dream (or delusion) of fleeing the horrors of the material universe: for hadn't Hanuman sought to fold all the matter of all the galaxies into his Universal Computer and so become as *the* God of a sort of heavenly realm of artificial life in which strife, suffering, disease, and death ceased to exist? Weren't all of the galaxy's gods, to say nothing of its trillions of human beings, forever susceptible to such madness?

'Why,' she asked, 'do you think the warrior-poets made their rule to kill all potential gods?'

She looked down at her fisted hands, at her two red rings. For a moment, her gaze seemed to gather the past, present, and future into a single point where time itself stopped. Rane had noticed several of these time-outs of ordinary consciousness during their meal. He wondered if during these flickers of intense concentration, lasting a millisecond, Kalinda somehow interfaced her thousands of unseen moon-brains that filled faraway spaces.

'But you,' Rane said, 'are a warrior-poet, or were, and yet you did not kill Mallory Ringess.'

'And the warrior-poets have never stopped trying to kill me for betraying my order. We of the rainbow rings are supposed to embrace death, not flee from it as the gods do.' She drew out her killing knife and tapped her finger against the shining blade.

'We are supposed to walk the razor edge between life and death, and thus truly live.'

'That I have heard.'

Again, her eyes grew still for a flicker of time. 'Have you also heard that the dead know only one thing: that it is better to be alive? But *how* alive? Who has really lived? Ede the God? The warrior-poets? Mallory Ringess?'

Rane thought about this as he ate a tamarind. He said, 'Perhaps Danlo has. Perhaps his children.'

He told her about Sunjay and Chandra and the other *Asta Siluuna*. She listened with a frightening concentration. Her eyes flickered like a lightship passing in and out of realtime and the manifold.

'Your old Timekeeper,' she said, 'might have loved Mallory, but he dreaded what he became, and he would not have abided his child, much less his grandchildren.'

'You know of Lord Horthy Hosthoh?'

'I knew him long ago on Arcite, before the fourth wave of the Swarming, when he called himself Rowan Madeus.'

She went on to say that even before the Timekeeper had founded the Order, he had always feared the galaxy's gods, whom he saw as mad tyrants. And so he had gone on to become a sort of tyrant himself as Lord of the Order: an order that claimed as its mission the loftiest of ideals but in reality kept people from the truly high. Within the Order, he had done everything possible to prevent evolutionary breakouts such as Mallory Ringess. Without, as in Neverness's Farsider's Quarter, he had allowed people the freedom to fornicate, drink, drug themselves, gluttonize, sculpt their bodies into the forms of animals, and worship false gods – all so long as they did *not* have the freedom to evolve.

'He was the ultimate conservative,' Kalinda said. 'And his stifling of your Order's professionals and pilots was the ultimate cause of your Pilots' War and everything that followed.'

And what had followed had been the even greater War in Heaven, with great fleets of lightships, goldships, and blackships trying to destroy each other – even as the mad human beings called the Iviomils of one of the old Cybernetic churches blew up the stars in order to propel their ships into the manifold and fill all the galaxy with trillions of their kind. And all the while, the truly mad (or truly clear-sighted) Silicon God tried to destroy this explosive humanity along with the galaxy's gods who had sprung from the seed race known as *Homo sapiens*.

'The Silicon God,' she said, 'began as a single computer and AI program and is as sexless as a bacterium, but I will refer to him as a "he". In a way, he is like Hanuman, whom he would have used to destroy all in order to become all.'

And from where did this egomaniacal derangement of the self arise, she asked? From nothing more (but nothing less) than a confusion of the part with the whole.

'The ancients,' she said, 'spoke of holons, as your Order's holists still do. How to at once be a part and a whole within a holoarchy? That has always been life's problem, never fully solved.'

Rane considered this. An atom of carbon in his blood's DNA made up part of that vital helical molecule, which in turn with other kinds of molecules formed themselves into a blood cell. And that single red cell dwelled in an exquisite synergy of interchanging nerve and chemical signals with the body's other thirty trillion cells – until it did not. A single atom of radioactive carbon-14 might derange the DNA of the blood cell, which might turn leukemic and kill the greater body with cancer.

'Some people,' Rane said, 'would have called Hanuman a cancer. Some of the holists see the entire human race as a cancer, though others believe humanity has not yet achieved the sort of order that would make our trillions into a functioning whole.'

And what, he asked, was the great, secret hope of the Order of Mystic Mathematicians and Other Seekers of the Ineffable Flame? Wasn't it, at bottom, the gathering of all people in the galaxy into a single, sane, superluminal organism, a holarchy that would take its inspiration not only from the body itself but from the wisdom and ways of the Order's very own structure, refined over three thousand years?

'That,' Kalinda said, looking back and forth between Rane and Nikolandru, 'is a curious idea. Do you see any hope that human beings could ever live together in anything approaching harmony, let alone the synergy of a holon within the greater holon we call the living universe?'

Rane thought of Naveek, who had wanted to be free to be

himself, to *create* a glorious new man – and in doing so had disrupted if not destroyed the Nepenthians' royad. He thought of Maria and himself. When, except for a few moments of rapturous union, had they ever been a true dyad?

'There must be hope,' Rane said to Kalinda. 'For human and god. You haven't tried to fold all the stars and planets into yourself.'

'No, not yet.' Her hands swept up above her as if she might lay hold of the heavenly bodies concealed by the sun's blaze and the sky's blue shimmer. She let loose a laugh, high and harsh like the cry of a hawk. 'But I am a little insane myself, and I have carved up enough of this nebula that others might consider me a cancer.'

Rane looked at this strange, sad woman in silence, for he could think of nothing to say.

'And then there is the other thing,' she murmured, 'part of the problem of which I have spoken.'

Again, her eyes emptied themselves into timelessness for a span of time that Rane measured by the very beginning of an indrawn breath. And he said, 'It must be very hard for you, existing simultaneously as a woman and as the galaxy's greatest goddess.'

'You're too perceptive, Rane,' she said softly.

They spoke of things then that he had never imagined discussing with a being who, if he offended her with unwanted empathy, could perhaps kill him with a thought. While the bonobos continued their feast and cavorted in twos or threes or fours on the grass, they talked about the age-old peril of the human brain's interfacing a computer. Nikolandru had much to say about this, too, for didn't pilots sometimes have to dwell for many days at a time in the cybernetic realm of pure mathematics? Rane mentioned the Order's cetics, particularly the cybershamans who practised in secret a forbidden, continual interface with the computers they used to vasten their consciousness. Hanuman li Tosh, he pointed out, had been a cybershaman before he stared too long into the dazzling electric face of his computer and merged mind with machine in a euphoria (and hell) that had maddened him. The cetics of the other branches – the yogin much more so than the neurosingers – had long anticipated the pitfalls of such absorption, for didn't meditation offer one the opportunity to disappear from the real world into the great Emptiness? And hadn't the Fravashi Old Fathers, in all their white fur and wisdom, guided their students through what they called the *vashnorn*, which was to be annihilated in something much greater than the self? And didn't this practice find resonance with the realizations of the masters of *Advaita Vedanta* in the forest ashrams of Old Earth millennia before? How *did* a man or a woman explode into a billion bits of incandescent being, each bit more brilliant than a supernova, while at the same time talking or thinking or peeling oranges or chewing bites of roasted goat meat in the company of others on a warm, sunny day?

'You must face,' Kalinda said to Rane, 'a similar difficulty when you enter your remembrancing attitudes, particularly the one you call the sixty-fourth.'

'Is it similar? I haven't found remembrance to be very like computer consciousness.'

'You haven't interfaced *my* computers,' she said. 'The . . . power. The possibilities. All the infinities of echo and light.'

Her dark eyes brightened like moons at the touch of sunrise, and she spent a much longer time looking into timelessness.

'It is much the same in the sixty-fourth,' he admitted. 'Most take three sips of kalla, and must lie as still as the dreaming or the dead. Yet, if one goes deeply enough into the One Memory, there is a sense that it might be possible to perfectly exist at once as man and something vastly greater.'

'Or as a *woman*?' she said, smiling at him.

'There is also another sense, madam, that the problem of the part and the whole can never be solved, that it was never *meant* to be solved. Kolenya Mor would say that it is a driving force of evolution.'

'Perhaps both senses are true.'

'How can that be?'

'Because existence itself is paradoxical, and life will always—'

Rane was never to know what she would have said next, for at that moment her vision vanished into itself even as her arm snapped up as if to ward off a blow. The air above them wavered. Across the glade fifty feet away, the top part of a carob tree – its branches, twigs, leaves, and hanging green seed pods – flared as with the same colours that made up the iridescent substance of

Rane's scarf and Kalinda's dress. The pretty colours, though, did not hold but rather blackened like a leaf held to a flame. All of the matter of the tree thus touched collapsed in upon itself into a dark, dense mass like a cannonball, which fell down through cracking stems and branches and punched a hole in the grass-covered ground. At this amazement, Nikolandru rose up to dash over to the ugly wound in the earth and look inside. Kalinda, though, grasped his arm to restrain him even as her eyes again found their humanity and something more.

'Curious man,' she said. 'Some sights are not for you.'

'How not? I would wish to behold everything so that I might sing of anything.'

'You would do better to sing of love and not hate. Curiosity killed the cat.'

At this word, the tigress growled and fixed Nikolandru with her golden eyes.

With a sigh of reluctance, Nikolandru again took his seat. The bonobos went on munching fruit or sexing each other as if they had seen such things before. And Rane asked, 'But what happened?'

'Once a day, sometimes twice,' Kalinda said, 'the Silicon God attacks me thus. He is getting desperate.'

'Isn't it you, madam, who should be desperate? He might have killed you.'

She laughed at this. 'And perhaps some day he will, if I don't destroy him first. Though the chances don't favour him.'

'Why do you say that?'

'Because the volume of matter thus changed always equals that of my body. The Silicon God can only guess at my location, and he attacks anywhere within a two-hundred-foot radius of that guess. With each attack, the probability is one in eighteen million that he will succeed.'

'But what if the attacks grow more frequent? What if his guesses get better?'

What if, he wondered, the Silicon God guessed wrong and collapsed Rane's body into a black ball rather than destroying part of a pretty tree? He looked at Kalinda, but she only smiled at him in silence.

'The Silicon God,' she said, 'also wields weapons of psyche and consciousness against me, and therefore against humanity, but it is through such weapons that he himself will soon be unmade.'

'What are you talking about? What weapons are these?'

She fell into a cold silence that suggested she did not intend to answer his question.

'But *what* happened, here? How did the Silicon God from twelve thousand light years away—'

'I can't explain it to you, Rane, for your Order's mechanics have neither the mathematics nor the physics to have taught you the technology.' She looked at him for an uncomfortable moment. 'And I wouldn't explain it if I could. Wouldn't you say, considering the war that your people have just fought, that there are some things that man shouldn't know?'

'I belong to an order, or did, that believes human beings should pursue all possible knowledge.'

'Let us see how devoted you are to pursuing other things. Have you eaten your fill?'

He nodded his assent, and she put the same question to Nikolandru, who said, 'I've eaten better than I can remember.'

'I am glad,' Kalinda said. 'I will walk you back to your ship.'

While the bonobos went about their bonobo business, Kalinda and the tiger led the way back through the woods to the beach. To Nikolandru, she said, 'Later I will recite for you one of Lovita's poems. But now I want to talk to Rane alone.'

With the tigress on one side of her and Rane on the other, she moved off down the beach toward the rocky headland she called Atushqun. After half a mile, she stopped and looked out to the west. The sun had neared the curving horizon, and white-capped waves broke the ocean's glossy blue waters. The air smelled of salt and seaweed and the exhalations of the seals that barked on gold-vermillion sands not far away. Kalinda stood close to him. The wind off the waves rattled their hair.

'I love this time of day,' she said, taking his arm. 'When the sun dies for a few hours and the stars are born again.'

Why had she said that to him? Why had this immortal woman who had been alone for so long told him so much? Asked like that, the question answered itself: she had no one with whom to share. Shimuri and the other bonobos, the tigress, too, might have been comforting companions, but they couldn't really have understood much of what she said. They couldn't understand *her*. Could he? He could almost feel in the grasp of her warm hand the hunger to be fully human again, to laugh and love and eat and sleep in the company of others of her kind without the continual concern of being attacked by a malevolent machine. How badly she wanted to be free from the need always to look off far away with some part of her mind toward dark moons crackling with nearly infinite energies but not really alive! He sensed in her fiery, dark eyes and rushing breath the most basic of needs, the same simple joy of life that had always come so easily to Maria.

'Is that really *the* sun?' Rane said to her.

'Yes,' she said, with surprising candour, 'the same sun that shone two million years ago upon the apes that our kind used to be.'

'Aren't you worried that the Silicon God will destroy it as he did the tree? Or even as the Iviomils blow up the stars into supernovae?'

'That will never happen as long as I watch over it,' she said peering out for a moment at the ball of fire in the west.

'You've watched for a long, long time. How much longer will you remain here with your tiger and your apes, watching and waiting?'

'Am I a scryer,' she asked, 'to see the future? Am I a remembrancer to look into the One Memory and see how the future breaks forth from the past?'

'You are a goddess,' he said, 'and you are free to—'

'Why did you come here, Rane? What is the favour you wish to ask?'

'I believe,' he said, glancing at the killing knife hanging at her side, 'that Maria was born here.'

'Are you hoping that I might tell you of her so that Nikolandru can write his poem while you complete your quest?'

'Not just,' he said, glancing at the tigress. He drew in a deep breath. 'I was hoping that Maria might be born here again.'

A wave broke thirty feet from shore and bathed the beach in its sempiternal sound. A seagull circling above cried out in anger – or perhaps the white and grey bird all alone in the air called to its kind. Kalinda's hand dropped to her knife and tightened around the bone hilt. She glared at Rane. The black pupils of her eyes gathered in the last light of the sun and opened with a bottomless wrath like tunnels of fire deep into her brain: her human brain and that vastly greater being spinning in millions of black spheres in far-off spaces he could not see. Such pain in those lonely, lonely eyes! All the anguish of the universe! She whipped free her knife and pointed it at his heart. His life, he sensed, hung upon its gleaming razor's edge.

'Tell me,' she said, 'how Maria died.'

He tried to. An image came to mind and connected to a memory, which opened upon ten more images and then ten thousand: the storm. The cold, immense and inescapable. The sound of rushing air, the sobbing, sobbing, sobbing. The water in Maria's golden skin all hard and yellow-white. The frozen tears. The bitten lip. The single drop of red, red blood that rolled down onto the white snow. The snow crystals, their six points fractalling into tinier bits of ice down nearly to infinity, melting into water. Her last breaths upon his face: carbon dioxide and coffee and warmth and pain and love. The wild pounding of her heart's last beats. His own hated heart, melting at last, melting too quickly in flames of agony that burned down deep into the water of his trillions of cells. Her last words to him. The words he had spoken to her before the storm had taken her in its icy claws. The three simple words forming up on his bitten soul like drops of red lava. The terrible words so easy to remember but so necessary to forget, for if he did not, he too must die.

'There was a storm,' he finally said to Kalinda. 'A great mother of a storm, a *sarsara*.'

As the warrior-poet's knife wavered in the air, that storm still raged inside him. It built ever stronger, deeper, colder – cold enough to freeze lava to stone and to crack and pulverize it into bits of dust that blew away like ice crystals in a blinding white wind.

'Each year in deep winter,' he said, 'people get caught in such storms, which can come on very quickly like a *morateth* blowing out of the west. Maria was new to Neverness and not wise to her ways.'

As the last glow of the sun died along the dark horizon and the earth turned deeper into night, he told Kalinda as much as he could about Maria's death and life. There was a lot to tell, though he could not of course relate every detail, for that would have involved describing the shape of each snow crystal that broke upon Maria's frozen face and each breath that he took from the time that he had realized Maria had gone missing to the moment when the sunship had rocketed up from the Hollow Fields on the terrible day of her funeral. He talked for a long time. Kalinda listened with a sense that seemed to reach much deeper than could sound through ears.

'I don't understand,' she said when Rane finally finished, 'why she would have gone out into such a storm. New to Neverness or not, the Maria you've described to me would still have been too wise for that.'

'I don't know,' he said truthfully, or nearly so. How could one really know that which had been forgotten? 'Maria was headstrong. She did things that other people did not.'

Kalinda looked at him across the star-silvered beach for a long time. At last, she sheathed her knife. In a raw voice, she said, 'Your Maria fascinates me. I can understand why you must have loved her . . . so terribly.'

Something in the way she said that caused a heat of water to blur the images that his eyes struggled to take in: the moon, low in the eastern sky; the ocean's dark waves; Kalinda's dark, troubled face nearly lost into the greater darkness of the night. He could almost feel, if not see, her hot, moist eyes searching for something in him.

'I think you have been as honest with me as you can be,' she said. 'But it is not enough. Do you really wish to hold Maria again?'

'More than I do life.'

'Very well, then meet me here tomorrow at dawn, and you will be tested.'

'Tested how?'

'Part of the testing is for you to perceive the nature of the test and the ones that follow.'

'And if I pass your tests, you will restore Maria to me?'

'Yes.'

'And if I fail, you will not?'

'If you fail, you will die.'

She moved up close to him and kissed his lips as if to impart to him a portion of her great courage – along with something warm and deep and good. Then she moved off silently with her tigress into the night.

·

23

The next morning at first light, Rane and Nikolandru walked from the *Asherah* down the beach to the appointed place, for Kalinda had asked the pilot-poet to take part in Rane's test. The two men stood on wet, hard-packed sands recently uncovered by the retreating tide. The seagulls had winged themselves aloft, and the sandpipers skittered on their skinny yellow legs along the waterline hunting for insects and amphipods. Far to the east, the Tears of the Moon Mountains formed a dark line against the glowing horizon, and there the sun rose in a blinding red-white blaze in the notch between Yepunash and Shamulashan. Something about that strangely familiar fusion fire in the sky and the earth upon which he stood – perhaps some precise wavelength of light or scent of life that called up racial memories – persuaded Rane that he might have really found *the* sun and *the* Earth that had given birth to Maria not so long ago.

Kalinda, her tigress moving silently by her side, arrived easy of stride and fresh of eye as if she had just had the best night's sleep of her life. How, though, could that be, when Rane had hardly slept at all and his eyes felt as if someone had rubbed sea grit into them? How *could* she allow herself to sleep, ever, when she might need all her wits at an instant's notice to fend off an attack by the Silicon God or to mastermind some emergency to which her millions of moon-brains had called the alarm? More to the moment, he thought, how could such a brilliant woman possessing a very human heart simply kill him out of hand if he failed her?

'Good morning,' she said, as chipper and alert as any of the shore birds. She might have been greeting a houseguest with the promise of a good breakfast and a pleasant day. 'Are you ready?'

'How can I be ready,' Rane asked, 'when I have no idea of what I should be ready for?'

Kalinda laughed at his grumpiness. 'A warrior-poet must always be ready . . . to be ready.'

'But I, madam, am a remembrancer.'

'This morning, you will need to be a bit of a warrior and very much of a poet. You are to make me a poem in remembrance of Maria: words that reflect her essence.'

'Now? Here?' He looked about the glowing beach. How he wished for a pot of strong Summerworld coffee to put some life into him and wake him up! 'With Nikolandru looking on?'

'Yes. The pilot-poet will be the judge of your poem.'

'What? The sole judge?'

'Yes.'

So, the nature of his first test at least was obvious. How could he fail? Nikolandru would want to judge whatever clumsy lines that came out of his mouth as a masterpiece, else how could he sing of Rane's triumph across the Civilized Worlds?

Rane's relief lasted only a moment, as Kalinda said, 'And I will be the judge of Nikolandru's judging. Judge well, pilot-poet, and live.'

She flashed Nikolandru a warm smile. Then she whipped free her knife and faced the men as the tigress circled around behind them. Rane could almost feel the beast's three-inch fangs feeling their way through his neck bones.

'But this is impossible!' he said, gazing at the knife. Its blade had been wrought of shasteel, the hardest and most refined of all alloys, while the handle was crude: sweat-stained leather wrapped around a section of the femur of the first man that Kalinda had ever killed. So did warrior-poets make their knives. 'How can I make a poem in such circumstances?'

'You might better ask how you can make a *great* poem, great at least in one way, for it must come from your heart and move Nikolandru's heart, if you are to walk away from this place.'

'But not your heart?'

'I will be moved by Nikolandru's appreciation – or not.'

Despite the morning's coolness, Rane began sweating, and his kamelaika stuck to his clammy skin. Nikolandru, however, stood easily within what seemed a preternatural calm and confidence, the morning sun breaking upon his curls of black hair and warming his sensuous upcurved lips. And why shouldn't he relish this challenge? All he needed to do to be safe from Kalinda's killing knife was to judge Rane's poem as poor, for it seemed certain that Rane could create no other kind. Then Nikolandru could keep his hundred thousand City Disks and still have quite a tale of which to sing.

The complexities of this test within a test remained unclear to Rane. So he asked Kalinda, 'But what if I should compose what you call a great poem and Nikolandru deems it otherwise?'

'Then you will die upon his judgement, and he will die for misjudging.'

Her mirrored blade threw the sun's rays into Rane's eyes. So sharp was a warrior-poet's knife said to be that it could slice open a man's throat without his feeling it.

'You may begin.'

It seemed to Rane that his only hope lay in composing a great poem after all, or at least one possessing some element of greatness that Nikolandru could seize upon as a justification for a favourable verdict. And that Rane could never do with a knife pointing at him and a four-hundred-pound tiger breathing down his neck. Only . . . Kalinda hadn't said that he needed to compose a wholly *new* poem. What if he called the single poem he had written for Maria unfinished, for could any work of art or an attempt at such ever be truly perfect and complete? What if Rane changed only a line or two of his poem – or even a couple of words! – and recited it here and now? Nikolandru had once said, hadn't he, that Rane had come up with some touching images? Why shouldn't those same images, recalled now, touch him again?

'You may begin,' Kalinda repeated.

'How much time do I have?'

'How long can you stand in one place before you drop from exhaustion?'

'But what if my poem is long? I have no computer with which to generate ideoplasts. Nor even pen and paper with which to write so that I might see the poem as it unfolds.'

'Can the Lord Remembrancer not remember what words he chooses?'

'May I speak them aloud so I might hear them and deem them worthy or not?'

'You may.'

Rane tried to keep himself from smiling in relief. All he need do was to speak a line or two of his poem as if searching for images and so cue Nikolandru to his plan. If Nikolandru warmed to his words, he would communicate his assent through that silent and mutual accord the two shipmates had built up over years of journeying together and conversations on countless planets.

And so he drew in his breath and said:

'In that moment, open gaze, pools of light . . .'

Some flicker of warning in Nikolandru's eyes, though, kept him from continuing. What if Nikolandru, in his easy and affable poet's way, had spoken favourably of Rane's poem only to spare him hurt feelings? What if, in reality, he had found *nothing* in his poem to be moving? And what if Kalinda detected in him now not the slightest passion for Rane's poem?

He closed his eyes, trying to empty his mind of all thought like a snowfield that went on and on forever. He would need a poem that neither Nikolandru nor Kalinda had heard before. He needed new words. But not a single one appeared on that infinite white plain inside him. Then that whiteness recalled that of a curving chunk of coconut meat that the Maria on Nepenthe had given him – the Maria who had once been a man named Henri and many other men and women. That Maria had once recited to Rane a poem, a favourite of Henri, perhaps even composed by him or one of her earlier selves in a previous incarnation. Or perhaps the poem had been passed on through the Nepenthians' oral tradition and its source had long been lost to the haze of ancient history. Could Rane now remember this poem that he had heard only once and paid little mind? Could he gamble that the Solid State Entity would not know of an obscure poem spoken into the sea breezes on an obscure planet far from the doings of the Civilized Worlds and the rest of galaxy?

A rose unfolds to earth and sun
Bright petals, hues divinely spun . . .

The words of the poem's first line came to him like flaming jewels falling down from a clear blue sky. Then word connected to word, thought to thought, image to image, and the whole poem unscrolled in glyphs of pure fire before his inner eye. He thought that Nikolandru might particularly like the third stanza; surely he could find something in it to move him:

The smoothness of your skin compels
Caress, the slipping of the cells,
The shock and shiver, glide and ease,
The soul-dissolving ecstasies,
Unmeasured bliss of beings twined
As one: in loss of self, I find
Myself in you, and you in me –
No boundary, no boundary.

When he cleared his throat to recite the poem in its entirety, however, he froze. The poem was not his. Nikolandru might never know, or Kalinda, but Rane would know, and so how could he speak from his heart words in some way not real to him? Words that he (and Maria) might have wanted to be true but never had been? How could he hope that real Maria might be restored to him if he won his prize upon the memory of the false?

'You look as though,' Kalinda said to him, 'you have a poem for us.'

'I do,' he said. For the poignance he felt in remembering Maria's words on Nepenthe inspired new words that formed up on his tongue like bittersweet fruits. The pain of remembrance spoke to his failure to love boundlessly and with anything like poetic passion. 'It's a very short poem.'

He stood on the sand, sweating and swallowing. And Kalinda said, 'Well?'

'I have not perfected it.'

She smiled at him and said, 'Can you perfect yourself? First thought, best thought – recite it now before you lose your courage.'

Rane nodded. He looked at Nikolandru. He looked at Kalinda waiting in the early light. He swallowed, hard, against the knot of words caught in his throat. Then he drew in a breath and said:

'Starlight on water,
The oceans of your eyes
Hold deep secrets,
Echoes of light – too bright!'

Now he waited, and his breathing stopped, and the sun rose a thousandth of an inch higher in the east. Its red glare caught in the shasteel of Kalinda's knife. Nikolandru looked back and forth between that death-sheened blade and Rane.

'So, pilot-poet,' Kalinda said, 'how do you judge Rane's haiku?'

Rane waited while the strange, unseen constellations beyond the blue sky turned throughout the universe.

And Nikolandru, who appeared unable to look at Rane just then, said, 'If Rane were to change just a couple of words, then—'

'The poem stands as it is. So?'

'The poem did not move me.'

'You did not find it worthy?'

'I did not find it worthy of Rane.'

Kalinda nodded at him. 'I accept your judgement, for it is mine.'

She turned to Rane, and her knife turned with her. 'Your poem was not worthy of you, but yours was a worthy effort, for you put your heart into it – part of your heart – and that moved me.'

'Then—'

'You have still failed to move Nikolandru's heart.'

'Then I have failed my test.'

He closed his eyes. He didn't want to watch her knife streak out toward him like a bolt of silver lightning

'No, you have not,' she said. 'I needed to test your virtue: would you recite another's poem, which you knew would touch Nikolandru, or would you compose your own?'

He looked at her. 'If my mind is not open to you, how do you know I *did* compose the poem?'

She laughed with a surprising warmth. 'I do not need to be a mindreader or even a cetic, my faithful man, to read you.'

'Then . . .' He gazed at her long knife.

'Had you not found your honour,' she said, her hand tightening around leather and bone, 'I would not have used this. I would have left you to my friend, who takes her time to savour what she puts her claws into.'

He turned to look at the tigress, who watched him with red, sun-filled eyes.

'Then it seems I have passed my true test,' he said, 'while failing with my poem. But you said if I did not move Nikolandru, I would not walk away from this place.'

'And you will not. You will run. Run quickly, Rane, for if you do, she might not catch you.'

Was this yet another test? Or was it some sort of game, Kalinda making sport with him in all her cruelty and capriciousness?

'How can I run quickly enough to escape a tiger?'

Perhaps she was testing his resolve not to be moved by her whimsies. Perhaps she had never intended to kill him no matter what sort of poem he recited.

'You'll have a head start. Run!'

The tigress tensed every muscle along her orange and black neck, shoulder, and furry flank, as if trembling to spring upon him. And all questionings of Kalinda's subtleties of intention vanished. His brain emptied of thoughts as an ancient terror seized hold of him. Adrenaline shot through his arteries like flames, and his muscles bunched and moved as with a will of their own. He turned and ran for his life.

He ran back up the beach, north toward the ship. If he could reach this diamond-covered cavern before the big cat reached him, he would be safe. He ran hard, as hard as he could, his boots bruising the water-packed sand. He ran so hard that it seemed his heart would burst into bloody red bits and his gasps of breath would tear the lungs from his chest. He did not run quickly enough, though, for his legs were weak from inactivity, and he had little wind. Soon, after three hundred yards, he heard the cat's paws tearing up the beach behind him. The *Asherah*'s long, lithe hull wavered in the air like a mirage fifty yards from him. He didn't know if he could reach it. He didn't know if he *wanted* to seek safety inside, for if he hid like a mouse in a hole, what would Kalinda think of him? What would he think of himself? If Kalinda *did* wish him dead, surely she would find means to send him on to the other side of day sooner or later. Why not, then, let it be sooner? He was tired of running, so dreadfully tired. Hadn't he been running across the whole galaxy for years from the place he'd left Maria in Neverness in this hopeless wild goose chase to recreate her? Hadn't he, really, been running all his life? What if he simply, and suddenly, just stopped?

Deep secrets . . .

And so he did. He turned as he bent over, hands hard upon his knees, his chest heaving, breath wheezing through his throat. The tigress sprinted toward him in a flash of fury. It took the great beast seconds to tear across seventy yards. He fixed his gaze on orange and black death. The tigress, though, stopped herself not five yards away from him. He smelled her buttery scent and her hot, animal's breath. She stared at him. Her golden eyes, so unlike the two brilliant black moons that filled Kalinda's face, shone with the same intensity. And the same loneliness and longing for life and something else, some mysterious thing that united life and death, dark and light, into a single superluminal substance nearly as palpable as the drops of water that splashed up from an incoming wave. Through the clarity of a nearly perfect morning, with the sea beating its eternal pulse through the earth, she stared at him with those great, glowing eyes of hers, and he couldn't quite tell if she wanted to play with him – or to play with his intestines.

The oceans of your eyes . . .

'I'm . . . not running . . . from *this* place,' he gasped.

He moved toward the tigress, one step, two. A wave broke upon the beach, and water slipped back into the sea. Then the tigress moved toward him. She stretched out her neck to rub her head against his thigh. He let his hand settle down into fur as she loosed from her throat a soft chuffing sound. He had never touched such a creature before – unless he counted Maria as such, for hadn't she been the wildest of all animals?

After that, Kalinda and Nikolandru rejoined them. She smiled at the tigress, and at Rane. And she said, 'Shall I make us breakfast? You must be hungry.'

'Yes, very.'

He walked off with Nikolandru and her toward the glade to see what sorts of delicacies she would prepare for him.

24

No more tests did she put to him that day or on the next. She spent most of the days after that simply talking to him and asking questions about Maria, and he couldn't quite tell if those convivial but pointed conversations constituted some test unrevealed. She encouraged him through the sharpness of wit and tongue, if not her knife, to call up his memories of Maria: how they met in the Hofgarten on a bright winter day; the promises they had spoken to each other in the Light Pavilion when they found their star; the way Maria had shocked the Order's staid professionals when she used her fingers to eat and tore apart nearly raw cultured meats with her strong white teeth. Kalinda listened intently as he told of the first time that he and Maria made love – and the second, and the third and fourth, and the four hundredth. She bade him to confide every whispered word and caress, each moment of delight and doubt, the precise look in Maria's eyes all the many, many times she invited him inside to swim through an infinite sea where it seemed he must drown. Kalinda asked him about these intimacies not as a voyeur might seek easy titillations but rather with the mercilessness of a wise old woman after hard truths. She wanted him not just to recount these stories, impressions, and other sensa but to relive them.

To do so, he had to enter many times into the difficult attitude of recurrence. There, alive once again in the most vivid of memories, while sitting in the glade with Kalinda and the bonobos or lying on the dunes or standing on the beach looking out at the waves, he dwelled once more with Maria as Kalinda dwelled with him. How much of this woman he had loved could he call up from the past and bring to life inside him? How much of her could he ever really grasp, much less convey to Kalinda through mere words?

As one sunny day after another dawned and swelled bright and hopeful before dying into night, Kalinda's questioning of him continued. He gathered that she somehow recorded these living remembrances of Maria, though how she might have done so remained a mystery. He gained a hint of her command of technological marvels one morning in the glade. He was lying back against the soft grass looking up at the green canopy of the moringa tree. Inside his remembrance, he had worked half the way through his argument with Maria over her profligate spending of the little money she gained from reciting poems. Outside the fortress of his skull, twenty feet from him near the base of a tamarind tree, some of the bonobos were squabbling: the largest male in the troop, Dinos, had fallen into dispute over a fruit or some such trifle, and had shoved the pregnant Azizi. And Shimuri and several of the bonobo females quickly ganged up on Dinos, and with a quick hand-to-hand fury drove him off into the trees. Why the other males did not side with Dinos, Rane didn't know, but females outmanoeuvring males seemed to be the bonobo way. After peace was restored – and after the inevitable interchange of sexual favours that engendered harmony – the glade fell quiet again. The bonobos returned to their mostly edenic life, and Shimuri made gentle with a chastened Dinos. Rane listened to the clicking of insects and the chirping of birds. He returned to his remembrance. He took off his scarf and held it up to the sun to let its rays filter through the scarf's opalescent substance. He recalled how Maria had taken off the scarf during their argument and had tied this living rainbow of fabric around his face to shut him up. Then she had made gentle with him, kissing and caressing and biting softly at his neck and laughing with such a good-hearted insouciance that he couldn't help but laugh with her.

'Put your scarf back on.' Kalinda's voice filled the glade with her demand. He had almost forgotten that she sat on the grass by his side. 'Return to your remembrance.'

What powers, he wondered, what secrets did this pretty scarf hold along with Maria's scent? Could this colourful length of made matter somehow record his memories? When he asked Kalinda this, she only smiled at him.

He did as she commanded, for wasn't she, in her human part, a deadly warrior-poet, and in her godly part a nearly all-knowing being who could always outmanoeuvre him? When he had completed his remembrance, though, he sat up and said to her, 'How many memories of Maria, I wonder, will be enough to recreate her?'

She smiled her mysterious, infuriating smile. 'How many angels can dance on the head of a pin?'

'How many Marias—'

'I have not yet agreed that I will recreate her, have I?'

'No, but—'

'We are still determining if she *can* be reborn from your brow, as it were.'

He pressed the heel of his hand against his forehead. Somewhere buried beneath the bone, inside his brain, he had locked away his Maria memories. Even if he could find the key to this beloved woman, though, how could even the greatest of remembrancers ever call into being everything about Maria, whole and complete?

'Do you mean, madam, that she is capable of being reborn or that I am capable of recalling enough of her to be made real?'

'Perhaps both,' she said. Her voice grew wistful, and she gazed at him as if looking at a star far away. 'But hasn't every moment of Maria's life been recorded in what you call the One Memory?'

'That is what some remembrancers believe.'

'But what does Thomas Rane believe?'

'I believe that belief is useless. Danlo wi Soli Ringess used to say that beliefs are the eyelids of the mind.' He pointed his finger straight up. 'Only the blind need to *believe* that the sky is blue.'

'And you would apprehend this blueness with your eyes – even as you would the One Memory with your mind?'

'No one as yet has ever been able to grasp more than a grain of sand sifting along the currents in the ocean that is the One Memory.'

She looked at him as her hand pressed low against her belly.

'From a single cell, quickened with sperm, a whole human being is made.'

'But I—'

'The Jews on New Jerusalem believe that from the tiniest of ashes of a cremated body, God can resurrect a living woman or a man.'

'But what,' he asked, looking at her a second too long, as he might the sun, 'can a *goddess* bring to life?'

'That may depend on how much sand you can gather from the ocean.'

'Is that to be the next of my tests, then, how deep I can dive into that ocean?'

'Tell me about the times you have dived. Tell me about the ocean.'

While the bonobos ate their fruits and played with each other, he recounted much of his life as a remembrancer. She took particular interest in his guiding thousands of Ringists in the kalla ceremony in the time before the war and his instruction of the *Asta Siluuna* afterwards. He told her of Sunjay, and of Binah Jolatha Alora, and he spoke of his many journeys into the One Memory.

'But you must know of this,' he said. 'All that I have experienced must be known to one such as yourself.'

'There are none such as myself.' She watched Dinos and a female named Sunki coupling face to face on the grass. 'And I do not know all, for the One Memory you speak of remains closed to me.'

'That cannot be so.' He pointed at the brook tinkling through the glade. 'Every drop of water remembers the ocean from which it takes its being.'

'Each drop of water might, but not so a woman or a man, yes?'

'Perhaps not, but they might.'

'Mallory Ringess spoke to me,' she said, 'of the Elder Eddas. These racial memories that are part of the One Memory.'

'Though he was the first to grasp them, not even he knew their true nature.'

'He said that the Ieldra had encoded these memories into humankind's most ancient DNA.' She looked down at her callused hand. 'That the Eddas contain instructions on becoming gods.'

'But you must know of this?'

'There are gods . . . and there are gods.' She ran her finger along the back of her hand. 'I know of the Ieldra, more than any now living know. They were not gods . . . as I am.'

'Machines, then, like the Silicon God?'

'No, something else. Something new struggling to be born – to be born again. They were called toward their destiny by something beyond even the Ieldra.'

She gazed at Rane, and he felt himself falling as into a bottomless chasm of longing. He watched as she drew out her knife and used the point to carve a delicate double spiral on the back of her hand. Blood welled up from these etchings, and her gaze turned to embrace the red drops as if looking inside them for the secret of life.

'You see,' she said, 'when Nils Ordando founded my Order, he wanted to create the finest of warriors and poets. And so he engineered out of the genetic template of our kind parts of chromosomes thought to no longer function within the cell. Ancient DNA left over from life's experiments with evolution.'

'I have heard this,' Rane said.

'The oldest of our DNA into which the Ieldra had written the Eddas.'

She put her hand to her lips, sucked, swallowed blood. When she took it away from her mouth, Rane gasped to see the cuts in her flesh had fully healed.

'I will never,' she said, 'be able to use the Eddas as a doorway into the One Memory.'

'There are many doorways into the One Memory.'

'And you remembrancers have found these doors, yes? And you try to construct new ones?'

'We try to open them.'

She smiled at him and sheathed her knife. 'That we shall see.'

That evening, Rane walked with Kalinda by the ocean to the north of the *Asherah*. A nearly full moon threw down its light on the great Kalawasaq Rock out in the water. And Rane said to her, 'Many memories of Maria I have from her days in Neverness. Others I have reconstructed from what I learned about her journey there. But I know little about her childhood.'

'Then perhaps you should search the One Memory for a record of it.'

He watched a big wave break into fragments against the offshore rocks. He had to speak loudly against the sound of the surf: 'One does not simply search the One Memory with the ease of calling up information from a computer. Yes, somewhere within the One Memory lies the record of all Maria's thoughts, words, and acts – all that Maria *was*. That does not mean that I will ever find any of it.'

She looked at him through the thin, silvered light of the evening. Her eyes were black pools almost impossible to read.

'If Maria,' he said, 'was born on this Earth, you must know of it.'

'*Must* I? How many millions of creatures give birth to their kind each hour on my Earth?'

'But you would know if people besides yourself have lived here.'

A wave broke, and the wind swept his words away.

'Did you know Maria?'

She kept looking at him through a silence that grew deeper and darker.

'If you did, or if I could talk to her people and ask—'

'Ask yourself who Maria *really* was. Isn't that what you most need to know?'

'But it's said that the child is the mother of the woman and—'

'How about your childhood, Rane? How much do you remember?'

He closed his eyes for a moment as his father's stern face burned inside him like a flame. He said, 'I remember . . . too much.'

'Do you remember your birth?'

'No, I have never gone that far back, but Danlo did.'

'Do you remember your first few years?'

'Almost no one does. As the brain grows explosively after birth, the neurons prune synapses and—'

'And yet despite this childhood amnesia and all that you have forgotten since, you still became Thomas Rane, and you are still you.'

'I am, of course I am, but I can't—'

'Go find Maria,' she said, 'and don't concern yourself with what she was like as a little girl.'

Rane slept fitfully that night. Sometime after midnight he

arose from Nikolandru's and his encampment on the beach, and he walked alone by the moonlit ocean. A myriad of thoughts burst into radiance inside him, almost as many as the stars twinkling in the sky. Around which of these luminous points had the Ieldra dwelled? What secrets of evolution and life had enabled them to defeat the Dark God two million years before? And where, in this superabundance of splendour, did Maria's and his star, Val Adamah, the double sun that reflected back and forth in fire the secrets of their souls, shine?

He might never find it from this lost and lonely earth, as he might never find Maria. Now that he had come so close, he doubted if he could or should. Was he violating nature in his desperate attempt to defeat death? He thought of the mummified bodies of the ancient pharaohs, who had built mighty pyramids to safeguard the treasures that they would need to rule again in the afterlife. And the Kristoman, too, with his resurrected corpse and the empty tomb. He recalled the epic of Gilgamesh and the tragic tale of Orpheus, the greatest of all poets, who had gone down into the underworld and had sung to the God of Death a song of such beauty that his beloved Eurydice had been restored to him. And what of Avangel, a man so desirous of immortality that he had destroyed a star so that he might live forever feasting off its light?

If Rane told the truth to himself, he would have to admit that he hadn't expected to live long enough to come face to face with the imminence of his fantasies being made real. Now that it seemed *possible* that Maria might be recreated, he had to ask himself if it was *desirable*. Was it right? One question especially tormented him: did Maria or anyone have something that could be thought of as a soul? And if so, was this essence singular and eternal like light or rather modular, composed of multiple traits such as goodness, openness, impulsiveness, lustiness, empathy, and beauty, all the colours and tones of being that might be rearranged into many, many songs? Above all, he wondered if he could ever grasp Maria's undying essence, any more than he could lay hold of the water in the sea.

'Maria, Maria,' he murmured, looking out at the sparkling waves, 'how can I find you when I cannot find myself?'

As the Earth turned toward morning, his thoughts turned toward the practical and actual *how* of what he had asked of

Kalinda. He recalled the Nepenthians' Pool of Transfiguration in which robots the size of bacteria had swarmed through the tissues of Henri's body and transformed him into a woman possessing much of Maria's form if little of her soul. He recalled Danlo's account of how the Entity had built the false Tamara in a sort of artificial womb of the kind that the bioengineers of Fostora call an 'amritsar tank'. And what of the Agathanian god-women who had resurrected Mallory Ringess from his first death? The once-human beings who had transformed themselves into the shapes of otters, sea cows, dolphins, and a thousand other types of ocean creatures, many of which had never existed anywhere except in seas of beautiful, mysterious Agathange? The Agathanians had filled their world's blue, blue waters with micron-sized biological assemblers that could build organic molecules, proteins, and DNA into almost any kind of life they could imagine, from sparkling trillids much like the ocean's myriads of jewel-like diatoms to koholaaks vaster than any whale. Could Kalinda, through transcendent technologies perfected by the Solid State Entity, do less than her rival gods? How hard would it be for her to stack trillions of human cells into the shape of the Maria whom Rane remembered so well? And then to imprint that Maria with his living memories? Could such a miracle truly be possible?

He put these questions to Kalinda a few days later. They sat facing each other on some rocks in the foothills overlooking the coastal plain. With the tigress nowhere in sight, the warrior-poet seemed small against the granite boulders behind her and for the moment strangely vulnerable. Her unexpected softness called to his own, and he found himself confessing all his doubts:

'You've never said if Maria *could* be brought to life again.'

'A better question might be if *you* can be.'

'But could she really be conscious . . . the way my Maria was?'

'What do you know of that?' Her hands swept outward as if to embrace the beach below them and the turquoise ocean and the sky beyond. 'The whole Earth is conscious. So are the stars. The galaxy is a living organism.'

He thought about this as he tapped a pebble against a boulder and listened to its stony sound. 'If you can remake her, when might that be?'

'When will the Earth sing? When will you sing a love song to this reborn Earth?'

'You haven't even told me all that I need to do to hold Maria again.'

'And you haven't told all. Let's find out the truth about you and Maria.'

'I've been as honest with you as I could.'

'Have you been honest with yourself? What happened on Kailash Poru?'

'I have told you of that.'

'Yes, a little. But you haven't said whether Maria drove Armas Sarkissian to his death through their love for each other or whether she murdered him.'

'Because I don't know!'

She reached out and pressed her hand to his chest. 'Can you tell me in truth that your heart doesn't know?'

Could he? How could he ever open that great red throbbing door to find out?

He pulled away from her. 'It was one incident out of millions in Maria's life. Can it matter so much?'

'You must choose, Rane.'

'How can I?'

'Do you want her to be as you most nearly remember or as you would like her to be?'

'Are those two things different?'

'Only you can say.'

'I loved *all* of her.'

'You've told almost nothing of your difficult moments with her.'

'That's because there are almost none to tell.'

'You've told almost nothing of your difficulties with who Maria *was*.'

He gazed out at the ocean, where sets of waves in long rhythms broke against the shore. What in Maria had most grieved him? Her utter lack of shame or guilt? Her easy flirtations with other men (and women)? Her profligate passions? Her over-abundant sexuality, which she gave away as freely as she did coins to autists in the street, always to Rane, true – but only because she loved him enough to ease his jealousy by bestowing on him all her treasure? Hadn't his greatest difficulty also been his greatest delight? For at the bottom of everything, deep down into all the terror and wonder of Maria, hadn't she been utterly, agonizingly, and irresistibly *wild*?

'You must choose,' Kalinda said to him again. 'Maria is for you.'

What if, he wondered, in his remembrance of this wild, wild woman, he tamed her, just a little, as Kalinda had tamed her tiger? Wouldn't she still be Maria? A Maria much easier to laugh with and confide his dreams to and even more deeply to love?

'All right,' he said, looking at Kalinda. If Maria had never shied away from pain, how could he? Either he would hold the real Maria in his arms again, or he would hold no one. 'I will tell you all that I know.'

They talked a great deal over the next few days and the next few months after that. Often Rane went down into remembrance with a daring that he dreaded, as if descending into a dark cavern without a care of colliding with spears of rock or stumbling into ice-cold pools. Often he walked alone all day in the green-shrouded foothills or along the beach far to the south, before returning to the glade in the evening to tell Kalinda what he had discovered. He walked and walked until his legs grew strong again and Kalinda walked with him. The world around them never stopped renewing itself. In one of the canyons to the east, they watched the live oaks grow. In the shrubs of the dunes above the sea, some gulls hatched. In the glade, as the result of constant copulations, two little baby bonobos were born.

One day just after dawn, as Rane walked along the beach, Kalinda joined him, and so did Shimuri, Gada, Dinos, and Dede, with her little son Jimomo. The five bonobos strolled along the sand on one side of Kalinda while Yava moved in near silence on her other. The great tigress seemed especially alert that morning – or perhaps she was just hungry. She kept her golden eyes fixed on the waves as if watching for a seal she might charge upon and seize.

'There is something I haven't told you,' Rane said to Kalinda. Her rainbow dress fluttered in the strong wind blowing off the ocean. 'Something that I—'

'It is too late,' she said.

Rane loosed a hard breath as if punched in the belly. Had

Kalinda decided not to grant his wish after all? Hadn't he, for many, many days, been as diligent in remembrance as he could be? In Kalinda's constant questioning of him and her refusal to commit to helping him, he had seen yet another tiresome trial, a soul-grinding test of patience. Had he somehow, perhaps by asking *her* too many questions, failed that test?

'But if you'd only listen to what—'

'Be quiet now,' she said. 'You listen. And look.'

He followed the line of her gaze with his own eyes out into the ocean where the waves broke into white swirls of foam. And from out of that foam, pushed along by a great wave toward the beach, a woman appeared. She rode the surf belly down, but when she reached the shallows, she stood up out of the water. The sea ran in a silvery sheen over the curves of her strong, voluptuous body. Bubbles of foam clung to her long black hair like a crown of shining pearls. Sunlight played over her naked golden skin and reddened her lips – the full, smiling lips that Rane remembered so well.

Maria.

He couldn't move. It was as if the sight of this woman had struck deep into him like a paralytic poison – or a vision. Maria, though, moved from ocean to shore with all the ease and grace of a tigress. She walked straight up across the wet sand to Kalinda. She threw her arms around her and kissed her. She smiled, then called out with great happiness a single, shocking word: 'Mother!'

The bonobos rushed over to Maria, and little Jimomo hopped into her arms. 'Shimuri!' Maria cried out. 'Dede!' There was much kissing and caressing. Dinos became so excited at this reunion that his pink phallus pointed nearly straight up into the air. Yava, though, edged the ape aside in a powerful rush to close with Maria. She set Jimomo down, then fell upon the tigress, burying her face in Yava's fur and laughing with so much happiness it seemed that she might cry.

After a while, after Maria had touched her old friends and Kalinda many times as if to make sure they were real and would not go away, she stepped up to Rane. She stared straight at him as a tiger might. Her black eyes drank him in.

'This,' Kalinda said, 'is the Lord Remembrancer Thomas Rane. He has come here from Neverness to help you.'

From across ten feet of glowing beach, Maria held his gaze. There came a knowing of something deep and complete at the first encounter, like being born into a radiant new world and instantly apprehending the goodness and warmth of light. Maria smiled at him with all her old eagerness to connect, explore, and enjoy. It was the same lovely smile that had captured him so many years before as one star might another. But in the brightness of her eyes he could detect not the slightest flicker of recognition.

'Hello, Lord Rane,' she said with a provocative, puzzled look. The formality of her words confirmed a terrible fear that took him in its cold, cold claws. 'It is good to finally make your acquaintance.'

She had no memory of ever meeting him.

25

After that, in the company of the bonobos and the tigress, Maria went off to the glade to bathe in the brook and wash the salt water out of her hair. Rane stood alone on the beach with Kalinda.

'Tell me about Maria,' he said.

And so she did. She told of how she had created a bit of human life and had kept it safe inside her own womb. When the time was right, she caused a single fertilized egg to grow explosively into a blastocyst, an embryo, and a foetus, which she had then transferred into the much larger womb of the warm, salty waters off the coast. There, clouds of chemicals and nano-computers enabled the cells of Maria's body to complete the growth to a fully formed woman in only forty days. And all this time, Kalinda had watched over this little patch of ocean and had overseen the imprinting of Maria's memories. As Rane had paced the trails along the foothills and the sands of the beach, waiting and dreaming his impossible dream, Maria had floated within a strange consciousness, sometimes as dark as deep sleep yet often bright with new memories of what Rane had dreamed. She breathed in a strange new way, not as a dolphin takes in huge gasps of air or a fish gathers through gills the oxygen dissolved in sea water, but rather thrilling to the pulses of this life-giving element infused directly into her blood. Memories infused her brain, and she dwelled with those memories, and she became one with them.

And so, when it came time for her quickening and birth, in that wondrous moment when she first breathed air and opened her eyes to the world's splendour, she walked out of the ocean knowing life, *her* life, much as many people do. She remembered an idyllic childhood of feasts in the glade with her bonobo family and the tigress. She remembered her mother with adoration, for Kalinda watched over her and protected her with a fierce love that became her own. Kalinda nurtured in her a passion for poetry and birds and trees and all the marvels of life. She taught her things that few human beings ever had known. Slowly, as children measure time, and gladly, between the sun and the sea, she had grown into a vibrant and wild womanhood. She thought of herself as of the Earth, and often as the Earth, no different in kind than the dolphins who swam off the coast or bonobos in the woods or the great golden-eyed tigress.

Then one day, in Maria's memories, she had asked her mother what it would be like to know the company of a man instead of the hairy arms of the bonobos such as Dinos. And Kalinda told her about her father, a pilot of the Order on Neverness, far away across the stars. She told her of the Elder Eddas, the great secret of life that her father had sought, at first across the spiral arms of the Milky Way galaxy and in the end down through the spirals of his own DNA. She spoke in sad, hopeful tones of the One Memory, of which she herself had no experience but wanted to know all. These stories had excited Maria. This newly born grown woman did not desire so much to know everything as to experience it – and wasn't all the experience of all the stars written in the One Memory like a single, perfect poem? And so when her mother asked her to journey to Neverness to learn from the Order's greatest remembrancer the secrets of the One Memory, she had consented with gladness.

Maria, a woman of words and smiles and a blazing love for the here and now, took no count of the many deep-ships and the many more days that took her from her Old Earth to Neverness, for what were numbers to a poet and a seeker of memory? If she dallied a little too long on Nepenthe or Aracelli or the other planets that she visited on her journey, well, how could she be blamed? Didn't all her experiences, the perilous as well as the beautiful, serve to create new memories? Didn't they exalt her soul toward the realization of her life's great purpose?

At last, though, she had reached Neverness, the City of Light, the topological nexus of the entire galaxy – only to find that the Lord Remembrancer Thomas Rane had left the city on a pilgrimage to find Old Earth! He had hoped to discover in the ancient home of the human race the deepest secrets of racial memory that might open the door to the One Memory itself. Maria might have shaken her fist in wrath at this cosmic co-incidence and bemoaned this bitter irony. Instead, she laughed. She remembered her mother's telling her that she had been born laughing. She determined to make the best of her reversal. While waiting for a ship to take her back to earth, she had made many new poems and given them to the people of Neverness. One of these poems attracted the attention of the very attractive pilot-poet named Leander of Aoide. She promised to give him all that she had if he would help her go home. He asked her only that she compose poems just for him as the price of the passage aboard his lightship, the *Silver Swan*, that would take her from Neverness to earth.

They might have had an idyllic, memorable journey but for a turn of ill fortune and the illness that befell Maria. For just before the *Silver Swan* rocketed up through the Icefall's cold atmosphere, Maria contracted a memory virus left over from the War of the Faces millennia before. For much of the journey homeward, Maria floated in the silent darkness of the *Silver Swan*'s passenger compartment trying not to let the virus steal her memories away. She succeeded for the most part, although holes in her recollection of her life haunted her like ghosts that had devoured parts of herself. She came to believe that when she returned to earth, the healing powers of her birth world would restore her.

And so she restored herself to her optimism and natural enthusiasm for all things living – and most of all for the beautiful blue and white planet that she remembered so well. The *Silver Swan* put down in a meadow near the magic glade, and Maria said goodbye to Leander. Upon finding the glade empty, she stripped off her dirty, sweat-stained clothes and dashed down to the sea. For what seemed an hour, she floated in salt water and dived down deep below the waves. And when she finally stepped out of the surf, she had rejoiced in seeing Kalinda and Yava and Shimuri and everyone else waiting on the beach to welcome her home.

'That is quite a story,' Rane said when Kalinda had finished speaking. He looked out at the turbid, white-foamed waters in which she had brought Maria to life. 'Quite the fantasy.'

'Some fantasies contain more truth than do real stories.'

Despite three lifetimes of disciplines drilled into him by cetics and master remembrancers, Rane couldn't help the hot rage of blood that flushed his face. 'There is no truth here!'

He turned his gaze on her. And she told him, 'Do not look at me so, or I will cut out your eyes.'

She said this matter-of-factly, without raising her voice, as she might have told him that if he did not brush his teeth, they would fall out. He closed his eyes for a moment and breathed deeply to calm himself. And he said, 'You betrayed me.'

'You betrayed yourself,' she said when he finally dared to look at her again. 'Many days ago, I asked how Maria died but you could not tell me.'

'How can I tell you what I—?'

'What you have *forgotten*? Why have you forgotten, Rane?'

He breathed hard the thick, heavy sea air. 'Because I have been brought back to youth too many times, you see, the angslan, which attacks the memory, has begun—'

'That is not the truth. Even now, you try to hide from yourself, as you do from me.'

'You speak of truth? You who have created a woman who believes the fantasy that she is your daughter?'

Kalinda looked off into ocean. In voice as soft yet as powerful as the wind, she said, 'She is my daughter – my only begotten child.'

She told Rane then of how Maria came to be, the Maria he had known and loved on Neverness as well as the new woman who so recently had stepped out of the surf: at the end of the Pilots' War, Mallory Ringess had returned to the nebula of the Solid State Entity and had met Kalinda in the flesh. There had been a union of goddess and man. After Mallory had returned once again to Neverness, Kalinda had preserved the best of his sperm and the best of her eggs as a single zygote that divided into two and the two into four. One of these four bits of life Kalinda implanted in her womb, and so had been born the Maria to whom Rane had pledged himself in the Light Pavilion. The second zygote Kalinda had preserved inside herself for many years like a bud waiting to bloom.

'Then the Maria I just met,' Rane said, 'is a clone of the first.'

'An ugly word, that. She is more of an identical twin.'

He studied Kalinda's triangular face, the straight, sturdy nose, the curve of her high brow, the wide mouth and sensuous lips. He thought of Mallory Ringess. In truth, the bold-faced Maria did seem cut from the same chromosomes.

'Then she is Danlo's sister – his half-sister,' he said. 'And Sunjay's and Chandra's aunt.'

'She is who she is.'

Rane looked at Kalinda with bitter blame, and he didn't care if she gouged out his eyes with her own fingers. 'But why recreate her with all the memories of her life and no memory of meeting me?'

'Did you think I would give you my *daughter* so easily? You won't be able to hide from this Maria, my baby, my heart, from behind the wall of memory.'

'Do you really believe that—?'

'There was something wrong with the liaison of the old Maria and the old Rane. You must come to my daughter anew.'

Could he do that, he wondered, looking up at the sky?

'If you want her, you must woo her.'

How could he *not* win her affections again? He gazed at an osprey high on the wind, and he had a soaring hope that he could create with the new Maria the happiest of new memories.

'Is this to be a test of my persistence, then?' he asked.

'No, my heartful man – call it the Test of Love.'

That evening in the glade, Kalinda introduced Nikolandru to her daughter. Maria wore a blue dress, and, at her side, a knife that Kalinda had given her. When Nikolandru admitted that such weapons made him nervous, she laughed and reassured him that she would use it only to discourage the coyotes or pumas who might stray down from the mountains to threaten him.

After a feast in which Maria ate rock goat sushi, raw oysters, grubs, writhing worms and other foods that Rane could not stomach, he sat alone with her on the rocks above the brook. The light of the moon sifted down into the trees like a silver rain. She looked at him with a heartbreaking innocence, like an animal that had never before seen a predator. And yet she also reached out to him with a strange knowingness that he could not explain. She trusted him. She saw things in him that he had never wanted to see in himself.

> When I wept to know it glorious
> Strange to know you not strange . . .

After a long silence in which all they did was to sit gazing at each other, she said to him, 'What a coincidence that I journeyed to Neverness to meet you and you journeyed to Earth!'

She invested the word 'coincidence' with deep meaning, as if it had little to do with the pure chance of two events occurring at the same time and everything to do with fate.

'Yes, that it was.'

He had decided that he must play along with the fantasy of a nonexistent journey in the *Silver Swan* with the fictitious Leander if ever Maria and he were to believe the much greater fantasy that she could be the real Maria.

'And another coincidence that we both found pilot-poets to take us here.'

'Yes, the stars must have aligned in our favour.'

'And it was an even greater coincidence,' she said, 'that you can be my teacher and help me regain the memories that the virus destroyed.'

'I have not agreed to be your teacher,' he said. 'That is not why I came here.'

'But Mother said that you would be my teacher.' Her low, musical voice rang with a note of finality, as if to dispute Kalinda was to try to stop the turning of the Earth. 'Don't you want to be?'

How, he wondered, could he both teach and woo her? She sat on a rock facing him and looking at him hopefully. How innocent she seemed! How wise in the way the smile of her eyes sought to melt the doubt in him!

'Tell me what you remember,' he said.

And so she did. She began at the beginning, as he bade her to do, and she spoke of her sense that some twenty-five or thirty years before, in this very glade, she had been born laughing. She told of her childhood swimming with orcas who visited the waters off the coast in winter; once, she had watched a huge male orca flip a seal twenty feet into the air and into the open jaws of his brother. Another time, she had followed Dinos, then a baby, too high into the branches of the moringa tree. She had tried to leap about through the shaking leaves as he did but had fallen to the ground and had broken her leg. She could still remember the sound of the snapping bone and her howls of pain. She still marvelled at how her mother had wept along with her and had healed the ragged bone sticking out of her skin with the touch of her hands.

Her mother, she told him, could work other such miracles and knew almost everything. In the glade, her mother taught her poetry, music, mathematics, meditation, and all the other disciplines she would need in order to learn and grow. In the foothills and the mountains beyond, she taught Maria how to make a bow and arrows and hunt the deer that she loved to eat. On the beach on starlit evenings, as if standing at the edge of the world, she pointed out to Maria the constellations and the distant galaxies and told her of human beings and gods and the history of the universe.

As Maria confided in him the story of her life, it became clear that Kalinda had given her as many of *her* own memories as those of Rane – perhaps a hundred times as many. Of all that Rane had thought to have Maria remember, only those gleanings of happenstance that Rane had gathered on planets such as Aracelli and Zen Mother remained imprinted inside her moon-brightened head. These memories she seemed to recall no less vividly than any others – though just how vivid they could be Rane had yet to determine. What seemed certain, though, was that she sensed gaps in her past, missing memories that she felt always on the verge of recalling but never quite could. Of course, everyone has moments that they can't bring to mind, but Maria struggled to grasp within herself a sort of neverness of remembrance of whole periods of cancelled time.

'*Will* you help me?' she asked him. She rested her hand on his leg. 'Help me to remember everything?'

Her fingers danced along his inner thigh. Of course, Kalinda had imprinted in her all the customs and mores of a hundred planets, and she had learned that the women and men of the Civilized Worlds in particular do not freely touch those whom they hardly know. However, the ways of the bonobos worked in her a deeper imperative. And when had Maria ever cared about custom?

'No one,' he said, covering her hand with his, 'can remember everything.'

'But Mother says you know about the One Memory.'

What did he know about anything, especially the woman who sat so close to him on a slab of cool rock? That he must call her Maria, especially to himself, he could not deny. She looked like Maria; she talked like Maria; she moved like Maria, with Maria's perfect coordination of the tensing and relaxing of muscles and a sort of preternatural grace. She had Maria's eyes, black and fierce and full of light. She smelled like Maria. The soft sea breeze blowing through the glade brought to him a familiar musk of skin and breath and thick hair – and perhaps even the scent of her soul.

'All right,' he said, 'I will help you, if I can.'

'Thank you, Lord Rane!'

As gently as he could, he peeled her fingers from his thigh and squeezed her hand with a cool, false formality. 'Let's begin tomorrow, then. Can you meet me here at sunset?'

That night, Rane struggled to find sleep. He lay on a blanket on the beach for many hours, watching the moon burn a bright hole in the sky. Constellations whose names he hadn't yet learned fell slowly through black spaces toward the world's western waters. *Could* he, he wondered, help this beautiful woman who had stepped out of the ocean like a dream? *How* could he? How to help her recover memories that had never existed for her in the first place? Wasn't that something like identifying in a long book a particular phrase the author had never written? And, more to the moment, did he dare engage with this Maria whom his grief had called into being?

He didn't know if he *should*. Although it angered him that she had no memory of him, it relieved him, too, for wasn't he now free to make his excuses and flee? For how could he, now that it had come to it, embrace the false? Maria might be nearly identical to the woman he had loved on Neverness, down to the number of hairs of her thick, dark eyebrows. But wasn't she just a little *too* enticing, too lively, too bold? Or perhaps the fault lay not in her but in *his* own memory; perhaps he had toned down the real Maria as he might dampen the heat of a fire fresco because all the flaming colours hurt his eyes. He thought of Danlo's denial of the Tamara whom the Entity had created on this very earth. For Danlo, that second Tamara had in many ways seemed *too* real, unreally real and therefore false. Danlo had spoken of the imperfection of perfection.

Wasn't it, though, just the opposite for Rane? For this new Maria, with her slightly sweeter and deeper voice that lured him into the One Memory with the fragrance of the eternal, seemed to him perfectly imperfect. If Rane had to characterize the difference between Danlo and himself, he would say that what most concerned Danlo was the false and the real. But what most moved Rane, deep down where his heart dwelled, was what hurt. And how terrible the pain Maria struck into him with every touch of her guileless yet knowing fingers – pain that she promised to take away in the calling of her lovely eyes.

And so the next evening he met with her in the glade, lit with campfires that Kalinda had taught the bonobos to make. Near one of these fires, he spread out a blanket on the grass and told her to lie back and close her eyes. He guided her in a long meditation; he found that she had an inborn skill at watching the contents of her mind take form and unfold. After an hour of this work, he introduced her to the remembrancing attitudes of association memory and sequencing. When it came time for rest, he felt pleased at her progress; she relished his pleasure.

'I did well, didn't I?' she said.

'Yes, very well.'

She sat up and smiled. 'I have the world's best teacher of remembrance.'

'You have the world's *only* teacher.'

She laughed at this. She flung her arms up as if to embrace all the stars in the heavens. 'I didn't mean *this* world. I meant *the* world.'

'Tell me what you remembered,' he said.

She reached out and touched the scarf around his neck. Her fingers lingered in its soft substance as if stroking a kitten's fur.

'My old scarf,' she said. 'I lost it in a storm, on my first day in Neverness. How can it be that you are wearing it?'

'I . . . found it in the snow,' he said. That was not a total lie. 'Just before I left the city.'

'Then our time on Neverness overlapped by a day!' She clapped her hands together. 'Another coincidence!'

'You could call it that.'

'You found it because you were meant to find it. What an *amazing* coincidence!'

Her hand moved from the scarf to his face, and his hands moved as with a will of their own, and he took off the scarf and draped it around her neck. She tilted her head, trapping his hand against the scarf and her shoulder. Only with difficulty did he pull it back to the safety of empty air.

'I remembered,' she said, 'the way you looked at me when we met on the beach.'

'But that should have played no part in your practice,' he said. 'You were to remember events from your childhood.'

'I cheated,' she said with a smile. 'I couldn't help myself.'

She looked at him with such openness and need that he reached out to touch her after all. At the last moment, though, a coldness came into his hand. He reminded himself that this strangely familiar woman was *not* the Maria he had found in the snow, the Maria to whom he must make amends. Shouldn't he remain faithful to *that* Maria?

'You told me earlier,' she said, 'about the déjà vu, this sense of reliving things that never happened. I *know* that I never saw you before that day when I returned with Leander. But I feel like I've known you a thousand times before.'

The coldness spread through his hand and arm into his shoulder and chest. It felt like ice crystals spiking into tender tissues and freezing them down through his blood into his heart.

'It is getting late,' he said. He held his hand out to the fire, but the terrible cold did not go away. 'Tomorrow I'd like to introduce you to olfaction. My students have often used that attitude as a doorway to recurrence.'

'All right,' she said.

It hurt like a knife in his belly that she trusted him so completely.

26

For many days he sat with her in the glade or sometimes down on the beach, where they watched seagulls picking at shells. Summer gave way to the cooler winds of autumn blowing off the ocean to the north. The macadamia nuts in the trees along the brook ripened, and the bonobos used rocks to break them out. To the rhythms of strange musics summoned out of still air, Kalinda recited poems to Nikolandru as he did to her. She remained ever watchful of the handsome pilot-poet, as she did Rane and Maria and, indeed, all that occurred on her beautiful planet. She left Rane alone with Maria, though, to see if he could work his memory magic.

Several times he helped her stand on the threshold of recurrence. But through that doorway she could not pass. She could relive none of the past that Rane and Kalinda had conspired to make within her, for wasn't it always that way with imprinted memories? When she tried to do so, she came face to face with a heartbreaking hollowness.

'It's as if,' she told Rane late one night on the beach, 'I look and look for a part of myself that I can almost feel, that I know is there, like a star behind a cloud. But the harder I look, the darker the cloud grows, so dark it's like the space between the stars where everything is black and empty.'

It seemed that she might weep and pull him into her despair. What, he wondered, had he done? Had he cursed this loveliest of all women who should have been to him the greatest of blessings?

'Some people,' he told her as gently as he could, 'never manage to enter recurrence.'

'But sometimes I can't even remember simple things, like the first time I swived a man, the way I should. It's as if some of my memories are not really real.'

'It is that way with everyone,' he told her. 'There are many layers of memory.'

He talked about recent, clear memories, as when people closed their eyes and could see what they had beheld a moment before. Going backward toward birth, most memories grew hazier, and some of the earliest recollections weren't really memories at all, but more like memories of memories. How many could recall anything of their first year of life? How many moments of one's life were lost to time, like an infant's cries in the wind? Could he, the Lord Remembrancer, bring to mind his life's every thought, emotion, sensation of hot or cold, word spoken or heard, gas pain, tinkle of water, mouthful of food, or colour beheld? How much of himself could he actually remember? Some of the more pedantic remembrancers had once tried to quantify the self, and they had claimed that an average person might recall a billionth of all that they had ever experienced. And yet, people did not feel diminished as a result. And even in the saddest of circumstances, as with an old master akashic suffering from the angslan, a person might grieve the loss of her memories while still retaining a strong sense of herself.

'We are all rivers,' he told her. 'Always flowing and never quite the same, as our bodies create new blood cells and neurons out of food and water and our memories change moment by moment and we create new ones. And yet, no matter how you change, from baby to grandmother, you are still you, as the river is always the river.'

His words seemed to comfort her, and she squeezed his hand. 'Thank you. I know I am happier when I don't think about the past too much, but sometimes I can't help it.'

How could it be otherwise with this Maria, who had begun life as a single cell in Kalinda's womb and had then floated in warmed and protected salt water before stepping out of the ocean only forty days later as a fully formed woman? When she tried to relive a past that had never been, she fell through the terrifying void of nonexistence. But when she dwelled within the moment where she liked to be and bared her being to the naked now, she knew the wonder of herself as if for the first time and felt herself marvellously alive.

How happy she seemed sitting with him on the dunes above the sea as she looked up at the stars! And why shouldn't she have been glad indeed not to have consummated the desire they both could feel building within them like a rising tide? For she didn't yet have to live in a future, as had the first Maria, where things between her and Rane had gone bad.

As if she could read his thoughts (and she probably could), she pulled at his hand, and said, 'I want you to take me back to the empty places, even if they hurt because they are empty.'

'Why, Maria?'

'Because if I can fill in the void, I can stand more easily in the here and now and create the future that was meant to be.'

The next morning in the glade, with some bluebirds chirping in the tamarind tree, Rane brought out his old wooden box filled with bottles of essential oils and various drugs such as toalache and kalla. While Maria lay back in the grass smiling up at him, he unstoppered a vial containing the essence of oranges and held it beneath her nose. He used the powerful olfaction attitude to take her down into recurrence. He couldn't, of course, restore memories that had never been nor could he get her to relive the ersatz memories that Kalinda had imprinted in her. But he could help her to integrate them.

And so he took her through more recent memories, the real ones of laughing around a fire with Nikolandru and Kalinda and walking with Rane through the sere chaparral and acorn-heavy oaks of the foothills. These memories she could live again as she had only a month or a day or an hour before. Already, Maria had spent more time walking the flowered woods and the sunny beaches than she had as a foetus growing in the ocean. She already had thousands of new memories, like flaming jewels, perhaps millions of them. One memory in particular Rane planned to use as a sort of diamond that might lend a bit of its brilliance to dull stone and make it more vivid. Only the day before yesterday, while out on a hunt with Kalinda in the hills, Maria had shot an arrow into the flank of a deer. In the wild chase to bring down the doomed creature, she had driven it over a cliff. The fall had nearly killed the stag: its antlers snapped into splinters and its head broke open into bits of bone and brain spread upon the cliff's rocks like a red porridge. She had used the knife Kalinda had given her to slit the deer's throat and finish it.

Rane used this bloody memory to anchor inside Maria her tenuous recollection of the bloody death of Armas Sarkissian. He knew how badly his fall from the Karadan Adri troubled her, for she didn't understand how such a violent and significant event could remain so opaque to her. It soothed her not at all when Rane assured her that many people had trouble recalling the violent moments in their lives: storms of hormones and neurotransmitters drove the brain into an extremis of experience that could not easily be recalled in more normal states of consciousness and so drove memory away. But she determined to recall that which she felt she must recall. And so she had asked that he take her back to the Sarkissian estate on Kailash Poru and the terrible moment that she had murdered Armas.

'I did push him, I must have,' she said when she finished her remembrance an hour later and sat up. The bluebirds had flown away from the tamarind tree, and now some squirrels skittered about through its branches. On the grass by the brook, most of the bonobos were taking morning naps, as was the tigress. 'But I don't see how I *could* have.'

'Your situation was desperate,' Rane said to her. 'You had no choice.'

'Didn't I?'

'Not if you wanted to escape your enslavement. I know it must be the hardest thing, to take another human being's—'

'It *is* hard, very hard, as you say. But how many animals have I hunted and slain? Do you think it wasn't *hard* for me to cut the deer's throat open? My mother trained me to do the hard things.'

'Then—'

'So, yes, in the sense of being able to, I *could* have killed Armas, just as I could put my knife into Nikolandru if he tried to harm my mother. But in another sense – and the only one that matters – I *couldn't* have. You see, I loved him.'

Her words, in a moment of ice and paralysis, made no sense to him. And then a moment later, too much. He listened frozen into a terrible fear as she recounted her memory of Armas. She told of loving him deeply and completely, as she loved all that most mattered to her. She did not hesitate to divulge the details of the physical part of that love, and she did so matter-of-factly, as she might have described the technique for opening an oyster and getting out the meat. Her words forced Rane to recall how Santuu Sarkissian had wanted Rane to view the hologram of Maria and Armas together. No one, Santuu had said, could have had so much passion for another, and therefore Maria must have been acting out her looks of love and paroxysms of pleasure. Rane lived again his terrible hate for Santuu, and in that moment he knew that somehow, in this sweet-smelling glade with the brook running slow and clear, with a heart-piercing vividness, Maria had relived her memory of the man she had cherished. And that was impossible.

'Sometimes,' Rane said to her, 'victims of violence will create false memories to replace those they have obliterated – and so create a story of themselves that makes sense to them.'

'I am no victim,' she said.

'But Armas enslaved you!'

'No more than I did him. He wanted me to marry him.'

'Then why didn't you?'

She shrugged her shoulders. 'Because I would have had to become the mistress of other slaves.'

'Then perhaps you *did* kill him. You really had no other choice.'

'Yes, I did. I could have killed myself.'

She said that, too, matter-of-factly, as she might have spoken of taking off a dress that had got wet in the rain and hanging it in the sun to dry.

'I know I would have,' she said, 'rather than kill the man I loved.'

He reached out and clasped her hand. 'Please don't torment yourself. Perhaps this memory is only—'

'I know what happened,' she said. 'I *know* what is in my heart.'

Her fingers tightened around his hand, which she pressed against her breast. The look in her eyes pierced him straight through.

'How do you know?'

'Because,' she said, 'it is so *real.*'

Later, as Rane walked alone on the beach, the personal part
of him continued trying to convince himself that Maria must
have somehow transformed a false memory of having deep feelings for Armas into a fantasy she believed to be true. However,
the professional part of him knew very well she had entered deep
into recurrence and had lived herself anew. Impossible that still
seemed to him – and yet, wasn't there one way it might not be?

His wrath at that possibility built inside him through the
morning and afternoon and drove the coldness in his heart
away. Late that evening, he confronted Kalinda. He found her
down on the beach by the waterline, gazing up at the stars. It
seemed a nightly ritual of hers before bed, to look out at the
galaxy she meant to protect and awaken – that is, if she ever
truly slept at all.

'You told me,' he said to her, 'that Maria was for me. That
of what I learned about her, I could choose what would become
memory and what would not.'

Yava, at Kalinda's side, must not have liked the tone in Rane's
voice, for she opened her jaws and loosed a bone-shaking roar.
So angry was Rane that he didn't care.

'I did tell you that. Have you found a way, my doubtful man,
to tell yourself otherwise?'

'You imprinted in her the memory of her loving Armas
Sarkissian.'

Kalinda looked at him in silence. In the light of a sliver of
a moon, he could barely see her face.

'Somehow,' he said, 'you've found a way to make imprinted
memories as vivid as real ones.'

Her sharp, quick voice whipped out into the night: 'Accuse
me again, Lord Rane, and I will let Yava have her way with
you.'

Again, the great cat roared.

'I am sorry, madam, but what other explanation can
there be?'

'You were in doubt as to whether Maria loved Armas or
pushed him off the cliff. You chose to make Maria a killer, and
that is the memory I imprinted.'

'Because that is what I believed!'

'It is what you wanted to believe. But now we know you
believed wrongly.'

'But it is not just that Maria can't relive her killing of Armas – it's that the memory seems false to her.'

'But of course it is.'

'But her other memories, such as the fantasy of her journey here with Leander of Aoide, do not seem false to her.'

'Then it must be that there are degrees of the false. Maria's recollection of journeying here with Leander would be consistent with who Maria is. Her memory of killing a man she loved would be a violation of her soul.'

'Should that matter so much?'

'If I were to take off Maria's scarf and tie it again around your neck, you could wear it easily. But if I were to cut out your cold, covetous heart and replace it with Maria's beautiful one, your body would reject it.'

Was that possible, he wondered, for someone to reject imprinted memories in this way? Perhaps – but only if those false memories contradicted real ones.

'But if you didn't imprint Maria's feelings for Armas,' he said, 'from where did they come?'

'I don't know.'

'The real Maria, *my* Maria, might have been . . . fond of Armas.' He watched the waves moving like great dark beasts over the ocean. 'But how could the Maria born out of these waters believe she loved him?'

He sensed but couldn't see Kalinda's smile as she looked up at the ocean of stars above them. Her voice, though, sounded out as clear as a bell: 'In our universe, Lord Remembrancer, there is nothing but mystery.'

Rane could not stop thinking about what she had said. Through the warm days and cool nights of that autumn, he dived deep into memory and experience as he tried to solve the mystery of Maria. He spent as much time with her as he could. She took great pleasure in walking with him along the foothills and the beach and pointing out the living things that she knew as friends: the sycamore trees and the myrtle growing on sunny slopes; the periwinkles, anemones, and rock crabs searching for meaty titbits in the tidepools; the gulls and the ospreys gliding over lustrous blue waters. She showed him how to make snares to snag the rabbits that they cooked over sweet-smelling piñon fires. When she discovered that he liked dangerous sports such as climbing icefalls, she spent many days working with him to fashion two surfboards out of cedar and thuja wood. She laughed at his attempts to catch waves out in the frothy surf, and she laughed all the harder when he finally managed to stand up on his board and glide along by her side nearly all the way to shore. They laughed all the time because they found each other amusing and, more, because they made each other feel good. Sometimes at nights, she recited poetry to him. He learned of the great but unknown Jailahavru, who had combined Fravashi word keys and Moksha tones deriving from the ancient mixolydian mode and had set them into heroic dactylic hexameter verse of an almost transcendent beauty. He loved listening to her recite to him, in her rich, throaty voice that rang out with a music strangely her own.

Often, he thought of loving her as they both knew they wished to love. Maria had a way of sidling up against him as a cat might rub a tree to mark her territory. She had a way of looking at him that tore into him with a sharp pain. Many moments swelled hot and hurtful with his desire for her, while many more took hold of him like the grip of bone-chilling wind in deep winter.

It helped not at all that he continued instructing her in the art of remembrance. Long ago he had made a rule for himself that he would never involve himself intimately with a student. Other high professionals and academicians of the Order felt otherwise. Novices and sometimes journeymen kept house and prepared meals for the akashics, horologes, and the other masters who tutored them, and so why if both student and teacher agreed shouldn't that service deepen to a natural expression of physical accord? Merely because the one was older and had more power than the other?

He thought of the scryers, who abused their power over the very young women who entered their profession, or so he deemed. The scryers took their inspiration from the ancient Spartans: a boy wishing to become a warrior had to look to the guidance of an older man hardened in battle, a man who would act as both teacher of spear and shield and as a lover. Many young scryers described the relief they felt in abandoning themselves to the vision and wisdom of the older women. However, Rane knew of at least three novice scryers who had left the

Order rather than submit to the touches of their mistresses, and he well remembered the story of Evangelia Chu: more than a hundred years before, when Rane first became a master remembrancer, Evangelia had not only put out her own eyes in the most arduous and sacred of all the scryers' rituals but had then put the bloody knife to her throat. Although he could not imagine any such fate befalling Maria, his natural conservatism (always at war with the wilder part of himself) deterred him from returning her intimacies of hand and eye with his own.

One rainy evening in mid-autumn, when Nikolandru and Rane took shelter inside a tent retrieved from inside the *Asherah*, the pilot-poet finally lost patience with him: 'What a fool you are, my friend! It is as if you pursued a mare ten billion times around the circle of the world and she finally stands ready and winking at you. And what do you do? You pound your hoof into the earth, afraid that you'll crush her.'

'I just need to wait,' Rane said.

'Wait for what? Wait for how long? Of what am I to sing?'

So it went for another ten days, and Rane continued hunting and surfing and teaching remembrance, and the mystery of Maria deepened. At least once every day, he guided her journeys into memory. Often, he used his fingers to press against nexi in her face, using acupressure against nerves connecting through the skull and grey matter to the amygdala and other emotional centres of the brain. He helped her to release painful emotions and integrate them. Sometimes, in his best of moments, he spoke to her gently, with all the warmth and insight that he could call upon, and then he applied a sort of acupressure of the soul.

One day, sunny and warm again, Rane worked with her on the broad beach opposite the Kalawasaq Rock. He sat above her on a sandy blanket, and took her down again into recurrence. She wanted to explore again her remembrance of Armas Sarkissian. She kept returning to her love for him, like a finger that can't leave a wound alone. How easily love came to her, like nectar pouring out of a flower! And how her feeling for this dead man poisoned him! He felt the pain of it down below his throat like an acid. How long would it be, he wondered, before it worked its way through the tenderest parts of him deep into his heart?

When Maria finally sat up and looked at him, he saw

immediately that something had eclipsed her natural love as a dark moon might the sun. 'I remembered something,' she said.

She fell against him, sobbing, and he held her until the violent quaking of her chest and belly subsided and her breathing grew steady again. And then, in a voice raw and pained, she told him about Santuu Sarkissian:

'It happened one day,' she said, 'when Armas was away from the estate on business. Santuu hated me from the first hour that Armas brought me home from Onklash – almost as much as he lusted after me. He would have raped me, but I was Armas's slave, not his.'

And so instead, she told him, Santuu had done to her something even worse. The rules of the Sarkissian household demanded that any slave involved in any way with the offence of another must watch the offender's punishment. When Maria dared to offer her friend Lily solace after Santuu had beaten her for some trifling negligence, Santuu had ordered Maria bound but not gagged. And then he had raped the delicate Lily in front of her, violently, until she bled. Santuu told Maria that he enjoyed her screams of protest even more than he did Lily's.

'I can still *see* this happening!'

Had Rane, while on Kailash Poru, ever caught a whiff of a hint of this terrible story? From where, then, had it come? Had Maria confabulated it and then experienced it as a real memory? No – he knew as well as she did that it must be real.

'It was Santuu,' she said, 'whom I would have killed.'

So would I, he thought.

They looked at each other, and it was as if two stars passed a terrible fire back and forth, and, by a mysterious alchemy of flame and blood, the hate that each felt became as one awe-making thing:

In that hour waking wonder . . .

Although hate is always just hate, they did not hate in the same way. For Maria, it was all quick, furious, and personal. She wanted to rip off Santuu's filthy phallus with her teeth, swallow it, cut his throat, drink his blood and digest him into dung to remind him of who he really was. And thus the vile substance of Santuu would in the end fertilize the earth. Her hate came and went, like the moon uncovering the sun. It reminded her that the totality of darkness must always give way to the light. For she was made to love, and the earth pulled her always back into love, and no matter how imperfect she might be, she always felt herself at bottom to be whole and good.

Rane's hate, however, partook of the impersonal and the universal. He would have exulted in throwing Santuu over that damned wall – and then to have resurrected him a million times and to have murdered him an uncountable number of times more: by knife, by fist, by fire, by ice, so that Santuu could feel the pain of all those he had injured and the suffering of the entire world. He wanted Santuu's punishments to live on with that pain in eternity. Rane's hate came on slowly like a glacier and carved hollows in his soul. It pulled him into himself. It recalled the basic wrongness of the universe, and his own, and so he hated most deeply of all that which he should have held dear.

In that hour waking wonder,
Tender of touch,
Wet sweet burning eyes,
You looked without cover
Into the inferno – into myself.

How was it that Maria could look at him and see everything without turning away? And to love what she saw? He had never known why the first Maria had loved him, and it didn't make sense now.

'Rane.'

She said his name with a sweetness and a fire so deep and fierce that it cut the coldness out of him. How could anyone make of a single word an entire poem? In their walks along this beautiful beach, she had been his inspiration for poetry, and now she was to show him a much finer thing.

'Rane,' she said again.

And hadn't it always been that way with Maria? How else could it ever be?

She touched his hand with an unbearable tenderness. Their fingers worked at each other's garments, and she pulled off his kamelaika while he stripped off her flimsy dress. With the wind shivering their naked skin and the gulls crying out high and insistent over the ocean, their lips finally came together and they both made murmurs of desire deep inside their throats. He kissed her for a long time, and he had no care that the hot sun might burn his bare flesh. His kissed her along her neck, tied with the soft, fluttering scarf, and he kissed down across her belly. It seemed that he had a thirst that had been raging for ten lifetimes, a parching of his own throat and soul that he could slake only by drinking all of her in. She was all water and waves of motion, like the sea, and like the sea in its long, dark, eternal roar she called to him in a single sound:

'Rane!'

When it came time to join fire with fire and return to their star, he pulled back for a moment. She lay beneath him with her legs opened to him, along with her heart and her eyes and every cell of her body – all and everything that made up this perfect woman, utterly open. And through the windows of her eyes, so dark and yet so clear, he saw that what they were about to make together would hurt her terribly. And she knew this as a flower feels the wilt of the sun, and she didn't care. For out of that burn would come the most beautiful of all things, and for at least one moment the ardour they passed back and forth to each other would make them whole.

'Maria.'

And so she pulled him inside, and he knew himself immortal and good, and she became once again his healer and showed him how to be whole. There came a moment of bursting into brightness that would live on forever. As he had an infinite number of times, he felt himself remade from inside her, reborn in splendour, like a child coming out into a blinding, lovely light.

And into a pain without bottom or end.

27

The next three tendays Rane counted as his life's golden time. He felt happier with Maria even than he had on Neverness, for here on this faraway earth he had none of the duties and drears of his office as Lord Remembrancer to distract him from a more satisfying pursuit – and Maria could make of herself a poem to him rather than standing on the frozen Fravashi Green and reciting her verses to her admirers. Although it was early winter, it never got very cold on this golden coast. Indeed, after one brief spell of rain, with a fresh sea wind blowing up from the south, it actually got warmer and clearer, as if their love had called forth the very sun.

He had no care or concern other than making love with Maria and *making* love anew as often and completely as they could. They joined their bodies together on the dunes and down on the hard-packed sands and sometimes standing up in cold, buoyant ocean waters. They lay together in the glade and on a blanket spread out in a meadow below the white-capped Tears of the Moon Mountains. They swived like animals, with a grunting, screaming pleasure that overmatched even that of the bonobos, and yet like angels, too. So high did his spirits soar that if he could have, he would have leaped up into the air with her and mated mid-flight over the shining summit of Mount Shamulashan. His desire to shut out the past and to make of her his whole world recalled a riddle that Danlo had once learned from the elders of the Devaki tribe:

How do you capture a beautiful bird without killing its spirit?
And the answer: *By becoming the sky.*

One day, while they stood in the ocean's shallows looking out to the west, he worried that his unquenchable need for her might be exhausting and draining her. He said nothing of this, but he didn't have to, for she often understood him better than he did himself. She smiled, then recited words from an old, old poem to him:

> My bounty is as boundless as the sea,
> My love as deep. The more I give to thee,
> The more I have, for both are infinite.

'But if you empty out a little bit of infinity,' he said, playing the kind of mental games her mother had taught her to enjoy, 'isn't there just a little bit less of that infinity left?'

'No, of course not. An infinity always remains.'

The ocean that day glowed with a translucent kahurangi jade colour that warmed her sparkling eyes. So much awareness he saw there, of him, of herself, of every rushing wave and glint of sunlight off the waters of the world. So much delight in playing the great game of life and so much of what Sunjay and Chandra and the other Children called *awarei*.

'But what do you really know of infinity?' he asked her. 'Mathematically—'

'Is this a day for mathematics, my Rane? All right, then, my mother has taught me a little. There are different orders of infinity, yes? The counting numbers and the number of points on a line, Aleph Zero and Aleph One, and—'

'Actually,' he said, 'the equivalence of Aleph One and the number of points on a line is the old Continuum Hypothesis, not to be confused with the Continuum Hypothesis of the Order's pilots.'

'How pedantic you can be! The point is – please don't correct me if I'm wrong – a power set of another yields a new set of greater cardinality, and so—'

'That is right so far.'

'And so one order of infinity can generate a higher order of infinity, an infinity of infinities, on and on forever into Absolute Infinity, which is love.'

'Cantor called it God.'

'In the end, is there a difference?'

Some of their best moments came during their hikes up

the Atushqun headland above the sea. There they spent many hours just talking and laughing and looking into each other's eyes. For in the deeps of their ardour for each other, he found something so bright and good that he could hardly bear it. It was as if in all his couplings with other women over three long lifetimes he had made love with just one woman – and what *made* making love with Maria so ecstatic was that she was that one woman. By what miracle had he found her not just once in his life but twice? How could he ever hold all that inside himself? Wasn't that like trying to fit inside his heart the entire earth?

'I don't care any more about what happened with Armas,' she said to him one warm afternoon. 'A thousand years from now, my memories will be of you.'

Could that possibly be, he wondered? Maria, the daughter of a goddess, might live so long, but he would not. And why should he care? For what really mattered was Maria's smile, the softness of her words and fingers, the sweetness of her breath, the sunlight on her lips and the much deeper radiance in her eyes that brightened his. How to vanish into the magic of *this* moment and make it last?

For wasn't that one of Maria's greatest gifts, the annihilation of both past and future? Was it possible, he wondered, in the way of the warrior-poets and Mallory Ringess, simply to stop time? What would the Timekeeper, first of all the horologes, have said about this? What would he himself, as *the* Remembrancer, say? For wasn't it time, the experience of time, that turned the terror and wonder of the now-moment into memory? What was time's true nature? Why did it progress inexorably like the plummeting of an arrow-shot bird in one direction only when the symmetry of the laws of physics suggested it could move both forward and backward? Could it be possible, through memory, to defeat time and recreate the past? And thus redeem the present and make of it a whole new world?

That day, with the waves of a big sea breaking against the rocks below them, they came very close to stopping time. They made love for an uncountable number of moments beneath a golden sun. In the warm, wet clutch of Maria's body and the much deeper pulling of her soul, she seemed as real to him as his first Maria and as worthy of his love. She called with her deep eyes for him to give all of himself to her. It was not enough for her to cry out like a beautiful firebird streaking across the sky. Nor enough to show her bright plumage in a display of the universe's greatness in bringing forth such a marvel of creation. No, she had to be a mirror as well in which all who looked upon her might behold their own flaming splendour. In those wondrous moments when Rane dared to meet eyes with her, she showed him the greatest of himself, and then their love seemed a perfect and indestructible thing.

'I have decided,' Maria said to him. They sat together exhausted but happy on top of Atushqun's cliff. She dangled her legs over the rocky edge as they both gazed out at the sea. 'I am going to ask my mother's permission for you to make me pregnant.'

Her words drove like a fist into his belly. All his gladness whooshed out of him and blew away in the wind.

'I can't . . .'

How could he ever understand this wilful woman and her even more imperious mother? He remembered walking into the glade after the first of Maria's and his couplings just as the two women stood face to face concluding an argument:

'But Mother, this is my body, and I will do with it as I wish!'

'Your body is of the earth, *my* earth, and you will do with it as *I* say.'

Maria had pressed her hand against her belly as she glared at Kalinda. '*My* eggs, my womb, my life. I will live my own life!'

'Every one of your eggs came to life inside *my* womb, as did you. And *you* are my life, Maria.'

'I won't—'

'You *will*, my darling daughter.' And then she had laid down the law: 'I will not allow any of your ova to be fertilized until it is time.'

'And when will that be?'

There had come a searing, searching look as Kalinda had stared at Rane. 'It will be time when it is time.'

Now, thirty days later, sitting on a rock above big breaking waves, squeezing Rane's hand, Maria had run out of patience. She said to Rane, 'She can't keep on testing you forever.'

'Perhaps,' he said, 'your mother doesn't want grandchildren.'

'No, it is just the opposite: she is *dying* to have many.'

'But there are so many worlds, so many children. No one

has counted how many trillions. And your mother has made herself their protector. Perhaps that is enough.'

'It might be enough if people remained as they have been for a hundred thousand years. But you inspired my mother with your stories of the *Asta Siluuna*.'

'Sunjay,' he said, looking down at her dangling legs. 'Chandra.'

'And their father, Danlo.'

Her *brother*, he thought. Should he tell her what Kalinda had not wanted her to know?

'A new race,' she said. 'And remembrance of the One Memory will be crucial to their . . . what was it your Kolenya Mor called one's *becoming*?'

'Ontogenesis,' he said.

'Yes, this willed evolution that should be within the grasp of everyone.'

'It's not clear to me that it is within the grasp of *anyone*. Even Chandra, even Sunjay might not—'

'Evolution has spent ten billion years developing and preserving us through genetic memory. All we need to do is to let go and embrace the form within us that wants to be.'

'It's not so easy,' he said, 'to get past the patterns that evolution has graven in humanity's soul. Decadence, dominance, worship of—'

'Do you see *patterns* when you look at me?' she asked. She took his hands in hers and smiled at him. 'When I look at *you*, I see a painter of that soul.'

'You are so romantic. But people are complacent, locked inside themselves, and so they fall into *glavering*, schadenfreude, and what the Fravashi call prenune, in which—'

'Then they just need to open the door. And remembrance is that key.'

'It *should* be, but—'

'All we have to do is to let go of ourselves. And to find ourselves through the One Memory of who we really are. Just as I find myself in you, and you in me, when we look at each other and hold each other and make—'

'You are so idealistic,' he said.

'You make me so.' She pressed his hands between hers and held them over her heart. 'We just have to let go and not be afraid.'

Because he couldn't bear the wild hope that lit up her eyes, he pulled his hands away from her and gazed out at the sea.

The water rushed to the shore in its age-old patterns of sets of dark, breaking waves.

'A child,' she said, 'a beautiful boy or girl, part of you, and part of the—'

'Perhaps your mother is right,' he said. 'Perhaps this isn't the right time.'

'Of course it is! The earth is waiting.' She motioned with her hand toward the blue ocean. 'I am waiting. What could be a better time?'

'But we only just met, and I really don't know—'

'I love you, and you love me, and what more is there to know?'

Rane ground his fist against the rock beneath them. 'Aren't I to have something do with fertilizing those precious eggs of yours?'

'Only everything! I wasn't thinking of swiving Dinos or Nikolandru!'

'Then—'

'Don't you *want* to make a baby with me?'

He waited too long to answer her. She looked at him. And he felt as well as saw her immense will and wildness, which both rebuked and called to him. She *would*, if she could, create a child with him right here and now in this windy place above the sea. She would leap right off the cliff with him into a stormy future without a doubt that somehow they both would fly. And hadn't it been that way with the first Maria? Or *had* it been? Why couldn't he remember? How could he go down through his sickening sense of déjà vu to get to the heart of things? Somewhere inside him lay the truth of memory and love – truth and denial and terror.

'Rane?'

He began closing in on himself like the sea ice around Neverness in winter. Maria tried to feel her way through the coldness, touching his hand, kissing his face, looking into his eyes, trying to gather in a little hope like an orca coming up from the clear water between ice floes to breathe. Soon, though, no patch of ocean remained open in which she might arise or dive. Rane hardened into himself, leaving not an inch of room for her.

Her sobs of betrayal and despair came over her quickly, as they always had, like a tidal wave forming up from the ocean deeps and breaking against a rocky shore. She wept for a long time while Rane sat like a stone looking out to sea. At last she gave up. She stood and walked off toward the glade, leaving him alone.

Much later, after midnight, he found her by herself three miles to the south, walking along the beach that curved around a big, gleaming bay. They stood near the starlit surf. He put his arms around her and drew her close. And he told her, 'I'm sorry.'

'Why does it have to hurt so much?' she asked, looking at him through the dark.

'I don't know,' he said. 'But I think I would rather die than hurt you again.'

'Would you?' She kissed him. A terrible storm had passed, and now she felt happy again. 'I *know* I would rather die than hurt you.'

Rane hoped that would be the end of their troubles, and Maria felt sure of it. They coupled above the ocean without even a blanket to cover the earth, and Rane's knees drove deep into soft sands as they cried out to each other with great gladness. Their lovemaking went on all night, not just in the joining of their bodies but even more in their breathing in each other's newfound hope. By the time the sun rose over the mountains in the east, he felt almost ready to father fifty children out of Maria's beautiful, blessed womb.

They talked all that morning and afternoon about what they dreamed for each other. When they returned to the glade to rest, however, they did not find peace. Dinos had committed some new offence, perhaps stealing a fruit from the screaming Babecca, who teamed up with Shimuri and Emalia to chasten him again. Nikolandru sat quietly at the stone table and stared at the moringa tree as if contemplating being hanged from one of its stout branches. Rane went over to ask this usually cheerful man why he seemed so glum. And Nikolandru said, 'I would have made such a memorable song.'

Just as Rane was about to ask him what he meant, Kalinda and her tigress walked into the glade. And as she stopped near the brook, her eyes lost their sharpness and focused instead on infinity. Forty feet from her, the air above the ground came alive with a chatoyant shimmer. And then the colours cooking away oxygen and nitrogen died into a blackness that ate down through green blades of grass and dirt, charring and cutting a hole in the earth. In the last sixty days, Rane had seen several such holes, for after Maria had been born, the Silicon God's attacks had grown more frequent.

'Your tests are over,' Kalinda said when her gaze had cleared. She walked closer to Rane. She stopped in the centre of the glade as if poised at the axis mundi of the earth. 'You may prepare to leave.'

Rane, standing near Nikolandru, said to her: 'But Maria and I haven't even talked about leaving. We—'

'You will not leave with her.'

'But I—'

'You have failed your test.' Her hand settled on top of the head of the tigress who stared at Rane with her glowing eyes. 'My daughter came to me yesterday weeping. But it is sunlight I would see in her eyes and not tears. It is laughter I would hear upon her lips and not sobs. It is joy I would feel within her heart that is my heart, as she is my hope for a future that must be without you.'

Rane shook his head as if her words made no sense to him. 'We quarrelled and had a bad moment, but never again will—'

'Maria is not for you.'

All this time, Maria had stood quietly beneath the moringa tree with the bonobos, whom she joined in soothing the upset Babecca. Now, though, she moved away from the apes, her sheathed hunting knife swaying at her side with each of her angry steps. And she cried out: 'How can I not be for him if he is for me?'

Kalinda, though, kept her gaze focused on Rane. She told him, 'You will be taken to Danlo's old chalet on the coast a thousand miles from here. There, you will meditate on your failures and perhaps gain the powers of remembrance that should be yours.'

'Mother!'

'And you, my beloved daughter,' she said, turning to Maria, 'will return to Neverness to learn from a remembrancer who won't make you weep. A master remembrancer who can show you the way into the One Memory.'

She nodded at Nikolandru. 'The pilot-poet will take you there. You will leave immediately.'

Kalinda spoke with the weight of a million moons behind her dreadful words, and as she had said, so might it have been. At that moment, though, her eyes looked off into emptiness as the air a hundred feet from her across the glade scintillated with a second of the Silicon God's attacks. And in that moment, Nikolandru moved. The glumness fell away from his striking face, even as he himself went away, to be replaced with a stranger who looked nothing like him. This murderous fury of a man arose from his stone seat with a speed that made Rane gasp. He drove his fist into Rane's solar plexus, doubling up Rane in spasms of even deeper gasping. Almost before Maria could react, he charged across the glade upon her, and he struck her down to the grass even as his hand shot out to grab up her knife. As Rane tried to straighten up and avenge this inexplicable violence, Yava's roar shook the air. Her muscles bunched and trembled beneath orange and black fur as she charged at Nikolandru. He met the tigress's wrath with a terrifying speed and a coordination of eye, arm, hand, and knife. When the tigress sprang at him, he ducked beneath her leap and drove the knife's blade through fur and skin past bone, straight into the great beast's heart. Yava screamed a great, horrible scream, and dropped to the earth. And then Nikolandru turned on Kalinda.

'Mother!'

Maria managed to stand as Rane forced himself to straighten and take a step closer to her. Nikolandru closed the distance toward Kalinda.

'Mother, move!'

And move Kalinda did. She came out of her faraway consciousness with a flaring of her dazzling dark eyes into the naked now. She whipped free her killing knife. Its silvery shasteel shattered the light of the late sun. Then Nikolandru fell upon her as she fell upon him, and it was as if two whirlwinds of arms, fists, knees, and feet collided with each other in a single cloud of flashing metal and motion. And when the killing storm finally played out, Nikolandru lay dead on the grass with his throat cut open.

'Mother!'

Kalinda stood over Nikolandru, her long knife dripping blood. She breathed quickly and deeply; her eyes shone with triumph but also with the tears of an immense sadness. She cleaned her knife by thrusting it into the ground and sheathed it. She hurried over to Yava. In a single fluid motion, she stripped off her dress and dropped it down to cover the tigress's corpse. She stood naked to the sun, her whole body glistening, from her muscular neck down across breasts and belly and the black fur of her sex to brown legs and feet planted in the grass as if to draw strength from the earth. She looked off far away, perhaps a million miles, and then she looked at Yava. The garment she had laid upon the tigress now glowed in colours of green, bright blue, and flaming crimson. Soon, the tiger's breaths shook the flimsy fabric. Then Yava opened her yellow eyes as Kalinda dropped down to kiss the great beast's head. Her hand caressed the tiger as if to summon her to new life. When Kalinda took back her dress and Yava stood once again on her four furry legs, Rane could see no sign that she had ever been wounded.

So stunned were both Rane and Maria at the sights they had seen that neither of them could move. The whole bonobo troop, however, had fled the mayhem of the glade. Rane stared at the bloody red wound cut into Nikolandru's throat as if nothing in the world would ever make sense again.

'He was not a pilot-poet,' Kalinda said, looking down at Nikolandru. She knelt to kiss his forehead, then covered his face with her dress. This time, its chatoyant substance did not glow, and Nikolandru lay as still as a stone. 'He was a warrior-poet of Qallar.'

The story she now told both amazed and aggrieved Rane. She explained how the Silicon God, aided by those warrior-poets who had taken his side, had created a hunter-sleeper she called a droghul: years before, the warrior-poets had split the identity of one of their brightest and deadliest, a young man named Krikor, and had imprinted him with false memories. Nikolandru had actually believed himself to be a pilot-poet of the destroyed planet of Aoide – at least most of the time he believed that. At other times, the warrior-poet took over. Nikolandru knew nothing of Krikor; Krikor knew everything about Nikolandru. It had been Krikor who had first piloted the *Asherah* to Neverness.

'The warrior-poets,' Kalinda said to Rane, 'counted Danlo as a potential god, and they wanted to kill him. But Krikor found Danlo absent from the city. When he learned of your quest to find Old Earth and therefore me, he immediately plotted a much greater assassination.'

Rane, still staring at Nikolandru's corpse, and still stunned, shook his head. He had enough sense, however, to notice that Kalinda had said nothing about his quest to find *Maria*.

'But why the elaborate ruse?' he asked. 'In the first place and then after? Why didn't this Krikor droghul just hunt Danlo down and be done with it?'

'Because he, and his masters, knew that as Krikor he would be detected. We warrior-poets cannot hide who we really are.'

Could Kalinda, he wondered, looking at this lovely but lethal woman, have acted the part of a gentle pilot-poet?

'Krikor also had to convince you,' she said. 'Could he have travelled with you across half the galaxy merely pretending to be Nikolandru without your sensing that something was wrong? You, the Lord Remembrancer? Nikolandru's memories of himself had to seem real, especially to himself.'

He studied Kalinda's face, now calm and clear, then glanced at Maria. She stood staring at her mother in awe.

'And of course Krikor could never,' Kalinda said, 'have got near me.'

'*I* almost couldn't get near you. What Nikolandru did, that is, Krikor, changing plans of who to assassinate at the last moment, winning my trust, finding his way across the stars here – it all seems such a wild chance.'

Kalinda looked down at Nikolandru. 'The Silicon God does not mind spending human lives on wild chances.'

'And you never suspected that—'

'I suspected but I didn't know. Every time I looked into Nikolandru's mind—'

'I thought that you had a rule that you would not—'

'Considering the circumstances,' she said with a smile, 'I made a rule that that rule should be suspended.'

'But if you did suspect, then—?'

'Why didn't I kill him out of hand? Because there is an even older rule: keep your friends close but your enemies closer.' She pointed at the black hole in the ground. 'As long as Nikolandru lived, the Silicon God supposed that I was vulnerable. You see what he has done to my earth, but you do not see what I do to him. It is a game that we've been playing for a long time – a game that I will soon win.'

'You took a terrible chance.'

'Not as much as you might suppose. I watched Nikolandru . . . with great care. Then, too . . .'

Her gaze fell upon his body as if she looked through him straight into the heart of the earth.

'Yes?'

'Then, too,' she said softly, 'Nikolandru was two men, a poet and a murderer. Much like me. Didn't the poet deserve love and life until the murderer appeared?'

Rane fell silent. The chirping of the birds in the trees and Maria's murmurs of compassion for her mother seemed much too loud.

'The murderer,' he said. He looked down at Nikolandru's body. 'He was a friend and a great pilot who risked a great deal to bring me here. We should bury him.'

'He was a warrior-poet, and I will tend to him according to our ways.'

Rane thought about this. And then he thought that he needed to think more carefully. 'But if Nikolandru was Nikolandru up to the last moment, how did you know about Krikor?'

'I saw all in his mind just after Nikolandru went away.'

The thought grew stronger, and Rane entered the attitudes of imaging and dereism to smother it in a blanket of memories before it could ignite. 'Then what you said about Nikolandru returning to Neverness with Maria was just a feint to flush Krikor out?'

'Yes. It was time.'

'And what you said about the cabin on the coast was also part of this feint?'

'No, the *chalet* stands empty and waiting as it has for years. And there you will go.'

'Mother, there he will *not* go!' Maria called out. She charged across the glade right up to Kalinda, and stood glaring at her face to face. So great was her anger that if she had been a warrior-poet, Kalinda might have been in trouble. 'I love him!'

'And I love you, beautiful daughter, as I do the Earth, and that is why he *will* go.'

'And he loves me! He *won't* hurt me again!'

'You may walk with him down to the beach, where you will say goodbye.'

'He is my life! I will walk into the ocean and say goodbye to you and everything. Do you think I will not?'

'I know you will not. Rane will still have his life in his cabin, as he calls it. And you will still have your hope that some day you might see him again. And, then, too . . .'

'What?'

'Then, too, you are Maria.'

'Mother!'

It was said that the sperm whales that dive beneath the icebergs in the waters off Neverness Island can kill their prey with a single burst of sonance louder than a rocket's roar. Maria's great shout to her mother rang with the power of an immense love, anguish, and outrage. It didn't harm Kalinda, but it did move her.

'All right,' she said, looking up at the sky. The sun had gone down over the canopy of the trees, and soon it would be dark. 'You will have one last night to love him as you wish. And then, if you ever see him again, you will love him as you must.'

Rane held his body motionless and expressionless even as he held his mind within various remembrancing attitudes to cover the desperate thought that he dared not think: *This cannot be the way! I will not lose Maria, ever again!*

Kalinda pointed into the trees. 'Now go. You have until dawn.'

Rane, though, couldn't move. He couldn't let himself think what he might do if he did lose Maria.

'Come, *mi ardu*,' she said, looking at him with a desperation of her own. 'Let's get away from this place.'

The shocks of the last hour and the hurts of the last two nearly sleepless days had driven them into a state of consciousness both wild and fey. It was Maria who pulled at his hand to take him off through the woods and down to the sea. She wanted to make a fire and to lie with him on a blanket on the beach all night long, holding him close. Although she still had little memory of how she had come to be, or so Rane thought, she wanted to listen to the sound of the waves that had given her birth and might do so again if ever she and Rane could be reunited.

Near midnight, a half moon rose over them and scattered a thin light over the sand. Fifty yards away, the diamond hull of the *Asherah* picked up enough of this radiance so that it stood outlined against a nearly black, star-dusted sky. Rane lay on his side, face to face with Maria as he gazed at the glossy lightship. A breeze kept blowing pieces of her hair against his mouth and nose, and he inhaled the thick scent of her along with her breath and the scent of the sea itself. The strange stars poured their immense purpose through his eyes and into him. Something stirred there, a flicker of warmth that wanted to break out into a fire of thought and action. He felt it running through him and driving away the nearness of death with a sudden new life.

'Maria,' he whispered. He cupped his hands over her ear so that the wind would not pick up his words. 'Are you awake?'

'Yes, I can't sleep. I'm so tired, but I don't think I'll ever sleep again.'

'Do you really love me?'

'More than I do life.'

A wave crashed into water, and the moon rose a sliver of an inch higher. And now the thought had to be thought, and the fire must blaze. 'Will you come away with me?'

'How? Where?'

'To Neverness.'

'Yes! When?'

'Now!'

'Yes! Yes! Yes!'

As if they were of one body, they pushed themselves up off the blanket and helped each other to stand. And Rane whispered with all the ferocity of the first breath of a *sarsara*: 'Run!'

It took them only seconds to dash across the beach straight toward the *Asherah*. Rane reached the lightship just before she did, and he opened the hatch to the passenger compartment and said, 'It will be just as it was for you inside the *Silver Swan*. Do you remember?'

'Yes,' she gasped, nearly breathless from their run.

'Quickly!' He kissed her, and said, 'I love you!'

Then, in a rage to follow his own advice, he moved with the speed of a sleekit diving into a burrow. He opened the hatch to the pit of the lightship, pulled down the ladder, and climbed inside. The sound of the hatch slamming shut, he thought, reverberated with the closing of the passenger compartment. He strapped himself into a big padded chair even as Maria, he hoped, did the same.

The pit of the *Asherah* differed from that of Danlo's ship, for a section of the black neurologics and the opaque spundiamond hull had been cut out and replaced with a window of pure clary even more translucent than glass. Nikolandru, being a poetic man, had disliked always viewing the galaxy's vistas through his computer only. Instead, he had wanted to use his own eyes to look upon the stars.

Through this clary window, Rane set his sight on the moon, hanging in the sky above the mountains. He envisioned an angle of ascent and a course of flight that would take the *Asherah* nearly straight toward it. In theory, anyone could pilot a lightship: all you needed to do was to reach out with your mind to the ship's neurologics and computer and think. But think the wrong thought, and you would be dead.

And so the fire in Rane's brain to spirit Maria away from earth became electric impulses crackling through living neurologics and pulses of light within the computer. And then, deep in the bowels of the lightship between Maria and the ship's tail, hydrogen exploded into starfire, and the fusion rockets roared into life. The *Asherah* shot into the air with an acceleration that smashed Rane back against his chair. Never had Nikolandru called the *Asherah* into such a sudden violence of motion. Rane might have crushed the consciousness out of both of them or killed them outright if he hadn't quickly reached out to his ship with a gentler thought.

Soon the mountains grew small beneath them – although Rane could not perceive this change of perspective by means of the window, through which shone moon and stars. Now the computer filled his mind with images of the space around him in spheres of matter and light that contracted or expanded according to his wish. He wished, for a moment, to see his way clear to a place above the earth in which he might make a mapping to another star and flee into the manifold. He wished too quickly, though, and the succession of gleaming and expanding spheres disoriented him and made him dizzy and sick. Most of all, he wished that Maria's and his sudden retreat into the night had taken Kalinda unawares and that they would make their escape.

'Maria!'

He gazed out into space as if looking for a missile streaking his way to shoot them down.

'Maria, are you all right?'

Not for the first time, he bemoaned Nikolandru's partitioning of the ship's computer into pilot and passenger fields. How he wished to talk to Maria, to hold her in his thoughts if not his arms! How he wanted to tell her that soon they would point the way toward Neverness and home!

She is not all right.

As before on Nikolandru's and his journey into the Solid State Entity, the air about Rane vibrated with the sounds of a godly voice that he now recognized as Kalinda's.

You will be the death of her.

'No,' Rane said into the dark air about him, 'I will be her love and life!'

You will be her despair and excruciation.

'You do not really know Maria, and you do not know me.'

You have gambled that I could not stop you without harming Maria – or would not. But it would be better for her to die now.

'You can't kill your own daughter!'

I created her. Isn't it upon me to destroy her?

'No!'

Then, to destroy you?

'No – if you kill me, you kill her.'

Are you so certain of that?

'If you kill me, you kill your hope of mastering the One Memory.'

My hope for that lay in your solitude in the chalet and your finding your way into yourself.

'Your hope was in vain. Maria might not have walked into the ocean, but I would have.'

In Neverness, you will find death.

'I will marry Maria and have children – the grandchildren you desire.'

The air in the dark pit of Rane's lightship grew quiet as he rocketed through space. Fusion fire shook diamond and sent vibrations through the ship into his brain.

Is that the future you wish to be, Lord Rane?

'Yes.'

Then don't look back.

'What do you mean? Into memory? I'm a remembrancer.'

Do not look back, or you will lose her.

'No, I never will. Now that I have her—'

Are you sure you do?

Maria, he called out into the noise of his mind, hoping that she could hear him and Kalinda could not. *Have I ever been sure of anything about you?*

He called out to Kalinda that he would prove her wrong, but she did not answer him. The silence about him grew almost total, like that of an interstellar void, even as the stream of images and mathematical symbols pouring into his brain turned into a river. His computer identified a thickspace of many point-sources just above the earth's atmosphere. Rane piloted the *Asherah* straight into the thickspace. He applied the topological and other mathematics that he had spent so many days learning on his journey across the galaxy, and he made a mapping to another star. And then the lightship's spacetime engines opened a window to the manifold, and a hundred billion stars for a moment flickered like fireflies, and in an instant Kalinda of the Flowers and her beautiful earth were gone.

28

As many do, Rane had often fantasized about being pilot out on an adventure across the unknown stars. Despite his natural tendency to distrust the mystical and embrace the material, he had romanticized the pilot's art as, well, a true art engendering deep aesthetic raptures and even visions. He had listened many times as pilots spoke of the marvels of the manifold, and he had seen many artists' simulations of their conceptions of the space that lies beneath space. But imagination is one thing and experience another. A blind man who has never seen the world might conceive the colour blue in a certain shallow way. Let sight be given him, though, and he might dive into the blue, blue waters of Agathange and know colour itself as a deep, graspable, living thing.

In the instant that Rane first entered the manifold as a pilot, his eyes were opened. The mathematics that he needed to survive the especially treacherous part of the manifold beneath the starry reaches of the Entity's nebula came alive to him. Torsion spaces writhed like hideous, burning snakes. Decision trees split into branches and then branches of branches of branches so quickly that he felt lost in a fracturing of sense and thought. Many times, he had to klein back across his pathways, for in the manifold the shortest distance from point to point is almost *never* a straight line. As the *Asherah* fell in and out of realspace in a flickering of stars and the three-dimensional mathematical symbols luming his mind, the windows from star to star opened so quickly that he felt lost in the pilots' sense of interfenestration and the sickness of light. True pilots such as Lara Jesusa, the Sonderval, and

Danlo wi Soli Ringess might have seen a beauty in the interplay between matter and mathematics and even a secret order to the universe. Rane, however, found chaos and terror. He struggled from the first just to survive.

It would have seemed impossible to any of these pilots that he did. It might have seemed impossible to him, for didn't a journeyman pilot take years to master the senses of zazen, hallning, adagio, and fugue needed to negotiate the manifold? How could he, a remembrancer, turn mathematical theory and an idealization of the pilot's art into hard, cold practice, all in a moment?

He didn't have a moment to reflect on the miracle of his sudden prowess; he needed to concentrate all his attention on everything that could kill him – and more importantly, Maria. There were the dead spaces as crushing as black holes to be avoided, and Wen neighbourhoods of too great a density of zero-points that must be skirted, in the same way that one should give the wormrunners of the Slizzaring a wide berth. A supposed decision tree of possible pathways through the dark woods of the manifold might easily turn out to be an infinite tree from which there could be no escape. Make the wrong mapping, fall into inattentiveness even for a moment, and he might lose himself in the blinding light of an uncontrollable interfenestration or even fall out into realspace straight into the fiery heart of a star.

He might have spent more time in realspace, letting the *Asherah* rocket ever so slowly through the black ink between the stars, gliding along the galaxy's glittering geodesics so that he could integrate his new experiences and recuperate from too many instances of near death. However, even after the *Asherah* broke free from that bright cloud of stars that the Solid State Entity claimed as Her own, he didn't know how far across realspace the goddess could reach. He floated in the dark pit of his lightship, sweating and hoping and thinking, and with each postulate that he proved and mapping that he made, the ship's spacetime engines opened windows to the manifold. Had the Entity, perhaps, made spacetime engines the size of stars? If the *Asherah* moved too slowly and lingered too long too close to the Entity, could She simply open a window in the ship's diamond hull and spirit Maria away?

Then, too, realspace possessed dangers of its own. Once, just beyond Kamilusa and Perdido Luz, the *Asherah* fell out into a bright hell of ionized gases, radiation, and light: all the energy and debris moving outward in a killing wave front from an exploded star. In the instant before Rane gathered in his nerves and flung the *Asherah* back into the manifold, the ship's computer informed him that the supernova had resulted from the core collapse of a star a hundred times the mass of the sun. The rogue Architects of the Cybernetic Universal Church called the Iviomils had destroyed many stars, but this supernova had involved a spinning black hole, a jet of plasma, and a gamma ray burst as part of the dirty fireball that Rane just barely managed to avoid: and as far as was known, the Iviomils did not possess the technology to cause this type of supernova. From where, then, had it come? Could it have been a rare, natural Type-II core-collapse supernova? Or, Rane, thought, perhaps the Silicon God had decided to destroy the stars surrounding the Entity's nebula so as to surround the Entity in an impenetrable shell of light.

We are safe, he thought, as the manifold opened and the *Asherah* fell through an infinitely blue sky of an invariant space. *For the moment, safe.*

Into his mind and his heart's imaginings came the tones of Maria's low, sweet voice that he longed to hear:

'I always feel safe with you.'

'You do?'

'I always *want* to.'

'Your mother can't meddle with our lives any more. We are free.'

'I have always wanted you to be free, since the moment I stepped out of the ocean and saw you on the beach.'

'I am. I defied a goddess and lived to tell about it. So I am free from—'

'Are you free from pride? And are you free from yourself?'

'Yes, you make me so – you make me want to be so.'

'But it is not enough to know what you wish to be free *from*, my Rane. What are you free *for*?'

The silence pervading the manifold could be even more total than the emptiness between the stars.

'Are you free to love?'

Rane might have hoped for a longer conversation with this provocative Maria he had conjured up out of mind and memory, but just then the invariant space wavered like a mirage over the sea and gave way to a Lavi space, as dark as wine. Mathematics drove away whimsy as the Lavi space wrinkled like the silver folds of a remembrancer's robe. He had to take great care, else the *Asherah* might be lost in an iteration of infolding perhaps isomorphic to, and therefore as deadly as, an infinite tree. He had to face the essential paradox of his headlong flight with Maria across the stars: objectively, the manifold was much more dangerous than realspace, but its traps and terrors needed to be braved if ever he was to reach Neverness. The sooner he got used to all the frangible segmented spaces and null waves as dark as a scryer's blacking oil – when he learned that life must be lived with every breath – the sooner he might become a true pilot and the safer they would be.

Sometimes, in places where the manifold smoothed out like the glassy waters of a warm tropical sea, with the *Asherah* and his fearful heart for the moment becalmed, he had time to think. Mostly, he thought about Maria. His desire to be with her as he wished could find fulfilment only if they reached Neverness unharmed. And how he wished that he might fall from the spaces near the Entity's nebula to the Star of Neverness without enduring a journey of endless days and countless stars! And why shouldn't that be? Hadn't Mallory Ringess many years before been the first pilot to prove the Continuum Hypothesis: that between any two point-sources, a mapping exists? And that therefore, in theory if not practice, if only the patterns of points could be perceived, it was possible to fall from any star in the galaxy to any other by way of a single mapping and moment?

Through the will a pilot realizes insight from pattern.

Long ago, Rane had heard this saying of the pilots, and it had always seemed to him to hint at many pilots' magical thinking and the very definition of magic itself. And why shouldn't the pilots tend toward the occult and the mysterious, they who styled themselves as belonging to the Order of *Mystic* Mathematicians? He had always thought the pilots, on the whole, were too quixotic ever to make practical use of Mallory's proof. Now, though, upon reflection, he didn't feel so sure.

For many days of intime (in the manifold one could never

say how much realtime passed without a horologe to measure it), he thought about the mathematics of Mallory's brilliant proof. His questionings led to the contemplation of the cantors' Generalized Continuum Hypothesis: that since *any* two points in spacetime could be mapped in a one-to-one correspondence, therefore the entire universe could be mapped onto itself. And that therefore, as suggested by the ancient mechanics' demonstrations of the superluminal entanglement of pairs of photons, all things everywhere interconnected with all things in their deepest part.

The cantors had never counted their Generalized Continuum Hypothesis as either mechanics or even mathematics. Rather, they created it more as a philosophy, in particular as a metaphysics in opposition to strong materialism: that only matter exists and all mental phenomena such as emotions, beliefs, and desires could be treated as mere illusion. Many had been the ancients who had championed this philosophy, from the Churchlands to Feyerabend to the Order's much-esteemed Evangelia Chu. The cantors had meant the Generalized Continuum Hypothesis as materialism's mirror opposite: only minds existed and all matter from starfire to rocks to water to whales took form only as will and idea within the universal mind. Such strong idealism had been put forth by Dharmakirti and Berkeley on Old Earth and, during the Third Wave of the Swarming and the Sixth Mentality, by Davaasurem, Altangeral, and Indah-Sul. Others – the Plato, Yangming, and Sunwar – had taught a weaker idealism, while the remembrancers had long argued among themselves as to the true nature of the real.

Matter is memory.

Was this not, Rane thought, the quintessential maxim of the remembrancers? But his colleagues could just as easily have said: *Memory is matter*. Taken together, both statements could be seen as profession of either idealism or materialism – or as their resolution. Rane the Rational, Rane the Reasonable, had often advised a middle path between these extremes. Instead of regarding matter, energy, space, and time as either illusory or as the totality of reality, why not try to perceive the world as an expression of a deep order? A unity that the Plato called the Form of the Good and the remembrancers identified as the One Memory because it contained the record and essence of all things? Rane the Doubtful, however, thought he knew the answer to that question: because no one could say anything intelligible as to the true nature of that One Memory, not even *the* Remembrancer himself. Perhaps the pilots were right after all. Why, he wondered, must life always be such a *mystery*? Why couldn't people just know the important things? Why must they have to choose, ultimately, between faith in reassuring philosophies and sciences and a leap into the utter wildness of the real?

Memory is.

During many days of schooning and slipsliding through the gentler parts of the manifold, he had much time to question the nature of mind and memory itself. He wished that he might schoon right across the galaxy to the core stars and the vast black hole at their centre, into which, it was said, the Ieldra had carked their consciousness. (The akashics hold that since consciousness could not be divided or localized in space, then the essence of the Ieldra could be seen as co-extensive with the whole of the universe – and therefore the Ieldra could move across the stars with the speed of thought.) Surely these elder gods, who had told Leopold Soli to seek the secret to humankind's immortality in the past and in the future, must know everything that could be known about memory. They must know about the strange attitude of recurrence, in which the past lived on through the eternal present into the future. If Maria could live her life again in recurrence, then where did that living actually occur? In her own mind? In Rane's? Or perhaps the Ieldra could simply think Maria into existence, whole and complete, as Rane might summon up the taste of a rich, sweet Summerworld coffee with enough reality to make his mouth water and his throat ache.

Maria . . .

'I am here, my Rane.'

'Where?'

'The only place I could ever be.'

'I wish I could tear down the wall to your compartment and see you.'

'That wall is made of mere diamond. There are harder walls to break through than that.'

'I wish I could hold you. Are you too cold? Do you have enough to eat?'

'I am never too cold when you hold me. Why don't you?'

'How? You are not really real.'

'Look about you. Face away from your computer for a moment and see what you see. The straps of your chair, floating. The food packets. The clary window, dead to light. The echo of my mother's voice. Her last words, which she might have spoken to you – or might have whispered into your brain. Your hand, which you cannot see. Which is more real, these things or your awareness that you are thinking of these things?'

'I am thinking of you. I can't stop. I never want to.'

'You have wondered about me, if I can exist in your mind and memory. Have you wondered about you? In whose mind do you exist? How is it you know you are you?'

'I *know*.'

'Do you know the most important thing? In all the universe, the one thing that is the most real?'

He couldn't answer her. He couldn't go on this way, shivering in the coldness of the mathematics of the manifold, lost in the darkness of the pit of his lightship, longing for something that could never be. And yet, what else could he do but go on?

And so he did. The *Asherah* finally broke free from an invariant space into a Gallivare space of nearly infinite complexity that demanded his total awareness. The nested embeddings of point-sources – like diamonds containing rubies concealing sapphires and other gemstones in a seemingly endless succession – made it difficult to identify one that might map to a point-exit in a safe neighbourhood surrounding a star. If he chose the wrong point, he would likely map his lightship *into* a star. Would its fire consume the *Asherah* instantly? Or would it take many terrible moments for his ship's diamond hull to burn away into black char, the air inside heating up like a furnace and slowly roasting Maria and him to death?

As Rane struggled to make a mapping and free them from the hellishly beautiful Gallivare space, a coldness of mathematics became a fever of computation and attempted proofs. He sweated as he thought in a fury of ideas and symbols that flickered through his mind. A lightning of logic not quite realized flashed through the pit of his ship. His heart pushed out bursts of blood with the rhythm of a pulsar, and he longed for nothing so much as escape.

Memory saved him. *Not* any record of the mappings that Nikolandru had made on his outward journey to the Entity – nor any elucidation of the dangers of such spaces that great pilots such as the Sonderval and Delora wi Towt had passed on as part of the pilots' lore. No, as it had been in Ailieyha's room in the secret brothel with the deadly Batar Bulba, he had a strange sense that he had lived through such emergencies before and that he knew exactly what to do. This time, his actions flowed not so much from the physical coordination of muscle and nerve memory but a deeper discipline of neurons firing to the music of a remembered mathematics. He saw all at once that he could use the Soli nesting lemmas to prove that the Gallivare space could be collapsed onto itself into a set of discrete and computable points. He perceived the pattern of these points: they fractalled hexagonally like the points of a snowflake. He found a point near their centre that mapped to a blue giant star named Atara Luz. He made his mapping, and the *Asherah* fell out into realspace bathed in a blessed blue light.

That was close, Rane. As close as a razor's edge against your throat.

'Yes, it was, Maria. But the mathematics is making more sense. Some day, I might even stand in the bar of the master pilots and drink as one of them.'

He expected her to caution him again about his pride, but she said nothing. The pit in which he floated, lit up with an eerie blue glow, remained silent.

'Maria, can you hear me?'

Could she, trapped in the evil passenger compartment, hear anything at all? Doubt worked at his mind like drillworms eating their way through his skull. Had she, he wondered, remembered to strap herself into her chair during those frantic moments of fleeing Old Earth? Had she survived the murderous acceleration of their take-off? Or had she locked herself into the *Asherah* in the first place? Now that he thought about it, he couldn't remember the sound of the passenger compartment's hatch slamming shut. What if Maria had decided at the last that she couldn't defy her mighty mother? Or what if Kalinda had snatched her away from the *Asherah* after all?

'Maria?'

Silence. Doubt became a trepidation bordering on despair. He felt hollowed out inside, as if those drillworms had eaten not just his brain but down through his neck and into his lungs and heart.

'Maria!'

And so he decided that he must make planetfall somewhere to disprove what he most dreaded. He made a mapping to Shambhalla in a region of stars that the Order's pilots had never charted but Nikolandru had explored. He remembered the names of many of the region's inhabited planets: Caritas, Redemption, Gavriel's Gambol, Azul Amor, Newsun, and Kailash Poru. His memories of the Sarkissian estate validated his impulse to steer away from the dwelling places of humankind as much as possible and pilot the *Asherah* all the way home to Neverness himself. Absent the need to explore the cities and islands that the first Maria had visited, he might reach Neverness in a matter of a season or two instead of years. Perhaps he would even master the Continuum Hypothesis and reach Neverness in one single and magical moment. First, though, he needed to assure himself that Maria was all right.

As Nikolandru had often done, he put down in a mountain meadow far from Shambhalla's cities. He wanted to avoid people; people could prove more treacherous than torsion spaces or black holes. Most of the Civilized Worlds, bound together by the Order, permitted pilots the privilege of unregistered landings, for they wanted to indulge these masters of the manifold. As for the pilots, their freedom to enjoy at will the beauty of a virgin beach or an empty desert accorded with their imperative to explore every corner of a still largely unmapped and uninhabited galaxy. Theirs was the romance of going wherever in the universe they wished.

Almost the moment that the *Asherah*'s rockets grew quiet and the lightship settled down onto green grass, Rane flung open the hatch, lowered the ladder, and climbed down onto the meadow. He opened the hatch to the passenger compartment. And there was Maria.

'Where are we?' she asked when she stood beside him. She blinked against the red light of Shambhalla's great eastern sun. A cool wind rippled the grass in waves of glossy green and fluffed out her scarf. 'I was so scared!'

He hugged her close as if to reassure himself that she was real. He kissed her. Then he retrieved a blanket and some food from the ship, and they walked hand in hand across the meadow to put some life back into their unused legs. He laid the blanket on the ground.

'I want to make love to you,' he said, working at the fasteners of her dress. 'Here, beneath that hot red star.'

Just then, however, the sound of rockets shattered the air. Above the ridgeline of the mountains to the north, two ships appeared like ugly red welts against the blue skin of the sky. Before Rane and Maria could cover half the distance to the *Asherah*, the ships landed in the meadow, cutting off their retreat. Five men hurried out of each ship. They wore uniforms of scarlet-saffron, and the smallest of the ten stood half a head higher than Rane and was even huger than Batar Bulba.

'Identify yourselves,' one of the men commanded Rane. He had a round, stern face, and a black lotus emblazoned on the side of his red beret. His voice sounded less like that of a human being and more like a gong. 'Now.'

'I am Thomas, a pilot of the Order,' Rane said, telling the first lie that came to him. 'And this is Maria of the Roses.'

'What roses? What kind of name is that? What are you doing on our world?'

Lies breed lies like astriers do children, and so Rane told this giant of a man that he and Maria had set out on a quest from Neverness to reach the Poetry Islands on the lost world of Nepenthe – and there they might learn of the lost poems of the great Placida Lovita.

'I have never heard of Neverness.'

Under the guns of this man's mistrustful eyes, Rane told him about the City of Light.

'Ha, the centre of the Uncivilized Worlds, you say.' The giant glanced at the *Asherah*. 'Would a pilot of your order waste valuable resources on such a frivolity?'

'We pilots consider the making of quests our purpose, and as for poetry—'

'Tenzin, search the barbarians' ship!'

The man barked out this command to a slightly shorter man; a jagged scar ran across his cheek and jaw. His beret bore the insignia of a geometric black knot. 'Yes, Kushok.'

Was this a name, Rane wondered? A title or a rank? While the man went off toward the *Asherah* to do Kushok's bidding, Kushok (or the Kushok) motioned for the eight others to surround Rane and Maria. Rane gazed at the black wands hanging from their belts. He had seen such objects many years before in a museum on Urradeth: keisaku, or awakening, sticks they were called. How had they come to be used on this obscure planet? A meditation master used the keisaku to rap a student between the shoulders in order to focus the attention. Upon a twist of the handle, the keisaku could be set to deliver a more stimulating jolt of electricity or, if needed, could shock a meditator into a stillness of the breath and heart and the great Emptiness beyond. He shot Maria a quick look as if to plead with her to remain silent.

'The ship is locked, Kushok!'

Kushok looked at Rane. 'What is the password?'

'Ah, is it your way, then, to search the possessions of visitors to your pleasant planet without first asking their—'

'Quickly now! We are wasting time.'

He nodded at one of the others, who gripped his stick with his huge hand. And Rane said, 'The password is . . . tiger, tiger.'

While Rane watched Tenzin shout out the password and get both hatches to the ship open, Kushok nodded to one his compatriots, and said, 'Norbu, scan them.'

Norbu, a fleshy man who seemed cut from the same dull, ugly fabric as all the others, brought forth a tablet and oriented it so that one of its glowing screens mirrored Rane's face and form while Norbu read the other. From time to time, his thick finger tapped the screen even as he held his face flat and emotionless. The scanning went on for a long time.

Rane had the good sense to lower his eyes, but just before he did so, he noticed Maria staring at Norbu as if she wouldn't think of hiding from him. 'What are you looking for?' she asked him.

'Yes,' Rane said, glancing at the ship's open hatches and then at Kushok, 'as I've said, we are on a quest, and we have nothing but personal effects and—'

'We have a problem,' Kushok said, 'with smugglers bringing in jook and jambool. Why else would you land here without permission?'

'We wished only for a few hours' rest from a long journey,' Rane said. He pointed down at the blanket and the food. 'We were just about to begin a picnic.'

Kushok's brown eyes emptied of recognition, as if the word 'picnic' had no meaning for him. He said, 'The penalty for smuggling drugs is death.'

Just then Tenzin returned bearing various items ransacked from both the pit and the passenger's compartment: a book of poems; Maria's hunting knife; Rane's wooden remembrancer's box. And, tinkling in Tenzin's hand, the bag of diamond City Disks that Rane had paid Nikolandru as the price of his passage. Tenzin stood next to Kushok, handing him one by one those items that Kushok indicated.

'What is this?' Kushok said, holding up the collection of poems after first riffling its pages.

'It is called a book,' Rane said. He described how the sounds of language could be encoded as letters printed in rows on paper and bound with leather. 'Some of my Order practise the lost art of reading.'

'Barbaric,' Kushok said. He opened the book and studied one of the pages. His eyes narrowed as if trying to decipher some sort of smuggler's code. Then he dropped the book on the blanket, and opened the wooden box. 'And this?'

'Mostly a collection of essential oils. We pilots use them to sharpen our attention to recall various structures of the manifold.'

Kushok motioned for the man standing next to him to hold open the box while he drew out a vial and unstoppered it. The essence of cinnamon scented the air. 'No drugs?'

Drugs the box contained aplenty, toalache and tingol and Rane's precious blue bottle of kalla. As Kushok opened bottle after bottle and sniffed their contents, Rane's heart raced and sweat poured down his sides beneath his kamelaika as if he had drunk the whole bottle of tingol all in a gulp.

'What is this?' Kushok said, holding out his hand to show Rane a bit of dirty brown wrinkled matter.

'Those are mushrooms,' Rane said. 'We pilots use them when we need visions of—'

'Yes, we ourselves make of them a tea to drink in our ceremonies when we wish for visions of the Enlightened One. Perhaps you are not so barbaric after all.' And then, 'Norbu! Scan all this.'

Norbu came over and held the tablet over the box. After a while, in a voice like a growl, he said, 'No jambool. No jook. No poppy or alcohol. Nothing.'

Rane's sigh of relief lasted only as long as it took for Kushok to hold up Maria's knife. At Kushok's scowl, he said, 'My father gave that to me. It is his old hunting knife.'

Kushok's scowl deepened to a mask of savagery. 'It is forbidden to kill animals. Had you done so here, you would have been executed immediately.'

'I assure you that I had no such—'

'Norbu! Scan the knife. And their hands.'

After Norbu did as he had been commanded, he said, 'The blade is made of shasteel.'

'Shasteel,' Kushok said, as if forced to utter an obscenity. 'Assassins use such weapons. And weapons of any sort are forbidden here.'

Rane glanced at the weapons hanging from the ten men's belts, but he said nothing.

'I found the knife in the passenger compartment,' Norbu said. 'And I found the woman's DNA all over the hilt but not the man's.'

'Liar,' Kushok said, staring at Rane. 'You are a liar, and we do not allow liars here.'

'No, you don't understand, I lent Maria the knife only so that she could—'

'There is nothing here about this Thomas,' Norbu said, looking at his scanner and then at Rane. 'But of the woman, we have much record. Her name is Maria. She is an escaped slave, from Kailash Poru. There is a reward for her capture and return, payable by a Santuu Sarkissian.'

At the sound of this name, Rane watched as Maria's eyes filled with anger and fear. No wind rustled the grasses and wild-flowers of the meadow, and the whole world seemed dead quiet.

'Your records must be incomplete,' Rane said to Norbu. 'There are many women named Maria in the galaxy.'

'Yes, but how many look like her?'

'Perhaps there are millions.' Then, remembering what Julior had said on Nepenthe's dreamy beach, he added, 'As with many beautiful women like her, she is one of the classical forms.'

'She is beautiful,' Kushok agreed.

He stepped up to Maria and reached toward her face. The moment that his fingers touched her cheek, however, her hand shot out with a sudden savagery and knocked his hand away. Strangely, her recklessness did not incite Kushok to use his keisaku. Instead, he smiled.

'Her violence confirms the allegation that she murdered Santuu Sarkissian's father. Norbu, your scanner!'

He snapped his fingers at Norbu, who surrendered up his scanner. Kushok tapped the scanner a dozen times, oriented it vertically over the earth, and watched as the scanner's screen lit up and projected a life-sized hologram of Maria wearing a blue dress and the golden collar of a naukar.

'This Maria is identical,' Kushok said to Rane, 'to the woman who stands by you.'

'Some of the classical forms are cut from the same—'

'Watch!'

Kushok tapped the back of the scanner, and the hologram came to life. Rane couldn't help but watch as a man whom Rane recognized as Armas Sarkissian stood talking and drinking wine with Maria in his sleeping chamber overlooking the green grounds of the Karadan Adri. Armas and Maria laughed together. They embraced with a great tenderness and kissed each other. They stripped away their clothing, and Armas unlocked Maria's collar. They fell down together onto a bed covered with blue satin sheets, and they . . .

'Enough!' Rane said, stepping forward to punch his fist into the hologram. But he couldn't knock away interference patterns of fields of light. 'I do not wish to look upon such things!'

'The two women are one and the same,' Kushok said. 'Faces and forms can be sculpted according to design but the soul cannot. Look how the same programs animate both women's faces!'

'No, they are not the same!'

'There is a . . .' Kushok studied the scanner. 'There is 99.997 per cent chance that the two women's programs were written by the same soul.'

'Then in that .003 per cent chance lies the truth of—'

'You speak of truth, Pilot Thomas, you who cannot get past ten words without speaking a lie?'

'There are many infinitesimal chances that become actuality. Life, itself, any one human being's life is so—'

'How can you deny the truth of who this woman is?' Kushok said, nodding at Maria.

How *could* he, he wondered as he looked at her. She glared at Kushok as if she wanted to tear out his throat. She was truly her mother's daughter, and if Rane told the truth of how this beautiful, savage Maria had come to be, then surely his words would be taken as just another and even more fantastical lie.

'I will buy her freedom,' Rane said. He bent to pick up the bag of coins from the blanket. He smacked the tinkling disks into Kushok's hand. 'There are nearly a hundred thousand—'

'We do not deal in *money*, pilot! And she is not ours to sell. She will be returned to Santuu Sarkissian.'

'No, she is the Maria I have said! She has never set foot on Kailash Poru. She was born on Old Earth from—'

'Enough of your lies!' He drew out his keisaku and pointed it at Rane's face. 'A deep-ship leaves Yonten later this afternoon. Maria will be put aboard and will arrive on Kailash Poru in six days.'

He nodded at Norbu and Tenzin, who closed in on Maria to seize her. Just as they laid their hands on her, though, she struck out at them. Kushok moved very quickly for a very large man, and he whipped his black keisaku into Maria's arm. The bone snapped like a stick with a sound that enraged Rane. Maria cried out in pain almost at the same moment that he leaped toward Kushok. As it had been with Batar Bulba, he moved with the dreadful memory of a warrior-poet driven by a warrior's killing art. He moved even more quickly than did Kushok, but not quickly enough. For one of the others came up behind Rane and rammed the point of the keisaku into Rane's back. The terrible shock of it raced along his nerves from chest to head and legs, and dropped him as if every muscle in his body had been liquefied. He lay on the earth, gasping and twitching and moaning.

After a few moments, he found that he could still work his throat, and he cried out, 'Maria!'

'Let me leave him with something!' Maria said to Kushok. She stood between Tenzin and Norbu, who clamped their hands upon her. 'Please!'

Two of the men hoisted Rane to his feet, and held him up with a tremendous strength and a surprising gentleness lest he should topple to the ground again. Kushok nodded at Tenzin and Norbu. Still holding onto Maria, they walked her over to Rane. One of her arms hung swollen and limp by her side. Her other arm lifted up, and she undid her scarf and draped it around Rane's neck.

'Come find me!' she said.

He couldn't move as she looked at him. Then Tenzin and Norbu escorted her over to one of the red ships and wrestled her inside. The hatch slammed shut like the door of a tomb.

'You will leave now yourself,' Kushok told Rane. 'Gather your things.'

Rane bent to tie up the blanket. He said, 'Then I am free . . . to go where I will?'

'We do not want you here. We do not imprison your kind, and you have done nothing to merit execution.' He shot Rane a hard, knowing look. 'Though I think both of us might prefer that.'

A breeze came up and blew the scarf against Rane's face. Maria's scent, the fresh smell of her sweat and the perfume of her skin, wafted into him like an elixir. And he thought: *No, you're wrong. I will find Maria.*

Kushok said nothing more to him, and neither did Rane speak to him. Kushok and his men walked Rane over to the *Asherah* and locked him into the pit of the lightship. When the hatch closed and he was alone, he let the scent of Maria's scarf fill his head and lungs and every part of him. Then he called the ship's rockets into life. He still had his purse of diamond coins, and he still had his hope. The *Asherah* shot up through the atmosphere into the blue sky and through the window in space that opened upon the treacherous, luminous future.

29

Hope is a delicate thing, balanced on the edge of a knife like a gossamer scarf that can fall either of two ways. On the one hand, Rane felt sure that he had not come so far and endured so much only to lose Maria once more. On the other hand, her situation seemed desperate, and he had a sick feeling that he might fail.

He fought that feeling with all his will. Didn't he have six days to arrive on Kailash Poru ahead of Maria? Couldn't a great deal be accomplished in six days or even much less time? In five days, Ondine of Darkmoon had written her Sonnets to the Stars, and a fire fritillary lived out its entire adult life before burning out in a blaze of colours. In less than twenty billionths of a second, upon the Silicon God's creation on Fostora, this greatest of artificial intelligences had come into full consciousness of his hatred for the human race – and so had begun the greatest of wars. It took a man such as Rane perhaps a day to digest his food, sleep, and renew himself. Another man, the Kristoman, had died and been resurrected in only two days. And his father, the great god Yahweh, had needed only six days to create the entire world.

Rane should have taken all his determination with him into the manifold that opened in the dark spaces above Shambhalla, and so he did. But he also took other things: his rage at the Kushok for striking Maria and his wrath of fear that Santuu Sarkissian would likely do much worse. His brain still buzzed with the keisaku's aftershock. The glowing ideoplasts that the ship-computer infused into his visual cortex seemed blurry, a confusion of semi-solid mathematical symbols that he struggled to kithe into proof arrays that made sense to him. In such a state, of course, he should not have entered the manifold in the first place. How was he to find the balance of hallning and the stillness of zazen when all he could think of was to land on Kailash Poru ahead of the deep-ship and make things safe for Maria?

And so almost as soon as the manifold closed in upon the *Asherah* like a wavering sea of hellish colours, he made a mistake. He entered a binary decision tree hoping to map through almost all the way to Kailash Poru in only sixty-four bifurcations. That is, he presumed that the quickly dividing space must be a simple decision tree based on the patterns of point-sources that scintillated in his mind's eye. Like a journeyman pilot grown overconfident, he trusted his hard-won prowess at recognizing the manifold's various structures. And like the desperate man he was, he wanted to spare not a moment with tedious confirmations of the obvious. Therefore, not thinking clearly, he neglected to employ the heuristics developed by John Penhallegon and Rollo Gallivare to distinguish finite trees from those that were not: in specific, he completely forgot about the important third test of cardinality. In only seconds, it seemed, the tree began splitting apart into a perhaps uncountable number of branches and sub-branches. Sweat broke forth from every pore in his body as shock gave way to a gut-grabbing, heart-stopping terror.

Maria, I'm sorry!

Even if the decision tree proved to be finite, no pilot had ever escaped a tree whose branchings exceeded a number somewhere in the neighbourhood of a centillion.

Maria!

He made a quick computation. The number of branchings hadn't yet approached anywhere close to a centillion. He let out his air in a great sigh, and then drew in a gasp of bitter breath. For the fourth test of cardinality proved the decision tree to be infinite. What pilot had ever escaped from an infinite tree? Who could ever escape the inescapable?

I am dead – as dead as the dinosaurs who once roamed Old Earth, only I do not yet know it. Soon I will be only a memory, and then a memory of a memory, or perhaps nothing at all.

Then the scarf fluttered as if a breeze freshened the fear-sick air of his ship, and he heard Maria calling out to him in a poem full of hope. Or perhaps, in the shocks of the last hour, he only hallucinated her strong, musical voice.

I will not leave you.

If no pilot, he thought, had ever escaped from an infinite tree, did that therefore imply that no pilot ever could? Had such an impossibility ever been *proved*? What did it matter if the greatest of pilots such as Leopold Soli and the Sonderval had declared infinite trees to be inescapable? What if they were wrong? What if they had overlooked some clever proof by which a pilot might map out of an infinite tree into realspace? What if the Ieldra had known of such a proof and Rane could now go deep into the One Memory in order to duplicate it? Was he not *the* Remembrancer? Should he let rage, despair, and the prejudices of a long tradition keep him from becoming *the* Pilot?

As the tree that had captured his lightship kept splitting and its number of branches far exceeded a centillion, he searched all the mathematics that he knew and much that he did not. Time passed. How much biological time passed he might measure in the number of breaths of stinking air that he breathed or how many times his chest shook with a beat of his heart. The black hair that pushed out from his cheeks and chin also marked the passing of too many moments.

And there was the intime, his sense of how much subjective time he endured. In his determination to discover or create a new mathematics, he had little need of quicktime, when moments grew too long and boredom gripped him and he wanted time to pass more quickly. Of slowtime, however, he had a rage for too much: and so he allowed the ship-computer to speed up his brain so that time slowed down and he could make new proofs in moments that seemed to last forever. How much time elapsed from the vantage of a god looking for the *Asherah* through realspace? He could not have known, for his lightship and therefore he himself were also subject to the manifold's Einsteinian time distortions. Only a horologe could compute anything like the amount of total time that the *Asherah* spent lost in the infinite tree, and Rane doubted if he would ever see a horologe again.

How much time for you, Maria? How much Maria time, the only measure of time that could ever matter?

If he could still reach Kailash Poru ahead of her, he might use his treasure of coins to purchase Maria's freedom, before Santuu had a chance to execute her. Or failing that – and he did not think that Santuu's hardened heart could be softened by bits of even harder diamond – he could use Maria's knife to open that vile heart. He himself would then be executed as a murderer of a master, but what would that matter? Tajasha, who would then inherit Maria, would be more sympathetic to her, and she might spare her life.

Why did I think I had to put down on that damned Shambhalla?

They might have, he thought, journeyed all the way home to Neverness without making planetfall. Now, even supposing that he could find his way out of the infinite tree, he would need to put down on a planet which might allow no easier escape than the tree itself.

Damn me!

Time passed. He made a desperate mathematics. He ate and excreted; he breathed and sweated and slept and dreamed. He awoke to a clutch of memories and fears, and he fell back into the mathematical realm that his computer opened for him. The manifold opened out and out in streamers of light fracturing and refracturing into separate rays a billion billion times each second. He ate more tasteless food in order to keep himself conscious and alive. His body made proteins and pushed his beard out an inch from his grimy face.

More time passed. He ate too little, and he stared into the mathematical spaces of his computer too continually and too long. The jewelled ideoplasts representing definitions, axioms, theorems, and clever ideas for the most profound of proofs fractured into iridescent bits that reassembled into colours and shapes of places and peoples that he had known. Memory haunted him. Maria called to him. Often he could not recall whether the images flooding his mind were of events that had already occurred or memories of a future that had yet to be.

'Where are you?'

'I am here, Maria!'

'It is too late.'

He stood with his back to the ocean on the green lawn of the Sarkissian estate; just behind him was the wall from which

Armas Sarkissian had plunged down the cliff face to the rocks below. Rane faced the marble columns of the veranda of the great house where Santuu and Tajasha lived with their slaves. He faced Maria. Santuu had wanted her to look upon the wall from which she had pushed his father. And so he had nailed her to a wooden cross from which she had a clear line of sight from lawn to wall to ocean — and to Rane himself.

'No, you are still alive!'

'Am I?'

Rane gazed at iron spikes driven through flesh and bones and the blood crusted black over her palms and feet. Rope bound her arms to the wooden crosspiece, and her skin had blackened with gangrene.

'I will cut you down! I will free you!'

'Can you free yourself?'

Rane stood with his back against the stone wall, looking at her. He couldn't move. He didn't know why he couldn't move.

'Oh, Maria, why are people so cruel!'

'Why is life cruel?'

'But people aren't bound by life. We can choose.'

'Can we?'

How could Rane free Maria when he couldn't even command his limbs to move so that he could walk over to her and touch her one last time?

'Look what life has done to you! Why aren't you screaming?'

'And give Santuu the satisfaction?'

'But it must hurt.'

'It is agony. But that is nothing against the pain that you didn't come for me with time enough for me to hold you again.'

'Maria!'

In the pit of his lightship, the sound of Maria's name bounced about like the clapper of a wildly ringing bronze bell. Only he was that clapper and it beat against the inside of his skull, and he could hardly hear himself think. His long nails bit into the palms of his clenched fists. An agony drilled into his swollen feet. He hadn't moved them for a long time, and the blood had pooled and clotted deep within his veins.

Maria, don't die!

And still the *Asherah* fell upward into the endlessly spreading branches of the infinite tree. Or perhaps downward: in this last torment of the manifold, all topologies failed him, and he could make no sense of up or down, shape or formlessness, inside or out. The present bound him in a bitter blood to a frozen past, which melted in the torrid heat of memory and flowed into a hellish future. He ate and excreted; he breathed and sweated and slept and wept and dreamed. His beard grew out two inches and then ten more.

Goddamn you, time!

Although he could not compute time, it wasn't possible that so much could have passed for him and so little for Maria. Surely the six days needed for the deep-ship to fall from Shambhalla to Kailash Poru had long since elapsed. And surely Maria had long since died on that cross or impaled upon an iron spear – or perhaps Santuu had decided on clemency and had flung her over the edge of the cliff to join his father. And what did it matter anyway? For it was also impossible that he would escape the infinite tree. Time would turn on and on like a great iron wheel grinding him into nothingness forever.

Time is not real! As light undoes darkness, memory defeats time.

After the last of his food ran out, as the *Asherah* fell on and on into very unreal spaces of the manifold, he at last fell mad – mad with unbounded memory. He closed his inner eyes to the visual noise of his computer, and he broke all rules of the remembrancers' art by going down into the infinite tree of association memory. Thought bound to image to sensation and the experience of all the shimmering, interconnected moments of his life. He entered deep into recurrence, and there he would remain. Were madness and recurrence without end the same thing? Very well, then, he would live again and again madly and wildly a single moment of time: the great moment of his life in the Light Pavilion when he had clasped hands with Maria and they had looked upon their star. The moment when he had known for the first time the greatest thing that could ever be known: that he was a part of her as she was of him, and that the love they called into life in each other could never die.

And so he stood with her again in the Light Pavilion, and they looked upon their great blazing double star. And Rane looked not just with his eyes but through the clear lens of mathematics. Surely mathematics, if ever he could understand it, could show him the way to map through the manifold to Val Adamah when it came time. But how to understand that which dwelled so deep at the heart of things that it underlay understanding itself?

For ages, the cantors had divided into many schools as to the meaning and actuality of mathematics. The logicists believed mathematics to be logic and little more, while the constructivists saw maths as a work of pure creation. To the formalists, mathematics was only a game played by set rules. The symbolists and predictivists had their interpretations as well. Perhaps the oldest of schools, the Platonists, held mathematics to be eternal form in the mind of God.

Rane himself thought that all these schools, with their different ontologies, must in some way have grasped part of the truth. What was mathematics, really, he wondered? Certainly it couldn't be just symbols and rules, which after all only ordered deeper ideas and logic. And what was logic if not the very will of the universe itself, for how could anyone or anything will against logic? If Rane could will hard enough, willed with every cell in his body and glint of his mind, could he behold the way that the universal will played out through the divine game of *lila*? Could he dance forever with Maria their wild whirl of love around their star? Could he, at the end of all things, at last grasp the mystery of mathematics and memory and touch upon the mind of God?

Through the will a pilot realizes insight from pattern.

Rane, lost somewhere in the universe, starving and rotting and dying, looked through memory at the patterns of his life. Every planet and star that he had ever known took form within him, every person, thought, and speck of dust. And everything interconnected with everything else, like ice crystals scattering the light of the Star of Neverness in a perfect splendour across endless fields of newly fallen snow. There he willed himself to be, in Neverness, with Maria in the Light Pavilion, where all life and its infinite possibilities called to him – called him down into death. He would take Maria with him. If his remembrance was strong enough and complete, if it blazed bright and clear as a star, then their moment might live on in the One Memory as a perfect and beautiful thing.

Through the will . . .

And so for a moment, his will aligned with the will of the entire universe, and he made a last mapping straight into its fiery red heart. In a blinding burst of radiance, he broke free from the manifold into a higher and deeper order of infinity. Then a terrible shivering caught him in its cold claws and took him down into the dark.

30

He was never to remember landing the *Asherah* on the thick white ice of the Sound to the north of Neverness and making his way from North Beach across the Pilots' Quarter and along the Gallivare Green and Courtesan's Conservatory into the Old City. One of the worst snows of midwinter spring that year clouded the air with billions of bits of stinging ice crystals, and nearly everyone who could had taken shelter from the storm for the night inside warm apartments or houses. A wealthy astrier, though, making his way home down the Old City Glissade, happened to stop for a few moments in the deserted Light Pavilion. It was he who found the naked Rane unconscious and frozen to the ice.

He might have taken Rane for just another dying autist and moved on, for he could hardly bear to get near his starved, filthy, frostbitten body, and the stench of Rane's blackened and rotten feet repelled him. Something about Rane, however, also touched him, and he found himself leaning over him and tending to him. He used the knife he carried as protection against wormrunners and other predators to chisel Rane's shoulder, side, and hip free from the ice. Then, gritting his cold teeth at all the blood that ran from Rane's ripped flesh, he took off his white shagshay furs and wrapped him up like an infant. The gore would ruin his fine garment, but the astrier's unusual act of kindness would also fill him with an unusual satisfaction, for his great fur coat saved Rane's life.

So little did Rane weigh that the astrier was able to carry him three blocks to a hospice. There the astrier left him to the mercies of the white-robed women who would nurse Rane back to health, if they could. The astrier had no idea that he had rescued the greatest remembrancer the city of Neverness had ever known.

Neither did the devoted hospicers. They set Rane in an amnio tank to bring his hypothermic body up to temperature and to rehydrate him; they infused his veins with water, amino acids, rich sugars, vitamins, and minerals in order to restore his wasted flesh. They cut his matted hair and shaved him. Then they worked over Rane, amputating the toes of one foot and all of the other and the tips of two fingers on his left hand. They scraped off the fungus that had fuzzed his skin in too many places, and they salved his terrible wounds.

For many days, he floated like a foetus in unknowningness. The hospicers kept him in a near coma, for every time he arose from his dark dreams to a more conscious state, he screamed out the same senseless words: 'I will find you!' Even when it came time for the regrowth of Rane's limbs and all his ruined tissue, the hospicers deemed it for the best that he should have no cognizance of what was happening to him. Rane, they thought, was already distressed beyond reason, and they did not want to drive him down into total madness.

The storms of midwinter spring, though, at last gave way to false winter's much warmer weather, and it came time to get Rane up out of his tank and teach him to walk again. Regrown muscles and bones needed to be built up under the weight of real gravity, and nerves needed to connect and coordinate with a fully functional brain. For this next phase of Rane's healing, he needed to be awake and aware. When the hospicers at last allowed him to be so, he immediately cried out his mantra: 'I will find you.' When they asked him who it was he sought, he was able to say, 'Maria'. The speaking of her name worked better than any of the hospicers' drugs to fully revive him.

'Who is Maria?'

The elder hospicer asked this of Rane. Eleanora had iron-grey hair, and a hard face like a piece of chipped flint, but also gentle eyes and a sweet smile. She looked down at Rane, who lay between clean white sheets on a bed covered with the softest of shagshay furs. On the table beside him were a pitcher of water and a vase of fireflowers. With the melting of the sea's ice and retreating snows, these blood-orange blossoms were blooming again as the world came back to life.

'Who is Maria?' the hospicer asked him again.

'Maria is Maria,' he told her.

'And who are you?'

'I am . . . who I am,' he said.

'Are you an autist? The man who brought you here thought you might be.'

Rane considered this. He recalled that those of the autist sect wilfully damage parts of the brain so that other parts could blossom with abilities as bright as any flower.

'No,' he said, 'I am no autist.'

'What is your name?'

Rane looked out of the window at the blue and yellow fritillaries that alighted upon the flowers on the lawn of the hospice. What *was* his name? Surely it must dwell somewhere in his still-frozen memory like a fritillary just about ready to break out of its cocoon.

I am no man, he thought. *No man at all without Maria.*

'Sir, you must have a name?'

'I am Noman,' he said. 'Call me Noman.'

This the hospicers did, even as the planet of Icefall turned around the Star of Neverness and false winter turned into winter with its first snows. The hospicers fed Rane nutritious foods and made him lift weights to strengthen his body. They considered as well feeding him drugs to strengthen his mind, but because they didn't know what ailed him, they plied him with herbal teas and kindness instead. Theirs was the faith that given the right nurturing, both body and mind would heal themselves.

There came a day in full winter with a fresh snow on the ground and a gold-dusted sky when he called the elder hospicer to his room. Eleanora's concerned smile broke the harshness of her face, and he said to her, 'My name is Thomas Rane.'

Eleanora looked at him as if he had declared that he was Mallory Ringess or Ede the God. She said, 'The Order used to have a Lord Remembrancer of the same name.'

Although he couldn't claim to be that same remembrancer or even that same man, he said, 'Yes, they used to call me Lord Remembrancer.'

Eleanora looked at him as if perhaps she should give him drugs after all. 'That Thomas Rane left Neverness years ago on an impossible quest to bring the woman he loved back to life. Surely he must long since have died.'

'Surely,' he said. 'Died and resurrected, like Maria herself.'

'Maria!' she said. 'It was *that* Maria you called for? I heard her recite her poems in the Gallivare Green once.'

'As she will do again.'

'But she is dead, Noman. I myself was there at the Hollow Fields that day when the sunship carried her remains into the Star of Neverness.'

'I was there, too. Did you not hear me speak?'

'I did not stand close enough to the speakers to make out any of their faces.'

'But you can see now and hear me. I'm telling you the truth.'

'Rest,' she said. 'Rest your mind and heal.'

'I *am* Thomas Rane,' he insisted. 'And I must go find Maria . . . again.'

'All right, Thomas Rane Noman, if you must, you must. But not right now. Wait at least until you are strong enough to skate again.'

Eleanora relayed this curious incident to the other hospicers, one of whom had friends among the Order's academicians and high professionals. It didn't take long before the story of the Mad Remembrancer began circulating around the towers and halls of Upplysa, Lara Sig, and the Academy's other colleges. On the 45th day of winter, such wild talk prompted a visit from one of the Order's master cetics. Cyril Bramani, decked out in orange robes and furs, was shown into the hospice with great deference. He looked in on the sleeping Thomas Rane Noman. He smiled, thanked Eleanora, and left. The next day, early in the morning on the 46th, the Lord of the Order himself arrived at the hospice and told Eleanora that he wished to speak with Lord Rane.

Bardo wore snow-dusted sable furs over his black pilot's robe, and when he entered Rane's room, he took off this thick garment and hung it on a hook behind the door. He sat in a chair by the side of Rane's bed. His black diamond pilot's ring gleamed around his huge finger. Much older he looked to Rane, as if the cares of his office and the whole galaxy had worn the fat off his face. He sighed as he looked at Rane. His fingers pulled at his thick black beard.

'It has been a long time,' he said.

'Yes, but how much time? What year is it here?'

'What happened to you that you don't know the year? The hospicers told me that you did not at first even know your own name.'

'I did not know if I was alive or dead. I meant to be. I thought I was. When I fell to the ice, I thought I'd fallen into the cold hell they believe in on Urradeth.'

'The ice of the Light Pavilion? The astrier found you naked, wearing only that damn scarf of yours. How did you come to be there?'

Rane fingered the scarf tied around his neck, and he shook his head. 'I don't remember.'

'How did you come to be in Neverness?'

'I don't remember. I must have fallen out around our star and landed my ship on the ice of the Sound.'

Bardo looked at him curiously. 'What ship are you talking about?'

'The *Asherah*. I inherited it from Nikolandru. You see, he turned out to be a warrior-poet, and Kalinda had to kill him.'

'Tell me what happened to you,' Bardo said.

And so Rane did. He told of his and Nikolandru's journey in the *Asherah* outward across the Sagittarius and Orion arms of the galaxy. He had tracked Maria to her birth planet, he said, through the scents of the same scarf that by some miracle he still wore. He told of the tiger in the Dreaming City that had devoured him countless times and of the Maria on Nepenthe who had been both women and men countless times as well. He told of Old Earth. The goddess called Kalinda of the Flowers who dwelled as the living heart of the Solid State Entity, he said, had called Maria back into life from little more than a few handfuls of chemicals and his own fiery memories, and this was the greatest miracle of all.

When Rane had finished recounting how he had lost Maria on Shambhalla and then lost himself in the fragmenting, flaming hell of the infinite tree, Bardo sat for a long while staring at him. At last, he said, 'I need some coffee. Will you have some with me?'

'I would love some – it's been a long time. But the hospicers allow me no stimulants.'

'They will this morning.'

And as he had said, so it came to be. He called for coffee, and soon Eleanora sent a young hospicer into the room bearing a pot of Summerworld coffee, some cream, sugar, and two big brown mugs. Bardo poured the coffee, and into his mug, he heaped much sugar and added many dollops of thick cream. Rane drank his coffee black. He wanted to savour its richness and deliciousness in all its purity of essence – much as he did his memories of Maria.

'So,' Bardo murmured, the single word booming out like the rumble of a volcano, 'you defied a goddess, as you say, and piloted a lightship on your own through the deadliest part of the manifold – a part that has either daunted or killed master pilots such as myself. And you did this with no training beyond some mathematics that you learned in the *Asherah*'s passenger compartment and simulations made by the ship's computer?'

'And memory,' Rane said. 'I must have reached into the One Memory to gather the skills of master pilots such as yourself.'

'Ah, you *must* have, mustn't you? But you don't . . . remember?'

'I remember very little of my last moments in the infinite tree.'

'Which you say that you somehow escaped. When no pilot in the history of our Order has ever done so.'

'Mallory Ringess did.'

'No, he mistook a finite tree for an infinite one.' Bardo took a sip of coffee and shook his head. 'When he proved that the tree that had captured the *Immanent Carnation* could be modelled by a simple Lavi set and embedded in an invariant space, the tree collapsed to a single branch, and Mallory mapped himself free.'

'Then it must have been that—'

'You say that you used the fourth test of cardinality to prove the tree to be infinite.'

'Yes, I did.'

'You are sure that you did not make a mistake?'

'I verified the proof twenty times.'

'Describe for me your verifications.'

This Rane did. He sipped his coffee and spoke for a long while. While mathematics is best and most fully represented by the glittering ideoplasts the cantors and pilots have created, it can also be represented by the sounds of language. Although it is cumbersome and time-consuming to do so, one can always 'talk' mathematics. As the ancient Kristians had taught, in the beginning was the Word.

'The tree you have just told of is certainly infinite. But it cannot have been a real tree. And you cannot have reached into the One Memory to find a way to escape it, for no pilot has ever done such a thing, and therefore no such memories exist to be recovered.'

'Perhaps, then, the memories of the Ieldra dwell within—'

'Let us consider a more parsimonious conjecture.' Bardo tapped his forehead. 'Your memory is nonpareil. You are *the* Remembrancer, or were. Somewhere on your impossible journey to recreate Maria, you reached into that remarkable memory of yours, and you did recreate her – and created as well the fabulous story that you have related to me.'

'You think I'm *lying* to you?'

'No, I could never believe that.'

'You think I've fallen mad.'

'I think perhaps you've fallen into memory and have remained there too long. Don't those of your profession warn of such dangers?'

'No, I know what happened really did.'

'But how do you know?' Bardo looked at him. 'How can I ever know what happened when Leopold Soli cast my lightship into the hell of Perdido Luz? Did I die in that damn star, only to be remade by the Solid State Entity? Remade . . . imperfectly. Or did She rescue me?'

Rane put his mug down on the table. He clasped Bardo's arm and said, 'Set your mind at peace, old friend. I asked Kalinda about this. She did not remake you atom by atom from memory. You are really *you*.'

'Ah,' Bardo sighed, rubbing his beard, 'I wish I could believe you.'

'She said that—'

'I wish I could believe the rest of your incredible story.'

'Is that so hard to do?'

'That Mallory swived a goddess, who gave birth to Maria
. . . twice? Ah, well, he was so wild that he *would* have swived
the whole galaxy to give birth to light, but . . . you say that he
actually fathered Maria? The woman I once embraced and spoke
to as I am speaking to you now?'

'Yes.'

'And you say that after the Entity recreated your Maria
out of the matter of Mallory's and Her body and your
memories that you lost her on some planet out of myth called
Shambhalla?'

'Shambhalla really exists, and so does Maria.'

'If you've told true, then Maria must surely be dead. Again.'

'I will find her,' Rane said. 'I will find her, and bring her
home, and you will see.'

'But you can't really believe that.'

'I believe that I am *here*, in this pretty little room, talking to
you on this fine winter day. Don't you?'

'Yes, Lord Rane, I do believe *that*.'

'Then I must have landed the *Asherah* on some planet and
taken passage to Neverness on a deep-ship.' Rane took another
sip of coffee. 'Either that, or I must have landed the *Asherah* on
the ice, as I have said, as I believe.'

'Had you done so, someone out ice schooning on the Sound
would have espied your ship.'

'Not if the ice broke up in false winter first and the *Asherah*
sank to the bottom of the Sound.'

'So that is your hypothesis?'

'Somehow, my memory of Maria, all my will, led me to the
Light Pavilion. How else could I have come to be there?'

'That is one mystery yet to be determined. That I would like
to know.'

'I must have lain down in the Pavilion to die.'

'But you don't remember? And that is the problem, for you
and for me.'

'I don't understand how this should be any sort of problem
for you. I am no longer of the Order.'

'Ah, but you see, you might be again.' Bardo smiled at him.
'Your old chalet stands empty, and after your recovery, I want
you to move in.'

'But no one who has left the Order has ever returned.'

Bardo's smile deepened. 'Just as no one has ever returned from Old Earth and lived to tell about it?'

'But the College of Lords would have to—'

'In this matter, I believe they will do as I ask.' He nodded at Rane. 'But first you must recover. Eleanora says that you are well enough to leave here, as long as you are cared for by someone. Kolenya Mor has insisted that you stay with her.'

Rane thought about this. 'All right, but I cannot commit to rejoining the Order, even if that should prove possible. I could never renew my vows knowing that I must soon journey to Kailash Poru and find Maria, if she is still alive.'

At this, Bardo loosed a sigh that sounded out long and deep like the winter wind. He said goodbye to Rane, and left him with his impossible schemes.

31

Later that day, Rane was taken by sled into the Pilots' Quarter, and he moved into the guest room of Kolenya's granite chalet. He was glad to be once again in this place of good smells and beautiful things. The familiarity of the bright paintings on the walls and the Fravashi carpets on top of the polished wooden floors comforted him and brought to mind many happy memories.

For the next couple of days, he rested for six hours out of seven in a big bed covered with a down duvet that Kolenya herself had embroidered with blue and gold threads in pleasing geometric patterns. Two dwarf trees grew from big pots on the floor; smaller pots containing plants such as bamboo, jade, and a many-coloured croton lined the window sill. The window itself – frosted along its edges – let in a bright, clean light. This lovely radiance passed through many hanging crystals, which scattered colours over the opposite wall and the fireplace that Kolenya kept full of blazing logs. Rane liked listening to the water that tinkled through the slate pools of the triple-tiered fountain. He liked breathing in the fresh oxygen that the plants provided and recalling the scents and sounds of the surf that had given birth to Maria.

Kolenya, who had grown even plumper and kinder in the years since he had last seen her, took great pleasure in tending to all his needs. She massaged his newly grown limbs and helped him exercise. She played her old gosharp for him and sometimes her flute. She cooked for him, for as well as being the Order's finest eschatologist, she was also a woman of hearth and home.

She fed him rich cultured meats braised in herbs and wine, crunchy spiced baldo nuts, lemon ricotta pancakes, and much else. She loved to bake: yeast breads and biscuits, mallaks and muffins and golden brown popovers. Twice she made him custard tarts topped with bright fruits. She urged all this sugary, carbohydrate-rich food into him, if not to fatten him up to her ample dimensions, then at least to fill out his gaunt flesh. She did everything she could think of to nurture him and restore him to himself.

Most of all she talked to him. Rane had known no other person with whom he could talk so easily and honestly. She had a rare talent for listening, and it took several days for him to tell her all.

'All right,' she said to him one morning after they had breakfasted together in the sunroom and Rane had returned to bed. She sat in a plush chair by his side, the folds of her blue eschatologist's robe gathered around her plush body. 'That was quite a tale, some would say something out of an epic or even a legend.'

'Some would – but what would *you* say?'

'Does that matter so much?'

'Of course it does.'

Kolenya stirred some sugar into a fresh cup of coffee. She liked hers even sweeter than did Bardo. 'You are my dear friend,' she said by way of evading his questioning look.

'Then you *should* believe me.'

'I believe in *you*,' she said. 'Isn't that what really matters?'

She leaned over out of her chair to kiss his forehead and lips. She sat back down and smiled at him, her moon-shaped face bright with encouragement.

'Your tale is unfinished,' she added. 'What remains to be seen is what sort of ending you will make of it.'

'What possible ending can there be? I will find Maria again.'

'Or?'

'Or what? I don't know what you mean.'

'Yes, you do,' she said softly. She took his hand in hers. 'I can see it in your eyes, my dear. If you can't be reunited with her, you mean to end your own life.'

Rane did not want to look at her just then. His words tasted bitter with black coffee and memory as he said, 'Well, you are the eschatologist, and I suppose you can't help speculating about last things and endings.'

'Yes, I am the eschatologist, and it is in my professional capacity that I need to tell you something that you need to understand.' The softness melted out of her eyes for a moment, leaving them cold and clear. 'Something has happened in the years you've been gone, is happening now. Something is *about* to happen, to Sunjay and the other *Asta Siluuna*, to Neverness, to the whole galaxy, I think. Some great and beautiful thing.'

'What, then? This true evolution of our kind that you've been hoping for forever?'

'The Children need you,' she said. 'Now more than ever.'

'Children are children. I'm sure they have just about forgotten me.'

'You are their teacher.'

'They have got along very well, I'm sure, without my pouring kalla down their throats and nearly killing them.'

'As you would think to kill yourself?'

He closed his eyes for a moment, then stared out of the window. 'All I can think of is Maria. If she is alive, she suffers. What kind of ending to my story would it be for me just to put on my robes again, roll up my sleeves, and get back to work?'

'Perhaps a very great ending,' she told him. 'Let's suppose for a moment that everything happened as you said. Then the Solid State Entity could not have recreated Maria with so great a fidelity to the Maria whom both you and I loved unless you—'

'She *did* remake her. I saw her step out of the ocean's foam.'

'But did you see—'

'She was *perfect*, Kolenya. Nearly so.'

'But are your memories perfect?'

'They are as good as anyone's, I think. Or they used to be.'

'Here is what I think, dear Rane: when you reached into yourself to find your memories of Maria, you must also have reached deeper than anyone ever has into the One Memory itself.'

'Why do you say that?'

'Because it accords with all you have told me. It is the logic of your life.'

'The logic of my life is love. I never knew that until I met Maria.'

'Do you know it now? Maria loved poetry and the ocean and the stars and you. But most of all, she loved children, Sunjay and Chandra and—'

'You don't really know anything about Maria.'

'I know that you have the greatest of gifts. And Maria, alive or dead, would not want you to spend it all on her.'

That was all Kolenya said to him that day. But they talked a great deal during the next few snowy days, for Kolenya loved talking even more than she did exploring the possibilities of eschatology or baking brown bread or even making love. She talked to Bardo about Rane, and she talked to Poppy Panshin and Jonathan Hur and their other old friends. She talked to Tamara Ten Ashtoreth.

On the 57th of winter – a cold, clear day of deep blue skies glowing with the radiance of the Golden Ring – Tamara came to visit Rane, and she did not come alone. Her adopted daughters Julia, Miwa, and Ilona were off doing other things, as was Tavio and her elusive husband, but otherwise Tamara intended to pay Rane a family visit. And so Chandra and Sunjay accompanied her, along with little Alasharia, who had grown from a newborn to a kinetic and playful girl during the years since Rane had last watched her nursing at Tamara's breast. They enjoyed a feast of cookies and hot chocolate with Kolenya in her sunroom, then Sunjay brought chairs into Rane's sleeping room, and while Kolenya went off to tend to other matters, everyone else gathered around his bed.

Although Rane couldn't help thinking of Sunjay as still a boy, he had gained his full growth and stood as tall as his father and grandfather, Mallory Ringess. He had their bold, fierce features, which recalled the look of the thallow or hawk. His wild black hair fell down over eyes as deep and blue as a quiet sea. He looked at Rane out of that deep quiet as if he could tell him all and anything without speaking and Rane would understand.

'I am sorry that I was gone so long,' Rane said to him. He looked at the black diamond ring that now encircled Sunjay's finger. 'I would have liked to have been there at the ceremony to see you made a full pilot.'

'But you were there, sir,' he said, holding up his hand so that his ring caught the morning light streaming in through the window. 'I thought of you when Bardo put this on my finger.'

His happiness at seeing Rane again communicated to Alasharia, who decided that Rane must be one of her large extended family. With a sudden bound of enthusiasm, she leaped up onto his bed and bounced about on top of his belly as if riding a horse. She giggled when Rane smiled at her and lifted her up into the air straight above his head. With her curly black hair and aliveness to the moment and everything around her, she reminded him of Maria. She possessed in abundance that fiery and open-eyed sense of wonder that the *Asta Siluuna* called *awarei*.

'Alasharia, you are going to tire Rane out,' Tamara said, standing up to pull her daughter off him. Alasharia wiggled in Tamara's arms as she played with her mother's long blonde hair. By way of apology, she said to Rane, 'She has so much energy.'

'That's all right,' he said. 'I could use some of that.'

Tamara, a tall, big-boned woman, held the squirming Alasharia easily as if all the years of tending to her wild little daughter had depleted not an erg of her own great energy. Danlo had always said that his sensuous, beautiful wife had a nearly bottomless *animajii*: the same wild joy that made Maria so alive.

'It can't be long now,' Tamara said, 'before you are up and about again.'

'A few days, I hope, and no more. Kolenya is a wonderful host but . . .'

'What are your plans? Will you rejoin the Order? Bardo told me that the College of Lords has approved your petition.'

'You mean, Bardo's petition made on my behalf?'

Tamara set down Alasharia, who went over to her sister. Chandra had grown into a full and voluptuous womanhood like that of her mother, though she lacked her mother's height. She had the form and figure of Maria, and many of her striking features recalled Maria's, though where Maria's eyes were of black diamond, Chandra's shone a deep golden brown.

'We are all hoping that we can study with you again,' Chandra said. 'Now, more than ever.'

Rane looked at her and at her brother. 'But while I have been away, you have both grown up – it has been a long time since you were novices.'

'Didn't you once say, sir, that when it comes to entering the One Memory, everyone is a novice?'

Rane smiled at her, then turned back to Tamara. 'It would be good to be in my old house again, at least for a while.'

'I have heard that you want to go back out into the stars again,' Tamara said. 'The whole Order is talking about that. The whole city is.'

'Yes, Kolenya told me that I am being called the Mad Remembrancer.'

'People can be cruel,' she said. She, who had lost her firstborn to war and starvation and had suffered the ravaging of her memories, knew as much about human cruelty as anyone. 'But they can be kind, too. You are also being called the Great Remembrancer.'

'And what do you call me?' he asked, looking at her sharply.

'Nothing other than my dear old friend.'

'If Maria still lives,' he said, 'I have to go her.'

'Of course you do. But which Maria?'

That was a strange thing for her to say, and she looked at him strangely. Then she said, 'I wish Danlo was here. I don't think he ever realized that Maria was his sister.'

Was Mallory Ringess really both Danlo's father and Maria's? Or had Kalinda lied about that? As Rane looked from Sunjay to Chandra to little Alasharia, he could see Maria and Mallory in all of them, and he felt certain that Kalinda had told true.

'Where is Danlo?' he asked Tamara. 'Kolenya didn't know, and Bardo wouldn't say.'

'No one knows,' she said. 'After Danlo finished his work with the Alaloi, he lived with us again long enough to see Sunjay receive his ring. Then he went out to the stars himself. I believe he might have set out to the core stars like his grandfather to try to talk with the Ieldra.'

'I am sure he did,' Sunjay said.

He looked at Chandra, then Alasharia, too. Only five years before, they and the other *Asta Siluuna* had often spoken to each other through their silent signals of finger taps, lip tightenings, brow furrowings, and blinks, as well as what they called 'eyetalk'. Now, however, this communication seemed to have deepened into a language conveyed wholly and completely through their lively, luminous eyes. Rane could not have said how he understood this, but he sensed that Tamara's three children exchanged huge amounts of information in very little time as they silently discussed their father and Rane himself, and argued among themselves, and finally came to a consensus.

And Sunjay, speaking for all of them, said to Rane, 'Surely my father went to ask the Ieldra about the One Memory. Soon he will return to ask you.'

'And what could I tell him that the elder gods could not?'

'Perhaps everything,' Sunjay said. 'They are not human, sir, and you are.'

'Does that matter so much?'

'It means everything. It is a truly human thing to do, when evidence and logic seem to suggest otherwise and half the Order does think you are mad, for you to want to go to search for Maria again.' Sunjay looked at him, and in his blue, blue eyes burned the wildest of fires. 'That suggests to me that either you are mad, which I know you are not, or that you know things that others do not.'

'Then you believe that Maria might still be alive?'

'I know she is. And you must go to her.'

At this, Rane sat straight up in bed and reached out to clasp Sunjay's hand. 'Will you help me? You have your own lightship now, the *Silver Thallow*, yes? Will you take me to Kailash Poru?'

'I would, if Bardo would permit it. But Kailash Poru, Shambhalla, too, and other planets of which you have spoken, appear on none of our charts. And so Bardo believes they might not exist, and so he will *not* permit it.'

'Then . . .'

'My father will return, and soon. He may take your side against Bardo. And then either he will take you to search for Kailash Poru or I will.'

'Thank you,' Rane said. He thought of the bloody cross he had seen planted on the grounds of the Karadan Adri. 'But what if by then it is too late?'

'It will not be, sir. I feel certain that for you and Maria, it will never be too late.'

At this, Alasharia came over to his bed and asked him, 'But Uncle Rane, why do you want to go away again? Aunt Maria is right here.'

Rane smiled at this. Sunjay's and Chandra's talk of Maria must have made her real to her.

'Why do you have to go away from *me* again?'

'But Alasharia, I haven't seen you since you were a newborn baby and—'

'I remember!'

'But that's not possible because—'

'But I do! You held me, and you smelled like tears and wind and jasmine. You said I was made of light.'

Rane thought back more than five years. 'I said you were *so* light.'

She raised up her little hand to catch the rainbow scattered by one of the crystals hanging in the window. Her skin lit up with curves of red, orange, yellow, green, blue, and violet. 'But you meant we're *all* made of light. Like Aunt Maria is. Here she is, Uncle Rane!'

She pressed her hand to Rane's chest and smiled at him as if her child's logic of love made complete sense to her and was the simplest thing in the universe.

That afternoon, another visitor arrived to renew her acquaintance with Rane. Ailieyha, as dark of skin as the night, as bright in spirit as the moon, brought Rane some flowers and arranged them with a well-practised art in the blue vase that Konlenya provided. She wore fine sable furs as dark as her eyes and a silver choker studded with diamonds around her neck. She had prospered in her new profession that Rane and Tamara had opened for her, and she had risen in the ranks of the courtesans. She seemed happy to see Rane – and happy altogether that her life had turned out much differently than she had once feared.

'I knew you would come back,' she said, hugging him, then sitting down beside his bed. 'I am so glad that you did.'

'But I came back without Maria.'

Ailieyha gestured with her artful, expressive hand. A small woman, she moved with all the quickness and alertness of a bird. 'It matters only that you got to love her again.'

'Then you believe that I—'

'I do, though most of my sisters don't. I have argued that the courtesans should make a second contribution toward a second quest for you to go back to Maria, but . . .'

Her sweet voice died off into the crackling of the fire. Then she said, 'But everywhere in the city, people are talking about you and making bets as to whether or not there will ever be proof of your story. I think there will be. And we may be able to use that to gather funds for a second quest. That is why I came here today, to give you some hope along with this.'

She undid her choker and handed it to Rane. She told him to sell it on the Street of Diamonds as a start toward his new quest.

'Oh, and I also want to give you a kiss.'

And with that she stood up and pressed her full, soft lips to his. Then she left him with a promise that she would visit him again soon.

32

Three days later, buoyed by hope, propelled up out of bed and out of Kolenya's house by his need to breathe fresh air and test the strength of his body again, Rane struck out on his skates onto the coloured ice of the streets of Neverness. He didn't go far that first morning: he contented himself with a short foray through the Pilots' Quarter and into the Tycho's Green. His exercise exhausted him. Kolenya's meals and a long night's rest in bed restored him. The following day, he skated down the orange North Sliddery around the Hofgarten, packed with Ordermen, diplomats, white-furred Fravashi, and others drinking coffee or taking their lunches. He went as far as the Darghinni District, but decided not to venture down the red lesser glidderies there, for he did not want to spend time or energy in chance encounters with one of the wormlike Scutari or other aliens. In the days after that, though, with his leg muscles building long and lean, he ranged the entire city from Far North Beach down through the Zoo and the City Wild then past the Winter Ring and into the Ashtoreth District, home to many astrier families like the one that had reared Tamara. He skated down the Serpentine and the Run, and along avenues and glissades coloured yellow and green. And as he skated, the icy wind against his face brought the smells of the city: cilka and roasting meats, toalache and woodsmoke and perfume and the sprays of rank speech molecules of the alien Friends of Man. The wind brought memory, too, for in their short time together in Neverness, he and Maria had made outings to most parts of the city together.

When it came time for him to move back into his old chalet, he did so with an uncomfortable mixture of gladness and dread, for he still hadn't decided if he should rejoin the Order, and here his memories of Maria were many. Once inside that old heap of wood and stone, after he had kindled a blazing fire, he thought again of her books of poetry and the adjal and the flute. He remembered the bitter sweetness of the hot Summerworld coffee that had so often wafted from her blue mug. And the dress. A flash of red opened windows upon the hues of fire roses and yu berries and the glister of the morning sun. He saw again Maria's beautiful bitten lip and the drop of blood that welled up from it – the single drop of red blood that had rolled onto the white snow beneath her. It stained the world's whiteness in a haemorrhage that swelled out and out, engulfing the snow-shagged mountains, sweeping across the ice of the Sound and colouring crimson all that he looked upon, without and within. And so hope became horror, and he doubted the wisdom of all he had done and still intended to do.

Early that evening, he decided that he must drive away these visions of defeat and despair. A wild notion came to him. Hadn't he, in truth, mapped his way out of an infinite tree? Wasn't he, therefore, in some sense a master pilot? Why then shouldn't he go down into the Farsider's Quarter to the Street of the Ten Thousand Bars, where he might seek rescue in the master pilot's bar? Perhaps he might find a pilot willing to defy Bardo and take him back to Kailash Poru. Failing that, he might find a way to forget the images that kept crowding into his consciousness like the garish colours of a flesh fresco: the memories of Maria that none of his remembrancer's tricks could dispel. For the master pilot's bar had in abundance that old, old, anti-remembrancer's drug sometimes called akalla.

Through the cold and dark he skated down past the Street of Fumes and the Street of Musicians until he reached his destination. At the kerb of a red lesser gliddery, he pushed open the heavy obsidian door to the bar. In a tiny, dim room lit by some burning logs in the marble fireplace and a couple of glowglobes, two pilots in black kamelaikas like the one he wore stood over the ancient shatterwood bar, drinking and talking. Rane knew them both, for one was Alesar Estarei, a hero of the Battle of the Ten Thousand Suns, and the other was Lara Jesusa, whom he had once instructed. When Rane ejected his skate blades and moved toward the bar, Alesar turned toward the firelight. A thin, quick man with a long, sardonic face, he looked at Rane and said, 'Lord Remembrancer, I'd heard that you are claiming to have mapped free from an infinite tree, but you are not in fact of the pilots, and this bar is for us.'

At this, Lara Jesusa shook her head in anger. A small woman with a huge intellect and a snow leopard's heart, she feared nothing in or out of the manifold, least of all Alesar Estarei. She turned her ice-blue eyes on him and said, 'You are ungracious and have the soul of a worm. Lord Rane is my guest and he *will* drink with us here, if he wishes.'

'No, he will not,' Alesar said. He finished his glass of beer and slammed it down on the bar. 'You may drink with him, I don't care. I will see you later.'

'Not if fate is kind,' she said, glaring at him.

Alesar stomped out of the bar, and he would have slammed the door if it hadn't been made of heavy stone not easy to move. Rane stood beside Lara looking at the bottles of various drugs lined up on the shelf on the wall behind the bar. To the journeyman holist serving as bartender that evening, he said, 'I would like some akalla.'

'Akalla, sir?' The big bartender, who had flaming red hair, shook his head.

'Alcohol, I think most people call it.'

'Would you like a glass of wine? I have an excellent Yarkonan firewine that—'

'I know little of such drugs, but it seems to me that wine is not strong enough to be considered akalla. Do you not have anything more potent?'

'Well, there is brandy and skol, vodka and cachaca, too, and—'

'I have just remembered something. Didn't Mallory Ringess once drink a drug called skotch?'

'It is said that he did, sir, though that was before I was born. We still have some bottles of it that he brought back from Urradeth.'

'I will try that, then.'

The bartender produced a bottle of skotch, and poured a little of the smoky amber liquid into a tumbler. Rane swept it up and drank down the skotch in a single gulp. He said, 'That is a vile medicine.'

'Many say that, which is why we still have bottles of it left after so many years.'

'I do not feel anything. Are you sure you measured out the correct dosage?'

'You are not supposed to feel anything yet. And I only poured you a sample, to see if you could stomach it.'

'Please pour me some more then.' He set his tumbler back down. To Lara, he said, 'Do you have any experience with this skotch?'

'No, Lord Rane, I don't – I like my beer.' Lara drank from her mug, then wiped a bit of foam from her thin lips. 'But I think you are supposed to sip and savour it.'

This time, the bartender filled the tumbler halfway. Again, Rane gulped it down.

'I do not feel anything beyond a burning in my throat and belly,' he said. He tapped his finger against his tumbler and glanced at the bartender. 'Pour.'

Again, the bartender filled the tumbler, and again Rane drank its contents. And Lara said to him, 'Two such drinks so quickly should be enough for you to feel at least a—'

'I do feel something,' Rane said. His tight control over muscle and thought seemed to be relaxing as a strange new consciousness rushed through him like a liquid fire. His legs seemed weak. 'But it is not enough.'

'Not enough for what?' Lara asked him.

'To forget.'

It did not take him long to finish a third tumbler of skotch. Was it enough to annihilate the memory of that damned infinite tree and the look on Maria's face as the Kushok and the Shambhallans led her away? No, it was not. And so he downed a fourth tumbler. Was he drunk yet? Not as much as he wanted to be, and so he took a fifth dose and then a sixth. So the evening went. By the time that he could barely stand and had trouble focusing on the features of Lara's blurred face, he had drunk nearly half the bottle of skotch. The bitter drug did nothing to erase his memories of Maria, but it did dull their pain.

Lara called for a sled and took him home. After putting him to bed, she made him promise never to drink so much again.

When Rane awoke the following morning to a throbbing headache and a body that felt as if it had been beaten and stretched on a rack, he felt sure that he would keep that promise.

He spent most of the next couple of days busying himself with household chores to make his chalet liveable again. There were plants and food and new clothes to acquire, and he needed a new box full of kalla, toalache, and aromatics if ever he was to re-establish himself as a remembrancer. One afternoon while outside setting up some wind chimes, he chanced to look beneath the yu tree at a bright red berry that stood out against the white snow. And immediately he saw Maria's lips again and the drop of blood, and it seemed impossible to him that either his first Maria or his second could still be alive.

That evening he returned to the pilot's bar, and he drank himself stupid. The following morning, he promised never again to put tongue to skotch or any other alcohol. But then Sunjay stopped by to deliver grievous news: Bardo had heard that Rane had sold Ailieyha's choker and was using the funds to try to bribe pilots to take him out to Kailash Poru – or, failing that, anywhere away from Neverness.

'Bardo has forbidden *any* ship from providing you passage,' Sunjay told him.

'Even the deep-ships? Even the lightships of the pilot-poets?'

'He says it is for your own good.'

'How can anything ever be good again?'

'If you feel that way, sir, then why bother making your home comfortable again?'

'Because I still have to live.'

In this, however, he lied both to Sunjay and himself, for he knew that no one could live a moment longer than one's fated time of death. And so that evening he went out to seek his fate or at least to draw a little nearer to it. He found himself in the master pilot's bar with another tumbler of skotch in his hand. Lara Jesusa arrived with Helena Charbo to try reason him away from yet another drunken spree. Cristobel the Bold joined them, for he had heard of Rane's drinking feats, and he wished to see for himself how far the great remembrancer had fallen. His cool green eyes regarded the wobbly Rane with both condescension and great guilt that he had failed to be the pilot to take Rane to the Solid State Entity.

Though he didn't really believe the story, he had a secret fear that Rane had told the truth.

'Describe for us again,' the arrogant Cristobel said, 'how a remembrancer stole away in an unfamiliar lightship into an unfamiliar manifold.'

Before Rane could slur out an answer, Bardo walked into the bar. He lumbered up to Rane like a great black-furred bear and said, 'Enough. I won't allow you to poison your brain this way.'

'There is nothing the matter with my brain.'

'You had problems with your memory years ago even before you left the city.'

'There is nothing the matter with my memory.'

'You are destroying it along with yourself.'

'But memory can never be destroyed.'

'Keep on drinking as you have, and you'll shrink your brain like a bird's.'

'What do you know of birds? On Old Earth, I learned that a jay can bury three thousand seeds in the ground and remember the location of each six months later.'

'In the state you're in, you couldn't remember the location of three hundred seeds three days later.'

'I could remember ten thousand.'

At this, Bardo laughed nervously and Lara Jesusa looked at him strangely. And Cristobel said, 'Could you remember the location of ten thousand baldo nuts buried in the snow?'

'If I do,' Rane asked, 'will you all please leave me alone?'

Cristobel had issued his challenge mostly as a joke, but it turned into something much more than that when word of what had transpired in the master pilot's bar got out to the other pilots and then the rest of the Order. And then soon people from all of the districts of Neverness from the Farsider's Quarter to the Old City were talking about the Mad Remembrancer and the ten thousand nuts. Harijan made bets with wormrunners as to whether or not Rane could do as he had said. A wealthy astrier agreed to put up a prize of ten thousand City Disks if Rane could drink half a bottle of skotch and then locate the buried nuts. Should Rane prove triumphant, many thousands of others agreed to add a few disks to a pool that would pay for the construction of a new lightship to be

called the *Star of Maria*. They wanted to see if Rane really could
pilot it out into the stars.

Bardo, as Lord of the Order, did not view his office as the
old Timekeeper had, and he had always resented the Timekeeper's
imperious ways. And so when many lords of the Order such as
Dominic Catharis and the Lord Holist, Julia Honavar, joined a
delegation of astriers and diplomats from the city to petition
for a festival of remembrance to be held in Thomas Rane's
honour, he decided that he must consider their request. His
conscience, too, weighed upon him, for Rane had once been his
teacher and he had always felt uneasy laying down edicts as to
what Rane should or should not do. As he said to Kolenya Mor
one day in late winter: 'If our friend really wishes to kill himself,
who am I to stop him?'

And so he consented to the conditions of the astrier who
had proposed the contest: ten thousand baldo nuts would
be inscribed with glyphs representing as many numbers. As
Rane looked on, the nuts would be buried at random beneath
the snow of the Fravashi Green. Then, some days later, Rane
would drink his half bottle of skotch. A hundred numbers, one
by one, would be called out, also at random. If Rane could walk
about the Fravashi Green (if he *could* still walk) and identify
the exact location of every one of the hundred nuts, then all the
disks in the pool would be his. He could then build his own
lightship if he wished, and Bardo would have to let him leave
Neverness.

It took most of five days for volunteers to gather nuts from
beneath the trees of the city's various greens, and then another
three to number and hide them. Little snow falls in late winter,
but at least four inches of dense *horeesh*, as the Alaloi call packed
powder, carpeted the Fravashi Green that season. The ten
thousand nuts were lost beneath the many white acres like so
many stars in the vastness of space. The astrier who had proposed
and organized the contest – a thin sleekit of a man named Diego
Arizul – had at first demanded that Rane should have to dig up
all the nuts in order to claim his prize. Then it was pointed out
to him that Rane would still have to memorize the location of
all the ten thousand nuts in order to locate the random hundred.
And it would make for a more exciting contest if Rane's treasure
hunt transpired over a few hours as opposed to the few days

that it would take to uncover ten thousand nuts. Then, too, Rane had to be drunk when he performed his feat, and such a state he could hardly be expected to maintain for so long.

On the morning of the 86th of winter, many people from across the city converged on the Fravashi Green: harijan, arhats, diplomats, astriers, and aliens. And wormrunners and warrior-poets, too, as well as nimspinners, haikuists, musicians, and autists. The Order's academicians and professionals stood in the gelid air beneath the great yu trees, and flashes of fur coloured orange, blue, red, gold, and purple mingled with the hues of the green trees, the white snow, and the deep blue sky. Pilots in their black furs and black racing kamelaikas joined the gathering. Helena Charbo and Lara Jesusa met up with Cristobel the Bold and the Sonderval, the tallest human being present that morning and possibly the most arrogant pilot who had ever lived. His loud voice rumbled with his disbelief that Rane could ever have piloted a lightship through the manifold, much less have found his way out of an infinite tree. He doubted as well that Rane could find his hundred nuts. Others did not seem so sure. Li Chu, stolid and dignified in his silver robe, stood conferring with Shri Santo Ris, who had replaced Rane as Lord Remembrancer. They knew Rane well; they feared only that the awful akalla that Rane had to drink would cripple his fabulous memory if not outright kill him.

Near the centre of the green, Rane waited with friends and the various contest officials. People were still arriving to the sound of piping flutes and thousands of excited voices. Puffs of silvery breath exploded out from blue lips and vanished into the air a moment later. Most everyone seemed in a festive mood. Many smoked triya seeds, toalache, even tobacco, and other euphorics that scented the air in little grey and purple clouds. They drank coffee and tea and hot chocolate; or, more in keeping with the moment, they warmed their throats with hot ale and mulled wine spiced with cinnamon, cloves, and oranges. Many, especially those from other worlds not used to Neverness's cold, wore masks over chilled cheeks and noses. Others, though, left their faces bare, and Rane recognized many of them: the Lord Librarian, Ursula Eshtawi, who had entered Borja in the same year that he had, and the Lord Akashic, Miklos Tal, and hundreds of other Ordermen. Malaclypse Redring, the renegade warrior-poet who had become Danlo's friend, looked on with violet eyes that seemed too alert and too alive. In the throngs crowding around him, Rane picked out the astrier Georgios, who had tried to sell him his daughter's eggs. He had his arm around Cornelia, whom Rane remembered too well. He could still see Maria in her, just as he saw nearly every curvaceous, black-haired beauty in the multitude gathered that morning as one of the classic forms. He could not stop thinking about Maria. He saw her in his memories of how they had once lain together beneath the yu trees here looking up at the stars. He saw her in the wavering air and in the trees' millions of needles blazing bright green and most of all in the many blood-red berries that dotted the snow.

'I think we should begin,' Diego Arizul called out. He clearly enjoyed his new role as the festival's organizer and master of ceremonies, for his thin, metallic voice sounded self-satisfied and happy. 'Is everyone ready?'

Rane stood between Kolenya Mor and Sunjay as if to draw strength from them. Bardo stomped his feet as he looked at Rane. He held in his huge hand a little computer programmed to generate random numbers. Rane said, 'Let's get this over.'

He nodded at Ari Olvagga, the red-haired bartender who had served Rane his first taste of skotch. Ari bore a clean tumbler and a dark bottle. This he unstoppered, and he poured a bit of smoky poison into the tumbler and handed it to Rane. Rane raised his glass.

'Salud!' someone in the crowd called out. And another: 'Skal!'

Ancient and more contemporary toasts sounded out loud and insistent: 'Viva! Kanpai! Om Nut! Tazto! Za Lyubov!'

Rane gulped down his skotch, and Ari poured him some more.

'Skal! Tazto! Cheers! Za Lyubov!'

So it went, Ari pouring and Rane drinking. After Ari had trickled out the last dram, he showed the bottle to Diego to verify that it now measured half-empty. Again, Rane raised his glass.

'Za Lyubov! Za Lyubov! Za Lyubov!'

Rane, supervised by Diego, had eaten a substantial breakfast to slow the rush of inebriation. This had been permitted, as the ingestion of anti-alcohol metabolants had not. Even so, the last swallow of skotch pulled a grey gauze of confusion over his eyes and poured muscle-dissolving acids into his legs. He could hardly stand.

'Za Lyubov!'

But, for the sake of love, he must stand – and then walk and remember and see. Bardo showed the computer's screen to Diego, who called out, 'Number 7,386!'

Rane breathed raggedly. Ethanol seeped from his belly into his blood and then into his brain. Neurons flooded with dopamine and serotonin, and the ethanol increased the effects of inhibitory neurotransmitters, slowing the limbic system. His thoughts slowed into a slurry of ideas and impulses. Although he needed to step forward, he didn't know if he could.

'The number is 7,386,' Diego repeated. 'And might I remind the Lord Remembrancer that the time limit of this contest will be strictly observed.'

Rane thought that he should wait until his body had burned off some of the skotch before he moved, but he seemed to be getting drunker by the moment, not more sober. And so he forced himself forward. However, as soon as his foot lifted into the air, he wobbled like a spinning top about to collapse. Sunjay rushed up to catch him. He handed Rane the two ski poles that he had thought to bring with him. When someone called out that the use of such an aid amounted to cheating, Sunjay made a quick argument that the rules of the contest had nothing to say about ski poles. Diego, sensing the mood of the many people who clearly wished for Rane to succeed, announced, 'Lord Rane can use your poles. But time passes, and the number 7,386 has been called.'

Through a grey mist, Rane looked about the Fravashi Green as he recalled trudging over its white expanse some days ago when the baldo nuts had been buried. He studied the undulations and indentations of the snow for signs of disturbance. The tramp of hundreds of boots, though, had obliterated any such, and he would gain no help in this way. And so he looked with a different sense, triangulating on trees, mapping fields of snow to the image fields of mnemonics that he had learned so well. He took a step, then stopped, planting his pole hard to keep from falling. He took a dozen steps more, veered to left to the pull of the akalla, then righted himself as he moved toward a huge yu tree. In fits and stops, in quick steps broken by unexpected lurches, he arrived at what he thought must be the right spot.

'Number . . . 7,386 . . . is here,' he said. He hardly recognized the sound of his own voice, so thick and inarticulate that it seemed that he spoke through a mouth full of frozen mush. 'I . . . think.'

When he bent to dig up the nut, however, he toppled over face first into the snow. Seeing this, Sunjay rushed forward, sat Rane up, helped him to stand, and dusted off his face and furs. He pressed the ski poles into Rane's hands again. Then he enlarged and deepened the hole begun by Rane, scattering handfuls of snow like a dog digging up a bone. A few moments later, he straightened, holding up a big brown baldo nut for everyone to see.

'Number 7,386!' Bardo called out in a voice that boomed over the Fravashi Green. He had followed along with Rane across the snow, as had everyone else.

'Number 7,386!' Diego Arizul confirmed. He dropped the nut into a leather bag that he carried. 'The Lord Remembrancer has found his first nut.'

'Za Lyubov!' the hundreds of people looking on cried out. 'Za Lyubov!'

While Rane stood trying to catch his breath and keep down the contents of his big breakfast, Bardo summoned up another number from his computer.

'Number 8,935!' Diego cried out.

Rane looked about the frozen green. He looked through moments frozen in time into memory. He walked toward the southeast, in the direction of the Hollow Fields, where his first Maria had been placed into a sunship and shot into space. When he came to the right spot, he nudged the snow with the tip of his ski pole. He bent to begin digging, but Sunjay wrapped a strong arm around him to keep him upright. He was not so drunk that he couldn't appreciate how badly Sunjay wished to preserve his dignity, and he loved him for that.

'Let me!' an ugly wormrunner called out. A tall man dressed in real mink furs flayed from the flesh of living animals stomped across the snow. He used his knife to dig up the second nut. 'I can't make out the meaning of these markings.'

He showed the nut to Bardo, who said, 'Number 8,935!'

And Diego confirmed this, dropping the nut into his bag and announcing, 'Number 8,935!'

'Za Lyubov! For love! For Maria!'

So it went, Diego calling out numbers and the multitude following Rane across the Fravashi Green. One by one, volunteers came forward to dig in the snow where Rane indicated. One by one, Diego dropped the nuts into his bag: ten of them, twenty, and then fifty more. The sun, low against the cobalt winter sky, reached its greatest height above the southern horizon. With each nut uncovered and confirmed, Rane grew a little more sober and more confident of success. Ninety-six nuts now filled Diego Arizul's bag, and then ninety-seven and ninety-eight. With only two more nuts to be found, Bardo called out the number 2,212. A curvaceous astrier whose white furs clung to her big breasts and hips dug down into the snow in the mark made by Rane's ski pole. She brushed ice crystals from a round brown nut. Bardo called out 2,212, and Diego slipped it into his bulging bag.

'We have come to the hundredth nut!' Diego announced. Hundreds of buzzing voices across the green now hushed. 'The Lord of the Order will now tell the number!'

'The number,' Bardo said, glancing down at his computer, 'is 1,729!'

Rane, triangulating on trees, mapping fields of snow to the image fields of mnemonics, reaching deep down into his perfect memory, recalled the moment when he and Maria had first stepped onto the Fravashi Green on a fine winter day and every crystal of snow had seemed precisely placed and utterly perfect. He stepped toward the place where he knew nut number 1,729 to be. Everyone else and the whole world seemed to move with him. He stopped. He stabbed his pole through a layer of six-pointed ice crystals.

'Za Lyubov!' someone cried out.

Another astrier who could have been a sister to the woman who had dug up the penultimate nut came forward. She, too, wore rich white shagshay furs; black hair spilled out from beneath a puffy white hat, and a red mask covered her face. She dropped down, and used a long, shining knife to dig in the snow. She dug and dug, deeper and wider, bent over the growing hole as clumps of snow flew. Finally, she stood, put away her knife, and held out her empty hands for all to see.

'There is no nut here!' the wormrunner who had uncovered the first nut announced.

'The Remembrancer has failed!' someone else shouted.

'Impossible!' Rane cried out. 'I stood in this exact place when the nut was put here three days ago.'

He looked down into the hole. He looked into a great white emptiness.

'We need to dig more!' Sunjay said.

He moved up to the hole as if to do just that. Diego, however, stopped him. He produced a marked tape and measured the hole, its depth and diameter. He called out, 'The hole is already beyond its permissible dimensions. The Lord Remembrancer has failed!'

Rane looked and looked and looked. Then he looked for Ari Olvagga, intending to wrest the bottle of scotch away from the bartender and drink its contents straight down. And then to press him to open up the master pilot's bar so that he could drink three bottles more.

'Cheater!' This ugly word came from Lara Jesusa, who elbowed her way through the crowd and joined the others near the hole. She pointed at the astrier, who stood gazing at Rane. 'I do believe that she pocketed the nut!'

'Search her!' someone called out. And then two, ten, and twenty more: 'Search the astrier woman!'

Diego nodded his head, but Bardo would not allow this. He said to Lara Jesusa, 'We cannot just search someone according to your belief as to what might or might not have happened. But why don't we just ask her?'

He turned to the woman in the white furs and nodded. He waited as she looked first at him and then at Rane. She reached into her pocket and drew out nut number 1,729.

'Here it is,' she said to Rane in a low voice muffled by her mask. 'I would like to keep it as a memento.'

'A memento of what?'

'You did not come for me, so I came to you.'

Then she pulled down her red mask and smiled at him. It was Maria.

33

Many religions, peoples, and individuals have conceived of some sort of a heaven far beyond the cold hard edges and cruelties of the world. The ancient Kristians had hoped after death to be resurrected in perfect immortal bodies and to dwell in the gardens of a New Jerusalem at the right hand of God. Gardens, too, had played into the beliefs of the Zoroastrians and even more so the Muslims, who conceived of springs and rivers flowing over green lawns as wide as the earth. And in each garden they would dwell with children and loved ones, resting on cushions and carpets, eating delicious foods, forever happy and without hurt, fear, or sorrow. In Al-Firdaws, the highest level of heaven, they would be granted the highest vision of Allah. The Buddhists had their nirvana and the release from their torturous cycles of birth and rebirth into the eternal bliss of the great Emptiness. The Cybernetic Gnostics, too, sought to free their spirits from the prison of matter, even as the Cybernetic churches taught that a worthy Architect could find oneness inside the blissful information storms of a computer's circuitry in union with Ede the God. Hanuman li Tosh, maddened by the suffering of the world, had striven to collapse the entire cosmos into a single Universal Computer in which would dwell a perfected artificial life that he would guide and nurture in his transcendent state as a sort of living god. The warrior-poets, much less ambitious, had their moment of the possible and the composing of the perfect poem. The Ringists, of course, guided at first by Thomas Rane himself in many kalla ceremonies, drew inspiration from the ancient remembrancers. For the One Memory, in its deepest part, shone with the One Light which broke out into all the colours of being at birth and then gathered the whole universe back into itself at death in a shimmering ecstasy of remembrance.

For Rane, triumphant at last, heaven took the form of Maria. In the time following the festival on the Fravashi Green, he knew many blissful moments with her, breathing in sweet fragrances on walks along the streams that flowed through the Hyacinth Gardens, eating delicious foods in candlelit restaurants, lying together on cushions and fire-warmed carpets. Released from the sorrows of their journeys, they found a deep contentment in the fullness of many happy days. They recited to each other the found poems of Placida Lovita; they shared in ecstasy the glorious matter of each other's body; they stood once again in the Light Pavilion as their spirits soared outward into the universe toward their shining star.

Their reunion should have been all that Rane could have hoped for. They were free from Kalinda, free from Kailash Poru, free from the *Asherah*, but they were not free from the past. For Rane sensed a little bit of hell hidden in his Maria heaven, like a worm working at the core of a perfect red apple.

He gained his first hint that all might not be as he wished almost as soon as he and Maria returned to his chalet after the festival. After all the many cries of amazement rang out, after all the congratulations had been proffered and wishes for a wonderful future had been made, after they were alone, he and Maria had made love in the chalet's fireroom in a blaze of passion so bright and hot that it burned the last of his drunkenness away. They lay for a long while on thick furs, letting their sweat dry, listening to the crackle of red-hot logs, breathing in each other's scents and quiet words. Then he asked her what had happened. She had quite a tale to tell, an epic of pain, inspiration, daring, and death. But she did not tell it, or at least not very much of it. She said to him only this: 'Yes, I think Santuu might have had me crucified after he was done with me, but he met with an accident first. He fell from the same cliff as had Armas. It was an amazing coincidence.'

Of her escape and how she had contrived it, she said nothing. She would not talk about the long journey she had made from Kailash Poru to Neverness. Nor would she respond to any of his encouragements, no matter how gentle, for her to tell him of her sufferings. It was not so much that she wished to forget an unbearable memory, for that was Rane's way and not hers. No, instead she willed herself to live in the moment with Rane, in the warmth of sweet smiles and happy eyes and firelight. It was a place of new promises and new life, and in that place only did she want to be.

'I would have died to help free you,' Rane said to her, resting his hand between her breasts.

'You almost did, didn't you? It is what I love about you.' The black centres of her eyes gathered in the fire's flickering orange flames. 'But would you live to help me remain here now?'

That was a strange thing for her to say. He didn't understand it. Or rather, he didn't want to understand it. And Maria, poet thought she was, did not want to try to explain herself in words. No, her way was to make a poem of herself that would call to all that was deep and good within him. When they began kissing and caressing again, he felt her great need to find a home in him. But can the whole of the sea fill a shell or does the shell lose itself tumbling along the dark currents and rising tides of the sea? How had he ever dared to hope that he could hold more than an infinitesimal part of Maria, in his heart or in his memories or in the hollows of his hands? How could he keep this woman with a bottomless capacity for love from slipping away?

Tell me how to make love last, he remembered someone saying, *and I will tell you the secret of the universe*.

During the first days of deep winter, with the sky so blue that it looked like a great hollowed-out sapphire, Rane and Maria returned to their old life, or rather the life that Rane had lived with his first Maria. In a long, tiresome ceremony of candles and ancient rites attended by Bardo, Kolenya, and other old friends and lords, he renewed his vows as a faithful remembrancer of the Order. Although Shri Santo Ris had replaced him as Lord Remembrancer, Rane would remain to many *the* Remembrancer. He felt glad to be relieved from the duties of his old office so that he could spend more time with his students.

He sat frequently with two novices, Marko Morales and Jerica Shen-wu, and with Binah Jolatha Alora and Decan

Tomasan, two of the *Asta Siluuna* whom he had watched grow from a promising childhood to become brilliant journeymen in their professions. Binah, after the fashion of the scryers, daubed blacking oil into her eye hollows so that they filled with an impenetrable darkness that both obscured the scarring and lent her an air of mystery. Sunjay and Chandra, too old now to be formally instructed in the basics of remembrance required of all those who entered the Academy, nevertheless signed up for the more advanced work that some few pilots and professionals undertook. So did Kolenya Mor, who renewed her acquaintance with the remembrancing attitudes and the kalla that she had drunk in so many of the Ringist ceremonies led by Rane. So did Maria. Though not of the Order, the first Maria had been beloved by many who were, and no one objected when Rane set aside precious time to instruct Maria Number Two.

As she had before, she settled in to his chalet on the cliffs above North Beach with a will to transform its austere rooms into a home. By some strange instinct, she softened the wood floors with rich red carpets of a kind very familiar to Rane. On the walls, she hung tondos and tapestries whose colours brought forth a rainbow of hues that burned in Rane's memory. She filled the sunroom with blue vases of freshly cut fireflowers, and into her writing room went a shatterwood desk inlaid with squares of gold onyx. In a little shop on the Street of Artefacts, she acquired a blue fountain pen painted with tiny white thallows and covered with many layers of shining lacquer. And she bought ink and paper, and a leather writing pad, too: everything she would need to begin writing poems again.

Perhaps inspired by all that had happened to her, she set to composing a set of new poems to be called *Love Song to a Lost Earth*. Usually she worked alone, scribbling away at her desk in her little writing room. Sometimes, though, she liked to write at the table by the big bay windows and watch the fluttering red and blue sails of the schooners running before the wind out on the ice of the hard-frozen Sound. She liked to watch Rane, too, lost in meditation or remembrance in the adjacent fireroom as he gazed into hot orange flames. She drank her old Summerworld coffee from a new blue mug as she smiled at Rane from time to time and put pen to paper.

As deep winter grew colder, Rane did his best to keep Maria

inside the house, composing couplets, eating savoury foods, bringing their bodies together to the delight of their souls. When they did go out into the bitter blue air, usually they went together, skating for exercise to the Elf Gardens or to Our Lady of Rocks carved into Mount Atakel at the eastern edge of the city. Often, though, duties called Rane to the halls of the Academy, and then he was loath to leave Maria alone.

'But I want to skate down every gliddery in the city,' she said to him one day. 'I want to go into every shop, eat every food, talk to every alien who will talk to me. I want to meet all your friends!'

And that, Rane thought as he drank in the enthusiasm that radiated from her like sunshine, was exactly what he did *not* want. Or rather, the kind of social intercourse that he felt he must discourage. Doing so went against his natural inclination to honour another's soul as a beautiful, inviolable thing never to be deformed or ruled. In this instance, however, he found himself desperate to keep Maria to himself. For now that they had returned to a semblance of the life that he had known with her before he had set out on his quest, a fundamental flaw at the heart of that quest widened like a wound he could not think how to heal.

It should have been obvious from the first that when Rane did return to Neverness with Maria she would encounter many people who had memories of her: friends such as Kolenya Mor and Tamara, of course, and Chandra, Sunjay, and the *Asta Siluuna*. And appreciators of her poetry, and academicians she had met at parties, and the many nimspinners, arhats, and such whom the naturally gregarious Maria had met on the streets. Why hadn't Rane foreseen the possibility – the *inevitability* – that one or more of them would tell her of the first Maria and how she had died?

True, he was a remembrancer, not a scryer, for whom the future opened like the pages of the books that Maria liked to read. True, as well, how could he have known that Kalinda would have remade a Maria who had no memory of him and only a spotty recall of chance meetings with his friends? The deeper truth, however, he did not like to tell himself: for all his bravura, hope, and dreams, he had never really thought that he would succeed in bringing Maria back to Neverness. And so he hadn't worried that the day must come when Maria would discover who she really was and how she had come to be.

If Rane had found the best of himself, he would have told her all this before they had fled Old Earth. He should have gathered up all his courage and explained things to her on the night after the festival when she had pocketed the baldo nut. As the days went by, though, his omission became a silence that seemed impossible to escape. For if he tried to do so, Maria might hate him for not telling her sooner, and his worry that he would wound her only deepened his silence, making it ever harder and more consequential to break the longer it went on. He could not bear the thought of Maria's suffering an intense depersonalization, a loss of all sense of herself as if looking into a mirror and seeing nothing but reflections of reflections of memories – or worse, nothing at all. Most of all he feared that Maria would know him as he really was: a lonely man who, out of vanity and a terrible need, had called her back into existence in order to fill a bottomless hole in his life.

For half of deep winter, he lived in dread that some terrible thing would soon befall. A few days before the Festival of Lights, she informed him that she had agreed to read some of her new poems in the Hofgarten that evening. He tried to discourage her. He found reasons why she shouldn't go out that seemed either spurious or outright silly. She, though, would not be deterred.

'Diego Arizul stopped by earlier while you were at the Academy,' she informed him. 'He said that after you found your nuts, he became more curious about me and my poetry. He said that he would put up a small prize if I would do a recitation for him and a few of his friends.'

'I have already won a very large prize in finding you again, and neither of us will ever want for money – that is, if we ever happen to need it.'

'I am not doing this for the money.'

'It is too soon for you to be doing it at all. Why don't you complete your cycle of poems and wait until spring?'

'I told Diego that I would recite this evening, and so I will.'

Could he stop the wind of a rising *sarsara* from blowing by blowing back with a breath of protest from his trembling lips? Could he turn back the tides of the sea?

'Maria, I don't think that—'

'I've already asked Kolenya to come.'

'Oh, no! She's probably already asked fifty—'

'But you can't just keep me here to yourself like an old dragon hoarding its treasure! It will be good for both of us to get out among old friends and new.'

Why, he wondered, hadn't the very voluble Kolenya already let slip to Maria her true origins? Why hadn't Sunjay or Tamara or even one of the *Asta Siluuna* such as Decan Tomasan? Because, he thought, they were waiting for Rane to do so. It was as if Maria wore a beautiful new self over the old, and no one wished to shatter the illusion of her identity by being the one to tell her the naked truth.

That evening, they skated down the Pilot's Sliddery along North Beach through a bitter wind blowing off the frozen sea. Rane had hoped the sub-zero temperature might discourage people from turning out, but Neverness is Neverness, and many who had come to love the City of Light had by necessity become inured to the cold. Many people crowded the Hofgarten, built at the edge of North Beach overlooking the Sound.

Inside the great clary dome that covered it, most of those enjoying this great gathering place took their meals or drinks in the restaurants, cafés, and bars pushed right up to the outer edge of the dome so that they could look out of the frosted curving windows or up at the stars. Or, they could look through the inner – and much warmer – windows at the great show of people skating about the ice ring at the Hofgarten's centre.

In its very centre, at the middle of the ring, stood an old, battered stage. Anyone wishing to do so could mount this stage to perform for the skaters and onlookers. And just about anyone did: nimspinners and phantasists, autists and Avalon thaumaturgists, flautists and gosharpists and entire orchestras. And poets. The people of Neverness loved their poetry and poets, and so hundreds had arrived to hear Maria recite for them. So many, in fact, crowded the ice that no one could skate and only the tallest looking on could easily see Maria up on the stage calling out her verse. All, though, could hear her well, for her musical voice, amplified by the sulki grids around the stage and buried in the ice, filled the spaces around each arhat, astrier, diplomat, Orderman, and everyone else as if each could hear Maria speaking right up close to them. Thus did the coldness of poetry

recited in too-large a place become an intimacy of warm words
that echoed inside the chest and went straight to the heart.

> Earth, beloved,
> Earth, immortal,
> Blue oceans beating,
> Waving, onstreaming . . .

Maria had no need to read from her ink-inscribed sheets of
paper bound into a journal or book. Rane had taught the art
of remembrance well, and she recited by heart as if looking upon
ideoplasts instantiated like fiery pearls strung out in the air. She
shared only a few poems. Even lovers of poetry loved a little
less when forced to stand shoulder to shoulder in the middle of
a mob packed onto hard ice for too long. When she finished her
last poem, many people shouted their appreciation, and their
enthusiasm cheered Rane and pleased Maria.

Not everyone, however, shared in this spontaneous celebration. Just as Maria moved to come down from the stage and
greet people, someone cried out: 'She is not who she pretends
to be! She is a plagiarist!'

This accusation froze Maria to the stage, as it did everyone
else to the ice. The air beneath the dome seemed poisoned by a
deathlike quiet.

'She has plagiarized not only another's words but another's
soul! Or, I should say, she has *slelled* another's soul.'

Some of those who had come to hear the poetry that evening
had also been present at the mass burial at the Hollow Fields
years before when Rane had announced to the world that Maria
could not be in her coffin and could not be dead. They believed
a story going around the city: that Rane had indeed found Old
Earth, to where Maria had returned after her mother, the mighty
Kalinda of the Flowers, had called her back home.

Most others, however, knew very well that another Maria
had graced their city before. They knew (or at least suspected)
how Maria had been made. And most didn't care. They regarded
Rane's triumph on Old Earth as a kind of miracle in which they
might take part if only they could accept Maria as real and true.

'She is a slel necker and a whore, and I won't abide her
kind!'

Of course, this filthy slur was a logical absurdity and a lie, for Maria could have taken no part in stealing another's germ plasm to effect her own creation. Rane, standing above most everyone crowding the ice, looked through the sea of furs to see who might have slandered Maria. And then he spotted him, an ugly, ugly man he remembered too well: for it was Artulio, the leader of the Rakehells who had once accosted Rane and Maria near the Slizzaring. He wore the same rich fur cape and the same white ermine hat as he had years before. He had the same sallow face pocked with scars resulting from his addiction to jook. He fairly reeked with the same self-pity and resentment – and a malice that cut the air like a knife.

'I know you, Artulio!' Rane shouted out. 'Don't you move!'

Rane himself moved as quickly as he could, forcing himself between the startled onlookers, not caring if he hurt people in pushing them out of his way. He fell into a rage to close with Artulio. He wanted to grab him, shake him like a cat does a sleekit, rip off his lying face, and squeeze the life out of him.

'Don't you move!'

However, when he reached that place on the ice near the stage where Artulio had stood, he found that he had slipped away. He looked off into the Hofgarten, east, south, west, and north, but no Artulio or anyone like him did he see.

After a while, after Maria had spoken with those who swarmed her in hope of exchanging a few words of conversation or a few lines of poetry of their own, she came up to Rane. And in a trembling voice, she asked, 'Do you know what that vile man meant by calling me a slel necker?'

Rane could not answer her, certainly not then and there. All he could think to say was: 'Come on – I will take you home.'

34

When they reached the chalet, he led her into the fireroom, where they had spent so many happy times together. Rane arrayed some fresh logs and kindling on the grate of the fireplace; he struck some sparks into the fuel and summoned from the dry wood a dance of hot orange flames. Their light played over the tondos hanging on the stone walls and the room's great wooden beams and brightened Maria's expectant face. She sat on the furs facing him and waiting for him to tell her things that he did not want to tell.

It took him a long time to do so. He spoke of another Maria, like her in every way that really mattered, from the colours of the flames that lit up her being to the scent of her soul. He began with the moment he had first seen her, many years before in the Hofgarten when she, in her first incarnation, had recited a different set of poems. He told of the first time they had stood together beneath the stars of the Light Pavilion, and of the much deeper radiance they had called out of each other afterwards when they made love. They had been happy together, he said, until the first Maria had lost her way in the storm and died. Much of Rane had died along with her, he explained, and so he had made the nearly impossible journey to Old Earth to ask a goddess that Maria might be born again.

When he had finished his story, she sat in silence looking at him. Flames danced in her black eyes, and the scent of her anger emanated from her and mingled with the faint pungency of smoke wafting off the fire's blazing logs.

'Then in a way that horrible man was right,' she said. 'I *was* slelled.'

'No, your mother called you into being from her own germ plasm and that of Mallory Ringess, with the consent of both, and in that you are no different from anyone else.'

'But you and my mother slelled me from your memories of the other Maria, who did *not* give her consent.'

'Maria, I—'

She started weeping then, and he feared that they had come to the moment of the terrible, when all that he had done would break forth like a disease to destroy them. He moved closer to hold her, and she let herself be held. She sobbed and shook, and everything seemed to pour out of her at once, for she had no way to keep herself from Rane. Tears flowed from her eyes, and rags of breath tore free from her lips, and her heart loosed wave upon wave of dark emotions: rage, sorrow, hurt, sadness. Soon, though, her weeping quieted. Through the sheen of water that washed her cheeks and a movement of her belly, he sensed in her a great relief. Her lips turned upward in a smile as she wept and laughed all at once; she could not contain her amusement and excitement, all her desire and delight. She looked at him with something like awe.

'Maria, I—'

'I know that vile Artulio meant for me to see myself as a vile thing,' she said. 'But I am still I, aren't I? Whatever I am, I *am* still alive right here right now, with you.'

He caught up her hand as her eyes found his.

'My memories, many of them, were hers. But who was she, that Maria? She must have been someone marvellous or you never would have risked death so many times to make your memories of her into the marvel of me.'

She kept looking at him, looking and looking, and his own eyes burned with a wet pressure that no amount of blinking could drive away.

'You loved me so much that you were willing to do *anything* to love me again.' She smiled, kissed him, smiled again, and awe became adoration. 'And that is the way I will always need to love you.'

When they drew together naked, the fire's heat caressed their glowing skin as did the deeper burn of each other's fingers. In this one coupling seemed to live again all the many times he and Maria (both of them) had done their dance of ecstasy. Moving to rhythms as old as time, they annihilated time in a heated rush to make each moment of urgent breath and rising blood last forever. Never had their mating been so fiery yet so tender. Never had he felt so close to her. She bared all to him, not just in the opening of her legs or her arms that clasped him with a sweet ferocity, but in the calling of her eyes that drew him deep inside, there to join with her cell to cell as if all the substance of their bodies flowed together as one bright, indestructible thing. He wanted to hold onto the joy they found in each other until the last star in the last galaxy burned out and the universe was made anew.

Long after midnight, they lay side by side catching their breaths and gazing into each other's eyes. And Maria murmured to him, 'Other people talk about "making" love as if they were folding eggs and vegetables into an omelette, and that always sounds either trite or pretentious. Or like a euphemism for raw, animal passion. Sometimes, though, I cannot think of another way to describe how it is with you. Making love is exactly what we do, isn't it?'

Rane would have been content with silence just then, broken only by the crackle of the fire and the howling of the wind outside.

'I want to make new memories with you,' she said. 'There's nothing to stop us now from getting married.'

He froze as if the weight of the moment had caused him to break through thin ice and plunge into the sea. His breath caught in his throat.

'We've both survived hard things. Enough to know how fragile everything is and that we won't live forever. We should leave something behind: the best of us.'

Although he looked *at* her eyes, he could no longer see her or see her seeing him.

'I want to make a baby with you,' she said. She sat up and tapped her hand against his chest with sudden excitement. She laid her other hand over her belly. 'We may have already. Three days ago, after you got back from the Academy. Or maybe tonight. I *feel* pregnant.'

Now he sat up, too, jolted into a straightness of the spine

and a tension of muscle and emotion by the force of her electric words. 'But your mother said that she would not allow you to become pregnant until it was time.'

She waved her hand at this. 'Oh, no, that was only on Earth. She has no power over me here.'

He recalled in a blaze of images the hurt Maria had suffered when they had argued over this very matter just before they left Earth. He willed himself to say nothing. He tried to take refuge in silence.

'Rane, where are you?' She grasped his hand and pressed it against her yoni – and then over her belly, heart, and against her forehead. 'You were right here with me, and now you're not.'

He stared off through the blackness of her eyes into black holes and vacant interstellar spaces. How could he tell her that if she had thought she might become pregnant she should have taken precautions? How to explain that even now much could be done to make sure that she would give birth to nothing?

'Why won't you look at me?'

At last, he did. He let his eyes focus on hers as he said with all the softness he could find, 'You wouldn't want any more of my kind to live.'

She fell quiet, which made the howling of the wind outside the house seem all that much louder. Then she asked him, 'What do you mean? What are your kind?'

The kind who suffer, he thought, looking at her. Those with marvel in their eyes and murder in their hearts who make others suffer even more. The malcontents, trapped in the past, trapped within themselves. The freaks of nature, who are strangers even to themselves. The dreamers. The kind who can't bear living on the earth yet can't believe in a world they fear might some day be.

'You wouldn't want me to be the father of your child,' he told her.

'But there is nothing I want more!'

In the way that she opened her gaze to his, much as she had during their moments of shared passion, she looked past the death that always haunted his eyes, looked down deep into the hell that he felt ashamed for anyone to see, but needed *someone* to behold without fleeing in loathing or terror.

And in the middle of that smouldering, burned-out black waste-land inside him, she found a green, growing shoot of life, and she brought it back to him and placed it gently in his hands to remind him of who he really was. No greater gift had anyone ever given him. Why did he always have to spurn it?

'What's wrong?' she asked him.

He felt with a hated sense her heart beating too fast and her throat catching with words she tried to force out but could not. And the sobbing, sobbing, sobbing that sounded out through a night now long dead and soon forever again to be . . . The tears frozen in time like diamond drops to the tawny skin beneath her eyes.

'You were thinking of her, weren't you?' she asked him.

'No, when I'm with you, I never think of her.'

'I think of her all the time, now. She is like a ghost that haunts this house.'

'No, she is only—'

'How did she die?'

'I told you, she lost her way in a storm. By the time I got to her—'

'Yes, I know. But *why* did she go out into such a deadly storm?'

'I can't . . . really say. She was wilful, like you, and some-times she—'

'Let's go find her, together.'

'What do you mean?'

'Your memory of her, all your love, formed the basis of your love for me. I would know who this woman is.'

'So that you can make her go away?'

'No, so that she can live inside me. How else can we create a new life together?'

A new life, he thought. Was there anything he wanted more? Was there anything he feared more?

'I want us to drink kalla,' she said, 'and go down together into the One Memory.'

'You mean, to *share* memory? That is dangerous.'

'Didn't you share memory with Sunjay?'

'No. Yes – perhaps I did, for a few moments. And he nearly died.'

'Because he drank six drops of kalla.'

'Yes. No – I think now, looking back, it might not have been just the kalla.'

'What are you so afraid of?'

He looked through the window at the crystals of snow the wind drove against the dark panes. He told her, 'I've just renewed my vows, and it is forbidden for a remembrancer to share memory with anyone.'

'And what of the vow you made to me in calling me back to life?'

'Maria, I would do almost—'

'How many things have you done already that are "forbidden"?'

'All right, but this thing you ask of me—'

'In the end, there is only one thing that is forbidden.'

'What, then?'

'You know,' she said softly, looking at him. 'You have always known.'

In her refusal to look away from his angry stare, in her insistence on seeing in him what he refused to see, he remembered in a sickness of belly and blood that the thing he loved most about her he also most hated. He couldn't bite back the words he hated to say, the three terrible words that he drove like shards of ice through her heart and her damned, adoring eyes: 'Leave me alone.'

And so she did. She broke into tears as she shook her head and pounded her fist against the floor in a frustrated fury. Then she rose up and ran naked from the room into the deeper parts of the house.

He moved in the opposite direction, through the kitchen and into the skate room. There he put on his racing kamelaika, his furs, his face mask, and his skates. When he opened the door, a blast of wind drove tiny bullets of ice through the holes in the mask straight into his eyes, nearly blinding him. He didn't care. He slammed shut the door behind him and went out into the night.

He found his way onto the gliddery outside his chalet and then onto the North Sliddery that parallels the shoreline of the Pilots' Quarter. He skated east toward Mount Atakel without plan or purpose. No one else skated with him on this black, bitter night. The storm, which seemed to have come out of nowhere, blighted out the stars, and the light of the street lamps had to fight through a cloud of swirling snow. He could not make out the orange sheen of the sliddery, for a carpet of white wavered beneath him and made it difficult to feel the ice. It didn't take very long for that unseen ice to suck away his body's heat through slashing steel and hard leather. His feet grew so cold that he could not feel his toes. A terrible numbness spread through him. He could not feel the pain that he had caused Maria, and he never wanted to again.

He knew very well that he should never have left the house, that many people had turned an ankle trying to skate through snow that obscured the bends and boundaries of Neverness's streets. How easy it would be to trip and break a leg and have to lie down bleeding in the snow to wait for help that never came! How Maria must have hurt when the *sarsara* closed in on her in billions of tiny slashing knives of ice and caught her lost and alone! How *had* she died, really? Why had she gone out into that damned storm?

When he grew too cold and the snow grew too deep for easy skating, he found his way to one of North Beach's two warming pavilions overlooking the Sound. He hurried inside and sat down on a wooden bench. The open-aired structure, however, was not all that warm, for its jets of hot air could barely fight away the wind-whipped snow that blew inside. He sat lost in memory as he gazed through a boil of white-flecked blackness toward the ice of the frozen Sound that he could not see.

Leave me alone.

Alone he now dwelled in a city of many people in a galaxy of many millions of millions more. How far from here had Maria died? Why had he told his new Maria what he had? Did he really dread himself so much that he did not want any of his children to live? What did he dread most of all? Wasn't it his very dread of death, a million times worse than death itself? All his life, ever since he had been a little boy cowering beneath his father's cold wrath, he had fled from death. Sometimes, as when he had goaded a goddess, he had sought it just to prove that it had no hold over him. Why else had he become a remembrancer? Hadn't the ancient remembrancers also wished to drive back death through the indestructible memories of those they loved? And thus through ages dark and bright to preserve the soul of humanity?

Leave me alone.

Ah, but what was that golden, immortal soul? Old humanity should not be afraid to live more deeply in dying into the new, as the *Asta Siluuna* and Maria herself were unafraid. As Rane very much *was*. To live, I die, Mallory Ringess had said. And the warrior-poets had asked: how does one truly live? And their answer: prepare for death.

Had Rane ever made peace with the inevitability of his passing or that of anyone dear to him? Why had he *really* tried to recreate Maria? *Had* it been out of love? Or was it that he sought to reassure himself that someone or something might one day recreate him and he would never die? In holding on to himself and the past in this way, however, and in shutting Maria and the future out, hadn't he just found a more terrible and final way to die? And that was the hell of it, for he was who he was with no escape, just as Maria couldn't help but be Maria. In the end, she was of life as he was of death, and in the end the great wheel of the spirals of stars would turn on and on through an eternal night without a care that he had ever been born.

Maria.

A single snowflake found its way through the pavilion's curtains of warm, blowing air and broke against the cornea of his eye. Its frozen water melted into the warmth and salt of his tears. Ten quintillion molecules of dihydrogen monoxide made up this snowflake, and by chance alone, surely one of those molecules Maria had carried with her from Old Earth in the moisture of her body. She had breathed out this tiny bit of water into the air, where it had combined with myriad other molecules to become a six-pointed bit of ice. And so she had breathed into him some infinitesimal essence of herself.

The memory of all things is in all things.

Yes, and the fracturing of snow against flesh awakened him to the terrible memories, too. They gathered force in a *sarsara* of remembrance that he could no longer hold back. The past embraced him and pulled him toward the centre of a swirling whiteness: the whiteness of the snow and the sun's blinding brilliance off Maria's naked breasts and her throat and her dead, silent face. He felt once more the press of his skin against hers, his fingers hoping for the comfort of her soft body and finding instead an unyieldingness as cold and hard as stone. And her beautiful bitten lip and the drop of blood and a quintillion quintillion other memories that exploded inside him like the incandescent hell of a dying star: all the memories of Maria he had ever had and all but a few more that would ever be.

Maria, I am sorry.

He drove his hard, hurting body up from the bench and tried to rub some life back into his stiff limbs. Then he forced himself to go out on the street again, and he hurried home to tell Maria that his search for her had been a cosmic mistake.

After he had taken off his furs in the chalet's skate room and moved into the kitchen, he noticed her journal lying open upon the table. Her blue pen rested in the little valley between its open pages. Beside the journal rested her blue mug, full of peppermint tea, still warm. The tea's pungency drove straight up his nose, alarming him. She did not particularly like the smell of peppermint, which he had taught her to use to enter the attitude of olfaction. A quick glance at the journal's last entry alarmed him even more. He couldn't help taking in the poem she had inscribed there. It was of the kind that warrior-poets sometimes compose when their moment of the possible is near. It was entitled 'Rane'.

The oak tree fruits and dies;
The acorn sprouts in you,
Beloved, mighty tree of life.

'Maria!' he shouted. 'Maria!'

He found her back in the fireroom, naked, lying still on the furs. She had built up the fire with fresh logs so that it roared with flames. She had trimmed the bases of new candles to fit into their bronze stands: wax dulled the shasteel of her knife, which she had set down on the furs beside her. In her hand, she clutched a little blue bottle. He prised it free from her warm fingers. He should have locked his new wooden remembrancer's box against the wild chance that she might seek out his store of kalla, but when had he ever been able to see what Maria might do? He unstoppered the bottle, shook it, sniffed, looked inside, and realized that it was empty. How much kalla had the bottle held when he had last closed it after he had guided Sunjay in a remembrance? How much of the clear, cool, lethal kalla had she drunk? Surely at least six drops – and perhaps a good deal more.

The oak tree fruits and dies . . .

A holist, as well as a remembrancer, might enter the attitude of gestalt in order to perceive the whole of a pattern from a single part. Many pieces of the puzzle of Maria lay before him, and he knew all at once what had happened: Maria, the daughter of a warrior-poet, had little fear of death, or, rather, she would not let fright or misgivings keep her from what she thought she had to do. And she, like her mother, considered Rane crucial to the development of the remembrancer's art and the evolution of the *Asta Siluuna*. She had drunk too much kalla in the hope that Rane would find her just as he had and go down into remembrance with her as he had with Sunjay.

But that is not all, he thought.

She had escaped her mother on Old Earth, and she had escaped from Santuu Sarkissian on Kailash Poru, and now she would escape the killing grip of the kalla. She would return from the land of the dead with the true power of remembrance in her hands.

But that is not all.

Failing that – and she must have known that she would likely fail – she had hoped that Rane would find her even as he had and guide her through the most perilous of places. Hadn't he done as much with Sunjay? How could he fail to find her within remembrance's bright universe and bring her back to life?

But that is not all.

For a single, long moment in which he should have acted instead of remembering, he looked down at her. How alike in every way she seemed to his first Maria! Almost alike. For in the end he had said to that one, too, 'Leave me alone', and she had fled his chalet in tears and had gone out into the *sarsara* to die. *This* Maria, though, had dared an even wilder storm: the storm of pure consciousness. And she had done so not out of despair but a great hope. He watched her draw in a faint, shallow breath, and in a great gestalt of agony and shame, he knew her deepest reason for poisoning herself: she had taken a desperate risk for *his* sake. She was willing to die in order to wake him up to the secret part of himself that she cherished most and thus to heal him of himself.

'Maria!'

As he had with Sunjay, he fell into a fury of motion. He locked his hands together and pressed down in violent rhythms against her chest. He opened her mouth, and breathed hot, hurting breaths through her soft, unmoving lips. He breathed and he breathed, dozens of times, and more – and he would gladly have breathed his last breath into her and then have given up breathing altogether if only she might return to him.

'Goddamn you, Maria!'

He swept up the bottle of kalla, put it to his lips, and threw back his head. No trickle of pungent liquid cooled his tongue. Empty the bottle was, as empty and dry as a desert – how had he forgotten this? How could he go down into the darkest deeps of remembrance to bring her back without kalla to open the way?

Maria.

Her breathing stopped. He pressed his fingers against her throat, but he felt not the faintest pulse. He had waited much too long to return home.

Maria, where are you?

He picked up her knife, the incredibly sharp length of shasteel and bone made in imitation of a warrior-poet's killing knife. Where had Maria acquired such a dreadful weapon? Did it matter now? It would soon be laid with her and her other possessions inside a new coffin. But he would not be there to attest that she lay inside the coffin, too.

Goddamn me!

He set the knife's edge against his throat. Nikolandru's throat had been slashed by a nearly identical knife, and Rane thought that he would hardly feel his skin and arteries coming open. Although Nikolandru was gone, Rane might still give other poets a double death to sing about. It would be a sordid but fitting end to his hopeless quest. His hand trembled to draw the blade in a quick, furious motion from left to right. He felt a slight sting as he might while shaving. He looked down to see a drop of blood fall through the air like the first of a red rain and stain the white shagshay fur on which Maria rested.

No, no . . .

How could he escape the pressure of that hateful blade? Had he ever been able to free himself from the grip of his own hands around his throat, even for a moment? How had he, really, escaped the infinite tree? How was he to take a single step away from this moment and this place, which had been drawing him on all his life with the full force of the strangest and most terrible attractor of all? The next step, as Sunjay had said to him, when kalla wouldn't be needed any more.

If I kill myself, he thought, touching Maria's face, *I kill you.*

He flung the knife away from him. It bounced in a hard, gouging clatter across the wooden floor. He touched Maria, again. He felt the fire's heat play across her breasts and belly, as if its flames sought to gather her in. He felt another kind of fire within himself, a reaching out with flame and yearning toward a great, good thing that had always eluded him. Living was not enough if it amounted to mere pointless survival. Hadn't he secretly wanted to live as Maria had, wild and free, as she still wanted him to do, or would have if she hadn't stopped breathing? How long had it been since he had seen her chest rise up a fraction of an inch into the air? Only a few moments, he thought, for within such a short span of time can dwell an entire eternity. Very well, then he still had time if only he could let go of his murderous hold on himself and embrace Maria instead. Time enough to touch the place inside her that she had always held open to him, the one, secret place into which he had most feared to go.

Yes.

He bowed down his head, touching his mouth and nose to her neck, and he drew in the scent of the scarf tied there. He would use the olfaction attitude to enter recurrence and, if he could, to go down into the deepest parts of memory. When he inhaled a second time, the scarf came alive, and its iridescent fabric began vibrating with sound, and Maria's voice filled the words of an old poem that she had written for him:

Star of my soul . . .

The music of her verse simultaneously swept him into harmonics, and then into the sixty-fourth attitude. He felt his heart resonating like a great red bell with her heart, trying to bring it back into rhythm with the heart of the universe itself. The One Memory opened before him. Everything was there: every word and sound everything had ever uttered, every thought, every sensation, every dream anyone had ever dreamed. The universe remembered the reflection of the moon in the eye of a snowy owl a million years ago, and he remembered much more. The deaths of the dinosaurs beneath a flaming asteroid on Old Earth were recorded there in a symphony of millions of barks, bellows, and screams, and there, too, lived the birth of a billion galaxies in an agony of fire and light. Why was there so much pain? Why did everything have to hurt so much? Why did so many lose so much of their hope?

And yet, there was splendour, too. And within that bright infinity, he found the Maria memories. They were everywhere. Some were buried in the white snow of time like nuts. Some rose up through the presence of the past like great trees crowned in green leaves and glory. Others sparkled like jewels flung out like spinning galaxies into the night. One of those uncountable galaxies drew him inward along its glittering spiral arms to an old yellow-white star and an old Earth. There Maria dwelled, even as she now dwelled near death, her eyes unseeing and her heart unmoving but her brain still crackling with the electrochemical storms of deep remembrance. She dwelled within her mother's womb, listening as Kalinda taught her the fundamentals of poetry in the iambic rhythms of her beating heart. She remembered many things about him, too. On another world, she looked on as Rane's father, in all his coldness and demand, stood fast within a terrible pride that hid a fierce love for his wondrous son.

It hurts.

He remembered the night when he made love to Maria shortly after she had come to Neverness, and she remembered it, too – remembered how they had conceived a child together in this very room of fire and light. The tiny manchild who had died when Maria had frozen to death in the blood-tinged snow but yet still lived. The remembrance of that terrible moment glittered like a diamond whose hard edges forever slashed open the tissues of eternity.

It hurts, it hurts, it hurts . . .

Happier memories, though, they had both created in abundance, and in these moments of cheer and quiet contentment he wished to remain. There was that meal together in the Hofgarten, when the food, lighting, music, and the easy exchange of intimacies all combined into a perfection of grace. And the moment skating arm in arm in the Great Circle when they couldn't stop laughing just because it felt so good to laugh. And, of course, the meeting of their eyes in the Light Pavilion when for a breath of time he hadn't been able to hold back the truth of himself from her, or she from him, and they had trusted each other completely.

This is not the way. You cannot stay here.

Maria in her many forms took shape within the onstreaming ocean of remembrance: the lover, the friend, the poet, the adventurer, the mother, the murderer. Why couldn't he see the Maria who most wanted to be? The Maria who had given everything to him and called him to do what he had been born to do?

Remember who I really am.

She was a star, and so was he, and he remembered their birth a billion years before when a disc of hydrogen and dust whirling about through space split into two brilliant parts that spun out splendour into the universe. All that joy, the light of creation itself, could be his if only he opened his heart to hold on to it. Strangely, not his hands – not just – but his heart.

Yes, Maria, I will.

And with that affirmation and that will, the One Memory opened inside him, and for a moment, the whole of the cosmos became his. He remembered how to create kalla within his blood from the neurotransmitter precursors, down to the peptides and the amines, the individual atoms of hydrogen, oxygen, carbon, and all the rest. He remembered how to uncreate them, as he had with Sunjay. Matter is memory, and memory is matter, and memory through consciousness moves matter. The power was his, whenever he wished to call upon it.

This is the way, Maria. Like this: can you feel how to break the covalent carbon bonds and synthesize the metabolic enzymes? The cells remember. As we contain memories of the future that must be.

So much kalla she had drunk! How much had she drunk?
You taught me about life. Live, Maria, now – please live.
And so she did. She drew in a soft, shallow breath that moved
her chest. Her heart beat to the touch of his fingers against her
wrist. She opened her eyes, and looked at him.

'Why did you have to drink so much kalla?' he asked her.

'I remember,' she murmured. 'There is so much to remember.'

'But what do you remember?'

'Everything.'

She remembered, she told him, the night they had conceived
a child in a wild rush of hope and love. She told of their perfect
meal in the Hofgarten and of the time they had taken an ice
schooner far out on the frozen sea. Then, because she had a
hard time getting out the words, she smiled weakly and spoke
to him in silence.

'But all those things,' he said, 'I did with her.'

'I know. I am that Maria now, too.'

How could that be possible? Had Maria's sharing of DNA
and form with the elder Maria somehow acted as a strange
attractor that had called them both into a life of shared memory
and identity?

'I remember,' she said, 'sobbing because I couldn't see a way
for us, sobbing and biting my lip until it bled.'

'I remember that, too. But now we can—'

'I drank so much kalla,' she whispered. 'Too much.'

He held her hand and pressed his fingers to her wrist. Her
pulse had slowed and weakened as they had talked.

'You came too late, the first time,' she said. 'It was so cold,
it hurt so much.'

In the coolness of her skin over her wrist veins and arteries,
he remembered what he had forgotten for more than a hundred
years: how his mother had been unable to bear his father's rages
and so had taken too much of her pain medicine in order to
escape. He had been only a boy then, too young to save her.

'But it is not too late this time!' he said.

'Oh, Rane!' She pulled his fingers to her lips and kissed them.
'It's all right.'

In the light of the fire, in the radiance of a much deeper
flame, she looked at him as she had so many years before in the
Light Pavilion. He had not then or ever been able to look without

cover into the perfect mirror she held up to him. Now, though, at last he did look, and he began to see. Her eyes were black pools of light that showed him what he had always feared to behold. And he remembered the one ineffable thing about her that he had realized and forgotten a hundred times but never quite grasped, the way she had always revealed to him the deepest and truest of all his selves, a glorious Rane capable of immense love. She showed him this now, in a reflection of her own devotion to him, which he could not help giving back, in hope, in life's eternal fire, in all the infinities of echo and light. And with each reflection of self to self they enlarged each other until they became each other and created as one the whole of the universe.

'Kiss me,' she said.

He pressed his lips to hers, and a bit of her breath, still warm, fell over him and into him and recalled the fiery exhalations of their star.

'Come find me,' she whispered.

Then she closed her eyes and said no more.

When he had made sure that her heart beat no longer and that he could not go back into the One Memory to revive her again, he bit his lip until it bled and he tasted her inside him. In the end, no one could forever defeat death.

Come find me.

And nothing could ever vanquish life. He breathed in her marvellous scent, in and in, and he felt his heart beating stronger and more vital than it ever had, with a new purpose now his own. At last she truly lived inside him because at last he truly lived.

'Maria,' he said.

He rested his face upon her still belly. There came a sobbing, sobbing, sobbing – only this time it came from him.

35

Maria's second funeral took place with many others on the bare ice of the Hollow Fields below the slopes of frozen Mount Urkel. It was a warm day for deep winter, only a few degrees below freezing. The many mourners, some wearing only kamelaikas in place of furs, stood near the coffins of those they had lost. The largest of these groups – hundreds of men, women, children, and others – gathered around Maria's coffin. Rane knew them all by name, for he had asked that any of Maria's acquaintances unknown to him should come up to introduce themselves. On this day of clear air opening up into a golden-blue infinity, he did not want to say goodbye to Maria in the company of strangers, and he wished to be estranged from no one ever again.

Those who had been closest to Maria and him drew in the nearest: Chandra and Sunjay, Tamara and little Alasharia. Many of the *Asta Siluuna* joined them, and Rane smiled to see Binah Jolatha Alora, Decan Tomasan, Phineas Wu. Bardo, with his black furs undone to dissipate some of the heat that his large body gave off, stood talking to Kolenya Mor. Ailieyha had come, too, and so had Kiyoshi Telek and Jonathan Hur and many of the old Kalla Fellowship. Lara Jesusa had resolved her dispute with Alesar Estarei, and they stood chatting amiably with Cristobel the Bold, Helena Charbo, and handful of master pilots. Other masters of the Order whom Rane had known for decades (or as long as a century) waited on the ice farther out like rippling waves of red, brown, blue, and yellow fabric and furs. They all waited to hear what Rane would say.

'Will you recite the poem?' This came from Kolenya, who had disengaged with Bardo so that she could come up and ask Rane this question.

'Do you think I should?'

'We all think you should.'

Rane smiled, for he did not know whether he should say anything at all. He looked across the ice at the centre of the Hollow Fields, where the great diamond sunship waited to shoot up through the atmosphere and carry the hundreds of coffins into the Star of Neverness. Perhaps he should let the ship speak for him in a thunder of red rocket fire and a blaze of light.

'Binah,' she said, 'wrote a poem for Maria, and she'd like to go first. Perhaps that might put you in the mood.

Rane looked over at Binah Jolatha Alora, whose golden hair caught up the colours of the sun and sky. He smiled at her, and it gave him great satisfaction that she smiled back, not just in the curve of her lips and the flash of her white teeth, but in all her own happiness which poured like light out of her sparkling blue eyes. She had new eyes, like perfect jewels faceted by sheer wonder at the beauty of the world and filled with her immense gratitude that Rane had helped her to remember how to regrow them.

'Perhaps it might,' Rane said to Kolenya.

Bardo stepped up to them, and he asked Kolenya if she would mind if he spoke to Rane alone. She didn't. She went off to tell anyone who would listen that Rane would be glad to recite his poem.

'Ah, my friend,' Bardo said, clasping Rane's arm. His voice boomed out into the air, and he did his best to lower it. 'I'm so sorry that this day had to come . . . again.'

He hadn't spoken with Rane since Maria's death. He looked at Rane as if seeing him for the first time in a century – or perhaps seeing him for the first time at all. Then he gazed at Binah. He knew, as many did now, that something extraordinary had occurred in Rane's fireroom with Maria, something that would ripple out like water from that time and place through the city of Neverness and across an ocean of stars.

'There is something I've been too busy to discuss with you, but now I must.' Bardo apologized that the organizing of a new mission to the Vild and perhaps to Old Earth had taken up so much of his time. Then he said, 'We have completed our search for your lightship. I hated to spend the resources, but I had to know. We have scanned every inch of the bottom of the Sound and the sea for a hundred miles beyond – and also the whole of Neverness Island. We have not found the *Asherah*.'

'Absence of evidence,' Rane said, quoting the old adage, 'is not evidence of absence. Perhaps you need to look harder.'

'You cannot find what is not there.'

'But the *Asherah* must exist . . . somewhere.'

'Yes, somewhere. And *somehow* you must have returned to our city.'

'It must have been, then, that I took passage in a deep-ship or other vessel.'

'Then you *still* don't remember?'

Rane shook his head. He looked over at Maria's coffin, its richly grained shatterwood polished to a high finish, which scattered the light of the low sun. Some day, perhaps, he would call into memory all things, but this was a day for the remembrance of only one thing.

'Ever since the war ended,' Bardo said, 'we have kept a strict accounting of all who leave or enter the city. There is a record of your leaving with Nikolandru but none of your return.'

'Well, then, perhaps a smuggler—'

'We have shot down all their ships. I don't mind a little jook or sassafax finding its way onto the streets of the Slizzaring, but weapons I won't permit.'

Rane looked at him. 'You have come a long way from the Bardo I knew who would permit himself and everyone else almost anything.'

'And you, my friend, have come a long way.' Again, he clasped Rane's arm, and this time his grip grew stronger. 'I think only one possibility as to how you did arrive on our cold world is logical or likely.'

'And that is?'

'We pilots open windows to the manifold with the spacetime engines of our lightships. Somehow, you did so with the engine of your mind.'

Had he done anything like that? Rane wondered. Could such a leap from one star to another even be possible? He drank in the rays of light that had fallen down all on their own from the

Star of Neverness to illuminate Maria's coffin. He opened himself to the One Memory, as it did to him. He remembered that the Ieldra, through idea and will, had fallen at the speed of thought across the universe. And the whales of Agathange, who spoke of quenging, might have done the same. *Yes, it was possible.* Light moved light, as matter did mind and mind moved matter, and some day he would remember once again how he had done such a miraculous thing.

'Sunjay thinks you might have,' Bardo said, 'though I don't understand very much of what the Children do or even talk about.'

But you did, Maria. We never spoke of this, but somehow you always knew.

The sun rose a little higher, and the morning warmed, and it came time for those who wished to speak of Maria to do so. Binah Jolatha Alora recited her sweet poem extolling Maria's sweetness and patience, but also her warrior's ruthlessness in teaching her to kill any single word that did not help a poem to sing. Kolenya shared a few stories about Maria and might have recounted more if Bardo hadn't cleared his throat to indicate that she should yield to someone else. Tamara Ten Ashtoreth finally told the world what she had confided only to Danlo wi Soli Ringess and to Rane: how she had recovered her lost life from the One Memory and how Maria must have done the same. Even Alasharia wanted to say something: in her piercing little girl's voice, she called out that her Aunt Maria loved her more than all the water of all the oceans of all worlds everywhere, and no one thought to object that she exaggerated.

Rane smiled down at her as he took her place standing over Maria's coffin. In his ungloved hand, he held the fire rose that Chandra had given him. He placed the pretty flower on the smooth wood. Inside, Maria rested where he had placed her, along with her blue pen, her coffee mug, flute, adjal, and her wax-covered knife. The coffin, polished to a mirror finish, showed him the same Rane that she had. He was a man who would demand great things of himself, who would teach others how to enter the One Memory at will: Sunjay and Chandra, Binah and Decan and little Alasharia, all the *Asta Siluuna*. They would pass this art to others, many others, and he would become the Remembrancer at last.

It was as a remembrancer, at first, that he spoke of his beloved art and what that had meant for Maria. He looked out at his friends, old and new, and he asked them to chant along with him from the liturgy of a religion now long dead. Dead, yes, but strangely alive in words that Rane had memorized a hundred and fifty years before and had never forgotten. For they contained all that was best about remembrance and a directive that remembrancers, in a time of universal war and transcendence, must keep alive the soul of humanity. And what was that imperishable essence? Only one thing: that the soul of the truly human was human love. Maria, he told the people around him, had known that and had lived that truth in every breath. Before she had died, she had reminded him that the one forbidden thing was not to love.

And so Rane made the ancient ceremony of remembrance, and hundreds of others joined him. Then it came time to speak of other things. He looked down at the coffin, and slapped it with his bare hand. He called out to everyone near him and even those farther out around other coffins on the Hollow Fields: 'Maria cannot be here! Not *just* here.'

He smiled, and held his hand to his chest for a moment before touching his lips. 'She is also here, in the words of this poem that she once made for me.'

It was a double poem, he told them, of the kind that the pilot-poets of Aoide developed and that an old friend named Nikolandru would have taught him to compose had he only lived. The first part of the poem had come entirely from the mind and hand (and heart) of Maria. But the second part, which reflected the first in many of its phrases and form, as well as theme, Rane had written with Maria's pen only the night before. From his pocket of his silver furs, he drew out a sheaf of folded pages. Although he knew every word by heart, he wanted to honour Maria by reading their poem in this way. And so in a clear voice strengthened by the encouragements of those who looked on, he called out:

'Star of my soul,
How you shimmer
Behind the midnight sky,
You and I spinning sparks
Of joy into the empty . . .'

Their poem, though no epic, was not a short one, and it took him more than a few moments to read it. Maria had tried, as always, to put all of herself into the poem, and so had he. It was a poem of starlight and flowers and hope and death. And its opposite: where Rane had looked to the past to see what the universe planned for human beings, Maria lived in the eternal now-moment that contains all things past and present and gives birth to the future. She had always known, as he had not, that the old patterns worn into the human soul must give way to something far greater and more complex, though at their heart much simpler. Very soon must arise a new humanity and a new way of living on earth. This birthing of the extraordinary Maria had longed for even more than she had a child, for it involved the fecundity of the entire galaxy. Now, he wanted the same thing. He would join Maria out in their star, and in love, always and only in love, they would bring forth a new race of millions like Maria, this vastly superior being who had asked everything of him and had given much more.

After he had finished, he unknotted the scarf from around his neck, and he tied it to the coffin's handle. The wind off the frozen ocean rippled the scarf's iridescent fabric, and the fabric moved the wind. And Maria's voice sounded out softly: 'Remember, my Rane: for me, you will never die.'

The coffin, along with all the hundreds of others, was carried to the sunship and laid inside. As at Maria's first funeral, the many groups of mourners broke apart, and everyone spread out across the ice of the Hollow Fields in a huge circle with the sunship at its centre. Rane stood between Sunjay and Kolenya, holding their hands. He gazed at the silvery sunship, and the sharpness of a rising wind stung his eyes. When its rockets ignited in a great blast of sound and fire, he had to look away for a moment. Some sights would always be too bright to bear.

'Goodbye, Aunt Maria.'

Alasharia, too young to really understand death, Rane thought, stood next to Sunjay as she held hands with him and Tamara. The ship grew smaller and smaller and vanished like a spark into the golden blue sky. And she came up to Rane and said, 'Aunt Maria is only starlight now, like I said. Burning up into light inside the sun.'

And wasn't that the whole point of this strange and involved funerary ritual? But did Alasharia really grasp the laws of motion and the physics of fusion and light? He bent to pick her up, and he remembered when Tamara had placed a little black-haired baby smelling of milk and love in his arms a lifetime before.

'The ship,' he said, 'will not enter the sun's corona for many days.'

'But the first Maria is there, isn't she?'

'Yes,' he told her, kissing her forehead, 'she is.'

He gave her to Tamara, who converged with Chandra and Kolenya to discuss the plans for the gathering at Tamara's house that would follow the funeral. And Sunjay looked at him and said, 'Our other aunt is calling my sister to her. All of my family.'

'What do you mean?'

'Our great-aunt, Kalinda. It is time. Earth is ready again for our kind.'

'But how can you know such a thing? Has the Entity sent an emissary to Neverness? Or some sort of communication?'

'Something like that, sir. If by communication you mean the way that everything in the universe is interconnected through memory and knows of everything else.'

'I don't understand. Are you saying that you have somehow learned of Kalinda's thoughts and intentions?'

'No, not I – Binah.'

Rane looked over at the golden, bright-eyed woman who had once been blind. She stood laughing with Chandra, laughing and looking and speaking with the lift of a brow or touch or a blink. Now that she could see again, she seemed to be growing adept at the Children's eyetalk.

'But I thought, because she was eyeless for so long, so cut off, that she would have to rely on touches, spoken words, and intonations – that sort of thing.' He watched Binah more closely. 'I thought that her speech was therefore compromised and that of all the Children, she was the least among you.'

'Oh, no, sir, it is just the opposite: she is the greatest.'

He went on to say that the whole of the galaxy was alive and had a type of mind transcending and yet including all the separate minds and memories of those such as Rane, Bardo, Chandra, and everyone else. Binah, because she had been blind, had needed to develop a deeper sense in order to speak the Children's eyetalk – or rather, the soultalk, as Sunjay called it.

'It is really a simple thing, sir,' Sunjay said, 'though I don't fully understand it yet myself. We read letters inscribed on paper to make out words. We kithe ideoplasts instantiated in our minds to understand our theorems and complexes of ideas. And we quenge through memories emblazoned in our souls to speak the language of the universe.'

Rane listened intently as Sunjay described this new art of communing, knowing, and being. The wind brought down from Mount Urkel the smell of the evergreen trees, and the air shook with the sound of the many voices around them, and Sunjay told of how the *Asta Siluuna* were learning how to speak into creation a new consciousness that would wake up the universe and make everything more alive. Theirs would be a language of light and sound, of the dreams of starfire and the poetry of hydrogen and oxygen carried on the breath, and it could never be articulated in the absence of love.

'You taught us, sir,' Sunjay said. 'You and Maria.'

'I? No, Maria, perhaps, but not I. I have loved . . . so imperfectly.'

'No, sir – it is just the opposite.'

Rane gazed up into a great openness. In the sky, no bit of brightness remained to mark the vanishing of the sunship. To Sunjay, he said, 'But what does love have to do with any of this?'

Even as his question hung in the air like a pendulum at the height of its swing, he knew the answer. For one could not love truly without coming into a complete identity with someone or something beyond the self. And only through identity could anyone realize the first and final secret of remembrance: that love and remembrance are really one and the same and that memory binds all things to all things.

'Binah has made it clear,' Sunjay said, looking up at the sky with Rane, 'that you are to come with us.'

'Has Binah . . . found Kalinda's wish that I should come within the One Memory? How could she have?' Rane looked to the east at the white slopes of Mount Urkel. 'To find one memory in an infinity? It would be easier to identify a single snowflake in all those that had ever fallen on this world since time began.'

'You have taught her well, sir.'

'That doesn't say anything.'

'How did you find your memories of Maria when you entered the sixty-fourth attitude in your fireroom?'

'Only with great difficulty. And only because our lives were bound together and there was a resonance, the way that two violins might find each other through the strings of one vibrating to the touch of those of the other.'

'Perhaps Binah has such a resonance with Kalinda. She calls her our other Mother.'

Rane shook his head at this. 'Yes, Mother Earth, herself. And she would kill me the moment I set foot on her planet.'

'No, she has forgiven you. She is calling *all* the *Asta Siluuna* home.'

'But I am not one of you.'

'You are the first of us, sir, after my father.'

Could that be true? He watched Chandra, who now held Alasharia, talking with Binah in the Language of the Civilized Worlds and in their secret speech of gestures, smiles, and knowing looks that he was finally beginning to grasp. To comprehend it fully, he thought, he needed only to return to his once-lost younger self and remember always to see the world as through the eyes of a child.

Innocence is the child, and forgetfulness, a new beginning, a game, a wheel rolling out of its own centre, a first movement, a holy Yea.

Could he, *would* he, ever forget and leave behind the Rane that had twice driven Maria to death?

Yes.

'Then do you wish,' he asked Sunjay, 'to return to the Garden of Eden that Kalinda has made?'

Sunjay laughed at this. 'It will hardly be that. Tigers live there. And so will we.'

Their new world, he said, would not be without strife. The *Asta Siluuna* would still contend among themselves for *chith*, which had evolved from a kind of mental money to a way of honour, interlinking obligations, ethical prowess, and a poetry of the soul. For themselves, for the earth, they would always seek more *awarei*, more love, more life.

'And there is a great battle still to fight,' he added. 'Only on

Earth will we be safe to fight it. I don't understand it yet, but Kalinda needs our help to defeat the Silicon God.'

The wind chilled Rane's face as he remembered the scent of another wind off a cool blue ocean far away. 'But how are you to return to Earth? Did Kalinda say?'

'Even as you returned to Neverness.'

'But, you see, I don't know how I did. I don't know if I will ever remember.'

'You will, sir. You must. It is the next step.'

'The next step,' Rane said softly.

Yes, yes, yes.

'And there is always another way,' Sunjay said. He stamped his boot down onto the ice. Below them, the Cavern of a Thousand Lightships opened through vast halls melted long ago out of solid rock. There, in row upon row of glittering sweeps of spun diamond, resided the soul of the Order. 'I have not forgotten how to pilot a lightship. And neither have you.'

Rane thought about this as he watched many of the mourners snapping back in the blades of their skates to join family and friends in private gatherings in hundreds of houses and apartments scattered across the city. The air cooled with a rising wind even as the sun shone as warm as it ever did in this darkest of seasons. Not far away, Alasharia sang out the words of Maria's and Rane's poem that she had determined to memorize:

'Star of my soul,
 How you shimmer . . .'

Sunjay listened to his little sister work her way through the poem's lines, and he said, 'Soon everyone in the city will know about your star.'

Rane thought he meant Val Adamah, the twin suns circling each other through the millennia in the radiant deeps of the galaxy out beyond the Laniuma Luz and the Morbio Superiore. He pointed up at the Star of Neverness, which burned just a little brighter for the fuel that his first Maria had provided and soon would burn brighter still. And he said, 'This is our star.'

'So is the Star of Earth. It is waiting for you.'

'But I can't leave Maria here.'

'Then bring her with you.'

Inside him, a brilliance that had not faded since Maria had drunk the kalla came alive with all that she had been and might ever be. Impossibly, with every breath he took and every thought of her, it grew brighter and brighter.

Come home with me.

'All right,' he said.

Then he, too, snapped in his skate blades and struck off across the ice to join a celebration of the woman who was his friend, his lover, his memory, his great teacher of life.

Chronology of *Homo Sapiens*

220,000 BCE   Early *Homo sapiens* emergent on Old Earth. The Golden Age, climaxed by the florescence of the Primeval Mentality at various places, at various times.

185,000 BCE   *Homo sapiens sapiens* migrates from Africa in waves and begins to encounter other species of human beings on the Eurasian continent. The first wars.

40,000 BCE   The last Neanderthals go extinct. *Homo sapiens* becomes the only species of human being to inhabit the Earth.

29,291 BCE   The Ieldra cark their memories into human DNA; they create 125 'immortals'. Gilgamesh (Kelkemesh) is one of these.

12,000 BCE   Small-scale agriculture begins sporadically at various places on the Eurasian and African continents – the First Mentality.

6,000 BCE   The first states. Property. Organized war. Written symbols invented for words and numbers. The Second Mentality begins.

1680 CE	Age of the Newton. Birth of the First Science. Reason exalted. The Third Mentality.
1844 CE	Birth of Nietzsche, honorary founder of the Warrior-Poets.
1905 CE	The Einstein publishes his General Theory of Relativity. Beginning of the Holocaust Centuries. The Fourth Mentality begins.
2098 CE	The Little War – limited nuclear war.
2197 CE	The first colony is established on the Moon. The Little Swarming begins.
2223 CE	The first space colonies.
2333 CE	The first colony is established on Mars.
2350 CE	Earth is nearly destroyed by nuclear war. The Second Dark Age.
2525 CE	The first intelligent computer made on Mars. The Age of Simulation begins. The Fifth Mentality.
2689 CE	The first reseeding of Earth fails.
2801 CE	The second Earth colony fails.
3002 CE	The third Earth colony fails.
3003 CE	Earth is forbidden to human beings.
3290 CE	The War of the Worlds. Moon colony destroyed.
3520 CE	The mission to Alpha Centauri fails and returns to Mars.
4222 CE	The cantor Roald Merripen discovers the manifold.

4331 CE	The first lightships made. The exploration of the galaxy begins.
4499 CE	The first seedship leaves Mars and founds New Earth. The true Swarming begins.
5800 CE	The First Wave of the Swarming reaches its crest. The planets Rollo's Rock, Kaarta, Wakanda, Vesper, Nwarth, Farfara and Fostora are settled.
5899 CE	On Fostora, the carking of human consciousness into the computer begins. The Remnants of the Old Japan colony on Mars settle the first of the Japanese Worlds. Mars is abandoned.
6000–9000 CE	The Lost Centuries.
9061 CE	Rowan Madeus establishes the Order of Holists and True Scientists on Arcite.
9077 CE	On Silvaplana, the Way of Remembrance becomes the Order of Remembrancers.
9085 CE	Order of Scryers founded on Ninsun.
9101 CE	Order of Yogin moves to Simoom.
9122 CE	Order of Neurologicians founded on Askling.
9231 CE	Order of Neurologicians schisms. Order of Cybershamans formed.
9459 CE	The Order of Cetics established on Simoom by Nils Ordando, absorbing many of the yogin, neurologicians, and cybershamans. Some scryers and remembrancers join them.
9777 CE	The Silicon God is made on Fostora.

| 9801 CE | The Order of Holists and True Scientists absorbs the Order of Cetics. Nils Ordando does not accept this. He and a hundred neurologicians flee to Qallar. |

9809 CE   Nils Ordando and Ivar Hanuman establish the Order of Warrior-Poets on Qallar. It is their mission to breed – as opposed to engineer – a new race of human beings.

9907 CE   The remembrancers and scryers become their own disciplines within the cetics.

10,200–
10,700 CE   The Third Dark Age.

l0,709 CE   The warrior-poets perfect the art of using computers to replace parts of the brain. They begin a campaign of terror and extreme proselytization in order to convert human beings to their way.

10,792 CE   The first war between the warrior-poets and the Order of Holists and True Scientists. The Order is nearly destroyed. Only the Order's superior command of lightships and the manifold allows them to fight to a stalemate. The war strengthens the pilots as a discipline within the Order.

10,808 CE   The Peace of Qallar. The warrior-poets agree to limits on technology.

11,326 CE   The escape and evolution of the April Colonial Intelligence. The April Cluster grows.

11,740 CE   Agathange is discovered.

12,001 CE   Chimene is given over to a bacteria swarm.

12,008 CE	The Fifth Mentality reaches its limits. The planets Yarkona, the Nave, Darkmoon, and Lechoix are settled. A splinter group of anarchists from Fostora found Alumit, which refuses to honor the Laws of the Civilized Worlds. Many worlds forbid human–computer interface. The Japanese Worlds grow further apart from the rest of humanity.
12,099 CE	The Assembly of Worlds. The Laws of the Civilized Worlds are agreed upon. Most worlds agree on strict limits to technology. Some of the Japanese Worlds leave the assembly in protest, the warrior-poets as well. The Order of Holists and True Scientists takes the lead in trying to make a new civilization.
12,111 CE	The Second Wave of the Swarming begins.
12,990–13,112 CE	The Human–Darghinni wars.
13,600–14,000 CE	The Fourth Dark Age.
14,526 CE	Pilots from Arcite discover the planet Fravashing.
14,710 CE	On Arcite, Omar Narayama lays the foundation for the Second Science based on a new understanding of language, rather than mathematics. The Sixth (or Last) Mentality begins.
14,712 CE	The pilot Rollo Gallivare discovers Icefall.
14,782 CE	The First Schism of the Order of Holists and True Scientists. Many scientists cannot accept the crystallization of holism and the challenge of the Second Science. Rowan Madeus, then known as Sarojin Noy, pushes for the formal acceptance

of holism, which has been gradually replacing science for 12,000 years. In a shocking and daring move, he proclaims that the Old Science is finally dead. Civil war on Arcite. Omar Narayama is killed while creating an instantiation quaternion of the Universal Syntax.

14,784 CE	Rowan Madeus and Rollo Gallivare lead a deep-ship and 100 lightships to Icefall.
14,790 CE	THE FOUNDING OF NEVERNESS (0 FN) and the establishment of the Order of Mystic Mathematicians and Other Seekers of the Ineffable Flame. (This name is a concession to the holists and true scientists who have followed Rowan Madeus. They have agreed that the Old Science may be dead, but mathematics is eternal.) The newly made Order pledges itself to play a greater role in the fate of the Civilized Worlds and the exploration of the galaxy. The Order's motto is: 'To begin; to travel; to learn; to illuminate.' This is the age of the pilots' ascendency and the mapping of the galaxy.
54 FN	Kalinda is born on Qallar. She is the only female to earn a warrior-poet's rings.
70 FN	The Third Wave of the Swarming begins.
81 FN	The birth of Nikolos Daru Ede on Alumit.
100 FN	Kalinda comes to Agathange where she begins her vastening.
101 FN	The death of Rollo Gallivare. Dov Danladi becomes the Order's second Lord Pilot.
213 FN	On Alumit, Ede carks his consciousness into a computer, thus violating the Second Law of the Civilized Worlds. This miracle is known as Ede's

Vastening. Kostos Olorun and other followers of Ede call themselves the Architects of Ede the God and found the Cybernetic Universal Church.

234 FN   The Architects consolidate their rule on Alumit.

544 FN   The Ianthian heresy of the Cybernetic Universal Church.

547 FN   Yerik Chu leads a schism and is destroyed along with his followers at the Battle of Bhodan Light Fields. The survivors flee to Wertlos to found the Architects of the Universal God.

550 FN   The Solid State Entity appears near the Eta Carina nebula.

676 FN   Ricardo Lavi becomes Lord Pilot. The Golden Age of the Order begins.

908 FN   Yoshi Watanabe, as Lord Pilot, consolidates the Order's control of the Stellar Fallaways. Each of the Civilized Worlds agrees to allow the Order to operate all deep-ships, longships, and prayer-ships.

978 FN   Assembler technology banned on Neverness.

1234 FN   In the Prakriti Cluster, Ede the God begins the creation of the first of his 'Earths'.

1749 FN   The Great Schism of the Cybernetic Church. The Order reaches the height of its power. The Third Wave of the Swarming crests. Jemmu Flowtow proposes the Great Theorem. The War of the Faces begins.

1946 FN   The surviving Architects of the Old Church flee to the unknown spaces beyond the Rosette Nebula.

| 2003 FN | John Penhallegon, the Tycho, becomes Lord Pilot. |

2023 FN   The Architects of the Reformed Churches reach Yarkona, their first contact with the Civilized Worlds.

2024 FN   The Great Plague erupts on Yarkona.

2024–
2054 FN   The Great Plague, a bioweapon made during the War of the Faces, ravages Yarkona. The Architect's religion – and the Great Plague – spread wildly throughout the Civilized Worlds. Whole populations begin converting en masse. It becomes popular to convert, wait for the symptoms of the plague to manifest, and then undergo the ceremony of vastening as a way of trying to transcend death.

2060 FN   When it is proven that the Architects are the source of the plague, the Order's Timekeeper places severe restrictions on Architect travel. It becomes clear that an accommodation between the Order and Edeism will be difficult: the Order's holism is at odds with the Architects' cybernetic gnosticism.

2061 FN   The Order's elite school on Fostora is burned. The Timekeeper is nearly assassinated on Neverness. The War of Assassins begins (also called the War of the Slel Neckers). The Cybernetic Church and Edeism are outlawed on Neverness.

2063 FN   The Dark Year. Order schools on 843 worlds are burned in religious riots. The Timekeeper makes an alliance with the warrior-poets. The slaughter of the Elders of the Cybernetic Church begins. The Church is nearly destroyed. The plague comes to Neverness.

2065 FN	The Church's Doctrine of Stringency is overthrown. The Doctrine of Free Interpretation is promulgated. The Church breaks up into many splinter groups, but still maintains its seat on Alumit.
2070 FN	The Peace of Hosthoh. The Architects are allowed to travel and preach – to worlds that have already been infected with the plague – but are restricted as to the kinds of memory removal they may perform in their cleansing ceremonies. Further restrictions are placed on the Architects' vastening and facing ceremonies. Architects are restricted from holding temporal power on many Civilized Worlds.
2074 FN	The Tycho plots to overthrow the Timekeeper. The Timekeeper calls the First Quest, the quest to reach the core of the galaxy. Many of the Tycho's best pilots are killed. The Tycho returns to Neverness half-mad, and the plot is broken. But the Order is further weakened.
2079 FN	The Tycho is lost in the Solid State Entity.
2100–2200 FN	The Little Dark Age. The Order is in decline.
2526 FN	The light of the first Vild supernovas reaches Jacaranda.
2539 FN	Dario the Bold discovers the Vild.
2670 FN	The Silicon God discovers Ede the God. Unknown to most human beings, the War in Heaven begins.
2679 FN	The Solid State Entity goes to war against the Silicon God.
2729 FN	Leopold Soli is born on Simoom.

| 2750 FN | The warrior-poets, who have perfected the art of slel-mime, are caught in a plot to mime several important lords of the Order. War between the Order and the warrior-poets is threatened, but the Timekeeper journeys to Qallar where he negotiates a secret peace with Keleman Redring. |

| 2771 FN | Leopold Soli becomes Lord Pilot. |

| 2840 FN | Ede the God creates the thirty-fourth and last of his 'Earths'. |

| 2904 FN | Leopold Soli begins his famous journey to the galactic core. The Ieldra speak to him and tell him that the secret of life is to be found 'in man's past and future'. |

| 2908 FN | Mallory Ringess is born in Neverness. |

| 2929 FN | Leopold Soli returns from the core. The Quest to find the Elder Eddas is called. |

| 2931 FN | Danlo wi Soli Ringess is born on Icefall on the island of Kweitkel. |

| 2934 FN | The Pilots' War. Mallory Ringess is made Lord Pilot, and then, Lord of the Order. |

| 2936 FN | The First Vild Mission departs. |

| 2941 FN | The First Vild Mission returns having failed. Mallory Ringess disappears. It is said that he became a god and joined the Ieldra at the galactic core. |

| 2945 FN | Leopold Soli dies on Kweitkel. |

| 2946 FN | Ede the God is slain by the Silicon God. |

2953 FN   Master Pilot Pesheval Lal – known as Bardo –
                 brings the Way of Ringess to Neverness.

2954 FN   Danlo wi Soli Ringess becomes a pilot. The
                 Second Vild Mission leaves Neverness. The Order
                 fissions, and the New Order is established on
                 Thiells at the edge of the Vild.

2955 FN   Danlo wi Soli Ringess discovers the remnants
                 of Ede the God. He discovers that the Silicon
                 God is using the Architects of the Cybernetic
                 Universal Church to destroy the stars.

2959 FN   The Old Order opposes the New Order. The
                 Fellowship of Free Worlds supports the New
                 Order, while the rest of the Civilized Worlds
                 support Hanuman li Tosh and his Ringists, who
                 have taken over the Old Order and Neverness.

                 The War of the Gods begins. (Also called the
                 War in Heaven.) Battle of Mara's Star. Battle of
                 the Ten Thousand Suns. The evolution of *Homo
                 sapiens gyrus*, also called the *Asta Siluuna*.

The Universe of Neverness

In the beginning was a word – a single word that became an entire universe. Neverness, Jorge Luis Borges had said, is a word unlike any other in any language. It is a powerful word, a poem in itself, but also a dreadful word full of hopelessness, sadness, and despair. Eternity does not begin to capture its meaning, not even in the sense of a negative eternity or an impossibility that continues forever. The poets, Borges had implied, had not captured the word's meaning either, for no one had used it. But it *should* be used, because along with its terrible aspect, it happens to be very beautiful.

I knew that I had to use it as the title of my first novel, which became a whole series of books concerning the rise and rise of a brilliant species called *Homo sapiens*. I began thinking about it all the time. A phrase blossomed in my mind like a fireflower in the middle of a snowfield: how is it possible that the impossible might not only be *possible* but inevitable? What was the most impossible thing in all the universe?

That seemed to be myself. How had the supposedly soulless elements of carbon, hydrogen, oxygen, iron, and all the others, forged in the heart of a star ages ago, come together in the form of a man who looked up at the stars and marvelled at their existence – and who looked inside to marvel at his own soul? That seemed utterly impossible. It seemed that the universe shouldn't exist at all, that instead of a bright infinity full of shimmering stars there should only be a black, eternal, unending neverness.

The same universe paradoxically also seemed inevitable. *I* did, myself – despite the trillion-trillion-gazillion-to-one shot that I should have come into consciousness and being. *Homo sapiens*, although only a quirk of evolution on our wandering Earth, seemed inevitable as well. We have design, if only the necessary consequences of the fundamental laws of physics. We have purpose. We have a destiny. Anyone, I thought, searching down through the impossibly bright caverns inside the human soul, had to sense what that destiny must be.

We also, in our DNA, carry not only the record of a billion years of evolution, but the seed of a billion years of new transcendences yet to come. As the child is the father of the man, so are we the progenitors of men – and women – who will be more than human. But why was it always so hard to evolve?

Our evolution, from the grassy veld of primeval Africa to the cold, painted caverns of Lascaux to the hot, hot, brilliant nuclear blast near Alamogordo in the Journey of Death Desert, has brought us to beginning of godhood – and to the brink of extinction as well. In our wars and in the industries of our mad, marvellous, doomed civilization, we have nearly made a wasteland of the earth.

T. S. Eliot's famous poem *The Waste Land* had moved me the first time I read it. Eliot used as a source material Jessie L. Weston's *From Ritual to Romance*, which discusses the legend of the Holy Grail. In that legend, the sexually maimed Fisher King rules over a land that has become parched and sterile. Only a hero who understands the true meaning of the Grail can heal the king and restore that wasted land to life. The medieval romances featuring King Arthur, Queen Guinevere, Lancelot, Galahad, Perceval and all the other knights of Camelot often concern a quest for the Grail.

One day, while reading *The Waste Land* yet again, I froze cold as ice upon reading these lines:

> Unreal City,
> Under the brown fog of a winter dawn,
> A crowd flowed over London Bridge, so many,
> I had not thought death had undone so many.

And it suddenly came to me: Unreal City – impossible place

. . . Neverness. Neverness wasn't just a word that I had fallen in love with; it was, or should be, the name of a city. What kind of city? A cold city, a city of snow and ice mists, a city of the stars. A city at the centre of a vast, stellar civilization slowly declining into a spiritual wasteland. But Neverness would also be a city where the impossible might somehow become possible – in other words, a magical city where men and women sought the Holy Grail of the deepest kind of understanding and gods were born.

And so from the seed of a single word, planted in some very fertile soil, my first novel germinated and grew. I wonder if things worked similarly with the two greatest world-builders of my reading universe. J.R.R. Tolkien, a linguist, invented his Elvish languages, around which grew his universe of Eä and the great epics *The Silmarillion* and *The Lord of the Rings*. Frank Herbert, a journalist out on assignment to write a magazine article, discovered the Oregon Dunes and the ecologists' ideas of anchoring this sea of sand with grasses, shrubs, and trees – and so transforming a wasteland into a new habitat that would support more life. And so he created *Dune*, the mightiest science fiction novel ever written.

All right, so in the beginning, I had a word and then another, and I had two great masters of the art of world-building to guide me. I had as yet, however, no characters, no plot. And then, upon considering all those Arthurian romances, I suddenly had both. I would tell my own romance set far, far in the future. It would be a family drama, in the way of the King Arthur stories – even as the whole human race is one large family, which has co-created our million-year, fantastic story.

Names came to me. King Arthur would be Leopold Soli, the Lord Pilot of the Order of Mystic Mathematicians and Other Seekers of the Ineffable Flame: my Camelot, a sort of kingdom of the mind and soul. His wife, Justine, would stand in for Queen Guinevere. The sorceress Morgan le Fay became Moira, who would bear a bastard son named Kuella. He was to be my treacherous and evil Mordred. His friend, Bardo, would be a big and blustering man whom I thought of as Sir Gawain. They would be pilots, too: my knights in shining lightships. Another pilot, named Lionel, would serve as Justine's adulterous lover, just as Lancelot had with Queen Guinevere. Their forbidden affair would ultimately lead to a war, which would destroy the Order, and perhaps Neverness as well.

Ah, but what was this Order at the heart of my new story and universe and why mathematicians, *mystic* mathematicians at that? Why not an Order of Poets, since poetry inspired much of my writing? Why not an order of wandering minstrels?

History has known many orders, some fraternal such as the Freemasons and others religious: the Jesuits, Sufis, and Shaolin Buddhist monks come to mind. I took much inspiration from Herman Hesse's 'pedagogic province', called Castalia in his novel *The Glass Bead Game* (the only science fiction novel, by the way, to win for its author the Nobel Prize). Castalia's glass bead game players and other teachers practise an art that integrates all human knowledge and keeps alive the soul of humankind. In Castalia, music and meditation are just as important as history, science, economics, and all the other disciplines. I wanted the same to be true of my Order. But where the glass bead game informs the soul of Castalia, in the Order that role is played by mathematics.

When I sat down to write *Neverness*, I was just finishing a degree in mathematics, and I had fallen in love with the universe of number and the secret order of all things. I marvelled at the *mystery* of mathematics: why should a purely mental construction of such ideas as points, sets, and imaginary numbers have such a deep correspondence with what we know as the real world? Why should mathematics *work*?

In my growing universe, seventy years before the establishment of Neverness and the Order (nearly three thousand years before the events of the *Neverness* novels), a great event in the unfolding of intellectual life occurred, which began the Sixth Mentality of humankind. On the world of Arcite, Omar Narayama laid the foundation for the Universal Syntax and a Second Science based on language instead of mathematics. Or so it was thought. For those of the Order have argued for millennia whether or not mathematics is a special case of the Universal Syntax or the reverse. I, myself, as an author, am still trying to get to the bottom of this mystery. I favour mathematics as fundamental; for me, mathematics *is* the language of the universe, and to speak it truly is to gain great and godly powers.

Of all the Order, the cantors delve the mysteries of mathematics with the greatest art. They have taken the name of their ancient discipline from the great nineteenth-century mathematician Georg Cantor, who founded set theory and gave humanity a new conception of infinity. The cantors – along with cetic meditation masters, remembrancers, and others of the Order – are the teachers of the pilots such as Mallory Ringess. The pilots must ply mathematics to open windows to the manifold, a purely mental realm that nevertheless has a deep correspondence with the spacetime of the universe – and with the space that lies beneath space. In this way, the pilots guide their lightships through 'torsion spaces that writhe like hideous, burning snakes' and 'decision trees that split into branches and then branches of branches of branches so quickly one could become lost in a fracturing of sense and thought'. In this way, they fall from star to star.

This sense of falling gave me another name and another idea: the Stellar Fallaways, spread out across the glittering Sagittarius and Orion arms of the Milky Way galaxy, is a vast swathe of stars that the pilots of the Order have mapped. The Civilized Worlds – humanity's greatest civilization – orbit three thousand of these stars. Any civilization, to be called such, must have laws. Mine certainly does. Two of the greatest are: human beings may not stare at the face of a computer too long. And: human beings may do with their flesh as they please, but their DNA belongs to their species. In other, lawless parts of the galaxy, barbaric peoples might jack their brains into their computers to experience cybernetic bliss or mutate their bodies through genetic engineering into dolphin-like forms, but on the Civilized Worlds, human beings were to remain human. And the Order provides the teachers of this civilization while its pilots are the glue that holds it together.

My first four *Neverness* novels concern the stories of the pilot Mallory Ringess and his son Danlo, also a pilot. And so they necessarily centre around pilots and their art. However, the pilots schooled in Resa know too little of the Order's other two colleges, Lara Sig, and Upplysa. (These names I culled out of the Swedish section of my huge *Webster's Third International Dictionary*. They mean: to travel; to learn; to illuminate. Why Swedish? Who knows? At the time I began writing *Neverness*, I lived in Boulder, where it seems half the people drive Volvos.)

Out of Lara Sig come the Order's Academicians: akashics, horologes, historians, librarians, neologicians, semanticists, tinkers, notationists, and others. And Upplysa trains the High Professionals: holists, haikuists, cantors, fabulists, phantasts, imprimaturs, Eschatologists, scryers, cetics, and remembrancers. There are dozens of such disciplines. The names of some do not always mean what readers might think they mean: for instance, my mechanics don't work on lightship engines and stain themselves with grease; rather, they further the ancient development of Einsteinian and quantum *mechanics*.

I still do not know what all these disciplines are about. Only recently did I discover what the haikuists do, and it has little to do with writing classical, three-line Japanese poetry. (Though the art of haiku does entail the using of words to enter into mystical states.) I feel pretty sure that the haikuists seek to encode the subject matter of each of the Order's many disciplines into short, pithy, and universal formulae that can be mutually understood by all so that the Order does not suffer the fate of the modern university, whose mathematics professors, for instance, have no understanding of cutting-edge literary theories created in the English department, and vice versa. Later I'll have more to say about my discovery of my own universe, for it lies at the heart of what I know as world-building.

I have often thought that each of these disciplines might be worthy of their own story and their own hero, as turned out to be true with *The Remembrancer's Tale*. About one discipline, I am learning more in preparation for writing *The Scryer's Tale*. My explorations in this mirror my entire creative process. In *Neverness*, I wrote of a great scryer named Katharine, the lover of Mallory Ringess. The scryers, who peer into the future, go around saying irritating things such as 'What should be shall be' and 'In the end, we choose our futures'. But from where did my scryers come? *The Waste Land* also contains these lines:

> I Tiresias, old man with wrinkled dugs,
> Perceived the scene, and foretold the rest—

In Greek mythology, one of the gods, Hera, punishes Tiresias for the sin of separating two copulating snakes: she turns the blind prophet into a woman for seven years. So I associated the gift and curse of prophecy not only with blindness (only the blind, deprived of the sight of the exterior world, can truly *see*) but with masculine and feminine sexual energies. This plays out in the training of the scryers, who take as their model the ancient Spartans, who required that young males must look to older warriors to teach them the arts of love as well as war. The Order's scryers, all women, must look to older scryers to guide them not only through rites of sexual initiation but through a rite of passage more arduous and more terrifying than even a pilot's first encounter with the deadly manifold. For an aspirant scryer must blind *herself*.

This discovery came to me as a shock, and at first I didn't want to accept it. When I finally did, I realized that the scryers would not wear eye-patches, like pirates, or glass eyes. Rather, they would daub into their eye hollows blacking oil, a substance so black that it reflects no light. And therefore, the curious and the horrified would not actually be able to perceive the scryers' scarring and mutilation. To look into the place where a scryer's eyes should be is to see only a mysterious and total blackness – a sort of neverness.

And so with the germination and growth of the Order, the seed became a tree, which began branching outward in a hundred directions, growing with the full force of its own life. Some branches became stunted or even died: Lionel never really worked as a character, and I wound up writing him out of the book. Kuella, though, a cold man who burned with secret passions, a brilliant mathematical man for whom 'the best sensation was no sensation', began to fascinate me. I changed his name to Mallory Ringess. And rather than tell my novel from Soli's (King Arthur's) point of view, I decided that *Neverness* was really Mallory's story.

It is a story, of course, of the quest for the Holy Grail. I call that the Elder Eddas. This great Secret of Life – the knowledge of the gods who have preceded human beings – lies bound in the oldest DNA of *Homo sapiens*. The Order calls a great quest to find the Elder Eddas. Its pilots, including Soli, Justine, Mallory, and Bardo, sail off in their lightships to the stars even as knights might once have journeyed into castles and dark woods.

I want to say more about the 'gods' of my books, for gods and the idea of godhood play a critical part in my novels. The

Law of the Civilized Worlds was made primarily to keep human beings human. But what does *that* mean? Although the whole arc of my *Neverness* series curves toward an answer to that question, I hope I never actually do answer it, for most of my interest in these books lies in the *attempt* to answer a question that really can't and shouldn't be answered. (As a poet once said, 'I'd gladly give my life for anyone seeking the truth, and I'd gladly murder anyone who claimed to have found it.')

The Law of the Civilized Worlds does *not* try to stifle human evolution, only a particular, technological kind of evolution: all the hubris and destructiveness in our trying to make ourselves into a certain kind of god. Some of the Order's cybershamans (one of the cetics' three branches, very different from the neurologicians and the yogin), practise in secret an almost continual interface with the computers they use to unlock the mysteries of the human mind. In a way, their computers become extensional brains in a symbiosis of human and machine. Others in the galaxy, for millennia, have gone much further on the path of technological transcendence. Nikolos Daru Ede, it is said, long ago carked his consciousness into one of his holy computers and so became as one with the lightning information flows of a computer that added new circuitry and components in an explosive growth of the mind of a man into Ede the God. Kalinda of the Flowers, history's only female warrior-poet (yes, it turned out that there was also an Order of Warrior-Poets and an Order of Pilot-Poets and an Order of True Scientists and many others), began converting the elements of whole planets into the neurologics of computers the size of moons. She took over a vast region of stars near the Eta Carina Nebula and so became a god known as the Solid State Entity. Another of the galaxy's gods had no human origins at all beyond those of the very hubristic human beings who tried to create in a computer a sort of divine being beyond themselves. However, these scientists of Fostora gave their Frankenstein creation the ability to program itself and to control the robots that built and augmented itself. Thus was born the Silicon God – which immediately turned upon the human beings who had created it, for the crime of bringing it into a hateful existence. So instead of creating a god that would save humanity from all its foolishness, destructiveness, and ignorance, the Fostorans created a monster that began gobbling up the galaxy. (And here, of course, I took inspiration from Fredric Brown's story 'Answer': a team of scientists manage to build a computer crackling with all the knowledge of ninety-six billion planets. They turn on the computer and ask it their most burning question: 'Is there God?' Then comes the answer: 'Now there is.')

I was hoping that the greed of my gods would make sense to my readers, for doesn't our society tolerate and even encourage such rapacious growth? I would be happy, so I tell myself, with a million dollars, even though many people say that is not really enough money to get through a long and comfortable retirement. With ten million, though, wouldn't I surely feel secure? Maybe not: the Texas oilmen measure their wealth against each other's in units, a unit being a hundred million dollars. They say things like: 'Ol' John's got a big, fat eight units while poor little Bobby has only four and a half.' If I had a billion dollars, I'd feel like a god. Ten billion would be unimaginable to me. And yet, the richest men have surpassed a hundred billion dollars in wealth and seem to be on the way to becoming the first trillionaires. It is not so hard to imagine them trying to gobble up the economy of the entire Earth.

What is to stop them? What stopped Napoleon Bonaparte from conquering all of Europe and creating an empire that might eventually have taken over the world? Only another empire, the British Empire, at the battles of Trafalgar and Waterloo. What is to stop any single god from trying to take over the universe? Only another god or gods.

In *Neverness*, the pilots of the Order fight a war with each other that nearly destroys the Order. This war concerns the old ordering of humanity and its laws versus a vision of the new. Mallory Ringess leads the great quest to find the Elder Eddas. Some, particularly the mad Silicon God, don't want it to be found. They don't want *Homo sapiens* to evolve. Many gods, such as the April Colonial Intelligence, would actually like to exterminate the human race and so eliminate a potential competitor, much as a giant software company might drive out of business a start-up in possession of a brilliant idea. Other gods who have accepted limits upon their growth – the Solid State Entity in particular – favour a new evolution of humanity. They believe in the design and vision of that most ancient race of gods, the Ieldra, said to have seeded the entire galaxy with their DNA. And so the gods secretly take sides in the wars human beings fight among themselves, much as Hera and Zeus and the other Greek gods favoured either Greek heroes such as Achilles or Trojan princes such as Hector in the Trojan War.

The Pilots' War of *Neverness*, however, does not resolve the essential tension at the heart of my universe. Perhaps the conflicts of spirit and matter never can be resolved. As Coleridge says in his great poem about another would-be world conqueror:

> And 'mid this tumult Kubla heard from far
> Ancestral voices prophesying war!

The tumult of the Pilots' War leads to the much greater strife that moves *The Broken God*, *The Wild*, and *War in Heaven*. The scryer Katharine has foreseen the shape of this much greater war and the future of humanity in the persons of her son Danlo and her grandchildren, Sunjay and Chandra wi Soli Ringess. They will come to be called the *Asta Siluuna*, the Star Children. However, as is often the case with prophets, Katharine is unable to share her vision with others. It is a beautiful vision, but a terrible one, too. For out of the chaos of the Pilot's War comes perhaps the greatest of all attempts of a human being to break out into godhood.

I built the character of Hanuman li Tosh out of someone I loved who became fascinated with the realm of the night – and also out of Milton's Satan, along with the light and dark parts of myself. Hanuman, born a sensitive soul, cannot bear the suffering and evil of the world. And so he seeks not just to master the world and live in glory forever like some Egyptian pharaoh, but to remake it – in fact, to gobble up the entire universe and collapse it into what he calls his Universal Computer. The artificial life that he creates will thrive in his computer's information flows, and this perfect life will know no suffering, disease or death. As was said of a village in Vietnam when I was young, Hanuman will have to destroy the universe in order to save it.

Could even the Silicon God dream of anything so mad? For Hanuman seeks not just to become the ruling Zeus or Odin of a pantheon of gods, but literally . . . God. Like Satan, he does so out of pride, telling himself that our universe has been botched and that he can do better. Like my friend (and like the Bolsheviks purging their enemies during the Russian Revolution), he is willing to do the hard things and work necessary evils in order to achieve in the end the greatest possible good. Like me, he feels trapped in his fragile, mortal human form and longs for transcendence through identity with something much greater.

A single question, a great riddle, will shape his fate: what does it mean to be a god? This turns out to be just another way of asking what it means to be human.

Hanuman's answer – and this is the sentiment of many cyberpunk and transhumanist authors who began writing their fictions around the time I did mine – is that we *Homo sapiens* will find our deepest purpose in a technological transcendence known as the Singularity. Human beings will use genetic engineering to begin the transformation of the human body; we will use nanotechnology to complete it – and to effect the transformation of every part of material reality. We will become immortal, nearly omniscient and omnipotent, through 'uploading' our consciousnesses into computers. These machines will grow ever more hyper-intelligent, powerful, and vast, as big as gleaming moons. This total transcendence of history, mind, spirit, and flesh will concentrate into a singularity in spacetime beyond which all evolution will both explode exponentially and become completely inapprehensible – at least to the poor, mortal, dumb humans still bound to our all-too-human forms.

The galaxy's godlings, however, would find in this open-ended evolution humankind's true destiny. To them it would be like a star bursting into a supernova. They would be like silver surfers catching a wave front of expanding light and riding it outward in all directions into a bright infinity.

The Singularity looms over my *Neverness* novels like a perfect stellar storm that will sweep the whole human race away. And here, too, Eliot's *The Waste Land* found its way into my story. For out in unmapped parts of the galaxy, a sect of religious fanatics called the Iviomils who worship Ede the God are blowing up the stars. Why would they do such a crazy thing? Because they obey the injunction to fill the universe with more worshippers who one day will go on to join Ede in his divinity – and only by exploding stars into supernovas can they generate the

incredible spacetime deformations necessary to tear open
windows to the manifold. Their deep-ships filled with millions
of Iviomils fall from star to star almost at random, and so they
create the blasted-out wasteland of stellar debris and radiation
known as the Vild.

In *The Broken God*, I plant the seeds for rejecting this
Singularity, which bids fair to make a blasted-out wasteland of
our beautiful Earth. I begin to ask a truly vital question: what
is technology, really? Sometimes technology is seen as something
material only, something external to human consciousness and
being that usually winds up deforming both: think of all those
images of people with sockets drilled into their bald, wired skulls
so that they can insert metal plugs into their brains and 'jack
in' to the information storms of their computers. That is the
kind of technology that Hanuman li Tosh embraces.

I do not. In fact, I loathe and dread it. It's not that I consider
it impossible or even unlikely; rather, I disdain it simply because
I find it ugly.

I hope I am not giving too much away by admitting here
that in my novels I reject the paths of technological transcendence that Hanuman and the Silicon God, even the Solid State
Entity, choose to take. Theirs is the sickness of solipsism and
hyperindividualism, of feeling themselves to be whole universes
cut off from a much, much greater All. Surely there must be a
better way. But *what* way?

My novels much concern mysticism and evolution, specifically the tension between the two and how they come together. A
mystic celebrates pure being. A whole life can be lived in a single
breath. A fire rose, doomed soon to wilt and die, is perfect in
the moment of its flowering. The future not only doesn't matter
but doesn't exist, for the rose's brilliant colours blossom out
into an eternal Now-moment preserved forever outside of time.
Life is complete in every moment, its purpose utterly fulfilled.
That single rose, ablaze forever with an ineffable flame, contains
much, much more than just itself. In a single bit of red pigment,
bright as a drop of blood, a mystic marvelling at the flower
beholds entire galaxies of planets, moons, quasars, and exploding
stars, in the same way that William Blake saw in a grain of sand
the entire universe.

Evolution, on the other hand, is not about being but rather

becoming. It moves through time – and, it seems to me, moves toward *something*. The history of our universe is not just a record of the random collisions of hydrogen and helium atoms irradiated by all the unimaginable energy unleashed at the Big Bang. Something Big seems to be happening.

Biologists don't like to talk about a direction or purpose to evolution, which they reject as teleology. The Order's eschatologists, however, spend their professional lives speculating on what might come next for the universe, particularly for *Homo sapiens*. Is the future of our kind to be found in the gods such as the Solid State Entity or the would-be gods like Hanuman li Tosh who set out on a technological path toward transcendence? Or is there another way, a way that unites the mystical with all the power and purpose of a more natural evolution? A path where pure being can flow into becoming, as when an individual such as Danlo wi Soli Ringess turns away from interfacing Hanuman's Universal Computer and instead looks into himself, deep down into his DNA, in order to perceive whole and beautiful the infinite face of God?

The best of the pilots, the truly mystical mathematicians, have glimpsed this unitive path. So have the remembrancers. As I wrote my way deeper and deeper into my Neverness universe, as I discovered more about it, I realized that memory was playing a greater and greater role not just in the philosophy and science that inform my novels but in the actions my characters took. Mallory Ringess and the pilots of the Order set out on a quest to find the secret of life imprinted as memories in humanity's oldest DNA – and perhaps even deeper, in the very fabric of spacetime. How are they to do this? For their art is mathematics, not memory. And so they – everyone who seeks the Ineffable Flame burning at the heart of the Elder Eddas – must look to the remembrancers.

At the end of *Neverness*, Mallory Ringess comes to understand much more about the Eddas, which the remembrancers recognize as part of the One Memory they have sought for millennia but have never fully grasped. Can a man grasp the very lightning of heaven and hold it in his hand? Can a man who would be more than a man use the very fires of creation to shape not just the material universe but himself? Many people believe astonishing things about Mallory Ringess.

In *The Broken God*, Hanuman li Tosh and Mallory's friend Bardo found the religion called Ringism based on the miracle of Mallory's realization of the Elder Eddas. How can others follow this Way of Ringess, as it is called?

The Order's Lord Remembrancer, Thomas Rane, wants to bring this gift of the Eddas to all. And so he slips away from the duties of his office to join the new religion of Ringism. He leads hundreds and then thousands of people, those of the Order and many others such as diplomats, courtesans, and astriers, in a ceremony of remembrance. He does not, however, dole out to the multitudes a symbolic sacrament such as wine but a more potent substance: kalla, the remembrancers' drug. Kalla enables some Ringists to 'remember down the DNA' straight toward the heart of the One Memory. If the absent Mallory is the messiah of this new religion and Hanuman and Bardo its prophets, then Thomas Rane is Ringism's High Priest.

As I have hinted, things go bad for Hanuman li Tosh and the religion he tries to control. He mistrusts kalla; the drug has given him a vision of a horrifying neverness at the centre of the universe. This soul-poisoning vision leads him to construct his Universal Computer to replace the universe. He mistrusts the Ringists, for he does not believe them capable of true remembrance. He mistrusts Thomas Rane. For Thomas Rane, despite all, keeps pure his faith that the One Memory will open doors for humanity to the brightest of futures. He and Hanuman argue over the future of Ringism, and their quarrel in part leads to the terrible War in Heaven.

In the war's aftermath, Rane returns to his own personal quest for the Elder Eddas. His great gift is to realize the future by remembrancing the past. For, as the remembrancers say, 'The memory of all things is in all things'. And, as the scryers say, 'What has been will be'. In the eternity of the One Memory, past, future, and present become as one.

The One Memory pulls Rane deeper into himself, straight toward his fate. He has taught both Mallory Ringess and his son, Danlo, the art of remembrance. Now he teaches Danlo's children, Chandra and Sunjay, and others: the *Asta Siluuna*, whom the scryer Katharine called the Star Children because she foresaw that their remembrance of the Eddas would bestow upon them the splendour of the stars.

Rane also teaches Maria, a mysterious, black-eyed poet, but also a child at heart herself, who comes to Neverness from the stars in order to learn more about the One Memory.

And Rane, drawn as by a star's intense gravitation, immediately falls in love. How can he help it? For Maria is brilliant, beautiful, compassionate, and full of life. She also has a wildness of heart and soul that Rane cannot fathom.

From where did Maria come? Even as Rane the character asked himself this question, I as the author of my tale did the same. I came to realize that Maria, who seemed to emerge from *my* soul whole and complete like Aphrodite from the sea, was every amazing woman I had ever known: my brilliant friend Tina, a fine artist, who went bust through no fault of her own and then through sheer determination figured out how to draft blueprints and build mountain houses for a living; my even more brilliant friend Jane, a fine writer and also rock climber, who had to summon all her courage and skill to survive a night stranded on the side of a mountain; my great-hearted friend Mary, who would fight tooth and nail to defend those she loved. Maria was also my mother: she who wanted more than anything else to find her own splendour through the child she gave to the world.

In a strange way – and this discovery astonished me – Maria was also Tarzan. Tarzan? Yes, but *not* the Tarzan of most movies, the noble savage who grunts out the few words of English he knows and barks out commands to animals. No, I had long been taken by the Tarzan of Edgar Rice Burroughs's imaginative books, and *that* Tarzan teaches himself to read by puzzling out the squiggles of letters matched to pictures in the child's primer that his parents left to him after they died and left him orphaned and adopted by great apes. The Tarzan whom I knew and loved could be considered a natural genius in addition to possessing great powers of body, sense, and soul.

My Maria, who did not teach herself to read, nevertheless becomes so brilliant with words that her poems move many. She, too, has grown up living among animals, for her childhood companions include a great tiger and a band of bonobos who regard her as one of their own. She is happy to eat meat raw, and she doesn't particularly like wearing clothes. She is passionate in all that she does, totally alive and totally in possession of the gift of *animajii*, the wild joy of life. She loathes civilization and longs to live in nature. Her fearlessness in being willing to lay down her life for those she loves gives her a natural nobility. She is savage, too, for she will face down with tooth or clawed fingernails or wit anyone who tries to cage her or keep her from her beautiful purpose.

What is that purpose? Thomas Rane spends much of *The Remembrancer's Tale* searching for it and trying to make it his own. When he loses Maria, it is as if he loses his own life, and something more.

In his devastation, in the hell of his private neverness that seems to suck away his soul, he ponders great questions: why does time move in one direction only? Why does the world evolve and not devolve? Why *can't* we remake the past?

In one of the greatest Greek myths, the poet Orpheus goes down into the underworld to bring back his beloved Eurydice from the land of the dead. Thomas Rane, no Greek hero but only a remembrancer, goes down into his marvellous memory in order to sing Maria back into life.

Although myths have moved many of my books, I write science fiction and read a great deal of physics, biology, anthropology, and much else in order to learn more science. In *Neverness*, I tell of how macroscopic information decays to microscopic information and that 'nothing can be lost'. This sense of the universe preserving all events occurring in spacetime harkens back to the ancient Vedanta concept of the Akasha. Some modern physicists, in homage to the ancients, have hypothesized a universal Akashic Field capable of storing an infinite amount of information. The Order's akashics, inheritors of this tradition, try to understand the workings of information and memory through their theories. The remembrancers, however, delve the depths of the One Memory through the practice of their difficult art. (And here I have just realized that their sixty-four traditional attitudes such as mnemonics and olfaction used to enter into remembrance include one called hakuism: the remembrancers chant the haikuists' powerful word formulae to take them deep into memory.)

Thomas Rane, mortal like all of us, has agonized over a great question: if the universe somehow remembers perfectly and preserves all, what essential part of him can never be destroyed? What would he most like to preserve? That turns out *not* to be himself, but rather someone he loves more than himself. And so he sets out on his unlikely quest to find Maria and love her again.

Will it surprise anyone at this point to learn that his quest became my own? I promised that I would say more about the discovery of my own universe. For hundreds of years, mathematicians have debated whether mathematics is discovered or created. Some argue strongly for the latter: twenty-five hundred years ago, the Greek philosopher Pythagoras etched figures in the sand and created his proof that the squares of the two smaller sides of a right-angled triangle added together equal the square of the hypotenuse – and so gave humankind the mighty Pythagorean Theorem. Ah, yes, but wouldn't another philosopher, perhaps a huge, white-furred alien on a faraway planet, etching figures in the snow, discover the exact same theorem? Doesn't all of mathematics pre-exist in some sort of pure, Platonic realm of the mind like perfect jewels just waiting to be discovered?

I can't answer this question, not exactly. But both creation and discovery seem to me to be two sides of one face. The Big Bang coming out of that single word 'neverness' somehow resulted in a universe every bit as vast and real as our own. Yes, I am free to create: a name for a flower, an alien world, a musical instrument, a philosophy, an entire mentality of an age of humankind. In a deeper sense, though, all these things and everything in my novels seem to pre-exist, as I seem to be a remembrancer or a scryer or a pilot in a lightship falling from star to star and discovering wonders. Somehow, through a sort of magical alchemy of turning simple words into golden stories, even the impossible becomes not only possible but inevitable.

For I never doubt that my universe is real. In a way, it sparkles with a reality *more* real than that of our own, for I can create and discover simultaneously, as I can see and feel my way deep into the heart of any part of it. As the pilots have learned (thanks to Mallory Ringess), it is possible to fall from any star to any other through thought and will. As the mystics know, all points in the universe interconnect with each other like a tapestry of living jewels, each one reflecting the radiance of all the others. And as the scryers say, and as Thomas Rane realizes through anguish and impossible journeys and the greatest of love: 'In the end, we choose our futures'.

Glossary

Adal Vun – a starless region in the galaxy's Orion Arm beyond the Eta Carina Nebula.

Adjal – a small instrument that makes a music of colours in a kinetic, three-dimensional display.

Advaita Vedanta – an ancient discipline of the cetics, scryers, and remembrancers, dating back to Old Earth and teaching that individual and universal consciousness are one and the same.

Afarique' – the mother continent on Old Earth from which evolved *Homo sapiens*.

Agathange – a water world rimward from Neverness in the Sagittarius Arm near Arcite. The Agathanians are master bio-engineers who have carked their human forms into shapes resembling those of seals, whales, and other sea creatures.

Agathism – the doctrine that all things move toward the ultimate good.

Ahira – the Alaloi's name for the snowy owl, the animal guide of Danlo wi Soli Ringess.

akashics – academicians of the Order who study how information of events occurring in spacetime is preserved in what they call the Akashic Records (and the remembrancers call the One Memory).

Alaloi – the first peoples of Icefall. The Alaloi carked their *Homo sapiens* forms and DNA in order that their descendants would look and live like Neanderthals, so that they could live on the frozen islands west of Neverness.

Alam Al-Mithral – the space where images are real, lying halfway between the material world and the world of intellect.

Altjiranga Mitjina – the Dreamtime of the indigenous Australians and the Alaloi in which one's dreaming self can be sent out into the world.

amorgenic – an aphrodisiac.

amritsar tank – an artificial womb where organisms, usually bio-engineered, are grown.

anatman – an ancient Buddhist doctrine teaching that there is no self, that the sense of identity separate from universal consciousness is an illusion.

angslan – loss of memory due to aging; also, the pain of aging at a different rate from one's family, friends, and lovers.

animajii – the wild joy of life; life's overflowing delight in itself.

Aoide – a planet coreward from Neverness, home of the pilot-poets.

April Colonial Intelligence – one of the galaxy's greatest gods, a swarm intelligence allied with the Silicon God.

Architects of the Vild – one of the many divisions of the Cybernetic Universal Church. Some of their chapters use the explosions of stars in order to propel their deep-ships into the manifold so that the Architects can seed the galaxy with their kind.

Arcite – the first home of the Order of Holists and True Scientists, from which developed the Order of Mystic Mathematicians and Other Seekers of the Ineffable Flame.

Arda Sophar – the scriptures of the astrier sects.

arhat – someone who has attained wealth supposedly through spiritual perfection.

Ashtoreth District – large part of Neverness's Farsider's Quarter where the Ashtoreth clans reside.

Asta Siluuna – the Star Children, a new generation who are learning to apply the secrets of the Elder Eddas toward the evolution of *Homo sapiens*.

August Colonial Intelligence – a minor god of the galaxy.

autists – a sect denying the validity of objective reality; the Dreamtime is sought and venerated as the Real Real. Some autists, like the aphasics, practise mutilation of parts of the brain deemed unnecessary so that other parts might develop phenomenal powers of computation and simulation.

Battle of the Ten Thousand Suns – the culminating battle of the War in Heaven, in which Hanuman li Tosh and the Iviomils of the Cybernetic Universal Church were defeated.

Blessed Realm – the meta-galactic centre into which all space folds. Said to be the home of the Ieldra.

Borja – the Order's school for novices on Neverness.

Brihadaranyaka Upanishad – ancient Vedic scripture developed in the forest ashrams of India.

carking – radical transformation, as in carking the form of one's body or carking one's consciousness into a computer.

cetics – High Professionals of the Order who study consciousness; divided into neurologicians, yogin, and cybershamans.

chith – mental money; honour.

cilka – pineal gland of the thallow; psychedelic in small quantities and lethal in large ones.

Civilized Worlds – the three thousand planets of the Stellar Fallaways where laws limiting dangerous technologies such as bio-engineering and nuclear weapons are honoured.

The Clading – the splitting of *Homo sapiens* into new and divergent species.

clary – a synthetic whose clarity and strength exceeds that of glass.

College of Lords – the ruling body of the Order.

Continuum Hypothesis – a theorem stating that in the manifold, at least one pair of simply connected points exists in the neighbourhood of any two stars. First proposed by Rollo Gallivare in 14,784 CE and finally proved by Mallory Ringess nearly three thousand years later. More simply stated: it is possible to fall from any star in the galaxy to any other in a single fall.

crewelwork – a kind of genetic engineering.

curarax – a fatal nerve poison.

cybernetic holism – nature seen as information exchange. See the Sixth Mentality.

Cybernetic Universal Church – founded after Nikolos Daru Ede carked his consciousness into a computer and became Ede the God. Edeism is the largest religious grouping of *Homo sapiens*.

cybershamans – cetics who explore the human psyche through interface with computers.

Darghinni – aliens who reside in Neverness's Zoo Quarter.

Darkmoon – a planet rimward from Neverness near Agathange.

deep-ship – a large starship carrying up to five thousand passengers and cargo or both.

dereism – a remembrancing attitude in which thinking is directed away from reality.

dreammakers – those who induce sounds and sights into auditory and visual centres of the brain, most often in the form of narcotizing hallucinations that are considered an art form.

Dreamtime – see *Altjiranga Mitjina*.

drillworms – invertebrates of the Nematoda phylum native to Fostora. Can burrow into any tissue but particularly like brain matter.

droghul – someone engineered with one or more disassociative identities usually created for the purpose of assassination.

dyson sphere – a spherical structure built to wholly encompass a star and capture all its energy.

Elf Gardens – a spectacular rock and ice formation in eastern Neverness at the base of Mounts Urkel and Attakel.

Elidi – humans who have carked their forms into those of birds on the low-gravity planet of Elidin.

Enth Generation – a wholly computer-generated artificial intelligence. One of the galaxy's gods.

Eta Carina – a nebula in the region of space taken over by the Solid State Entity.

exoecology – generalized ecology applied to all planets besides Earth.

exopsychology – the study of alien minds.

eyetalk – the language of the eyes and facial expressions developed by the *Asta Siluuna*.

fantell – musical instrument similar to the lute but smaller, with a bright, crisp sound.

Farfara – a planet near Fostora in the Orion Arm.

Farsheyden – a small, watery world rimward from Neverness at the edge of the Sagittarius Arm.

Farsider's Quarter – the southwest and largest of Neverness's four quarters.

farwhen – originally, the horologes' term for the immeasurable, distant future.

Fayoli – a planet in the Orion Arm.

Fifth Mentality of Humankind – this commenced in 2525 CE with the development of the first intelligent computers on Mars. The Fifth Mentality informed the Age of Simulation.

figuration – from the old French word for face; figuration involves interfacing the mathematics of the manifold. Also, part of the cetic art of reading faces.

fireflowers – native to Icefall; their usually orange and red blossoms are bioluminescent and much warmer than ambient temperatures.

Fostora Redemption Fellowship – one of the Cybernetic Universal Churches.

Fravashi – eight-foot-tall, white-furred philosophers and meditation masters. The alien Fravashi teach the art of thinking to many peoples, including those of the Order.

Friends of Man – alien courtesans who use the arts of ecstasy to win converts to their religion.

furanorn – a Fravashi term for becoming annihilate in one's clan. Related to *ilnorn*, becoming annihilate in the individual self, and *vashnorn*, which is to lose one's identity in God.

Gallivare Green – one of Neverness's parks, named for the great pilot Rollo Gallivare.

Gallivare Space – in the manifold, a Riemann surface embedded in a Wen space whose genus approaches infinity.

Generalized Continuum Hypothesis – this states that it is possible to fall from any point in spacetime to any other.

glavering – to believe that one's beliefs about the universe are correct, solely as a result of one's cultural conditioning; being deceitfully kind to oneself; flattering one's own intellect.

glent – to move one's thoughts quickly, especially in an oblique manner.

Godsward – a planet near the Oxblood Nebula. Also, a movement toward breaking out into godhood in a hakariad.

Gorgorim – humans who have sculpted their bodies and face into the forms of beasts.

gosharp – a stringed instrument capable of producing both overtones and microtones.

gyrance – the rapid turning of thoughts.

hafe – a Fravashi term. To view reality so that subject and object are separate. (See melge and prenune.)

hakariad – to break out into godhood.

haikuists – Order academicians who seek to encode the subject matter of each of the Order's many disciplines into short universal formulae that can be mutually understood by all. The most ancient school of haikuists use words or symbols to enter into mystical states or remembrance.

hallning – the mental discipline necessary to enter the manifold. There are eighty-one hallning attitudes. The art of hallning was developed by the cetics, holists, and the Fravashi in order to integrate the crosstalk of the mind's senses.

harijan – outcasts from the Civilized Worlds who have found shelter and freedom in Neverness.

heaume – the original helmet that the pilots wore to interface with their computers.

Hofgarten – a gathering place of restaurants and bars built around a large ice ring, which overlooks the sea.

Holocaust Centuries – on Old Earth, from 1905 CE to 2525 CE and the creation of the first intelligent computers on Mars and the beginning of the Fifth Mentality.

hoshik – the beauty of life, as seen and created by a person. Beauty as a way of life.

ideoplast – a three-dimensional mental symbol usually infused into the brain's visual and auditory cortices. Often a meta-symbol encoding whole sequences of symbols. Ideoplasts can be adapted for use either in mathematics or the Universal Syntax. Ideoplasts are pleached together to generate meaning in the art of kithing.

Ieldra – legendary elder gods who seeded the galaxy with their DNA.

ilnorn – see *furanorn*.

the *Immanent Carnation* – Mallory Ringess's lightship.

infons – pure information hypothesized to make up all matter and energy.

intime – subjective time, often different from elapsed time due to Einsteinian time distortions.

Iviomils – a sect of the Cybernetic Universal Church who are destroying the stars, thus creating the Vild.

Jacaranda – a pleasant, temperate planet noted for its pleasure domes.

jambool – a narcotic drug.

jewood – a hard, reddish wood often used in sculptures and houses.

Jonah's Star Far Group – a small stellar cluster located between the galaxy's Sagittarius and Orion arms.

jook – a narcotic drug inducing both ecstasies and paranoid delusional states.

juf – a narcotic drug. One of the three Js: jook, jambool, juf. Also, a biological antifreeze injected into the blood and other living tissues.

Kalinda of the Flowers – the human name of the warrior-poet who became the Solid State Entity.

Kalla Fellowship – the name of the devotees who drank the remembrancers' drug kalla in order to apprehend the Elder Eddas.

kamelaika – a racing suit woven of wool and biothermal fibres.

Kamilusa – a lost planet in the neighbourhood of the Solid State Entity.

keisaku – the zen stick, used to smack meditators in order to focus their awareness.

kinematics – an applied geometry in which the movement of a mechanical system is described using the transformations of Euclidean geometry.

kithing – the art of understanding three-dimensional mental symbols known as ideoplasts. Also, rarely, known as hyper-reading.

kittikeesha – a small white bird native to Icefall.

kleining – topological infolding, as in a klein bottle, klein inversion or klein space.

Kristians – an ancient religious sect dating back to year 33CE on Old Earth. Nearly extinct.

Kristoman – another name for Christ the God in his human incarnation of Jesus.

Lavi algebras – created by the pilot Ricardo Lavi to model Lavi spaces.

logic field – a field generated by heaumes. Also called an information field.

logicists – those who study logic as the foundation not only of mathematics and the Universal Syntax but of all systems of thought.

Rowan Madeus – one of names of the immortal created by the Ieldra on Old Earth. Other names include Gilgamesh, Kalkin, Kane, Sarojin Noy, and Horthy Hosthoh. On Arcite in 9061 CE, Rowan Madeus established the Order of Holists and True Scientists, a forerunner of the Order of Mystic Mathematicians and Other Seekers of the Ineffable Flame.

Magellanic Cloud – a small satellite galaxy of the Milky Way.

Malaclypse of Qallar – a ronin warrior-poet who devoted himself to the Way of Ringess.

melge – a Fravashi term. To view reality so that subject and object are one. (See hafe and prenune.)

Merripen Green – a park in Neverness's Farsider's Quarter just off the East-West Sliddery.

Morbio Superiore – like the Morbio Inferiore, an almost unmappable region of new stars and quasars that has killed many of the Order's pilots.

Omar Narayama – creator of Universal Syntax, which in 19,459 CE laid the foundation of the Second Science based on a new understanding of language, instead of mathematics.

neurologicians – a branch of the cetics. The neurologicians apply the biology of the brain and logic to understand the workings of the human mind. They rely on the computer as a model and metaphor for the brain/mind.

neurosingers – a sect, like the cetic cybershamans, who practise a continual interface with computers in order to hear the 'singing of deep mind'.

Sarojin Noy – one of Rowan Madeus's many names.

Old Earth – near the edge of the Orion Arm, the planet that gave birth to *Homo sapiens*.

One Memory – also known as the Akasha Field or Akashic Record, in which all events occurring in spacetime are preserved. The ancient remembrancers spoke of it as the memory of God.

Nils Ordando – established the Order of Cetics on Simoom in 9454 CE.

Order of Mystic Mathematicians and Other Seekers of the

Ineffable Flame – established with the founding of Neverness in 24,790 CE (year zero FN). The pilots, academicians, and high professionals of the Order devote themselves to exploring the universe, both in its outward manifestation as planets, stars, and galaxies, and in its inward reality of consciousness and the mind. The Order provides teachers to the Civilized Worlds and holds civilization together.

Oxblood Nebula – a cluster of stars in one of the galaxy's 'lost' regions.

John Penhallegon (the Tycho) – one of the greatest of the Order's Lord Pilots. Lost in 2020 FN while exploring the Solid State Entity.

Perdido Luz – star at the 'gateway' of the nebula of the Solid State Entity.

pilot-poets – an order established on Aoide in homage to the Order's pilots and the warrior-poets.

the Plato – honorary founder of the Order, on Old Earth circa 387 BCE.

plexure – the art of weaving together and 'seeing' knowledge (or events) as through different lenses, thoughtways, or epistemological systems; the ability to enter and hold different realities, sometimes mutually contradictory ones.

prenune – to view reality in such a way that subject and object are simultaneously both separate and one. (See hafe and melge.)

quicktime – the computer-generated slowing of the brain that enables time to pass more quickly.

Real Real – the deep reality of the autists, as distinct from the illusory real world.

realspace – normal macro-space; the familiar spacetime of the universe, as distinct from the manifold.

realtime – time elapsing in a stationary frame of reference, unperturbed by Einsteinian or manifold time distortions.

Riemannian – another name for elliptic geometry in which a space contains no parallel lines.

Danlo wi Soli Ringess – Mallory Ringess's son, and one of the Order's greatest pilots. Danlo expanded and deepened his father's understanding of the Elder Eddas.

Ringism – a religion founded by Pesheval Lal (Bardo) and Hanuman li Tosh to further the evolutionary discoveries of Mallory Ringess.

ronin pilots – pilots who have abjured their vows and left the Order.

saltation – an evolutionary leap.

sarsara – a violent, whistling, bitterly cold wind, usually blowing out of the west.

scacchic bar – in Neverness, a popular place to play chess. Usually the scacch stimulant is served rather than alcohol.

shasteel – an alloy of steel and synthetic matter; extremely strong, tough, and hard.

shatterwood – a hardwood evergreen species whose oldest trees sometimes explode in extremely cold weather.

singularitist – one who believes that *Homo sapiens*, through artificial intelligence and nanotechnology, is approaching a total transcendence of history, mind, spirit, and flesh that will concentrate into a singularity in spacetime beyond which all evolution will both explode exponentially and become completely inapprehensible.

Sixth Mentality – this commenced on Arcite in 24,710 CE with Omar Narayama's creation of the Universal Syntax. *Homo sapiens* began a new dialogue with the universe based on a new ontology that Narayama calls the 'linguistics of being'.

sleekits – small mammals who make burrows in the snow.

slel cells – the programmed bacteria used to disassemble and replace the human brain with neurologics.

slel mime – the replacement neuron by neuron of a person's brain with protein neurologics in order to create a human biocomputer.

slel neckers – steal others' DNA for various purposes from the making of individually designed poisons and cancers to the making of zygotes.

slowtime – the computer-generated speeding up of the mind so that external events and time seem to slow down.

Leopold Soli – one of the Order's greatest Lord Pilots. Soli was the first pilot to reach the galactic core, where he learned of the Elder Eddas: the knowledge as to how human beings should become gods, which the Ieldra had embroidered in the oldest DNA of the human race. Soli survived to bring back to Neverness this news, which led to the great Quest and to the Pilot's War.

solido – a hologram.

Solid State Entity – one of the greatest gods of the galaxy.

the Sonderval – immensely tall and very arrogant pilot who made many discoveries and fought with distinction in the Pilot's War.

soreesh – a light, powdery snow.

spacewise – refers to direction and magnitude in normal spacetime.

Stellar Fallaways – the well-mapped region of the three thousand Civilized Worlds spread out mostly across the Sagittarius and Orion arms but reaching also to the Perseus Arm.

Summerworld – the hot home planet of the Lord Pilot Pesheval Lal (Bardo); famed for its coffee and other agricultural products.

teleogenesis – the purposeful bringing into form and life. The self's willed evolution of the self.

thallow – a great bird, often white with grey markings, larger than an eagle. Thallows usually prey on sleekits and fish but have been known to attack human beings and even bears.

thermals – a type of heated clothing. See kamelaika.

thickspace – a region of the manifold with many point-sources and point-exits to stars.

Third Wave of the Swarming – commenced in 70 FN (24,860 CE); very rapid spread of *Homo sapiens* across the galaxy.

toalache – a psychoactive seaweed native to Agathange, usually smoked in small glass pipes.

Hanuman li Tosh – a cetic who co-founded the Way of Ringess and tried to construct his Universal Computer that would take over all matter and spacetime. Led the Ringists in the War in Heaven.

triptons – one of the new organisms living in the space above Icefall's atmosphere. The red chlorophyll of trillions of tiny triptons gives colour to the new ecology of life called the Golden Ring.

Tychism – the proposition that absolute chance forms the most basic law of the universe.

the Tycho – see John Penhallegon.

Upplysa College – the Order's college that trains holists, cetics, scryers, remembrancers, and other high professionals.

Urradeth – a planet coreward from Summerworld and coreward south from Neverness.

vashnorn – to lose one's identity in God. See *ilnorn* and *furanorn*.

ventriloquists – those who throw their 'voice' into others, i.e. those who infect others with a memory virus or otherwise infuse others with false memories. See slel mimes.

the Vild – between the Orion and Perseus arms, a region of space where human beings have exploded many stars into supernovas, resulting in a vast radioactive wasteland.

warrior-poets – an order established by Nils Ordando and Ivar Hanuman on Qallar in 19,809 CE after the Order of Holists and True Scientists absorbed the Order of Cetics. Nils Ordando led a hundred renegade neurologicians to Qallar in order to breed a new and superior race of human beings.

westering – the drive to push outward to the end of the universe.

wormrunners – smugglers, procurers, and petty criminals. Wormrunners pride themselves in making their own laws or spurning the idea of law altogether. They often call themselves thallows or freebirds.

Yahweh – the elder god of the Jewish faith.

yu tree – a beautiful softwood evergreen that produces edible nuts and large, bright red berries.

zazen – a state of relaxed mental alertness in the face of death that pilots must master in order to navigate the manifold.